SILKEN PREY

ALSO BY JOHN SANDFORD

JOHN SANDFORD
SILKEN PREY

**SIMON &
SCHUSTER**

London · New York · Sydney · Toronto · New Delhi

A CBS COMPANY

First published in the US by G. P. Putnam's Sons, 2013
A division of the Penguin Group (USA) Inc.
First published in Great Britain by Simon & Schuster UK Ltd, 2013
A CBS COMPANY

1 3 5 7 9 10 8 6 4 2

Simon & Schuster UK Ltd
1st Floor
222 Gray's Inn Road
London WC1X 8HB

www.simonandschuster.co.uk

Simon & Schuster Australia, Sydney
Simon & Schuster India, New Delhi

A CIP catalogue record for this book
is available from the British Library

Trade Paperback ISBN 978-1-47112-963-6
Hardback ISBN 978-1-47112-962-9
Ebook ISBN 978-1-47112-966-7

Printed and bound by CPI Group (UK) Ltd, Croydon, CR0 4YY.

For Summer, Colin, Mac, and Gus

1

queak.

 Tubbs was half-asleep on the couch, his face covered with an unfolded *Star Tribune*. The overhead light was still on, and when he'd collapsed on the couch, he'd been too tired to get up and turn it off. The squeak wasn't so much consciously felt, as *understood*: he had a visitor. But nobody knocked.

TUBBS WAS A POLITICAL.

In his case, political wasn't an adjective, but a noun. He didn't have a particular job, most of the time, though sometimes he did: an aide to this state senator or that one, a lobbyist for the Minnesota Association of Whatever, a staffer for so-and-so's campaign. So-and-so was almost always a Democrat.

He'd started with Jimmy Carter in '76, when he was eighteen, stayed pure until he jumped to the Jesse Ventura gubernatorial revolt in '98, and then it was back to the Democrats. He'd never done anything else.

He was a political; and frequently, a fixer.

Occasionally, a bagman.

Several times—like just now—a nervous, semi-competent black-mailer.

TUBBS SLEPT, USUALLY, in the smaller of his two bedrooms. The other was a chaotic office, the floor stacked with position papers and reports and magazines, with four overflowing file cabinets against one wall. An Apple iMac sat in the middle of his desk, surrounded by more stacks of paper. A disassembled Mac Pro body and a cinema screen hunkered on the floor to one side of the desk, along with an abandoned Sony desktop. Boxes of old three-and-a-half-inch computer disks sat on bookshelves over the radiator. They'd been saved by simple negligence: he no longer knew what was on any of them.

The desk had four drawers. One was taken up with current employment and tax files, and the others were occupied by office junk: envelopes, stationery, yellow legal pads, staplers, rubber bands, thumb drives, Post-it notes, scissors, several pairs of finger-nail clippers, Sharpies, business cards, dozens of ballpoints, five or six coffee cups from political campaigns and lobbyist groups, tangles of computer connectors.

He had two printers, one a heavy-duty Canon office machine, the other a Brother multiple-use copy/fax/scan/print model.

There were three small thirty-inch televisions in his office, all fastened to the wall above the desk, so he could work on the iMac and watch C-SPAN, Fox, and CNN all at once. A sixty-inch LED screen hung on the living room wall opposite the couch where he'd been napping.

Squeak.

This time he opened his eyes.

TUBBS REACHED OUT for his cell phone, punched the button on top, checked the time: three-fifteen in the morning. He'd had any number of visitors at three-fifteen, but to get through the apartment house's front door, they had to buzz him. He frowned, sat up, listening, smacked his lips; his mouth tasted like a chicken had been roosting in it, and the room smelled of cold chili.

Then his doorbell blipped: a quiet *ding-dong*. Not the buzzer from outside, which was a raucous *ZZZZTTT*, but the doorbell. Tubbs dropped his feet off the couch, thinking, *Neighbor*. Had to be Mrs. Thomas R. Jefferson. She sometimes got disoriented at night, out looking for her deceased husband, and several times had locked herself out of her own apartment.

Tubbs padded across the floor in his stocking feet. There was nothing tubby about Tubbs: he was a tall man, and thin. Though he'd lived a life of fund-raising dinners and high-stress campaigns, he'd ignored the proffered sheet cake, Ding Dongs, Pepsi, Mr. Goodbars, and even the odd moon pies, as well as the stacks of Hungry-Man microwave meals found in campaign refrigerators. A vegetarian, he went instead for the soy-based proteins, the non-fat cereals, and the celery sticks. If he found himself cornered at a church-basement dinner, he looked for the Jell-O with shredded carrots and onions, and those little pink marshmallows.

Tubbs had blond hair, still thick as he pushed into his fifties, a neatly cropped mustache, and a flat belly. Given his habits and his diet, he figured his life expectancy was about ninety-six. Maybe ninety-nine.

One big deficit: he hadn't had a regular woman since his third wife departed five years earlier. On the other hand, the irregular women came along often enough—campaign volunteers, legislative staff, the occasional lobbyist. He had always been a popular man, a man with political stories that were funny, generally absurd, and sometimes terrifying. He told them well.

As he walked toward the door, he scratched his crotch. His dick felt sort of . . . bent. Chafed. A little swollen.

The latest irregular woman was more irregular than most. They'd had a strenuous workout earlier that evening, a day that had left Tubbs exhausted. Hours of cruising the media outlets, talking to other operators all over the state, assessing the damage; a tumultuous sexual encounter; and finally, the biggest blackmail effort of his life, the biggest potential payoff . . .

He was beat, which was why, perhaps, he wasn't more suspicious.

Tubbs checked the peephole. Nobody there. *Probably Mrs. Jefferson,* he thought, who hadn't been five-two on her tallest day, and now was severely bent by osteoporosis.

He popped open the door, and,

Surprise!

TUBBS REGAINED CONSCIOUSNESS on the floor of a moving car, an SUV. He was terribly injured, and knew it. He no longer knew exactly how it had happened, if he ever had, but there was something awfully wrong with his head, his skull. His face and hands were wet with blood, and he could taste blood in his mouth and his nose was stuffed with it. He would have gagged if he had the strength.

He could move his hands, but not his feet, and with a little clarity that came after a while, he knew something else: he was lying on a plastic sheet. And he knew why: so the floor of the car wouldn't get blood on it.

The images in his mind were confused, but deep down, in a part that hadn't been impacted, he knew who his attackers must be, and he knew what the end would be. He'd be killed. And he was so hurt that he wouldn't be able to fight it.

Tubbs was dying. There wasn't much in the way of pain, because he was too badly injured for that. Nothing to do about it but wait until the darkness came.

The car was traveling on a smooth road, and its gentle motion nevertheless suggested speed. A highway, headed out of St. Paul. Going to a burial ground, or maybe to the Mississippi. He had no preference. A few minutes after he regained consciousness, he slipped away again.

Then he resurfaced, and deep down in the lizard part of his brain, a spark of anger burned. Nothing he could do? A plan formed, not a good one, but something. Something he could actually do. His hands were damp with blood. With much of his remaining life force, he pushed one wet hand across the plastic sheet, and tried as best he could to form the letters *TG*.

That was it. That was all he had. A scrawl of blood on the underside of a car seat, where the owner wouldn't see it, but where a crime-scene technician might.

He pulled his hand back and then felt his tongue crawl out of his mouth, beyond his will, the muscles of his face relaxing toward death.

He was still alive when the car slowed, and then turned. Still alive when it slowed again, and this time, traveled down a rougher road. Felt the final turn, and the car rocking to a stop. Car doors opening.

His killers pulled him out of the backseat by pulling and lifting the plastic tarp on which he lay. One of them said, "Skinny fuck is heavy."

The other answered, "Hey. I think he's breathing."

"Yeah? Give me the bat."

Just before the darkness came, Tubbs sensed the fetid wetness of a swamp; an odor, a softness in the soil beneath his body. He never heard or felt the crunch of his skull shattering under the bat.

Nothingness.

2

Lucas Davenport was having his hockey nightmare, the one where he is about to take the ice in an NCAA championship game, but can't find his skates. He knows where they are—locker 120—but the locker numbers end at 110 down one aisle, and pick up at 140 on the next one.

He knows 120 is somewhere in the vast locker room, and as the time ticks down to the beginning of the match, and the fan-chants start from the bleachers overhead, he runs frantically barefoot up and down the rows of lockers, scanning the number plates. . . .

He knew he was dreaming even as he did it. He wanted nothing more than to end it, which was why he was struggling toward consciousness at eight o'clock on a Sunday morning and heard Weather chortling in the bathroom.

Weather, his wife, was a surgeon, and on working days was always out of the house by six-thirty. Even on sleep-in days, she hardly ever slept until eight. Lucas, on the other hand, was a night owl. He was rarely in bed before two o'clock, except for recreational purposes, and he was content to sleep until nine o'clock, or later.

This morning, he could hear her laughing in the bathroom, and realized that she was watching the built-in bathroom TV as she put on her makeup. She'd resisted the idea of a bathroom television, but Lucas had installed one anyway, claiming that it would increase their efficiency—get the local news out of the way, so they could start their days.

In reality, it had more to do with shaving. He'd started shaving when he was fifteen, and had never had a two-week beard. Even counting the rare days when he hadn't shaved for one reason or another, he'd still gone through the ritual at least twelve thousand times, and he enjoyed it. Took his time with it. Found that the television added to the whole ceremony.

Now, as he struggled to the surface, and out of the hockey arena, he called, "What?"

She called back, "More on Smalls. The guy is truly fucked."

Lucas said, "Have a good day," and rolled over and tried to find a better dream, preferably involving twin blondes with long plaited hair and really tight, round . . . ZZZ.

Just before he went back to dreamland, he thought about Weather's choice of words. She didn't use obscenity lightly, but in this case, she was correct: Smalls was really, truly fucked.

LUCAS DAVENPORT WAS TALL, heavy-shouldered, and hawk-faced, and, at the end of the first full month of autumn, still well-tanned, which made his blue eyes seem bluer yet, and made a couple of white scars stand out on his face and neck. The facial scar was thin, like a piece of pale fishing line strung down over his eyebrow and onto one cheek. The neck scar, centered on his throat, was circular with a vertical slash through it. Not one he liked to remember: the young girl had pulled the piece-of-crap .22 out of nowhere and shot him and would have killed him if Weather hadn't been there with a jackknife. The vertical slash was the result of the tracheotomy that had saved his life. The slug had barely missed his spinal cord.

The tan would be fading over the next few months, and the scars would become almost invisible until, in March, he'd be as pale as a piece of typing paper.

LUCAS ROLLED OUT OF bed at nine o'clock, spent some time with himself in the bathroom, and caught a little more about Porter Smalls.

Smalls was a conservative Republican politician. Lucas generally didn't like right-wingers, finding them generally to be self-righteous and uncompromising. Smalls was more relaxed than that. He was conservative, especially on the abortion issue, and he was death on taxes; on the other hand, he had a Clintonesque attitude about women, and even a sense of humor about his own peccadilloes. Minnesotans went for his whole bad-boy act, especially in comparison to the stiffs who usually got elected to high office.

Smalls was rich. As someone at the Capitol once told Lucas, he'd started out selling apples. The first one he bought for a nickel, and sold for a quarter. With the quarter, he bought five more apples, and sold them for a dollar. Then he inherited twenty million dollars from his father, and became an overnight success.

Weather loathed Smalls because he advocated Medicaid cuts as a way to balance the state budget. He was also virulently pro-life, and Weather was strongly pro-choice. He was also anti-union, and wanted to eliminate all public employee unions with a federal law. "Conflict of interest," he said. "Payoffs with taxpayer money."

Lucas paid little attention to it. He generally voted for Democrats, but not always. He'd voted for a nominally Republican governor, not once but twice. Whatever happened, he figured he could live with it.

ANYWAY, SMALLS HAD LOOKED like he was headed for reelection over an attractive young Minnesota heiress, though it was going to be close. Her qualifications for office were actually better than Smalls's; she looked terrific, and had an ocean of money. If she had a problem, it was that she carried with her a whiff of arrogance and entitlement, and maybe more than a whiff.

Then, on the Friday before, a dewy young volunteer, as conservative as Smalls himself, and with the confidence that comes from being both dewy and affluent—it seemed like everybody involved in the election had money—had gone into Smalls's campaign office to drop off some numbers on federal aid to Minnesota for bridge construction, also known as U.S. Government Certified A-1 Pork.

She told the cops that Smalls's computer screen was blanked out when she walked into the office. She wanted him to see the bridge files as soon as he came in, so she put them on his keyboard.

When the packets hit the keyboard, the screen lit up . . . with a kind of child porn so ugly that the young woman hardly knew what she was seeing for the first few seconds. Then she did what any dewy Young Republican would have done: she called her father. He told her to stay where she was: he'd call the police.

When the cops arrived, they took one look, and seized the computer.

And somebody, maybe everybody, blabbed to the media.

Porter Smalls was in the shit.

SUNDAY MORNING, A TIME for newspapers and kids: Lucas pulled on a pair of blue jeans, a black shirt, and low-cut black boots. When he was done, he admired himself in Weather's full-length admiring mirror, brushed an imaginary flake from his shoulder, and went down to French toast and bacon, which he could smell sizzling on the griddle even on the second floor.

The housekeeper, Helen, was passing it all around when he sat down. His son, Sam, a toddler, was babbling about trucks, and had three of them on the table; Letty was talking about a fashion-forward girl who'd worn a tiara to high school, in a kind of make-or-break status move; Weather was reading a *Times* review about some artist who'd spent five years doing a time-lapse movie of grass growing and dying; and Baby Gabrielle was throwing oatmeal at the refrigerator.

There were end-of-the-world headlines about Smalls, in both the Minneapolis and New York papers. The *Times*, whose editorial por-tentousness approached traumatic constipation, tried to suppress its glee under the bushel basket of feigned sadness that another civil servant had been caught in a sexual misadventure; they hadn't even bothered to use the word "alleged."

Lucas was halfway through the *Star Tribune*'s comics when his cell phone buzzed. He took it out of his pocket, looked at the caller ID, clicked it, and said, "Good morning, Neil. I assume you're calling from the Cathedral."

Neil Mitford, chief weasel for the governor of Minnesota, ignored the comment. "The guy needs to see you this morning. He should be out of church and down at his office by ten-thirty or so. He's got to talk to a guy at ten-forty-five, more or less, until eleven-thirty or so. He'd like to see you either at ten-thirty or eleven-thirty."

"I could make the ten-thirty," Lucas said. "Is this about Tubbs?"

"Tubbs? No, Tubbs is just off on a bender somewhere. This is about Smalls."

"What about Smalls? That's being handled by St. Paul."

"He'll tell you. Come in the back," Mitford said. "We'll have a guard down at the door for you."

LUCAS CHECKED HIS WATCH and saw that he would make it to the Capitol right on time, if he left in the next few minutes, and drove slowly enough.

"Wait," Weather said. "We were all going shopping."

"It's hard to tell the governor to piss up a rope," Lucas said. "Even on a Sunday."

"But we were going to pick out Halloween costumes . . ."

"I'd just be bored and in your way, and you wouldn't let me choose, anyway," Lucas said. "You and Letty will be fine."

Letty shrugged and said to Weather, "That's all true."

SO LUCAS IDLED UP Mississippi River Boulevard, top down on the Porsche 911, to Summit Avenue, then along Summit with its grand houses, and over to the Capitol.

The Minnesota Capitol is sited on a hill overlooking St. Paul, and because of the expanse of the hill, looks taller and wider than the U.S. Capitol. Also, whiter.

Lucas left the car a block away, and strolled through the cheerful morning, stopping to look at a late-season butterfly that was perched on a zinnia, looking for something to eat. The big change-of-season cold front had come through the week before, but, weirdly, there hadn't yet been a killing frost, and there were still butterflies and flowers all over the place.

At the Capitol, an overweight guard was waiting for him at a back door. He and the guard had once worked patrol together on the Minneapolis police force—the guard was double-dipping—and they chatted for a few minutes, and then Lucas climbed some stairs and walked down to the governor's office.

The governor, or somebody, had left a newspaper blocking the doorjamb, and Lucas pushed open the door, picked up the paper, and let the door lock behind him. He was standing in a darkened outer office and the governor called, "Lucas? Come on in."

THE GOVERNOR WAS A tall, slender blond named Elmer Henderson, who might, in four years, be a viable candidate for vice president of the United States on the Democratic ticket. The media said he'd nail down the left-wingers for a presidential candidate who might prefer to run a little closer to the middle.

Henderson might himself have been a candidate for the top job, if he had not been, in his younger years, quite so fond of women in pairs and trios, known at Harvard as the "Henderson Hoagie," and cocaine. He certainly had the right pedigree: Ivy League undergraduate and law, flawless if slightly robotic wife and children, perhaps a half billion dollars from his share of the 3M inheritance.

He was standing behind his desk, wearing a dark going-to-church suit, open at the throat, the tie curled on his desktop. He had a sheaf of papers in his hands, thumbing them, when Lucas walked in. He looked over his glasses and said, "Lucas. Sit. Sorry to bother you on a Sunday morning."

"It's okay." Lucas took a chair. "You need somebody killed?"

"Several people, but I'd hesitate to ask, at least here in the office, on the Lord's Day," the governor said. He gave the papers a last shuffle, set them aside, pressed a button on a box on his desk, and said, "Get in here," and asked Lucas, "You've been reading about Porter Smalls?"

"Yeah. You guys must be dancing in the aisles," Lucas said.

"Should be," said a voice from behind Lucas. Lucas turned his head as Mitford came through a side door, which led into his compact, paper-littered office. "This is one of the better political moments of my life. Porter Smalls takes it between the cheeks."

"What an unhappy expression," the governor said. He dropped into his chair, sighed, and put his stocking feet on the desktop. "But appropriate, I suppose. He's certainly being screwed by all and sundry."

"And it kills the Medicaid nonsense," Mitford said, as he took another chair. "He was carrying that on his back, and anything he was carrying is tainted. *You want to pass a bill sponsored by a kiddie-porn addict? What kind of human being are you?*"

"Grossly unfair," the governor said. He didn't seem particularly worried about the unfairness of it. He'd been looking at Mitford, but now turned to Lucas. "You know what the problem is?"

"What?"

"He didn't do it. Wasn't his child porn," the governor said. "I talked to him yesterday afternoon, over at his house, for a long time. He didn't do it."

"I thought you guys were blood enemies," Lucas said.

"Political enemies. I went to kindergarten with him, and knew him before that. Went to the same prep school, he went to Yale and I went to Harvard. His sister was a good friend of mine, for a while." He paused, looked up at the ceiling, and smiled a private smile, then recovered. "I tell you, from the bottom of my little liberal heart, Porter didn't do it."

"He could've gone off the rails somewhere," Lucas suggested.

The governor shook his head. "No. He doesn't have it in him, to look at kiddie porn. I know the kind of women he looks at. I can describe them in minute detail, and nobody would call them kiddies: he likes them big-titted, big-assed, and blond. He liked them that way in kindergarten and he still likes them that way. Go look at his staff, you'll see what I mean."

"Can't always tell . . ." Lucas began, but the governor held up a finger.

"Another thing," he said. "This volunteer said she walked into his office and put some papers on his keyboard and up popped the porn. If it really happened like that, it means that he had a screen of kiddie porn up on his computer, and walked away from it to a campaign finance meeting, leaving the door unlocked and the kiddie porn on the screen. The screen blanked for a while, but was still there, waiting to be found. Vile stuff, I'm told. Vile. Anyway, that's the only way her story works: the screen was blanked when she walked in, and popped back up when she put the papers on the keyboard. Porter was near the top of his class at Yale Law. He's not stupid, he's not a huge risk-taker. Do you really believe he would do that?"

"Even smart people—"

"Oh, horseshit," the governor said, waving him off.

"Suicidal . . ."

"Porter goes to the emergency room if the barber cuts his hair too short," the governor said. "He wants and expects to live forever, preferably with a big-titted, big-assed blonde sitting on his face."

Lucas thought for a moment, then conceded the point: "That thing about the volunteer—it worries me."

"It should," the governor said. He kicked his feet off the desktop and said, "I want you to look into this, Lucas. But quietly. I don't want to disturb anybody without . . . without there being something worthwhile to disturb them with."

"One more question," Lucas said. "This guy is a major pain in your party's ass. Why . . . ?"

"Because it's the right thing to do, mostly," the governor said. "There's something else, too. This sort of shit is going too far. Way too far. Most Republicans aren't nuts. They're perfectly good people. So are most of us Democrats. But this kind of thing, if it's deliberate—it's a threat to everybody. All you have to do is *say* 'kiddie porn' and a guy's career is over. Doesn't make any difference what he's done, what his character is like, how hard he's worked, it doesn't even matter if there's proof—once it gets out in the media, they'll repeat it endlessly, and there's no calling it back. You could have the Archbishop of Canterbury go on TV tomorrow and say he has absolute proof that Porter Smalls is innocent, and fifty other bloggers would be sneering at him in two minutes and CNN would be calling the bishop a liar. So we're talking about dangerous, immoral, antidemocratic stuff."

"You're saying the media is dangerous, immoral, and antidemocratic?"

"Well . . . yes," Henderson said. "They don't recognize it in themselves, but they're basically criminals. In the classic sense of that word."

"All right," Lucas said.

"And, of course, there's the other thing," the governor said. "The less righteous thing."

Lucas said, "Uh-oh."

Mitford said, "We're already hearing rumors that he was framed. That there were hints *before* anyone found the porn that something was coming on Smalls. If it turns out that some overzealous young Democratic hacker did it, if this is a campaign dirty trick . . . then there could be a lot more trouble. If that's what happened, we need to know it first. The election's too close to be screwing around."

The governor added, "But the preliminary investigation has to be quiet. Invisible might be a better word."

Mitford said, "Totally quiet. That fuckin' tool over in the attorney general's office wants to move into this office. He thinks prosecuting Smalls is one way to do it. If he finds out that you're digging around, he'll paper your ass so fast you'd think you were a new country kitchen. You'll be working for him."

"You don't sound as *offended* as the governor," Lucas said to Mitford. "About Smalls being framed."

"I'm paid to keep my eye on the ball, so that's what I do," Mitford said. "Short term, there's no benefit to us, saving an asshole like Smalls. If we get a reward, it's gonna have to be in heaven, because we sure as shit won't get it now. If the party found out we were trying to help Smalls, then . . . well, you know, we're thinking about the vice presidency. On the other hand, if *we* did this, meaning *we* in the all-inclusive sense, and if that comes out, say, the Friday before the election . . ."

"I can't afford to lose the state House," Henderson said. He wasn't running. He still had two years to go on his second term.

"But Smalls is in the U.S. Senate," Lucas said. "How could that affect the state House?"

"Because our majority is too narrow. If it turns out that we tried to sabotage a U.S. Senate race, with child porn, Smalls will eat us alive in the last few days before the election. He could pump up the Republican turnout just enough that we could lose those extra three or four close-run seats. If we lose the House, and the Senate stays Republican, which it will, they'll spend the next two years dreaming up ways to embarrass me."

"We can't have that," Mitford said. "I mean, really."

"But. If Smalls owes us, even under the rose, he'll pay up," the governor said. "He's that kind of guy. He won't go after us . . . if he owes us."

"ALL RIGHT," LUCAS SAID. He stood up. "I'll do it."

"Excellent," the governor said. "Call me every day."

"But what if he did it?" Lucas asked.

"He didn't," the governor said.

Lucas said, "I'm going to tell Rose Marie about it. I can't . . . not do that." Rose Marie was the public safety commissioner and an old friend.

The governor was exasperated: "Jesus Christ, Lucas . . ."

"I can't not do that," Lucas insisted.

The governor threw up his hands. "All right. When you tell her, you tell her to call me. I'll need . . . Wait. Hell no. I'll call her right now. You get going on this. I'd like to get something pretty definitive in, say, mmm, three days. Two would be better."

"Man . . ."

"Go." Henderson waved him away.

ROSE MARIE ROUX HAD been a cop, then a lawyer and prosecutor, then a state senator, then the Minneapolis chief of police, and finally, the commissioner of public safety under Henderson. She had jurisdiction over a number of law enforcement agencies, including the Bureau of Criminal Apprehension. She viewed Lucas as both a friend and an effective tool for achieving her policy goals, not all of them involving crime-fighting. She'd gotten him his job at the BCA.

Rose Marie's husband was ten years older than she was, and when he'd retired, he talked her into dumping the suburban Minneapolis house in favor of a sprawling co-op apartment in downtown St. Paul. Lucas gave the governor a few minutes to talk to her, and then, as he walked back to his car, called her himself.

"You at home?"

"Yeah, come on down. I'll buzz you into the garage."

LUCAS HAD BEEN TO the apartment often enough that he knew the routine; buzzed into the garage, he parked in one of the visitors' slots and took the elevator to the top floor. Rose Marie's husband opened the door; he was holding the *Times* in one hand and a piece of jelly toast in the other. "She's out on the deck," he said.

"You raked the leaves off the deck yet?"

"Thank God for the penthouse—not a leaf to be seen," he said.

Rose Marie, wrapped in a wool shawl, was sitting on a lounge chair, smoking a cigarette; nicotine gum, she said, was for pussies. She was a short woman, going to weight, with an ever-changing hair color. Lucas liked her a lot.

When Lucas stepped out on the deck, she said, "I appreciate what you did, bringing me into it. This will be interesting, all the way around. Although it has a downside, of course."

She crushed the cigarette out on a ceramic saucer by the side of the chair. As Lucas sat down facing her, she asked, "How much do you like your job?"

"It's okay. Been doing it for a while," Lucas said.

"If this kind of thing happens too often, you'll get pushed out," Rose Marie said. "It's inevitable."

Lucas shrugged. "I do it because it's interesting. This assignment's interesting. If I wasn't doing this, I'd be chasing chicken thieves in Black Duck."

Rose Marie said, "I keep thinking about what I'm going to do when this job is over. If Elmer makes vice president, he'll take care of both of us. If he doesn't, then I'm unemployed, and you probably will be, too."

"That's a cheerful thought," Lucas said.

"Gotta face facts," Rose Marie said. "We've both had a good run. But I don't feel like retiring, and you're way too young to retire. We're both financially fine, but what the fuck do we do? Become consultants? I don't feel like running for anything."

"I haven't spent a lot of time worrying about it," Lucas said.

"You should," Rose Marie said. "Even if Elmer makes vice president, I'm not sure you'd want what he could get you. I'd be fine, because I'm basically a politician, I could work in D.C., or for his office here. But you . . . I don't know what you'd do. I don't think you'd want to wind up as some FBI functionary. Or Elmer's valet."

"No."

"Well. Sooner or later, your name will be connected to this job," Rose Marie said. "Whether or not it pans out. If the attorney general doesn't jump you for the prosecution, Porter Smalls will come after you for the defense. A lot of people in the Department of Public Safety and over at the BCA don't like this kind of thing, the political stuff. And you've been doing a lot of it. When I'm not here to protect you, when Elmer's not here . . ."

"Ah, it's all right, Rose Marie," Lucas said. "I've been fired before. Stop worrying about it."

"Yeah." She peered at him for a moment, then asked, "What are you going to do? About Smalls?"

"Try to keep it quiet, as long as I can," Lucas said.

"How are you going to do that?" she asked.

"Haven't worked it out yet. I've got a few ideas, but you wouldn't want to hear them."

"No. Actually, I wouldn't."

"So. Moving right along . . ." Lucas stood up.

Rose Marie said, "I'll talk to Henry. Make sure he has a feel for the situation." Henry Sands was director of the BCA and had been appointed by Henderson. If he knew Henderson was behind Lucas's investigation, he'd keep his mouth shut. Unless, of course, he could see some profit in slipping a word to a reporter. He didn't much like Lucas, which was okay, because Lucas didn't much like him back.

"Good," Lucas said. "And hey—relax. Gonna be all right."

"No, it won't," she said. "I can almost guarantee that whatever it is, it won't be all right."

LUCAS STARTED BACK DOWN to the car, still thinking it over. Rose Marie was probably right about the political stuff. Even if you were on the side of the Lord, the politics could taint you. Which created a specific problem: there was at least one man at the BCA who'd be invaluable to Lucas's investigation—Del Capslock. Del had contacts everywhere, on both sides of the law, and knew the local porn industry inside out.

The problem was, Del depended on his BCA salary, and all the benefits, for his livelihood. He had a wife and kid, and was probably fifteen years from retirement. Everybody in the BCA knew that he and Lucas had a special relationship, but that was okay . . . as long as Lucas didn't drag him down.

Lucas didn't particularly worry about himself. Back in the nineties, he'd been kicked out of the Minneapolis Police Department and had gone looking for something to do. He'd long had a mildly profitable sideline as a designer of pen-and-paper role-playing games, which had gone back to his days at the university. After he left the MPD, he'd gotten together with a computer guy from the university's Institute of Technology. Together they created a piece of software that could be plugged into 911 computer systems, to run simulations of high-stress law-enforcement problems.

Davenport Simulations—the company still existed, though he no longer had a part of it—had done very well through the nineties, and even better after the September 11 attacks on the World Trade Center. Instead of one simulation aimed at police departments, they now produced dozens of simulations for everything from bodyguard training to aircraft gunfight situations. When the management bought Lucas out, he walked away with enough money to last several lifetimes.

He was rich. Porter Smalls was rich. The governor was *really* rich, and for that matter, so was Porter Smalls's opponent; even the volunteer who'd started the trouble was rich, or would be. Rich people all over the place; gunfight at the one-percent corral.

Anyway, he was good, whatever happened. If the Porter Smalls assignment turned into a political quagmire, he could always . . . putter in the garden.

Del couldn't.

Lucas popped the doors on the 911 and stood beside the open door for a minute, working through it.

Del was out of it. So were his other friends with the BCA.

Which left the question, who was in, and where would he get the intelligence he would need? He had to smile at the governor's presumption: get it done, he'd said, in a day or two, and keep it absolutely private. He didn't care how, or who, or what. He just expected it to be done, and probably wouldn't even think about it again until Lucas called him.

3

ucas decided to go right to the heart of the problem and start with Porter Smalls. He called the number given him by Mitford, and was invited over. Smalls lived forty-five minutes from downtown St. Paul, on the east side of Lake Minnetonka.

His house was a glass-and-stone mid-century, built atop what might have been an Indian burial mound, though the land was far too expensive for anyone to look into that possibility. In any case, the house was raised slightly above the lake, with a grassy back-yard, spotted with old oak and linden trees.

Lucas was met at the door by a young woman who said she was Smalls's daughter, Monica. "Dad's up on the sunporch," she said. "This way."

Lucas followed her through a quiet living room and down a hall, then up a narrow, twisting stairway. Lucas noted, purely as a matter of verifying previous information, that she was both big-titted and big-assed, as well as blond, so Henderson's description of Smalls's sexual preferences were showing some genetic support.

At the top of the stairs, she said, "Dad's out there," nodding toward an open door, and asked if Lucas would like something to drink.

Lucas said, "Anything cold and diet?"

"Diet Coke," she said.

"Excellent."

"Is Mrs. Smalls around?" Lucas asked.

"If by 'around' you mean the Minneapolis loft district with her Lithuanian lover, then yes."

"Maybe I shouldn't have asked," Lucas said.

"No, that's all right," she said cheerfully. "It's been in the papers."

SMALLS WAS SITTING ON a draftsman's stool on the open sun-porch, looking out over the lake through a four-foot-long brass telescope. He was wearing faded jeans and an olive-drab, long-sleeved linen shirt under an open wool vest.

Lucas thought he looked less like a right-wing politician than like a professor of economics, maybe, or a poet. He was a small man, five-seven or five-eight, slender—no more than a hundred and fifty pounds—and tough-looking, like an aging French bicycle racer. He wore his white hair long, with tortoiseshell glasses over crystal-line blue eyes.

Lucas knocked on the doorjamb and said, "Hello," and Smalls turned and said, "There you are," and stood to shake Lucas's hand. "Elmer said you'd be coming around."

"You want me?" Lucas asked.

"I'll take anything I can get, at this point," Smalls said. He pointed at a couple of wooden deck chairs, and they sat down, facing each other. Before going to the telescope, Smalls had apparently been reading newspapers, which were stacked around the feet of his chair. "What do you think? How fucked am I?"

Lucas thought about Weather and said, "My wife was watching TV this morning, as she was getting ready to go out, and the story came up, and she said, 'Smalls is truly fucked.'"

Smalls nodded. "She may be right. She would be right, if I were guilty. . . . Your wife works?"

"She's a surgeon," Lucas said.

"And you made a couple of bucks in software," Smalls said.

"Yes, I did. You've been looking me up?"

"Just what I can get through the Internet," Smalls said. He reached down, picked up an iPad, flashed it at Lucas, dropped it again on the pile of paper. "You think you can do me any good?"

"If I proved you were innocent, *would* it do you any good?" Lucas asked.

Smalls considered for a moment, staring over the lake, pulling at his lower lip. Then he looked up and said, "Have to be fast. Nine days to the election. If you don't find anything before the weekend, I couldn't get the word out quickly enough to make a difference. I need to be at the top of the Sunday paper, at the latest. My opponent has more money than Jesus, Mary, and Joseph put together, along with a body that . . . never mind. Of course, even if I lose, it'd be nice if I weren't indicted and sent to prison. But I don't want to lose. I don't deserve to lose, because I'm being framed."

"The governor tells me you didn't do it," Lucas said.

"Of course I didn't," Smalls snapped, his glasses glittering in the sun. "For one thing, I'm not damn fool enough to leave a bunch of kiddie porn on an office computer, with all kinds of people walking in and out. The idea that I'd do that . . . that's *insulting.*"

"We talked about that," Lucas said. "The governor and I."

"And that rattlesnake Mitford, no doubt," Smalls said.

Monica came out with a bottle of Diet Coke and a glass with ice. She'd overheard the last part of the conversation, and said, "I promise you, Mr. Davenport, Dad's *not* a damn fool."

Lucas poured some Coke, took a sip, said "Thanks" to Monica and asked Smalls, "What do you know about this volunteer? Has she got anything against you? Did you have any kind of personal involvement with her?"

"No. That's another thing I'm not damn fool enough to do. Not since Clinton. If I were going to play around, there are lots of good-looking, smart, discreet adult women available. I really wouldn't have a problem."

"People sometimes get entangled—"

"Not me," Smalls said. He started to say something more, but then looked up at his daughter and grinned and said, "Monica, could you get me a beer? Or wait, no. I don't want a beer. This talk could get embarrassing, so . . . sweetie . . . could you just go away?"

"You sure you want to be by yourself, with a cop?" Monica asked.

"I think I can handle it," Smalls said. She patted him on the shoulder and walked back into his house, and down the stairs. When she was gone, Smalls said, "She's a lawyer, too. A pretty good one, actually." They both thought about that for a second, then Smalls said, "Look: I've done some fooling around. Got caught, too. Not by the morality police. It was worse than that: the old lady walked in on me."

"Ouch."

"Twice. The last time, she had her lawyer with her."

"Ahh . . ."

"So I *can* be a fool, but not the kind of damn fool I'd have to be if I were guilty of this kiddie porn stuff," Smalls said. "I think before I jump. The women I've been involved with, they're pretty good gals, for the most part. They knew what they were getting into, and so did I. That sort of thing, for a guy at my level, is okay. Elmer couldn't get away with it, anymore, but I'm not quite as visible as the governor. The other thing is, political people are pretty social, and they knew what the situation was between Brenda and me. So, looking outside was considered okay, as long as it was discreet."

"I get that," Lucas said. "I guess."

"But some things are not okay," Smalls said. "Going after volunteers—the young ones—is not okay. A relationship with a lobbyist is not okay. I wouldn't look at kiddie porn, even if I were bent that way, which I'm not. If I were interested in drugs, which I'm not, I wouldn't snort cocaine or smoke pot around witnesses, at a party. I wouldn't chisel money from my expense accounts. You know why I wouldn't do any of that? Because I'm not stupid. I'm not stupid, and I've seen all that stuff done by people who were supposedly smart, and they got caught, and some of them even went to jail. If I were to do any of that, and get caught, I'd feel like an absolute moron. That's one thing I won't tolerate in myself. Moronic behavior."

"All right," Lucas said. "So this volunteer . . ."

"To tell you the truth . . ." Smalls was already shaking his head. "I believe her. I think she's telling the truth."

"Yes?"

"Yup. It sort of baffles me, but I believe her," Smalls said. "I'm not a hundred percent sure of her, but mostly, I think somebody planted that porn on my computer. People are always going in and out of my office. I think somebody went in there, called it up, and walked back out. Then she walked in . . ."

"But how'd they know she'd toss the files on the keyboard?"

"How do we know this was the only time they tried it?" Smalls asked. "Maybe they did this ten times, just waiting for somebody to touch the keyboard. But the thing is, her story is too stupid. I keep coming back to stupidity, and whoever did this to me isn't entirely stupid. But the way *she* says it happened, this volunteer, this girl . . . it's too stupid. If *she's* the one who did it, I'd think she would have made up a better story."

Lucas shook his head. "Unless your office is a lot more public than I think it is—"

Smalls held up a hand: "Stop right there. Wrong thinking. The thing is, it *is* public," he said. "It's a temporary campaign office, full of rented chairs and desks and office equipment. I hardly ever go there, but technically, it's mine. I have another office, the Senate office. In that office, my secretary would monitor people coming and going. Nobody would get in the private office without her knowing, and watching them every minute. There's classified stuff in there. In the campaign office, there are staff people going in and out all the time."

"You think a staff person might have been involved?" Lucas asked.

"Had to be. There are undoubtedly a couple of devoted Democrats around—just as . . . and this is off the record . . . just as there are a couple of pretty devoted Republicans over in Taryn Grant's campaign staff."

"Spies."

"If you want to be rude about it," Smalls said. "So you get a couple of young people as spies, and some of them are a little fanatical about their status, and about helping one party or the other win. So, yeah, somebody on the staff. That's a good possibility. A probability."

"The computer didn't have any password protection?"

"Yes, of course it did. Want to know what it was? It was 'Smallscampaign.'"

"Great."

"Yeah."

Lucas asked, "Do you know what happened to it? Your computer?"

"The St. Paul police have it," Smalls said.

"You think you could get access to it?" Lucas asked.

"Maybe. Probably. I don't know if I could get to the computer itself, but we should be able to get a duplicate of the hard drive, which would give you everything relevant," Smalls said.

Lucas nodded. "Okay. You're innocent, right?"

"Yes."

"So: call your attorney," Lucas said. "Today. Right now, on Sunday. Tell him that you want to duplicate the hard drive to start preparing a defense. Take it to court if you have to, but get the hard drive for me. If you have to go to court, you argue that you will be irreparably harmed, with only a week to the election, if you're not allowed to see what you're accused of. You'll get it. When they give you access, call me, and I'll send somebody down to monitor the copy process."

"Somebody from your company?"

"No. It'll be a computer expert named Ingrid Caroline Eccols—everybody calls her ICE, for her initials," Lucas said. "She's an independent contractor, and she knows this kind of thing, inside and out."

"A hacker?"

"Not exactly," Lucas said. "She does a little bit of everything. She's worked for law enforcement agencies, from time to time, and the St. Paul crime lab folks know her. I think she may have worked on the other side, too. I do trust her, when she says she'll take a job. The key thing is, when it comes to copying the drive, she won't miss anything. There won't be any games. She'll get everything there is to get."

"John Shelton is my attorney," Smalls said. "I'll get him going. You get this ICE."

"Another thing: I need a list of everybody who works for and around the committee. Send it to my personal e-mail." Lucas took out a business card and a pen, wrote his e-mail address on the back of it, and handed it to Smalls.

"I'll do it this afternoon," Smalls said.

"Do it right away," Lucas said. "I need all the help I can get from you, or I'll spend a lot of time sitting on my ass."

"Let me tell you another little political thing," Smalls said. "The Democrats have me right where they want me. My opponent is young, good-looking, about a hundred times richer than I am, and is running a good campaign. Her problem was, I was going to beat her by six points, 53 to 47 or thereabouts, before the child porn thing happened. She might have cut a point off that. Now, she's going to take me down, probably 52 or 53 to 48 or 47. My core constituency will sit on its hands if they think I'm guilty of this child porn thing. I'm already hearing that."

"I knew some of that," Lucas said.

"But here's the thing," Smalls said, leaning toward Lucas: "The Democrats don't need to get me indicted, or to be guilty. They just need the accusation out there, with the attorney general running around, looking under rocks. If I'm innocent, they'll be perfectly happy to apologize for all of this, about an hour after I lose the election. 'That really wasn't right about old Porter Smalls. . . .' So to do me any good, you pretty much have to find out what happened. Not just that I'm probably innocent. 'Probably' won't cut it. We need to hang somebody, and in the next five days or so."

Lucas didn't say that his mission wasn't to save Smalls's career; he just said, "Okay."

"Damn. I'll tell you what, Davenport, you may have done the worst possible thing here," Smalls said.

"Hmm?"

"Elmer says you're really, really good. You've given me a little hope. Now I've got further to fall."

ALTHOUGH IT WAS SUNDAY, Lucas decided to stop back at the BCA headquarters, on his way home. He walked through the mostly empty building up to his office, where he found an e-mail from Smalls, saying that he'd talked to his attorney, who would go after the hard drive that afternoon. He asked Lucas to put ICE in touch with the attorney. Lucas called ICE, who said she'd take the job, "though I don't like working for a wing-nut."

"You're not working for a wing-nut," Lucas said. "You're working for democracy in America."

"For two hundred dollars an hour. Let's not forget that."

LUCAS SPENT AN HOUR at BCA headquarters, looking at e-mailed reports on investigations that his people were running, but nothing was pressing. Del, Shrake, and Jenkins were trying to find a designer drug lab believed to be in the Anoka area, and Virgil Flowers was seeking the Ape-Man Rapist of Rochester. Lucas wrote notes to them all that he'd be working an individual op for a couple of weeks, but he'd be in touch daily.

While he was doing that, an e-mail came in from Smalls, saying that he wouldn't have the list of campaign employees and volunteers until late in the day. Lucas then tried to call the young woman who'd discovered the porn, and was told by her mother that she was at a friend's house at Cross Lake, and wouldn't be back before midnight. Lucas arranged to meet her the next morning at her home in Edina.

That done, he made a call to the St. Paul cops, got shifted around to the home phone of a cop named Larry Whidden, of the narcotics and vice unit. Whidden was out in his backyard, scraping down the barbecue as an end-of-season chore. Lucas asked to see his investigative reports, and Whidden said, "As far as I'm concerned, you can look at everything we got, if the chief says okay. It's pretty political, so I want to keep all the authorizations very clear."

Lucas called the chief, who wanted to know why Lucas was interested. "Rose Marie asked me to take a look," Lucas said. "To monitor it, more or less. No big deal, but she wants to stay informed."

"Politics," the chief said.

"Tell you what, Rick," Lucas said, "how did you get appointed?"

"What's that supposed to mean?"

"Politics," Lucas said. "It is what it is."

"Funny. Okay. But I'll tell you what, this whole thing ranks really high on my badshitometer. If Smalls is guilty, he could still do a lot of damage thrashing around. If he's innocent, he's gonna be looking for revenge, and he's in exactly the right spot to get it."

"All the more reason for somebody like yourself to spread the responsibility around," Lucas said.

"I'd already thought of that," the chief said. "I'll call Whidden."

Whidden called Lucas five minutes later and said, "I can go in later and Xerox the book for you, but you're gonna have to wait awhile. I got my in-laws coming over. Why don't you come by at six? You want to look at the porn, I can have Jim Reynolds come in."

SO LUCAS HAD RUN out of stuff to do. He tried to think about it for a while, but didn't have enough material to think about. He called home, and nobody answered—they were still out shopping for superhero costumes for Sam. He left a message that he'd prob-ably be home at seven o'clock. That done, he went out to a divorced guys' matinee, to catch the Three Stooges movie he'd missed when it came by in the spring. The divorced guys were scattered around the theater as always, single guys with popcorn, carefully spaced apart from each other, emitting clouds of depression like smoke from eighties' Volkswagen diesel.

Despite that, Lucas laughed at the movie from the moment a nun got poked in the eyes and fell on her ass; took him back to his childhood, with the ancient movies on the obscure TV channels. And Jesus, nuns getting poked in the eye? You'd have to have a heart of pure ice not to laugh at that.

HE WAS OUT OF the movie at five-thirty, called ahead to St. Paul, and at five-forty-five, he parked at the St. Paul Police Department, in the guest lot. He walked inside, had a friendly chat with the po-licewoman in the glass cage, and was buzzed through to the back, where he found Whidden leaning against the wall, sucking on a Tootsie Pop.

Whidden said, "This way," and led him down to Vice, where he took a fat file off an unoccupied desk and said, "Copy of what we got. Want to look at the porn?"

"Maybe take a peek," Lucas said.

He followed Whidden down to the lab, where Jim Reynolds, a very thin man in a cowboy shirt, was looking at a spreadsheet. He saw Lucas and Whidden, stood up and said, "Over here," and to Lucas, "Thanks for the overtime."

"No problem. Christmas is coming."

Reynolds took them to a gray Dell desktop computer. "Smalls is getting a court order for a copy of the hard drive," he told them. "It'll be here first thing tomorrow."

"He's denying any knowledge," Lucas said. "What do you think?"

"I've usually got an opinion," Reynolds said. "But this thing is a little funky. I don't know."

"Funky, how?"

"The circumstances of the discovery," Reynolds said. "When you get into it, you'll see."

Whidden said, "I'm sixty-five percent that he's guilty. But, if I was on the jury . . . I don't think I'd convict him."

Reynolds brought up the porn file: the usual stuff, for kiddie porn: young boys and girls having sex with each other, young boys and girls with adults. Nothing new there, as kiddie porn went.

Lucas asked, "How much is there?"

"Several hundred individual images and thirty-eight video clips," Reynolds said. "Some European—we've seen them before—and some, we don't know where it comes from. We haven't looked at it all, but what we've seen, it's pretty bad stuff."

"What about this volunteer, the whole thing about throwing some papers on the keyboard?" Lucas asked.

"We've tested that, and that's the way it works," Reynolds said. "You're looking at the porn, you walk away. In two minutes, the screen blanks. Touch a key, and it comes back up with whatever was on the screen. In this case, the porn file."

THERE WASN'T MUCH TO talk about, so Lucas thanked Whidden for the file, and Reynolds for the demonstration, and drove home. He arrived twenty minutes before dinner would be ready, and when Weather asked him if there was anything new, he said, "Yeah. I've been asked to prove that Porter Smalls is innocent."

"Shut up," she said.

PORTER SMALLS'S LIST OF campaign staff members came in, more than forty of them, both paid and volunteer. After dinner, Lucas spent a while digging around on the Internet, looking for background on them. He found a few things on Facebook, but quickly realized that nobody was going to post "Guess who I framed?"

He'd just given up when ICE called. "I talked to your wing-nut's lawyer, and he says we'll get a copy of the hard drive tomorrow, around ten-thirty, eleven o'clock," she said.

"I was told you'd get it first thing," Lucas said.

"Well, I was told that the attorney general's office wants a representative there, and they're bringing along their own computer guy. They couldn't get him there any sooner."

"I need to talk to you as soon as you've got it, but don't tell anybody you're bringing it to me. Let them think it's for Smalls's attorney and nobody else," Lucas said. "Could you bring the stuff here, to my place?"

"I'll have to see what the attorney says, but I don't see why not."

"Call me, then," Lucas said. "One other thing: I'm researching a bunch of people, I really need to get background on them. But all I get from Google is a lot of shit."

"You know that old thing about 'Garbage in, garbage out'?" ICE asked.

"Yeah?"

"Google is now the biggest pile of garbage ever assembled on earth," ICE said. "Give it a couple more years, and you won't be able to find anything in it. But, hate to tell you, I don't do databases. I do coding and decoding and some hardware. But I don't do messaging or databases. I don't even Tweet."

"You got anybody who's good at databases?" Lucas asked. "I really need to get some research done."

"Yeah. I do know someone. So do you. He probably knows more about databases than anybody in the world. Literally."

"Who's that?" Lucas asked.

"Kidd."

"What kid?"

"Kidd the artist," ICE said.

"Kidd? The artist?" Lucas knew Kidd fairly well, and knew he did something with computers, in addition to his painting. They'd been jocks at the University of Minnesota around the same time, Lucas in hockey and Kidd as a wrestler. Weather owned one of Kidd's riverscapes, and had paid dearly for it—a price Lucas would have considered ridiculous, except that Weather had been offered three times what she'd paid, and had been told by an art dealer that the offer wasn't nearly good enough.

ICE said, "Yeah. Believe me, he does databases."

"He's really good?"

"Lucas, the guy's a legend," ICE said. "He not only does databases, he does everything. There's a story—it might not be true—that Steve Jobs was afraid that Microsoft's new operating system would crush the life out of Apple. This was back in the late nineties, or maybe 2000. So Jobs asked Kidd to help out, and Kidd supposedly said he'd see what he could do. The next Microsoft release . . . well, you've heard of Windows ME?"

"Sort of."

"It did more damage to Windows' reputation among consumers than anything before or since," ICE said. "It sucked. It worse than sucked. Supposedly, Kidd had a finger deep in its suckedness." She hesitated, then said, "Of course, that might all be a fairy tale."

Lucas said, "Well, I guess I'll give him a call."

"Say hello for me," ICE said. "Tell him if he ever ditches his wife, I'm around."

"That way, huh?"

"He is *so* hot . . . don't even get me started."

HOT? KIDD?

Lucas had never thought of Kidd as hot, or even particularly good-looking. He certainly didn't know anything about fashion— Lucas had never seen him in anything but jeans and tennis shoes and T-shirts or sweatshirts, sometimes with the sleeves cut off. Weather gave money to the Minneapolis Institute of Art, quite a lot of money, and they'd once gone to a function that specified business casual dress, and Kidd was there . . . in jeans, running shoes, and a sweatshirt, but with the sleeves intact. He said it was casual, for his business.

Still, in regard to his hotness . . . Weather seemed to enjoy Kidd's company. A lot. Sort of like she enjoyed the company of Virgil Flowers, another predator, in Lucas's opinion. And Kidd had a wife who was herself so hot, in Lucas's view, that she was either far too good for the likes of Kidd, or . . .

Kidd had something that Lucas didn't recognize. Not that there was anything wrong with that, Lucas thought.

LUCAS DUG KIDD'S PHONE number out of his desk and called him. Kidd picked up: "Hey, Davenport," he said. "Wasn't there, didn't do it."

"How's Lauren?" Lucas asked.

"Who wants to know? And why?"

"Just making small talk," Lucas said. "I need to talk to you . . . about computers. A friend told me that you understand databases."

"What friend?"

"Ingrid Caroline Eccols." There followed a silence so long that Lucas finally asked, "You still there?"

"Thinking about ICE," Kidd said. "So, what's the situation?"

"I'd rather explain it in person," Lucas said. "But time is short. Would you be around tomorrow, early afternoon?"

"Yeah, but ICE isn't invited."

"She's a problem?"

"I couldn't even begin to explain the many ways in which she could be a problem," Kidd said.

"Okay. She's not invited," Lucas said.

"Can Lauren sit in?"

Lucas hesitated, then said, "It's a very confidential matter."

"She's a very confidential woman," Kidd said. "And if it's that confidential, I'd rather she hear about it. You know, in case I need a witness at some later date."

"Then fine, she's invited, if she wants to be there."

"Oh, she'll be there," Kidd said. "She thinks you're totally hot."

TOTALLY HOT.

Everybody was hot, everybody was rich. Better than chasing chicken thieves in Black Duck, Lucas thought, as he settled at his desk with the file from Whidden.

The file looked pretty good, until he opened it. Once opened, half of it turned out to be printouts of 911 conversations, repetitive reports on the seizing of the computer from the campaign offices, and reports of conversations and interviews with office personnel, most of whom knew nothing whatever, and an interview with Brittany Hunt, the volunteer who found the pictures.

Hunt was twenty and had been working as a volunteer since June, and would return to college—Sarah Lawrence—the following winter, having spent half a year working on the campaign.

She knew only slightly more than the completely ignorant office employees. She'd had a report on the ten-year cost of proposed bridge repairs, for which Smalls had gotten appropriations from the feds. She'd walked into his office a little after ten o'clock in the morning, and since Smalls himself had ordered the report, she'd placed it where he'd be sure to see it, and know that she'd fulfilled his request: she dropped it on his keyboard.

Instantly, she said, a picture flashed up, and she'd reflexively looked at it: at first it seemed like a jumble of dead people, and then she realized that it was a group sex photo, and that two of the people in the photo were children.

She called Dad, and Dad dialed 911. The rest was history. Lucas learned almost nothing from the report that he hadn't gotten from Smalls, except that Sarah Lawrence women freely used sexual references that Lucas heretofore thought confined to pornographic films.

He finished the file, and went into the kitchen in search of orange juice. Weather and Letty were leaning on the kitchen breakfast bar, programming something into Weather's cell phone. Weather looked up and asked, "Well? What was in the file? Did he do it?"

Lucas got a bottle of orange juice from the refrigerator and twisted its cap off. "File was useless. One good thing: I'm not far behind the St. Paul cops."

"I'm shocked that you're behind at all," Weather said.

"Me too," said Letty. "Shame."

"Thank you for your support," Lucas said. "You'll find me in the garage, sharpening my lawn mower blade."

Letty looked at Weather and asked, "Is that a euphemism?"

"I hope not."

Lucas ignored them, finished the orange juice, put the bottle in the recyclables, and went off to the garage.

They could taunt him all they wished; but Kidd's scorchingly good-looking wife, Lauren, thought he was totally hot.

4

Taryn Grant came back from a campaign loop through Rochester, Wabasha, and Red Wing, and found Doug Dannon, her security coordinator, waiting inside the door from the garage. Her two German shepherds, Hansel and Gretel, whimpered with joy when she walked in, and she knelt and gave them a good scratch and got a kiss from each of them, and then Dannon said, "I've got some news. Where's Green?"

Alice Green was a former Secret Service agent. She was not in the loop on the shadow campaign. Taryn said, "Alice is with the car. . . . What happened?"

"The word around the Smalls campaign is that there's a new state investigator looking into the porn scandal," Dannon said. "I don't know if they've taken it away from St. Paul, but Smalls is pretty happy about it. He thinks something's gonna get done. There are rumors that Smalls talked to the governor, but nobody knows what was said."

"The governor? He's supposed to be on our side." Taryn bent sideways and gave Gretel another scratch on the head.

"Don't know—don't know what's happening. Maybe Connie can get something."

Connie Schiffer was Taryn's campaign manager.

"What about the investigator, the new guy?" Taryn asked.

"I've been looking him up on the Internet. He's a killer. His name is Lucas Davenport, he's been around a long time," Dannon said. "Works for the Bureau of Criminal Apprehension. There's a ton of newspaper clips. He's killed a bunch of people in shoot-outs. He seems to be the guy they go to, when they need somebody really smart, or really mean."

"But what could he find out?"

"Worst case, he could find the thread that leads from Tubbs to Smalls," Dannon said. "Everybody's looking for Tubbs, but they don't know about the connection. We can't do anything about it. They'll probably come and talk to you, Taryn. If they think there's something fishy about the porn, this campaign is where they'll look. If they find out that Tubbs is connected, and Tubbs never shows up . . . then they'll be asking about murder."

"But Tubbs will never show up," she said.

"No. No chance of that," Dannon said.

TARYN GRANT, DEMOCRATIC CANDIDATE for the U.S. Senate, suffered from narcissistic personality disorder, or so she'd been told by a psychologist in her third year at the Wharton School. He'd added, "I wouldn't worry too much about it, as long as you don't go into a life of crime. Half the people here are narcissists. The other half are psychopaths. Well, except for Roland Shafer. He's normal enough."

Taryn didn't know Roland Shafer, but all these years later, she sometimes thought about him, and wondered what happened to him, being . . . "normal."

The shrink had explained the disorder to her, in sketchy terms, perhaps trying to be kind. When she left his office, she'd gone straight to the library and looked it up, because she knew in her heart that she was far too perfect to have any kind of disorder.

NARCISSISTIC PERSONALITY DISORDER:
- Has excessive feelings of self-importance.
- Reacts to criticism with rage.
- Takes advantage of other people.
- Disregards the feelings of others.
- Preoccupied with fantasies of success, power, beauty, and intelligence.

EXCESSIVE FEELINGS OF SELF-IMPORTANCE? Did that idiot shrink know she'd inherit the better part of a billion dollars, that she already had enough money to buy an entire *industry*? She *was* important.

Reacts to criticism with rage? Well, what do you do when you're mistreated? Shy away from conflict and go snuffle into a Kleenex? Hell no: you get up in their face, straighten them out.

Takes advantage of other people? You don't get anywhere in this world by being a cupcake, cupcake.

Disregards the feelings of others? Look: half the people in the world were below average, and "average" isn't anything to brag about. We should pay attention to the dumbasses in life?

How about, "Preoccupied with fantasies of success, power,

beauty, and intelligence"? Hey, had he taken a good look at her and her CV? She was in the running for class valedictorian; she looked like Marilyn Monroe, without the black spot on her cheek; and she had, at age twenty-two, thirty million dollars of her own, with twenty or thirty times more than that, yet to come. What fantasies? Welcome to my world, bub.

THAT HAD BEEN more than a decade ago.

Taryn was now thirty-four. She still had those major assets—she was blond, good-looking, with interesting places in all the interesting places. She'd graduated from Wharton in Entrepreneurial Management, and then from the London School of Economics in finance. Until four years earlier, she'd worked in the finance department at Grant Mills, the family's much-diversified agricultural products business, the fifth largest closely held company in the U.S.

She'd spent six years with Grant Mills, six years of snarling combat with a list of parents, uncles, and cousins, about who was going to run what. She might have won that fight, eventually, but she'd opted out. There was a lot of money there, but she couldn't see spending her life with corn, wheat, beans, and rice.

She'd quit to start Digital Pen LLC, which wrote apps for smartphones and tablets. She employed two hundred people in Minneapolis, and another hundred out on the Coast, and had stacked up a few more tens of millions, on top of the three-quarters of a billion in the Grant Mills trust.

But even with Digital Pen, she'd grown bored. She'd turned the company over to a hired CEO, told him not to screw it up, and turned her eyes to politics.

Taryn had watched the incumbent U.S. senator, a Republican

named Porter Smalls, stepping on his political dick for five consecutive years. She thought, *Hmmm*. She had an interest in the Senate, as a stepping-stone, and it was clear from early on that the main Democratic candidates would be the usual bunch of stooges, clowns, buffoons, apparatchiks, and small-town wannabees—and a witch—who couldn't have found Washington, D.C., with a Cadillac's navigation system and a Seeing Eye dog.

Taryn had everything she needed to buy a good, solid Senate seat, and start looking to move up. She'd pounded the field in the Democratic primary, taking fifty-one percent of the vote in a four-way race; the witch had finished third. She'd been a weekly visitor on both local and national talk shows, was good at it, and people started referring to her as a "rising star."

She liked that. A lot. As anyone with narcissistic personality disorder would.

There was one large, juicy fly in the ointment. Three weeks before the election, she was losing. The thing about Smalls was, he was *likable*. Okay, he'd screw anything that moved, and in one case, allegedly, a woman who said she'd been too drunk to move. But then, what did that mean, anymore?

SO TARYN, WORKING ANONYMOUSLY through the shadow campaign, had hired Bob Tubbs to do his thing, to win the election for her. Tubbs didn't know the man who passed him the 100K in twenties and fifties.

But Tubbs was a political, and had been around a long time, and knew how to follow a trail. It took a while, but he eventually followed it back to Dannon and thus to Taryn.

He showed up at her house at midnight.

He wanted more money.

Like this:

DOUG DANNON WAS A sandy-haired man of medium height with a trim, sandy mustache and a wedge-shaped body, marked with a few shrapnel scars from nearby explosions. On the particular night that Tubbs showed up at the door, he was sitting on a twenty-thousand-dollar German woven-leather couch that was soft as merino wool, his feet on a seventy-five-thousand-dollar Persian carpet as delicately brilliant as a French cathedral's stained-glass window. He looked out through the faintly green, curved-glass porch windows at the billion-dollar woman, who looked like a million bucks.

She was topless, and the bottom of her bathing suit was not larger than a child's hand. She'd just pulled herself out of the deep end of the heated pool, after forty laps, and stood shaking off the water. Tall and blond and tanned, she had muscular thighs and small breasts tipped with erect pinkish-brown nipples.

Hansel and Gretel sat on the pool's flagstone deck, watching everything. The dogs made people a little nervous. Agitated, they could tear a rhinoceros apart, and they loved Taryn more than life itself.

Taryn knew Dannon was there behind the glass, watching, and that Ron Carver was someplace in the house, but paid no attention to that set of facts. Carver, who worked security with Dannon, was also part of the shadow campaign. Carver had suggested to Dannon that she could do this—swim topless, and occasionally nude, while they were in the house—because she was an exhibitionist.

Dannon thought that was probably true.

He was wrong.

She did it because, in the larger scheme of things, Dannon and Carver were irrelevant. The fact that they'd seen her nude meant nothing, because they meant nothing. They were tools; it was like being seen by a hammer and chisel.

TARYN HAD BEGUN TOWELING off when Carver came into the living room carrying a glass of bourbon; in fact, a glass of A.H. Hirsch Reserve, Dannon knew, which Carver had been regularly pouring from Taryn Grant's liquor closet. Carver had a deal going with the housekeeper, who would order additional bottles as necessary. Taryn need not know.

Dannon disapproved: but Carver had told him that he needed a bit of booze on a daily basis to keep his head straight and the Reserve was what he'd chosen.

"If she smells that on your breath, when you're working, she could fire you," Dannon said.

"Ah, she's so loaded she couldn't tell that she wasn't smelling her own breath," Carver said. He was a large man, thick through the chest and hips. A small head, with closely cropped brown hair, made his shoulders look especially wide. He had a 9mm Glock tucked into a belt holster in the small of his back, and, because he was slightly psycho, a little .380 auto in an ankle holster.

Dannon was less psycho, and carried only a single gun, a .40-caliber Heckler & Koch, butt-backwards in a cross-draw holster on his left hip. Of course, he also carried a Bratton fighting knife with a seven-inch serrated blade guaranteed to cut through bone, tendon, and ligament, on the theory that you should never bring a fist to a knife fight.

"Look at the ass on that bitch," Carver said, sipping at the Reserve.

"I don't want to hear that," Dannon said.

"'Cause you're totally pussy-whipped," Carver said, watching the billion-dollar woman arching her back, thrusting her breasts toward them, as she pulled the blue-striped pool towel across her back. "Though it is a pretty sweet billet. Kinda boring, though. Other than the fact we get to watch her rubbing her tits."

"Plenty of jobs outta Lagos," Dannon said, watching Taryn through the glass.

"Fuck Lagos. The goddamn Africans got gun guys coming out of their ass. They don't need me around."

"I knew this guy from Angola, black as a lump of coal," Dannon said. "Smart guy. Hired into the Bubble as a security guard. The first day he's there, some asshole raghead points his taxi at the Haleb gate . . ."

More been-there-done-that Baghdad bullshit, but Carver listened closely, because he liked war stories. In this job, so far, there hadn't been much to do but remember the Glory Days and collect the paycheck. Before he'd gotten kicked out of the army, he got to carry the SAW, the squad automatic weapon. It was twenty-two pounds of black death, loaded, and took a horse to carry. He was the horse, and happy about it.

OUT IN THE ENCLOSED pool, Taryn Grant finished drying herself and pulled on a robe. Carver was right: she was drunk, Dannon thought. She'd always taken a drink, and this night, at a campaign stop in a Minneapolis penthouse, she'd taken at least three, and maybe more, and two more back at the house, before she went for her swim; and she'd taken a drink with her, to the pool.

He'd talked to her about it, and she'd told him to shut up. She could handle it, she said. Maybe she could. In Dannon's experience, alcoholism was the easiest of the addictions to control. Look at Carver, for example.

TARYN WAS PICKING UP a pack of magazines when the front gate dinged at them, then a quick, more urgent *buzzzzz*. Somebody had hopped the gate.

Dannon snapped at Carver, "Get the camera. I'm on the door."

He started toward the front door, and as he went, pushed the walkie-talkie function on his phone. Taryn's phone buzzed at her and didn't stop, a deliberately annoying noise, impossible to ignore. She picked it up and asked, "What?"

"Somebody's inside, on the lawn, hopped the gate," Dannon said. He pulled his gun. "Get in here with the dogs and stay on the phone."

"I'm coming," she said. This is why she had security.

Carver was on the same walkie-talkie system, and said, looking at the video displays in the monitoring room, "Okay, one guy, big guy, coming up the walk. He's not lost, he's walking fast. Wearing a suit and tie. Hands are empty."

"I'm inside, locking the doors," Taryn said.

"Guy's at the door," Carver said. "I don't know him."

The doorbell rang and Dannon popped the door, gun in his hand; looked at the man's face and said, "Ah, shit."

"Hello, mystery man."

TARYN HAD BEGUN DOING research for her Senate run two years earlier. She did the research herself—narcissistic personality disorder aside, she was a brilliant researcher, both by training and inclination. Much of the research involved selection of campaign staff, from campaign manager on down. She shared the research with Dannon, whose personal loyalty she trusted, because Dannon was in love with her.

Because of that loyalty, and because of his history as an intelligence officer, she'd had him set up the shadow campaign staff—spies—to keep an eye on her opponent, Smalls. He'd also identified other possible assets: among them, Bob Tubbs.

Tubbs was a longtime Democratic political operative, and had been considered for a staff job with the regular campaign, to be eventually rejected. "He's been involved in some unsavory election stuff, so I want to keep our distance," Taryn told Dannon. "But also, it's good to keep him on the outside, in case we need somebody on the outside . . . somebody who could handle something unsavory."

The regular campaign staff, including the regular campaign manager, had no idea that the shadow staff existed.

When it had appeared that Taryn would lose despite a good, solid campaign, Dannon had met with Tubbs to discuss other possibilities. He hadn't identified himself, except as "Mr. Smith . . . or Jones, take your pick."

Tubbs probably wouldn't have talked to him, if it hadn't been for the 25K in the paper bag, and the promise of another twenty-five thousand dollars if Tubbs found a solution to the problem.

Tubbs hadn't even needed time to think about it. "Porter Smalls has a history of sexual entanglements," he'd told Dannon at that first meeting. Then he'd told him how that might be exploited. And that he'd need a hundred thousand dollars to pull it off. "It's danger-ous. People have to be paid," Tubbs had said.

They met twice more: Dannon had demanded details, and

names. At the last meeting, he'd handed over the other seventy-five thousand.

"Time is getting short," he'd told Tubbs. "By the way—we expect results. We are not people to be fucked with."

"You'll get them," Tubbs had said. "We're already rolling."

TUBBS WAS A POLITICAL.

And this one time, a blackmailer.

As he walked toward Taryn Grant's door, a rippling chill crawled up Tubbs's back. He was about to commit a felony, blackmail, *real blackmail*, not for the first time in his life, but never before like this: the payout would be life-changing. A man had to take care of his own retirement funding, these days. Not that another felony would be a problem, if he got caught. He was already in it, up to his ears.

He reached out and rang Taryn Grant's doorbell. He knew she was home, because he knew her schedule.

The door popped open, and,

Surprise!

"Ah, shit," said the man inside.

"Hello, mystery man," Tubbs said.

TARYN GRANT WAS THERE with her two security men, in a robe, her hair still damp from the swim.

Tubbs said, "Look, I'll tell you right up front. You saw what happened this morning. And I realized, my political life could be over. They could figure this out. I'm willing to go down for it and to keep my mouth shut, but I need a little more cash. I need to fund my retirement."

Taryn asked, through gritted teeth, "How much?"

"You've got more money than Jesus Christ," Tubbs said. "I'd like . . . a million. That's what I want. I swear to you, if there's a fall coming, I'll take it. And I'll never come back for another nickel."

"Fuck you," Taryn said. The snap in her voice caught the attention of the dogs, whose ears came forward, their noses pointed at Tubbs.

"Miz Grant—" Tubbs began.

Dannon cut him off, and said to Taryn, "Let's take this out to the pool."

"What are we talking about here?" Tubbs asked, looking from one of them to the other.

"We're talking cameras," Dannon said to him. "There aren't any cameras around the pool."

Tubbs nodded, and they trooped through the house, into the pool enclosure, Hansel leading, Gretel following. The pool had a wide deck with grow lights around the edges, shining sixteen hours a day on orchids, bromeliads, and palms; a tropical jungle in Minnesota. Tubbs looked around and said, "Nice."

Taryn didn't want to hear *nice*. She said, "You motherfucker. You've been well paid."

Tubbs said, "Not well paid for what's happening. There'll be cops all over the place. I've got another person I've got to pay off, and this is like . . . this is a political Armageddon."

Taryn had left an unfinished drink next to the pool, a screwdriver, half vodka and half orange juice, and she picked it up and threw back the rest of it, then said, "You don't know what you're messing with. You don't do this: you get bought and you stay bought."

"I just put you. in the U.S. Senate, and I know you're already thinking about moving up from that, *and I did it,*" Tubbs said, his voice climbing into the alto range. "You're losing. You'd be a loser if it weren't for me. You'd just be—"

"Shut up," Taryn shouted.

Dannon realized that she was drunker than he thought. He wrapped an arm around her and said, "Come talk to me for a minute."

She didn't want to go. She wanted to stay in Tubbs's face. But Dannon pulled her along, and halfway down the pool said to her quietly, "If you give it to him, he'll be back for more."

"So . . . what?"

"So, slow him down," Dannon said, leaning close to her, close enough to smell the chlorine. "Tell him you'll work something out. We need to get him out of the house so we can talk, come up with an action plan."

"He's not going away, he's never going away," she said. "God-damnit, how'd he track us down?"

"Well, there was really only one place that money could have come from, ultimately. Maybe he saw me in the background on one of the TV shots, or at a rally," Dannon said, glancing back at Tubbs. "Doesn't make any difference: he knows."

"I'm going to tell him to fuck himself," Taryn said.

Dannon hooked her arm as she started away. "Don't do that. Just delay, buy some time. Buy some time . . ."

Taryn pulled free, strode back down the pool, reaching for control.

As she came up, Tubbs said, "Don't try to screw me over. Don't try. Just give me the money, and it's done with. Don't drag your feet. You guys scare me a little, so I'm going to hide out somewhere, until the election's over. My offer here has a time limit: I want a million in a week, or I'm going to have to make an offer to the Smalls campaign."

"I need more than a week, it takes a while to round up that much cash," Taryn said, and despised herself for the begging tone in her voice.

"But that's what you've got," Tubbs said. "A week. I don't care how you get it. I'm sure you could fix something up in Vegas, through one of the casinos. Just get the fuckin' money, girlie, and get it to me."

It was the *girlie* that did it.

She turned to Dannon, now with an icy grip on herself, and said, "We'll get the money somehow. Get him out of here."

THEY GOT HIM OUT of there, with the promise of the money inside a week. When he was gone, Taryn had turned to the two security men and said, "This won't work."

Carver drawled, "No shit, Ms. Grant. He'll be back in your face like a rat. Even if you lose, he'll be back. If you win, it'll be five million, ten million, he'll be coming back forever. There's not enough money to fill that black hole."

Dannon said, "But if he talks . . . if he tries to turn us in, he'll implicate himself. He'll be right there in prison with us."

Taryn shook her head. "No. I'll tell you how this would go down. We refuse to pay, he goes to Smalls and says, 'I can get you your Senate seat back. I want a million dollars and immunity, or I never say a thing.' So Smalls takes it: he's got the cash, he could fix things with the prosecutors. Tubbs gets the money up front, then he confesses, points the finger, cries for the TV cameras. He does the right thing, says his conscience couldn't handle it. And we're done. The prosecutors won't care about Tubbs—he's small change. We're the ones they'd come for."

They all chewed on that for a while, then Dannon looked at Carver and said, "What do you think?"

Carver said, "You *know* what I think, Doug. He isn't going away, so I think we make him go away. If we're careful, we can pull it off—but I'd like a little appreciation for doing it."

Taryn looked at him: "How much appreciation?"

Carver shrugged and said, "Whatever you think."

She touched her lip, half turned away, considering: even rich people hate to give away money. Then she turned back and said, "A hundred thousand each. All cash. As soon as it's done."

Carver said, "Hooah!"

Dannon was less enthusiastic: "We'll need to do some recon. We'll need to fix it so that we've got alibis."

"You know about those things," Taryn said. "I'm out of it. If you get caught, I'll say I had no idea."

The two men nodded. Dannon said, "If we get caught, there's no reason to drag you into it. You could help us more from the outside, than if you were inside with us."

"I hope that's clear," she said, looking at Carver.

He said, "Clear."

"Then kill him," she said.

DANNON AND CARVER HAD buried Tubbs north of the Cities, in a marsh along the Mississippi. Taryn had helped: they'd put Tubbs's body in the back of Carver's SUV, and drove to the town house complex where both men were living. They parked in back, and Carver called Dannon, and then Dannon called Taryn, and a few minutes later, Taryn called Dannon back. They then went on to bury the body, while Taryn drove to their apartments and sent e-mails to herself and to a friend of Carver's, from their laptops in their respective apartments. All of that could be time-checked, if it ever came to that.

Then . . . nothing much had happened until the St. Paul papers reported that the police were looking for Tubbs, and feared foul play. And now the report that a new investigator was on the job.

When Dannon broke that news—that the new guy, Davenport, was a killer—she said, "Ah, God," and "Let's talk later. I need to go for a swim, and Alice'll be here in a minute. Let's talk tonight."

"I'm not sure we should talk later," Dannon said. "I think we ought to *stop* talking about it and focus on our ignorance. We don't know what happened with the porn, we don't know what happened with Tubbs, we don't know anything. If you can convince yourself of that, that you don't know anything . . . it'll be much easier to sell it to the cops."

"Focus on our ignorance." She didn't quite grasp the concept. She'd never been ignorant.

"Yeah. Just rewind back before we talked to Tubbs and think what your head was like," Dannon said. "Then think about the newspaper stories and think about your reaction to them. What you would have thought about them, if you didn't know what really happened. Then, when the cops come, if they come, you're confused about it all. A little scared. You ask questions, you suggest answers, you're all over the place. But basically, ignorant. Just delete Tubbs from your mind. You don't know him. You never knew him."

"I'll have to think about it, but I can do that," Taryn said.

"Of course you can," Dannon said. "But don't think about ways to trick them or outsmart them. Just focus on your ignorance. You don't *know* anything, but you're willing to speculate, and you'd like some information from them—to hear what they think."

"What about you and Carver?"

"We can handle it," Dannon said. "We've spent half our lives lying to cops, of one kind or another. Nobody else on the staff knows. Might not be a bad idea for us to stay away completely . . . unless they ask for us."

"Let's do that," Taryn said. "Maybe you two could start doing some advance security work."

"I'll talk to Ron," Dannon said. He heard high heels, and said, "Here comes Alice."

TWENTY MINUTES LATER, TARYN was sitting on the edge of the pool, wearing a conservative one-piece bathing suit. Alice Green, a lithe, handsome woman in her late thirties, relaxed in a chaise, reading the *Star Tribune*, while the dogs sat at her feet. The dogs were the world's most efficient burglar alarm. If anyone tried to enter the pool area, the dogs would be looking at them. If Taryn told them to attack, they'd tear that person apart, no questions asked.

Taryn slipped into the water, shivered, and started swimming laps. The exercise blanked her mind for the first two hundred yards, but after she got into the rhythm of it, she began reliving Tubbs's visit, and what happened next: not to obsess about it, but to cultivate her ignorance, as Dannon called it.

The two men had been gone for four hours, altogether, and when they'd come back, muddy and tired, they told a sleepless Taryn that they'd gone way up the Mississippi toward St. Cloud, found a fisherman's track that led to the river, and carried the body well off the track and buried it deep.

"Just about killed ourselves out there in the dark," Carver said. "He's gone. Put a few concrete blocks on top of him, just in case."

"In case of *what*?" Taryn asked, fascinated in spite of herself.

"Well . . . body gases," Carver said. "The ground was a little wet, you wouldn't want him popping up."

A few miles back toward the Twin Cities, they'd detoured down a side road, and threw Carver's carefully cleaned baseball bat into the roadside ditch. "Couldn't find it again ourselves, even if we had to," Dannon said, as they drove away in the dark.

TARYN KEPT SWIMMING, TWENTY laps, thirty, touching the lap counter at the west end of the pool after every second turn.

She had to think seriously about Carver and Dannon. Dannon was well under control—he'd been her security man for four years, and for all four years had hungered for her. Not just for sex. He was in love with her. That was useful. Carver was cruder. He didn't want her total being, he just wanted to fuck her. If she wasn't available, somebody else would do. So her grip on him was more precarious.

And the problem with Carver was, he was more of an adventurer than Dannon.

Dannon was happy to handle her security, and was good at it. He read about it, he knew about alarms and randomizing patrols and evasive driving, and all the rest. He took courses. She'd had a lover, a semi-dumb guy as anxious to get into her money as into her pants, and when she was done with him, he wouldn't go away.

Dannon had talked to him, and the guy had moved to Des Moines. No muss, no fuss.

On the night Tubbs was killed, Taryn had given each of the men a hundred thousand dollars in cash and gold, as a "thank you."

Dannon had carefully stashed his in a safe-deposit box. Carver, on the other hand, had asked for a day off. "The money just burns a hole in my pocket," he confessed. "I'd like to hop a plane for Vegas, if you don't mind."

That had been a Friday night. He'd left Saturday morning and had gotten back Sunday night, most of the money gone. Dannon said later he'd blown it on hookers, cocaine, and craps and felt that he'd gotten his money's worth.

So Carver sought risk, while Dannon tried to minimize risk. That made Carver a loose cannon, and given her involvement, she didn't need any cannons to be loose.

She thought for a few minutes about what would happen if, for example, Carver tried to squeeze her for money, as Tubbs had. He might suspect that Dannon would come after him, because Dannon was in love with her. But would that frighten him? Could Dannon take him? And if it got all bloody, and somebody tried to make a deal with the police, to trade her in . . . what would happen?

She had to think about it. Was Dannon loyal enough to take out Carver if she asked him to? Was Carver smart enough to set up a booby trap that would snap on them, if they took him out? Might he already have done so?

But thinking about it was hard. Ever since Tubbs had gone away, she'd had trouble tracking. But she had to track.

Because now, she was winning the election, up three points and climbing.

SHE HIT THE COUNTER at the end of the pool, and a big red LED "40" popped up. Forty laps, a thousand yards, a little more than half a mile.

She climbed out of the pool, and Alice, who'd been watching the counter, was waiting with a towel.

"You'd have been a good agent," Alice said. "Smart, terrific condition."

"Thank you," Taryn said. "I'm not sure I could handle the guns. I don't like guns."

"We had a saying in the service," Alice said. "Guns don't kill people, people kill people. Guns just make it really, really easy."

"Too easy, if you ask me," Taryn said. "When I get to the Senate, I'll try to do something about that. I always feel bad when I read about people being killed. It's usually so senseless. You know, 'The bell tolls for thee,' or whatever."

5

When Lucas woke Monday morning, the first thing he did was check the window: blue sky. Excellent. Another good day. People had been talking about bad weather coming in, but he didn't know when it was supposed to arrive.

And, thank God, they were through the weekend. Working on a Sunday was a pain in the ass, with everybody gone. Today, there'd be a lot going on: no more matinee movies.

He'd start with the volunteer who found the porn, he thought as he got dressed. He picked out a medium-blue wool suit that he'd thought would look awful at the time the salesman suggested it, but that had become one of his cool-weather favorites. He tried several ties, finally choosing a red-and-blue check with a turquoise thread in it, which went nicely with his eyes. Black lace-up shoes from Cleverley of London, for which he'd been measured during a European trip two years earlier, finished the ensemble.

The volunteer's family, the Hunts, lived in Edina, an affluent Minneapolis suburb. Lucas took the Porsche, because it would feel at home there. He took ten minutes driving across town, and after a few minutes of confusion caused by the Porsche's outdated navigation system, found the Hunts' home: another sprawling brick ranch, at the end of a woody cul-de-sac.

BRITTANY HUNT MET LUCAS at the door, her mother a step behind. Lucas was amazed: they looked almost exactly alike, and that was like Doris Day in 1960. Lucas hadn't yet been born in 1960 to get the full Doris Day effect, but he'd seen her often enough on late-night television. . . .

"I'm Brittany," Brittany said, offering her hand in a firm shake. "I'm the one who outed him."

"I'm her mother, Tammy," her mother said. "Friends call me Tam." She had perfect white teeth and sparkled at Lucas, and she smelled of Chanel on a Monday morning at home.

They led the way inside and a sliding door banged shut in the back. A man in an open-necked white shirt and khakis padded through the living room and thrust out his hand and said, "Jeff Hunt."

They wound up seated on a semicircular couch in a conversation pit in front of a flagstone fireplace. Lucas said, "So tell me what happened."

Brittany told him, and it was exactly what she'd told the St. Paul cops. When she finished—she'd stood by the computer until the cops got there—Lucas turned to Jeff and said, "You called the cops right away?"

"Instantly," he said. "First of all, you can't let people get away with this kind of stuff. Second of all, I was worried about Brit. What if he'd come back and found her standing there, with that stuff on the screen? I mean, this is the end of everything for him. What if he'd gotten violent?"

"I don't understand why they haven't arrested him yet," Tam said. "He's such a monster. I mean, children."

"There are some questions," Lucas said. "But unless something changes, it looks like the Hennepin County attorney is planning to take it to the grand jury next week, unless the attorney general takes it away."

"The AG is gonna run for governor, and he'd love to bag Smalls, so I bet he takes it," Jeff said. Jeff was yet another attorney. "If he does, it'll go to a grand jury for sure. If he loses the case, he can blame the grand jury for the indictment. If he wins, who cares about the grand jury?"

Lucas said, "Well . . ."

THEN BRITTANY CHANGED EVERYTHING.

"What a weird summer," she said. "Child porn on Porter's computer and then Bob Tubbs vanishes."

Lucas looked at her for a moment, then said, "Bob Tubbs? What did Bob Tubbs have to do with this?"

"Well, nothing," she said. "But, you know, he was around. You ever met him? Big tall blond guy? He used to call me *chica*, like the Mexicans do."

"He worked for Smalls?" Lucas asked.

She shook her head. "I don't know the details, exactly, but he was a lobbyist for the Minnesota Apiary Association."

"You mean, archery?" Jeff asked.

"No, *apiary*, Daddy. You know, honey bees. There was some kind of licensing thing going on," Brittany said. "The state was going to put on a fee, and some of the bee guys said they wouldn't bring their hives into Minnesota if that happened, and Tubbs thought that the bees were interstate commerce and so only the feds were allowed to regulate it. Or something like that. I don't know. I wasn't interested enough to follow it. But Bob was around."

"What about Bob?" Tam asked Lucas.

Lucas said, "He's one of our local political operators. He disappeared . . . what, it must have been Friday night?"

"Same day the porn file popped up," Jeff said.

"I'm not sure that's right, though," Lucas said. "I just heard about it from a St. Paul cop. Tubbs's mother claims he's been kidnapped. A couple people have said he might be on a bender somewhere. He did that once before—vanished, and turned up a week later in Cancún, dead drunk in a hotel room. But, I guess he hasn't been using his credit cards, doesn't answer his cell phone, his passport was in his desk, and his car is sitting in his parking garage."

"Boy, that doesn't sound good," Jeff said.

Lucas looked at Brittany. "How'd you even know about him?"

"It was in the paper," she said. "This morning. People are looking all over for him."

Tam's hand went to her throat: "You think . . . dead?"

"Don't know," Lucas said. "My agency isn't involved. It's just, you know, what I hear."

WHEN LUCAS LEFT, ten minutes later, Brit, Tam, and Jeff came out on the porch to wave good-bye. He waved, and sped back to St. Paul.

As Lucas was on the way to his office, ICE called and told him that she had the copy of Smalls's hard drive. "Got everything, gonna take you six months to read it. There's about a million e-mails. And old albums. He's got every Bowie album ever made."

"Let's try not to judge," Lucas said. "Anyway, I'm not going home, I'm coming there. Wait for me."

When Lucas got to the St. Paul police parking lot, he found her waiting in a black six-series BMW convertible. She handed Lucas a hard drive about the size of a paperback and said, "Who do I bill?"

"Send it to me personally," Lucas said. "I'll get it back later. Anything happen out of the ordinary?"

"Purely routine," she said. "Tell Kidd that it was Windows 7 . . . not that he won't know."

She didn't ask if she could come along, to visit with Kidd.

WHEN SHE WAS GONE, Lucas went inside, badged his way back to the homicide unit, and found Roger Morris peering at a brown paper bag with a small grease stain at one end.

"Is that a clue?" Lucas asked.

"It's my lunch," Morris said. "I'm thinking about eating it early."

"Why?"

"Because I'm starving to death, that's why," Morris said. "My wife's got me on a food-free diet."

"You *are* looking pretty trim," Lucas lied, since he needed a favor.

"Bullshit. I only started yesterday," Morris said. Then his brow beetled, and he said, "Say, you don't work here."

"I need to see the Tubbs file."

"Ah, man," Morris said. "Of the twelve million things I didn't need to hear this morning, that is number one. Davenport wants to see the Tubbs file."

"You're working it?"

"Nothing to work."

"So let me see the file," Lucas said. "I may have some suggestions."

"That's my greatest fear," Morris said. "After the contents of my lunch bag, of course."

LUCAS PAGED THROUGH the thin file, sitting at Morris's desk, peering at his computer. Tubbs hadn't been seen after Friday evening. Tubbs's mother had called St. Paul on Saturday afternoon to report him missing. Not much had been done—a couple cops went around and knocked on his apartment door, and asked a few questions of his neighbors, who hadn't seen him. His mother had shifted into high hysteria on Sunday, complaining to St. Paul that her son must have been kidnapped.

According to Mrs. Tubbs, Tubbs was supposed to pick her up and go shopping on Saturday, but hadn't shown, and hadn't called to say he wouldn't make it. Mom said he'd never done that in his life. On Sunday, he was supposed to take her to Mass, but hadn't shown up then, either. She couldn't get him at home or on either of his two cell phones, and she'd been trying since Saturday morning.

The cops checked with AT&T and found that he hadn't used either his home or his cell phones, nor had he used his credit cards, which was when they began to take the old woman's complaints seriously: Tubbs had never, in a credit card record going back ten years, gone two days without using one. He paid for everything with a card, his mother said. He hardly used cash at all, because you couldn't deduct invisible business expenses, and almost all of Tubbs's expenses were business.

On Sunday afternoon, Tubbs's mother let the cops into his apartment for a look around. One of the cops said that it was apparent that he'd recently been sexually involved, as there were stains on the bedsheets. Samples had been taken. There was no sign of forced entry, or violence.

On Monday morning, there were a couple of stories in the local newspapers, based on calls by Tubbs's mother. The stories hadn't shaken him loose, nor had he begun to use his credit cards.

"You think he's dead?" Lucas asked Morris.

"That's what I think," Morris said.

"What about his apartment?"

"What about it?"

"Close it out yet?" Lucas asked.

"Not yet," Morris said. "You want to look around?"

"Yes."

"You'd have to get an okay from Tubbs's mother, but you'll get it. She's frantic," Morris said. "Why are you interested?"

"If I told you, you'd have to change your name and move to New Zealand," Lucas said.

"Seriously . . ."

"I'm a little serious," Lucas said. "I'm doing a political thing and you really don't want to know about it. And it probably has nothing to do with Tubbs. If it does, I'll tell you, first thing."

"First thing?"

"Absolutely," Lucas said.

Morris reached out and touched his lunch sack, and said, "She made me a BLT. With motherfuckin' soy bacon."

"Jesus, that's not good," Lucas said. "Motherfuckin' soy bacon?"

"That's the way us black people talk," Morris said.

"What about Tubbs's apartment?" Lucas asked.

"I've got a key," Morris said. "Let's call the old lady. If you find anything . . ."

"First thing," Lucas said.

Morris called Tubbs's mother, explained that a high-ranking agent from the state Bureau of Criminal Apprehension would like to check out the apartment, and was immediately given an okay. Morris gave him the key, said, "Use it wisely," and agreed to send an electronic copy of the Tubbs file to the BCA, where Lucas could look at it.

Lucas thanked him, and headed across town to the river, not to Tubbs's apartment but to Kidd's.

KIDD OWNED HALF A FLOOR in a redbrick restoration condo overlooking the Mississippi. Lucas had visited him a few times, and had watched the condo grow. Kidd had started with a single large unit, added a second one a few years later, and finally, during the great real estate crash, picked up a third unit for nearly nothing. He also owned a piece of the underground parking garage, where he kept a couple of cars and a boat.

Lucas rode up to Kidd's floor in a freight elevator that smelled of oranges and bananas and paint and maybe oil, walked down the hall and knocked on Kidd's hand-carved walnut door, which Kidd said he'd copied from some Gauguin carvings. Lucas wouldn't have known a Gauguin carving if one had bit him on the ass, so when told about it, he'd just said, "Hey, that's great," and felt like an idiot.

LAUREN OPENED THE DOOR, a slender woman, not tall, with red hair and high cheekbones and a big smile: "Lucas, damnit, you need to come around more often. Why don't you jack up Weather and let's go to dinner? I need to get out. So does she."

She pecked him on the cheek and then Kidd came up, chewing on a hot dog bun with no dog. He was wearing jeans and a paint-flecked military-gray T-shirt stretched tight across his shoulders. And gold-rimmed glasses.

"New glasses," Lucas said.

"Yeah. When I'm working, I walk away from the painting, then I walk right up close, and then I walk away again," Kidd said. "You know, figuring it out. I began to realize I wasn't seeing the close-up stuff so well."

"Getting old," Lucas said.

"I'm a year older than you," Kidd said. "I just turned fifty."

"Yeah . . . I'm not looking forward to it."

Kidd shrugged. "Forty-five was a little tough. Fifty, I didn't notice."

"Didn't even remember," Lauren said, nudging Kidd with her elbow. "Jackson and I popped a surprise party on him, and he didn't even know what it was for, at first."

Jackson was their son, who was five, named after some dead New York painter. They drifted into the living room, and Lucas told them about Letty and Sam and the baby, and they talked about schools and other domestic matters. Then Kidd asked, "So what's up?"

Lucas: "You've read about Porter Smalls?"

Kidd: "Yeah. Good riddance."

Lucas: "He might be innocent."

Lauren: "Oh, please."

Kidd: "Huh. Tell me about it."

LUCAS TOLD HIM ABOUT the computer, and Kidd listened carefully, eyes fixed on Lucas's face. Kidd was a couple of inches shorter than Lucas, but was wider across the shoulders, and narrower through the hips: a wrestler. He'd lost an athletic scholarship when he'd dragged an abusive coach out of his office and forced his head through the bars of a railing around the field house balcony. They'd had to call the fire department to get the coach free, and around the field house, Kidd had been both a hero and a persona non grata. Not that it mattered much: the Institute of Technology hired him as a teaching assistant, and paid him more than he'd gotten from the scholarship.

When Lucas finished with what he knew about Porter Smalls, Kidd said, "I need to see the hard drive."

Lucas took it out of his jacket pocket and handed it to him.

Kidd said, "Mmm. How long did she have it before she gave it to you?"

"Half an hour," Lucas said. "Maybe a little more."

Kidd turned the drive in his hands, then said, "She could have done anything to it."

"She didn't mess with it," Lucas said. "She'd understand the consequences."

"Which would be?"

"She'd make an enemy out of me," Lucas said. "She wouldn't want that. And she knows what's at stake here."

Kidd thought for a couple seconds, then nodded, a quick jerk of the head. "Okay," and then, "Come on back to the shop."

Lucas asked, "So you're in?"

"We're in," Kidd said.

KIDD, LAUREN, AND JACKSON lived in the original oversized unit, which had a long living room overlooking the river and the Port of St. Paul, and a couple of bedrooms and bathrooms; and Kidd used the other two units as studio and computer work space. He still did some computer-related consulting, he said, as Lucas followed him back to the computer space, though ninety percent of his time was now spent painting.

Lucas stuck his head into the studio—Kidd had three landscapes under way—and then asked, "Lauren doesn't work?"

"Not so much, anymore," Kidd said. "Pretty much a full-time mom."

"What'd she do when she was working?"

"Insurance adjuster," Kidd said.

His computer desk was an old oaken library table, ten or twelve feet long, with a half-dozen computers scattered down its length. Three printers sat on an adjacent table, and a heap of cameras sat next to them. He said, "Let's see what we've got here."

LUCAS CONSIDERED HIMSELF computer literate in the sense that he could hook up computers and printers and Wi-Fi systems, and that he could use Microsoft Word, Excel, and Access, and Google and a few other programs; and he'd once owned a software company, though he had nothing to do with coding the software.

But he had no idea what Kidd was doing, other than whistling while he worked. Kidd started by plugging ICE's hard drive into an unbranded desktop computer. He brought the system up, poked at some keys, looked at some numbers, then wandered across the workshop to a bin full of DVDs, flipped through them, chose one, brought it back, and loaded it into the computer.

"What's that?" Lucas asked.

"It's an inventory program. It searches for certain kinds of apps and . . . whoops. There we are."

"What?"

"I don't know. Let's look at it."

Kidd's fingers rattled on his keyboard, and a program popped up in reader form. Lauren came in, looked at Lucas, and raised an eyebrow, and he shrugged. Lucas knew nothing about the program, except that it wasn't very long.

After reading through it, Kidd said, "If this is what it looks like, you're right—Smalls didn't do it."

It was too fast. Lucas was astonished: "What is it?"

"Watch." Kidd pulled the DVD out of the computer, restarted the machine, and when it was up, rattled his fingers across the keyboard again. The screen instantly went blank.

"Good work," Lauren said.

They looked at the blank screen for a moment, then Kidd reached out, picked up a computer manual, and dropped it on the keyboard. A pornographic picture popped up.

"Aw, that's rotten," Lauren said. "Kids."

"That's the file," Lucas said. "How'd you do that?"

"Somebody wrote a little script—"

"A script?"

"Not even a program," Kidd said. "Just a few lines of shell commands." He paused. "How technical do you want this?"

"Just tell me what it does," Lucas said.

"What it does is, it tells the computer, 'If someone presses these keys all at the same time, show these photos.' It's more complicated than that, but it's not . . . mmm . . . complex."

"Show me."

"Well, first, you have to get the script and the porn file—it's actually a bunch of files, but they're stored in a wrapper format—on the computer. That's the tricky bit. You have to run the script once—just type the name or double-click it—and it installs itself so it starts on bootup."

"Like a virus," said Lucas.

"Not really. You have to do it intentionally. A virus would do it by itself. Anyway, if the script is running, it's just waiting for you to press four keys: QW with one hand, and OP with the other. If you do that, it sends the porn file to the default photo viewer—that's actually *called* Photo Viewer in this case. It also activates the screen-saver. The next person who touches the keyboard or the mouse cancels the screensaver and, *presto*. Porn right in your face."

Kidd held the four keys and the screen blacked out. "The porn is floating under there. If I hit anything to cancel it, the porn's right there. But. If I hit the escape key, and only the escape key . . ."

He did it, and they were back at the Windows home screen. He tapped on the keyboard, and nothing more happened.

"What you have is a script that will take you right to the porn, blank the screen, and set it up for instant retrieval," Kidd said. "But if you need to ditch the program, you hit the escape key—specifically the escape key and nothing else. I can think of no earthly reason to set that up, if you were just looking at the porn. The only reason to do it . . ."

"Would be to set up a booby trap," Lucas finished. "But—wouldn't any computer investigator find that? The script? I mean, as soon as that turned up . . ."

Kidd looked at him and said, "No."

"No?"

"No, they wouldn't find it. My tool here chased it down. The script itself is actually fairly well hidden. My tool found it because it's not part of any standard Windows boot protocol," he said. "Here's another thought. Whoever did this, whoever wrote and installed this script, knows his or *her* way around coding. This is a very tight little piece of work. I don't think it's something a politician would write, unless he came out of the computer industry."

"You said his or *her*. You italicized the *her*."

"ICE could do it—she could write this in four minutes," Kidd said.

Lucas thought about it for a second, then said, "Nah."

"Okay."

LAUREN SAID, "WAIT A MINUTE. You're moving too fast. If this guy is like a . . . thrill freak . . . then he might get off looking at porn while there are other people across the desk. Then if he needed to dump it really fast, he could do it. One touch . . ."

Kidd shook his head. "I see what you're saying, but it doesn't feel like that to me. That feels backwards. He's got this complicated four-key press to get the file up . . . but he doesn't need to do that. If you know the file is there, you can bring it up fast enough. Just like any work file. But the script is designed to bring it up and simultaneously hide it. Why is that?"

Lucas and Lauren both shrugged, and Kidd said, "Because it was designed so that somebody could go into his office for a few seconds and bring it up as a booby trap."

Kidd continued: "If he was only out for thrills, he'd probably just bring it up the regular way. No reason not to. Then he'd write the script so that *any key would kill it*. If he was getting his thrills by looking at it in his office, with other people present, and then somebody unexpectedly stepped behind his desk, he'd want to kill it with any key. Now, you kill it with the escape key. But if you needed to kill it in a big hurry, you wouldn't want to have to reach out and hit the escape key—specifically the escape key—and nothing else, to kill it. You could fumble that."

They all thought about that for a while, then Lauren said, "Maybe."

"Find something else," Lucas said, flicking his fingers at the computer.

"That'll take a little longer," Kidd said. "I suspected something like this script was there. Anything else . . . I'll have to dig into the file."

"How long will that take?"

"Dunno," Kidd said.

"Gotta be fast," Lucas said.

"I'll make it a priority," Kidd said.

"There's one other thing," Kidd said. "Do you have any idea *how* this was put in there?"

"Not yet."

"That's gonna be a problem. If the machine is on the Internet, it's theoretically vulnerable. Even if it's on a local network. It's not likely, but it's possible. But if it's not that, and it doesn't look like it, you've got a different problem. To install this quickly, you'd have to know the machine's password. Just to run something the first time, nowadays, you need to do that."

"That's not a problem. Apparently everybody in the office knew it. It's 'Smallscampaign.'"

Kidd shook his head: "People never learn."

Lucas had another thought: "Can you tell me if the script was written at the same time the porn file was created?"

"Good thought," Kidd said. He rattled the keys for a while, peered at the screen, and said, "Yeah. They were. And . . . uh-oh."

"What?"

"Interesting." He said it like computer freaks do when they're preoccupied.

"*What?*" Lucas asked.

He got a minute of silence, then:

"This is an unusual collection," Kidd said. "When people create a porn collection, they almost always collect the pieces separately, because everybody's tastes are different. But here, every file was downloaded all at once. That's unusual."

"But what does that mean?"

"Don't know. It's possible that he made the collection on a different computer, put it on a thumb drive, and carried it over to his office, but it's also possible . . ."

"That somebody brought it to his office and loaded them all at once," Lucas said.

"Man, it feels like something dirty happened here," Kidd said. "This is just not right."

"Keep pushing," Lucas said.

"I'll call you," Kidd said.

Lucas took Smalls's employee list out of his pocket. "When you get tired of checking out the porn thing, could you look up some people for me? I don't know how to do this, and ICE said you're really good at databases."

WHEN LUCAS LEFT KIDD'S apartment, he called the governor: "We have some early indications that Smalls was set up."

"Could you prove it in court?"

"No. Couldn't prove he was set up, but we might get him acquitted . . . but that's purely a negative thing. Doesn't say he's innocent."

"Keep working," Henderson said, and he was gone.

LUCAS HEADED BACK to the BCA building to look at the St. Paul homicide file on Tubbs. That done, he'd go over to Tubbs's apartment. Then he'd harass the hell out of Kidd until he'd unwrapped the hard drive from top to bottom.

The case was getting interesting.

Eight days to the election, and counting.

6

The St. Paul file on the Tubbs disappearance didn't quite convince Lucas that Tubbs had been murdered, but he thought it probable. The physical evidence was nonexistent, and the circumstantial evidence ambiguous, although the longer Tubbs remained missing, the more likely it was that he was dead.

The circumstantial evidence included the fact that Tubbs called his mother on an almost daily basis, and hadn't called her since he disappeared; that his credit cards hadn't been used, and that he used the cards for even the most minor purchases, including daily bagel breakfasts at a Bruegger's bagel bakery on Grand Avenue; and that he'd missed a number of appointments that would have been important to him.

On the other hand, he'd disappeared once before, so completely that he'd made the newspapers. Ten years earlier, he'd flown to Cancún for a wedding, intending to come back two days later. Instead, he'd apparently gone on an alcoholic bender and had not surfaced for a week. Before he showed up, it had been widely speculated that he'd gone swimming alone and had been eaten by a shark.

He'd never disappeared again, and after that alcoholic episode, he'd signed up with Alcoholics Anonymous. Abstinence only lasted a few weeks before he'd started drinking again, but he'd controlled it, as far as anyone knew.

Still, there was the possibility that he was facedown in a motel room somewhere.

Lucas didn't believe that, but it was possible.

WHEN HE'D FINISHED READING the file, Lucas put on his jacket, got his keys, stopped at a candy machine for a pack of Oreos, then drove south to University Avenue, and over to Tubbs's apartment building.

He'd just found a parking spot when his cell phone rang. He looked at the screen: Kidd.

"Yeah?"

"How bad do you cops hate Smalls?" Kidd asked.

"I don't hate him at all," Lucas said. "I didn't vote for him, but there was nothing personal about it."

Kidd said, "When I started looking him up, I found out that he doesn't like public employee unions. Any public employee unions, including police unions. He wants to outlaw them. He debated the head of the Minneapolis union on public television, the *Almanac* program."

"He's a right-winger," Lucas said. "This is a surprise?"

"No, what's a surprise is, I think the porn file might have come out of a police department," Kidd said.

Lucas wasn't sure he'd heard that right: "What are you talking about?"

"A part of it may have come out of evidentiary files. There's some text with most of the photos, the usual pedophile bullshit. Then there's one says, 'Left to right, unknown adult male, unknown adult male, Mark James Trebuchet, thirteen, unknown female, Sandra Mae Otis, fifteen.' That's the only one with text, but there are about five photos related to that one. I looked them up, those kids—I had to do a little excavating in the juvenile files—and found out that both of them were involved in a prostitution ring busted three years ago by the Minneapolis cops. I assume evidentiary photos wouldn't just be turned loose on the Internet."

"Ah, fuck me," Lucas said.

"I thought you'd be pleased," Kidd said.

"Fuck me. I gotta think about this," Lucas said. "If anybody— anybody—got wind of this, the whole goddamn state would blow up."

"No, it wouldn't. The whole goddamn media-political complex would get its knickers in a twist, and then, after a lot of screaming and slander, life would go on," Kidd said. "You gotta keep some perspective."

"I'll tell you something, Kidd—that might be true if you're an artist," Lucas said. "But if you're a cop, what you see is endless finger-pointing, investigative commissions, legislative inquiries, accusations of obstruction of justice, perjury . . ."

". . . misfeasance with a corncob . . ."

"Yeah, go ahead and laugh," Lucas said. "Listen, keep working this. You think the Smalls file came out of Minneapolis?"

"I have no idea—but those two kids were involved with Minneapolis police. I could dig out the complete juvenile files, if you need them."

"Do that. Uh, how do you do that? I thought they were sealed."

Kidd slid past the question: "Oh, you know. Anyway, what I can't figure out is why the photos of these kids would be inserted in the middle of a child-porn file . . . unless maybe the cops got the file when they busted the prostitution ring. And then annotated it? I don't know, that sounds weird."

Lucas thought for a moment, then asked, "This girl in the picture, Sandra, you said she was fifteen? And this was three years ago?"

"Sandra Mae Otis, and yeah, the caption says she was fifteen," Kidd said.

"Huh. Look, I'm in my car. Are you in a place where you could look up her birth date? Like in the DMV files? See if she's eighteen yet?"

"Wait one," Kidd said. Lucas heard his keyboard rattling, and ten seconds later Kidd said, "She's eighteen . . . as of last March. March tenth."

"What's her address?"

Kidd read it off, then said, "I'm checking that address on a satellite photo. . . . Hold on a second . . . it looks like a trailer park."

"I know the place," Lucas said. Then, "All right. I don't know what access you have to Minneapolis police files, and I won't ask, but if you should stumble over what looks like the Smalls file . . . let me know."

"I'll do that," Kidd said. "Why was Sandra's age important?"

"Think about it for one second," Lucas said.

Kidd thought about it for one second, then said, "Ah. She's an adult now. You can twist her arm until it falls off, and nobody can tell you to quit."

"Perzactly," Lucas said. "And that's what I'm going to do . . . if that's what it takes."

———

TUBBS LIVED IN A prosperous-looking, two-story redbrick apartment building, set up above the street. Still thinking about the porn file, Lucas let himself in with the keys he'd gotten from Morris, skipped the elevator for a flight of carpeted stairs, and let himself into Tubbs's apartment. The living room and bedroom were acceptably neat, for a bachelor who lived alone, and smelled faintly of food that was made in cans and cooked in pots, and also of scented candles. The office was a mess, with stacks of paper everywhere.

Lucas spent only a few minutes in the living room, bedroom, and the two bathrooms, because they'd have been gone through by St. Paul detectives and the crime-scene crew, and they wouldn't have missed anything significant. The office would be where the action was at, because Lucas knew something the St. Paul cops hadn't known: a possible connection to the Smalls problem.

St. Paul had taken out Tubbs's computers, so there wasn't anything to work with but paper. He skipped everything that looked like a report, and started shuffling through individual pieces of paper.

A half hour in, he found a Republican Senate campaign schedule, a half-dozen sheets stapled at the corner and folded in thirds—the right size to be stuck in the breast pocket of a sport coat. The outside sheet was crumpled and then resmoothed, and the whole pack of paper had been folded and refolded, so Tubbs had carried it for a while. There was no equivalent schedule for the Democrats, although Tubbs had been one.

Lucas carried the schedule to a window for the better light and peered at the sheets: there were penciled tick marks against a half-dozen scheduled appearances by Smalls. Interesting, but not definitive. Tubbs had been following Smalls's campaign.

He called Smalls:

"What was your relationship with Bob Tubbs?"

"Tubbs?" Smalls asked. "What're you doing?"

"Trying to figure out why he was tracking your campaign."

"Tracking . . . Well, I don't think you could draw any conclusions from that," Smalls said. "That's what he did for a living."

Lucas read off the list of the appearances Tubbs had been tracking. "Any reason why he'd pick those four?"

After a moment of silence, Smalls said, "The only thing I can think of is that I was out of town on all of them."

"Of course," Lucas said. He should have seen it.

"My God, Davenport, the papers say Tubbs has disappeared," Smalls said. "What does this have to do with the porn thing?"

"I don't know—but I was told that he went through your campaign office from time to time," Lucas said.

"Not while I was there," Smalls said. "But, you know . . . political people hang out."

"What about Tubbs? Did he hate you?"

"Oh, not really. We didn't particularly care for each other," Smalls said. "He was pretty much a standard Democrat operator. He also lobbied some, so he had to suck up to Republicans as well. He was just one of those guys doing a little here, a little there. He was supposedly a bagman for one of our less revered St. Paul state senators. Don't know if that's true or not, but I suspect it was."

"Did he do dirty tricks? Could he have come up with this porn idea?"

"Well, you know, yeah, probably," Smalls said. "He'd do opposition research, try to find a picture of you picking your nose, or waving your arm so that if it was cropped right, you looked like you were doing a Hitler salute."

They talked for a few more minutes, and when Lucas got off the phone, he started taking the apartment apart. It hadn't occurred to him until Smalls mentioned the possibility that Tubbs had been a bagman, and that he might have been involved in dirty tricks, but the fact was, nothing the least bit discreditable had been found in the apartment by either the St. Paul cops or the crime-scene people. No porn, no cash . . . and looking around, Lucas hadn't found any employment contracts, no car titles, no leases, no legal papers of any kind.

Tubbs might well have a safe-deposit box somewhere, but Lucas thought there was a good chance that he'd have a hidey-hole somewhere in the apartment, somewhere he could get at important papers quickly. After a quick survey, in which he didn't spot anything in particular, he unplugged a lamp and carried it around the apartment, testing all the outlets. Fake electric outlets, though opening to small caches, were both innocuous-looking and easy to get at. In this case, all the outlets worked.

He rapped on the wooden floor and got a hard return: the building was a steel-reinforced concrete structure, so there were no holes in either the floor or the ceiling, which looked like genuine plaster. An access panel on the back wall of the bathroom looked promising, because it appeared to have been removed a few times—probably at least once by the crime-scene crew. He found a screwdriver in a tool kit that he'd seen in the kitchen, and removed the panel, and found sewer pipes and the usual inter-wall dust and grime. He put the panel back on and moved to the closets, checking for fake side panels.

Lucas had designed his own home, and worked daily with the

contractor who built it, almost inch by inch. He was standing in a closet when he thought, *Sewer pipes?* He went back to the bathroom and took the panel off again. Two white six-inch PVC sewer pipes were coming down from above—but Tubbs's apartment was on the second floor of a two-story building. Where were the pipes coming from? Couldn't be Tubbs's own bathroom because, unless there are big pumps involved, sewage flows *down*, not up.

He sat on the toilet seat, looking at the two large pipes, and it occurred to him that the access panel didn't give access to anything. You couldn't do anything except look at the pipes. He reached out and shook one of them: solid. Shook the other: also solid.

But when he tried twisting one of them, it turned, and quite easily.

THE PIPES WERE ABOUT fourteen inches long, with screw-in caps. He unscrewed the cap on the first pipe, and there it all was: the personal papers that had been missing, along with a gun—an old revolver with fake pearl stocks—and three thumb drives. The second pipe contained more paper, all curled to fit in the pipe, the kind of thing that Lucas might have been looking at in a corruption investigation. There were tax records, testimony clipped from lawsuits, bills of sale, corporate records, and $23,000 in stacks of fifty-dollar bills, held together by rubber bands.

He put back the gun and all the personal papers, and the money. He took everything else, and called Kidd.

"I've got three thumb drives and I need a quick survey, just to find out what's on them."

"How big are they?" Kidd asked.

Lucas looked at the drives and said, "Two two-gig, one four-gig."

"You could put the equivalent of several thousand books on those things, so the survey might not be quick," Kidd said.

"I just need an idea—and I need to know if that porn file is on one of them," Lucas said. "I doubt that there are several thousand books on them."

"Well, shoot, look . . . I guess. We could check for the porn fairly quickly. Come over in an hour. I'll put a little search program together."

"Would two or three hours be better? I've got something else I could do."

"Two hours would be better," Kidd said. "We're expecting some guests and I'm in the kitchen, being a scullery maid."

"See you then: two hours."

Lucas put the pipes back together and screwed the panel back on, walked back to the car, and headed north up I-35.

SANDRA MAE OTIS LIVED in a manufactured home in a manufactured home park off I-494 north of St. Paul. She also ran an illegal daycare center.

Otis was sitting on the stoop smoking when Lucas pulled into the driveway: she had bleached-blond hair, black eyebrows, and small metallic eyes like the buttons on 501 jeans. She regarded him with a certain resignation as he got out of the car, flicked the butt-end of the smoke off into the weeds, turned and shouted, "Carl, knock it the fuck off," and looked back at Lucas.

As Lucas walked up, a little boy, maybe three, dressed in a Kool-Aid-spotted T-shirt and shorts, and crying, came out and said, "Carl hit me, really hard."

Otis said, "I know, Spud, we'll get him later. You go on back in

there and tell him that if he hits you again, I'll put him in the garbage can and let you beat on it." Back to Lucas: "How long have
cops been driving Porsches?"

"Personal car," Lucas said. The musky odor of weed hung
around her head.

She looked at him for a minute, then said, "So give me some
money if you're so rich."

Lucas opened his mouth to say something when another small
boy, a couple years older than the first, came out crying, rubbing an
eye with his fist, and said, "Spud says you're gonna put me in the
garbage can again."

"Yeah, well, don't hit him," Otis told the kid.

The kid said, "Sometimes Spud really pisses me off."

"But don't hit him," Otis said. "You see this guy? He's a cop and
he's got a big gun. If you hit Spud again, he's going to shoot you."

The kid stepped back, his mouth open in fear. Lucas blurted,
"No, I won't."

But the kid backed away, still scared, and vanished inside. Otis
said, "So what do you want? I'm not responsible for Dick's debts.
We're all over with."

Lucas looked around for something to sit on: the stoop would
never touch the seat of his Salvatore Ferragamo slacks. There was
nothing, so he stood, looming over her. "Three years ago, you were
picked up and taken to juvie court as part of a prostitution ring that
was busted over in Minneapolis."

"That's juvenile and it doesn't count," Otis said.

"It does count, because it's probably messed up your head, but
that's not exactly what I want to talk about," Lucas said. "Sometime
in there, when these people were running you, they took pictures

of you and Mark Trebuchet and three adults in a sex thing. Did they sell those pictures?"

"I don't know if they had time, before they were busted," Otis said. "They were busted, like, two days after the photo shoot. I think the photographer bragged to the wrong guy about it."

"Now, who was this? Who's 'they'?" Lucas asked.

"The Pattersons. Irma and Bjorn."

"The Pattersons ran the business?"

"Yeah. They're doing fifteen years. They got twelve to go. And if you're a cop, how come you didn't know that?"

"Because I'm operating off a telephone," Lucas said. "Our guys just found the pictures . . . but the pictures were in court? You, and the two men and the woman and Mark?"

"Yup."

"Did the cops get them off the Internet? The evidence photos?"

"I don't think so. The Internet was already getting too dangerous, with cops all over the place. The Pattersons were really scared about that, telling their clients to stay away from the 'net. They mostly printed them out and sent them around that way," Otis said. "They said they were for my *portfolio*. They said I was going to be a movie star. Like that was going to happen, the big fat liars."

"So what happened in court?"

"Well, I had to testify about what we did. The sex and all. And about the pictures. They wanted us to identify the adults, but, you know, we didn't know who they were," she said. "I'd seen them around, but I didn't know their names. I think they took off when the Pattersons got busted."

"Were there a lot of other pictures put in at the same time? In court? Of you?"

She frowned. "No. When the Pattersons took the pictures, they took a lot of them. I can remember that flash going off over and over and really frying my eyeballs. And this guy I was blowing, he had like a soft-on all the time, I had to keep pumping him up. But the cops had, I don't know, four or five pictures. Or six or seven. Like that. I think all they had were like these paper pictures, and they took them right off the Pattersons' desk."

A little girl, maybe Spud's sister, came out of the house and looked at Lucas and then at Otis and said, "I pooped."

"Ah, Jesus Christ, you little shit machine," Otis said. "All right. You go back in, and I'll come and change you."

The girl went back in and Otis asked, "You done?"

"Yeah, but don't go anywhere, okay?" Lucas said.

"Where in the fuck would I go?" Otis asked. "I'm living in an old fuckin' trailer. My next stop is a park bench."

Lucas turned away, then back and said, "This place can't be licensed."

"Are you kidding me?" she asked. "I'm working for minimum-wage dumbasses who either leave the kids with me or lock them in a car. I'm all they can afford, and I'm better than a car. Maybe."

Lucas said, "All right, but don't put Carl in the garbage can anymore, okay?"

"Carl gets what Carl deserves," she said. "But they all like chocolate ice cream. I could get some for tomorrow, Porsche cop, if I had an extra twenty bucks."

"How many kids are in there?"

"Seven," she said. "Unless one of them has killed another one."

Lucas took a twenty out of his wallet. "Get them the ice cream," he said. "You spend it on dope, I'll put you in something worse than a garbage can."

———

BACK DOWN I-35 TO Kidd's place.

Lauren came to the door, said, "Hi," and then, as Lucas followed her inside, said, "We've got a couple of friends staying with us for a few days, with their kids. It could be a little noisy."

"I just need Kidd to take a look and give me an estimate on what's inside these things," Lucas said, showing her the thumb drives.

Kidd was sitting in the front room with a black couple, and Kidd said, "Hey, Lucas," and to the couple, "This is Lucas Davenport, he's a cop. Lucas, John and Marvel Smith, from down in Longstreet, Arkansas. John's a sculptor, Marvel's a politician. John does some stuff that you and Weather ought to look at."

"I'll do that," Lucas said. He shook hands with John Smith, an athletic guy with some boxer's scars around his eyes, and smiled at Marvel, a beautiful long-legged woman with a reserved smile; like she might be wary of cops.

Kidd said, "So let's see what you got. . . . Back in a couple of minutes, guys."

On the way back, Lucas gave Kidd a thirty-second summary of how he'd gotten the drives. "This Tubbs guy—I believe he's dead. Murdered. I mean, we all thought so, but now I'm pretty sure of it."

"That's disturbing," Kidd said.

In the computer lab, Kidd plugged in all three thumb drives at the same time, quickly figured out that one set had been formatted under an Apple OSX operating system, and the other two with different versions of Windows.

He put in a piece of his own software and tapped some keys,

and a file popped up. "There it is," he said. He opened it, and they saw the first photos of the Smalls porn files.

"How'd you do that?" Lucas asked.

"I've got the number of bytes from the file off the Smalls machine, and looked for a file of close to the same length. This one was exact, which is a rare thing."

"Goddamnit—Smalls is clear."

"Not necessarily," Kidd said. "Remember—the file could have gone the other way, too. From Smalls to Tubbs. Maybe Tubbs stole it, and was blackmailing Smalls."

"You sound like a defense lawyer," Lucas said.

"Thanks." Kidd did some other computer stuff, popping up files with all kinds of various corporate papers, real estate records, legislative committee meeting transcripts, court records.

"Cover-your-ass files," Lucas said.

"Might be more complicated than that," Kidd said. He went to the door and called, "Hey, Marvel? You got a minute?" And he said to Lucas, "Marvel's okay."

MARVEL CAME DOWN THE HALL, and Kidd showed her into the lab and said, "Look at this file. It's from here in Minnesota. Do you see anything?"

Lucas was a little nervous having the woman looking at the file, but she was from Arkansas, and Kidd probably wouldn't have asked her to look at it if she might become a problem. He kept his mouth shut.

The file Marvel was examining was one of the smaller ones, fifteen or twenty pieces of paper that had been scanned into PDF files, as well as three or four fine-resolution JPEG photos. Using a mouse, Marvel clicked back and forth between the images. John and Lauren came into the lab, leaned against a wall to watch.

Marvel took five minutes; at one point, the kids made a noise that sounded like they'd killed a chicken, and Lauren ran off to see what it was. She'd just come back when Marvel tapped the computer screen and said, "See, what happened was, this guy, Representative Diller, got the licensing fees on semi-trailers reduced by about half, so they'd supposedly be in line with what they were in the surrounding states. He said he wanted to do that so the trucking companies wouldn't move out of Minnesota. But what you see over here is a bunch of 1099 forms that were sent by trucking companies to Sisseton High-Line Consulting, LLC, of Sisseton, South Dakota. Over here is the South Dakota LLC form and we find out that a Cheryl Diller is the president of Sisseton High-Line Consulting. And we see that she got, mmm, fifty-five thousand dollars for consulting work that year, from trucking companies."

"So if these two Dillers are related . . ." Lucas began.

"I promise you, they are," Marvel said.

Kidd said, "Marvel's a state senator. In Arkansas."

Marvel added, "This shit goes on all the time. On everything you can think of, and probably a lot you can't think of."

Lucas said to Kidd, "So what these are, are blackmail files."

"Or protection files, if they're all the same kind of thing," Marvel said. "Whoever owned these files might have been involved in these deals, and kept the evidence in case he ever got in trouble and needed help."

Lucas looked at the computer screen for a moment and then said, "All right. Give me the drives back, Kidd. You guys don't want to know anything about this."

Kidd pulled the drives out, handed them to Lucas, and said, "You are *so* right. Do not mention my name in any of this."

"I won't," Lucas promised. "Can I print these out on my home printer?"

"Probably," Kidd said. "What kind of computer are you running?"

"Macs," Lucas said.

"Most of the files are on government machines, Windows," Kidd said. "I'll loan you a Windows laptop, a cleaned-up Sony. If anyone asks, you paid cash at Best Buy a couple years ago."

BACK IN THE CAR, the laptop on the passenger seat, Lucas called the governor and said, "I need to talk to you alone, tonight. Without Mitford or anybody else around."

"That bad?"

"Worse than you could have imagined," Lucas said. "The problem is, I can't get out of it now."

"I've got a cabin on the Wisconsin side of the St. Croix, north of St. Croix falls. I could be there at six, if it's that bad."

"Tell me where," Lucas said.

He got directions to the cabin, again told the governor to come alone, then went home, said hello to the housekeeper, who said that Letty wouldn't be back until six o'clock, that Weather had been called to do emergency work on a woman whose face had been cut in an auto accident, and she'd be late, and that the kids were fine.

Lucas took the thumb drives back to his den, hooked the Sony up to his printer, then had to download some printer software that matched the Sony to his printer. He took a few more minutes to re-familiarize himself with Windows, and started printing. There were thirty-four files on the three drives, not nearly filling them, but it took two hours to get them all printed out.

He didn't print the porn file.

While the printing was going on, he paged through the porn file, image by image, and found the photos that Kidd thought came from police files. He looked at the captions, which had apparently been printed onto sheets of paper that had been attached to the bottom of paper photos—the kind of photos you would give to a jury. Kidd was right, he thought: they were evidentiary photos.

When the printing was done, he used a three-hole punch to put binder holes in Tubbs's files, and bound them book-style between cardboard covers. Then he started annotating them, figuring out who was who, and trying to figure out what was going on in each file. Virtually all of them were evidence of payoffs to state legislators and a variety of state bureaucrats.

Some of the evidence was explicit, some of it was simply suggestive. Some of it would have led to criminal charges, or to clawback civil suits. Almost all of it would have ended careers.

A LITTLE AFTER FIVE, he went out to the Lexus SUV that he drove outside the Cities, and took off for Wisconsin. He was not in a mood for the scenic tour, so he went straight up I-35 to Highway 8, then east through Chisago City and Lindstrom and past Center City to Taylors Falls, then across the St. Croix into Wisconsin, north on Highway 82, off on River Road and finally, down a dirt lane lined with beech and oak trees to a redwood house perched on a bluff over the river. The front door was propped open with a river rock.

The governor was sitting on a four-season porch, already closed in for the winter, that looked over the river valley. When Lucas banged on the screen door, he called, "Straight through to the porch. Get a beer out of the kitchen, or make yourself a drink."

The kitchen was compact: Lucas snagged a Leinie's from the refrigerator, popped the top with a church key hung on the refrigerator with a magnet, and walked through the house to the porch. The house was larger than it looked from the outside, and elegant, and smelled lightly of cigar smoke. A side hallway led toward what must've been two or three bedrooms. A library featured pop fiction and a big octagonal poker table with a green baize surface; the living room was cluttered with couches and chairs and small tables. An oversized television hung from one wall.

Henderson was wearing soft tan slacks and a white shirt with the sleeves rolled to the elbow, and boat shoes. He said, "Give me one sentence to crank up my enthusiasm for being here."

Lucas sat on a wooden chaise with waterproof cushions, took a sip of the beer, thought for a few seconds, then said, "Bob Tubbs had the porn before it was unloaded on Smalls, and was probably murdered to shut him up."

The governor stared at him for a few seconds, then said, "Oh, shit."

Lucas pushed on: "I went into Tubbs's apartment, legally, with the approval of Tubbs's mother and the investigator from the St. Paul Police Department. I searched the place, and pretty much because of my superior intelligence . . ."

". . . goes without saying . . ."

". . . I found Tubbs's hideout cache, which St. Paul hadn't found," Lucas said.

"Why didn't they find it?" Henderson asked.

"Because he hid it in a weird place, and when they opened it up, they found just what they expected to find." He told Henderson about the pipes, and how he belatedly realized that they'd hardly be draining upward.

"And in the pipes . . ." Henderson prompted.

"I found a gun, a wad of papers, plus some money, cash, and three thumb drives. I opened the thumb drives and found exactly the same porn file—exactly the same—as the one the cops found on Smalls's computer. There's a remote possibility—remote in my mind, anyway—that the file went from Smalls to Tubbs. That Tubbs found out that there was a porn file on Smalls's computer, went in, stole it, and is, or was planning to, blackmail Smalls. So Smalls, or one of his henchmen, killed him. There's a much better possibility that it went the other way—from Tubbs to Smalls's computer. We know that Tubbs occasionally dropped by Smalls's campaign office."

"Let's look at the first possibility," Henderson said; he was a lawyer. "Why don't you think Tubbs was blackmailing Smalls?"

"Because there's nothing on the file, or in the other documents on the thumb drives, that mentions the porn or Smalls. He'd have no way to tie it to Smalls—all he had was the file itself. Why would anyone believe it came from Smalls, or anyone else, for that matter? If he tried to go public with it, Smalls would just blow it off as an egregiously vicious smear by a Democratic operative who'd been involved in other dirty tricks."

"Is there any reason to think it *could* be a blackmail file?"

"Only one that I could think of," Lucas said. He patted his bound copies: "Because it seems likely that Tubbs may have been involved in other blackmail operations. Maybe not for money, maybe for influence. So he might have been a practiced blackmailer."

Henderson nodded: "So what's the other side? Why do you think it went Tubbs to Smalls, that Tubbs planted it on Smalls's computer?"

"Couple of reasons," Lucas said. "If it had really been Smalls's file, he probably would have paid Tubbs off. He'd have done it in a way that Tubbs couldn't come back on him—filmed it, or done it with trusted witnesses. That way, if the file ever showed up again, Tubbs at least would go down for blackmail."

He continued: "The other reason is, just look what happened. A guy who does dirty tricks is involved, somehow, with a really dirty trick, which could change an important election. He might have been paid for it. Maybe a lot. So if you take the simplest, straightforward answer to a complicated question . . ."

"Occam's razor . . ."

Lucas nodded. ". . . the file was going from Tubbs to Smalls. A straightforward political hit."

"So, what you're saying is, Tubbs probably took the thumb drive to Smalls's office, and when Smalls was gone, inserted the file."

"Yes. Or more likely, an associate of his did. Whatever happened, for either side, Tubbs was probably murdered to shut him up. Neither one of us is going to be able to avoid that . . . fact," Lucas said.

"I wouldn't avoid the fact," Henderson said, "but that doesn't mean that I don't think it could use some management."

"I agree," Lucas said. He added, "The thumb drives included a lot of other stuff. I printed it out—it's all documents, with a few photos. I annotated them, best I could, and bound it up."

HE HANDED THE BOOK to Henderson, who weighed it in his hands and then turned to the first page. He thumbed through it for a few minutes, then, in a distracted voice, asked, "You know how to make a G-and-T?"

"Sure."

"Could you get me another? Lean hard on the G."

Lucas went and made the drink, and then brought it back, and the governor took it without looking up, and Lucas pulled off his shoes and leaned back on the chaise and drank his beer and stared out into the dark over the river valley. He could see stars through a break in the trees: winter could arrive any second, although there was no sign of it.

A minute or so later, Henderson chuckled and said, "Jean Coutee . . . I wondered where she got that Jaguar. Poor as a church mouse, all workingman's rights and anti-this-and-that . . . and she took the money and bought a fuckin' Jag."

And fifteen minutes after that, Henderson sighed and shut the book, and handed it back to Lucas. "Am I in there . . . anywhere?"

"No."

"I don't mean as a crook, because I'm not. But am I mentioned? Am I going to court?"

"You're not even mentioned," Lucas said.

"Okay. That's okay."

"There's another thing that worries me," Lucas said. "That porn file. There're a lot of photos and most of them have some text. But one of the files seems likely to have come from a police evidence file. From Minneapolis."

"What? Police?"

"I don't know the connection, or how it got in the bigger file," Lucas said. "I suspect it came from the police. The question is, did the Minneapolis cops, or probably one cop, give the file to Tubbs, in an effort to destroy Smalls? If they did, is it possible—"

"That a cop killed Tubbs? So that he wouldn't rat them out if he got caught?"

"Or maybe they realized he wasn't reliable," Lucas said. "The thing is, Smalls and the cops, and Minneapolis in particular, did not get along. Smalls wanted to outlaw public employee unions. The unions saw him as a deadly enemy. When I look into this, that's going to be one aspect of the case," Lucas said.

"Which makes it even a bigger stink bomb," Henderson said.

"It'd be good to keep you out of this . . . in an operative sense," Lucas said.

"Absolutely."

"I might have to perjure myself, but only lightly and not really significantly," Lucas said. "The only two people who'd ever know would be you and me. . . ." *And Kidd and Lauren and Marvel and John, but they should be safe enough,* Lucas thought. He wasn't telling any real lies, he was just warping time a bit.

The governor didn't quail at the idea of perjury, he simply asked, "What are we talking about?"

"I put everything back. The St. Paul cops don't know I've already been to the apartment. I put everything back, and call the lead investigator, and tell him that I've been there for an hour. When they arrive, I'll be sitting there, looking at the paper. . . . I'll insist on taking it to the BCA computer lab. Nobody there knows what I've been up to. They'd find all this stuff, and the porn, Smalls would be cleared, a couple of crooks might go down. I noticed that one of them is a pretty close ally of yours."

"Fuck him," Henderson said. "He's a goddamned criminal, sucking on the public tit. I never saw that in him. But where's the perjury in this?"

"Might not be any. I'd tell them exactly what happened when I entered the apartment, where I looked and what I did, and here's the evidence. I wouldn't have to mention that it was my second trip there . . . that I took the stuff out, copied it, and then put it back. After all, the docs are all in the public record."

Henderson nodded, and closed his eyes. Then he said, "The murder."

"I'd want to stay on that," Lucas said.

"I'd insist. This thing will leak five minutes after you call St. Paul, and there's gonna be a shit storm. I'll be outraged, and you'll be my minister plenipotentiary to the investigation. That'll give us a reason for these . . . conferences."

"That'll work, I think," Lucas said.

They sat there for a minute, then Henderson said, "There's the elephant in the room . . . that we haven't talked about."

Lucas nodded: "Who did it. Who killed Tubbs."

"If he's dead."

"Yeah, if he's dead. But . . . it feels like it."

"*Why* it was done . . . should lead you to who did it," Henderson said. "A lot of people hate Smalls, but the most obvious beneficiary is Taryn Grant."

"But hiring a killer is a problem, no matter how much money you have," Lucas said. "The best model for that is the movie *Fargo*— idiots hiring idiots. From what I've read about her, she's not an idiot."

"She's not," Henderson agreed. "But it could be somebody working on her behalf. Or somebody who *thinks* he's working on her behalf. A psycho."

"I'll talk to her," Lucas said. "As the investigation spreads out, she'd be an obvious person to interview. I'll take a look and see what we can find out about her."

"Another thing: we need to manage the news release. We know it'll leak, we need to be out front on that."

"That's what Mitford's for," Lucas said. "Just make sure he gives me a heads-up before the shit hits the fan."

"I will. Now about your book . . ." Henderson said. He patted the bound printout that Lucas had given him.

"Into the grinder," Lucas said.

AT TEN MINUTES AFTER nine o'clock that night, Roger Morris, the St. Paul homicide detective, wearing a purple velour tracksuit and Nike Air running shoes, stuck his head into Tubbs's apartment and called, "Where are you?"

"In the bathroom," Lucas called back.

Morris found Lucas on his knees, looking at papers he was pulling out of two white plastic sewer pipes. Morris tipped his head back and closed his eyes and said, "Fuck me with a parking meter. We missed it."

"Yeah, well . . . I looked in there and wondered, why would you drain a sewer *up*, in a two-story building?" Lucas said.

"So what is it?"

"Papers, money, and three computer thumb drives," Lucas said. "You can have the money and the papers. The thumb drives . . . finders keepers. I've got a guy waiting for me at the BCA computer lab."

"*We* got a computer lab—"

"Ours is better," Lucas said. "This stuff just might blow the ass off the legislature. . . . These papers, the ones I can read, suggest that some of our beloved politicians are on the take."

"That's a motive on the Tubbs killing," Morris said. "Seriously, man, it's my murder investigation—"

"I want those thumb drives at the BCA," Lucas said. "You'll get the contents—I'll drive you over there, and we'll give you a receipt. I'll tell you what, Roger, I'm only looking at Tubbs for one reason: the kid who found that porn said Tubbs had been hanging around the Smalls campaign, and might have had the opportunity to put it on Smalls's computer. I looked close at the Smalls porn, the stuff from your computer lab, and there's some involvement there that you don't want to deal with. I don't want to deal with it, either, but you *really* don't."

"Like what?"

"Like one of the photos may have come out of the Minneapolis cops," Lucas said. "Maybe the whole file did. Maybe some cops were trying to get rid of Smalls. Maybe Tubbs was killed to seal off the connection."

"No, no," Morris said. A few seconds later, "You don't have to drive me—I'll follow you over. I want that receipt. You can keep the papers and the money, too. But I want copies of every single goddamn document on my computer tomorrow morning."

"Fast as I can get it to you, Roger," Lucas said. "I promise."

7

ucas got the contents of Tubbs's hidey-hole into the BCA lab, and the tech there, called in on overtime, loaded up the files and began printing out the documents. When he found the porn file, he asked, "What about this trash?"

"Aw, man," Lucas said. They dialed into the file, and he switched to full drama mode: "Aw, Jesus Christ."

He'd given Morris a receipt for the pile of evidence and Morris had gone home with the promise of complete access in the morning. Now Lucas called him at home and said, "You might want to get over here."

"What happened?"

"We pretty much confirmed that Tubbs–porn connection," Lucas said. "He's got the file on one of these thumb drives."

"I'll be there in ten minutes," Morris said.

WHEN MORRIS ARRIVED, THE first thing he asked Lucas was, "If this file was a setup, if Tubbs did it, and if Tubbs was killed the same day the file was found . . . that night . . . then he'd have had to go to Smalls's office that morning. Right? He couldn't have put it on the day before."

"That's right," Lucas said.

"I'll tell you what: you can check us on this, but we backtracked Tubbs, to see who he'd talked to, and where he'd been, the day he disappeared, and that night. He didn't go to Smalls's campaign office. We've accounted for all his time back a couple of days, and he wasn't there."

"Then . . . he had to have an associate."

"Who might've gotten scared when he saw how crazy this whole thing got," Morris said. "It might've started out as a dirty trick, and all of a sudden, people are talking about multiple felonies and Smalls is going nuts on TV. He figures if it comes out, who put the file on Smalls's computer, he's heading for prison. So he talks to Tubbs, one thing leads to another . . . and *bang.*"

"That seems reasonable," Lucas said, because it was.

They talked about the possibilities as Lucas walked Morris up to the lab, where Lucas said to the lab tech, "You need to call the St. Paul computer lab guy. There's got to be some trigger for the porn file booby trap. Between the two of you, I want you to find it tonight, so Roger and I know what it is when we come in tomorrow."

"That's a tall order," the tech said.

"That's your problem," Lucas said. "It's gotta be there: find it."

To Morris: "I want to show you this one group of photos." He ran through the file, found the pictures of Otis and the others in the group sex, and tapped the caption. "These were the pictures that were presented in court. Unless you believe that the Minneapolis cops are posting this stuff on the Internet, then they had to come out of the Minneapolis computer system. In fact, I was told by this girl"—he tapped Otis's face—"that the photos presented in court were on paper, and were seized when the cops raided the porn operation. I'm thinking . . . this had to come out of Minneapolis's evidence file. I mean, look at the caption: that's cop stuff."

Morris rubbed his forehead: "You're saying somebody in Minneapolis helped Tubbs set up Smalls?"

"It's a possibility," Lucas said.

"Then . . . *that* guy could be the killer," Morris said.

Lucas shrugged.

Morris watched Lucas for a moment, then switched directions: "Have you looked at the document files?"

"I'm getting them printed now," Lucas said. "It looks like it's the same as the other papers—blackmail stuff, cover-your-ass files, whatever. A lot of corrupt bullshit."

Morris considered for a moment, then said, "We need a conference. We need the heavies on this. I'll call you tomorrow at eight o'clock—"

"Nine would be better," Lucas said.

"Nine o'clock, and we'll both have lists of who should be in the conference."

"It's a plan," Lucas said.

He and Morris spent a half hour flicking through the document files, and then through the porn files, looking for any other clue to its origin, but found nothing new. When they were done, Morris said, "Nine o'clock tomorrow."

LUCAS WENT HOME: he'd successfully covered his ass, he thought. Now it should be a straightforward murder investigation, and they already had several pieces of the puzzle.

Morris was a competent investigator, and more than competent:

but he didn't have everything that Lucas had, and Lucas couldn't give him some of it. He really had to stay on the case, Lucas thought. He *wanted* to stay on it. It was getting intense, and he liked intense.

Liked it enough that he got up early to think about it. And at nine o'clock the next morning, in jeans and T-shirt, he'd already finished a Diet Coke and a plate of scrambled eggs, and his list of who should be at the conference. His list: Henry Sands, director of the BCA; Rose Marie Roux, commissioner of public safety; Rick Card, St. Paul chief of police; Morris; and himself. He was trying to remember who would call whom, when his phone rang. He picked it up, looked at the screen.

The governor: "Everything cool?" Henderson asked.

"Yes. We're going bureaucratic, to blur everything over. The St. Paul homicide detective on the Tubbs case, and I, are going to convene a conference with Sands and Rose Marie and the St. Paul chief, lay it all out, and then just start a straight criminal investigation. Maybe parcel some of it out to the attorney general . . . but we'll see what Rose Marie has to say about that. You should stay clear."

"Keep me informed."

MORRIS CALLED A MINUTE LATER, with his list. He had the same list as Lucas, less Rose Marie, and with the addition of the Ramsey County attorney.

He agreed with Lucas on Rose Marie, but Lucas argued against the county attorney: "That guy is owned by Channel Three. If he's in the conference, we might as well put it on television."

"Man, my computer guy printed out those document files and left them for me, and I gotta tell you, it's gonna be political, and it's gonna be ugly. The names in these things . . . they scare the shit out of me. I think we need lawyers. Lots of lawyers. The more the better. These docs aren't for cops."

"I'll take a look as soon as I go in this morning," Lucas said. "But we're cops, so it's okay to have a conference about a possible crime. Nobody can criticize us for that. Then we let Rose Marie and Rick figure out who to bring in, for the political stuff. We can just focus on the murder."

They went back and forth, and eventually Morris said, "I knew you had a sneaky streak, but I didn't know it was this sneaky. But okay, let's do it your way. I'll declare a big-ass emergency and try to get a conference at noon or one o'clock, here in St. Paul."

"Do it," Lucas said.

THE MEETING WAS SET for eleven o'clock, the only mutual time they could all find, in the chief's office in St. Paul. Lucas had a couple of hours, so he called Brittany Hunt, the volunteer who'd discovered the porn file. She was driving to the Mall of America. She was no longer employed, she said, but not too worried about it.

"I talked to my adviser and she said that exposing a criminal like Smalls was a lot more important than my campaign work." She was worried about meeting Lucas without her father present, but he told her that he just had a couple of quick questions that weren't about her at all. "I need to gossip," he said.

She agreed to make a quick detour and meet him at a sandwich shop off Ford Parkway, five minutes from his house. He changed into a suit and tie, then drove over to the sandwich shop, where he found her eating a fried egg sandwich on a buttermilk biscuit. Lucas got a glass of water and sat down across the table from her.

"I was famished," she said.

"So eat." Lucas leaned toward her and pitched his voice down. "Tubbs . . . did he have any special friends in Smalls's campaign?"

She cocked her head and licked a crumb of biscuit off her lower lip, then asked, "You mean, was he sleeping with anybody?"

Lucas said, "Well, any kind of close friend."

She said, "You know . . . I don't know. But I can tell you how to find out. There's a guy there, Cory, mmm, I don't really know his last name, he works in the copy room. He's the biggest gossip in the world. He knows *everything*."

"Cory."

"Yes. He's not really part of the campaign staff, he was hired to do the printing and copying. They do a lot of that. He knows *everything*. Ask Helen Roman. She's the campaign manager, she'll know where to find him."

"Sounds like a good guy to know," Lucas said.

"Yeah. If you like gossip, and we all do." She burped, then looked toward the counter. "I could use another one of those sandwiches. I haven't eaten since the day before yesterday."

SMALLS'S CAMPAIGN OFFICE was off I-94 on the St. Paul side of the Mississippi, ten minutes away. Lucas went there, found Helen Roman, the office manager, who said that Cory Makovsky worked in the distribution center, at the end of the hall. Lucas went there, where he found Makovsky talking excitedly on his cell phone. When Lucas tried to get his attention, Makovsky held up a finger, meaning "Wait one," and gushed a revelation "He'd just seen it online from *People*, there really isn't any doubt that she's pregnant," into the phone.

Lucas looked pointedly at his watch, and Makovsky frowned and said to the phone, "Hang on a sec," and to Lucas, *"What?"*

Lucas said, "I'm an agent with the BCA. Did you murder Bob Tubbs?"

Makovsky took that in for a few seconds, then said hastily into the phone, "I gotta get back to you, Betty."

When Lucas had Makovsky's attention, he asked, "Did you kill him?"

Makovsky, who'd gone a little pale, said, "Of course not. Who told you I did?"

"Nobody. I just wondered," Lucas said. Then: "I was told you might have some information I need. Do you know if Bob Tubbs had a special friend of some kind . . . a lover, maybe . . . in Senator Smalls's campaign office?"

Makovsky's eyes widened, and his voice dropped to a whisper: "Is that the story Smalls is putting out?"

"No—that's the question I'm asking. Did Tubbs have a special friend?"

"I don't know," Makovsky said, with real regret in his voice. "I realize I should know, but I don't. I could ask around."

"Could you do that?" Lucas asked. He dug a card out of his pocket, wrote a number on the back, and said, "If you hear anything, call me."

"I'll do that," Makovsky said, his eyes bright. Lucas believed him; and two minutes after he called Lucas, the word would probably be tweeted, or Twittered, or whatever that was. Probably to *People*.

WHEN HE LEFT the campaign office, Lucas had ten minutes to get down to the St. Paul Police Department, just enough time to retrieve his car and be marginally late. When he got there, he found he was the first person from outside the department to arrive.

The chief, Morris, and a lab tech were sitting around, drinking coffee, talking about a recent controversial tasing. A Bloomington cop's wife had woken angry in the middle of the night, and had used his duty Taser to tase her sleeping husband in the area sometimes called the *gooch*. He was now claiming a major disability—sexual dysfunction caused by a city-owned instrument—and was seeking to be retired at full pay. He was twenty-seven.

"I'll tell you what," Morris said, holding his coffee cup with his pinkie finger properly out in the air, "That boy won't be sleeping easy with a woman again, no matter who she is."

Commissioner of Public Safety Rose Marie Roux walked in and caught the last of that, and she asked, "Who was that?"

"Talking about the Bloomington tasing," Lucas said.

"Oh, yeah," she said. She took a chair, and plopped her purse on the chief's desk. "The guy who got it in the gooch."

Henry Sands, the BCA director, showed up a minute later, took the last chair, and Rose Marie asked, "So what's up? Or, I sorta know what's up, but what's new, and why is it an emergency?"

Morris said, "Lucas and I found a bunch of stuff in Bob Tubbs's apartment—you all know Tubbs, and know we're investigating his disappearance as a possible murder. Well, the stuff we found suggests that Tubbs planted the kiddie porn on Senator Smalls's computer. There's the theoretical possibility that he found it on Smalls's computer, and was using it to blackmail him, but Lucas and I don't believe that. . . . We think he was killed to eliminate him as a witness to whoever supplied the porn to get Smalls. It's possible that the kiddie porn came through the Minneapolis Police Department, so the killer could be a cop."

"Holy shit," the chief said.

"Plus," Morris continued, "in the same hideout where we found the kiddie porn—the porn was on a thumb drive—we found a bunch of other papers and copies of public documents which pretty much prove that seven serving state senators and representatives have committed a wide range of felonies, along with six former senators and representatives who are no longer in office, and a half-dozen bureaucrats who were paid off for arranging contracts."

There was a long silence while the VIPs looked at the ceiling, sideways, and at the carpet, then, "That's just the fuckin' cherry on the cake, isn't it?" Rose Marie said to everybody, the disgust showing on her face. "That's just the fuckin' cherry."

"What we need from you all," Morris concluded, "is for you to tell us what to do. I mean, we have to continue the Tubbs investigation. We can be pretty sure now that he was murdered—we've got a hell of a pile of motives. But there's a lot of political stuff."

"I need to see copies of everything," Rose Marie said.

"Got it at the BCA," Lucas said. "I can send it over."

Card said, "I need to see it, too."

"I've got a copy for you," Morris said.

Rose Marie held her index finger in the air, asking for silence as she thought for a moment, then: "Here's what I'd suggest. The corruption stuff goes to the attorney general, and he can have some of his under-employed young lawyers look at it. And we need to talk to Senator Smalls's attorneys right away. Smalls may be a suspect in the murder, if the porn was taken *from* him and he was being blackmailed. But if I understand you correctly, you think there's a much greater possibility that Tubbs put the porn on Smalls's computer, in which case, Smalls is being unfairly demonized as a pervert a week before a critical election. We have to tell him what we know, and then let Smalls do what he can with it."

Lucas chipped in: "I don't think the porn was taken from Smalls.

It's a logical possibility, which is why we mention it, but . . . it's like one percent. I think he was framed."

"Okay. More reason to talk to him soon," Rose Marie said.

Sands said to Rose Marie, "You can handle the politics. I think that's proper. But the Tubbs murder . . . and what comes out of it, a definite finding on how the porn got on Smalls's computer . . . is that St. Paul? Or is that us? St. Paul has been handling the case, and Detective Morris seems to have done an excellent job so far."

The chief never tried to catch that hot potato—he just let it fly by.

"It's you," he said. "I'll be goddamned if this department is going to investigate the Minneapolis department. That seems to be one of the critical questions, where the porn came from, and you guys have jurisdiction in Minneapolis. We don't."

"That's true," Sands began. "However—"

Rose Marie jumped in: "Henry, give it to Lucas."

Sands took a deep breath and said, "We've got federal funding being talked about right now. No matter what happens here, whether Smalls or Grant wins the election, we're gonna piss somebody off. The funding comes right through the Senate Office Building."

The chief said, "We got the same problem, big guy."

"Yeah, but it's a few pennies, relatively," Sands said. "I'm talking about another building and putting a major lab out in Worthington."

Rose Marie said again, to both of them, "Lucas has it. Everybody agree? Lucas has it."

The chief sat back and smiled, and Lucas said, *"Okay."*

ROSE MARIE, SANDS, AND LUCAS walked out to the parking lot together, and after Sands took off, Rose Marie said to Lucas, "You should call Elmer and see if he's the one who wants to break the news on Smalls. If he doesn't, I will—but we need to move now. We need to catch the five-o'clocks."

The five-o'clocks—the early-afternoon news.

"I'll call right now," Lucas said. He clicked up the governor's number on his cell phone, and Henderson answered on the third ring. Lucas told him what the group had decided, and Henderson said, "Tell Rose Marie to take the press conference. I'll call Porter now, and tell him what's coming."

He clicked off and Lucas relayed the word to Rose Marie. She said, "I'll set up a press conference for three o'clock. I'll be calling you from my hairdresser's for the background: just e-mail me a few tight paragraphs on the whole thing. Goddamnit, I was hoping Smalls would go down."

"Maybe he still will," Lucas said.

"Maybe," she said. "Taryn is cute, smart, and she's got more money than Elmer."

"Okay . . ."

"So how are you going to handle the investigation? Now that it's public?"

"Don't know yet," Lucas said. "I'm thinking about it."

LUCAS WALKED OVER to his car and climbed in, and his phone went off: Porter Smalls. Lucas answered and Smalls said, "Thank you. I just talked with Elmer. I owe you big-time and I don't forget."

"That makes me a little nervous," Lucas said. "I don't want to be owed: this is my job."

"I don't care. I owe you," Smalls said.

When Smalls got off the phone, Lucas called Kidd: "Did you ever get a chance to look at that list of campaign members?"

"Should be in your e-mail," Kidd said. "There are only a dozen who might be serious contenders. There are two people of particular interest. Daniel MacGuire and Rudy Holly. MacGuire is gay and has run a gay Republicans group, but Smalls has been against gay marriage, so . . . And MacGuire is also a depressive and has anger-management issues, and is taking medication for both. Holly is a conspiracy theory guy, going back to the Clinton years and that whole blow-job business. I've seen some stuff he's put on some conspiracy sites, and the thing is, he's nuts."

"Any lonely middle-aged women in there?" Lucas asked.

"Yes. You're thinking, what?"

"Tubbs wasn't crazy, he was calculating. Somebody had to set the booby trap the morning that the volunteer tripped it—and that wasn't Tubbs, because Tubbs has been backtracked by a pretty good cop: he wasn't at the campaign office that morning. The question is, did he have a lover? Or a very close friend? Somebody he could trust with this?"

After a moment of silence, Kidd said, "Ramona Johnson. She would be your best bet. Divorced four years ago . . . let me see here . . . until about five months ago, she was complaining on Facebook about the lack of eligible men and the problems of middle-aged women. Then she shut up."

"Ramona Johnson."

"Yes. There's one more possibility. A Sally Fey. She's younger, she's thirty-one, and she has a new beau, but she's not talking about it. From what I've seen of her and her e-mails . . ."

"You've got her e-mails?"

"Forget I said that. From what I've seen of her, she's a very shy, quiet type, and she's a little mousy. Doesn't do much with her hair," Kidd said. "But you can see the hope in her eyes."

"You can see her eyes?"

"Try to stay on track," Kidd said. "If the right guy said the right things to her . . ."

"Tubbs could do that. He had a reputation as a ladies' man," Lucas said.

"So put Fey on the list." He spelled her name, and Lucas wrote it down.

WHEN HE GOT OFF the phone with Kidd, Lucas used his cell phone to check his e-mail, looked at the list that Kidd had shipped him. Twelve names, half men, half women. Would it be an ideologue or a lover?

He'd track down as many of the people on the list as he could, and ask them the hard question. Did you set the booby trap? If the answer was no, Lucas would say, "You realize that Tubbs was killed for what he knew. If you're lying, you could be next."

If the answer was still no, the next question would be, "If you didn't set it, who did?"

It *could* work.

8

T aryn Grant's phone buzzed, a call, not an alarm. She was lying on her bed, waking up from a much-needed afternoon nap. She stretched, yawned, picked up the phone, and said, "Hello?"

"What are you doing?" Her campaign manager, Connie Schiffer.

"Took a nap. I just woke up."

"Good. We need you sharp. You're ready for tonight?" A fundraiser at the Wayzata Country Club. Taryn didn't actually need the funds, but if people gave you money, they tended to support you, to feel a connection.

"Absolutely."

"You're bringing the gorgeous David?" David Wein, a commodities broker who would someday inherit his father's firm. A small firm. David was a corn expert, but was also thoroughly grounded in soybeans, and sometimes dabbled in sugar beets. He looked good, though he was always called David, and never Dave.

"Tonight, anyway," Taryn said.

There was a *tone* in her voice and Connie instantly picked it up: "Ooo, if you're done with him, could I have him for a week or so?"

"Then, when you were done with him, he'd go around comparing our . . . attributes . . . with the boys in the locker room," Taryn said.

After a few seconds of silence, Connie said, "Wait—you're saying that would be a bad thing?"

Taryn laughed and said, "You're *such* a slut. I like that."

"Yeah, well, I'm now walking out to the turbo after spending the last two hours at KeeKee's. I spent four thousand, three hundred and sixty dollars on ridiculously overpriced clothing sewn by poverty-stricken foreigners. I'm all shopped out and we need to talk."

"I have to run through the shower and gel up," Taryn said.

"Fifteen minutes," Connie said.

"If I'm not quite ready, I'll tell Dannon to let you in."

"Mmm . . . Dannon . . ."

Taryn laughed again, pushed *End*. She switched to the walkie-talkie function and was instantly answered by Dannon. She said, "Connie will be here in a few minutes. We've got Push at four o'clock and Borders at five, that'll take another hour. Then back here to dress for the party tonight. David will pick me up."

He said, "I've got the schedule," and "Alice is in the house. Carver will be here at five."

TARYN WENT INTO THE bathroom and examined her eyes for circles, jumped in and out of the shower, then went to work on her face. She used only minimal makeup during the day; her natural Scandinavian complexion was good enough, most of the time.

The problem with politics was that it went on well into the night. The night before, she'd gone to a reception in Sunfish Lake with fifty of the faithful, and it had gone late. When the party ended, a dozen of them had gathered in the homeowner's recreation room and had gotten down to the nut-cutting.

Her lead over Smalls was holding, and the numbers of leaners—people who were not fully committed yet, but who were inclined to vote for her—was increasing. She was going to win, and if she won, if she took off Porter Smalls, she wanted to hit Washington with a bang.

The people in the rec room had had some ideas about how she could do that; two of them were former U.S. senators themselves.

THEN, THAT MORNING, SHE'D been up at five o'clock, and had hit a series of assembly plants at the morning shift changes, and quickly returned to the Twin Cities for the local morning talk shows. She'd done two of them, but one was way the hell out west, and the other was almost downtown. It'd been hectic.

After the talk shows, she spoke to the Optimist Club in Forest Lake, another short out-of-town trip. She could feel a tickle in the back of her throat, and worried that she might be losing her voice. Schiffer had given her some kind of double-secret lozenge used, supposedly, by the president, to keep the voice going. She'd pop one as soon as she was done with her face.

Taryn looked at herself in the mirror: maybe a shadow there in the eyes, from too many twenty-hour days. Maybe from Tubbs? No: that was dwindling in the rearview mirror. She had more important things to worry about.

And nobody had heard a thing from the cops.

She'd been a little surprised by the campaign. She'd known politics was harsh, but had no idea exactly how harsh it was. There seemed to be one polestar, one overriding objective, one singular focus: to win. Nothing else really counted. Just winning.

She liked that. It fit her.

She went back to work on her face.

DANNON HAD JUST FINISHED his backyard checks when Schiffer arrived in her plum-colored Porsche Panamera. He let her in, and she went to the living room, carrying a legal briefcase full of paper, which she began digging through. Dannon asked her if she wanted a drink, and she took a lime-water, which he got for her.

Schiffer was a short, sturdy, dark-eyed woman, twice-divorced, with no regrets about either the marriages or the divorces. She had a degree in mechanical engineering from Duke, but after a month working for a lobbying firm in Washington, D.C., she'd never again looked with desire on an open-channel crimper. One thing led to another, and at forty, she was one of the country's best professional campaign managers.

She was sitting on the soft-as-wool leather couch, looking at a miniature legal pad, when Taryn came down from the bathroom, wearing black slacks and a white angora sweater, with gold earrings and a modest gold necklace.

"Dannon said he'd be in the monitoring room. Alice is outside," Schiffer said.

Taryn nodded and dropped into a chair opposite Schiffer. "So what's up?"

"Things are developing and it's almost all good," Schiffer said. "I talked to Ray Jorgenson, just in passing, and he says that Smalls is toast. That doesn't mean we can let up: we have to go after him even harder. Push his head under. Kick him while he's down."

"I thought we were doing that," Taryn said.

"We are, but we can always do more. Ben Wells is giving a talk to the Minneapolis chamber, and if we could commit to a twenty-five-thousand-dollar donation in two years, and if we can plant a question with somebody, he's willing to go off on Smalls. You know, an unscripted spontaneous statement, spoken in real but slightly saddened anger. He'd call for Porter's withdrawal."

Wells was a Republican congressman, who might like a shot at Smalls's Senate seat someday, after he grew up. Taryn asked, "Would it help twenty-five thousand dollars' worth?"

"Yes. It'd absolutely curdle the Republican vote," Schiffer said. "But Wells wants a call from your father, since you wouldn't be able to make the donation. You know, being . . . a loyal mainstream Democrat."

"I'll talk to Father tonight," Taryn said. "He'll want me to kick the money back to him somehow, but that's not a problem."

"Good. Then let's make it happen." Schiffer drew a line through an item on the yellow pad.

THEY SPENT FORTY-FIVE MINUTES plowing through the minutiae of the campaign. Taryn was running as a law-and-order Democrat, as conservative as she could be and still get the nod from the party. The party understood the problem with taking down Smalls, and hadn't really expected her, or any other Democrat, to win, so it was willing to overlook a little political incorrectness. On the other hand, she couldn't be too incorrect.

Walking the line was both interesting and delicate.

Schiffer said, "About the gorgeous David. If you really are thinking of breaking it off with him—or in him—I'd suggest that you wait for three weeks. Everybody understands that it's a nice, adult relationship, and Smalls has banged enough strange women that he won't mention it, but you probably wouldn't want to call it off right now. It'd make you look flighty. Or unsteady. Or fickle."

"Okay. I've about had it with David's act, but he doesn't know that," Taryn said. "I'll keep him on until the excitement dies down."

"Excellent." Another item checked off on Schiffer's list. "Now, over at Push. We fully support Push and we'll find money for it somewhere. The problem is that the Republicans are unnecessarily locking up money or sending it off to their already-rich friends . . ."

". . . and as a longtime successful businesswoman, I know how that works," Taryn recited, "I adamantly oppose socialism for the rich while the less-well-to-do have their funding cut off . . ."

". . . for important neighborhood programs like Push," Schiffer said, "which keeps the drug dealers out of our neighborhoods . . ."

". . . especially black ones with cornrows, who wear hoodies and those funny low-crotch pants and listen to that awful hopscotch music, or whatever it is."

Schiffer recoiled: "Oh, Jesus Christ, Taryn, don't give me a heart attack," she said, clutching at her chest. "Remember: no sense of humor. How many times do I have to tell you that: *No sense of humor*. Humor can get you in all kinds of shit and we've got this won, if we don't get funny."

"Then we go to Borders," Taryn continued. "I don't drink too much and I tell everybody that I don't want their money but I do want their love, and—"

"*No humor,*" Schiffer said. "You don't want their money, but you do want their respect—"

"I got it, I got it," Taryn said. "You need to take a couple of aspirin, Connie."

Schiffer shook a finger at her: "I lost the first race I ran because I didn't nail down those details. I let my candidate speak honestly. I let him be funny and intelligent: that was the last time I'll make *that* mistake. Now listen to what I'm saying, goddamnit. You want to be a U.S. senator? You want to go higher than that? Then you stay on program."

Taryn nodded: "Yes. I know and I agree. I like to tease you, but I'm on program."

Schiffer relaxed. "I know. You're a natural at this, and with training, you'll get even better. You'll get that big-time polish. Some people spend twenty years in the Senate and *never* get that. You could. You could be a contender."

"If I stay on program."

"Absolutely."

They both knew what they were thinking, though neither said it: Taryn Grant had what it took to be president. She had the business background, she understood economics and finance, she had the money wrapped up, she looked terrific, she had a mind that understood the necessary treacheries: a silken Machiavelli.

THEY DID PUSH at four o'clock, and Borders at five, and Taryn stayed on program. Dannon hovered in the background, with what looked like a G&T in his hand, which was really water with a slice of lemon. Alice Green stayed outside with the cars.

Taryn knew she'd done well with the richie-rich crowd. They were, her involvement with the Democratic Party to one side, her people. She'd known many of the younger ones since childhood, and had slept with two of them.

So she was a little surprised when, after she'd given her talk on shared values, Schiffer had appeared as she began circulating through the Borders living room, and had taken her arm in a nearly painful grip and hustled her out to a hallway.

"We've got a problem," she said.

"What?" Taryn thought, *Murder.*

"Smalls didn't do it. Didn't do the porn," Schiffer said. "One of the governor's people, Rose Marie Roux, has been on television saying that it's possible that he was framed. Smalls had a spontaneous press conference demanding that the people who did this be caught. There's an implication there . . . that it could have been an opposition trick. That would be you."

"When did this happen?" Taryn asked.

"Top of the five-o'clock news. Everybody has it. We need to come up with a reaction and we need it fast."

"Let me finish the hand-shaking," Taryn said. "You go sit in the corner and think."

TARYN WORKED THE CROWD for another half hour, then swirled out of the room, calling out good-byes. Schiffer was waiting at the door with Green. Taryn had four vehicles, the largest and most ungainly and only American one being the large silver GMC Yukon Denali, which she'd acquired the day before she launched her campaign. She didn't want the right-wingers asking why she didn't "Buy American"; and if some leftie asked about the environmental impact, she'd ask, "What, you don't believe in Minnesota's ethanol economy?" In any case, the Porsche, Jag, and M5 stayed under wraps.

Leaving the house, she kissed Ellen Borders on the cheek,

squeezed her husband's biceps, pointed Green, who usually rode with her, at the security car, trading places with Barb Siegel, the media fixer.

Schiffer drove, and Dannon and Green fell in behind, discreet in the gray BMW sport-utility escort vehicle.

In the car with Schiffer and Siegel, Taryn closed her eyes and said, aloud, *"We understand that this news is a preliminary statement, but we certainly hope that Senator Smalls is found not responsible for this distasteful child pornography discovery. But, as long as we have to talk about unpleasant things, let me say that I bitterly resent Porter Smalls's implicit suggestion that his political opponents may be involved with this situation. I'm his only political opponent at the moment, so that was aimed at me. I'll tell Senator Smalls this: I've long been involved in child-care issues, and have devoted quite a lot of my hard-earned money to charities that help children. Need I point out that he has not been? That he should suggest this . . . just totally creeps me out."*

"Not 'hard-earned money,'" Schiffer said. "You inherited too much, and not everybody knows you founded your own company. Say, 'devoted a lot of my time.' And get rid of the 'totally creeps me out.' That sounds Valley girl, and you already look too Valley girl."

Taryn nodded. *"Where was I . . . That he should suggest this, I can only characterize as vicious. As distasteful in the extreme. And, frankly, as creepy. I would remind him that this child pornography was on his personal computer, in his personal campaign office, and if somebody placed this pornography on his computer . . ."*

"Personal computer . . . and 'creepy' is good, because he is a little creepy," Siegel said.

". . . if somebody placed this child pornography on his personal computer, and it wasn't his, then it was one of the people in his campaign

office—the office that he's supposedly running. And I will tell you—I've checked, and none of my people has ever been in Porter Smalls's office. Furthermore, I'd note that what Commissioner Roux said tonight didn't say that Porter Smalls was innocent of the child pornography charge, just that there seem to be other possibilities."

"No. No. Quit after the part where you say, 'the office he's supposedly running,'" Schiffer said. "When you're done, I'll get some of the TV people together and make the point, off the record, that he's not been shown to be innocent. They'll run with that."

"The more we can hook his name to child porn, the better it'll be for us, even if he's innocent," Siegel said. "If there's a headline every day that says, 'child porn' and 'Porter Smalls,' then that wouldn't be all bad."

"It was better the other way," Schiffer said, "because we had him beat. Now this adds a complication."

"I *will* beat him," Taryn said. "Where are we doing the press conference?"

"I thought the front lawn, inside the gate," Schiffer said. "There's a nice sort of amphitheater thing there on the lawn."

"You think we could get them around by the pool?" Taryn asked.

"Well, we could, but why would we?"

"Because it looks rich. The point is, if this hurts me, I'll be hurt with the more conservative voters out here," Taryn said. "The richer ones. I want to make the point, 'I'm one of you.' I've got the liberals no matter what."

Schiffer thought about that for a moment, and then said, "Yeah. That's good."

Taryn said, "That fuckin' Roux. What the heck was she doing?"

"Didn't even get a heads-up," Schiffer said. "Well, when you get to Washington . . ."

THEY WERE ALMOST to the house when Schiffer said, "You know, I read a lot of history. One thing that I've noticed is that people who go a long way in politics seem to have some kind of destiny. Opponents die, seats open up when they need them, they get an appointment that's critical . . . This thing with Smalls. This is a test, but you *will* beat him. It's your destiny. You do ten years, work really hard at it . . . You'd be a hot, smart, rich, law-and-order Democrat, with loads of experience, and still *young*. . . . I mean, who knows where you could go."

Taryn didn't laugh. No false modesty here; just a rich young blond woman with a burning case of narcissistic personality disorder. She did say, "We may be getting ahead of ourselves. Let's get Smalls out of the way first."

"I'm just saying: it's your destiny," Schiffer said, looking across at Taryn in the dark. "You'd be a fool not to ride it hard as you can."

9

Lucas spent the afternoon chasing campaign committee members from Kidd's list. By early evening, he had found and interviewed ten of the twelve.

Two were out of town, one of those two would be back the next day, the other, not for a week and a half, having begun a hunting trip to Northern Ontario. Lucas was curious about that, because the timing seemed odd. He had a conference with Cory Makovsky, the gossip in the distribution center, who said, quietly, "He's being fired."

"Ah. When was he last in here?"

"Couple weeks ago. He was in charge of lawn signs, and the word is, there were a lot fewer lawn signs than the campaign paid for. Of course, it's hard to know for sure, but the rumor is, we're short about ten thousand signs at two dollars each. He went north before Bob Tubbs disappeared."

Lucas crossed the sign guy off his list.

LUCAS ARRANGED THE INTERVIEWS through Helen Roman, the office manager, who also found Lucas a small room with a desk and two chairs. He lined up those people who were working that day, the ten-of-twelve. He asked all of them the same questions, explaining that he was investigating the presumptive murder of Tubbs, but he focused on the four names isolated by Kidd.

MacGuire, a big, square guy with short curly red hair, denied any knowledge of anything that Tubbs had been doing, and was out-front with his gay issues. But, he said, he had no real problem working with Smalls, as conservative as Smalls was. "Senator Smalls is conservative on social issues, and I lean the other way, except on guns—I'm pro-gun, to use the shorthand. But I'm *very* conservative on financial and economic issues. Something has to be done to get the country back on an even economic keel. That's what I work on for the senator. Social issues, I'm not so involved with that. He is against gay marriage, and I'm for it, but we joke about it, you know? He's not really anti-gay, per se—he's got several gays on his staff, men and women both, and when one of them got married to her partner, he sent along a nice wedding present. So . . . it's complicated. But I think of him as a friend. And there are a hell of a lot of worse guys in the Senate than Smalls, and Taryn Grant doesn't seem a hell of a lot more understanding about gay issues than he is."

Lucas dug for opinions about other staffers, and MacGuire shrugged him off.

"This whole thing is a mystery—I have no idea who'd want to set the senator up. I mean, on the staff. Maybe we've got a spy somewhere, I don't know. But it's not me."

"We need to know who it is, if he or she is there," Lucas said. "That person's life could be in danger from the same people who killed Tubbs . . . unless he or she did it. Then, that'd mean you're working with a cold-blooded killer."

"Okay. I'll think about it," MacGuire said. "I'm not lying to you here, I really don't know—but I'll think about it, and ask around."

RUDY HOLLY, the conspiracy theory guy, thought Tubbs had been taken off because he'd been behind the dirty trick involving the porn. "The Republicans in this state rarely do well . . . but now, all of a sudden, they are doing well. The Dems are frantic. I believe that there's a force out there, funded by union money, that is putting pressure on people . . . probably set up the porn thing, then killed Tubbs to cover up. It seems so obvious. . . ."

He went on like that for a while, and before he was done, Lucas had dismissed him as being ineffectually goofy, although his ideas about the killing were roughly the same as Lucas's own. Holly said he had no idea who on the staff might have been involved with Tubbs, or might be working as a spy.

SALLY FEY SHRANK in her office chair when Lucas asked the question, her shoulders turning in, her neck seeming almost to shorten, as though she were trying to pull her head into a turtle shell. She looked up at Lucas and said, "Robert and I had an ambiguous relationship. . . ."

She was twisting her hands, as she spoke. She was a slight woman, who might have been attractive if she'd done anything to make it so. But she didn't: her clothing—she wore dresses—might have come from the 1950s. She wore neither jewelry nor makeup, but did wear square, clunky shoes. She looked at Lucas from under her eyebrows, and at an angle, as though she were worried that he might strike her.

Lucas tried to be as soft as he could be; it wasn't his natural attitude. "Ambiguous . . . how? Was this a sexual relationship?"

"Yes. Twice. I mean, we . . . yes, we slept together twice. When
he went away, wherever he went, it's hard to believe that he might
be dead, because he was so upbeat when I last saw him. . . . Anyway,
I thought maybe the police would ask me about him, but nobody
did, and I didn't know what to do about that. I was scared. . . . I
didn't know what happened to him, and when he didn't call me
Saturday or Sunday, I thought he wasn't interested anymore."

"When was the last time you heard from him?" Lucas asked.

"Friday night, about . . . nine o'clock," she said.

"And when did you last see him?"

"Friday night . . . about nine o'clock. I didn't stay over." Her eyes
roamed the small office, meeting Lucas's eyes only with difficulty.
"I just . . . visited for a while, and went home."

"Then people began looking for him, and you didn't say anything?"

"Well . . . yes. I did think I should," Fey said. "But one day came
and went, and nothing happened, and nobody seemed to really
know where he was, and some people thought he was drinking . . .
and I just . . . let it go. I really didn't have anything to contribute,
and I thought I might get in trouble."

"Did he ever ask you . . . or suggest to you . . . that he might
want to pull some kind of dirty trick on Senator Smalls?"

"Oh, no, he would never have done that," Fey said. "I mean, he
might have tried to pull a dirty trick, but he wouldn't have spoken
to me about it. I *like* Senator Smalls and Robert knew that. The
senator and I have common interests. He likes classical piano and
he likes Postimpressionist art. If Robert had asked me to do a dirty
trick on Senator Smalls, I would have refused and I would have told

Senator Smalls. Robert teased me about that. About me being loyal."

Lucas worked her for a while, but in the end, believed her. "Are you friends with Ramona Johnson?" Lucas asked.

"Ramona? Well, yes, I guess. We don't socialize or anything, but we're friendly."

"What is her attitude toward Senator Smalls?"

"Well . . ." Fey's eyes flew off again. "Oh . . ."

"Nobody will know who said what in here," Lucas said. "Did Ramona have some kind of grudge against Senator Smalls?"

"Oh, no, I wouldn't think so," Fey said. "Just the opposite. I had the impression, mmm . . ." She trailed away.

"You think they had a relationship?"

"I, mmm, I thought it . . . possible," Fey said. "*Please* don't tell her I said that."

JOHNSON WAS THE LAST of the ten people he'd question that day. Before he called her in, he phoned Smalls and said, "I have a somewhat delicate personal question to ask you."

"Ask."

"Ramona Johnson?"

"No. Though the thought has crossed my mind," Smalls said.

"Would she have felt . . . neglected, or spurned?"

"I don't believe so. . . . No. I don't see it. You think she had something to do with the porn?"

"I don't think anything in particular. I'm just trying to get everybody straight, and to cross-check what I can. Looking for motives," Lucas said. "If you wanted to talk to somebody on the committee staff about art or music, who would you have talked to?"

"You've interviewed Sally Fey . . . and she's the one I would have talked to. I didn't sleep with her, either."

"Okay. That's what I needed."

"Wait a minute," Smalls said, "I've got a question for you, before you hang up. Have you heard any rumblings from the AG's office?"

"I haven't heard a thing. Should I have?"

"Mmm. I don't know," Smalls said. "He had that guy over at the St. Paul police when this ICE woman copied the hard drive. Now there's a rumor around that he wants to know what we found that brought about Rose Marie's announcement."

"I think she told him."

"I've heard that he wants it in detail," Smalls said. "He wants to know how it all came about. But all I've got is a rumor."

"I haven't heard a thing," Lucas said.

RAMONA JOHNSON was a fleshy, dark-haired woman with intelligent eyes and a smoldering, resentful aggression that piqued Lucas's curiosity. He began by asking about her career, first as a researcher and then as a senior staffer. She had three degrees, she said, both a B.A. and a master's in political science, and an MBA in business. She'd spent most of her life bumping against various glass ceilings, she said, and was presently planning a number of political initiatives involving Republican women's work issues—glass ceiling issues.

She had nothing to do with Tubbs, she said, and resented the fact that she'd been asked to talk to a police officer investigating his disappearance. "I know you think you're just doing your job, but there are more and more police-state aspects to the way our various security apparati are conducting themselves. Really, your questions are no more than a fishing expedition."

"That's what most investigations *are*," Lucas said. "So, you had nothing to do with Tubbs lately. Have you *ever* had anything to do with Tubbs?"

"No," she said. "I've always been Republican policy, he's always been Democratic operations. We've worked on opposing political campaigns, of course, and we sometimes go to the same parties. I've known him for years, but we've never been . . . intimate. I don't mean that just in a sexual way, either. I mean, we've never really shared confidences."

"You know that possession of that child porn is a crime, and that the use of the child porn in an effort to smear Senator Smalls would be another crime, and that Tubbs, if we could find him, if he's not dead, could be looking at years in prison? As would an accomplice?"

"Is that a threat?" she asked.

Lucas shook his head: "No. I'm telling this to everyone. I want everybody to understand the stakes involved. We're naturally more interested in the possible, the likely, murder of Mr. Tubbs than we are in an accomplice who might not even have understood what he or she was getting into. We'd be interested in discussing a possible immunity, or partial immunity, with that person, if we could find him or her. We'd also want that person to know that if Tubbs was murdered, then he or she might be next in line."

"But that's not me," Johnson said. "Why are you telling me?"

"Because if it's not you, I'd expect you to talk to your friends about this. I want the word to get around. There almost certainly is an accomplice, and we really need to talk to that person . . . for her own protection."

"Well," she said, "not me. Are we done?"

Lucas spread his hands. "If you've got nothing else . . . we're done."

———

WHEN SHE WAS GONE, Lucas took out his cell phone, went online and looked up the plural of *apparatus*, and found that it was *apparatus*, or *apparatuses*, and not *apparati*. He said, "Huh," turned the phone off and thought about Johnson.

She was the most interesting of the staffers he'd spoken to, because of the underlying self-righteousness, anger, spite . . . whatever. She wore it like a gown. He'd seen it often enough in government work, people who felt that they were better than their job, and better than those around them; a princess kidnapped by gypsies, and raised below her station.

He was still thinking about Johnson, looking at the blank face of his phone, when it lit up and rang at him. Rose Marie calling.

"Yeah?"

"We've got a problem," she said. "That goddamn Lockes is about to serve subpoenas on all of us, to find out what happened that led to the press conference."

"Aw, man . . . Can't you threaten him or something?" Lucas asked.

"Elmer is going to talk with him, but . . . Elmer's going away in two years, one way or another. Lockes wants his job."

"Is he going to subpoena the governor?"

"I don't think so—but he knows you were asked by the governor to look at the case," Rose Marie said. "There's nothing to do but be upfront about it."

"The problem is, I used a couple of personal friends as information sources and computer support," Lucas said, referring to Kidd and ICE. "If I have to name them, they could be pretty goddamn unhappy."

"That will probably come up, but as technical people, they shouldn't have too much of a problem," Rose Marie said. "If they're called, they just tell the truth, and go on their way. They were asked to help out in a law enforcement investigation, and they did."

"Aw, shit," Lucas said.

ICE would not be much of a problem; she'd worked with law enforcement, and had testified in court hearings about her work. But he dreaded calling Kidd, who'd always seemed to Lucas to be a reclusive sort, an artist, a fringe guy who, as it turned out, also knew something about computers. He shouldn't have used him, Lucas thought: Kidd looked and talked tough, but might actually be too brittle for a rough-and-tumble political fight.

He called Kidd, and was surprised by the reaction: "Don't worry about it," Kidd said. "I'm a guy you knew from back when, who's worked in the computer industry, so you got me to take a look. I don't mind showing up to tell him that, as long as I don't have to wear a suit."

"You got a suit?"

"Yeah, but I only wear it when I marry somebody," Kidd said. "Listen, I'm pretty friendly with Jed Cothran and Maury Berkowitz. If you think this guy could cause you some real trouble, I could give them a ring. If they lean on him a little, with the governor, I don't think he'll be inclined to a show trial, or anything. If that's what's worrying you."

Lucas was surprised a second time: Cothran and Berkowitz had been Minnesota U.S. senators, one from each party. "How do you know those guys?"

"Ah, back in the day, I used to sell do-it-yourself political polling kits. This was back before everything was run on polls, and everybody hired a pro. They were customers, young guys on their way up. They sorta became friends."

"I had no idea," Lucas said. "I don't think you need to call them—I was just worried you'd think I sold you out or something. Lockes won't be interested in you. He'll figure you for a technician. He's more interested in the . . . political interplay. You might not even be called. In fact, the governor might be able to head the whole thing off."

LUCAS WENT HOME. Ate dinner, messed around with the kids, told Weather what had happened that day, including the possibility of a subpoena. "Why does everybody seem to think that Lockes is a horse's ass?" she asked.

"Because he's a horse's ass," Lucas said.

A little after nine o'clock, as Lucas was browsing his financial websites, Horse's Ass's minions arrived with a subpoena. There were two of them, one of each gender, and he knew the woman. Sarah Sorensen was a mid-level assistant attorney general, a bland, brown-haired woman who was wearing an animal-rights baseball cap. She gave Lucas the paper and introduced the male half of the delegation, Mark Dunn, who looked around and said, "This is a nice property."

There was a *tone* about the comment that suggested that a cop shouldn't be living quite so well, and Sorensen picked it up and said curtly, "Lucas founded Davenport Simulations. You may have heard of it."

Dunn said, "Of course," and shut up.

Sorensen said to Lucas, "The subpoena is for tomorrow, but

we'd like to have a little pre-interview here, if you have the time. We'd like to get this over with as quickly as possible—tomorrow, if possible. We need to know if we've contacted everybody necessary to get a complete picture."

Sorensen already had the names of all the people in the meeting at the St. Paul Police Department, plus the governor, and Neil Mitford, the governor's weasel, and ICE. Lucas added Kidd's name to the list, feeling guilty about it, even though Kidd hadn't seemed bothered by the prospect.

Sorensen said, "This Ingrid Eccols—ICE, you call her—and Mr. Kidd are essentially computer technicians?"

"That's correct," Lucas said. "We contacted them because we had rather pressing time limitations, with the pornography allegations pushed up against the approaching elections. We got a copy of the hard drive the way we did, through Senator Smalls's attorney, because it was convenient and fast. You understand that we didn't change anything, that we were operating only from a copy of the computer hard drive, that the original was preserved."

"We understand that," Sorensen said.

"We were trying to cover as much ground as quickly as we could, so I called in a couple of personal favors from people I knew to be knowledgeable about computers. And, what popped out, popped out."

Dunn said, "Excuse me, but I don't understand exactly what popped out."

"A kind of booby trap which would reveal the porn to anyone who touched Senator Smalls's keyboard . . . and would allow it to be hidden quickly, should Senator Smalls return before the trap was triggered," Lucas said. "During that investigation, Robert Tubbs's name came up, and further investigation—"

"We have that file," Sorensen said.

"Then you know what I know," Lucas said. "The only thing not in the file is what I was doing today, which was interviewing staff members with Senator Smalls's campaign committee to try to determine whether Tubbs had an accomplice. I interviewed ten members of the campaign, and all of them denied any connection to Tubbs."

Sorensen asked, "And you believe all of them?"

"I don't really believe *any* of them," Lucas said. "I can't afford to—but I think all but one are telling the truth. I just don't know who that one is."

Sorensen said, "Okay. If you can give me the phone number for Mr. Kidd, I think that's all we'll need before tomorrow. Ten a.m., if that's good with you."

AT TEN O'CLOCK the next morning, Lucas showed up at the attorney general's office, wound up waiting until after noon, as Rose Marie Roux, Henry Sands, Neil Mitford, Rick Card, and Roger Morris were called in, one by one, and questioned. The interviews were being done in a conference room with a long table, a dozen chairs, five lawyers including Lockes, the attorney general, Sorensen, and Dunn. A court reporter sat at the far end of the table with a steno machine and a tape recorder.

Lucas was sworn, and told the same story he'd told Sorensen the night before, but in more detail. Lockes, a narrow, dark-haired man who looked like he ran marathons, probed for the reason Lucas had taken the assignment directly from the governor.

"The governor told me that he knew Senator Smalls personally, a lifelong . . . relationship, if not exactly a friendship," Lucas said.

"He said that Senator Smalls swore to him that he was innocent, and had been set up, probably by somebody on the campaign committee staff—possibly a spy working for the Democratic Party. The governor was inclined to believe him, judging from his knowledge of Smalls's character. The governor was then concerned on two fronts: First, one of simple fairness, if Senator Smalls was telling the truth. Second, he worried that if it was, in fact, a dirty trick, it could come back to haunt his party during the elections."

"But why did he come to you, specifically, rather than speak to Rose Marie Roux or Henry Sands?" Lockes asked.

"Because speed was required. Urgently required. The governor was familiar with my work, and once he decided to move, he informed Rose Marie, who informed Henry, and he talked to me, all within a very short period of time. I'm not sure of the exact sequence there."

Dunn asked, "Do you routinely take political assignments directly from the governor?"

"No. And I object to that characterization," Lucas snapped. "The governor realized that a crime had been committed and that an important election could be affected by it."

"He didn't *know* that a crime had been committed," Dunn said.

"Of course he did," Lucas said. "If Senator Smalls was knowingly in possession of child pornography, then he'd committed a crime. If somebody planted the pornography on Senator Smalls, then a different crime had been committed. It had to be one or the other, so the crime was there. As a senior agent of the BCA, he asked me to find out the truth of the matter, and as rapidly as possible, with the least amount of bureaucratic involvement, in an effort to resolve this before the election. I'd emphasize that he was looking for the truth, not just to clear Senator Smalls. It'd be far better for the governor's party if Smalls was guilty: it would give them an extra Senate seat in a very tight political situation."

Lockes said tentatively, "There's been some mention of possible involvement by the Minneapolis Police Department."

Lucas shook his head. "That's purely conjecture at this point." He explained about what appeared to be an evidentiary photograph among the rest of the pornography.

"And this could tie in to the disappearance of Mr. Tubbs," Lockes said.

"Again, conjecture at this point," Lucas said.

"But if there's anything to all of this, if Tubbs doesn't show up somewhere . . . then we're talking about a murder."

Lucas nodded: "Yes. I'm treating it as a murder investigation."

Dunn started to jump in. "If the governor asked—"

Lockes held up a hand to stop him, then said to Lucas: "You're a busy man, with a murder out there. You better get back to it."

Lucas stood and said, "Thanks. I do need to do that."

And was gone.

HE CALLED THE GOVERNOR, outlined his testimony, and Henderson said, "Lockes told me he was going to wind it up today. Your computer pals are testifying later this afternoon, and that should be it. I don't know what he's planning to do, but after talking to me and Smalls, I suspect he smells dogshit on his shoe. If he wants to run for this office in two years, he doesn't need both me and Smalls on his ass. He's gonna have to get through a primary."

"What about Smalls? Could he be a problem?"

"No. He owes us big, and he knows it, and Porter does pay his bills," the governor said. "If it turns out Tubbs did it to him . . . well, Tubbs is probably dead. Not much blood to be wrung out of that stone, even if he wanted to."

"Is he going to win the election?"

"Neil says no—but I'm not sure. Porter's always been pretty resilient. On the other hand, his opponent is pretty hot, has an ocean of money, and a lead, with momentum. Not much time left. So . . . we'll see," Henderson said. "By the way . . . do you know her? Have you interviewed her?"

"No, I've never met her," Lucas said. "Seen her on TV."

"She'd be the main beneficiary, of course, if Smalls went down."

"I'll be talking to her, unless something else breaks before I get there," Lucas said. "Today, I've got one more of Smalls's staff members to interview, and I need to talk to my computer people about their testimony. Make sure everything is okay."

"Stay in touch," Henderson said.

THE AFTERNOON was like walking through tar: Lucas tracked down and interviewed the last of Smalls's volunteer staff, and the interview produced nothing. He talked to ICE and Kidd after their testimony, and learned that it had been perfunctory. He talked again with both Rose Marie and the governor, and updated Morris on the state of his investigation.

"That's not much of a state," Morris said when he was finished. "Investigation-wise, that's like the state of Kazakhstan."

"Tell me about it," Lucas said.

"What's next on the menu?"

"Dinner. It's just nice enough outside to barbecue. The housekeeper's out there now with ten pounds of baby-back ribs, sweet corn from California, honey-coated corn bread, baked potatoes with sour cream and butter, and mushroom gravy."

"You sadistic sonofabitch," Morris said. "I already finished my celery."

10

aryn Grant wore cotton pajamas at night, and had just gotten into them, in a dressing room off the hallway in her bedroom suite, a few minutes before midnight, when she heard—or maybe felt—footsteps on the wooden floor coming down to the bedroom. The security people were the only others in the house, and weren't welcome in her bedroom wing.

Something had happened, or was happening. She took down the Japanese kimono that she used as a robe, pulled it over her shoulders, and headed toward the door, just as the doorbell burped discreetly. She pressed an intercom button: "Yes?"

"It's me, Doug. I need to talk with you."

She popped the door and nodded down the hall: "In the sitting room."

"Yes," he said, and led the way.

The sitting room had three big fabric chairs arrayed around a circular table; the walls were in the form of a five-eighths dome—as though a big slice had been taken out of an orange—and kept their voices contained.

"What happened?" she asked, as she settled into a chair facing him.

"I talked with our source at the AG's office. The police unraveled how Tubbs set up the computer, and they've tied his disappearance to the porn. I've got a lot of details, if you want to hear them, but the main thing is, the police will probably want to interview you, since you had the most to gain from the porn attack. You'll need to figure out a response. The guy coming to interview you will probably be this Davenport, who I told you about."

"Give me the details," she said. "All of them. I'll forget them later."

Dannon spent twenty minutes on the briefing, reviewing what had happened that day at the attorney general's office, and the results so far of investigations by Davenport and a St. Paul homicide cop named Morris. "We've had one piece of great good luck: when they found Tubbs's hideout spot, there was no mention of the porn or any dirty tricks, other than the porn file itself. They did find some cash, and it may have been from us, but we were careful there, and it's untraceable."

When he was done, Taryn asked, "The fact that you talked to this guy at the AG's office, could that come back to us?"

"No, I don't think so—not in a way that could hurt us," Dannon said. "I left the impression that we were desperate to work out the political implications of what was going on, this close to the election. Of course, when he took the money, he was technically committing a crime, so he won't be inclined to talk."

"Unless he suddenly starts feeling guilty," Taryn said.

"Not a problem with this guy," Dannon said. "He believes he's on the side of Jesus, helping us beat Smalls. He knows taking the money was a crime of some kind, but he doesn't think he's really done anything wrong. He sees the money more as compensation for his time. A consultation fee."

"Amazing how that works," Taryn said.

"Yeah. Anyway, it all brings up the question about Tubbs's girl," Dannon said. "Davenport is going through the whole campaign committee office, grilling everybody, looking for his accomplice. I don't think she knows anything about us."

"Do you know who she is? What her name is?"

"Yeah, but I'm not going to tell you," Dannon said. "I don't want her name in your head, if you're asked about her."

She looked at him for a moment, thinking about that, then nodded and said, "Okay. I see that. But how could she know about us? Tubbs didn't know for sure. Not until he got here."

"Tubbs *knew*, he just didn't have any proof," Dannon said. "He didn't know my name or anything about me. We made the assumption, incorrect, in retrospect, that if the payoff was big enough, he'd keep his head down, that he wouldn't even want to know where the money came from. But once he started looking, it was just a matter of time before he found us."

Taryn stood and wandered around the sitting area, working it out. "The real problem is, if he mentioned anything to this woman, even his suspicions, those would sort of harden up if she talked with the police. You know what I mean? If Tubbs was alive, but he hadn't gone looking for you, and they found him and put him under oath, he'd have to admit that he couldn't identify the person who paid him. But if this Davenport finds his girl, his accomplice, and she just tells him what Tubbs *thought*, that takes on its own reality. And Tubbs won't be around to cross-examine, to say he didn't know where the money came from."

"That's true," Dannon said. "But: right now, they can't know Tubbs's motive. Not for sure. As far as they know, he might have done it on his own hook. If we *do* something about her, that would confirm to Davenport that there's somebody else operating here. If he finds her and she says she doesn't have any idea why Tubbs planted the porn, then it stops with Tubbs. But if *she* turns up dead, then there's gotta be somebody else. See what I mean?"

"I do," she said. "It's a conundrum."

"I've been thinking about it," Dannon said. "Davenport's already raised the question of whether somebody in the Minneapolis Police Department might have been involved with the porn. Well, there is somebody. When Tubbs first got back in touch with me, with the porn idea, I asked him where he'd get it. He said he knew a vice cop in Minneapolis who had a file of it. I don't know if it's for the cop's own viewing pleasure, or just one of those things that cops do. Anyway, I pushed Tubbs on it, saying I had to vet the guy before Tubbs made an offer. Tubbs told me the guy's name is Ray Quintana. If word ever gets out that he supplied the porn, he's in a world of hurt. So I'm thinking . . . I could call Quintana, mention that Tubbs's girl could be a problem for him, and maybe he could figure out a way to do a little investigating for us. As a vice cop, looking into this porn allegation. Talk to her. Let us know if there's a problem."

"This is turning into a rat's nest," Taryn said. "One complication after another."

"Yes. And maybe the best way out would be to do nothing. Deny, deny. They'll be looking at you for sure, but there's no way to connect us to anything. We've never had any formal contact with Tubbs—you never met him, you don't know him, Connie doesn't know him. . . . We could just sit tight."

"Maybe even put out the word that we suspect Smalls of some

kind of disinformation campaign." Taryn stood and walked a few steps down the hall, then back, and a few steps up the hall, and back.

"I don't know how you'd work that—"

She waved a hand at him: "I do. That's not your concern. The real question mark is Tubbs's girl. If this Davenport cracks her, and she points at us, we can deny . . . but the word'll get out and the implications of it all, like Tubbs's disappearance . . . I'll lose the election."

"But you won't go to prison."

"But I want to win. That's the whole point of the exercise," Taryn said.

They sat in silence for a minute, then Dannon said, "What do you want me to do?"

"Think about it," she said. "You're smart. And I'll think about it overnight. We'll talk tomorrow morning. It's all a balancing of the various risks, and the various goals. It's like a calculus problem: and there is an answer."

THE HOUSE HAD WI-FI throughout, and when Dannon was gone, Taryn fired up her laptop, went online, and looked up Lucas Davenport. Google turned up thousands of entries, most from newspapers and television stations statewide, covering criminal cases on which he'd worked over the past twenty-five years.

There were also what appeared to be several hundred business-oriented entries from his involvement with Davenport Simulations.

Those caught her attention, and she dug deeper. Davenport, it seemed, had been a role-playing game designer as a young man, and then, with the rise of the machines, had created a number of simulations for 911 systems. The simulations were in use nation-wide, and after the World Trade Center attack, Davenport Simulations had moved more extensively into training software for security professionals. By that time, she found, Davenport was out of the business, having sold it to his management group.

The local business magazines estimated that he'd gotten out with around forty million dollars.

So he was smart and rich.

And the first batch of clips demonstrated that he was, without a doubt, a killer.

Somebody, she thought, that she might like.

SHE HAD A RESTLESS NIGHT, working through it all, and in the morning beeped Dannon on the walkie-talkie function and said, "I'm going to get an orange juice. Meet me by the pool in three minutes."

Three minutes later, she was asking, "This Quintana guy, the Minneapolis cop. If we asked him to check around, he wouldn't have any idea where the question was coming from, right?"

"Well, he'd have an idea," Dannon said. "It's possible that he and Tubbs speculated on it, but there's no way he could know for sure."

"Then I think we ask him to look up this woman, Tubbs's girl, and ask the question. He should be able to come up with some kind of legal reason for doing it—that he heard about the attorney general's review and thought he ought to look into the Minneapolis department's exposure, something like that. Some reason that wouldn't implicate him. Just doing his job."

"I thought about that last night—I couldn't decide. I'm about fifty-fifty on it," Dannon said.

"So I've decided," Taryn said. "Do it, but be clever about it. Don't give yourself away. Call from a cold phone."

"I can be careful," Dannon said, "but it's still a little more chum in the water. We could be stirring up the sharks."

"It's a small risk, and we need to take it," she said. "Make the call. Let's see what happens."

11

A few years earlier, Kidd had become entrapped in his computer sideline when the National Security Agency, working with the FBI, tried to tear up a hacking network to which he supposedly belonged. Kidd's team had managed to fend off the attention, and after several years of quiet, he'd begun to feel safe again.

Part of it, he thought, might be that he and Lauren had finally had to deal with the fact that they loved each other. Then the baby showed up, though not unexpectedly . . .

He *wanted* to be safe. He wanted all that old hacker stuff to be over. If you want something badly enough, he thought, sometimes you began to assume that you had it. He and his network had some serious assets, and hadn't been able to detect any sign that the feds were still looking for them.

Still, he was sure that if the government people thought they could set up an invisible spiderweb, so they'd get the vibration if Kidd touched the web . . . then they'd do that. They'd give it a shot.

So Kidd had had to stay with the computers, watching for trouble, although now, painting six and seven hours a day, he was working so hard that he hadn't time to do anything creative with the machines; and he was making so much money that he didn't have to.

He and the other members of his network understood that even monitoring the feds could be dangerous. Computer systems were totally malleable, changing all the time. Updating access code could lead to serious trouble if it was detected. In addition to that problem, the number of major computer systems was increasing all the time, and security was constantly getting better. So care was needed, and time was on the government's side.

The most powerful aspect of any bureaucracy, in Kidd's eyes, was the same thing that gave cancer its power: it was immortal. If you didn't seek it out and kill it, cell by cell, it'd just keep growing. Bureaucracies could chase you forever. You could defeat them over and over and over again, and the bureaucracy didn't much care, though some individual bureaucrats might.

The bureaucracy, as a whole, just kept coming, as long as the funding lasted.

As PART OF his monitoring efforts, Kidd had long been resident in the Minneapolis Police Department's computer systems, which had useful access to several federal systems. The federal systems had safeguards, of course, but since the basic design of the system had been done to *encourage* access by law enforcement, the safeguards were relatively weak. Once you had unrestricted access to a few big federal systems, you could get to some pretty amazing places.

None of which concerned him when he went out on the network from a Grand Avenue coffee shop eight hours after he'd testified for the attorney general. In his testimony, he'd represented himself as a former computer consultant who was mostly out of the business, and was now concentrating on art. That was true.

Which didn't mean he'd misplaced his brain.

So he got a grande no-foam latte and sat at a round plastic table at the back of the shop and slipped into the Minneapolis Police Department's computer system. Instead of going out to the federal networks, he began probing individual computers on the network. He was looking for a group of numbers—the number of bytes represented by the photo collection.

The collection was a big one, and though there'd be thousands of files in the department's computers, the actual number of bytes would vary wildly from file to file. If he found a matching number, it'd almost certainly be the porn file.

He'd thought he had a good chance to find the file; and he was right.

"THE PROBLEM," he told Lauren later that night, "is that I found four copies of it. I know which computers have accessed the files, but I don't know who runs those computers."

"Sounds like something Lucas should find out for himself," she said.

"Yeah. But how's he going to explain that he knows about the files? Without explaining about me?"

"Maybe that's something you should talk to him about," she said.

Kidd looked at his watch: "You think it's too late to call?"

"He said he stays up late."

Lucas answered on the third ring. "Hey, what's up?"

"I have a certain amount of access to the Minneapolis police computer system," Kidd began.

"I'm shocked," Lucas said. "So . . . what'd you find?"

"I found the porn file. I found it in four different places, but I don't know who controls the files. The files themselves have four different names. The thing is, I don't want to be connected to this one."

"Because then the cops will know you're inside," Lucas said.

"That's right."

"So how'd you do it?" Lucas asked.

Kidd explained, briefly, Lucas thought about it for a moment, then said, "How about this? I get a warrant, or a subpoena, or just an okay, whichever works. I show the file to ICE, and she finds that number. That byte number. We go over to Minneapolis and jack up their systems manager and ICE finds the files, like you did, using that number, all on the up-and-up."

"That would be perfect," Kidd said. "Let me give you the number you're looking for."

"You're not in the BCA system, are you?" Lucas asked.

"Of course not," Kidd said.

"Then how'd you get this phone number?" Lucas asked. "You're calling on my work phone."

"You called *me* on this phone—so your number was on *my* phone," Kidd said. "Jesus, don't you trust anyone?"

Lucas said, "Oh . . . maybe."

Kidd gave Lucas the number he'd be looking for, and hung up. Lauren said, "He suspects you're in the BCA system, huh?"

"Naw, he was just kicking the anthill, to see if anything ran out," Kidd said. "He's got no clue."

"I'd stay out of there for a while, anyway," Lauren said. "Just in case."

———

"KIDD IS INTO EVERYTHING," Lucas told Weather, as they got in bed. "He's all over Minneapolis and I know damn well he's in the BCA computers, too. He says he's not, but he's lying."

"Don't you trust anyone?" she asked.

"You and Letty," Lucas said. "Most of the time. Of course, I always check back and verify."

THE NEXT MORNING, he called ICE, described the file to her, and asked, "How do I find out how many bytes are in it?"

"Why do you want to know?"

"Because when I was working at the company, the guys there could find specific files by the number of bytes they had in them. I'd like to know how many are in this one, then I can take it over to the Minneapolis cops' system and look for it there."

"That'll work," she said. "Okay, you got the file up? I'll walk you through it."

She did, and eventually had Lucas write down the same number that Kidd had come up with, although he didn't tell her that. When he had the number, she said, "Do you trust the Minneapolis cops?"

"If somebody puts a gun in my ear," he said. "Why?"

"Because what if their systems guy plugs the number into his machine, says, 'Nope, not here.' You're far too ignorant to argue. Then what?"

"I've got that figured out—that was easy," he said.

"Yeah? What're you going to do?"

"I'm gonna take you with me."

———

THERE WAS BUREAUCRACY to be worked through. When Lucas talked to Rose Marie, she was unhappy about the necessity of jacking up the Minneapolis cops, even though she'd known it was coming. "We're doing everything right out in front of the media now, and I'm not going to have you serve a search warrant on Minneapolis," she said. "Talk to Robin and get him straight, we'll bring in their own Internal Affairs unit, and we'll talk about all the cooperation we're getting."

Robin Connolly was the Minneapolis chief of police.

"What if Connolly says no?" Lucas asked.

"He won't. He'll want to be out front on this, he'll want to be informed. If he does say no, I'll call him. I'll tell him that I'll personally stick the search warrant up his ass and then cut him out of the loop on the return."

"You're so grandmotherly sometimes," Lucas said.

Which didn't mean that Connolly didn't throw a fit when Lucas called him and told him what he wanted to do.

"What the hell are you talking about? You think we planted the porn file on Smalls? You're nuts, Davenport. I'm not going to . . ." blah blah blah.

Lucas said, "Rose Marie will be calling you in a minute or so. Maybe she can explain things more clearly than I have."

"Fuck a bunch of Rose Marie," Connolly shouted. "I'll put wheels on that bitch and roll her right into the Mississippi."

Lucas called Rose Marie, who said she'd call Connolly. Connolly called back five minutes later and said, "It might be possible that we can work something out."

"Is Rose Marie in the Mississippi?" Lucas asked.

"Fuck you."

LUCAS CALLED ICE and asked her to gently and with great diplomacy set up an appointment with the Minneapolis systems manager. While he was waiting for ICE to get back to him, he called the duty officer and asked him to get him a good phone number for Taryn Grant. He was sitting in his office, with his feet up on his desk, waiting for callbacks and thinking about how he'd sequence his various visits, when Del stopped in, took a chair, and said, "I bought a Harley."

"Oh, Jesus . . ."

"What? I had one before."

"You were in your twenties," Lucas said. "If you had to lay one down now, they'd be picking you up with a sponge."

"I'm not going on any big rides. . . . It's gonna be a warm-weather bike, just rolling around town on the local streets," Del said. "Besides, most Harley guys are my age. Or older."

"And you know what? They're getting picked up with sponges."

Jenkins came in and when Del told him about the Harley, they slapped hands and Jenkins said, "I'd have one myself, if they weren't such pieces of shit."

"Says the owner of a personal Crown Vic."

Shrake showed up a few minutes later, and they talked about the Harley, and Shrake said, "That fuckin' Flowers used to ride, right after he got out of the army. He had some sorta crotch rocket, though, not a Harley. I remember him showing up at crime scenes on it, when he was working for St. Paul. He had hair down his back, he looked like Wild Bill Hickok."

After another couple of minutes, Jenkins said to Lucas, "I'm hearing rumors that the Geheime Staatspolizei doesn't like the fact that you're working directly for the governor, and bailing out Smalls. I hear you're about to slap a search warrant on the Minneapolis cops, and that's got everybody steppin' and fetchin'."

In Jenkins's personal lexicon, the Geheime Staatspolizei comprised the BCA's top management. It was also the proper name of the German Gestapo, though he probably wasn't pronouncing it correctly—not that Lucas knew for sure.

Lucas explained that a compromise had been worked out with Minneapolis, and that he'd be working in cooperation with the city's Internal Affairs unit.

"That doesn't help much," Del said. "I'll tell you what, my friend. You're not doing yourself a lot of good around here, hanging out with the politicians. The knives are coming out."

"Fuck 'em," Lucas said. "It's a murder case. I'll break it and the tunes will change."

"No, they won't," Shrake said. "Everybody will agree that you did a great job and then they'll stab you in the back. It's the tall poppy syndrome."

"I'll take care," Lucas said.

"You already haven't," Del said.

WHEN THEY'D GONE, Lucas got Taryn Grant's office phone number, called it and spoke to a secretary, who went away for a moment, then came back and said, "Ms. Grant is in her car. I'm forwarding your call directly to her."

When Grant came on—she had the kind of voice he'd always liked, low and husky, like Weather's—he said, "I'm working on the investigation of the child pornography found on Senator Smalls's computer, and also the disappearance of a political operative named Bob Tubbs. I need to talk to you about the situation."

"I've already made a public statement to the media."

"I know, I saw it. But I have a few questions for you, and I also need to brief you on the status of the investigation," Lucas said. "Time is so short, before the election, we want to be sure everybody is informed."

"I'll be home between six and six-forty-five tonight, but then I have campaign visits to make."

"I'll see you then," Lucas said. "If you could give me your address . . ."

ICE CALLED: "I talked to the systems manager over in Minneapolis, and we're on for three o'clock. I'm familiar with their equipment. I didn't tell him exactly what we are going to do, you know . . . just in case they might try to ditch it."

"Good. The chief knows what we're doing, so they might be able to figure it out, but they don't have the number, as far as I know."

WHEN LUCAS got to the Minneapolis Police Department's ugly, obsolete, purple-stone headquarters in downtown Minneapolis, ICE was sitting with her feet up on the systems manager's desk, talking about old times at what was once called the Institute of Technology at the University of Minnesota.

A sergeant named Buck Marion sat in a corner, reading a free newspaper; Marion was with the Minneapolis Internal Affairs unit, and nodded at Lucas. One of Marion's predecessors had gotten Lucas thrown off the Minneapolis police force, for beating up a pimp.

Lucas listened to ICE and the systems manager ramble along, then shook his head, and ICE asked, "What?"

"Nothing like a long, rambling C++ story," Lucas said, not trying to hide a yawn. "Fascinating."

"We're intellectuals," ICE explained. "Anyway, Larry's going to help us look for the files. We were waiting for you." Larry Benson was the systems manager.

"Then let's do it," Lucas said.

ICE explained that they wouldn't be using the specific byte size, but would enter a narrow range that the file should fall into, even if an item or two were missing. ICE leaned over Benson's shoulder and fed him the file size number, and he entered the number range into his system. They all watched as the system thought it over, and then spat out twelve returns. "Twelve returns," ICE said. "Interesting."

Lucas almost blurted out that Kidd had found only four. Before he could, Benson said, "Let's take a look."

He opened them, one by one, on top of each other. Eight of them were irrelevant. Four of them, just as Kidd said, showed an identical opening set of child porn. "Man, I hate to think this shit is floating around in there," Benson said. "One file . . . it's pretty open access, if you know what to look for."

"Any way to tell *who* has accessed them?" Lucas asked.

"Not really. Well, I can tell you pretty sure in one case, but not the other three. Tom Morgan, Lieutenant Morgan, opened them, let me see, about eight times, all in about a four-day period a little more than three years ago, in August."

Lucas said, "There was a trial right then. Probably for trial purposes. He was one of the people who testified."

Benson said, "The other three sets of files were accessed by three different machines. Each machine accessed only one file, but multiple times."

Marion: "Who's assigned to the machines?"

Benson shook his head. "They're office machines. Maybe somebody uses them most of the time, but the rest of the time, anybody could do it."

ICE reached out and tapped the computer screen. "Look at this: this machine accessed the file four hundred and eighteen times over three years. They never quit looking at it . . . they're *still* looking at it."

ICE AND BENSON STARTED working through it, and Marion said to Lucas, "This is gonna be a disaster. I don't know what's gonna happen if it turns out that a hundred guys were looking at this stuff."

"Maybe it won't be necessary to bring it up," Lucas suggested.

"It'll be necessary," Marion said. "The chief will be inside my shirt, wanting to know what we found. You've probably got to tell your boss. Once that's done, it'll get away from us. If it was only us four . . . but it's not."

Lucas said, "You're probably right. I'm sorry."

ICE said, "All right. Machine One is in Vice, and that machine apparently dealt with the original files, and that's where a variety of files was grouped into one, and that's where the first duplicate was made. The duplicate had the same name as the original, but with a version number, Version Two. That was probably a legit backup. Machine Two is also in Vice, and somebody made a second duplicate on that machine, and saved it under a completely new name. That's the one that has been accessed by Machine Three, the four hundred and eighteen accesses. Machine Three never made a dupe. Machine Four accessed the original file, but only twice. Machine Four is in Vice."

"What's the latest date?" Lucas asked.

"Machine Three has had sixteen accesses in the last month," ICE said. "Both of the Machine Four accesses were last year."

"We've got to nail them all down," Marion said.

Lucas said, "This whole Smalls-porn thing feels improvised to me. It doesn't feel like something that was planned out a year ago. So . . . it probably came off Machine Three. Where's that one?"

Benson said, "It's here, in the building. Down in Domestics."

"How many people in Domestics?"

Benson shrugged, but Marion said, "About twelve or fifteen, counting the shrinks. Seven sworn officers, two or three support people, and the shrinks. Some of the shrinks are part-time, but they'd have access."

"Is there any way to see who signed on the machine and what they did? What they looked at?" Lucas asked.

Benson shook his head. "The only way you could figure that out, would be if Machine Three was in somebody's locked office. But Domestics is an open bay, with people coming and going. The only way to tell would be to observe . . . figure out who was on that machine at what time."

"But all this is in the past," Lucas said. "How would we do that?"

"We can't," Benson said.

"What we can do," Marion said, "is bust some balls."

"Gotta be soon," Lucas said. "Smalls is about halfway off the hook, but the media doesn't like him, so he's only halfway off. They're already saying that Rose Marie never said he was innocent."

"I need to talk to the chief," Marion said to Lucas. "What're you doing this evening?"

"Talking with a really hot chick," Lucas said.

"*Hot chick* . . . that expression is so disco, so 1979," ICE said, with disdain.

Marion, Benson, and Lucas all looked at each other, and then Lucas shrugged and said, "Not for cops."

THEY HAD BENSON SAVE the files and the information they'd turned up to a new, confidential file, and then ICE took off, after Lucas thanked her: "You'll get the bill at your office," she said.

Marion went to see the chief, and Lucas walked down to the training office. Tom Morgan, the lieutenant who'd put together the original file, and had testified in the child porn case, was now the training officer. The new job could either be a matter of grooming a cop for a move upward, or a dead end for a guy who wasn't going anywhere; in Morgan's case, Lucas didn't know which it was.

Morgan was poking at a computer keyboard when Lucas knocked on his doorjamb. He turned in his chair and his face fell, and he said, "Lucas. Goddamnit, I was afraid you'd show up here."

Lucas said, "Really."

"Yeah, everybody in the building is hiding out, afraid you're gonna want to talk to them. The word's all over the place."

"I only talked to the chief . . . and Marion. And Larry Benson . . ."

"Might as well have driven down the hall in a sound truck," Morgan said. He reached back, caught a wheeled guest chair, and shoved it toward Lucas. "Sit down and tell me about it."

Lucas explained the situation, and when he was finished, Morgan said, "Well, that's about what I heard. I'll tell you what, though. When we busted that place, the Pattersons', they weren't putting the files on the Internet. They were too smart to do that. If you wanted pictures from them, you'd get them by FedEx, and they'd be on paper. The Internet was only used for contacts. When we got them, we scanned the paper photos into the system, because that was the only way we had to coordinate them with everything else, for the court case. But they were a separate file. Nobody had access but the people who were working the case. And they should never have been aggregated with other files."

"What are the chances that somebody saw an opportunity for a little private enterprise? Put the files together and then sell them?" Lucas asked.

"I'd say . . . slim to none," Morgan said. "The thing is, the files were down in Vice, and nobody had access to them but us vice guys. And one thing we all knew, and most cops know now, is that cops and snitches are all over the place on kiddie porn. They're everywhere. Guys spend their spare time browsing the 'net, looking for it, looking for a bust. You buy kiddie porn off the 'net, you're gonna lose your job, probably get divorced, and probably go to prison. The vice guys . . . they wouldn't mess with it. It's more dangerous than dealing drugs. Way more. And there's less money in it."

"So you're saying whoever took it wasn't trying to make a buck, and it didn't get loose somehow."

Morgan shook his head: "Nope. Sad as I am to say it, I'd bet those pictures came straight out of here. Straight out of our system."

Lucas asked, "You hear any rumors of guys looking at porn?"

"Lucas, you know how it is. You worked here, for how long? You hear some guys might be looking at porn, some guys might be getting their knobs polished by the street girls, that some guys have a little too much cash, that some cocaine's gone astray . . . you hear all that crap. And most of it's crap. Backbiting bullshit."

That was true enough. The brotherhood of cops was fairly tight from the outside, but from the inside, it was more like a bureaucratic knife fight.

They talked for a while longer, about various possibilities, then Lucas looked at the wall clock and said, "I gotta roll. Thanks for the conversation."

Morgan asked, "Is the stuff gonna hit the fan?"

"Not if Robin handles it right," Lucas said. "What you need is a lot of promises and a big cloud of smoke . . . and then hope something blows up somewhere, and makes the media stampede that way."

12

Dannon and Taryn were both on their feet, in the library, feeling the stress, and Dannon said, "We don't know anything. We're amazed that people are talking to us. Who *is* Tubbs?"

She nodded. "I worked on it last night before I went to bed. I can do it. But I have to have my head in the right place."

"I'll be outside with Carver. Green will be in the monitor room. We want him to see Green, but not us."

"Yes," she said. She frowned. "What are we talking about, anyway?"

"Exactly." He nodded, and left.

A minute later, her walkie-talkie function buzzed, and Alice Green said, "We've got a Porsche at the gate."

LUCAS WATCHED THE GATE roll back and caught the two clear lenses, and two black glassy spots, one of each on the stone gate pillars, on either side of the driveway. Camera lenses and infrared alarm sensors. The security would be excellent. And the hard drives on the security cameras could be gotten with a search warrant: something to know.

The house was a long and sprawling ranch, built of a yellowish stone and clapboard, with a fieldstone chimney climbing out of one end. The lot itself, just the part he could see, was the size of a football field, dotted with mature oaks, maples, and firs.

The chimney, Lucas thought, would lead down to a really gorgeous wood-burning fireplace, with logs as long as a big man's arm. Lucas liked fireplaces, he just didn't like burning wood—he had few allergies, but burning wood always seemed to set off his nose, and he'd wake in the morning with a sore throat.

He had designed his own house, and had put in a fireplace, though of a fussier, arts-and-crafts style, green tile surround and black steel—and a really, really good set of fake iron logs, which concealed the gas jets. Instant fire, with the push of a button. He'd been told he should feel guilty about that, but he didn't.

Taryn Grant's house was bigger than his, but not enormously so, at least in appearance; nothing like a southern mansion, which was what he'd half expected. Lucas had been all over the contractor on the fine details of his own house, and so he noticed them in Grant's, like the copper flashing on the downspouts, the cabinetry-level detailing in the woodwork around the garage doors. He supposed that in this neighborhood, no house would be worth less than a million and a half; but looking at Grant's house, he suspected that given the size and the detailing, three million might be closer to the mark.

Though if she were as rich as people said she was, that amount would be insignificant to her.

————

He walked up to the front door, which opened as he approached it. A slender woman, probably in her mid-thirties, waited behind it. She had dark red hair, high cheekbones, and she wore a delicate turquoise necklace that chimed with her eyes. She looked a little like Kidd's wife, Lauren, Lucas thought.

She smiled and said, "Agent Davenport? I'm Alice Green. Ms. Grant is waiting for you in the library."

Which sounded just slightly snotty. Lucas thought, *I've got a library, too*, and then Green turned away from him and he saw the semiautomatic pistol clipped to the back of her slacks.

Lucas said, "You're security?"

"Yes," she said, looking over her shoulder. "I can stay with Ms. Grant where men can't. Like ladies' rooms."

"Ex-cop or something?"

"Secret Service," she said.

"La-di-da," Lucas said. Green tilted her head back and laughed and said, "Yes," and her reaction made Lucas like her.

Green led the way through the house. Through a side door, Lucas saw a gorgeous brick-floored porch with white-plastered walls and green-glass windows that looked out on a huge enclosed swimming pool. The house didn't look much larger than his from the front, he realized, but was nearly as deep as it was wide.

The library was modest in size, with dark wood shelves filled with books that looked like they'd been read. Grant was sitting on a wine-red couch, and stood up when Lucas stepped into the room, putting aside a magazine. She smiled and said, "Agent Davenport . . ." and put out her hand.

Lucas shook it as he took her in. She was tall and solid, with muscles showing in her neck and forearms; bigger than she'd seemed when he'd seen her on television, but just as pretty. She was wearing a red blouse and black slacks, with a simple gold-chain necklace that looked old.

"Pleased to meet you," Lucas said. "I won't take too much of your time."

"I'd say take as much as you need, but I really am jammed up," she said, as she gestured at an easy chair, and sank back onto the couch.

Lucas took the chair and asked, "Do you know Bob Tubbs?"

"Bob Tubbs? I've heard of him. He works for the party. Has he done something . . . ?"

"You know he disappeared?"

A wrinkle appeared in her forehead. "Disappeared? I'm not tracking this very well . . ."

Lucas decided to slap her: "Basically, I'm wondering if your campaign employed Tubbs to sabotage Senator Smalls's campaign by planting child pornography on his computer," he said.

Another wrinkle in her forehead, and she sat back and said, "Well . . . no."

Lucas had been watching her face for a flinch or any kind of frightened reaction, and what he saw was the beginning of rage. He opened his mouth to ask another question, but before he could, Grant jabbed a finger at him.

"Wait a minute! Wait one fuckin' minute, here, buster," she

said. "Who are you working for? Are you hooked up to Smalls's campaign?"

"I'm hooked up to the Bureau of Criminal Apprehension, Ms. Grant," Lucas said. "We believe that Mr. Tubbs planted the pornography on Senator Smalls's computer. We believe Mr. Tubbs has been murdered to cover up that crime. There's only one reason for him to have planted the porn, and that's to sabotage Senator Smalls's campaign."

"Murdered? Did you say murdered?" The anger faded a bit, overridden by something else. Fear?

Lucas said, "Yes. He's disappeared, and we think there's a reason for it. We think he planted the porn, and then had to be gotten rid of, to cover it up."

"Well, I mean we, I mean . . . We didn't have anything to do with that, if it's even true." Now the anger came clawing back: "And you didn't answer the question. Are you hooked up with Smalls's campaign? Have you ever worked for him? What are your politics? We are less than a week from Election Day, and you come to me with *this*? An accusation I can't refute, because you can't refute a complete negative? When you put this in the paper and on TV—and you will, won't you?—it'll kill me. Sabotage and murder? Are you kidding me?"

The anger was real and was getting hotter and Grant got to her feet and bent toward him: "Answer the question."

She was nearly shouting, and Lucas saw movement at the corner of his eye, and two huge German shepherds ghosted into the room, focused on him.

He said, "The dogs . . ."

She half turned to the dogs and said, "Hansel, Gretel, *easy*," and the dogs' gazes softened.

Green, who'd left the room, stepped in and said, "Ms. Grant . . . can I help?"

Grant said, "No, I'm okay, Alice. Agent Davenport has gotten me a little upset." She sank back on the couch and said, "Well? What contact have you had with the Smalls campaign? Have you taken any money from him?"

Lucas was getting angry himself, and strained to contain it: but some leaked into his voice. "No. I've spoken to Senator Smalls about who had access to his computer, and I've taken information from him. I do not know him, except for the contact involved in this investigation. Personally, I'm a registered Democrat, and my wife has contributed to the campaigns of a number of Democratic candidates, including yours, I believe, though I have not. There's no politics in this, Ms. Grant. What there is, is a vicious sabotage attempt, which would have reduced Senator Smalls's reputation to tatters, and very probably a murder. So, if we could get back to the reason I'm here: you say you knew nothing of the pornography, and you didn't know Bob Tubbs?"

She seemed to go through a brief internal struggle, then controlled it: "As far as I know, I've never met Mr. Tubbs, although it's possible that he was at some of my campaign events—I know he worked for the party, and there've been a lot of people I don't know at my events. So I may have seen him, though I wouldn't recognize him. I have not knowingly spoken a single word with him. I'm not heavily engaged with the party—my candidacy is mostly self-generated. And the pornography, I know nothing about it."

Green had lingered in the doorway, listening, and one of the dogs moved up to Lucas and put its head on his knees, looking straight in at his groin. Lucas said, "Ms. Grant, you wanna move the dog?"

"Make you nervous?"

"Makes me angry," Lucas said. "If this dog bites me, I shoot it. Then I shoot the other one if I have to, then I throw you on the floor, cuff you, and drag your ass down to the Hennepin County jail and charge you with aggravated assault on a police officer. Then you *will* go to jail."

"Gretel won't bite unless I tell her to," Grant said. But she said to the dog, "Gretel, back," and the dog eased away from Lucas.

Green said, "Ms. Grant, I'll be in the nook."

"Thanks, Alice," Grant said, and to Lucas, "I don't like you, and I suspect you don't like me, but try to be fair. Don't stick yourself into this campaign. Don't sabotage me."

"I'm not trying—"

"Whether you're trying or not, that's the effect," Grant said. "Wait a week or ten days, let the election take place, then do your worst. But give me a chance. I've worked very hard for it."

"So has Senator Smalls."

"Smalls should be okay, after Rose Marie Roux's press conference. I'm the one who has the problem now," Grant said. "And listen: even *I* think it's possible that you're right, to some extent. It's possible that somebody who was trying to help me—this Tubbs person—might have put the porn on Smalls's computer. But I know nothing about that. There are dozens of people working in campaigns, all kinds of people who don't like Smalls, and some of those people are a little nuts. So it's possible that somebody went after him, but it's just as likely that they were trying to hurt him, as trying to help me. A lot of union people hate him—especially public employee union people—and the pro-choice people go crazy when they talk about him. Look at them!" She tightened up a fist and smacked it into her thigh, and said it again. "Look at them!"

"We'll look everywhere," Lucas said. "So let me go through this. You didn't know Tubbs, and though you may have shaken hands, or had some slight contact with him, you've never had any kind of substantive talk with him."

"No, I haven't. And let me ask you this—how do you know that Tubbs didn't put the porn on the computer, and then take off? How do you know that he hasn't deliberately put himself out of reach?" she asked. "Win or lose, after the election's over, nobody's going to care much about the porn."

Lucas said, "It's not just that he's gone, it's that he left a lot of cash behind, and he also isn't using his credit cards," Lucas said. "He hasn't used them once since he was last seen on Friday night, and he uses them all the time."

"But you don't *know*," she insisted.

"No, I don't."

"Then don't fuck with me on the basis of guesswork," Grant said. "At least, not until the election is done."

Lucas stared at her for a moment, and she didn't flinch. He asked, "What about your campaign manager? Did she know Tubbs? Who, in your campaign, is in charge of dirty tricks?"

"There are no dirty tricks in this campaign, for the simple reason that anything you can accuse Smalls of doing, he's already admitted. Has he been unfaithful to his wife? Yes. He's talked about it on TV. Made a lot of money as an attorney, screwing over widows? Yes, he's talked about *that* on TV. What kind of dirty trick would work with him?"

"Well, child porn," Lucas said.

"That's absurd," Grant said. "If anybody even hinted at something like that, I'd not only fire him, I'd do everything I could to destroy him."

"I need to talk to your campaign manager," Lucas said.

"I will give you her number, and you can ask her yourself," Grant said. "She wanted to be here today, but I made her go away. I didn't want her . . . using this discussion in some way . . . in the campaign."

Felt like a threat, smelled like a threat, Lucas thought. "Like how?"

"I don't know, but I don't know you, and neither does Connie, and she might have asked a little more about your background to see exactly why . . . you're here."

"I think I've made that clear," Lucas said.

She leaned back on the couch. "Well, you have. But in my position, which is very delicate right now, Connie would say that we couldn't ignore the possibility that you're lying. She'd want some research."

Lucas asked, "How many armed security people do you have? Is Alice Green the only one?"

He saw a quick flash of uncertainty in her eyes, which vanished as quickly as it came; and quite possibly was a trick of his imagination. She said, "Year-round, there are three, working various hours. During the campaign there are eight, because they have to travel with me. This house is extensively wired for security. There are two safe rooms, I can get to them in a few seconds from anywhere in the house, and, of course, Hansel and Gretel are full-time. They're here overnight. If I put them on guard, they stop being dogs and start being leopards."

"Okay," Lucas said. He thought for a moment, and then stood up. "I'm done. I apologize if I upset you, but this is a very serious matter."

She waved a hand at him and said, "Just be fair."

———

THE DOGS TOOK HIM through the door to the living room, where Green was sitting with a magazine that she wasn't reading.

"I'll show you the door," Green said.

On the way, Lucas said, "Chicken."

"I beg your pardon?"

"You didn't want to hear that," Lucas said.

"I'm not paid to hear that," Green said. She hesitated, then said, "Do you have a card?"

Lucas gave her a card, taking a second to scribble his cell phone number on the back. "Call anytime," he said.

"Give me an hour," she said.

ON THE WAY OUT to the highway, Lucas thought about Grant's behavior, and came to a conclusion: she was either totally innocent, or totally nuts. A normal person, guilty, could never have pulled off that performance. But he'd known a number of crazies who could have. . . .

Green called an hour and a half later. Lucas had gone back to the office, having already missed dinner, to check messages and track his agents on their regular assignments. He was most interested in the Ape Man Rapist of Rochester, who was attacking women as often as twice a week, but Flowers reported no progress. Lucas had just turned off his office lights when Green called. He answered: "Yes? Alice?"

Green said, "I don't know where Ms. Grant stands on all of this, but I need to talk to you. We need to keep this private."

"Is she there now?" Lucas asked.

"She's up on a stage. I'm at the back of the room . . . keeping an eye out." Lucas could hear a voice in the background, and then a rumbling sound: applause line, he thought.

Green continued: "I wanted to tell you, she works harder than anyone I've ever met. I find her admirable, if a little chilly. But I don't want to have anything to do with any possible crime, and one of the other security men here . . . his name is Ronald Carver, conventional spelling . . . is pretty rough. I suspect that if you put enough money in front of him, he'd kill somebody for you, and do a thorough job of it. This man Tubbs, the man who disappeared? I'm not saying it's Carver, but if you needed that done, if you needed Tubbs to go away, you'd try to find somebody just like Carver."

"What's his background?" Lucas asked.

"Ex-military special operations of some kind. A master sergeant, which is up there. The head of security, Doug Dannon, is the same kind, ex-military, but much more restrained. His problem is, he's in love with Taryn, so . . . I don't know what he'd do for her. But whatever has been done, I don't know about it, and didn't have anything to do with it. I'm not going to spy on Ms. Grant for you, but I wanted to say this. I hope you keep it under your hat."

"I will. But it's an odd thing to tell a cop you don't know," Lucas said, not quite trusting her. "What if I *was* working for Smalls?"

"I still have friends with the Secret Service," she said. "I had them look you up. I know as much about you as Weather does."

"Well, maybe not," Lucas said, picking up on Green's use of his wife's first name.

"Anyway, you're not working for Smalls," Green said. Longer applause in the background. "I gotta go."

"One more question," Lucas said. "I saw a lot of cameras out there, which must go to what, a hard drive? Or the cloud?"

Long wait, and then Green said, "Oh, God."

"What?"

Another long wait, then Green said, "I wish you hadn't asked that. I wouldn't have called you at all, but . . . Ah, damn. I work in the monitoring room, sometimes. There used to be a monthlong video-record sent out to the cloud. I noticed this morning that the wipe time has been reduced to forty-eight hours."

"Forty-eight hours. Why?"

"I don't know. There's no reason to, and it worries me. The cameras only record when they pick up motion, so it's not that much, and a hundred bucks a month would mean nothing to Ms. Grant. But somebody reduced the wipe time to forty-eight hours, and I was thinking, you know . . . if you were worried that somebody might get the archived recording with a search warrant, and if there was something on it that you didn't want anybody to see . . . I mean, the change was made on Monday—about forty-eight hours after Tubbs disappeared."

Lucas said, "You've got a suspicious mind, Alice."

"Developed by government experts," she said. "I gotta go. Right now. Good-bye."

13

On the way out the door, Lucas stopped at the BCA men's room, where he found Jenkins, shirtless and shaving. He went to a urinal and over his shoulder asked, "What? You lost all your money gambling and now you're homeless?"

"Got a date," Jenkins said. "She likes it when my cheeks are smooth like a baby's butt."

"So she doesn't get beard burn on her thighs?"

"That's disgusting, but given a person of your ilk, I'm not surprised," Jenkins said.

Lucas finished up at the urinal and walked over to wash his hands and said, "Say you've got a hot, rich politician running for office, but she's losing, then her opponent is hit with a scandal involving child porn on his computers, then the guy you think put it there suddenly disappears and the politician turns out to have armed security people, including a couple of guys with thick necks who were in special operations in the army. What we unsophisticates call 'trained killers.' What do you think?"

Jenkins paused, half of his face covered with shaving cream, the other half bare and shaven; he asked, "You got that much for sure?"

"I'm being told all that," Lucas said.

"Have you hooked Tubbs to Grant?"

"Not yet . . . but Tubbs was probably involved in dirty tricks, and she needed one, bad. And he had a whole bunch of money, cash, in a hideout spot."

"You steal any of it?" Jenkins asked.

"No, no, I didn't."

"Huh," Jenkins said. "Little cold cash is always useful."

"But that would be illegal," Lucas said.

"Oh, yeah, I forgot," Jenkins said. "Listen, we told you, you gotta be careful. Now you gotta be more careful. If Tubbs was found dead with a gunshot wound or his head bashed in, that's one thing. The killer could have been anybody. But if he disappears with no sign . . . then whoever disappeared him knew what he was doing, and that's another thing entirely. You don't find that kind of guy standing around on a street corner—a killer who knows how to organize it, and carries it out clean."

"My very thought."

Jenkins took another thoughtful scrape through the shaving cream, rinsed the blade, then asked, "Would winning the election be worth the risk of murdering somebody? Of getting involved in a conspiracy to murder somebody?"

"That's the problem," Lucas said. "I don't think any rational person would, and Grant seems pretty rational. Either that, or she's crazier than a shithouse mouse. I talked to her today, pushed her a bit, and she pushed back. Never showed a wrinkle of worry, which means she's either innocent or nuts."

"Go for innocent: it cuts down the number of problems," Jenkins said.

"Another thing: I'm told one of these special forces guys is in love with her . . . which creates the question, exactly what would he do to see her win? Would he even tell her what he was planning to do?"

"Remember that guy who went around robbing those ladies' spa places?" Jenkins asked. "You know, manicure stores? Couple years ago?"

"Yeah, but I can't remember why he did it."

"He did it because he figured that there wouldn't be many guys around to deal with. No macho problems. It'd just be a bunch of women, and the places were almost all cash. He was getting a couple thousand bucks a week, paying no taxes, taking it easy," Jenkins said. "Anyway, he was ex–special forces. I tried to get his military records, and couldn't. Never did. We didn't need them, as it turned out, because one of the places he hit made some great movies of him . . . but the point is, I couldn't get the records. That's gonna be a problem, if these guys are really ex-army. Especially if they're former special ops."

"Maybe I won't need them," Lucas said.

"Oh . . . I think you probably will. There's nothing harder to break, IMHO"—he actually said the letters, I-M-H-O—"than a murder done by a guy who's well organized, doesn't feel much guilt, and you can't find the body. I've had two of those, and I'm batting five hundred. The one guy I got, it was luck. This is probably gonna be tougher. So you will need all the background you can get on them. . . . Grant wouldn't hire stupid people."

"I knew that talking to you would cheer me up," Lucas said.

"Yeah, well . . ."

Jenkins went back to shaving, and though it was late, Lucas headed back to his office. He wasn't exactly inspired by Jenkins, but he could make a couple of quick checks.

He found employment records for Carver and Dannon in the quarterly tax reports filed by Grant with the state, which gave him their full names and addresses—they both lived in the same town house complex off I-494 west of the Cities. They didn't show up in the property tax records, so they were probably renting. He couldn't get directly at the income tax records, though he had a friend who could; but he hesitated to use her when he didn't have to, and he didn't really need to know how much they made. The DMV gave him their birth dates, which was what he really needed.

With that, he went out to the National Crime Information Center. Carver had once been arrested, at age eighteen, for fighting, apparently while he was still in high school. The charges had been dismissed without prosecution. Dannon came up clean.

There was almost nothing else, on either of them. Jenkins had been right: he'd need the army records. He picked up the phone and called Kidd.

"I already owe you for the help with the porn and the Minneapolis connection . . . but I've spotted a couple of guys who I'm interested in, and I can't find anything about them in the records that I can get at. Could you get military records?"

After a moment, Kidd said, "I hate to mess with the feds."

"I can understand that," Lucas said. "The thing is . . . these two guys are ex–special operations, apparently, and would have the skills to take out somebody like Tubbs. What I'd like to know is, did they have a record of killing in the military? Did they have a criminal history there? Did they get honorable discharges? I've got no way of getting that."

Kidd said, "I'll tell you what. I'll take a very conservative, safe approach. If I can get the stuff without a problem, without setting anything off, I'll do it. I won't take any risks. But if you use it, how'll you explain it?"

"You could dump it to my e-mail, anonymously. I'll figure out a way to explain it that'll keep you clear."

"I'm already not clear—people already know that I'm involved in this thing," Kidd said.

"What if I put in an official request for the records, with the army?" Lucas suggested. "They'll take it under advisement, but they won't give them to me. If you could find a way to ship the re- cords out of the army's database, like there was a slipup . . ."

"Oh, boy . . ."

"I'll start calling the army the first thing in the morning. If you can help me out, that'd be good. If you can't, you can't."

"Oh, boy . . ."

"And there's another thing," Lucas said. "Something I doubt you could do."

"Lucas, my man, you originally just wanted a little help protect- ing the American Way . . ."

"I know, I know. But here's the thing. Taryn Grant's got this ter- rific security system. Cameras all over the place, inside and out. At one time, the photography went out to the cloud, saved for a month. In the last couple of days, somebody cut that to forty-eight hours. They did that about forty-eight hours after Tubbs disap- peared. I'm wondering, what if Tubbs showed up at Grant's place, and ran into something with one of these security guys?"

"You want me to find the recordings?" Kidd asked.

"If you can."

"Do you know which cloud?" Kidd asked. "There are lots of clouds."

"I don't know jack shit," Lucas admitted.

"Do you know her cell phone number?"

"Well . . . yeah, I do know that."

"Give it to me," Kidd said. "It's a start, if she monitors the system from her phone."

LUCAS WENT HOME.

Weather and Letty were curious, and Lucas kept them updated on his cases, but he had nothing to tell them. He did describe the meeting with Grant, and Weather said, "She sounds more interesting than I would have expected. Educated."

"She is. And she may have gotten a guy murdered."

"And she may not have," Weather said. "Something for you to think about."

LUCAS SPOKE TO the governor later that evening. The attorney general, the governor said, was all over the papers taken from Tubbs's apartment. "I suggested he investigate them thoroughly, at least until the election was over and done with. That way, he'll have the full attention of the press. He saw the wisdom of that."

"So I don't have to worry about him being in my hair . . ."

"At least not for a week," Henderson said. "What'd you think of Grant?"

"Smart and tough," Lucas said.

"She could be president someday, if you don't drag her down."

"What's that supposed to mean?" Lucas asked.

"I'm just sayin', my friend. Keep me up to date."

LUCAS GOT TO THE OFFICE early the next morning, conscious of the time difference between Minneapolis and Washington, and began calling the Pentagon. He spent two hours talking to a variety of captains, majors, and colonels—somehow missing lieutenant colonels—and got nothing substantial, except the feeling that everybody dreaded making a mistake. He did get pointed to online request forms, which he dutifully filled out and submitted, and backed those with direct e-mails to the captains, majors, and colonels, reiterating his requests for information.

When he was done, he had no information, but had laid down a solid record of information requests. Now if Kidd came through . . .

Lucas thought about spies, and with no particular place to push, eventually drove over to Smalls's campaign headquarters and talked to Helen Roman, Smalls's campaign secretary, who sent him down the hall to a guy named John Mack, the deputy campaign manager. He was, Roman told him, in charge of operations.

Mack said that he knew Bob Tubbs by sight, and may have said hello at the candy machine, but had never had a real conversation with him. "He's a bit older than I am—we're not contemporaries. I don't know what we'd have in common. We're not even with the same political party."

"Even without knowing him, but just knowing what he did . . . knowing what *you* do . . ."

"Maybe I should take the Fifth," Mack said.

"C'mon, man, gimme a little help . . . Give Smalls a little help."

Mack repeated that he didn't know anything about spying, but just as an intellectual exercise . . .

Tubbs's accomplice would have had one of three motives for

trying to dump Smalls, Mack said: (1) financial—he might have been paid; (2) ideological—he wanted Smalls dumped because he hated his politics; or (3) personal—he (or she) was a close friend or lover of Tubbs; or he (or she) was a personal enemy of Smalls.

If it were (3), it seemed likely that the accomplice would also be older. Perhaps not exactly Tubbs's or Smalls's contemporary, but most of the volunteers were college kids, and unlikely to be close enough to either man to do something as ugly as dropping the child pornography on Smalls, simply at Tubbs's say-so.

Could be (2) ideological, Mack said, although the volunteers were vetted before they were given any real responsibility. "But the thing is, if they planted this thing in Porter's computer, they don't have to have any responsibility. All they need is access," Mack said. "I have no idea how many office keys are floating around, but it's quite a few, and the place is empty late at night."

Or he said, it could be (1) financial . . . though if it were financial, how would Tubbs have made the approach to the accomplice, or spy? He could probably have done it only through personal knowledge of the accomplice, and that would loop right back to (3): a personal relationship.

So Lucas was probably looking for somebody a bit older, Mack said, or a reckless, ideologically driven youngster, whom Tubbs would have to have known. Was it possible that Tubbs had recruited a spy for Taryn Grant's campaign, then enlisted him to do the pornography dump?

"Grant says she didn't know Tubbs, and she seems smart enough that she probably wouldn't lie about it . . . especially if we could find out about it," Lucas told Mack. "Anyway, I believed her. She probably *didn't* know him."

"I'll tell you what—if an operator like Tubbs knew about a spy

in our campaign, other Democrats would know about it, too,"
Mack said. "I think you might be going around threatening the
wrong people."

"I wasn't threatening you," Lucas said.

"Then why am I sweating?"

LUCAS WAS MULLING IT all over as he walked out to his car, and as
he popped the door lock, took a call from Marion, the Minneapolis
internal affairs cop.

"Just an update: I've been tearing up Domestics this morning. I
don't have any proof, but I've got a half-dozen names, and whoever
copied that porn for Tubbs is probably on the list."

"How'd you get the names?" Lucas asked.

Marion explained that he'd started with the people he'd considered least likely to be involved, and with the threat of felonies hanging over their heads, they'd been cooperative. He'd been looking
for people who'd been seen using the Domestics computer at unlikely times, alone or in small groups, or had been unhappy to be
seen using it and had quickly signed off when a new face turned up
at the office.

"There are five guys and one woman who may—and I say
'may'—have been looking at the porn repeatedly. I think all six
probably were . . . kind of like a little club down there that knew
about it. Two of the shrinks had heard rumors about child porn on
city computers. That's where I got the names."

"What're you doing next?" Lucas asked.

"I've got to talk to the chief about that, but I'm inclined to try to
figure out who was the least likely to have dumped the porn to
Tubbs, and offer him immunity for information."

"When are you going to do it?"

"After I talk to the chief, I'll have to get with the lawyers . . . I'm thinking it couldn't be any earlier than this evening, and most likely tomorrow."

"Keep talking to me," Lucas said.

ON THE WAY BACK to his office, he called Smalls:

"How's the campaign going?"

"Not well: that bitch has got everybody she knows whispering that the porn was really mine."

"I thought she told the TV people that her campaign wasn't doing that, and she'd fire anybody who did," Lucas said.

"Well, of course she said that," Smalls said. "She's lying through her teeth."

"How do you know that?"

"Because that's what *I'd* do."

Lucas said, "Okay. Listen, we're making more progress, but we need to find Tubbs's accomplice in your office. That'll break the thing wide open. If this was done for ideological reasons, if it was done by a spy, then somebody in your campaign has got to have doubts about that person. It's not that easy to hide your basic beliefs . . . especially if you're a college kid. So, I need somebody, not you but maybe your campaign manager, to talk to everybody about who that might be. We're trying to catch a spy. I'm going to work it from the other end, the Democratic side, see if I can get them to cough somebody up."

Smalls was silent for a moment, then said, "I can do that. In fact, if we leak to the TV people that we're looking for a spy . . . that might help convince them that there really was a dirty trick."

"Whatever," Lucas said. "I'm not really trying to get you re-elected."

Smalls laughed and said, "Gotta be killing a good liberal like you."

"Ah, I'm not that political. Anyway, if you could do that, I'll start on the other side."

"Four days to the election," Smalls said. "If it ain't done by Sunday, I'm screwed."

LUCAS CALLED KIDD: "Anything happening?"

"Not yet. It's delicate."

FROM HIS OFFICE, he called Rose Marie Roux and asked, "What Democratic Party operator would be most likely to know who is spying on who?"

"Well, that'd be Don Schariff, but don't tell him I said so. Why?"

"I'm going to jack him up," Lucas said. "Where can I find him?"

Schariff had an office at the DFL headquarters—Minnesota's Democratic Party was technically called the Democratic-Farmer-Labor Party—and Lucas found him there, by phone, and said he wanted to come over.

"Should I be worried?" Schariff asked.

Lucas said, "I don't know. Should you?"

"I'm wondering if I should have a lawyer sit in?"

Lucas said, "I don't know. Should you?"

The DFL headquarters was a low white-brick building in a St. Paul business park across the Mississippi from downtown that possibly looked hip for fifteen minutes after it was built but no longer did. Lucas talked to a receptionist, who made a call. Schariff came out and got him, and said, "We're down in the conference room."

"Who's we?" Lucas asked.

"Me and Daryl Larson, our attorney," Schariff said. He was a stocky, dark-haired man with a neatly trimmed beard and dark-rimmed glasses. He was wearing a white shirt with a couple of pens in a plastic pocket protector. In any other circumstance, Lucas would have been willing to arrest him on the basis of the pocket protector alone. "I asked, and everybody said when you're talking to a cop . . . especially one investigating the Grant-Smalls fight . . ."

"Okay," Lucas said.

Larson was a tall, thin man whom Lucas knew through Weather's association with the St. Paul Chamber Orchestra. Larson raised money for the orchestra, usually by wheedling rich wives; it'd worked with Weather. When Lucas stepped into the room, Larson put down the paper he'd been reading and stood to shake hands. "Lucas, nice to see you. How's Weather?"

"Broke. She's broke. She's got no money left. She's wondering how we're going to feed the kids."

"Hate to hear that," Larson said, with a toothy smile. "I'll call her with my condolences."

The pleasantries out of the way, they settled into the conference chairs and Lucas outlined some of what he knew and believed about Tubbs's disappearance. He finished by saying, "You guys are probably not going to want to talk about this, because when the media puts Tubbs's disappearance together with the porn trick . . . it's gonna look bad."

"I think we can agree on that," Larson said for Schariff, who'd kept his mouth shut. "But how does this involve Don?"

"I've been told, by somebody who knows these things, that Don knows a lot about the, mmm, tactical maneuverings of the party, and everybody involved in these things."

"I don't do dirty tricks," Schariff said.

Larson put up a finger to shut him up, and said to Lucas, "Go on."

"So the technical fact of the matter is, the booby trap on Smalls's computer had to be set the same morning it went off. Tubbs wasn't there that morning. Hadn't been there for a few days," Lucas said. "So, he had an accomplice. That accomplice might have been acting out of pure greed . . . Tubbs might have paid him. But it's equally likely that it's an ideological thing, that Tubbs knew that there was a spy among the volunteers and got the guy to set the trap. Since Don knows most of the party's operators . . . well, we thought he might also know who the spy is. If there is one."

"Getting information like that isn't a crime," Larson said.

"I didn't say it was—but framing Smalls is. Anybody who helped the spy put that stuff on the computer, or knows about it and doesn't say so, is also in trouble. Conspiracy and all that. Prison time," Lucas said. "I'm not trying to be impolite here, but you see where I'm going."

Schariff said, "Well, I—"

Larson put the finger up again and said, "No." Then to Lucas, "Don and I have to talk. I'll call you later today."

"How about in ten minutes?" Lucas asked. "Things are getting really tight with the election."

"Later today," Larson said. And he wouldn't budge.

OUT ON THE SIDEWALK, Lucas took a phone call from Ruffe Ignace, a crime reporter for the *Star Tribune*: "We're getting all kinds of different signals on Smalls. Smalls says he's been cleared by Rose Marie Roux, and she says she's made her statement, which, when you look at it, doesn't quite clear him. In the meantime, people are whispering to our political people that the porn was his. Which way should I lean?"

"I'd have to go off the record on that," Lucas said. "Better yet, why don't you call Rose Marie directly?"

"She tends to blow me off," Ignace said. "Anyway, could we stay a little bit on the record? A highly placed source in the investigation?"

"I'm the only one investigating, so that won't work," Lucas said. "I need to go completely off."

"Shit. All right, we're off the record," Ignace said. "Which way should I lean?"

"Smalls was framed. . . . He's innocent."

"Thanks. We're almost even now. You only owe me a little bit."

"Call me back in one minute," Lucas said. "I might have something else for you."

"You in the can?"

"No, I'm in a parking lot, leaning on my car," Lucas said. "I need to think. One minute."

Lucas leaned against the car and thought about it. One minute later, Ignace called back and Lucas said, "Still off the record, okay?"

"Okay. Against my better judgment. The public's trust in both government and the media would be so much higher if we identified—"

"Yeah, yeah, yeah. We're off the record. Call Don Schariff—S-C-H-A-R-I-F-F—at DFL headquarters. He's got some kind of title there, but I'm not sure what. Anyway, he's involved with DFL intelligence gathering—"

"Spies."

"Yeah. Ask him if Bob Tubbs—"

"The guy who disappeared . . . *Holy shit*, Tubbs? Tubbs dumped the porn on Smalls?"

"I didn't say that," Lucas said. "Schariff might possibly have some information for you. But he'll probably deny any involvement with Tubbs."

"You're saying the Republicans killed Tubbs?"

"Somebody did, but I don't think it was the Republicans," Lucas said. "I think there's a cover-up going on. But it's possible that Tubbs is just lying low, until the election is over."

"Not from what I hear," Ignace said. "I hear the St. Paul cops think he's dead. I hear you do, too."

"Yeah, I guess I do," Lucas said.

"All right, we're more than even. You need anything from me?"

"Not right now. But wait at least an hour before you call Schariff. I just talked to him two minutes ago, and if you call him right now, he'll figure I talked to you. So wait."

"You talking to Channel Three?"

"No. You've got it exclusively. So wait."

"I can do that," Ignace said. "I can probably get one of our political guys to tie Schariff to Tubbs. They must've worked together a hundred times. *Hot dog*. But say it out loud: Tubbs used the porn to frame Smalls."

"I can't say that," Lucas said. "But I can say that you sometimes, against all odds, seem like a very, very smart guy."

"You can kiss my odds," Ignace said. "But no, wait. Thanks, Lucas. I owe you big. If you're ever indicted for anything, I'll take your side."

———

LUCAS WENT BACK TO his office, called his agents, got updates—still nothing on the Ape Man Rapist of Rochester—and waited for something from the DFL.

Larson, the lawyer, called back two hours later. He was angry: "Lucas, I'd call you a miserable motherfucker if I didn't need Weather's money. You talked to Ignace, over at the *Strib*. You got him on Don's case. He's going to publicly connect Don to Bob Tubbs and Tubbs to the Smalls scandal."

"I'm not talking to anybody," Lucas lied. "I'm just trying to get a little cooperation from people who might know why a guy got murdered."

"You lying motherfucker . . . pardon the language. Don't talk to Ignace again: don't, or I'll find some way to screw you. I promise."

"Do your best, Daryl. But if I find out Don knew something that he's not giving me, he's going to prison," Lucas said. "He'll be part of the conspiracy if he tries to cover it up."

"There's no cover-up," Larson said. "If there's a spy in the Smalls campaign, she was placed by Grant's campaign, not by us."

"You said, 'she,'" Lucas said. "So you know something."

"I'll tell you exactly what we did," Larson said. "We got everybody together, and we tried to figure out who was working for Smalls, all the volunteers, and then we showed the list to Don. He looked it over and said there was one volunteer, a young woman, Bunny Knoedler, who he was surprised to see working for the opposition."

"Bunny?"

"Yes. Knoedler. K-N-O-E-D-L-E-R."

"How surprised was he?" Lucas asked.

"He said she worked on a couple of our campaigns out-state that Tubbs was involved with," Larson said. "Don said she seemed like a pretty dedicated DFLer."

Lucas said, "If this works out, Daryl, I'll send you a hundred dollars myself."

"Fuck you, Lucas . . . but do say hello to Weather for me."

LUCAS LOOKED AT HIS WATCH: getting late. He walked down the hall, saw Shrake on the phone at his desk, went that way. Shrake saw him coming, held up a finger, said, "Uh-huh. Uh-huh. Well, send me the paper. Okay. I gotta go." He hung up and said, "You're quivering."

"You got some time?"

"Ah . . . no. Not if you want me to keep pushing the Jackson thing," Shrake said.

"All right. Where's Jenkins?" Lucas asked.

"He's getting his oil changed," Shrake said.

"He's . . ."

"No, no, not that," Shrake said. "He was going down to a Rapid Oil Change, getting the oil changed in his car."

"Call him, tell him to get back here," Lucas said. "I need to terrorize a young woman, and I want one of you guys to come along."

"Well, hell, that's right up his alley," Shrake said. He picked up his phone and dialed.

With Jenkins on the way back, Lucas called Smalls and asked the question. Smalls made a call and came back immediately: "The girl is working until nine o'clock on the phone bank. Is she the one who did this?"

"Don't know—but we got a tip that made us want to talk with her," Lucas said. "Don't do anything that would let her know we're looking at her."

"In other words, keep my mouth shut."

"I'm far too polite to say that to a U.S. senator."

JENKINS SHOWED UP and said, "I was next in line."

"That piece of shit you drive won't know the difference," Lucas said. "You could fill it up with a water hose. Let's go."

Lucas briefed Jenkins on the way over. They got to Smalls's headquarters a little after four o'clock, and the secretary, Helen, pointed out Bunny Knoedler, a tall, dark-haired, blue-eyed girl with bow-lips, who looked like she might have been Lucas's daughter.

The phone room was just another office, divided up into a half-dozen booths with acoustic tiling on the walls, to hush up the multiple voices. Knoedler was sitting in a booth with two hard-wired phones and a list, and was dialing a number when Lucas leaned over her shoulder and pushed down the hang-up bar on the base set.

She turned and looked up at him and said, "What . . . ?" and he could see in her eyes that she knew who he was.

"We need you to come back into Senator Smalls's office," Lucas said. Jenkins loomed behind him, as though to keep her from running.

"What . . . what?" she asked.

"I think you know what, but we have to talk about it," Lucas said. "Come along."

She put the phone down, and with the other phone-bank people suddenly gone silent, followed them out of the room, sandwiched between Jenkins and Lucas, like a perp walk.

Smalls's office was empty—not even a computer anymore—and Lucas pointed Knoedler at a chair. He and Jenkins remained on their feet, looking down at her. "You're a Democratic spy," Lucas said. "A friend of Bob Tubbs, and you worked with him on out-state campaigns. He planted you here to watch Senator Smalls's campaign."

She was scared, and started to reply. She said, "I—"

Lucas put up a hand to stop her. "We're going to read you your rights. But I want to tell you, in addition to your rights, if you lie to me, that's a crime. You have the right to remain silent, to say nothing at all, but you can't lie to me. At this point, we're looking for information."

Lucas looked at Jenkins and nodded, and Jenkins started the routine. "You have the right to remain silent . . ."

When he was finished, Lucas asked, "Did you understand all of that? That you have a right to an attorney?"

"I haven't done anything illegal," she said, looking at the two of them, looming.

She hadn't asked for a lawyer. This was delicate: Lucas didn't want to talk about illegalities. Instead, he said, "Bob's mother is worried sick about him, but we don't know whether he's just lying low, or if he's been . . . killed. We're afraid that he has been. If he's still around, we desperately need to know that."

"I . . . I . . . I don't know," she said. "I mean, I'm worried, too. He was the guy I was supposed to talk to, if I found anything out. Then he just stopped answering his phone. I was calling him every night, and then . . . he was gone."

She'd just admitted being a spy. "Do you know where he got the pornography?" Jenkins asked. "Did he get it from a police officer?"

"The pornography . . . He didn't have anything to do with that," she said. "That's crazy. He didn't do dirty tricks."

"We know you're a little new with this political campaign stuff," Lucas said. "But I'm here to tell you, Bob was involved in a few tricks in the past. And you're sort of a dirty trick, spying on the Smalls campaign."

"Everybody does it," she said. "Everybody. Smalls has a spy in the Grant camp, too. Just ask him. Ask him under oath."

"Okay," Lucas said. Smalls had already as much as admitted that.

He looked at Jenkins, who was the asshole. Jenkins said, "I dunno. I doubt that everybody does it. Gotta be some kind of a crime. And she's not all that new with this stuff—she's worked those out-state campaigns."

"It is *not* a crime," she said, showing a little streak of anger. "It's not illegal. I wouldn't do anything illegal."

"We know that you were close to Bob," Lucas said. "We know that Bob needed somebody to help set the computer so the pornography would pop up—"

"I had nothing to do with that!" she said, her voice rising. "I would never do something that dirty. That's rotten. That porn . . . that belongs to Smalls. Everybody knows about his attitude toward women, and sex . . ."

"Come on," Jenkins said, the scorn rough in his voice.

"I didn't . . ."

They pushed her for another five minutes, and she claimed that she worked afternoons and nights, and hadn't been around when the trap must've been set. They pushed on that, and she eventually admitted that she thought that Tubbs had been in the office at night, two days before the trap popped. They pushed on that, and finally she said the magic words.

"Look," she said. "I want a lawyer. Right fuckin' now."

Jenkins looked at Lucas and lifted his eyebrows. Arrest her? Lucas shook his head; he wasn't ready for that. He said, "We'll want to talk to you again. Do not go away. Do not try to avoid us. I'm tempted to arrest you, and put you in jail overnight, but I'm hoping that you understand that we need to know what happened, more than we need to haul in the small fish. You're a small fish. Do you understand that?"

She nodded, and said, "Lawyer."

Lucas offered to provide one, a public defender, but she said she'd get her own. "Are we done?"

"Yes. But don't run—"

"I'm not going to run, but I want you to take me out of the office," she said. She looked out through the glass window on Smalls's office door. "They're gonna be a little pissed at me."

"That's the least of your problems," Lucas said. "Come on. We'll take you out."

SHE WAS RIGHT: when they walked out of the room, the other volunteers started hissing, and somebody called, "Put her ass in jail." At the door, Knoedler flashed a finger over her shoulder, and Jenkins laughed and said, "That's really classy, sweetheart."

They saw her into her car, and as she backed out of the parking space, Lucas asked Jenkins, "What do you think?"

Jenkins shrugged and said, "Don't think she knew about the porn. But I wouldn't be surprised if she let Tubbs into the office, late one night, after everybody else had gone home."

Lucas nodded. "Maybe. Which would make her a part of it. The thing is, the DFLers swear that they didn't put her on Smalls, and I believe them because if they did, too many people would have to know about it. I'd find out, and they know that. So, they're telling the truth. It had to be Tubbs, working alone, or Tubbs working for Grant. We need to keep going back to her, if nothing else breaks."

"Maybe give Knoedler limited immunity," Jenkins said.

"Don't want to give her immunity, if she set the trap," Lucas said.

Jenkins shook his head: "I gotta tell you: I kinda believed her about that. She got pretty hot about it and that looked real. Besides, she knows we can check."

Lucas rubbed his nose and looked after her taillights, two blocks down the street. "Yeah. It did look kinda real," he said. "Goddamnit."

HE CHECKED ANYWAY, and Roman, the secretary, said that Knoedler hadn't been scheduled to work, because even the volunteers were limited to eight hours a day. "But people, you know, are enthusiastic, and they come and go all the time. She could have been here, and I doubt that anyone would have thought it unusual, or even noticed."

14

auren had put together a munchie plate and Kidd was munching on the last of the celery with pimento cheese as he bypassed the privacy option on Taryn Grant's bedroom security camera.

The camera was inactive, which meant nobody had walked through the bedroom in the past thirty seconds.

He was working off a laptop that was, technically, operating out of a Wi-Fi system in the federal courthouse, which was just up the street. He'd taken the precaution of building a repeater into the building several years earlier.

With nothing moving on the screen, he wandered away from the laptop to look at a landscape he was working on, a view of the Mississippi a few miles above the Coon Rapids Dam. The color of the autumn leaves and the dark river was all accurate enough, he thought, but didn't work for the painting: and accurate color was not a driving aspect of his work.

He pulled on a paint-spattered apron, selected a handful of tubes of oil paint, squeezed some paint onto a glass palette, and began mixing color. An hour later, he was still adjusting the color on the river's surface when the laptop screen flickered to life and Taryn Grant walked into the bedroom.

Kidd stepped over to the laptop as Grant kicked off her shoes, then unzipped the back of her dress, pulled it over her head, and tossed it on the bed. A slip followed, leaving her in her bra, underpants, and genuine nylon stockings held up with a genuine garter belt.

She walked off screen to the left, and Kidd said, aloud, "Come back, come back . . ."

Thirty seconds later, the screen went dead.

She had to come back through the bedroom, though, and Kidd pulled a drawing stool over to the laptop bench, sat and waited. Seven or eight minutes later, naked as the day she was born, fresh out of the shower, Grant walked across the bedroom, wiping down her back with a long white terrycloth towel. She was, Kidd thought, a healthy lass.

As Kidd watched, she tossed the towel on her bed and walked over to a side table, reached behind it, and must have pushed a button or moved a lever—a built-in bookcase on a sidewall smoothly rotated away from the wall. Grant stepped over to the safe and after punching in a string of numbers on the safe's keypad, she pulled open the heavy steel door and started taking out jewelry cases.

Kidd turned to the studio and shouted, "Hey, Lauren. C'mere. Quick."

Lauren popped into the doorway a minute later, said, "I've got to get Jackson . . ." Jackson was at school.

"Look at this," Kidd said, pointing at the monitor.

She looked and a frown line appeared on her forehead and she said, "What is this? Is that Taryn Grant? Kidd, what the heck are you doing?"

"Hey. Look what *she's* doing."

Lauren peered at the monitor. "She's . . . whoa, look at that."

Grant had opened one of a half-dozen jewelry cases she'd put on the bed, and tried on a heavy necklace of knotted gold. She looked at herself in the mirror, then took off the gold, dropped it back next to the case, and opened another case. This necklace was smaller, more demure . . . and sparkled with diamonds.

Kidd tapped a corner of the screen: "She took it out of the safe."

"Can we get a look at it? The safe?"

"I can rewind a bit, look at that corner . . ."

He stepped back through the recording, to the point that the camera had stopped recording. "The camera triggers on movement, and runs for another thirty seconds."

There was a jump, and then the unclothed Grant walked into the screen again, from the left side, and Kidd said, "Yow," and Lauren said, "Yeah, yow. You are in no way qualified to handle something like that."

"*That*, my little pumpkin flower, holds not a candle to your own self," Kidd said.

"Thanks, but to be honest, you're not qualified to handle *me*. I have to tone down my whole . . . Okay, here goes."

Lauren watched as Grant opened the bookcase, and then the safe.

"That's a Robinson Steel-Block," Lauren said, peering at the safe door. "Can we rerun and get closer on the keypad?"

Kidd rattled some keys and the corner of the screen that showed the safe shifted to occupy the entire screen; a few more keystrokes and the recording stepped back and showed the bookcase opening. Grant's hand appeared and she hit the key sequence.

Kidd said, "Jesus, an eight-number code."

"You won't get into a Robinson with a jackknife," Lauren said. "Run that again."

Kidd ran it again and Lauren said, "I think it was 62649628. Or it could have been 95970960. I'll need to look at it some more. Is there an alarm when the safe opens?"

"I'd have to do a little more exploring to figure that out . . . but I doubt it," Kidd said.

"Okay. I want to look at the way she pushed that button again."

They ran the file a dozen times, and Lauren watched Grant's arm and fingers as she pushed the button, or moved the lever, that shifted the bookcase. Eventually, she decided that it was a simple button-push, probably wireless, and that the button was mounted on the back of the side table. "You can see that she feels for it, for a second, and then her middle finger pushes it . . . not a slide motion. It's a button, and she pushes it once: it's not a coded sequence."

Kidd started the live video again, and Grant, now back in her underpants, garter belt straps hanging loose down her legs, hooked her bra and started trying on the jewelry again, including a lot of colored gemstones.

"Look at that, I think that's a ruby," Lauren said. "My God, the thing's the size of a drain stopper."

Eventually, Grant chose what looked like a multiple string of pearls.

"The stuff she looked at, the stuff she rejected—assuming it's all top-of-the-line, and given her money, I'd bet it is—we're looking at a million bucks with just what we saw. There's more in the safe. She was looking for the right necklace. She wouldn't have taken everything out, the rings and bracelets."

"I made a million last year," Kidd said. "We don't need the money."

"That's your money, not mine," Lauren said. "I like to have my own money."

"You can be such a silly shit," Kidd said.

"Whatever. I'm going to want to look at a few key photos," Lauren said.

"Me too," Kidd said. "Like when she puts on her nylons . . ."

"Hey . . ."

". . . my little rutabaga flower."

Lauren patted his chest. "Put that video somewhere safe. I'm late to get Jackson. We'll talk after he's in bed tonight."

KIDD TOLD LUCAS that Lauren had worked as an insurance adjuster, which was true enough: after Lauren called on her rich clients, their insurance needed adjustment. She mostly stole money, for the simple reason that it was . . . money. She'd also steal jewelry, if it was the kind that could be melted or broken down into unidentifiable stones.

Kidd had once needed to get some information on a man who was peddling defense secrets, and had used Lauren to hit his safe, as a cover for his own break-in. The safe couldn't be cracked in place: it was too good. So Lauren had simply used a power jack to rip the safe completely out of the wall, had Kidd throw it out the window of the man's condominium, and had whipped him into carrying the brutally heavy safe, at a fast jog, which was all he could manage, several hundred yards to their car. She'd taken the safe to a machinist friend, who'd cut it open.

Kidd could feel an incipient hernia when he even thought about that night. . . .

She hadn't only stolen for the income, though: she had done it because she liked it, and often because her victims deserved it. The kind of people who were most vulnerable to her were almost always assholes, running some kind of illegal or immoral hustle. She chose them because most would not go to the police. Politicians were a favorite target—no politician had ever called the FBI to report that a hundred thousand dollars in twenty-dollar bills had been taken out of his freezer.

Lauren also had a taste for cocaine and cowboys, both of which she'd given up when she and Kidd had decided a child would be nice. Not that the taste had necessarily gone away.

WHEN JACKSON was put to bed that night, and Kidd was lying on the living room couch reading deep into *George Bellows*, a hefty volume produced by the National Gallery of Art, in conjunction with a retrospective exhibition on the American painter, Lauren came in and said, "Move your feet."

Kidd sat up and Lauren plopped on the couch and asked, "Why'd you show me that?"

"You said last week that you were feeling stale. Then when we were over at the Roosavelts' place, I noticed you casing the place."

"I was looking at the new décor, with Suki," Lauren said.

"Right." The Roosavelts had decorated their new eight-thousand-square-foot penthouse with, among other things, a big Kidd landscape, and Kidd and Lauren had gone over to see what the installation looked like.

"Hey . . ."

"I need to know what's going on in your head," Kidd said.

"A lot of stuff," Lauren said. "But to get back to Taryn . . . You think I should crack her house?"

"No. I want you to think about it," Kidd said. "All about it. About what would happen if you were caught, about the effect it would have on Jackson and me, and what would happen if you weren't caught. How would that change things? Or would it change anything?"

Lauren said, "I don't know. I don't know what would happen. But ever since you showed me the video . . . it's like I've got a fever."

"You had the fever before then. I could see it. If you hadn't, I wouldn't have shown you Grant's bedroom."

"Yeah . . ." She stood up and wandered over to the window and looked out at the river, where it disappeared around the bend and rolled off to the Gulf of Mexico. "Yeah, you're right. I've been looking at places."

"I was afraid of that," Kidd said.

"I've never been caught," Lauren said, turning back. "I've never been printed."

"You didn't have that much riding on it before," Kidd said.

"You're right. I didn't."

"I quit," Kidd said. "As much as I could, anyway."

"You could quit because you never wanted to do it that much— industrial espionage, sneaking around in factories . . . it all seemed so weird," Lauren said. "You didn't need it, because you're basically a painter, not a thief. But I'm basically a thief. That's what I do. That's my painting. I'm not basically a housewife."

"But nobody's going to put me in jail for painting . . ."

"That *Times* critic might," Lauren said. "He said you were a throwback to a bygone era and that your prices were absurd for something as old-fashioned as paintings."

"I'm trying to be serious," Kidd said. "About everything. That's why I showed you the video. I want you to think about your life."

She turned away from him and bobbed her head. "All right. I'll do that. I *will* do that, Kidd."

THEY TALKED for two hours. Lauren was mostly right—Kidd was basically a painter, but there was one spot in his heart that would never go away, reserved for the beauty of computers and their languages.

Much later that night, Kidd was back in the studio when a computer chirped at him. He went over and looked at it. Military records depository. He touched a key and the computer on the other end hesitated. "Open sesame," Kidd said, feeling the rush.

The army's computer opened up.

15

ucas was lying on a couch reading the Steve Jobs biography, which he'd been meaning to do for a long time, when his cell phone rang. He looked at the screen, which said it was two minutes after eleven o'clock, and "Caller Unknown."

"Hello?"

"Don't say anything. This is a wrong number. Look at your e-mail. Don't call me back before tomorrow night."

Click. Kidd was gone; the call had lasted six seconds.

LUCAS GOT OFF the couch and padded back to his study, sat down at the computer, and brought up his e-mail. He had incoming mail from the military records depository.

He clicked on it, and found two PDF documents. He clicked on the first and found a thirty-page document on Ronald L. Carver, Sgt. E-8 U.S. Army, marked "Secret." Lucas had never been in the army, and thought E-8 was a rank, but wasn't sure. He went out on Google to check: E-8 was a master sergeant.

The document was a mass of acronyms and it took him an hour

to work through the thirty pages, going back and forth to Google, searching for definitions, making notes on a yellow legal pad.

Weather stuck her head in and said, "You're not coming to bed?"

"Not for a while." She was up late; not working in the morning. "Something came up."

"Don't drink any more Diet Coke or you'll be up all night."

She went away and Lucas went back to Carver. Scanning the document, he'd figured that Carver had spent three years in Iraq and two more in Afghanistan. He had a Silver Star and a Bronze Star for bravery under fire, and had been wounded at least twice, with two Purple Hearts. Neither wound had been serious. Both had been treated in-country, and he'd returned to active duty in less than a month, in each case.

Then something happened, but Lucas couldn't tell what it was. Carver had been reprimanded—exact circumstances unspecified—and very shortly afterward had been honorably discharged.

Reading through the document a second time, he determined that Carver had been through a number of high-level training courses: he was a Ranger, he was parachute qualified, he'd taken a half-dozen courses in anti-insurgency warfare, and had spent a lot of time on "detached duty" in both Iraq and Afghanistan.

Working through military sites he found through Google, he determined that Carver had made the master sergeant rank about as quickly as was possible. Then he was out.

Lucas leaned back in his chair and processed it. He thought Carver had probably been some sort of enlisted-ranks combat specialist, what the Internet military sites called an "operator." Lucas suspected that he'd killed a lot of people—his training all pointed in that direction.

But the reprimand could cover a lot of territory. Carver, he thought, might very well have killed either the wrong person, or too many of them. With Carver's medals, experience, and training, Lucas thought it unlikely that he'd been kicked out for rolling a joint.

IN A LOT OF WAYS, the records for Douglas Damien Dannon were parallel to Carver's. Dannon had been in the military for six years, leaving as a captain, honorably discharged. There was nothing in the records to indicate that he'd been pushed out.

Like Carver, he'd spent most of his service time in either Iraq or Afghanistan. He'd won the Bronze Star for bravery under fire, had been wounded by a roadside bomb during the initial invasion of Iraq. After a couple of years as an infantry lieutenant, he'd been assigned to a mobile intelligence unit, and then later, to an intelligence unit at a battalion headquarters. Lucas wasn't sure exactly what that meant, and spent some time looking up words like *battalion*, *company*, *brigade*, and *division*.

A battalion was apparently a mid-level unit, in size, and his particular battalion had apparently been deeply enmeshed in combat in Iraq. Dannon had gotten good efficiency marks, but Lucas wasn't sure how exactly to evaluate them. In his own bureaucracy, good efficiency marks were subject to interpretation by insiders, and could damn with praise a little too faint.

BY THE TIME LUCAS went to bed, a little after two in the morning, he'd learned enough to know that Grant's security detail could plan and carry out a murder with calculated precision and had no large problem with qualms. They would have the means, the training, the personalities that would allow them to get it done.

If they were responsible for Tubbs's murder, catching them would be the next thing to impossible.

Next to impossible, he thought, as he drifted away to sleep. *Next to . . .*

He opened his eyes, listened to Weather breathing beside him, then crept out of bed again, taking his phone with him, into the study, where he called Virgil Flowers. Flowers answered on the third ring and asked, "What happened?"

"I need you up here tomorrow, early. Ten o'clock or so."

Flowers groaned. "You had to call me in the middle of the night to tell me that? I thought the Ape Man was out again."

"Sorry. I was afraid you'd be out of there at five o'clock, in your boat," Lucas said. "I'm running out of time up here, and I need you to look at some paper. You're the only guy I know who could do it."

"What?"

"You were an army cop," Lucas said. "See you up here."

Lucas hung up, went back to bed, and slept soundly.

THE NEXT MORNING, Weather dropped a newspaper on his back and said, "Ruffe."

"What'd he say?"

"He said that the state—meaning you, though he doesn't use your name—is investigating the possibility that Tubbs was killed to cover up the dirty trick on Smalls. The Democrats are furious, while the Republicans are outraged."

"So . . . no change," Lucas said.

"Watch your ass, Lucas," Weather said. "The whole thing is about to lurch into the ditch."

A COUPLE OF HOURS later, Virgil Flowers, a lanky man with long blond hair, put the heels of his cowboy boots on Lucas's desk and turned over the last page of the two documents, which Lucas had printed for him. Flowers said, "You're right. These are two goddamned dangerous guys. Carver, especially, but this Dannon wouldn't be a pushover, either. He'd be the brains behind the operation."

Lucas had called Flowers in for two reasons: he was smart, and he'd been an MP captain in the army, before joining the St. Paul Police Department, and then the BCA. He normally worked the southern third of the state, except when Lucas needed him to do something else.

"I was struggling with the gobbledygook," Lucas said, tossing the papers on the desk. "I figured as a famous former warlord, you'd know what it was all about."

"I met a few of these guys in the Balkans," Flowers said. "They're scary. Smart, tough. Not like movie stars, not all muscled up with torn shirts. A lot of them are really pretty small guys, neat, quiet— you'd think you could throw them out the window, but you'd be wrong. Some trouble would start up, you know, and they'd get assigned a mission, they'd be really, really calm. Sit around eating crackers and checking their weapons. Contained. The army cuts them a lot of slack, because they're very good at what they do . . . which, basically, is killing and kidnapping people."

"An uncommon skill set," Lucas said.

"Yeah. I didn't have a lot of contact with them," Flowers said.

"They had their own compounds. They're secretive, a lot of them get killed—they have an unbelievable mortality rate. Even with that, they stay in the military. Some of them call the army 'Mother.' I think they get hooked on the stress and the camaraderie. Or maybe the sense that they're doing something really important, which they are. If they leave the military, they tend to get in trouble as civilians. Some of them, after they leave, wind up as military contractors, or working for military contractors, right back where they started. Roaming around the world, with a gun in their back pocket."

Lucas said, "Bob Tubbs, if he was working for the Grant campaign, might have posed some kind of danger to them. Maybe he wanted more money. Maybe he couldn't keep his mouth shut, maybe he wanted credit for taking down a senator. Who knows?— but he may have represented some kind of danger. And you've got these guys right there—"

"You don't have a fuckin' thing on them, do you?" Flowers asked.

"Not a fuckin' thing," Lucas said. "Which is why I brought you in. I want you to tell me: if a guy disappears without a trace, and you have these two guys hanging around . . . what are the chances?"

"You don't need me to figure that out. You already have," Flowers said, kicking his feet off the desk. "You just want me to say you're right."

"Am I right?"

"Probably. What are you going to do about it?"

"Will I ever get any evidence against them?"

"Not unless something weird happens," Flowers said. "Listen, let me tell you. Strange things happen in combat areas. Unpleasant things have to be done . . . and somebody has to do them. But those things can't be pulled out in the open. The do-gooders would be screaming to high heaven and careers would be wrecked. You know, 'That's not how we do things in America.' Well, you know, sometimes it is. Look at bin Laden: he was executed, not killed in a gunfight. Everybody knows that, but he was so big, there's a national collective agreement not to mention it. When something like that happens, people like Carver are holding the gun. There was no way to hide the bin Laden thing, but in other cases . . . they have to hide what they did. The army *knows*, but it doesn't know. Even the do-gooders in the Congress *know*, but they don't want to hear it. It's like the guys in Vice, or Narcotics. They're like *you*, really. Sometimes, strange things need to get done."

"Okay."

"Now, I don't know what Carver did that got him kicked out, but it was serious, and he was lucky," Flowers said. "I'd say it's about ninety–ten that if he'd done the same thing as a cop, whatever it was, he'd have gone to prison. Whatever he did, he had to go—but at the same time, the army took care of him."

"What if I subpoenaed some colonel in here to get specific about what he did?"

Flowers snorted. "Never happen."

Lucas said, "We go to federal court—"

"It would take you ten years before you saw the guy's face, and then he wouldn't be able to remember anything specific," Flowers said. "I'm not kidding you, Lucas. It wouldn't happen."

"So what do I do?" Lucas asked.

Flowers stood up and yawned and stretched. "I don't know. Sneak around. Plot. Manipulate. Lie, cheat, and steal. Do what the army did—settle it off the record. Or, forget it."

"I got one senator, one governor, and one would-be senator pointing guns at my head."

"If they take you down, can I have your job?" Flowers asked.

Lucas didn't smile. He said, "Careful what you wish for, Virg."

Virgil: "Hey. I wasn't serious."

"I am," Lucas said.

Lucas took Flowers to lunch, and they talked about it some more, and about life in general. Flowers had recently come off a case where he'd run down four out of five murderers. Three of them had been killed—none of them by Flowers—one was in Stillwater for thirty years, and one was walking around free. Flowers had been unhappy about the one who walked—and Lucas had argued that he'd done as much as he could, and that overall, justice had been served, even if the law hadn't gotten every possible ounce of flesh.

Now Flowers was arguing the same thing back to him. If Dannon and Carver had killed Tubbs, Lucas wouldn't find out about it except by accident. If justice were to be done, it would have to be extrajudicial.

"You think I should push them into a gunfight?" Lucas asked, only half-jokingly.

"Oh, Jesus, no. It'd be fifty-fifty that you'd lose," Flowers said. "If you took on both of them, it'd be seventy-thirty."

Lucas said nothing.

"Of course, if you *did* lose, at least you'd die knowing that I'd be here to take care of Weather," Flowers said.

"It's good to know you have friends," Lucas said.

WHEN FLOWERS LEFT—he said he was headed for the St. Croix River to check out possible environmental crimes, which meant that he was going fishing—Lucas went back to the BCA and shut his office door, sat in the chair where Flowers had been sitting, and put his feet up in the same spot.

If Dannon and Carver had been involved in the murder of Tubbs (if Tubbs *had* been murdered—the small possibility that he hadn't been wriggled away at the back of his thoughts), there were two possibilities: that one of them had done it on his own, and the other didn't know about it; or, more likely, that both of them were involved.

What about Grant? Did she know? He considered that for a while, and finally concluded that there was no way to tell. If she did know, or if she suspected, she'd be the weak link. He'd be tempted to go after her under any normal circumstances, but the circumstances were anything but normal. With a razor's-edge election coming up, any suggestion by a police official that she might know about a murder could tip the balance. And with no evidence on which to base the probe, that police officer could be in a lot of trouble if his suggestion didn't pan out.

For practical purposes, he'd have to confine his investigation to Dannon and Carver.

He thought about them for a while—about what Flowers had seen in their records—and then picked up his phone. The woman on the other end said, "It's been a while."

"You got time for tea?" Lucas asked.

"A social occasion? Trading information about old friends, and who's been up to what?"

"We can do that, too."

They took tea at a Thai place on Grand Avenue. Sister Mary Joseph was exactly Lucas's age; they'd walked hand in hand to kindergarten, when she was simply Elle. She might well have been, Lucas thought, when he thought about it, the first female he'd loved, though they'd gone through life on radically different paths. She'd chosen the nunnery and he'd chosen the craziest possible contact with the world.

But their paths had continued to cross: she'd become a professor of psychology at the University of St. Patrick and the College of St. Anne, and because of Lucas, had taken an interest in criminal pathology. She'd worked in most of the state's prisons, including those for the criminally insane.

Lucas got to the Thai place first, and she came in ten minutes later. In the early years she'd worn a full habit, and had persisted for years after most nuns had gone to modern dress. She'd finally changed over, and now wore what Lucas called "the drabs": brown or gray dresses and long stockings with a little brown coif stuck on top of her head like the vanilla twist on a Dairy Queen cone.

She slid into the booth opposite him and asked, "What's the problem?"

"How you doing, Elle?"

"I'm doing fine, but I'm running a little late."

Lucas told her about Dannon, Carver, and Grant, about what he thought and what Flowers thought. He paused while she ordered a cup of chai, and he got a second Diet Coke, and then continued. When he finished, she took a sip of tea, then said, "You know there are no guarantees."

"Of course."

"Go after Dannon," she said. "Dannon is the thinker and probably a manipulator. He'll try to figure a way out. Carver would consider that unmanly. He'd clam up, and if necessary, take one for the team. He'd sit there and say, 'Prove it.' Dannon might *say* the same thing, but he'd be looking for a way out."

"Dannon wouldn't take one for the team."

She made a moue, then said, "There's one exception. If he is, in fact, in love with Ms. Grant, he might take one for her . . . if she's involved. If he thinks Carver acted alone, he might also turn on Carver. Not because he wanted to, but to protect Ms. Grant."

Lucas said, "A hero."

"Yes. In his own eyes. Have you considered the possibility that Ms. Grant was involved in the killing?"

"I have, but there's no way to know. I can see Dannon or Carver doing it, but Grant, with all that she's got going for her, and the campaign . . . it seems nuts."

"Yes, but step back," Elle said. "Consider that fact that if they were going to take the risk of playing this dirty trick on Senator Smalls, she almost had to know about it—that something was up. Maybe not the details. When Tubbs disappeared, she most likely would make an . . . assumption. She probably would have asked some questions. Whether anybody would answer her, I don't know. That depends on all the different personalities involved."

Lucas explained that he didn't feel that he could go directly after her: that it would be unfair if she was innocent, and that too much was on the line.

"So go after Dannon . . . but ask that she be there when you question him. He might not give up much, but keep an eye on her. On her reaction. Is she astonished that anyone would think that Dannon could do it? Or is she worried? Does she try to protect him, or does she throw him under the bus? Does she feel like she can't throw him under the bus? That could tell you a lot, and it'd be a private session. Nothing leaking to the press."

ELLE WAS ON HER WAY to a piano recital, so Lucas walked her back to her car, and they agreed she'd come over to Lucas's house the following week for dinner. When she was gone, he wandered along the street, looking into windows, thinking about the possibilities, and a couple of blocks down the street took a call from the governor: "I saw the piece in the paper this morning," Henderson said. "Was that you, trying to break something loose?"

"Not necessarily," Lucas said. "Listen, what would you think about the idea of suspending the investigation until after the election? If Grant is involved, we could take her down even if she got elected. But I'm starting to worry about the fairness of it all."

"Let me worry about that," the governor said. "Do you have any indication that the Grant campaign was involved in . . . Tubbs's disappearance?"

"No proof. But Grant has a couple of killers working for her." Lucas filled him in on Dannon and Carver.

"Okay. You keep pushing, but no more press," Henderson said. "No more talking with Ruffe. No comments to anyone. I will have a press conference, and I will tell everybody that I spoke to the lead investigator in the case—that would be you—and that while you have established that the child porn was an attack on Senator Smalls, and that he almost certainly is innocent, that there is, at this point, no indication that the Grant campaign was involved. I will say that it appears likely that Tubbs was working alone, out of a personal animus toward Smalls. I'll ask Porter to back me up. He'll do that."

"Why do you think he'd do that? He's pretty goddamn angry," Lucas said.

"Because I'll call him before the press conference, and I'll tell him what I propose to say, and tell him if he doesn't back me up, I won't have the press conference," Henderson said. "The press conference will get him in the clear in tomorrow morning's papers and TV, which he desperately needs."

"All right. I'll keep it quiet."

"Attaboy. This thing is going to work out, Lucas. For us. It really shouldn't matter whether we get the killer this week or in two weeks. What matters right now is to try to square up this election. Let's focus on that: you do what you do, and let me try to get things straight with the voters."

"That sounded like something your weasel wrote," Lucas said.

"Who do you think taught him his stuff? If anything new erupts, call me, first."

A LITTLE LATER, as he was driving back to his house, he took another call, this one from Kidd. "I'm not too far from your place. You got time for a walk?"

"I'm on my way there, now," Lucas said. "What's up?"

"Let's talk about it when I get there. Radios make me nervous."

Lucas realized he was talking about cell phones, and said, "See you there."

Lucas had just pulled into his garage when Kidd showed up, driving a Mercedes SUV. Lucas said, "Fat ride. That's spelled P-H-A-T."

Kidd: "Wrong century, pal. Phat was about 1990."

"That's the second time one of you computer people told me I was outdated."

"Well, you gotta keep up," Kidd said. He paused, looked up at the sky, then said, "You know, I take that back. Really, maybe you don't need to keep up. Maybe keeping up is for idiots."

"Let's take that walk," Lucas said.

They strolled up Mississippi River Boulevard, taking their time. Kidd asked, "You get anything out of those army docs?"

"I had one of my guys look at them—he's ex-army, an MP captain. He said Dannon and Carver are dangerous guys."

"He's right," Kidd said. He had his hands in his pockets and half turned to Lucas. "I want to tell you some stuff, but I don't want it coming back to me, or showing up in court. It's for your information—and I'm giving it to you because I trust you, and because you may need it."

"You didn't stick up a 7-Eleven store?"

"Worse," Kidd said. "I stole military secrets."

"I got no problem with that," Lucas said. "What'd they say?"

"After I pulled those docs out of the record center, I did some more digging around," Kidd said. "It turns out, there's a classified report on what happened with Carver. There was no way I could get it to you by 'mistake.'"

"Okay."

"The short version of it is, he and a squad of special operations troops flew into a village in southern Afghanistan in two Blackhawks, with a gunship flying support. They were targeting a house where two Taliban leadership guys were hiding out with their bodyguards. They landed, hit the house, there was a short fight there, they killed one man, but they'd caught the Taliban guys while they were sleeping. They controlled and handcuffed the guys they were looking for, and had five of their bodyguards on the floor. Then the village came down on them like a ton of bricks. Instead of just being the two guys with their bodyguards, there were like fifty or sixty Taliban in there. There was no way to haul out the guys they'd arrested—there was nothing they could do but run. They got out by the skin of their teeth."

"What about Carver?" Lucas asked.

"Carver was the last guy out of the house. Turns out, the Taliban guys they'd handcuffed were executed. So were the bodyguards, and two of them were kids. Eleven or twelve years old. Armed, you know, but . . . kids."

"Yeah."

"An army investigator recommended that Carver be charged with murder, but it was quashed by the command in Afghanistan— deaths in the course of combat," Kidd said. "The investigator protested, but he was a career guy, a major, and eventually he shut up."

"Would he talk now? I need something that would open Carver up."

"I don't think so," Kidd said. "He's just made lieutenant colonel. He's never going to get a star, but if he behaves, he could get his birds before he retires."

"Birds?"

"Eagles. He could be promoted to colonel. That's a nice retirement bump for guys who behave. But, there's another guy. The second-to-the-last guy out. He's apparently the one who saw the executions and made the initial report. He's out of the army now. He lives down in Albuquerque."

"I've got no time to go to Albuquerque," Lucas said.

Kidd shrugged: "That's your problem. I'm passing along the information. He's there, he apparently had some pretty strong feelings about what he saw. They might even have pushed him out of the army. Up until then, he looked like he'd probably be a lifer. Same general profile as Carver's, but a few years younger. He was an E-6, a staff sergeant."

"You got a name and address?"

"Yeah, I do. Dale Rodriguez is the name." Kidd dug into

his hip pocket, pulled out a sheet of white paper. "Here's the address."

Lucas took the paper, stuck it in his own pocket. "How do I explain finding this?"

"On those docs you got from the army records center, Carver's last unit is listed. If you search for the unit on Facebook, you'll find a half-dozen different guys listing it as part of their biographies. Rodriguez is one of them."

"Ah. I've got a researcher who is good with Facebook and all that."

"You might have to get in touch with all of them as a cover for contacting Rodriguez."

"That can be done," Lucas said.

"And keep me out of it."

"You're gonna have to tell me someday how you come to have access to all this information. Government secrets. It can't be legal," Lucas said.

"Probably not entirely legal," Kidd said, scuffing along the street. "I've been doing this forever, from before there was an Internet. My access just grew. From the early hacking days, fooling around, back in the eighties. Now . . . I do databases. When I do computers at all, which isn't that often anymore."

"With a specialty in revealing secrets."

"Not really," Kidd said. "Sometimes I go looking for information, and I stumble over stuff that should be out there, in public. Secrets that shouldn't be secrets. Some stuff *should* be secret—I'm not going to give away any biowarfare docs—but a lot of other stuff is criminal and gets covered up."

"I'm seeing some of that right now, on the local level," Lucas said.

"Yeah. Embezzlement gets covered up, nepotism, favors for special groups or corporations that can run into billions of dollars . . .
special access. At the federal level, a lot of it gets classified one way
or the other. I see no reason to honor that. It's crime, plain and
simple."

16

Dannon was waiting by the door when Taryn got back, late, from a campaign rally. She was getting beat up: she'd been to East Grand Forks, on the North Dakota border, early that morning, had flown to International Falls, on the Canadian border, in the afternoon, and in the evening, had been in Duluth, on the Wisconsin border, where the cars met her and brought her back home.

The campaign had been shifting: it was all TV, and appearances that were sure to make TV, especially in those cities where they could still move votes. No more one-on-one talks, no more gatherings of the influential money men. It was too late for that. Now, it was all the downhill rush to Election Day, three days out.

When Taryn came in the house, trailed by Carver, Alice Green, and Connie Schiffer, the campaign manager, Carver peered at Taryn, hard, and she gave a terse nod and said to Green, "We're all done, Alice. You can take off. Six o'clock tomorrow morning."

Green said, "Thank you, ma'am. Six a.m. You try to get some sleep." Green turned and left.

"Good advice," said Schiffer to Taryn. "My butt is worn-out. And that goddamn Henderson."

"At least he gave us a little break," Taryn said. The governor had emphasized, at his press conference, that Tubbs had probably been working alone. Smalls, at a later press conference, hadn't challenged that assessment, and had said that it was time to get the election back on track. "Henderson seemed like he was trying to get everything back to neutral."

"I'd prefer a neutral in our favor," Schiffer said. "But you've got to be ready for the questions, tomorrow, about this Knoedler girl."

"Yeah, yeah . . ." Taryn waved her off: they'd talked about it in the car. "If you think of anything else, call me on the way home: I'll be up for another half hour."

"No Ambien," Schiffer said. "We don't need you stoned or sleep-walking if we wind up on one of the earlier shows."

Taryn nodded and said, "Take off." And to Carver and Dannon, "Set up the security. I'm going to look at the schedule and think in bed for a while."

Schiffer left, pausing to say, "We're still good. We've got four points, but we can't take any more erosion. Two points and we're tied and we lose control."

"Gotcha."

As SCHIFFER WAS LEAVING, Dannon asked Carver to do a serious look around the yard. One of the radar buzzers had been going off, Dannon said, and he hadn't been able to isolate why.

"Probably another goddamn skunk," Carver said. He pulled his jacket back on and went to look.

When he was gone, Taryn turned to Dannon and asked, "What?"

"I talked to Quintana," Dannon said. "He says that Davenport somehow figured out where the porn came from. He and the internal affairs officer at the Minneapolis Police Department are digging around, and Quintana says his name is going to come up. He thinks he can stay clear—but before he knew that Davenport was digging around, he went over to the Smalls campaign headquarters and talked to . . . the woman who set up the trap."

"Not this Knoedler girl?"

"No."

"That's a relief," Taryn said. "Might as well tell me the name of the real one."

Dannon shook his head. "Not yet. Really, it's a psychological issue—it's hard to fake surprise or confusion if you're not surprised or confused. Anyway, Quintana is afraid that if Davenport finds the source, she'll tell him that Quintana already talked to her. And there's no good reason he should have . . . or that he should have talked to her specifically. So if she mentions Quintana, they'll know he was likely the source of the porn, and he's in very deep shit. Like, going-to-prison deep shit. At that point, we don't know what happens. He didn't make any threats, but I gotta believe that he'll cooperate if he's given a break. Quintana doesn't know who I am, but he's a cop, and if I'm dragged into this, he might recognize my voice."

"What are you saying?" Taryn asked, one hand on her hip, her fist clenched.

Dannon hesitated, then said, "I think this woman . . . has to go away. If she goes away, she can't give up Quintana."

"Oh, Jesus Christ."

She stared at him for a moment, and he said hastily, "Don't worry about it. Don't think about it."

"One question. Why not Quintana himself?"

"Harder target. He might already be on edge, he carries a gun, he's been in a couple of shootings. If something went wrong . . . Anyway, I've been out scouting around. The woman is easy, and it'll be clean."

She continued to stare at him, he didn't flinch, but felt it, and then she said, "I have a personal question for you. I . . . it seems like I've seen certain things in you. Do you . . . have some feelings for me? Something I should know about?"

He shrugged again, and then said, as though he didn't want to, "Well . . . sure. For quite a while."

"I've had some of that myself," Taryn said. "There's nothing I can do about it right now—I have to be steady with David, for appearances' sake. I can't seem like I might be flighty, or that I play around. I wanted you to know that David is on his way out. He doesn't know, I'll wait until after the election to tell him. But then, you and I . . . we'll talk."

"Only talk?"

She gave him her best smile. "I don't know what will happen. But I need somebody like you . . . and for more than a bodyguard." She looked at her watch. "We'll talk about this. . . . Right now, I need some sleep."

Dannon was left standing in the living room; as she turned into the hallway to the bedroom wing, she flashed another bright smile at him. He'd never expected that. And he never expected the result: his heart was singing. He'd heard about that happening, but he'd never before felt it.

He walked around for a while, enjoying the glow. The glow never really faded, but he moved on to thinking a little wider, a little broader . . . and after a while, he made an executive decision.

LATE THAT NIGHT:

Dannon walked down the street, moving carefully, watching the car lights. Cop cars had a peculiar look to them: if they weren't going fast, they were going slow. They were big, and they were sedans. He didn't want to be seen anywhere near this particular house.

He was nearly invisible in a black cotton jacket and black slacks; there were almost no lights around, and lots of little clumps of hedge and old trees and crumbling concrete pillars that had once been decorative.

He was told that it was a bad neighborhood, though he'd been in much worse; in fact, he'd been in a dive an hour before that he thought he might have to shoot his way out of. Still, this wasn't exactly a well-lit park: he had yet to see a single soul on the street.

Though wickedly aware of his surroundings, he didn't look around; looking around attracted the eye. People who saw him would ask themselves, "Why's that guy looking around like that?" He'd learned not to do it.

He came up to the house—he'd passed it a few minutes earlier, moving much faster, checking it out—but now he crossed the woman's lawn, avoiding the concrete steps that led up the front bank. The storm door was unlatched, which made things that much easier. He opened it, quietly, quietly, took off one glove, slipped the lock-pick into the lock on the main door, worked the pins, kept the tensioner tight, felt it click once, twice and then turn. He put the glove back on.

He opened the inner door, slowly, slowly, and stepped inside, leaving the door cracked open. He took the pistol out of his pocket, waited for his eyes to fully adjust, saw a movement at the corner of his eye. A cat slipped away into the dark hallway, looking back at him.

When he was sure that nothing was moving, he took a telephone from his pocket, selected a quiet old song, "Heart of Glass" by Blondie, and turned it on. The music tinkled out into the dark, quiet, pretty . . . disturbing.

A woman's voice: "Hello? Is there somebody there? I'm calling the police."

He thought, *No, she isn't.*

"Hello?"

The hallway light clicked on, and the music played on.

He heard her footfalls in the hallway, and then she appeared, wearing a cotton nightgown.

Dannon shot her in the heart.

For Taryn.

He didn't look at the woman's face as she stepped back, stricken, put her hand to her chest, and said, "Awwww . . ." He reached out with his plastic-gloved hand, hit her in the face with the barrel of the pistol and she went down. Her feet thrashed, and he waited, and waited, and she went still. He stepped over her, walked down the hall to the bedroom, turned on the light, and took her purse, and tipped over a small jewelry case, took her cell phone, which was on the bed stand.

He'd been inside for about a minute, and the clock in his head said he should leave. He went back through the hall, checked the woman's still body.

She was gone, no question of it. He fished a plastic bag out of his jacket pocket, shook out a glove, carefully rolled her body back, slipped the glove beneath it, and then let the body roll back in place. Okay. This was all right.

Ninety seconds after he entered the house, he was out. He walked two blocks to his car, started up, then cruised as quietly as he could past the woman's house. As he passed by, he picked up a cigarette lighter and a cherry bomb from the passenger seat, lit the cherry bomb, and dropped it out the window. He was a hundred yards up the street when he heard it go off.

He did that because, at that moment, Carver was at Dannon's town house, sending an e-mail to Grant, under Dannon's name. When he'd done that, Carver would go back to his own town house, wait a few minutes, then make a phone call to a Duluth hotel, to see if they'd found a Mont Blanc pen. Then he'd go browse pens on Amazon and eBay. There'd be time stamps on all of that, if the cops came looking.

Two minutes after that, he dropped the thoroughly clean gun into a nearly full trash dumpster behind a restaurant. It would be at the landfill the next day. He took the money and credit cards out of the purse and threw the purse into a patch of weeds.

The plastic bag went in another dumpster, a mile from his apartment. The credit cards went down a sewer, the cash in his pocket.

Clean hit.

17

Lucas was up early the next morning, went for a run, got home and called his part-time researcher, a woman named Sandy. He told her that he needed her to work on a semi-emergency basis. He wanted all the names she could find for Carver's last military unit, and said he was especially interested in people who were no longer with the military. "Check the social media—all your usual sources. If you find anybody, I want to know what they're doing."

He'd just gotten out of the post-run shower when Turk Cochran called from Minneapolis Homicide.

Cochran said, "Hey, big guy. The word is, you've been snooping around city hall, trying to figure out if somebody over here supplied Porter Smalls's kiddie porn."

"You calling to confess?"

"Yeah, I did it with my little laptop. No wait, I meant my little lap dance, not laptop. Is this call being recorded?"

"What's up, Turk?" Cochran hadn't called simply to crack wise.

"What I meant to say is, some really bad person broke into Helen Roman's house last night and shot her to death. I was told that this particular murder might be of interest to yourself."

"Helen Roman?" For a moment, Lucas drew a blank. He *knew*

that name. . . . *"Helen Roman?* Smalls's secretary? Somebody killed her?"

"That's what I'm saying. Looks sorta like a robbery, but sorta not like a robbery. You want to take a look?"

"Tell me where. I'll be there." Lucas had taken any number of calls about murders: this one had his heart thumping.

HELEN ROMAN'S SMALL HOUSE was on the outskirts of what the Minneapolis media called "North Minneapolis." That was the approved code designation for "black people," usually referred to, further down in the story, as the "community," as in "community leaders asked, 'How come you crackers never talk about white junkies getting aced in East Minneapolis?'"

Lucas left the Porsche at the curb, said hello to a patrol sergeant he'd known for twenty years or so, and crossed the lawn to the small front porch, where Cochran was sitting in an aluminum lawn chair. Cochran was a big man, fleshy-faced with a gut, and the lawn chair was his, kept in the trunk of his car, so he'd have somewhere to sit when he was working around a crime scene.

"Why's it *not* like a robbery?" Lucas asked.

"Didn't take enough stuff," Cochran said. He was wearing gray flannel slacks, a red tie, and a blue blazer; he looked like a New York doorman. "She had quite a bit of takable stuff, lying around loose. The thing is, when something like this happens, either the shooter runs, instantly, or he stays around long enough to accomplish the mission. It's not very often that they stay around for fifteen seconds. It's either nothing, or five minutes. But why am I telling *you* that?"

"I would not be confident in that generalization when applied to a specific case," Lucas said.

"Jeez, you know a lot of big words," Cochran said. "If I understood them all, I agree—*somebody* might stay around for fifteen seconds, like this guy did, but not often."

"You got a time for it?"

"Right around one in the morning. Actually, since you ask, about five after one. A guy was watching TV up the street, heard a shot. If that was *the* shot. The thing is, he said it sounded like a shotgun: a big BOOM. I asked him if he knew what a shotgun sounded like, and he said yeah, he's a turkey hunter. But: the medical examiner's guy tells me that it looks like Roman was shot by a small-caliber weapon, probably a .22. Inside the house. Windows and doors all closed. I'm not even sure that could be heard, five houses away."

Lucas said, "Huh." And, "So you haven't figured out the *boom*."

"No, but who knows? Maybe that *was* the shot. The ME's guy says it looks pretty consistent with a one-o'clock shooting, the condition of the blood and the body temp."

"Who found the body?"

"A woman named Carmen West," Cochran said. "She puts up lawn signs for Smalls around the north end."

"Sounds like dangerous work," Lucas said.

"You mean because Smalls is a right-wing devil, and right-wing devils are not liked on the north side?"

"Something like that. Anyway . . ."

"Roman was supposed to be at work at six o'clock this morning," Cochran said. "Last days of the campaign, and all that. When she didn't show by eight, somebody at the office phoned West and asked her to knock on Roman's door. West said the door was open. . . . She looked in, and saw Roman in the hallway. Called 911."

"All that seems legit?"

"Yeah, it does." Cochran pushed himself out of his chair. "Come on in, I'll show you around."

Lucas followed him up to the porch and Cochran said, "Notice the door."

"Nothing there," Lucas said, checking out the door.

"It wasn't forced," Cochran said. "We can't find *anything* forced. Either the door was unlocked, which seems unlikely for a single woman, or the guy had a key. We talked to the neighbors, who said she didn't have a housekeeper, and her only relative—an heir—is her daughter, who lives in Austin, Texas, and was there this morning and took our call."

"Roman didn't have a boyfriend?"

"Daughter says no. She said they talked once or twice a week."

LUCAS HAD BEEN TO all kinds of murder scenes in his career, and this was like most of them: that is, like nothing in particular. Another house with a worn couch and a newer TV and personal photos on the wall. A kitchen smelling of last night's single-serving pepperoni pizza, dishes in the kitchen sink, waiting to be washed, but now with nobody to wash them.

And, of course, a dead body in the hallway.

Roman was flat on her back, her hands crossed on her chest. She had a slash across her face, which Cochran thought might have come from a gun sight. Her eyes were closed, which was better than open, for the cops, anyway; for Roman, it made no difference. "It looks like the shooter encountered her in the hallway, hit her with the gun, then shot her," Cochran said.

"Or vice versa."

"Could be. Can't tell her posture when she was hit, because the bullet's still inside. No exit, no trajectory." As he spoke, Lucas heard a gust of laughter, from somewhere behind the house: children playing.

"Goddamnit. I need to talk with her," Lucas said, looking down at the body. "I mean, we could have either a multiple murderer, or a freakin' weird coincidence."

"I might be able to help you with that, with the one-or-the-other," Cochran said. He squatted, carefully, dug inside his jacket for a pencil, and pointed the pencil at a patch of black fabric under one of her arms. "See that? That's a man's glove. It's pinned under her. There's only one glove, nothing else like it in the house. We're thinking . . ."

"Could be the killer's."

"Yeah. Either pulled off, or dropped out of a pocket," Cochran said. "Anyway, there's gonna be all kinds of DNA in it. If we get lucky . . ."

If they got lucky, they'd get a cold hit from the Minnesota DNA bank. All felons in Minnesota were DNA-typed.

"How soon?"

"Tomorrow morning. It'll be our top priority," Cochran said.

"I may send you a couple of swabs."

"Yeah?"

"Maybe," Lucas said.

LUCAS SAW A TOTE BAG sitting by the corner of the bed, and what appeared to be the silvery corner of a laptop poking out of it. "Would you mind taking the laptop out and turning it on?"

Cochran said, "No, I don't mind. . . . It doesn't seem too connected to the shooting scene. But it should have been stolen." He slipped the laptop out and said, "This isn't good."

"What?"

"It's a Mac PowerBook, like mine. The first screen you come to is gonna want a password."

"Let's give it a try," Lucas said. Cochran didn't want to put it down on anything the killer might have touched, so they carried it back outside, and he handed the laptop to Lucas and sat down in his lawn chair. Lucas sat on the stoop below him and turned it on. When they got to the password, Lucas asked, "What was the daughter's name?"

"Callie . . . Roman."

Lucas typed "Callie" into the password slot, and the computer opened up.

"Christ, it's like you're a detective," Cochran said.

Lucas went to the e-mail and started scrolling backwards. He found a BLTUBBS on the second page down, turned to Cochran and said, "It's not a robbery."

"Do tell?"

"Well, maybe not. But if it is, we really are ass-deep in coincidence."

He found a half-dozen messages from Tubbs in the past three weeks. Tubbs and Roman had been talking about something, but the messages were never specific. "Call you this evening . . ." and "Where will you be tonight?"

The replies were as short and nonspecific as the questions. The only thing that might mean something was a note from Tubbs that said: "Got the package. Talk to you tonight. Call me when you get home." The message was sent four days before the porn popped up on Smalls's computer. The last access of the pornography on the Minneapolis police computers had been five days before.

Lucas asked Cochran, "Cell phone?"

He shook his head. "No cell phone, but she didn't have a land-line, either. The killer took the cell. Like he should have taken the computer," Cochran said. "You want to give me the whole run-down on this?"

LUCAS SHUT DOWN the computer and handed it back to Coch-ran, stood up, dusted off the seat of his pants, leaned against the porch banister, and told him about the investigation, leaving out only what was necessary. When he was done, Cochran said, "You never talked to her? I mean, you talked to her, but you didn't inter-view her?"

Lucas rubbed his face and said, "Man, it's like the old joke. Ex-cept the joke's on me."

"What joke?"

"The one about the guy who rolls a wheelbarrow full of saw-dust out of a construction site every night."

"I don't know that one," Cochran said.

Lucas said, "The security guy keeps checking and checking and checking the wheelbarrow, thinking the guy had to be stealing something. Never found anything hidden in the sawdust, and no-body cared about the sawdust. Couple of years later, they bump into each other, and the security guy says, 'Look, it's all in the past, you can tell me now. I know you were stealing something. What was it?' And the guy says, 'Wheelbarrows.'"

Lucas continued, "I was convinced that the person who set the trap had to have been planted on the Smalls campaign, which meant somebody new—a volunteer, or a new hire. I interviewed all the likely suspects. But she's one of his oldest employees. I talked to her every time I went there, and it never occurred to me to question *her*."

"She was the wheelbarrow."

"Yeah. She was the fuckin' wheelbarrow. Right there in front of my eyes."

"Fuckin's right," Cochran said. "C'mere. I got a special surprise."

He heaved himself out of his chair and Lucas followed him back into the house and into the bedroom. Cochran took a plastic glove out of his jacket pocket, pulled it on, and opened the bottom drawer on the bedside table. He took out a framed photograph and turned it in his gloved hand so Lucas could see it in the light from the bedroom window.

Helen Roman, at least ten years younger, sitting on Porter Smalls's lap in a poolside chaise, somewhere with palm trees. Drinks on the deck below the chair.

Lucas looked at Cochran, who nodded: "Jilted lover?"

"At least. Several times by now," Lucas said. He looked around the bedroom, and out the door into the lonely little dilapidated house, and thought about Smalls's resort out on the lake. "She must have been pissed. You know what I'm sayin'?"

WORD OF ROMAN'S DEATH was going to get out soon enough, but Cochran hadn't begun any notifications, other than the daughter. The woman who found the body had been sequestered, and hadn't called the campaign or anyone else.

Lucas told Cochran that he was going to talk to Smalls, and Cochran nodded, but when Lucas called, Smalls's phone clicked over to the answering service, as Smalls had warned him it often might. He turned it off when he was speaking, and he'd said he'd be speaking almost constantly in the week before the election. Lucas phoned Smalls's headquarters and was told that the senator was, at that moment, appearing at a Baptist megachurch in Bloomington, on the south side of the metro area.

Lucas got the address, plugged it into his nav, and took off. On the way, he called Grant, and was again forwarded to the answering service. He'd gotten Grant's campaign manager's number, called that, and got Schiffer. "Where's Ms. Grant?" he asked, after identifying himself.

"Is there a problem?"

"You might say so. I need to meet with Ms. Grant and her security people, especially Douglas Dannon and Ronald Carver. I assume Ms. Green will be there as well?"

"Well, Carver isn't with us. . . . I suppose we can call him, if it's urgent."

"It's urgent. Where are you?"

"I'm in Afton. We're setting up for a rally in the park and a luncheon. Taryn's in Stillwater right now, she'll be going to Bayport in, mmm, fifteen minutes, and Lakeland at eleven-fifteen and Afton at noon."

"How about Afton at eleven-thirty?"

"I'll tell her to push everything up a bit, if it's really urgent. We'll be in the park. Look for the TV trucks."

"It's urgent. I'll see you at eleven-thirty in the park."

He made one more call, to the governor, who answered with a "What now?"

"Somebody murdered Porter Smalls's secretary last night," Lucas said. "Smalls had a sexual relationship with her and broke it off. Years ago, though. She was probably the one who set up the trigger on the computer."

Long silence. Then, "Jesus, Lucas, who killed her?"

"I have some ideas . . . but now I don't know what's going to happen," Lucas said. "I wanted to let you know, though: the whole thing might be headed over the cliff, again."

"Think I'll go to North Dakota. There are some border issues to deal with."

"Not a bad idea," Lucas said.

THE MEGACHURCH HAD PARKING for perhaps a thousand cars, and on this Sunday morning, there were probably twelve hundred jammed into the lot. Lucas walked into the entry and saw Smalls standing at a rostrum at the front of the church.

He'd apparently finished his talk and was answering questions. Lucas threaded his way through the crowded pews to the front, and stood waiting until Smalls saw him. When Smalls turned his way, Lucas tipped his head toward the back, and Smalls nodded at him and then said, "You know, folks, I could stand here and talk all day, but I've got another rally I've got to go to. You can reach me online with any more questions, and I can promise, you'll get an answer. Let's take two more questions. The lady in front, with the green blouse . . ."

Five minutes later, led by a security man, with another one trailing behind, and his campaign manager walking beside him, Smalls headed for a side door. Lucas walked that way. Smalls waited at the door until he caught up, and then led the way into a back hallway.

Lucas said, "We need to talk privately."

Smalls said, "It can't be good news."

"No . . ."

Smalls said, "Hang on," and walked back to the people who'd come through the door behind them, spoke to one, who pointed down the hall. Smalls walked back to Lucas and said, "Come on. I'd like Ralph to come along."

Ralph Cox was his campaign manager. He was a tall, ruddy-faced man with curly black hair and overlong sideburns. Lucas nodded to Smalls and said, "That's up to you," and followed Smalls down the hall to an office. Smalls opened the door, and the three of them stepped inside.

Lucas pushed the door shut and asked, "You had an affair with Helen Roman?"

After a long pause, Smalls said, "Years ago."

"Did she think that it might lead to something permanent?" Lucas asked.

"What's going on? Is she the one who pushed the porn?"

"Would she have reason to?" Lucas asked.

Smalls wet his lower lip with his tongue, then said, "She was . . . disappointed when I broke it off. Pretty unhappy. I tried to make it up to her by overpaying her on the secretary's job. There might have been some bad feeling at the time, but . . . that was years ago."

Cox asked, "What happened? Have you arrested her?"

"She was murdered last night," Lucas said.

Smalls staggered, as though he'd been struck. He reached behind himself, found an office chair, and sank into it. "My God. Helen?"

"She was struck in the head, the face, then shot with a small-caliber pistol," Lucas said. "It looks at least superficially like a robbery, but I think . . . it's related. I opened her computer and found notes from Tubbs. They're cryptic—follow-ups on personal conversations. They don't mention porn. They don't even mention you. But Tubbs mentions that he's got some kind of package, and that's just a couple of days before somebody dropped the porn into your computer. Anyway, they had some kind of relationship. . . . I mean, maybe not sexual, but at least conversational. And it seemed like, conspiratorial."

Cox said to Smalls, "We've got to get on top of this, and *right now*. We've got to give it a direction. There are two possibilities— that Tubbs and the Democrats led her into it, for purely political reasons, and that she was killed by a coconspirator, or that she dumped the porn to ruin you, because she was bitter about the broken relationship. We've got to hit the Tubbs angle hard. We've got to steer it—"

"Shut up for a minute. You can talk about that later," Lucas said to him. Back to Smalls: "You said she was disappointed. How disappointed? You think she might have done the porn?"

"I don't know . . . maybe. Maybe she was a little resentful. I didn't think so for a long time, but in the last couple of years, she's been getting more and more distant."

"Ah, Jesus Christ on a crutch," Cox said.

Smalls: "Watch your mouth, Ralph. We're in a church. If they heard you . . ."

"Sorry. But for God's sakes, Porter, if this comes out the wrong way, the TV people will dig up every woman you've ever slept with, and from what I understand, there's a lot of them."

Lucas said, "Could we—"

Cox jumped in again. "I'm gonna leave you guys to talk. I gotta call Marianne and get something going. We got no time for this, no time."

And he was out the door.

"Who's Marianne?" Lucas asked.

"Media," Smalls said. He pushed himself out of his chair. "I'll tell you, Lucas, this is pretty much the end, for me. Ralph can do all the media twisting he wants, but it ain't gonna work."

"There's something else going on," Lucas said. He hesitated, thinking that he might be about to make a mistake. "It's possible that if Tubbs was working for the Grant campaign that he was killed to break the connection between the porn and the Grant campaign. And that the same people who killed him, killed Roman."

Smalls waved him off, with a hand that looked weary. "Yeah, yeah, but I'll tell you what, Lucas. Political campaigns don't have killers on their staffs. End of story."

Lucas looked at him, didn't say a word.

Smalls peered back, then said, "What?"

Lucas shrugged.

"What, goddamnit? Are you . . . Grant doesn't have a killer . . . ?" He was reading Lucas's face, as a politician can, and he said, "Jesus Christ, what'd you find out?"

"Watch the language," Lucas said. "This is a church."

"Don't hassle me, Lucas. This is my life we're talking about."

"Grant has these two bodyguards," Lucas said. "They were involved in some very rough stuff in Iraq and Afghanistan. One of them was pushed out of the army for something he did there. He killed a bunch of people he shouldn't have—executed them. Including a couple of kids. I talked to an ex-army guy, a BCA guy now, who understands these things, and he said these guys essentially specialized in killing and kidnapping."

Smalls took off his glasses, rubbed his face with his hands. "I . . . This is really hard to believe."

"I know. I'll tell you what, when you spend your life doing investigations, you become wary of coincidences. Because they happen. It's possible that there was a dirty trick, followed by two killings, at a critical moment in a political campaign, and it's all purely a coincidence that the person who most benefits had two killers standing around. I personally am not ready to believe that."

"What're you gonna do?"

"I'm gonna go jack them up. But they're smart, and I have no evidence. None. If they tell me to blow it out my ass, well . . ."

"Killers," Smalls said. "I tell you, politics has gotten rougher and rougher, but I never thought it could come to this. Never. But maybe . . . Now that I think about it, maybe it was inevitable."

LUCAS TOOK OFF FOR AFTON. Afton was a small town, one of the oldest in Minnesota, built on the wild and scenic river that separated Minnesota from Wisconsin. The river was gorgeous in the summer and early fall and at mid-winter, after the freeze; less so in the cold patch of November or the early rains of March. But this day, though November, was particularly fine.

Lucas went to the University of Minnesota on a hockey scholarship, but since you couldn't major in hockey—and his mother peed all over the idea, suggested by the coaches, that he major in physical education—he wound up in American studies, a combination of American literature, history, and politics. He did well in it, enjoyed it, and since it was commonly used as a pre-law major, he thought about becoming a lawyer like a number of his classmates.

After all the bullshit was sorted through, a levelheaded professor suggested that he try police work for a year or so. He could always go back to law school, or even go to law night school, if he didn't like the cops—and the time on the street would be invaluable for certain kinds of law practice.

Lucas joined the Minneapolis cops, and never looked back: but the four years in American studies stuck with him, especially the literature. He thought Emily Dickinson was perhaps the best writer America had ever produced; but on this day, heading east out of the Cities, then south down the river, he thought of how some of the writers, Poe and Hemingway in particular, used the weather to create the mood and reflect the meanings of their stories.

Poe in particular.

Lucas could still quote from memory the first few lines of "The Fall of the House of Usher": *During the whole of a dull, dark and soundless day in the autumn of the year, when the clouds hung oppressively low in the heavens, I had been passing alone, on horseback, through a singularly dreary tract of country, and at length found myself, as the shades of the evening drew on, within view of the melancholy House of Usher. . . .*

And Lucas thought what a literary conceit that all was: he'd gone to a murder scene on a beautiful fall day, and heard children laughing outside. And why not? The murder had nothing to do with them, and old people died all the time.

Now he, the hunter, was headed south to tackle a couple of probable killers, a fairly grim task; but over here, to the right of the highway as he went by, a man was washing down his fishing boat, preparing it for winter storage; and coming down the road toward him, a half-dozen old Corvettes, all in a line, tops down on a fine blue-sky day, the women in the passenger seats all older blondes, one after the other.

And why not? Life doesn't have to be a long patch of misery.

There was plenty of room for blondes of a certain age, to ride around in seventies Corvettes, like they'd done when they were girls; a few beers at Lerk's Bar, and then a dark side street with a hand up their skirts. That was still welcome, wasn't it?

He'd made himself smile with all the rumination. He really ought to lighten up more, Lucas thought, as the last of the Corvettes went past. Hell, what are a couple more killers in a lifetime full of them? And he liked hunting, and what better day to do it than a fine blue day in the autumn of the year, with not a cloud in the heavens, when riding through a singularly beautiful tract of country, in a Porsche with the top down?

Fuck a bunch of E. A. Poe.

And his Raven.

THE GRANT CARAVAN had pulled to the side of the street in what passed for downtown Afton. A small crowd was hanging around in the park across the street, and a cable TV station was setting up a small video camera in front of a bandstand. Grant and her people were apparently in an ice cream parlor.

Lucas dumped the Porsche and started across the street to the parlor. As he did, Alice Green came out the front door and moved to one side, and nodded toward Lucas; then Grant came out the door holding an ice cream cone, squinted at him in the sunlight, and licked the cone as he came up.

Lucas thought, Some women shouldn't be allowed to lick ice cream cones, because it threw men into a whole different mental state. . . .

Schiffer came out of the ice cream parlor, also licking an ice cream cone, with markedly less effect; she was followed by a tall, bullet-headed man with fast eyes who Lucas suspected was one of the bodyguards; his eyes locked on Lucas. Then another man came out, smaller than the first, but with the same fast eyes, and the same quick fix on Lucas. Lucas wanted to put a hand on his .45, but instead, called, "Ms. Grant—glad you had the time."

"What's so urgent?" she asked.

"These two gentlemen," Lucas said, flicking a finger at Carver and Dannon. "Are they Misters Carver and Dannon?"

Grant turned, as if checking, then turned back and said, "Yeah," and nibbled on the cone, which looked like a cherry-nut, one of Lucas's favorites.

"Then let's find a place where we can talk," Lucas said.

"Courtyard," Green said, nodding toward an empty outdoor dining space to the left of the ice cream parlor. "You don't want to talk to me?"

"Not at the moment," Lucas said. "You might keep people away? Even other staffers. This is sort of private."

Green nodded; Schiffer said, "I'm going to listen in."

They moved over to the empty space, Green hovering on the periphery, listening. Lucas said, "One of Porter Smalls's secretaries was murdered last night. Shot to death in her house, in Minneapolis. I went through her laptop and she'd been corresponding in a fairly cryptic way with Bob Tubbs before he disappeared, and just before the pornography popped up on Smalls's computer."

He'd been watching Carver and Dannon, and nothing moved in their eyes, which Lucas thought interesting, because he thought something should have.

Grant said, "Well, that's awful, but what does it have to do with us?"

"Tubbs is dead, I'm almost certain of it, at this point, and now

Helen Roman has been murdered. It was all done very well, from a professional-killing standpoint. Most people who kill for money are fools and idiots and misfits. This doesn't appear to be the work of fools."

Grant said, "Yeah, yeah," and made a rolling motion with one forefinger—*moving right along*—as she simultaneously took another nibble of the cherry-nut.

"Well, it's possible that she put the porn on Smalls's computer to get revenge on him," Lucas said. "They'd had some personal disagreements, apparently. But if that was what it was, a personal matter, why would anybody kill her? Or Tubbs?"

"Well, I don't know," Grant said. "Are you sure she was killed for that reason? Because it had something to do with Smalls?"

Lucas was forced to admit it: "No. Not absolutely sure. But pretty sure. The other possibility is that the people who paid for the porn to be dumped on Porter Smalls, knowing that doing so involves a number of felonies, are breaking the link between themselves and the pornography. Breaking the link very professionally. I did the obvious: I looked for professional killers. The only ones I could find"—Lucas nodded at Carver and Dannon—"are employed by you."

"What!" Schiffer blurted, not a question.

Lucas had been watching Carver and Dannon again, and again, their eyes were blank; if they'd been lizards, Lucas thought, a nictitating membrane might have dropped slowly across them.

"That . . ." Grant waved her arms dismissively. "I really do have to talk to somebody about you. Professional killers? They're decorated war veterans. Were you in the military? Did you—"

Dannon interrupted her, and said to Lucas, "We had nothing to do with anything like that. We're professional security guys, end of story. If you have any evidence of any sort, bring it out: we'll re-fute it."

"I want to have a crime-scene guy take DNA samples from you," Lucas said. "Doesn't hurt, nothing invasive—"

"DNA?" Grant sputtered. "You know what—"

"It's okay with us," Dannon said, and now there was something in his eye, a little spark of pleasure, a job well done. Lucas thought, *This isn't good.*

Grant snapped at Dannon: "Don't interrupt. I know that you had nothing to do with this, I know the DNA will come back nega-tive, but don't you see what he's doing? When the word gets out that my bodyguards have been DNA-typed in a murder case? This guy is working for Smalls—"

"No. I'm not," Lucas said. "I guarantee that nothing about the DNA samples will get out before the election. I'll get one guy to take the samples and I'll read him the riot act. He will not say a word, and neither will I. If word gets out, I'll track it, and if it's my guy, I'll see that he's fired and I'll try to put him in jail."

Grant, Schiffer, Carver, and Dannon exchanged glances, and then Grant said to Dannon, "You've got no problem with this?"

"No. It's probably what I'd do in his place." He showed a thin white smile: "Because, you know, he's right. We *are* trained killers."

He poked Carver in the ribs with an elbow, and Carver let out a long, low, rambling laugh, one of genuine amusement, and . . . smugness. Lucas thought, *They know something.*

WITH THEIR CASUAL ACQUIESCENCE to the DNA tests, Lucas was left stranded. He asked some perfunctory questions—where were you last night at one o'clock? (At our apartments.) Did anyone see you there? (No.) Any proof that you were there? (Made some phone calls, moved some documents on e-mail.) Can we see those? (Of course.) Did you know either Tubbs or Roman? (No.)

Lucas walked away and made a call, asking them to wait, got hold of a crime-scene specialist, and made arrangements for Carver and Dannon to be DNA-typed.

He went back to them and said, "We'd like you to stop in at BCA headquarters on your way back through St. Paul, anytime before five o'clock. You'll see a duty officer, tell him that you're Ronald and Douglas—you won't have to give your last name or any other identifier—and that you're there at my request, Lucas Davenport's request, to be DNA-typed. A guy will come down to do the swabs. This will take one minute, and then you can take off. The swabs will be marked Ronald and Douglas, no other identifiers."

Carver and Dannon nodded, and Grant said, "What a crock," and tossed the remains of her ice cream cone into a trash can. "If you're done with us, I'm going to go shake some hands. I'll tell you what—nothing about this better get out."

"It won't," Lucas said. To Carver and Dannon: "Don't go anywhere."

Grant led her entourage across the street, with Green lingering behind. She said to Lucas, "Interesting."

"They did it," Lucas said. "You take care, Alice."

"I can handle it," she said.

"You sure? You ever shot anyone?"

"No, but I could."

Lucas looked after Dannon and Carver: "If it should come to that—and it could, if they think you might have figured something out—don't give them a chance. If you do, they'll kill you."

18

Ray Quintana was a fifty-one-year-old Minneapolis vice cop, a detective sergeant, and having thought about it, he figured that he'd thoroughly screwed the pooch, also known as having poked the pup or fucked the dog. He didn't know who'd been calling him about Helen Roman, but he suspected that whoever it was had gone over to Roman's house the night before and killed her.

Quintana wasn't a bad cop; okay, not a terrible one. He might have picked up a roll of fifties off a floor in a crack house that didn't make it back to the evidence room; he might have found a few nice guns that the jerkwads didn't need anymore, that made their way to gun shows in Wisconsin; he might have done a little toot from time to time, the random scatterings of the local dope dealers.

But he'd put a lot of bad people in jail, and overall, given the opportunities, and the stresses, not a bad guy.

When Tubbs had come to him, he'd put it out there as a straight business deal: Tubbs had heard from somewhere unknown that the Minneapolis Police Department had an outrageous file of kiddie porn. Quintana had known Tubbs since high school; Tubbs had been one of the slightly nerdy intellectuals on the edge of the popular clique, while Quintana had been metal shop and a football lineman.

Tubbs had said, "I'll give you five thousand dollars for that file. Nobody'll ever know, because hell, if I admit it went through my hands, I'd be in a lot more trouble than you."

Quintana had asked him what he was going to do with it, and Tubbs had told him: "I'm gonna use it to screw Porter Smalls. I'm gonna get Taryn Grant elected to the U.S. Senate. When that happens, I'll be fixed for life. I'll remember you, too."

Had Grant hired him?

"I don't know—I'm being funded anonymously," Tubbs said. "But that's obviously where it comes from. I got the cash, and enough to split off five thousand for you."

How much had Tubbs gotten?

"That's between me and Jesus," Tubbs said. "I'm taking all the risk. You get more than it's worth, and if you don't want the money—well, I'll get another file. I know they're floating around out there."

Quintana wanted the five grand. Hadn't really needed it, but he *wanted* it.

Quintana's problem now was that Marion from Internal Affairs was on the trail, as was Davenport. Quintana knew Davenport, had worked with him, both on patrol and as detectives; Davenport scared him. Eventually, he thought, they'd get to him. Tubbs hadn't exactly snuck into city hall. They might even have been seen talking together.

Quintana was thinking all of this at his desk, on a Sunday morning, staring at the wall behind it, over all the usual detective litter. He was so focused that his next-door desk neighbor asked, "You in there, Ray?"

"What?"

"I thought you were having a stroke or something."

Quintana shook his head. "Just tired."

"Then what are you doing in here? It's Sunday."

"I was thinking I shoulda gone to Hollywood and become an actor. I could have made the big time."

"Man, you *have* had a stroke."

He went back to staring.

His delivery of the porn file could get him jail time. Worse, he suspected that whoever was calling him had killed Roman. Even worse than that, he'd talked casually with Turk Cochran when he'd come in from Roman's place, and Cochran said that Davenport thought it might be a pro job.

Even worse than that . . . Quintana suspected the same pro might be coming to shut *him* up.

If Quintana kept his mouth shut, he might be killed as a clean-up measure. If he kept his mouth shut, Davenport could plausibly come after him as an accessory to murder, especially if word got out that he'd interviewed Roman, or had been seen with Tubbs.

That all looked really bad.

There was a bright side: Tubbs was presumably dead, and Roman certainly was. That meant that any story that he made up couldn't really be challenged. If he could just come up with something good enough, he would probably stay out of jail, and might even hang on to his pension. At least, the half that his ex-wife wasn't going to get.

But what was the story? How could he possibly justify handing

the file over to Tubbs? He thought and thought, and finally concluded that he couldn't.

So he thought some more, and at one o'clock in the afternoon,
picked up the phone and called the union rep at home, and said he
needed to talk to the lawyer, right then, Sunday or not.

The union guy wanted to know what for, and Quintana said he
really didn't want to know what for. At two o'clock, he was talking
to the lawyer, and at two-thirty, they called Marion. The lawyer,
whose name was James Meers, said Quintana needed to talk with
Marion and probably with Davenport, as soon as possible. Immediately, if possible.

Lucas took the call from Marion, who said, "We got a break."

He'd set up the meeting for four o'clock.

LUCAS PARKED HIS PORSCHE in one of the cop-only slots next to
city hall and threw his BCA card on the dash, which usually managed to piss somebody off; but they'd never towed him. The attorney's office, where the meeting would be held, was a block or so
away, in the Pillsbury building. As he walked along, he spotted Marion, whistled, and Marion turned, saw him, and waited.

"I thought somebody liked my ass," Marion said.

"Probably not," Lucas said. "You know what Quintana's going
to say?"

"Well, since it's you and me . . . I suspect it might have something to do with the porn. We've been looking at possibilities, and
his name's on the list. He had access to the relevant computers both
in Vice and Domestics."

"Ah, boy. I've known him for a long time," Lucas said. "Not a bad
cop—give or take a little."

"You know something about the take?" Marion asked.

"No, no. If he's taken anything, he's smart enough that nobody would know," Lucas said. "That's what's odd about this deal—why in God's name would he give a porn file to anyone? Especially when it was going to be used like this? You know, a public hurricane. That doesn't sound like the Ray Quintana we know and love. He's always been a pretty cautious guy."

"Mmm. Got a pretty clean jacket, too," Marion said. He looked up at the Pillsbury building. "I guess we'll find out."

QUINTANA AND MEERS were waiting, Quintana was in a sweat, and showing it. Meers was a soft-faced blond with gold-rimmed glasses in his mid-thirties, who looked like a British movie star, but Lucas couldn't think which one. A guy who'd been in a tennis movie. When Lucas and Marion were seated, he said, "Ray's got a problem. I don't think it has to go any further than this . . . it's not criminal, or anything, but he sorta screwed up."

Marion looked skeptical, lifted his hands, and looked at Quintana. "So what is it?"

Before Quintana could say anything, Meers added: "He also has some valuable information for you, he thinks. The fact is, he didn't have to do this—he's doing it voluntarily, this meeting, and he's not even going to try to deal on the information. He's just going to give it to you, because he's a good cop. I hope you keep that in mind."

Marion looked at his watch: "Are we done with the introductions?"

Lucas was the good guy: he looked at Quintana and asked, "How you doin', Ray?"

"Ah, man, I messed up," Quintana said.

"What happened?"

Quintana leaned forward in his chair, his hands clenched in his lap, and spoke mostly to Lucas. "About two weeks ago, Bob Tubbs came to see me. I knew him all the way back in high school, and we'd bump into each other from time to time. We weren't friends, but you know, we were friendly. So, he comes to see me in the office. He sits down and says he's got a big problem."

Quintana told it this way:

Tubbs said, "You guys have an extensive file of kiddie porn somewhere in your computers. Here in Vice, and down in Domestics. I don't care about that, but there's one picture in there that I need to see. I need to see it off the record."

Quintana: "What's this all about?"

Tubbs: "A very large person in the state legislature is banging a girl on the side. Young, but not too young. But now it turns out that she might have been involved in some kind of porn ring and probably prostitution, and was busted by you guys. I need to look at her picture. I can't get at it through regular sources, because she was underage when she was busted, and the file is sealed."

Quintana: "Why do you need to look at it?"

Tubbs: "Because this guy is in a pretty tender spot. He's in the process of getting a divorce. His wife's lawyer is a wolverine, and if she gets a sniff of this chick—and maybe she already did—they're going to make an issue of it. Then, it's all gonna come out. He needs to know if this girl's the one involved in porn and prostitution and all that. I've seen his girlfriend. Now I need to look at the file."

Quintana: "Even if she was, what would he do about it?"

Tubbs: "Put her ass on a plane to Austin, Texas. He's got a buddy in the Texas legislature who'll give her a job, and his old lady won't be able to find her."

Quintana: "Why doesn't he do that anyway?"

Tubbs: "Because it'll cost an arm and a leg. If she's not the one, he won't do it. The other thing is, he doesn't want to ask the girl, because he's afraid it'll change things. And she might decide to ask for a little cash herself. If she's the one. All he wants to do is *know*."

Lucas asked, "You gave him the file?"

Quintana shook his head. "No. All I did was sit at the computer and call up the file. I knew what he was talking about, the girl, because it went back to Tom Morgan's case three years ago.

"I showed him the picture, and he asked me to enlarge it, the best shot of her face. He looked at it and then he said, "Close, but no cigar. She's not the one."

Marion: "Then what?"

"I closed the file and he said thanks, and he went away."

Marion: "Didn't give you a little schmear?"

"No, no. Nothing like that," Quintana said. "Look, this was a fast favor for a guy. Didn't look at the porn, didn't do any of that. A favor for a guy big in the legislature. You know how that works."

"You believed all that bullshit?" Marion asked.

Quintana shook his head: "It looks bad now, but yeah, I believed him. Like I said, I knew him forever."

Lucas said, "If you didn't give him the file, how'd he get it?"

Quintana shook his head. "I don't know for sure. But I've got my suspicions."

"Like what?"

"He was standing behind me when I signed on," Quintana said. "He might have seen my password . . . it's . . . this sounds even stupider . . . it's 'yquintz.' And I mean, he was right there. Once you've got the password, you can get in even from outside, if you need to. After I signed on, I looked up the file. He saw that, too."

Marion said, "Unbelievable."

Quintana ran his hands through his hair. "Yeah, I know. Oldest goddamn trick in the book," Quintana said. "I never saw it. I mean, all he wanted to do was look at one face."

Lucas mostly didn't believe it, but was willing to buy it if he got anything that would aim him at Carver and Dannon. He asked, "What was this information you got?"

"Yesterday I was working over on Upton—we think there might be a high-ticket whorehouse over there, don't tell anybody. Anyway, I was sitting in my car taking down tag numbers and taking pictures of these girls coming and going, and I get this phone call. The guy says that he bought the pornography file from Tubbs and Tubbs said he got it from me. I say, 'That's bullshit, I didn't give him anything.'

"The guy says, 'Well, he said he got it from you, and I think he might have told a woman over in Smalls's office. And he might've told her about me, too. She's the one who put the porn in. Nobody knows who I am, but somebody needs to go over and talk to this woman, this Helen Roman. Like a cop. Needs to ask her where the porn came from, and where it went.'

"I said, 'I didn't give anybody any porn. Who is this, anyway?'

"He said, 'A guy who doesn't like Porter Smalls.'

"I said, 'I don't like Porter Smalls either, but I didn't give a thing to Tubbs.'

"The guy says, 'Look, all you have to do is check with her.'

"I say, 'Not me.'

"Then the guy hangs up," Quintana said.

"And you've got the phone number," Lucas said.

Quintana nodded: "I do." He dug in his pocket and handed Lucas a slip of notepaper, with a phone number on it.

Lucas took the paper, and Marion said, "I'm gonna need that."

Lucas nodded, took out a pen and a pocket notebook, and wrote the number down, and passed the original slip back to Marion. "I'm going to run down the number and look at the activity on that phone," Lucas said. "If this is real, it could be a serious break."

"I just hope I get credit for it," Quintana said.

Meers said, "That's pretty much the story. A simple request from a friend, to help out a guy in the legislature. If you go after a guy for that, we wouldn't have a police department left."

Marion said, "You know the problem, though: it's not important unless it becomes important. Ray's now all tangled up in what could be a double murder case. One way or another . . ."

Quintana said, "Come on. If I hadn't told you, you'd never have found out. I could've lied. Instead, I came right in, as soon as I worked it out. I even gave you what Lucas said could be a break. A *serious* break."

Marion looked at Lucas and asked, "What's the BCA think?"

Lucas said, "This is all on you guys. Do what's best: I don't care. I just want the phone number." He looked at Quintana: "Where's the phone they called you on?"

"In my pocket." He fished it out: an iPhone.

"I'm going to need to take it with me. I need to take it to our lab, we'll get in touch with your . . . Who's your service provider?"

"Verizon."

"We'll get in touch with Verizon, and when we know where our targets are, we're going to want you to call them," Lucas said.

Quintana shook his head. "You can take my phone, but these

guys are way too smart to be using their own phone. I'd give you ten to one that it's a disposable."

"That's why we need to catch them with it. We'll be monitoring the call and the location it comes from," Lucas said. "I'll probably get back to you tonight. Where you gonna be?"

"Without my cell . . . I'll probably go home if Buck is done talking to me. I've got a landline there."

"Okay. You sit there, wait for my call," Lucas said. "You go along with all of this, I'll testify on your side in any kind of proceedings."

Quintana nodded. "I'll do that."

He passed Lucas his cell phone, and Lucas said, "If you'll all excuse me . . . I gotta run."

As he headed for the door, Quintana called, "You believe me, right?"

Lucas paused at the door, then said, "No, not the whole story. Not even very much of it. But I believe the phone number."

THEN HE HAD a lot to do. From his car, as he headed back across town to the BCA, he called Jenkins and told him to find Shrake: "I know it's Sunday, but I need you to babysit some people for me. Only until tonight. I need to know where they are, all the time."

"How complicated is this going to be?"

"Not complicated. You have to tag a campaign caravan." He told Jenkins to find out where Taryn Grant was going to be, described Dannon and Carver. "It's those two guys you've got to stay with. I want you to go separately so if they split up, you can follow both of them. But they should stick pretty close to Grant for as long as I need you to watch them."

"Good enough," Jenkins said.

LUCAS HAD TO MAKE some calls, first to the director, and then the deputy director, and between them they found a technician who was willing to come in and set up the phone monitoring system. When he got there, the tech came up to Lucas's office and said, "We don't usually need a subpoena for Verizon, if we just want a location, but I'll check with them first. That's not usually a problem, though."

"Then get it going," Lucas said.

He was a little cranked: if this worked out, there'd be somebody in the bag by midnight. He called Jenkins: "Where are you guys?"

"Grant's up in Anoka. We're on the way. Then she's going to St. Cloud for an eight-o'clock appearance and then back home. Probably back in the Cities between ten and midnight."

"Keep me up to date," Lucas said.

Lucas called Quintana: "It'll be late—I'll probably come get you around nine or ten o'clock."

Lucas needed something to eat. He called Weather to find out what the food situation was, and was told that the housekeeper was making her patented mac & cheese & pepperoni. "I'll be there," he said.

He was pulling his jacket on when Virgil Flowers called: "I was talking to Barney and he didn't know what you were up to, but he said you might use my help. I'm down in Shakopee. I can either go home, or head your way."

"My house," Lucas said. "Helen's making her mac and cheese and pepperoni."

"What happened to that vegetarian thing you guys were doing?"

"Ah, that only lasted a month or two. Besides, pepperoni isn't meat—it's cheese made by pigs," Lucas said. "Anyway, we'll be going out later. I'll tell you about it when you get there."

He called Weather and told her that Flowers was coming to dinner, and she said, "We got plenty."

Which was true: the mac and cheese and pepperoni usually went on for the best part of a week.

LUCAS GOT HOME, changed into jeans, a wool vest over a white dress shirt, and an Italian cotton sport coat, blue-black in color that would be excellent, he thought, for nighttime shoot-outs. It hadn't yet been tested for that. When he got back downstairs, Flowers had come in, wearing a barn coat, jeans, and carrying a felt cowboy hat. His high-heeled cowboy boots made him an inch taller than Lucas.

"There better not be a fuckin' horse in my driveway," Lucas said.

A bit later, Lucas took a call from the BCA tech, who said they were set with Verizon, and they could give him a real-time location as soon as Lucas called the other phone, which, as it happened, also used Verizon. There'd been no calls on the phone for two days; the last call had been to Quintana's number.

They all ate together at a long oblong dinner table, Flowers and Letty happily gabbing away—Flowers, a part-time writer with a developing reputation, had done a biographical piece about Letty that had been published in *Vanity Fair*, with photographs by Annie Leibovitz. They were all now dear friends, Annie and Letty and Virgie.

Leibovitz had taken a bunch of pictures of Lucas, too, but the magazine had used only one. Lucas thought it made him look like a midwestern prairie preacher from the nineteenth century. As for the friendship, he thought Letty and Virgie were getting a little too dear. The issue came up before dinner, and Weather told him he was losing it if he thought Flowers had untoward ideas about Letty.

"When it comes to being around women, I wouldn't trust that guy further than I could spit a Norwegian rat," Lucas had grumbled.

"Why? Because he reminds you so much of your younger self?" she'd asked.

"Maybe," Lucas had said. "But not that much younger."

"He's not interested in Letty," Weather had declared.

"Okay," Lucas said. "How about in you?"

"Don't be absurd," she'd said, ostentatiously checking her hair in the mirror.

AFTER DINNER, Lucas and Virgil went to Lucas's study, with Letty perching on a side chair, and Lucas briefed him about the situation. "Basically," Flowers summed up, "we've got nothing, but if their phone's GPS says that they're in a certain spot, you think that's good enough for a search and seizure."

"I know it is, because there's been another case just like it," Lucas said. "It was in LA, but the federal court refused to order the evidence set aside."

"And so this could prove that these two highly trained killers were involved with the porn, and we know for sure that they've got guns."

"Uh-huh."

Virgil thought about that and said, "Okay."

They'd sat down to eat at seven, had finished with the food and talk at eight, and at eight-thirty, sitting in the den, Lucas took a call from Jenkins. "This is going to wind up sooner than I thought," Jenkins said. "She finished talking, the TV is pulling out, now she's going around mixing with the kids, but that's not going to last long, once the TV is gone. I think we'll be out of here in fifteen minutes, and then it's an hour back to her place."

He said to Flowers, "Let's go. Excuse me—I meant, 'Saddle up.'"

"Yeah," Virgil said, getting his hat.

"Don't let him push you around," Letty told Virgil. "That hat looks good on you. Not everybody could pull it off, but you can."

"Thank you, sweetheart," Flowers said, and he and Lucas were out the door.

They took Flowers's truck, and as they backed out of the drive-way, Lucas noticed that Flowers was smiling.

"What's the shit-eating grin about?" Lucas asked.

"Ah, I love pimping you about Letty. And Weather, for that matter."

"I don't mind, as long as you keep your hands off Helen and that mac and cheese and pepperoni," Lucas said.

JENKINS CALLED TO SAY that Taryn Grant's caravan consisted of three cars. The first carried what appeared to be three lower-ranking campaign people, one of whom was probably the media liaison. The second car was a big American SUV, and carried Grant, a short, heavyset woman, and one of the bodyguards; from Lucas's description, he thought it was probably Carver. The third car carried the other bodyguard, Dannon, and a thin woman who was apparently also security.

"Alice Green, ex–Secret Service," Lucas said. "Where are you guys?"

"Shrake is out front, I'm a quarter mile back, with four cars between us."

"Stay in touch," Lucas said. "Let me know for sure when they hit 494."

Quintana lived in Golden Valley, a first-ring suburb west of Minneapolis. He was standing on his front porch when Lucas and Virgil arrived. He got in the backseat, and Lucas introduced Flowers. Quintana said, "I appreciate the chance."

"Like I said, it's up to Minneapolis what they do about this," Lucas said. "But you kinda blew it, Ray."

"I know that," Quintana said. "But tell me you don't do a little off-the-record relationship stuff. I thought Tubbs might be something for me: a guy to know."

"I understand that," Lucas said. "I don't buy all that other stuff."

"Ahhh . . ." Quintana shut up and looked out the side window.

After a couple minutes of silence, Virgil said to Lucas, "At least we know he's not lying to us now."

"How's that?" Lucas asked.

"His lips aren't moving."

Quintana began laughing in the backseat, and then Lucas and Virgil started.

THEY PULLED INTO a mostly empty strip mall parking lot a mile from Grant's house. The streets were good between the mall and her house, and they could be there in a couple of minutes. They talked about Tubbs and Roman, but not about Quintana's problem.

"I wish that motherfucker Tubbs wasn't dead," Quintana said. "Then I could kill him myself."

Lucas asked Flowers how his most recent romance had been going.

"I think it's gone," Flowers said. "We're apparently friends, now."

"That's not necessarily the kiss of death," Quintana said from the backseat, and they talked about that for a while.

Jenkins called when the caravan got off I-94 and headed south on I-494, and then when it got off I-494 and headed west. Lucas called the tech and said, "I'm making the call."

And at that moment, as he hung up on the tech and prepared to call the unknown phone, another call from Jenkins came in. "Man, we got a problem. We got a problem."

"What?"

"I got a cop car on my ass, and so does Shrake. The caravan has pulled over ahead of us. Shit! They made us. I gotta talk to this cop."

"Goddamnit, where are you?" Lucas asked.

He got the location, and told Flowers to go that way, and then made the call on Quintana's phone and handed it to Quintana. It rang, and rang, and rang, with no answer. The tech called and said, "We've got a location for you. The phone's at Hampshire Avenue North and Thirtieth."

"What?"

"It's at Hampshire Avenue North and Thirtieth. There's a park there."

Lucas asked, "Where in the hell is that?"

"Well, if you're at Grant's house, it's about eight miles east. As the crow flies."

"Sonofabitch," Lucas said.

"What're we doing?" Flowers asked.

"Got no choice, now. We'll try to shake them, see if anything comes loose," Lucas said.

He turned around in his seat and said to Quintana, "I'm going to point out these guys and tell you to look at them. Like you'd seen them before. I want you to take a long look, then come over and mutter at me. Don't let them hear what you're saying."

"I never saw them," Quintana said.

"Ray, for Christ's sakes, I'm trying to shake 'em. We're doing a pageant."

Quintana cracked a smile. "All right."

"What do you want me to do?" Flowers asked, as they turned a corner and saw the lights on the squad cars.

"Well, given the way you're dressed, you could ask me if I want them hog-tied," Lucas said.

"Don't take it out on me," Flowers said. "I'm not the one who . . ."

". . . poked the pup," Quintana said.

"Shut up," Lucas snarled, no longer in the mood for humor.

WHEN THEY CAME UP on the lights, the street was full of cops and politicians. Flowers turned on his own flashers, and a cop who started toward them stopped and put his hands on his hips. Lucas, Flowers, and Quintana got out, and the cop waited for them to walk up, and then asked, "Any chance you're the BCA?"

"BCA and Minneapolis police," Lucas said.

At that moment, Taryn Grant, who was in the street with a half-dozen campaign workers and her security people, came steaming toward them and shrieked, "I knew it was you. I knew it."

"Shut up," Lucas said, but without much snap.

"This is the last straw." She was wildly angry; her blond hair had come loose from whatever kind of spray had been keeping it neat, and was fluttering over her forehead. Her campaign manager, Schiffer, took her arm and tried to pull her back, and Grant pulled free.

Dannon, Carver, and Green had come up behind Grant. Lucas turned to Quintana and said, "Take a look."

Quintana, with the unpleasant grittiness of a vice cop, stepped up close to Carver and looked him straight in the face for a long beat; then stepped over to Dannon and did the same thing. Neither man turned away, but they didn't like it.

"Who's this guy, and what does he want?" Dannon asked.

"I'm a cop," Quintana said. "You got a problem with that?"

"I don't like somebody standing two inches in front of my face breathing onions on me," Dannon said. "So back off."

Quintana did. Carver nodded at Flowers and asked, "Why's there a cowboy with you?"

"Lucas might've wanted you hog-tied," Flowers said. "He thought I'd be the guy to do it."

Carver stared at Flowers for a minute, then asked, "You in the military?"

"Yeah, for a while."

"Officer?"

"Yeah."

"MP?"

"Yeah."

"I thought so," Carver said.

Quintana had stepped over to Lucas and said, in a low tone, "I can't hardly believe it, but I think it really is that second guy I talked to." He looked back over his shoulder at Dannon and Carver and said, "The smaller one. He's got that funny accent—Texas. Like George Bush."

Dannon stepped toward them and said, "We gave you those DNA samples."

Lucas nodded and squared off with Grant. "We've got two days before the election and this whole thing is coming to a boil. We're watching everybody, because we don't want anybody else to show up dead: there have been two murders so far. We don't need a third."

"We don't have anything to do with any murders," she shouted, and Lucas could see little atoms of saliva spray in the headlights of Flowers's truck.

"We can't take any chances—*you* could be a target," Lucas said. "We had no plans to stop you. We were making sure that everybody got home all right."

"Fuck you," she shouted.

LUCAS TOLD SHRAKE and Jenkins to go home, and back in Flowers's truck, Lucas asked Quintana, "How sure are you?"

Quintana shrugged. "Hell, Lucas—he *sounded* like the guy. It's not like he's some random asshole and I'm trying to pick him out of a hundred people by the tone of his voice. He's your suspect, and I can tell you he's got that accent, and that was right, and his tone was right, and the way the words came out, that's exactly right. He sounded exactly like the guy on the phone. You say you're looking for professional killers and you find two professional killers, and then I listen to one of them . . . what are the chances that it's not him?"

"Slim and none, and slim is outta town," Lucas said. "I want you to go back to the office and write this down. A standard incident report and e-mail it to me. I'll talk to Marion and tell him you're working with me."

"I appreciate it," Quintana said, and he looked like he did. "In the meantime, I might move out to a motel for a couple of weeks."

"Stay in touch," Lucas said to Quintana, as Flowers pulled away from the curb. "I don't want to wonder what the hell happened to you."

Flowers asked, "We're going to Hampshire and Thirtieth?"

"Yeah, if we can find it."

Lucas called up the Google Maps app on his iPhone, and fifteen minutes later they pulled to the side of the road, houses on one side, a park on the other. Dark as tar on the park side.

Flowers got a flash and Lucas dialed the phone. They walked up and down the road, and then Virgil heard it buzzing down in the weeds. It took a minute or so and a couple of calls to find it. Flowers bagged it and handed it to Lucas.

"Have them check the battery," Flowers said. "They probably had to pull an insulating tab off. Maybe they forgot to wipe it."

"Fat chance," Lucas said. "But I'll do it anyway. I'm pulling on threads, 'cause threads are all I've got."

19

Taryn fixed herself a lemon drop, with a little extra vodka, as soon as she was back in the house; Dannon helped himself to a bottle of beer, Schiffer had a Diet Pepsi, Carver poured a glass of bourbon, Green got a bottle of Evian water. Schiffer said to Taryn, "All right, enough is enough, if you want to call the governor in the morning, go ahead and do it. But right now we've got more important stuff on the table."

"He thinks we killed somebody," Taryn shouted at her. "He thinks—"

"You know you didn't, so he's got no proof. You gotta keep your eye on the ball," Schiffer shouted back, the two women face-to-face. "We've got one more day of campaigning. We can still lose it."

Taryn looked at her over the glass, then asked, "Where are we?"

The media woman, whose name was Mary Booth, stepped up: "While you were up north, we're seeing a new Smalls ad. It ran prime time, Channel Three at seven o'clock, it's been on 'CCO and KSTP. We'd bought out the KARE slots so it wasn't there."

"Yeah, yeah, yeah, what is it?" Taryn asked.

"Well, all that neutrality thing is done with. He knows there's no time left, so he dropped the bomb—he says you planted the porn on him," Booth said. "He doesn't come right out and say the words, but he talks about the Democrats and opposition dirty tricks, and he gets angry. I'd say it's quite effective."

"Let's see it," Schiffer said.

They gathered around the living room TV and the media woman plugged a thumb drive into the digital port and brought the advertisement up: Smalls was dressed in a gray pin-striped suit, bankerish, but with a pale blue shirt open at the collar. He was in his Minnesota Senate office, with a hint of the American flag to his right, a couple of red and white stripes—not enough of a flag display to invite sarcasm, but it was there.

He faced the camera head-on and apparently had been whipped into a bit of a frenzy before they started rolling, because it was right there on his face: ". . . spent my entire life without committing an offense any worse than speeding, and now the Democrats and the opposition plant this dreadful, disgusting pornography on me, and yes, my fellow Minnesotans, they *still* think they're going to get away with it. They're still pretending to think that I might have collected this . . . crap, even though they know the name of the man who did it, a longtime Democrat dirty trickster named Bob Tubbs. They're laughing up their sleeves at all of us! Don't let them get away with it! This is not the way we do these things in Minnesota."

When he finished, Schiffer said, "Not bad."

Taryn was on her second drink: "What do we do?"

"We bought a lot of time tomorrow afternoon and evening. We can pretty much blanket the state. Mary, Sandy, and Carl will write a new advertisement overnight in which you are warm and understanding—but also a little angry. Maybe we'll say something about how we have to be rational and careful . . . hint that he's a little nuts. I'll call you in the morning about wardrobe. I'm thinking maybe something cowgirl, maybe . . . what's the name of that stables you ride at?"

"Birchmont," Taryn said.

"Get you out there in jeans and a barn coat, the one you wore out to Windom, and a jean jacket, cowboy boots . . . let your hair frizz out a little . . . and we do something along the lines of, 'We don't know where the porn came from, and if we find out, no matter who put it out there, we will support any prosecution. In the meantime, let's turn back to the serious issues in this campaign. . . .'"

As she was talking, outlining a possible quick advertising shoot, Booth's phone rang and she pulled it out and looked at it, while still listening to Schiffer. She saw who was calling and declined the call, but then a second later, a message came in, and she looked at it, and interrupted Schiffer to say, "I gotta take this," and stepped away.

Taryn was saying . . . "You don't think they'll mock me for the cowboy outfit?"

"They won't have time to, and it'll look really down-home and honest," Schiffer was replying . . .

. . . When Booth came back and said, "Oh my God, the *Pioneer Press* is on the street with a front-page story that says this dead woman, the woman that got murdered, had a long affair with Smalls and that the police are investigating a possible domestic motive for her murder."

They were all struck silent for a moment, then Taryn said, "Davenport said they had a personal conflict. He didn't say they had an affair."

Schiffer said, "Whatever, this could do it for us. It'll play right through Election Day. I still think the horse thing will work for us. Maybe we're a little more sympathetic about Smalls's problems."

Taryn finished the second drink and said, "While still hinting that he's nuts . . . let's do it. This is all so ludicrous that we shouldn't let anything go."

Schiffer raised her voice and said, "All right, everybody, let's clear out. Mary, you get the guys and get going on the ad. You can sleep tomorrow night. Everybody else . . . Taryn, I'll call you at nine o'clock. I'll cancel the Channel Three thing, that was the only morning show . . ."

As SCHIFFER WAS PUSHING everybody out, Taryn tipped her head at Dannon, saying, "Follow me," and drifted back to the bar. Dannon followed and she said, quietly, "Who's got the overnight?"

"Barry."

"Send him home. You and I need to talk. Carver's going to be a problem."

Dannon sighed, pulled a bottle of lemon water out of the refrigerator and poured his second drink over a couple of ice cubes. "Did he say something to you?"

"Yeah. When people clear out . . ."

"Okay," Dannon said.

He started back toward the group in the hallway, and she caught his sleeve and said, "One other thing. I'm so . . . angry, confused, cranked up . . ."

"It's been unreal . . ." Dannon began.

"And I really need something that David doesn't have, to mellow me out. . . . I'd like to see you back in the bedroom. You know. Send Barry home."

———

DANNON HAD UNUSUAL SKILLS in the area of death and dismemberment, but he was like anyone else when it came to sex. He'd slept with twenty women in the past twenty years, but had never really desired one. He'd wanted the sex, but hadn't been particularly interested in the package that it came in.

Taryn was an entirely different thing. He'd wanted her from the first week he'd known her. He'd seen her naked or semi-naked two hundred times, out in the pool, so that was no big thing, but seeing her naked when he was finally going to consummate that years-long desire was an entirely different thing.

As soon as the words "bedroom" came out of her mouth, he began to sweat: you know, would everything work? He kicked Barry out, made himself do all the checks, and had another beer, thinking that the alcohol might lubricate the equipment.

He needn't have worried: he walked back to the bedroom with the fourth drink in his hand, and as he walked in, she was coming out of the bathroom, naked except for her underpants, which were no more than a negligible gossamer swatch the size of a folded hankie, and she said, almost shyly, "I've been waiting . . ."

And then he was on her, like a mountain lion, and the equipment was no problem at all. He couldn't remember getting out of his clothes, didn't remember anything until she screamed, or moaned, or made some kind of sound that seemed ripped out of her, and she began patting his back and saying, "Okay/okay/okay/okay."

And it was okay for about ten minutes of stroking her pelvis, stomach, breasts, rolling her over, stroking her back and butt, and rolling her again and then they were going once more and he blacked out until he heard once more that scream/moan and "Okay/okay/okay . . ."

He collapsed on top of her, lying there sweaty and hot, until she said, "Whew," and "We should have done this years ago."

THEY TALKED FOR A WHILE, this and that, the campaign and Schiffer and Carver and Alice Green . . . Dannon told her for the first time why he and Carver were so casual about the DNA check: there was no DNA from Tubbs, because the cops didn't know where to look for it, and there was none with Helen Roman, either, because great care had been taken. "Besides, our DNA profiles are already in the army and FBI files. When there's a chance that some suicide bomber is going to blow you into hamburger, the army wants to be able to identify the scrap meat. We've all got DNA profiles."

Taryn said, "Ah: so it didn't make any difference."

Taryn rolled out of bed and went to a side bar, pulled open the top drawer, and took out a bottle of vodka, two or three drinks down from full. She asked, "You want more water?"

He said, "Sure."

She got some ice from the bar's refrigerator and poured the water over it, and made another lemon drop for herself, with enough lemon to bite, brought the drinks back to the bed and put his cold glass on his belly below his navel. He said, "Jesus, cold," and picked it up, and she laughed, almost girlishly, rolled onto the bed next to him, careful with the drink, and said, "Carver."

"What'd he say to you?" Dannon asked.

Taryn rolled toward him, one of her breasts pressing against his biceps; she wetted a finger and circled one of his nipples in a distracted way, and said, "This afternoon, before we went over to that school, he said that he hadn't signed up for all this. That's what he said, 'signed up.' I asked what that meant, and he said that he hoped I'd be more grateful than I had been so far. I said that I would be, that if he'd hold on until I was in the Senate, I could take care of him in a lot of ways: money, another army job, get his record wiped out, whatever he needed. He said, 'Money's good,' and said we could talk about the other stuff, then he asked when he'd get a down payment."

"What'd you say to that?"

"I said too much stuff was coming down right now: that I assumed he'd want a big brick of cash that he wouldn't have to pay taxes on, but even for me, it takes a while to get cash together. Almost nobody uses it anymore, except dope dealers, I guess."

Dannon said, "Got that right. I can't remember the last time I saw somebody buying groceries for cash, except me."

"He said, 'Well, better get on that. I'm gonna need a big chunk pretty soon. I got a feeling that when everything settles down . . . my services might not be needed.' I said, 'You've got a job as long as you want it, and you'll get paid as much as you need.' He laughed and said, 'I kinda don't think you know how much I need.'"

Dannon said, "That's the problem with Ron. He's hungry all the time—more pussy, more dope, more money. There won't be an end to it."

"I know, but I don't know what to do about it."

Dannon said, "Ron and I . . . he was enlisted, I was an officer. We're not natural friends. I'm not being arrogant here, lots of the enlisted guys are sharp as razors: but that's the way it is. He doesn't think, except tactically. How exactly to do one thing or another. He thinks three days down the road, but not three months or three years. He'll get us in trouble, sooner or later."

Taryn said nothing, waiting, watching Dannon think.

He said, finally, "There's something else."

"What?"

"I'm kinda worried that from Ron's perspective, *I'm* the problem," Dannon said. "He'll figure he can handle you. But you and me together . . ."

"You actually think . . . he might come after you?"

"I think it's inevitable," Dannon said. "It'll occur to him pretty soon. After it does, he won't wait. That's the three-days-thinking problem again. He'll think about it, then he'll move."

"Oh, dear."

"I think he has to go away," Dannon said.

"You mean . . . someday?"

"No. I mean right away. I know it'll be a political problem, but . . . I know this guy down in Houston. For ten thousand dollars, he'll fly Carver's passport to Kuwait. He's got a deal with one of the border people there."

"I don't understand," Taryn said, though she had an idea about it.

"Simple enough. Ron goes away. I FedEx his passport and ten grand—I've actually got the cash in my safe-deposit box—"

"I'll pay you back."

"I got this. My guy in Houston flies the passport to Kuwait and walks it across the border into Iraq. We call up this Davenport guy, say that we're worried because Ron didn't show up for work on Wednesday and he doesn't answer his phone. We don't know where he's gone."

"And Davenport thinks it's possible that he's run for it."

"Yeah, because they send out a stop order on him, and because of his background, and what they think—that he killed Tubbs and Roman—they include the border people and the airport security, and *they* report back that his passport left the country, and then crossed the border into Kuwait and then out of Kuwait and into Iraq."

"Don't they take pictures, you know, video cameras of everybody going through the airport?"

"Sure. But IDs aren't synced with pictures. They ask for your passport when you check in, but going through security, they only ask for a government ID. This Houston guy shows Ron's passport to the airlines and the security people, who check him through. The cops look at the security video, and they never see Ron, so they figure he ran some kind of dodge, and got through behind security. It's easy enough to do. Listen, all kinds of people from this country are carrying all kinds of stuff into Kuwait and then across the border into Iraq. This is a very *established* deal. . . . This Houston guy, it's his thing. It can be done."

"If you're sure . . ."

"It'll hurt, politically, but once it's done, we're really secure," Dannon said. "We'll be the only two who know the story. You're already a senator before the shit hits the fan, another guy goes missing . . . but, if Ron's passport goes into Iraq, what's Davenport going to do?"

"How soon?"

"Tomorrow," Dannon said. "We can't afford to wait. I can't give Ron a chance to move on me." He was on his back and Taryn snuggled her head down onto his chest and he stroked her hair. Without Ron, he thought, the future had no horizon. . . .

TARYN WAS PRETTY TIRED of the sex by the time Dannon went to sleep. She listened to him breathe, then slipped out of bed, pulled on a robe, and padded through to the living room, closing the bedroom door behind her, poured some vodka over a couple of ice cubes, sat on the couch, and thought about it.

Dannon, once he'd gotten rid of Carver, was going to be a problem. She could see it already: he was looking at a permanent relationship. He was looking at love. When she got to Washington, an heiress and businesswoman already worth a billion dollars or so, a U.S. senator . . . any permanent relationship wouldn't be with an ex–army captain who carried a switchblade in his pocket.

That their relationship wasn't going to be permanent would quickly become obvious. Then what? What do jilted lovers do, when they're men? What do jilted alcoholics with switchblades do?

Something to think about. Dannon, like Carver, would have to go away. But how? She sat on the couch for another hour, and another two vodkas, thinking about it: and what she thought was, *Best to wait until we get to Washington.*

THE NEIGHBORHOOD AROUND TARYN'S was quiet and dark and gently rolling. The highest nearby spot was between two pillared faux-plantation manors on five-acre lots, screened from the street by elaborate hedges. From the top of that low hill, any approaching cars could be seen three blocks away.

Lauren was behind the wheel of Kidd's Mercedes GL550, a large luxury vehicle and one that fit well in rich neighborhoods. Kidd sat in the passenger seat, looking at a hooded laptop that was plugged into an antenna and amplifier focused on one of the manors. Kidd was riding on the manor's Wi-Fi; and Lauren, looking over his shoulder, said, "We're not Peeping Toms."

"I'm not peeping, I'm trying to figure out who in the hell that is," he said, watching the scene in Taryn Grant's bedroom. "I think it's her security guy. The only security guy, if we counted right. I can't find anyone else."

"It's perfect," Lauren said. "They're both fully occupied."

"You're scaring the shit out of me," Kidd said.

"I'm so excited I'm gonna have an orgasm myself in the next two minutes," Lauren said. "Trade places. I'm going."

Kidd didn't bother to argue. He got out of the car—no interior lights, they had custom switches, and the switches were off—and walked around to the driver's side, as Lauren clambered into the passenger seat.

She was wearing trim, soft black cotton slacks, a silky white blouse, a red nylon runner's jacket with reflective strips front and back, and black running shoes. She had a thin black nylon ski mask in her pocket. The ski mask could be instantly buried; and no burglar in his or her right mind would be out with a red jacket, a shiny white blouse, and all those reflective strips.

Kidd started the SUV and they eased on down the hill toward Grant's house. As they rolled along, Lauren turned the jacket inside out: the lining, now the outer shell, was jet black. She pulled it back on, and was now dressed head to toe in black. A hundred yards out, Lauren said, "I'll call." Kidd tapped the brakes—no red flash on the custom-switched brake lights—and when they were stopped, Lauren dropped out and quietly closed the car door.

Five seconds later, with the hood over her head, she vanished into the woods between Grant's house and the neighbor's.

THE GROUNDS WERE PROTECTED by both radar and infrared installations, but Kidd had switched off the alarms on the rear approach, and had fixed the software so that they couldn't be turned back on without his permission. Lauren had one major worry: that the dogs would be turned loose. If that happened, she was in trouble. She had a can of bear spray, which should shut them down, but she had no idea how effective that would be.

For the time being, the dogs were in the house—one of them in the living room, where it could see the front hallway and the hall coming in from the garage; and the other outside the bedroom door.

Inside the tree line, she pulled a pair of starlight goggles over her head. They were military issue, and she'd had to pay nine thousand dollars for them six years before. With the goggles over her eyes, the world turned green and speckled: but she could see.

She began moving forward, like a still-hunter, placing each foot carefully, feeling for branches and twigs before she put weight down. Long pauses to listen. Fifty yards in, she crossed a nearly useless wrought iron fence. Any reasonably athletic human could slip right over it; Grant's dogs could jump it with three feet to spare, and a deer would hardly notice it. Once over the fence, she took nearly fifteen minutes to cross the hundred yards to the edge of Grant's back lawn. By that time, she knew she was alone. She took out her phone, a throwaway, and messaged Kidd, one word: "There."

One word came back. "Go."

Kidd was back on top of the hill, back on the manor's Wi-Fi. Nothing inside the house had changed. Grant's lawn was dotted with oak trees and shrubs, and Lauren stuck close to them as she closed in on the bedroom. There were motion and sonic alarms outside the bedroom windows, but Kidd had them handled. When she was below the windows, she took out a taped flashlight with a pinprick opening in the tape. She turned it on, and with the tiny speck of light, looked at the windows. Triple glazed, wired, with lever latches. Fully open, there'd be a space three feet long and a foot high that she'd have to get her body through. She could do that. . . .

She pulled back, listened, crept down the side of the house. A light came on in the living room and she froze. Nothing more happened and she felt her phone buzz. She risked a look: *Grant moving.* She listened, then began to back away from the house, heard a crunch when she stepped in some gravel, froze. Moved again ten seconds later, backing toward the woods.

From her new position, she could see the lighted living room, and Taryn Grant looking out the window. She was wearing a robe and had what looked like a drink in her hand. A dog moved by her hip, and Lauren thought, *Bigger than a wolf.*

The phone vibrated. She was into the tree line, and stopped to looked again: "Dogs may know . . . dogs may be coming."

She thought, *Damnit,* and texted, "Come now," and began moving more quickly. She crossed the fence, which should give her some protection from the dogs, and made the hundred yards out quickly, but not entirely silently. At the street-side tree line, she knelt, stripped the goggles and mask off, stuffed them in her pockets, and then Kidd was there in the car.

She was inside and pulled the door closed and they were rolling and Lauren looked out the window, toward Grant's house, but saw no dogs. "She let them out?"

"I think so—into the backyard, anyway. Didn't seem like there was any big rush. Maybe she was letting them out to pee."

"That's probably it," Lauren said. "I never saw them. They didn't bark."

"They don't bark, not those dogs," Kidd said.

"I know." She took a breath, squeezed Kidd's thigh. "I haven't felt like this in years. Six years."

They came out of the darkened neighborhood to a bigger street, and Kidd went left. They could see a traffic light at the end of the street, where the bigger street intersected with an even bigger avenue.

Kidd asked, "What do you think?"

"Piece of cake," Lauren said.

20

The next step was not obvious. Lucas had Quintana's belief that he'd spoken to Dannon on the phone, but that was not proof. Nor would it convince a jury to believe that a crime had been committed, not beyond a reasonable doubt. He needed a scrap of serious evidence, something that he could use as a crowbar to pry Grant, Dannon, and Carver apart.

He was also bothered by the sporadic thought: What if Tubbs showed up? In most killings, there was some physical indication that violence had been done. With Tubbs, there was nothing.

THE NEXT MORNING he did what he usually did when he was stuck, and needed to think about it: he went shopping. Nothing was so likely to clear the mind as spending money. He idled over to the Mall of America and poked around the Nordstrom store, looking for a good fall dog-walking jacket.

He didn't have a dog, but a good dog-walking jacket was useful for a lot of other things. He had the exact specification: light, water-resistant, knit cuffs and waistband, modern high-tech insulation, warm enough for late fall and early winter days. And, of course, it had to look good.

He'd drifted from jackets to cashmere socks, especially a pair in an attractive dark raspberry color, when his phone rang: Cochran, from Minneapolis Homicide. Both Dannon and Carver had shown up to give DNA samples, and Lucas had sent the samples to Minneapolis.

"Turk, tell me we got them," Lucas said.

"No, we don't. We got James Clay," Cochran said. "We got a cold hit from your DNA bank."

James Clay? "Who the hell is James Clay?"

"Dickwad from Chicago. Small-time dealer," Cochran said. "Moved up here five years ago when he got tired of the Chicago cops busting him for dope. We've been chasing him around for the same thing. We got him on felony possession of cocaine, got DNA on that case, he went away for a year. Since then, we've caught him holding twice, and both times, it was small amounts of marijuana, so he was cut loose."

"Jesus Christ, that can't be right," Lucas said. "Roman wasn't killed by any small-time dope dealer."

"Sort of looks that way—of course, it's possible he was paid to do it, though I doubt anyone would hire him," Cochran said. "I'll tell you, the dope guys say he's exactly the kind of punk you'd want for a killing like this. He thinks the house is empty, goes in, she surprises him, he freaks out, whacks her with his gun, then shoots her, with some piece-of-crap .22."

"Aw, man . . . Turk . . ."

Cochran said, "Listen, Lucas: he's an old gang member, probably done two hundred nickel-dime burglaries, funding his habit, been shot at least once himself. He'll steal anything that's not nailed down. If all this election stuff hadn't been going on, it'd be exactly who you'd have been looking for."

"Is Clay still alive?"

"Far as we know. He was last night. He was hanging out at Smackie's," Cochran said.

"If he was paid to kill Roman, he'd be dead himself, and we wouldn't be finding the body," Lucas said. "He sure as hell wouldn't be hanging around Smackie's."

"Lucas, what it is, is what it is," Cochran said.

"You gonna find him?" Lucas asked.

"Sooner or later. Sooner, if he goes back to Smackie's."

"We need him right now," Lucas said. "You know Del?"

"Sure."

"Del knows all those guys. If you don't mind, I'm gonna go get him and look around town."

"Hey, that's fine with me. If you find him first, give me a call— I'll do the same, if we find him."

Lucas walked out to his car, calling Del as he went. Del picked up and Lucas asked, "Where are you?"

"In my backyard, looking at a tree," Del said.

"Why?"

"We got oak wilt," Del said. "We're gonna lose it."

"Look, I'm sorry about your tree, but I need help finding a guy. Right now. I'm going to get some paper on him. Meet me at my place."

"Half hour?"

"See you then."

LUCAS WAS TEN MINUTES from his house, driving fast. On the way, he called his office, talked to his secretary, told her to call Turk, get the specifics on James Clay, including any photos, and e-mail them to him. "I'll be home in ten minutes. I need it then," he said.

The house was quiet when he got home. Letty was in school, Sam in preschool, the baby out for a stroll with the housekeeper.

He went into the study, brought up the computer, checked his e-mail, found a bunch of political letters pleading for money, and a file from his secretary. He opened it, found four photos of James Clay along with Minneapolis arrest records and a compilation of Chicago-area arrests from the National Crime Information Center.

Clay had somehow managed to make it to thirty-one, despite a life of gang shootings, street riots, drugs, knife fights, beatings, burglaries, and strong-arm robberies. His last parole officer wrote that there was no chance of rehabilitation, and that the best thing anyone could hope for was that Clay would OD. He sounded pissed.

The photos showed a light-complexioned black man with cornrows, a prison tattoo around his neck—ragged dashes and a caption that said, "Fill to dotted line"—and three or four facial scars, along with a nasty jagged scar on his scalp. A photo taken from his right side demonstrated the effects of being shot in the ear with a handgun with no medical insurance. Some intern had sewn him up and sent him on his way, and now his ear looked like a pork rind.

Lucas was reading down the rap sheet when Del knocked on the door. He walked through the living room to the front door and let him in: "What kind of shape are you in at Smackie's?"

"They won't buy me a free beer, but they know me," Del said. He was dressed in jeans, a dark blue hoodie, and running shoes. "Is that where we're going?"

"Yeah. To start with." He picked up all the paper on Clay and thrust it at Del. "I'll drive. You read."

They took Lucas's Lexus SUV, which had gotten a little battered during the last trip to his Wisconsin cabin, when a tree branch fell on the hood. Lucas couldn't decide whether to get it fixed, or wait until he was closer to trading it in. Something else to think about.

On the way up Mississippi River Road, headed to Minneapolis, Lucas filled Del in on the problem. Del was reading Clay's sheet, and said, "The name sounds familiar, but I don't know the guy. Any reason to think that he might be holed up somewhere, with a gun?"

"Turk apparently went in to Smackie's looking for him, so if he had any friends there, somebody might have told him to start running. If he gets down to Chicago, it could be a while before we find him."

"I see his mother lives here," Del said. "There's a note on the probation report."

"I hate that. The mothers always turn out to be worse than the children," Lucas said. "You remember that one mother, those two brothers—"

"I heard about it. Shrake thought it was fun."

"Sort of was, I guess," Lucas said. "Especially when he fell off the roof into that thornbush. He was crying like a Packers fan at the Metrodome."

They crossed the Marshall/Lake Bridge into south Minneapolis, and four minutes later left the car on the broken tarmac of the Pleasure Palace Bar & Grill parking lot. An "A" had fallen off the sign over the bar's door, so it now said "Ple sure Palace," but it didn't make any difference, because everybody who was nobody called it Smackie's.

The bar was painted Halloween colors of black and orange, supposedly because it was once all black, and when the new owner decided to paint over the flaking black concrete blocks, he ran out of orange halfway through; either that, or got tired of doing the work. The bar had two long, low, nearly opaque windows decorated with neon beer signs and stickers from various police and fire charitable organizations.

Del led the way inside. Smackie's was dark, and smelled like boiled eggs floating in vinegar, and maybe a pickled pig's foot. Fifteen men, and four women, half of them black, half white, were scattered down a dozen booths, looking at beers or the TV set mounted in a corner or nothing at all. A bartender was leaning on the back of the bar, eating an egg-salad sandwich. As they came up to the bar, he swallowed and said, "Del." Nobody else looked at them, because Lucas was so obviously a cop.

Del said, "I didn't know you were back."

"Almost a month," the bartender said.

Del said to Lucas, "He had a hernia operation."

"Fascinating," Lucas said. He pulled out a picture of Clay. "You seen this guy?"

The bartender took another bite of the sandwich, chewed, then said, through the masticated bread and egg, "Yeah, the Minneapolis cops already been here. They're looking for him, too. He was here last night, pretty late, then he went away. Haven't seen him since."

"Does he live around here?" Lucas asked.

"Every time I've seen him, he was walking, so probably around here somewhere. The Minneapolis cops were asking if his mother comes in here."

"Does she?" Del asked.

The bartender shrugged. "I don't know. I never seen him with any old ladies, and we don't get many old ladies in here."

"Is he in here pretty regular?" Del asked.

"Yeah, most days."

Lucas tipped his head toward the people in the booths: "Any of these people know him?"

The bartender looked past him, then shook his head. "I wouldn't say so. I don't pay that much attention to who sits with who. We got a waitress comes in later this afternoon, she'd know better than me."

"But you think he comes from around here."

"Yeah, unless he takes a bus. I seen him coming from the direction of the bus stop."

Del looked at Lucas and shook his head. Not that many people would take a bus to a dive like Smackie's. It wouldn't be worth the money, since almost any other place would be better.

Del said, "We'll check back," and he and Lucas started for the door. They were almost there when the bartender called, "Hey, guys. C'mere."

They walked back to the bar and the bartender flicked a finger at the window on the left side of the bar. The glass was dark green and dirty, not easily seen through, but they could see a very short man walking down a street toward the bar. The bartender said, "You owe me."

Del: "That's him?"

"Uh-huh."

THEY WATCHED THE SHORT MAN until he crossed the street and started toward the bar entrance. Lucas looked around and said, "Better take him outside," and Del said, "Yeah," and they went to the door, waited for a few seconds, then pushed through into the daylight. Clay was only fifteen feet away. He saw Lucas, and quick as a rat, turned and started running.

His feet were churning like a machine, Lucas noticed as he took off after the other man, but his legs were so short that he was only making about two feet per churn; Lucas caught him in a hundred feet. He didn't want to make the mistake of having a knife or gun pulled on him, so when he was close behind, and Clay turned to look at him, he hit Clay on the back of the neck and sent him sprawling, hands first, into the street.

Clay rolled over and looked up the muzzle of Del's pistol. "How you doin', James," Del said. "You're under arrest for murder."

"They're lying to you," Clay said. He was very short, maybe five-two, and thin.

"Who's lying to us?" Lucas asked.

"The Chicago cops. I had not a single fuckin' thing to do with any of that."

"Tell the Chicago cops that," Lucas said. "Roll over on your face, keep your arms out . . . you know the routine."

Lucas patted him down, took a short folding knife out of Clay's back pocket, handed it to Del. Del cuffed him, and they stood him up and Lucas held on to the cuff link while Del gave him a more thorough pat-down.

A young white kid, maybe ten, rode up on a fenderless half-sized bicycle, an unlit cigarette dangling from his lower lip. He stopped and asked, "You guys cops?"

"Yes," Del said. "You go on home, son."

"Blow me," the kid said, and rode away.

"That's righteous, that's righteous," Clay shouted after the kid, who gave him the finger.

"I guess he doesn't like any of us," Del said.

They put Clay up against Lucas's Lexus, and Lucas called Cochran. Cochran came up and Lucas said, "We got Clay for you."

"What? How'd you do that?"

"By accident, mostly." He explained about Smackie's.

Cochran said, "All right. I'll come down there myself and pick him up."

"Good. Because I hate to write reports," Lucas said. "He's your guy."

LUCAS HAD BEEN BOTHERED by Clay's reaction to the arrest. He told him, "You stand right there. If I've got to chase you down again, it won't be any patty-cake slap on the neck like last time. You understand that?"

Clay said, "Hey, man, you gotta listen to this. I never—"

"Shut up," Lucas said.

He and Del moved off ten steps, and Lucas said, "If he killed Roman . . ."

"I know," Del said. "He's been around. If he killed her, it should have been nothing but, 'I wanna lawyer.'"

"Maybe he's stupid," Lucas said, glancing at Clay.

"He *is* stupid, but not *that* stupid," Del said. "Doesn't take that much firepower to remember 'I wanna lawyer.'"

"Yeah." Lucas scratched his chin. "I'd like to ask him something . . . see his reaction."

"You give away too much, you're going to piss off Turk."

"Little rain falls in everybody's life," Lucas said.

Lucas ambled back to Clay and said, "You're toast. We got the

DNA. Why'd you do it? You get paid? Or was it because it looked easy?"

"What'd I do?" Clay asked, and Lucas got the impression that he really was confused.

"Gimme a break," Lucas said. "You been around. You know what the deal is. You're a smart guy—you killed that old lady and you took her purse and her other stuff. What'd you do with the gun?"

Clay's eyes had widened, and he shook his head. "What are you talking about, man? I never killed no old lady. What the fuck you talking about?"

"Up on the north side? Middle of the night? This coming back to you, now? One shot, right in the heart? Did you think she was like, attacking you? That she had a gun?"

"What? I never killed nobody. Nobody." He looked from Lucas to Del and shook his head.

"Where you living, James?" Del asked. "You living with your mom?"

"I gotta place. Look, I'm doing all right. I got a part-time gig with this guy. . . . I didn't kill nobody. I don't got a gun."

Lucas pushed him, and Clay said he took messages around town for some guy, whose name he didn't know. Translated, that meant that he was delivering dope; in any case, he had a job.

"When we go up to your place, we're going to find the other glove, won't we?" Del asked.

"Other glove? Hey . . . you got my glove?"

"You're missing one, right?" Del asked.

"Yeah, I missing one. How'd you know that?"

"A little birdie whispered it to me."

"Somebody took my glove. Or maybe I dropped it," Clay protested. "I was wearing it up to Smackie's. I was walking home, it gotten cold, I takes my gloves out, and I only got one. I say, 'What's this shit?' I go back to Smackie's, but there's no glove, and nobody saw it. . . . You saying you found my glove?"

"Yes. Under the old lady's body," Del said.

"Man, you're crazy. You're fuckin' insane, man." He looked at the two of them, then said the magic words: "I wanna lawyer."

Del looked at Lucas and said, "Turk's gonna be pissed."

COCHRAN WASN'T COMPLETELY UPSET with the preemptive interrogation for the simple reason that he had the glove with the DNA, and a glove with DNA was about all a jury required. He and another cop picked up Clay, listened to Lucas's unformed doubts, said "Thank you," and headed off to the Hennepin County jail.

"What're you going to do?" Del asked.

"Probably piss off Turk some more. I'm going to talk to Jamie Moore, see if he'll get Clay to talk to me again."

When Turk was gone, Del started back to Smackie's.

"Where're you going?" Lucas asked.

"See if the bartender knows about that glove," Del said.

"Good." Lucas went along.

The bartender, however, didn't know about the glove. "But I'm behind the bar. You have to ask Irma."

"The waitress?"

"Yeah, the waitress."

"You got a phone number?" Del asked.

He did, and they got it, and went outside to make the call.

Irma was on a bus, on the way to work. Lucas put her on the

cell-phone speaker, identified himself, and said, "We just arrested one of your customers, a guy named James Clay," Lucas said.

"I don't know that name," she said.

"He's a short guy with some scars on his face, tattoo around his neck, deals a little dope," Lucas said.

"Colored guy?"

"Yeah. Got cornrows," Lucas said.

"Okay, yeah, I know who he is."

"He says the other night, he was in your place, and he lost a glove in there, and didn't find out until after he left, but then he went back to look for it. You remember anything like that?"

"Well, yeah. He asked me if I seen a glove on the floor, but I didn't."

"Okay. How about this? Was there a guy in there, maybe five-ten, six-foot tall, sort of blond, blond mustache?"

"Oh, yeah. All the time."

Lucas's heart jumped. But: "All the time?"

"Hey, this is Minneapolis. I see about thirty guys like that. All the time."

That wasn't good. Irma said she'd be at work in forty-five minutes, and Lucas said he might stop by with a photograph.

ON THE WAY BACK to Lucas's house, he told Del what he'd learned about Grant's bodyguards, and explained why he hadn't involved Del from the start: the danger of messing with politicians.

"I appreciate the thought, but I can take care of myself," Del grumped.

"No, you can't, not anymore," Lucas said. "If I get fired, I'm okay. Even with this depression, or whatever you want to call it, I make more off my investments than I earn from the BCA. If you get fired, what're you gonna do? Get a job as a bank guard? Stick up liquor stores? There aren't a hell of a lot of openings for guys with your job description: 'Hang around bars and bullshit people and sometimes arrest them.'"

"It's a little more complicated than that," Del said.

"Del . . ."

"Yeah, yeah. You're right," Del said. "I'd probably wind up running a bar and hating it. Or be a repo man for somebody."

"Repo? You'd wind up hanging yourself off your kid's swing set."

SANDY, THE RESEARCHER, called as they were pulling into Lucas's driveway: "I found a half-dozen men from Carver's former unit. . . . One guy, down in Albuquerque, says he was with Ron Carver on the night he got in trouble. His name is Dale Rodriguez. He's willing to talk about it."

Lucas looked at his watch: one o'clock in the afternoon. "Check on flights to Albuquerque, e-mail me when you find out when they are."

"For today?"

"Yeah. And write up your notes on the Albuquerque guy, and e-mail those, too."

He rang off and punched up Flowers. "Where are you?"

"Home." Home was in Mankato, ninety miles south of the Twin Cities.

"Start up this way. Bring gear for an overnight," Lucas said. "You may be flying, but you won't need a weapon."

"Where am I going?" Flowers asked.

"Albuquerque, if we can get you a flight."

"You gonna brief me?"

"If we have time. Otherwise, take your laptop and I'll send you a long note when you're in the air."

"You want me to hang around?" Del asked after Lucas rang off.

"Unless you need to deal with that tree."

"The old lady's got that covered," Del said. "Tell you what: print out a picture of this Dannon and Carver, and I'll run them up and show Irma."

LUCAS DID THAT.

Del left, and Lucas checked his e-mail, found the airline schedule from Sandy, and called Flowers. "There's a four-twenty flight. Can you make that?"

"Yes. I took my grab-bag and I'm on my way," Flowers said. "Probably won't have time to swing by your place, though."

"That's okay. It's an interview with a friendly," Lucas said. "Be good if you could do it tonight. I'll try to set it up."

He called Sandy: "Do you have phone numbers for the Albuquerque guy, this Rodriguez guy?"

"Yes, I do. When I talked to him, he said he was going off to class at a tech school there. He said he'd be back late in the afternoon. They're an hour earlier than us."

"Good. We're gonna need a ticket for Flowers on the four-twenty. Tell Cheryl to fix that, will you?"

"Okay, and I'm sending my notes on Rodriguez . . . now."

Lucas rang off and three seconds later, his e-mail pinged at him, and Sandy's file came in. It was short: name, address, cell-phone number. She'd asked Rodriguez about Carver and he'd wanted to know why, and she'd said that there was a murder investigation going on, and that Carver was a "person of interest." Rodriguez said that Carver "oughta be in jail," and when Sandy asked why, Rodriguez said he'd shot some people in Afghanistan and shouldn't have. Sandy had said that might be relevant, and asked Rodriguez if he'd talk to an investigator. He'd said he would. Sandy noted, "He didn't seem all that reluctant. He sounded angry."

Which was all good, in Lucas's view. The army had buried the file, and Carver might have felt safe, but if Lucas threatened to revive it, he might be able to drive a wedge between Carver and Dannon.

HE CALLED JAMIE MOORE, the public defender, and said, "You're gonna get a client named James Clay, who is being checked into the Hennepin County jail about now. Turk Cochran's got him on a murder charge."

"That's profoundly interesting," Moore said in a dead voice.

"I need to talk to him," Lucas said. "Off the record."

"What's in it for him?" Moore asked.

"They got him on that Helen Roman killing, Porter Smalls's secretary. I don't think he did it. I want him to detail where he was when the murder happened, and then I'm going to backtrack him, see if his story holds up."

"What does Turk have on him?"

"Cold hit on DNA. Found a glove under the victim's body," Lucas said. "Pretty conveniently under the victim's body. But unless James gets a break, he's done. You know what it's like to argue with DNA."

"Let me check around," Moore said. "Unless you're telling me a big fat one, I'll get Dan to go over there and sit in with you."

"Aw, not Dan, for Christ's sakes, I hate that little snake," Lucas said.

"Really? All right, let me look around. . . . I got Nancy Bennett. How about Nancy?"

"She's fine. Also a snake, but a much better-looking one."

"Give her an hour. She'll have to do a little pre-interview, find out what's what."

"He's already asked for an attorney."

"Give us an hour."

Lucas spent forty-five minutes writing a long memo to Flowers, who'd get it either in the airport lounge or in the air. He sent along Sandy's memo on Rodriguez, and asked Flowers to get anything on the type and level of violence in which Carver had been involved, and what had happened on the last mission. He wanted details.

Forty minutes after he'd called the public defender, Moore called back and said, "Nancy's at the jail. She'll wait for you."

Del called: "Irma says she doesn't know if they were in there. She doesn't think Carver, she's not sure about Dannon, because she says there's a lot of guys who look like him. In fact, there's one sitting here right now."

"Okay. It was worth the try. Listen. Meet me at the Hennepin jail."

BENNETT AND CLAY were waiting in an interview room when Lucas and Del walked in. Bennett was a tall, thin, dark-haired woman wearing a jacket-and-pants combination that wouldn't show dirt. Clay saw Lucas and said, "This is the sucker who hit me."

"Is that right?" Bennett asked.

"Yeah. He was running. I used just enough violence to restrain him," Lucas said. "He got an owie on his wrist."

"Coulda got hurt," Clay said.

Bennett ignored that and said to Lucas, "I don't want to hear any bullshit about who did what to whom. Listen to what he has to say and take off. I got other things to do."

"We'll listen, anyway," Lucas said.

She nodded at Lucas, then said to Del, "Those look like last month's jeans, Del. You forget to change on the first?"

Del said, "Don't be a twit."

"A what?"

"A twit."

She showed a sliver of a smile. "Well played."

CLAY, ACCORDING TO CLAY, had spent Saturday evening, from around eight o'clock until the next morning, at a recreational facility called Joan What's-Her-Name's, and Del asked, "The red house?"

"That's it."

"How many people were there?"

"You know . . . coming and going," Clay said.

"How many were staying?"

"The usual ones. The one called Mike, and Larry. Larry was there, lost his shoes somewhere, spent the whole time walking around in his socks. Chuck. This really, really white guy named Joe. He was so white it hurt my eyes to look at him. . . . A guy named Dave went through, he was a white guy, too, another guy named Bill was passed out on the couch the whole time. A couple of chicks . . ."

They were playing cards, he said. They tried to get the chicks to play strip poker. "She strips and then you poke her, heh-heh."

Nobody else laughed, so he shrugged and said, "They didn't play, they just wanted to, you know, get high."

He'd been there all night, he said. He'd gotten high with what he brought with him, because he didn't have any money, and then went to sleep on the floor in a back room. There was somebody else in there with him, but he didn't know who. "All I know is, I was sleeping under a window with a crack at the bottom and when I got up in the morning, I was freezing and it felt like my bones was breaking."

Larry was still there when he woke up, still high; Bill was still passed out, and might have been dead. Somebody should check. Chuck was lifting a weight in the kitchen: it was a dumbbell, and there was only one, so he was changing hands with it, and was drinking Campbell's Tomato Soup straight out of the can.

They pulled as many details as they could from him, and when they were done, Lucas turned to Bennett and said, "We're going to check on this. See if the deputies will put him in the drunk tank by himself, at least until we go into this place. Tell Jamie we'll send him a note."

"You believe him?"

"He's pretty obviously a miserable dirtbag liar and a piece of low-life scum, but, he had a lot of detail," Lucas said.

Clay said, "Hey, I'm sitting right here."

Lucas said, "Just kiddin'."

BACK OUTSIDE, Del called a friend on the Minneapolis narcotics squad and asked about the chance of a raid that evening on Joan What's-Her-Name's, and was told that it'd be a problem: too many people were off, and overtime and everything. Del asked if Minneapolis would mind a BCA raid, and after a little talk, everybody agreed that it would be okay. One of the Minneapolis guys, who was working anyway, would ride along.

Lucas told Del, "Set it up. Late as you can—we'd like to get the same cast of characters, if we can."

"Probably go for eleven o'clock," Del said.

Lucas went home for supper and found Virgil Flowers sitting at his kitchen table, a black felt cowboy hat to one side; he was drinking a Leinie's.

"How was Albuquerque?" Lucas asked. Flowers should have been arriving there in an hour.

"You got me a ticket on Delta," Flowers said. "What do you *think* happened?"

"The plane broke?"

"Exactly. They're bringing another one in from Chicago. Revised departure time is ten o'clock, assuming that the replacement plane makes it this far. They're probably bringing it in on a truck. Anyway, I won't be interviewing anybody tonight. Since your house was close by . . . and I hadn't had dinner . . ."

"We're having meat loaf," Weather said.

Flowers said, "Mmmm, mmm."

AT DINNER, Weather asked Lucas for a summary of the case. He put his fork down and said, "Nothing's clear. One of Grant's bodyguards, or both of them working together, probably killed Tubbs and probably killed Helen Roman."

"Are you going to clear it up tomorrow?"

"No. I might *know* something tomorrow, but whether I'll have a court case . . . whether I'll *ever* have a court case . . . that, I can't say."

"If you find out tomorrow before four o'clock, call me," Weather said. "Otherwise, I'm going to vote for Taryn Grant."

"I already did," Flowers said. "I mailed in my ballot last week."

Lucas said, "The thing that plagues me is, she might *know* something. She might even be involved."

"Do you care that much? You're as cynical about government as anyone I've ever known," Weather said.

"I'm not *that* cynical," Lucas said. "I'm cynical about the fact that there are so many little payoffs going around all the time, so many little deals, that the legislature is greased by corruption."

"I think you overstate the problem."

"No, he doesn't," Flowers said. "The legislature runs on corruption. But a killer in the U.S. Senate . . . an actual murderer? The prospect is the tiniest bit disturbing."

21

Flowers went to Albuquerque, and Lucas went on the raid, which wasn't that much of a raid, as raids went.

The target house, the "red house," halfway down Minneapolis's south side, was owned by an obscure real estate investment group and rented to a thirty-one-year-old woman named Joan Busch, who was known by half the Minneapolis cops who worked the neighborhood. She'd once been a minor terror in the clubs, according to the Minneapolis vice cop who rode with them, but had gotten older and given up fighting.

She sold dope when she had it—marijuana—but more often, simply provided people with a warm place to party, as long as she could party along. She had a fifteen-year-old daughter who lived with a guy allegedly named Crown Royal, but, more importantly, brought in a child-support check.

"Nasty woman. Nasty," the vice cop said. "But, she won't let guns in her place, because she's afraid somebody'll shoot her nasty ass."

Lucas and Del were in Lucas's Lexus, with the vice cop, driving circles around the neighborhood, waiting. Lucas had supplied the BCA's SWAT team, which had scouted the location. The raid was supposed to go at eleven o'clock, but, as usual, things came up, and people ran late, and when Lucas turned the corner at eleven-forty, he saw the first of the SWAT guys go through the front door.

"There we go," he said.

"That door's been busted down so many times, you could open it by breathing on it," the vice cop said.

They parked directly in front of the house, behind a SWAT van, and Lucas, Del, and the vice cop ambled across the lawn and up the porch steps. Joan Busch was sitting on a ratty brown couch, looking both high and discouraged. Five men and a woman were facing a couple of different walls, hands on the walls, and had already been patted down. One man lay behind a couch, unmoving. The whole place smelled like weed, like an old motel room might smell of cigarette smoke.

"What happened to him?" Del asked, nodding at the unconscious man.

"He was like that when we came in," the SWAT leader said. "He's breathing, but he's not waking up. We've got an ambulance on the way."

"Must be Bill," Lucas said.

All seven of the house's inhabitants were stoned to some degree; when Lucas checked IDs, he found a Michael and a very, very white guy named Joe. The other woman, whose name was Charlotte Brown, said that she lived upstairs. Lucas told her to sit on the couch next to Busch, and then, after talking to the vice guy, they cut loose everybody except the two women, and Michael and Joe.

The freed men were taken outside one at a time by the vice guy, so that he could tell them that they were being released on his say-so, and that they owed him big time. A few minutes later, an ambulance showed up, and the unconscious guy was trundled out.

When that was done, Lucas and Del took the other four into the kitchen, one at a time, for questioning.

Michael and Busch were confused about the night that Clay was supposed to be in the house. They thought they might remember him, but were not sure exactly of the when: "That sucker comes and goes," Busch said. "In and out all the time."

He'd never come in the house with a gun, Busch said, "Because he knows if he do, that's the end of him. I throw his ass out and never let him come back. Cops don't mind a little weed, but they death on guns."

Brown, though, remembered something about Clay trying to start a game of strip poker. "I said, 'You so short, why'd I play strip poker with you?' and he said, 'Only my body short, 'cause all my growth went somewhere else.' Made me laugh, but I said, 'I ain't playin' strip poker with *nobody* in this house.'"

She said he was still there when she went upstairs, sometime well after midnight, but was gone when she came back down about noon.

Joe remembered him, too. "He was sleepin' on the floor when I got up. He was snorin' like a chain saw, you could hear him out in the street."

That was at six o'clock in the morning, or thereabouts. "I got to be to work at eight o'clock so I set my phone at six o'clock so I could go home and get washed up. The phone went off and he never moved, he snored right through it."

How high had Clay been the night before?

"He had this piece of hash he wanted to trade for a couple rocks, but nobody would trade him—I didn't have any myself—so he took out his pipe and smoked it," Joe said. "He was pretty high, best as I remember, but I don't remember too clear."

Was it possible that he could have gone away during the night and come back?

"Well, it's possible, but I don't know why he would," Joe said. "He didn't have any money to buy anything. All he had was that little piece of hash, wasn't bigger than about a nickel."

"How do you know he didn't have any money?" Del asked.

"'Cause somebody had one little rock and wanted twelve dollars for it, and he said he could only pay later and they said, 'Bullshit,' and he turned his pockets out, and he didn't have but eighty cents or something. And that little piece of hash."

"He have a gun?"

"Not that I seen."

WHEN THEY WERE FINISHED with them, they got their names, addresses, cell phone numbers—they all had phones—and told them not to leave town for a while. "Be the first chance you have to get a guy out of trouble, instead of in," Del said.

Out on the sidewalk, Lucas said, "Turk *will* be pissed. Clay's stoned on hash at two o'clock in the morning, and he's sound asleep at six. He's got no gun, and he doesn't have enough money even to catch a bus, so how does he get to North Minneapolis from way down here?"

"That's if everybody's remembering the right night," Del said. "Between the four of them, they couldn't *count* to four."

"I promise you something, Del," Lucas said. "Helen Roman wasn't killed by that dumbass. She was done by a pro. A guy who isn't a small-time burglar, and who never had to make a killing look like a burglary. She was killed by Carver or Dannon."

"Hey, I believe you," Del said. "But a jury would have its doubts. Especially when the defense attorneys start rolling out the military hero stuff, and they will."

"Yeah," Lucas said. "They will. We need somebody who's inside it."

"Dannon or Carver."

"Or Grant," Lucas said.

LYING IN BED THAT NIGHT, Lucas realized that it wouldn't be Grant. Grant was either completely innocent, or completely guilty. For her, there could be no middle ground.

As a rich woman, with her potential election to the Senate, she couldn't admit to the slightest knowledge of anything, without losing everything. A criminal trial would be brutal, and if she were convicted, she'd be looking at life in prison—thirty years in Minnesota. Even if she were acquitted in a criminal trial, the civil trials by the murder victims' relatives might still effectively destroy her, as O.J. Simpson had found out.

Logically, if she were guilty, nothing that Lucas could do would pry her open. And if she were innocent, she wouldn't know anything.

Therefore, Dannon or Carver.

With Dannon, he had Quintana's belief that Dannon was the man behind the phone call. The phone call indicated knowledge of at least the planting of the pornography on Smalls's computer, and from there, inductively, the murders of Tubbs and Roman.

With Carver, he had nothing about the specific case, but he did have the army records that suggested that Carver could kill, and in a cold way: the army case involved the execution of bound prisoners. On the other hand, the army killings involved levels of stress and circumstance about which Lucas knew nothing. Might those killings have been somehow justified? That was, he thought, possible.

Sister Mary Joseph—Elle—thought he should go after Dannon, because he was the thinker, and if you convinced him he was in trouble, he might decide to negotiate. On the other hand, she thought, Carver would simply stonewall.

But the army records, and the possibility that publicity might force the army to reopen the case, were a powerful pry-bar. In a sense, Carver had already been found to have murdered people, and if that were pushed into the open, he might already be eligible for a long, unpleasant prison term.

He rolled around, thinking about it, and rolled some more, got up, drank some milk, sat in his underwear in the living room, and finally went back to bed.

Pry-bar. Carver.

ELECTION DAY.

In the dawn's early light, he rolled out of bed when he felt Weather moving, and she said, "You had a bad night."

"Push coming to shove," Lucas said.

"When are you going to push?" she asked.

"Today, I think. There's no time left."

"Take your gun with you," she said. And, "God, I hate it when I think things like that. Take your gun with you, because somebody might try to kill you and you might have to kill them."

"Yeah. Well." He had nothing to say; and he would take his gun. He always did.

"How're you going to start?"

"By trusting somebody I have no really good reason to trust," he said.

WHILE WEATHER WENT IN the bathroom, Lucas walked downstairs to his study and called Alice Green. She came up on the second ring, sounding a little sleepy:

"Yes?"

"Lucas Davenport, the much-loved cop."

"I think Taryn talked to the governor about you," Green said. "Tried to get you fired."

"Yeah? What'd he say?"

"Not to be vulgar, but the phrase 'Go shit in your hat' comes to mind."

"With a person of the governor's refinement, I'm sure that phrase never occurred to him," Lucas said.

"This is probably not the time to discuss it, but I wouldn't mind being on his security detail," Green said. "I understand he doesn't have female security at the moment."

"I could ask him, Alice, but I don't think it's extremely likely," Lucas said.

"He's got something against women?"

"No, but his wife does," Lucas said. "You're far too good-looking to pass the test."

"Nothing to be done about that, I guess, unless you want to come over and punch me in the face," Green said.

"What I'd like to do," Lucas said, "is meet you somewhere to talk, before you go on the job today."

"Will this get me fired?" she asked.

"Maybe. I'd try to keep you out of it, but if it's a murder . . ."

"The thing is, disloyalty in one job might keep me from getting *any* other job."

"I'm trying to tell you the truth," Lucas said. "I can't absolutely guarantee that it wouldn't get out."

After a moment, she said, "There's a Caribou Coffee halfway between my place and Taryn's. I could meet you there at seven-fifteen. I'm on the job at eight."

"I'll see you then," Lucas said.

ALICE GREEN WAS DRESSED in green when Lucas arrived: a green blouse the color of her eyes, a much darker green jacket in a kind of knobby fabric, and black slacks that appeared to be form-fitting until you looked closely. She was paying for a cup of coffee, and Lucas looked closely, and realized that everything she wore was functional, nice-looking but tough, rather than luxurious, and well suited to a fight; the jacket was long enough and loose enough to conceal a pistol.

She paid, walked toward a far corner; saw him, nodded, but kept going. Lucas got a Diet Coke and checked the other customers before he walked over to her table, where she was blowing on a paper cup full of dark coffee. She said, "If anybody I know comes in, I'll have to shoot you."

Lucas sat down: "I need to talk to Carver, alone, I think. I've found a lever that might convince him to talk with me. I'll call him unless you think it would be a terrible idea."

She considered for a moment and then said, "Well, it would be a terrible idea, but talking to either one of them, Dannon or Carver, would be a terrible idea. I assume you've got your back against the wall."

"It's my last shot," Lucas said. "I'm almost certain that Dannon was involved in placing the porn on Smalls's computer. If Tubbs and Roman were killed to cover that up, then it's at least possible that he was acting alone and Carver could give me some insight into how to get him. Or, it's possible that Carver cooperated, but would take a plea. Also, I've got something on Carver that might convince him to cooperate. So, I'm looking at Carver."

"I doubt that he'll crack," Green said. "He'll stonewall. So will Dannon, for that matter. There's not much choice there."

Stonewall. She picked the same word as Elle had. "If you *had* to make a choice . . . which one would you choose?" Lucas asked.

She thought for a moment, sipping at the coffee, and finally said, "If I had to choose, I guess I'd have to agree with you: I'd go with Carver, if you've got some leverage. He's not as smart as Dannon. It's barely possible that you might confuse him enough to get something. I don't think that would be the case with Dannon. Also, Dannon's got another reason to stonewall: Taryn has started sleeping with him. If you take him down, she'd go down, too. At least, he'll see it that way. So he'll stonewall."

"It'll be tough either way," Lucas agreed.

"I'd say you've got no chance with Dannon, no matter how involved he is, and you've got a five percent chance with Carver. Or two percent."

"Off the top of your head . . . what are the chances that Grant knows what they did? That she's involved, that she directed it or approved it?"

Green shook her head: "She's a smart woman. I'd be surprised if she was involved. But . . . and I say *but* . . . she's obviously a sociopath. It wouldn't bother her that people died to get her into the Senate. It *would* bother her that she could go to prison for it. She's made that calculation, too. That's why she gets so angry when she sees you."

Lucas nodded, and said, "Okay," then leaned forward, his forearms on the table. "If I drive a wedge between Dannon and Carver, what would happen?"

"I don't know. They're colleagues, but not exactly friends," Green said. "Dannon is somewhat . . . disparaging . . . when it comes to Carver, because Carver was a sergeant, an enlisted man, and Dannon was an officer. He treats me more as an equal because I was with the Secret Service. Carver feels it. It pisses him off."

"What's Carver's relationship with Grant?"

"He's become . . . overly familiar. I don't know what happened, but yesterday I heard him call her 'honey,' when he thought they were alone. I pretended not to hear."

"She's not sleeping with him, too?"

"Oh, no. She's definitely the officer type. In fact, I'm a little surprised by the thing with Dannon. When I say 'officer type,' I'm talking generals, not captains. But, maybe it's just sex."

"All right," Lucas said. "Do you have a phone number for Carver?"

"Yes. He's already at the house, by the way. He'll be with Taryn until three o'clock, when he gets a couple hours off, to get ready for tonight. If you need to meet with him privately, you could call him while she's speaking. She has four brief appearances today, mostly for the television cameras, and for a couple of blogs. Then they'll head back and watch the results come in."

"Any idea about times?"

She took a piece of paper out of her bag and pushed it across the table. "I made a copy of her schedule. I'd call at one of the first two events—the schedule there is pretty hard. Later in the day, the time-table tends to slip."

"All right," Lucas said. "Thank you. Uh, do you have Carver's double-secret cell-phone number?"

"I do." She pulled back the paper with the schedule on it, took a pen out of her bag, and wrote the number on the paper. "Don't tell him where you got it."

"I won't," Lucas said.

"Did you find out what Carver did in the army? Is that what you've got on him?"

Lucas's eyebrows went up. "You know about that?"

"I don't know what it is, but I know something bad happened," Green said. "I suspect people wound up dead. I tried to find out, but I'm told it's all very classified."

"How about that," Lucas said.

She gazed at him for a moment, then said, "But you know?"

He smiled: "That's classified."

She smiled back. "You're a piece of work, Davenport. If it weren't for Weather, I'd take you to bed."

"If it weren't for Weather, I'd go," Lucas said.

THE EXCHANGE KEPT LUCAS warm all the way out to the car. He'd jump off a high building before he betrayed Weather, but a little extracurricular flirtation kept the blood circulating; not that all of it went to the brain.

Green asked Lucas not to call Carver until at least Grant's first appearance of the day. "I want it to be in Carver's head that I was around when you called. A little psychological insurance that he doesn't think of me, when he wonders how you got the number for his phone. He's a scary guy."

"I can do that," Lucas said. "And you lay low. It should be over in another day or two, one way or another."

She said, "I feel like it's gotta happen today. Everything is coming down to today. Taryn's snap polls say she's up, but it's really, really close, and Smalls may be narrowing the lead. It feels to me like everything's going to end tonight, when the votes come in."

22

After leaving Green, Lucas went back to BCA headquarters in St. Paul and rounded up Del, Shrake, and Jenkins. After talking with Henry Sands, the director, he got the green light to borrow four more male and two female agents from other sections. They'd work in two shifts; he would have preferred to use Virgil Flowers to lead the second shift, but Flowers was still in New Mexico. Instead, he assigned the second shift to Bob Shaffer, a lead investigator with whom he'd worked on other cases.

He got the working group together in a classroom and briefed all nine of them on the entire Smalls/Tubbs investigation, and told them about his planned approach to Carver.

"One of the problems we're facing is that these two guys are probably tougher than any of us, and very experienced in killing, very cool about it," Lucas said. "What I'm going to do is try to drive a wedge between them, which could create an explosive situation. *Could* create an explosive situation—but it might not do anything at all. There's no way to tell what will happen. We're going to spend today, tonight, and tomorrow monitoring Carver, and Dannon, too. If nothing happens before then, it's probably a bust."

When he was done, one of the agents, Sarah Bradley, raised a hand and asked, "If you really get Carver jammed up with this army case, and if he's armed, what happens if he goes off on you?"

"He's too experienced to go off on me, I think," Lucas said. "If we hook up at a restaurant or coffee shop—that's what I'm thinking—it'd be too public. He might leave ahead of me, go storming out of the place, and then try to back-shoot me, I suppose, but I don't see that, either. He'll want to think about it."

"But this army thing—it sounds impulsive, like he cracked," Bradley said. "If he cracked then, he could crack again."

Lucas said, "That's not the feeling I got. I got the feeling that the army was talking about a cold series of executions. He thought he could get away with it. Either that nobody would know, or that none of his platoon would tell, or that if somebody did, he'd be covered. He was partly right—they kicked him out but didn't prosecute. The point is, it seems to me that he . . . thought about it. At least a bit."

"That's what you *think*, but not what you *know*," Bradley said. "I'm not so much worried about *you*. If he shoots you in the coffee shop . . . then he'd have to kill the witnesses. And he could do that. He's essentially already done it once."

Lucas hadn't considered that, and said, "Huh."

"You'd be better off with a couple more guns in the shop," Bradley said. "Probably Jane and me. He doesn't sound like the type to be looking at women as potential combatants: he'd be too macho for that."

Jane was the other female agent, Jane Stack.

Lucas said, "Let me think about it."

Shrake said, "Sarah's exactly right. The rest of us look too much like cops, except Del, and he'd recognize Del. Let's put Sarah and Jane in."

Lucas eventually agreed, and divided the group in two. "I don't know when I'll be talking to him, but I expect it'll be late afternoon or evening. As soon as I find out, the first shift sets up. We'll monitor the meeting—I'll be wearing a wire—and then we'll take him all the way through the day, until he goes to bed. This could be a very long night, with the election. As soon as we're sure that the night's over, Bob and his guys will pick him up, take him all day tomorrow, and then the first shift picks him up again tomorrow evening. We're all clear on overtime. As soon as we leave here, the first shift should go on home, or wherever, get your shopping done, get something to eat . . ."

When the bureaucratic details were handled, they broke up. Del, Shrake, and Jenkins followed him back to his office, where they talked some more about the surveillance aspects. A tech would put a tracking bug on Carver's vehicle, and Del would try to get one on Dannon's, if he could do it without being seen.

"The big question is: Is he gonna talk, or is he gonna stonewall, or is he gonna shoot, or is he gonna run?" Jenkins said.

"That's four questions," Shrake said. "It irritates me that you can't count."

THEY WERE STILL AT IT when Flowers called from Albuquerque. Lucas put him on the speaker phone.

"I talked to Rodriguez, and he seems like a pretty straight guy. He's going to school here, he's got a wife and a couple of kids. He's willing to make a formal statement if we need it. It's about what we thought, with a couple of other things . . ."

"Do tell," Jenkins said.

Rodriguez told Flowers that military intelligence sources had pinpointed what they thought would be a meeting between two rival Taliban chieftains in a border village. How that intelligence was developed, Rodriguez didn't know for sure, but he suspected the original tip came from a paid Afghani source in the village, and that had been backed up by electronic intelligence—the army had been monitoring the relevant Taliban cell phones.

In any case, Carver's unit, which included Rodriguez, and was basically made up of a couple of officers and a bunch of NCOs, had been dropped five kilometers from the meeting site. The soldiers had followed a little-used ridge path into the village. The house where the meeting was to take place had been spotted by the informant, who'd placed a tiny multi-mirrored reflector, similar to those used on golf course pins, on the roof of the place.

When the attack team had gotten close enough, they'd illuminated the village—which was made up of forty or so houses built on the edge of an intermittent stream—with infrared light, and had spotted the sparkle of the reflector.

They'd entered the house at three o'clock in the morning, in a raid pretty much like any police raid. They'd found the Taliban asleep on an assortment of beds and air mattresses and on the floor.

One of the men had tried to resist and was shot and killed. The others had not resisted and were frisked and cuffed at both the hands and the feet and made to lie facedown on the floor, Rodriguez said.

When they'd launched the raid, they'd simultaneously called for helicopter support, which was waiting. But within minutes after the men in the house had been subdued, the raiders began taking heavy fire from neighboring houses.

"The choppers included a gunship, and Rodriguez said that from the air, they could see what looked like muzzle flashes from dozens of weapons," Flowers said. "That was not supposed to happen. They realized pretty quickly that they weren't going to be able to haul a bunch of bound prisoners out of there, so they decided to run for it."

The attacking team did a hopscotch retreat back along the ridge, to where they could be picked up by the Blackhawk transport helicopters, with the gunships keeping the Taliban shooters out of their hair.

"Rodriguez and Carver were supposed to be the last men out of the house," Flowers said. "Carver carried a SAW—that's a light machine gun—and he went last because he could really lay down a big volume of covering fire. Rodriguez went, but then he heard smaller-arms firing from the house, and ran back because he thought some of the Taliban had gotten inside and Carver would need help. What he found was, Carver had executed the prisoners, shooting them in the head with his personal sidearm, a nine-millimeter Beretta. Rodriguez didn't have time to investigate, or anything, this all happened in a few seconds, and then they were running for their lives. When they got back to their base, he reported what he'd seen. He was kinda freaked out. Carver denied it, said that some Taliban had broken through the back of the house, and if any prisoners were dead, they were killed in the firefight. Rodriguez said that the gunships had video, and the video didn't show an attack on the back of the house, but it could have happened. Eventually . . . well, you know what happened. The army got rid of Carver and Rodriguez both."

Rodriguez could have stayed in, Flowers said, but after reporting Carver's action, thought he'd never be trusted again by the special ops people. "That's all Rodriguez was interested in—special ops. He didn't want to be in a regular outfit. But he said that he'd heard other things about Carver—that Carver had always been the first to shoot, that there was at least one other incident—Rodriguez called it an incident—in which civilians had been killed, and nobody had done anything about it. Rodriguez says that Carver was a killer, and that a lot of other people knew it, and that quite a few of them didn't like it. So, they got rid of him."

"Covered it up," Lucas said.

"Yeah, that's what it amounted to, although I don't know what kind of investigation could have been done, given the situation," Flowers said. "Still, I think you might be able to threaten Carver with exposure, tell him that he'll wind up in Leavenworth, and he might believe you. I'm not sure that there's any possibility of a real follow-through on that. At least, not in time to do any good in your case."

"All right," Lucas said. "You recorded all of this?"

"Yeah, of course. If you want me to, I could stay here, transcribe it, and get Rodriguez to sign it."

"Do that," Lucas said. "But try to get back tonight or tomorrow morning. We might need to stick the document up Carver's nose."

"Probably gonna be tomorrow morning," Flowers said. "I don't think I'll get the docs done in time to catch the afternoon plane."

"Then get the docs," Lucas said. "I'll see you tomorrow."

DEL, SHRAKE, AND JENKINS watched Lucas make notes, and five minutes later call Carver. Carver came up on the phone almost instantly. He said, "Yeah."

"This is Davenport, the cop that's been following you around."

"How'd you get this number?"

"I'm a cop," Lucas said. "I need to talk to you. I need to talk to you right away, and somewhere private, where Dannon and Grant aren't around."

"I don't think I want to do that," Carver said, and the line went dead.

"Well, shit," Lucas said.

"You're a smooth talker," Del said.

"I wonder if he's got a smartphone," Lucas said. He sent a text: "Six executed in Afghanistan. Want to hear the governor talking about it on TV? Take the call."

He sent it, and got back "delivered" a second later. Ten seconds after that, Carver took the second voice call and said, "What kind of bullshit is this?"

"You know what kind of bullshit it is. It's Leavenworth bullshit," Lucas said. "Now, you need to take a little time off this afternoon, go out for a cup of coffee. There's an obscure Caribou Coffee a couple miles from Grant's house. Give me a time."

After a moment of silence, Carver said, "Three o'clock."

"Good. And I'll tell you, Ron, we are going to put some serious shit on you. We're also going to give you a way out. All of that gets canceled if you talk to Dannon or Grant. They're the targets in this. We've already got a guy willing to swear that Dannon set up the porn deal for Grant. You can walk, or you can get added to the list. I'll see you at three, and we'll decide which it is."

Lucas clicked off without giving him a chance to answer.

THEY HAD TIME to kill, and with one thing and another, killed it. The two women were going in with briefcases and spiral binders and carefully coordinated suits: real estate agents. Lucas would be wearing a wire, monitored from a van with a plumber's logo on the side, and a real phone number for anyone who needed plumbing services. Jenkins and Shrake would be nearby, but out of sight in separate cars, listening to the conversation on their own radios.

When Carver arrived, a tech who was riding in the plumbing van would try to place a battery-powered GPS tracker on Carver's car, if he could do it without being seen. When Carver left, he'd be tracked by Jenkins and Shrake, who would be well out of sight, running on parallel roads where they could. Lucas and the two women would follow in separate cars.

Del would watch Dannon. If he had an opportunity, he'd place another GPS tracker on Dannon's vehicle.

Since Lucas had been in the same coffee shop that morning, talking to Green, he knew the layout of the place. He told the two women agents, Stack and Bradley, to park as close as they could to the coffee shop's door, hoping that would push Carver away from a parking place that he could see from the shop, and give the technician a good chance to install the tracking bug.

The women were to take a table on the left end of the semicircular seating area, out of sight from where Lucas would take a table, on the far right end.

AND THAT'S WHAT they all did.

The two women went in at ten minutes of three, ordered a Northern Lite Salted Caramel Mocha and a large Americano, and two cranberry scones, put their briefcases on the floor by their ankles, tops open, guns right there, and opened a notebook full of pictures of houses.

Lucas arrived five minutes later, and as he did, Shrake called: "He's here, across the street behind the BP station. He's watching you."

"All right. I'm going in. If he pulls out a deer rifle, shoot him," Lucas said.

"Will do."

Lucas went in, saw the two women at the table on the right, got a Diet Coke and another scone, and walked down to the left, an empty table near the restroom door. His phone rang and Shrake said, "He's coming," and a second later, "He's parking on the side."

Carver slouched along the outside walk, pushed through the door. He was wearing a dark blue nylon shell over a cotton sweater, black slacks, and boots. He looked around the room, his gaze pausing on each of the people at the tables, on the servers, and finally to Lucas. Lucas nodded. Carver turned away, stepped up to the counter, got a large cup of black coffee, and Lucas thought, *Scalding hot coffee.*

Carver was a big guy, thick through the chest, but moved easily, comfortable with his size. Lucas wondered, if it came to a fistfight, if he could take him; and he decided he could. Lucas watched as Carver got his coffee and crossed to Lucas's table, put the coffee on the table, and sat down and asked, "What is this bullshit?"

Lucas said, "I know goddamned well that either you or Dannon killed Tubbs and Roman. I thought about it for a while, and decided that it'd be either Dannon by himself, or both of you together. I don't know where Grant comes in, if she's even aware of it. I need somebody to talk to me about it. I picked you."

"I have no idea of what you're talking about—"

"I hope that's not true, because whether or not it is, I'm going to hurt you. I got the records from the investigation into the shootings in Afghanistan, and I've got a guy who can put them on the political agenda. I think I can get the army to pull you back in—they can do that, for crimes committed under their jurisdiction—and I think I can get you sent to Leavenworth. I'm not sure I can do all that, but I think I can. And I will, unless you talk to me."

"There's nothing to talk about," Carver said. "The army cleared me. Those people were killed by Taliban firing through the windows, blind firing—"

"The report says there are witnesses who say otherwise. We've got video shot from an Apache . . . is that right? An Apache? A helicopter gunship? They have night-camera video from every angle on that house you raided, and nobody's shooting into it, not in a way that would hit people lying on the floor."

"It's that fuckin' Rodriguez, isn't it?" Carver said. "Listen, I gave him a down-check on an evaluation, stalled him out at E-6, and he never got over it. Said he was going to get me. Now he's talking to you, right?"

Lucas spoke right past him: "I can offer you a deal. You give me anything that points at Dannon, or Grant, for that matter, and we'll let sleeping dogs lie. Nobody will mention the word 'Afghanistan.' I can't offer you immunity for anything you've done here in Minnesota, only a prosecutor can set that up, but I can offer to testify in your behalf, in any court case that comes up, to say that you cooperated and aided the investigation."

Carver looked at Lucas over the coffee, which he hadn't touched, and finally said, "That's it? That's all you got?"

"I can't tell you what else we have—but one reason we came to you, is that we can hang the child porn thing on Dannon, and the two killings that follow the child porn. All by itself, the porn will get him twenty years. We need one more little thing to get him for the whole works—we're still processing the Roman scene, and we've got quite a bit of DNA. That takes a while to come back. If it comes back Dannon, he's done. If it comes back Carver, and you've been stonewalling us . . . then that's done. No deal. No way."

Carver shook his head: "First of all, as a suck-ass small-town cop, you got no idea of what you're getting into with the army. They cleared me, and if you try to prove otherwise, they'll hand you your ass. And I don't give a shit about any governor. The army's bigger than any governor, and they'll hand him *his* ass, too. Not because they're protecting me. Because those generals, they'll be protecting themselves."

"I'm willing to find out," Lucas said.

"Then you're gonna have to," Carver said. "Second of all, even if I knew something, I wouldn't tell you, because you can't even give me immunity. The best I could hope for, if I knew about these killings, would be what? Life with parole? Twenty years? Say I keep my mouth shut, and you're right about the governor and all that, and the army pulls me back . . . nothing they do could be worse than what you're talking about. To tell you the truth, given what happened that whole night . . . *heroes in a firefight* . . . I don't see any way they convict me of anything."

"So."

"So, you can take your deal and stick it up your ass," Carver said. He leaned back in his chair, as though satisfied with his decision.

"From what the army investigators say about what happened in Afghanistan, I don't suppose the murders of a couple more people would bother you—nothing for me to work with, there," Lucas said.

Carver rolled his eyes up and sideways, as if to say, *Please,* the way New Yorkers say it. As if to say, *Now you're wasting our time.*

"That's like asking me if I feel bad when somebody gets killed in a car accident. I mean, I gotta tell you, if I don't know them, I don't feel bad. It's like that with this Tubbs guy. Don't know him, never saw him. If I could snap my fingers and he'd come walking through the door, I'd do it. But feel bad, if he's dead? No. Sorry."

"All right. I got nothing more," Lucas said.

Carver looked at him for a moment, then pushed his chair back and stood up. As he turned, Lucas said, "I might have a deal for Dannon, too. If he takes it, I'll put you away forever. Thirty years, no parole. You'll be an old man when you get out."

"Fuck you."

"Whatever," Lucas said. "You got my phone number. The deal is open until Dannon talks to me. At that point, you're done."

"Double fuck you," Carver said.

"Keep your eye on the TV. You could be a star," Lucas said.

Carver walked away.

23

Kidd finally boiled it down to a single line: he said, "I think it's moronic."

"I know what I'm doing," Lauren said.

"I'm not sure of that. As far as you know, they'll have a dozen extra guards around the place to keep the starfuckers away," Kidd said.

"They'd be out front. I'll be going in from the dark side, right down the neighbor's tree line," Lauren said. She'd been studying satellite pictures all day, including several taken within the past week, with resolution good enough to see the hubcaps on cars. "I'll have my starlights. The security alarms will be off, the dogs will be locked up, all kinds of people will be walking around the place, and most of them will be either rich or important, so nobody will be inclined to question them."

"Jesus." Kidd dragged his fingertips through his eye sockets.

"One last time," Lauren said. "I swear to God, I do this, and I'm done. I'll go back to being the little housewife."

"You're not a little housewife."

"Yes, I am. I'm not a famous painter. I'm not a famous computer hacker," Lauren said. "People say, 'You're *that* Kidd's wife? You lucky woman.' You know—get your cookies in the oven and your buns in the bed, while Kidd takes care of the important stuff."

Kidd had to laugh, and she said, "Now you're laughing."

"I'm laughing because it's so fucking stupid. Why can't you be a rock climber or something? A scuba diver? You're smart—go to college, get a degree, become a famous . . . whatever."

"Right. Whatever. Even the Famous Kidd can't think exactly what that might be."

They were in the living room, in a couple of easy chairs overlooking the Mississippi. The weather was changing: not only from one day to the next, but from autumn to winter. The sky was gray, overcast, with thick clouds the color of aluminum, not a hint of the sun. Cold. On really bad days, Kidd sat in front of the window and drew the scene, with a pencil or a crayon and a sketchbook, and the scene changed every time. Lauren pushed herself out of her chair and walked to the window, pressed her forehead against the cool glass.

After a moment, Kidd walked up behind her and draped an arm over her shoulder. "All right. Let's do it."

"Thank you. You can't tell me this doesn't light you up, at least a little bit," Lauren said.

"The biggest problem is Jackson," Kidd said. "We can't both get caught. If they grab you . . ."

"You have to run," Lauren said. "But they won't grab me. . . . I absolutely will not push. I'll go in with my finger on the abort switch. The first second that trouble shows up, I'll go right back down the tree line. You get me, and we roll."

"One last time," Kidd said.

She turned back to him, her face bright. "I'm really stoked, Kidd. I'm high as a kite."

DANNON WAS DRIVING, TARYN was in the backseat. Schiffer, the campaign manager, was in the front passenger seat with two cell phones, three ballpoint pens, one red, one green, and one black, and a blue-cloth three-ring binder. Inside the binder was an inch-thick stack of paper, much of it given over to a listing of every voting precinct in Minnesota, all 4,130 of them, with the results of the last Senate campaign, which had been won by Porter Smalls.

Thirty precincts had been designated as critical signposts. For those precincts, the far right column was kept in red, green, or black ink; red for those precincts where exit polls suggested Smalls would exceed his total in the last campaign, green for those in which he was running behind, and black for those in which there was no discernible change.

Of the thirty, as of three o'clock in the afternoon, he was running behind his previous total in seventeen of the twenty-six where they had been able to gather enough responses to report. In the other nine, there was no discernible change. He was running ahead in none of them. All by itself, that would have been good; but what was happening was actually better than good. People who voted before five o'clock tended to be more conservative than those who voted after five o'clock.

Taryn had been scheduled to make four appearances during the day, set up to capture the noon and early evening news: going in, they'd thought they might need the small extra boost from those television appearances. Porter Smalls had ended his campaign with a breakfast at the St. Paul Hotel in St. Paul, so wouldn't be much of a factor on the news. Besides, the news departments at TV stations in Minneapolis were generally liberal, and would give Taryn a publicity break if they could get away with it.

In the front seat, Schiffer said into one of her phones, "I don't want to know about helium. I want some of the balloons to go down, instead of up. Is that too much to ask? Get it done."

On her second phone she said, "Well?" She listened for a moment, then grunted and wrote a number in the right column in green ink. She said, "Keep it going," and hung up and turned to Taryn.

"Eighteen of twenty-seven, and we're running stronger in our precincts than Sterling did last time."

"You want to make a call?" Taryn asked.

"I never believe it until I see the actual numbers . . . but yeah. You got it. You're the new senator from Minnesota."

Taryn said, "Yes!" and Dannon slapped the steering wheel and cried, "Oh, my God, it makes my dick hard!"

Taryn said, "Douglas . . ."

"I'm sorry, it's . . ."

Schiffer: "Don't worry about it. Makes my dick hard, too."

At four-fifteen they arrived at St. Mary's Park for a rally timed to the evening news. Del was there, too, wearing a navy blue suit that was a couple sizes too big for him, with a wrinkled white shirt and a blue-white-and-chocolate-striped nylon tie whose wideness would have made him proud in 1972. His hat had a snap brim and a feather. He looked like a flake and nobody paid any attention to him.

He got on his cell phone and told Lucas, "Dannon's still with her. Man, I think she's gonna win. She's not saying so, but it's coming through."

"Carver's still sitting there, I don't know what he's doing, but it's something," Lucas said. Carver had gone from the Caribou Coffee to a Starbucks, not far away.

"I'll call you back if anything happens," Del said. "It looks like they're gonna be here for a while. A couple of TV trucks just came in. I'm gonna stick that bug on their truck."

"Make sure you can do it clean."

"Do that," Del said.

LUCAS WAS ON THE STREET, ten miles away, in a parallel parking spot, ready to roll out in front of Carver, if he came that way. He couldn't actually see Carver, but Jenkins could, from a dry-cleaning shop across from the Starbucks. From his vantage point, Jenkins said it looked like Carver had gotten two or three cups of coffee at twenty-minute intervals and spent the rest of the time crouched over an iPad.

"I don't think he's reading the Bible," Jenkins said, on his handset. "But whatever it is, he's all over it."

"Maybe he's buying plane tickets," suggested Shrake, who was on the same net. Shrake was a half-mile up the street, ready to follow if Carver broke that way.

"That worries me," Lucas said. "We don't have enough to pull him in. If he gets on a plane, all we could do is wave good-bye."

"I haven't seen him take out a credit card," Jenkins said. "I'm more worried that he's waiting for his dry cleaning."

"This guy isn't dry cleaning, he's strictly wash-and-wear,"

Shrake said. "He's all Under Armour and nylon shells and combat boots."

"Sounds like you," Jenkins said. Then: "Hey. He's up. Looks . . . He's headed out." A minute later, "He's turning your way, Lucas. You better move."

"Got him on the monitor," Shrake said.

Lucas rolled away and said, "I'm gonna jump on 94, bet he's headed back to Grant's."

CARVER HAD SPENT an hour with his iPad, part of the time doing what Lucas had feared: checking planes from Minneapolis to the East Coast—New York, New Jersey, Philadelphia, Miami. He'd also checked in with old acquaintances working with contractors who supplied private security personnel in Afghanistan and several other nations in the Middle East and Africa; he asked about job openings.

Time, he thought, *to get out of Minneapolis.*

He spent the last minute or two on his cell phone. He was in-house for the party that evening, which Schiffer had said would go until ten-thirty or so, and then they'd head downtown to the Radisson Hotel for the victory party, if there was a victory party. The house party was reserved for political big shots and large donors.

He punched Dannon's number, and Dannon came up: "Yes."

"Is she winning?"

"Yes. Looks like it's in the bag. You at the house?"

"No, but I'm heading that way now," Carver said. "I need to talk to you. Privately. Right now. I got hit hard by Davenport."

Dannon said, "We're doing the last show. We'll be back there by five-thirty."

"I'll be waiting," Carver said.

———

KIDD AND LAUREN HAD a bad moment when they turned Jackson over to the babysitter. The babysitter was a middle-aged nurse who was grateful for the extra under-the-table cash money from Kidd; five hundred a month, with babysitting services on a moment's notice. She worked the day shift, and was available anytime after three o'clock in the afternoon, seven days a week. She adored Jackson, and Jackson liked her back.

But leaving Jackson, a thin child, tall for his age, strong, with a happy smile morning to night . . . Kidd got desperately tight in the throat, and Lauren said, "I know: but we're doing it. I need this, Kidd."

So they left him.

AT 45 DEGREES NORTH, the night comes early in November. They rolled out a few minutes after seven-thirty into the kind of autumn darkness that comes only with a thick cloud layer, no hint of starlight or moonlight, and no prospect of any. Lauren drove.

She was already dressed in her black brushed-cotton suit. Her hood, and her equipment, were locked in a concealed box behind the second row of seats. They chitchatted on the way across town, through enough traffic to keep things slow; Jackson wasn't mentioned.

They were a mile from Grant's place at eight-fifteen. The day before, they'd spotted a diner with a strong and reliable Wi-Fi and no protection, with parking on the side and in back, out of sight from the street. Kidd signed on from a laptop and dialed up another laptop, which was hooked into his cell phone, back at the condo.

His phone made a call to a friend who, at that moment, was playing a violin in a chamber quartet at the birthday party for a St. Paul surgeon's wife. Kidd let the call ring through to the answering service, left a message that suggested handball on Friday.

"Done," he said, when he'd hung up. An alibi. Both of their desktop computers would be roaming websites all through the evening, and they'd send out a couple of e-mails.

"Let's see what's going on."

Kidd signed on to Taryn's security system. All the cameras were operating, the interior cameras showing perhaps two or three dozen people in suits and dresses with cocktails, all apparently talking at full speed. The bedroom was dark, which was perfect. If it hadn't been, Lauren would have had to come in through a dead-ended hallway, at a seating area, that would have been more exposed to a visitor, but was free of cameras. This way, she could go in through the en suite bathroom. Outside, the cameras showed several uniformed men behind the fence along the line of the street, and a few people standing in the street, looking at the house.

"The uninvited," Lauren said. "Check the backyard."

Kidd cycled to the backyard cameras. They saw one guard, moving along the perimeter of the huge lot. A side camera showed the dog kennel, with both dogs sitting inside, alert, apparently watching the guard.

"There's the competition," Kidd said.

"Not if they're penned up," Lauren said. "They can't see my entry point. As long as they're not set loose . . ."

"They've got noses like radar," Kidd said.

"Yes. Keep an eye on them. If they turn them loose, I'll call it off."

They watched for fifteen minutes, until Lauren said, "Okay, we've got it."

Just before Kidd killed the image from the cameras, they saw a security man in a coat walk through the picture. "Mean-looking guy," Kidd said. "I think that's Carver."

"I'll stay away from him," Lauren said.

"Yeah. Far away." He reached out, put his hand on top of her head and turned her face toward his, and kissed her and said, "Let's call it off."

"No. I'm going in," Lauren said. "Tomorrow, I'm back to little housewifey."

"Fuck me," Kidd said, as he started the car. "Fuck me."

DANNON AND CARVER got together before dark, and Carver laid it out, exactly as it had happened: Davenport was blackmailing him for information.

"He's gonna get me, man," Carver said. He didn't seem scared, Dannon thought: he looked wired, like he might before a bad-odds mission. "He says that the governor will go on TV and talk about what happened in the 'stan. He says they can force the army to take me back and put me on trial. He said it was a massacre like that one in Vietnam, and there's no way that Obama could let it go."

"That's bullshit, man," Dannon said. "That whole thing is buried so deep, and the guys who buried it all have stars now. They'd never get you."

"That's what I told him," Carver said. "I think he's going to do it anyway. I'm telling you, he's a crazy mean cocksucker. He's got nothing unless I talk, except the 'stan, and he'll use it to bust my balls."

"If you talk, he'll bust more than your balls. He'll put you in the penitentiary forever," Dannon said.

Carver said, "I know. I been thinking about it ever since I talked to him. He can't do anything fast enough to keep me off a plane. I'm thinking I fly to Paris, take the train to Madrid, and fly out to Panama. Confuse the trail. I got a buddy there, runs a fishing place over on the Pacific side. By the time they get to Panama, if they even bother to chase me, I'll be deep in-country. I'll be wearing a sombrero and talking taco."

"Ah, man . . ."

"You got something better?" Carver asked.

"I need to think about it," Dannon said.

"Listen. I know you're sleeping with Taryn, so you can talk to her. You put this on her, right now. Tonight. I need cash. A lot of it. I got the passport, I know how to travel, there's nothing I want in the apartment that I can't get in a duffel bag or two. Maybe you could clean the rest of it out for me later. But I need cash."

"How much? You mean, traveling money?"

"I mean traveling money, and hiding money," Carver said. "Living money."

"What are we talking about, Ron?"

Carver hesitated, then said, "It's like Tubbs said. If you want to retire . . . I need a million."

"Jesus Christ, man, she can't come up with a million overnight."

"Sure she can. I've seen her wearing a half-million in diamonds. They're right there in her safe," Carver said. "I'll take diamonds. What's that one, that big green one? The Star of Kandiyohi? That's probably another half-million—I've heard people talk. And I know she keeps cash around. I need enough cash to get to a place where I could sell the diamonds or whatever else she wants to unload. And then I'm gone. . . . I want to be in Paris tomorrow night."

"I don't know," Dannon said. "I'll talk to her, maybe figure something out. A million is pretty goddamn rich, though. Pretty goddamn rich, man."

"How many millions has she got?" Carver asked. "A thousand millions? Isn't that right? I've heard people say that, that she's a billionaire. It takes one one-thousandth of what she's got to get me out of the way, stashed down south? She'll never hear from me again, she can go be a senator or a president or whatever."

Dannon nodded. "Okay. I'll talk to her. *I'll talk to her.* You gotta take off for the hotel pretty soon. Get us set up there. I'll try to get an answer tonight, and I'll talk to you at the hotel."

"Good. I appreciate it, man." Carver ran his hands through his thick hair, then shook it out. "Isn't this a bunch of shit? That guy, Davenport, you watch out for him. Maybe you ought to come with me. I mean, Paris. We could be in Paris tomorrow night."

"City of Light," Dannon said.

"What?"

"City of Light. That's what they call Paris."

"City of Cheese. That's what they oughta call it," Carver said. "I never noticed the light, but they sure got a shitload of cheese."

24

ucas drove past Grant's house with the driver's-side window down, along the street lined with towering pines and blue spruces. He could hear, distantly but clearly, Aretha Franklin singing "Think."

From the street, he could see that the front door was open, and he could see people inside; and he could see guards along the front lot line. Another dozen people were milling outside the front fence, one of them with a large handwritten sign that said, "Yay for the New Senator." As Lucas continued down the street, he saw, in his rearview mirror, a TV truck turning the corner.

She won, he thought. The TV people would be looking at exit polls, and would know which way the wind was blowing, even if they wouldn't say so until the polls closed. He continued around a curve, turned into an intersecting street, followed it down its twisting length to a slightly larger street, took a right, and followed the new street out to an even larger, straight street. Just around the corner, he pulled up behind Del, got out, and walked to the passenger side.

Del popped the door and Lucas got in. Del was eating a cheese and bratwurst sandwich, with onions, and Lucas said, "Maybe we oughta talk outside."

"Gotta man up," Del said. "Besides, only two more bites, and it's cold out there."

"Nothing's happening," Lucas said.

"Well, they're in there together. I wonder if Carver said anything?"

"I gotta believe he did, 'cause if he didn't, this is a huge waste of time," Lucas said.

"Yeah, and it's your fault," Del said. He finished the sandwich, dug a napkin out of a brown paper bag, burped, wiped his fingers and chin. "Goddamn, that was good."

"I thought Cheryl had you off that crap. Had to be ninety percent cholesterol."

"Ah, we compromised. I can have one a week. Gotta make it count."

Shrake called on the handset: "You hear the one about the guy walking around with his dog at night, and runs into his old pal with *his* dog?"

"Big waste of time," Lucas said. "But, no, I haven't."

"I'll tell it to you sometime," Shrake said. "Right now, I should probably mention that I went by Grant's place, and Carver was walking out to his truck. He was talking to Dannon. I think he's moving."

Lucas said, "I'm on it," said good-bye to Del, who was monitoring the main vehicle, the one Dannon had been driving, and walked back to his truck. Carver started moving two minutes later, and Lucas and Shrake and Jenkins and Bradley and Stack followed him downtown, and watched him turn into a parking ramp that fed the Radisson Hotel, where the victory party would be held.

BRADLEY AND STACK FOLLOWED him in. They were dressed for the party, Bradley with a big pin that said "Taryn" and Stack with a bunch of credentials around her neck that looked like news credentials. They'd both changed their hair a bit and Bradley had gotten a pair of black-rimmed glasses. Neither looked like the real estate ladies from that morning. The three men waited in the street, and five minutes after Carver drove into the garage, Bradley called on her cell phone and said, "He's in the ballroom, he's talking to security. Looks like they're setting up for tonight."

"Has he looked at you?" Lucas asked.

"No."

"Good. Stay out of sight," Lucas said. "You don't want him to see you more than a couple of times."

Annoyed, she said, "Yeah, I've done this before."

"I know you have . . . but I worry."

IN WHAT WOULD HAVE BEEN an expansive family room, if Taryn had had a family, all the white folks and the necessary number of blacks and browns were cuttin' a rug, if a lot of really stiff heirs and fund managers and entrepreneurs and politicians could, in fact, cut a rug.

Taryn had had a few drinks and was dancing with everyone, lit up like a Christmas tree, feeling the rush. Dannon had tried to catch her eye, but she'd resolutely moved on to the next Important Person.

KIDD COULD SEE HOW pumped Lauren was, so he didn't bother to argue any further, though he drove slowly. Eventually, however, they'd arrived at Grant's house, and there was no way to put it off. He hit the switch that killed the taillights, let the car roll to a stop, said, "Luck," and Lauren slipped out the door and into the night.

Lauren had always had a taste for cocaine, given up only when pregnancy was a prospect, and not touched since then; but now, as she slipped out of the car, over the curb and into the trees that marked the edge of the neighbor's lot, she felt as high as she ever had on coke, with the same preternatural awareness, her senses reaching out through the trees to the political party three hundred yards away.

Lauren was in her black suit, with a black nylon backpack. She'd opened a pair of sterile surgical gloves in the SUV, before getting out, and Kidd had helped her get into them as a surgeon would, with no contact on the outer surface that would spread germs . . . or DNA.

Once back in the trees, she pulled on her starlights and moved slowly toward Grant's place. There was a lot of light from that direction, and none from the house to the other side. The light threw India-ink shadows behind each tree. Ten feet from Grant's property line, she found a particularly deep shadow and lay down in it for five minutes, without moving; watching and listening.

She saw a guard moving across the yard, away from her; he apparently had been assigned to the backyard. She decided she needed to time him. She took out the cold phone and called Kidd. She said, "I'm at Target. I'll be a while. Call you when I'm ready to go."

"Okay. Everything's fine, here."

Target was the edge of the yard, where she lay. Cell phones are radios, and hobbyists listen to the calls. . . .

She hung up and lay back in the weeds. Three minutes, four minutes. The backyard guard had disappeared around the corner of the house, where the dog kennel was, and now reappeared, having walked all the way around the house. He was an older guy, hands in his pockets, peering here and there, but not obviously ready to act.

When he'd gone halfway around the house again, Lauren took a breath, punched in Kidd's number, said, "I'm gone." She crossed the four-foot-high wrought iron fence that marked the property line, and, keeping a tree trunk between herself and the house, crossed halfway to the house. At the tree, she paused again, watching and listening, and saw nothing.

Ten seconds, and she moved again, paused at another tree, then ran lightly across the yard to the house and lay down in a spreading arborvitae shrub at the house's foundation. She pushed the star-lights up and off, and stowed them in her pack. She smiled at a thought: the thought that the guard would hear her heart pounding in the bush.

A minute passed, then another, and she lay completely covered and unmoving, on her stomach, so she could make a fast dash for the side tree line if she had to, like a sprinter coming out of the blocks. The target window was straight above her head.

She hadn't felt like this in six years, and she nearly giggled.

A minute later, the guard ambled by, his head turned away from the house. When he was out of sight, she started counting seconds under her breath. At the same time, moving automatically, she stood up, looked through the window into a darkened bathroom. Kidd was watching the security cameras, and hadn't seen anything, so she stuck a couple of suction cups to the window, pulled a glass cutter from her leg pocket, and putting a lot of weight behind it, scored the first layer of glass. At "forty" she hit the glass with the back end of the cutter, and heard it crack along the score line. She pulled on the suction cups, but the glass was stubborn, and she hit it again. This time, it came free, and she lowered it to the ground. She was at sixty.

At one hundred twenty, she hit the second layer of glass twice, and pulled it free. The noise—a series of sharp but not particularly loud cracks—was unavoidable. The last sheet of the triple-pane glass would have to be done more carefully, because it had a foil alarm strip around the perimeter. Kidd thought all the alarms were off, but it would be best not to break it. She wasn't sure she had time, so she lay back in the bush, and at the count of two-twenty, the guard came past the house again.

When he was gone, she stood up again, and carefully cutting inside the foil strips, she yanked the last pane of glass off, and lay down again. She dialed Kidd and said, "Let's get coffee." He said, "I'll see you there."

He knew she was ready to enter; and she knew that there'd been no alarm yet.

Yet. Big word.

SHE PULLED A SHORT strip of thick, soft plastic tarp out of her pack, and waited again for the guard to pass. When he did, she put the tarp over the edges of the cut window glass and carefully boosted herself through the window. She stepped on a toilet seat, moved quickly to the water-closet door, into the main bathroom and to the bathroom door. She opened it, just a crack.

The bedroom was dark. She could hear the distant vibration of voices and the deeper thump of rock music, but nothing from the bedroom. She dialed Kidd and said, "In." He made no reply, but he was there, live, and if something broke, he'd start screaming.

She took a moment to remove the tarp from the window, then moved quickly through the bedroom, groped for the button that would open the bookcase panel, found it, opened it, put the phone to her ear. Was the bookcase button booby-trapped? Kidd said nothing, issued no warning. The safe was there, in the dark: she felt for the keypad, found it, tried a combination, turned the lock handle. It didn't budge. No panic: she had a sequence to run through, one of four possibilities. She hit it on the second one.

There must have been twenty small jewelry cases in the safe. She threw them in the pack, felt deeper into the safe, picked up something heavy and cylindrical . . . a roll of coins. Heavy: gold. She felt around, found a dozen more rolls. And cash: stacks of currency. Christ, this was good. She threw everything into her bag, and then closed the safe, and pushed the bookcase button . . .

And Kidd started screaming: "Hide hide hide . . ."

She punched off the phone and at the same moment, she heard them: somebody coming down the hall, arguing, coming fast. No time, not time even to get to the bathroom . . .

The bookcase was sliding back in place as she bounced once across the bed to the far side, pulling the pack along, hit the floor, then slipped under the bedskirt and pulled the pack with her, under the bed. At the same moment, the bedroom door opened, and a streak of light cut across the carpet.

DANNON FINALLY GOT TARYN out of the crowd. She was about two-thirds drunk, he thought, as he hustled her along by her arm, all the way to the bedroom, a few curious partiers looking after them. They pushed through the door, but didn't bother with the light: they needed privacy, not illumination.

"What is it?" Taryn snarled. "This is my night, you can't—"

"Shut up and listen, goddamnit, this is more important than any of that political bullshit," Dannon said, shaking her. "Carver got hit by that goddamn Davenport. Davenport found out what Carver did in Afghanistan, and supposedly is going to get the governor to say something about it, on a talk show or something—that Carver massacred some people."

"Did he?"

"Well, that depends on how you look at it," Dannon said.

"So he *did*," Taryn said.

"*Listen*. Davenport is trying to get Carver to turn on us. Offering him immunity. Carver's freaking out. He wants you to give him a million dollars in diamonds and cash, tonight. He's going to run for it. He thinks he can hide out in Panama."

"That sounds crazy," Taryn said.

"It's not entirely crazy, except that he won't stop with a million. He'll spend it in six months. He'll buy a goddamn fishing trawler or something, something that won't work out, and he'll keep coming back. Or he'll get in trouble and he'll tell everybody that a U.S. senator is a pal of his, and he'll be coming to you for a little influence peddling . . . and more money. It's the same deal as with Tubbs."

"Is there any chance that Davenport would give him immunity?" Taryn asked.

"Oh, hell, yes. If he could bag you and me? Hell, yes."

"So . . ."

"I'm gonna take Ron out tonight. I'll work out some kind of excuse to get him down to his vehicle, and I'll hit him—"

"The car will be full of blood—"

"No-no. I can do this. There won't be a speck of blood. We've already got the perfect graveyard. I'll get my pal to carry his passport across the border into Iraq . . . and we're good. Good forever."

A PHONE RANG; for a freaking split second, Lauren thought it was hers and she slid her hand down her leg to the side pocket, but then heard Taryn say, "Wait . . ." and then, as the phone continued to ring, Taryn said, "Damn it, where is it? Okay."

She'd been rummaging through her purse, Lauren thought. Then Taryn answered the phone and said, "We're in the back . . . probably pretty soon. Yeah, I've stopped, don't worry about it. Okay, we're coming out."

Lauren heard what sounded like a woman dropping a purse on a tabletop, and the door swung open.

Taryn's voice: "Do it. Do it."

Then they were gone, still talking, their voices diminishing as they went down the hall. Lauren started breathing again, slipped out from under the bed. The room was no longer entirely dark. She could be seen by the monitors if she stood up. She crawled across the carpet, pulling the pack, to the bathroom, which wasn't covered by the cameras. At the bathroom, she slipped inside, and as she was closing the door, saw Taryn's purse on the dresser on the opposite wall.

Thought about it, then went to the window, looked and listened, and satisfied that the guard wasn't right there, dropped the pack into the arborvitae. Then she went back to the bathroom door, got down on her knees, and then on her stomach, and slipped across the floor, staying close to the wall where the camera wouldn't see her. It would see her if she stood up at the dresser.

She stayed on the floor to the outer door, reached out and slowly, slowly closed the door. As soon as it was dark, she stood, went straight to the purse, dipped inside, found Taryn's iPhone, then hurried back across to the bathroom. She peered out the window, then pulled back: the guard was right there, on the lawn, still looking away from the house, toward the trees.

He went on by, slowly, and as soon as he was out of sight, she dropped the tarp across the cut edges of glass, pushed through the window, dropped behind the bush, on top of her pack. She stuffed the tarp into it, took the starlights out and put them on. She wouldn't wait now: she called Kidd, said, "Running," and took off, zigzagging between trees, into the tree line, then through the trees toward the street.

At the tree line, she knelt, pulled off her starlights, and stuffed them in her pack, and then the darkened car rolled up. She was inside then, and Kidd did a U-turn and asked, his voice tight, "How'd it go?"

"Pretty routine," she said. "Hey, slow down. I've got to text a guy."

"What?"

"Give me Lucas's cell phone number."

LUCAS WAS IN HIS LEXUS, alone, waiting for Carver to move again, when his phone burped at him.

Thinking Weather or Letty, he pulled it out and found a message from an unknown number:

Dannon will kill Carver tonight at the hotel and bury him in the perfect graveyard. Best wishes, Taryn.

Lucas said, "What?"

25

ucas sat for a minute looking at the message, didn't understand how it could possibly be right, then called the BCA duty officer on his own phone and asked him to do a lookup on the number: he came back a minute later and said, "Billed to Taryn Grant."

Lucas said, "Sonofabitch," to nobody. He couldn't think what he had to lose, so he redialed the number, and was instantly switched to an answering service, which meant that the phone had been turned off. He said, "Davenport . . . you sent me a message. Call me back."

He waited four or five minutes, then his phone burped: Del.

"Grant and Dannon and the campaign manager just came out of the house, and it looks like they're putting a caravan together," Del said. "I guess they're headed downtown. I've been monitoring Channel Three, and they are leaning pretty hard on her winning. They haven't called it yet, but they will before midnight."

"Last time I saw, it was pretty close," Lucas said.

"Yeah, but the suburbs are in, and the Iron Range isn't—she'll be two-to-one, up there."

"Okay. Listen—are you sure Dannon is with the convoy?"

"Pretty sure. I saw him getting in the truck, he's driving. That Green chick is in the second truck, and there are a couple more . . ."

"Okay. I'm gonna want you to buzz Grant's truck once it gets on I-94. I need to confirm that Dannon's in the truck. When you're sure, get your ass down here as fast as you can."

"I can do that."

Lucas rang off, waited for another call from Grant. Nobody called, until Del came back again and said, "I ran their convoy. Dannon's driving."

"Get down here. I'm outside the Radisson parking garage. Drop your car, and hook up with me."

DEL ARRIVED TWENTY MINUTES later, walking up the street in a gray hoodie, hands in the front pocket, looking a little like a monk. Lucas popped the lock on the passenger side, and Del climbed inside. "You sounded stressed," he said.

Lucas called up the message from Grant and passed the phone over to him. Del read it and said, "This don't compute."

"I had Dave look up the number. It's hers."

"Did you . . ."

"I called her back," Lucas said. "She'd turned off the phone."

"This is messed up. This isn't right," Del said. "I mean, even if it's true . . . she wouldn't send this message."

"That's what I can't figure out," Lucas said.

"What're you going to do?"

"Get past the first flush of the party . . . have Sarah and Jane keep an eye on Dannon and Carver . . . and maybe when things have settled down a little, I'll go in and get Taryn alone and brace her."

"You've been friendly with Green. Is there any possibility . . . ?"

Lucas groaned: "I should have thought of that. Maybe they're all using phones paid for by Grant."

"But why did she sign it 'Taryn' instead of leaving it alone?"

"Dunno." Lucas took his cell back and messaged Green: "Did you send me a note about C&D a few minutes ago?"

Del said, "She's driving, it might take a while for her to get back."

"She's a woman, it won't take—" Lucas's phone chirped, and he looked at the message screen. It said, "No," and the incoming phone number was wrong.

He texted back, "Are all your phones billed to Grant?"

Another ten seconds. "No."

"Any new info on C&D?"

"No."

Del said, "Something's happening, and we don't know what it is."

They thought about it, and then Del said, "You gotta make a call, here. Do we take it in and show it to Carver?"

"There's no way he'd believe it: he'd figure we're trying to ramp up the pressure," Lucas said. "It'd completely blow the fact that we're watching them full-time."

"But if he gets killed . . ."

"Yeah."

"I'm not worried about him, man, I'm worried about *you*," Del said. "If it got out that you got this message, and then didn't do anything about it . . ."

Lucas thought about that, then got on the radio to Bradley and Stack. He had to wait until the women got out of sight, where they could use their handsets. When they were both up, he said, "We've got a problem, and I can't really explain it. But: we need to be all over Carver and Dannon. I need to come and talk with Taryn as soon as possible."

Bradley said, "Wait, wait . . . you won't be able to talk to her for a while. Channel Three and Eleven called it for her. It's a mob scene in here. . . . She'll be up on the stage, making a speech . . ."

Lucas could hear a wall of noise in the background, and he said, "Okay. Call me as soon as she gets offstage. But you and Jane *must* keep track of Dannon and Carver."

"That's almost impossible, Lucas," Stack said. "We can keep track of them, kinda, but they keep going backstage with these politicians, these out-of-bounds areas, and then they'll pop out somewhere else. If we stay right on them, they'll spot us for sure."

"Do what you can. Call me when Taryn gets offstage. The minute she gets off."

The party rocked on.

Lucas rang off and Del said, "Maybe you ought to have them identify themselves, and tell Carver and Dannon that they're bodyguards and they aren't going away."

"Then we're right back to where we started," Lucas said. "With nothing—and with them knowing that we're on them like a cheap suit. If we go to them directly, we'll lose it all."

"Is that better or worse than somebody getting killed?"

Lucas had to think about that, and finally said, "I want them."

They sat in the street for an hour, talking to Stack and Bradley, and were finally told that the noise and tumult were beginning to wind down. Most of the good food and booze was gone, and the less needy of the party faithful were beginning to leak out the doors, Bradley said. Taryn was thanking some fourth-level party worker and his big-hair wife, a guy who'd raised a quarter million or something.

DANNON WAVED CARVER into the back where the food service people were working, where the hotel functionaries were counting bottles and security guards were taking breaks, got him back to a side room with the soft-drink and candy machines and said, "She can't get you all of it, not right now. She can get you a good part of it, if you'll take gold."

Carver was truculent: "What's a good part of it?"

"Quarter million, give or take, in cash," Dannon said. "She's not sure of the exact amount, but it started at a half million that she stacked up over the last six years, for the campaign. As it turned out, she only needed about half the cash. The good thing is, it's all cold, in case we had to make some payoffs. Then there are two hundred gold Eagles, no serial numbers or anything else. Right now gold is selling for seventeen hundred an ounce, which is another three hundred and forty grand. That's close to six hundred thousand that we can get our hands on tonight. The diamonds . . . She won't give up the diamonds. They've all got sentimental value for her. She says that as soon as we get clear of the campaign, she'll put another four hundred thousand on you, in Panama. You might have to make some arrangements—"

"Like what kind of arrangements?" Carver asked, but he'd brightened considerably.

"You might have to get a piece of land down there with your own money. Like, pay a hundred grand for a piece of oceanfront, or whatever, under a different name. She pays you half a million for it.

That keeps things straight with the tax people. It'll all be handled through front companies."

"Well, shit, we can do that," Carver said.

"Sure. It's not rocket science," Dannon said.

"When do I get it?" Carver asked.

"When do you want it?"

"Tonight, if we can do it," Carver said. "I can be on a six o'clock plane for New York."

"There are going to be people around the house, people coming back with Taryn," Dannon said. "I've got the numbers for the safe. We could do it right now—take your truck, you can drop it at Hertz on your way out of town. We were going to turn it back in tomorrow anyway."

"Good. Good. Can we go now?"

"Let me talk to Schiffer."

LUCAS AND DEL were still sitting in the street. Everything was running behind schedule; Taryn had been expected to speak at 11:30, but that got pushed to 11:45. She was supposed to talk for ten or fifteen minutes, but the thank-yous went on and on. Finally, at 12:30, Stack called Lucas and said, "It's winding down. She won't be here long after she finishes speaking."

"When was the last time you saw Carver and Dannon?"

"They've been going in and out of the back," Bradley said. "But Dannon's here right now, he's talking to Schiffer."

"Carver's right at the edge of the stage," Stack said. "He's talking to some guy in a suit. . . . Wait, he's going into the back again."

"I'm coming in," Lucas said.

Lucas took the stairs to the ballroom where the party was; people were going out through multiple folding doors, most of them with yellow credential tags around their necks that said, "Taryn VIP"—party invitees. There were guards at the door doing perfunctory credential checks, but there were more people leaving than arriving. A TV guy carrying a light stand hustled by, and a guard put a finger out to Lucas, a gesture asking for a credential, and Lucas showed him his BCA identification. The guard's eyebrows went up and he waved Lucas through.

Inside, a few hundred balloons, red, white, and blue, were scattered around the floor and floating around the ceiling, and a drunk young man was popping them with what looked like an Italian switchblade while his friends laughed at him. The carpet smelled like spilled champagne.

Taryn seemed to be getting ready to leave the stage, waving fairly randomly at the crowd, laughing; strobes popped in her face and her teeth flashed in the brilliant white pops.

Four sixty-inch TV screens were sitting on high stands at the edges of the ballroom, and Lucas paused to check the numbers: Taryn was up more than sixty thousand votes and the Iron Range was still coming in large; there were a few Republican counties yet to report out west, but they'd make little difference. It wasn't a huge victory, but a clear one: Smalls was toast.

CARVER AND DANNON took the back stairs to the parking ramp. Carver said, "Man, I wasn't sure she'd go for it. You gotta get in on this, dude. She's not gonna fuck you forever, and money is definitely better than pussy."

"Shut up," Dannon said.

"True love, huh?" Carver said, and he laughed.

Dannon was checking the garage. An older couple was getting into a Prius a hundred feet away, and a Chevy Tahoe was rolling toward the exit. He could see a man standing in the elevator lobby, apparently waiting to go up. They got to Carver's truck and Carver went to the driver's side, got inside, and Dannon took the pistol from his waistband and held it in his right hand, waited as Carver unlocked his door.

When the locks clicked, he opened the door with his left hand and then climbed inside, keeping his right hand out of sight. Carver looked at the dash as he started the car, and Dannon pulled the door shut with his left hand, and Carver shifted into reverse to back out, looked over his left shoulder, checking for traffic . . .

Dannon brought the .22 up and shot him in the temple. Carver's head bounced off the side window and Dannon shot him again, the .22 shots deafening inside the truck, but hardly audible outside. Carver slumped, his face not even looking surprised. Dannon pushed the gear shift back into Park, took a plastic bag out of his jacket pocket and pulled it over Carver's head, and cinched it around his neck. If Carver weren't quite dead, the plastic bag would do the job; and it would keep blood out of the car, though there shouldn't be too much in the way of blood, with the small-caliber bullets going straight into the brain.

That done—it took fifteen seconds—he got out, climbed in the backseat, and pulled Carver into the back, and tried to wedge him down onto the floor. Carver was too big for that, so he got out again, moved the passenger seat fully forward, and pushed Carver's head and chest down on that side, folding his legs onto the other side.

The back windows were darkened, but Dannon walked around to the back of the truck, took out one of the blankets they kept there, for when passengers wanted to sleep on trips, and spread it over Carver's body.

He closed the door and walked back to the driver's side, looking in the side windows as he went: Carver was invisible.

Two minutes after the shooting, he backed the truck out of the parking slot and started toward the exit. He was forty-five minutes from the perfect graveyard.

LUCAS WORKED HIS WAY to the front of the ballroom. Taryn was still talking to people on the stage, but Schiffer had a hand on her back and was moving her toward the stairs. Lucas moved close, where Schiffer could see him, and fixed his eyes on her face and sent her a telepathic message to look at him, and, as usually happened, a few seconds later she glanced his way, recognized him, and frowned. He jabbed a finger at Taryn, and then did it again.

She turned away, but he knew she'd seen him, and as they got closer to the edge of the stage, she said something sharp in Taryn's ear, and Taryn frowned and looked down and saw Lucas, turned and said something to Schiffer that he couldn't hear.

Lucas kept working toward the end of the stage where a crowd was waiting to talk to and touch Taryn as she came off. She moved slowly down the stairs, then through the crowd, shaking hands and patting shoulders. Lucas kept moving to stay directly in front of her, and eventually she got to him and she said, to the side of his face, so only he could hear, "Now you're in real trouble, governor or no governor."

"Why did you send me that message about Dannon and Carver?" Lucas asked.

She pulled her head back and said, "What?"

She didn't send it, Lucas thought. It was right there on her face.

"Do you have your cell phone? You sent me an urgent message from your phone."

She said, "What? Why would I . . ." She turned to look behind her and called, "Marjorie . . . Marjorie."

One of her campaign people, a short woman in a blue dress, shouldered her way through the crowd; she was carrying a clipboard, a huge tote bag, and two purses.

Taryn said to her, "Give me my purse."

The woman handed the purse over. Someone in the crowd tugged on Lucas's jacket, and he half turned and saw Bradley there. She put a hand to her ear, miming a handset, and mouthed, "Right now." Bradley eased back into the crowd and Taryn was saying, "Where's my phone? Marjorie, where's my phone?"

"I . . . I . . . I don't know." Marjorie looked frantic. "I never saw a phone."

"It was in there," Taryn said. "I put it there."

"You did not send me a text message?" Lucas asked her, virtually speaking into her ear. They looked like they were dancing.

She said, "No, no . . ."

Lucas backed away, and Taryn looked after him, puzzled, then dug through her purse again, while talking to Marjorie, and Schiffer began to urge her through the crowd. Lucas got to the edge of the ballroom and stepped behind one of the TV-set stands, put the handset to his face and said, "This is Lucas: What's up?"

Shrake came back instantly: "Carver's truck is moving, it's leaving downtown. Jenkins and I are on it, but we're gonna need help."

Jenkins said, "I was parked in the bottom of the garage, near the exit. I don't think it's Carver in the truck: I think it's Dannon."

"Where's Carver?"

"Don't know."

Del came up: "Dannon's truck is still in the garage. Maybe they switched vehicles."

"Okay," Lucas said. "Jane, Sarah, have you seen Carver?"

Stack came back. "I haven't, not since before you came up. He went in the back . . ."

Bradley said, "I saw Dannon maybe ten minutes ago, going into the back."

Lucas said, "Okay, you guys take off, help Shrake and Jenkins. Chase them down. Lights and sirens until you get close, then hang back and follow, okay?"

"Gotcha," Stack said.

Lucas asked, "Del, you're pretty sure Dannon's truck is still in the garage?"

"Yeah," Del said.

"Okay. Work your way up the parking ramp, see if you can spot him or Carver or the truck. I'm going into the back, see if I can chase them down."

"What's going on?" Del asked.

"I don't know—but Shrake, Jenkins, don't lose that car. Don't let it get too far ahead of you, either. I want you to be able to see it, if it stops."

"That's a risk," Shrake said. "He could spot us."

"I trust your professionalism that that won't happen," Lucas said.

"Thanks a lot," Jenkins said. "Shrake, I'm right behind you. Take a right."

"Taking a right," Shrake said.

"We need to get those goddamn women up here," Jenkins said.

"We're coming, we're coming," Bradley said.

LUCAS BADGED HIS WAY into the back. Taryn and her closest campaign people, including Green, were going through in a cluster, heading for a back elevator that would take them to the parking ramp. Taryn never looked back but Green did; she nodded and went on. Lucas hurriedly checked the back area—no Carver—and then took the stairs down to the parking ramp.

He arrived just as the elevator did. Green took the lead, and they walked over to the truck that Dannon had been driving, and Green took the wheel. Schiffer got in the passenger side and Taryn in the back, and the rest of the crew broke for different vehicles, and Lucas, still not seeing Carver, ran toward the truck carrying Green.

As he did that, Del pulled onto the floor and paused. Lucas ran up to Green's window and she rolled it down and Lucas asked, "Where's Carver?"

Green said, "He and Dannon headed back to the house. We're having an after-party, they're setting up there."

Lucas was unhappy about that, but nodded, and Taryn called, "Where's my phone?"

"Don't know," Lucas said, and he turned and walked down the ramp toward Del's car, putting the handset to his head: "Jenkins . . . I've been told that Carver and Dannon were going together out to Grant's house. Are you sure they weren't both in the car?"

"Man, they had to stop at the pay booth, and I was right there. There was a lot of light behind them, coming through the windows. There was only one guy in the car, and that was Dannon. Unless Carver was on the floor or something."

"Goddamnit," Lucas said. "You think you could buzz him?"

"Yeah. Once."

"Is Shrake close enough to pick him up after you buzz him?"

Shrake: "We're on 94 North, I'm about a quarter mile behind Jenkins. I could do it for a while, but he's driving right at fifty-five. If I hang back here, he could get suspicious. We need Jane and Sarah right now."

Bradley: "We're getting on the ramp now. . . . We're coming."

Lucas said, "Jenkins, go ahead and buzz him. We need to know if both of them are in there."

Lucas walked down to Del's car and Del opened the passenger-side door and asked, "What are we doing?"

"I can't find Carver. Nobody's waiting for him, because they think he already went."

"Is it possible he split?"

"You mean, called a cab or took a bus?"

"Okay, that doesn't seem likely," Del said.

Lucas looked at the phone message again: *Dannon will kill Carver tonight at the hotel and bury him in the perfect graveyard. Best wishes, Taryn.*

"He could be dead," Lucas said.

"That would take balls the size of the Goodyear blimp," Del said.

"I might have put Carver in the shit," Lucas said. "I was trying to drive a wedge between them, but what if he said something, or made some kind of threat, and they decided they needed to get rid of him immediately? What if he tried to blackmail them? What if he gave them a deadline?"

"Then . . ." Del said.

Lucas said, "Let's go back to my car."

"You're going after them?"

"We're both going," Lucas said. "We don't need to track Green.

But if Dannon killed Carver, he's going to dump him. We need to be there—we need everybody to be there."

"I could drive," Del said.

"They're too far ahead of us," Lucas said. "I need to drive."

"Goddamnit. I hate it when you drive," Del said. "I get so puckered up that I've got to pull my asshole back out with a nut pick."

"Thanks for the image," Lucas said. "Let's go."

26

They left Del's car in the garage and took off in Lucas's Lexus, lights and siren, Lucas turning the corner and busting the red light and then off through traffic to I-94, Del braced against collision, hanging on to his seat-belt strap with one hand, the other hand braced against the dashboard.

"Ask them where Dannon is at," Lucas said, as they rolled onto the interstate.

Del got on the handset, and Shrake came back with a mileage marker and Del said, "They've got seventeen miles on us."

"But they're going fifty-five and we're going ninety-five." Lucas did some math in his head and said, "We'll be catching up two-thirds of a mile every minute, so we'll catch them in more or less twenty-five minutes. That's not fast enough."

He dropped the hammer and the big Lexus groaned as it edged past a hundred miles an hour, then to a hundred and five.

"How do you do that?" Del asked.

"Do what?"

"That math?"

"The same way you would have done it, if you'd had nuns

beating fractions into your head in third, fourth, and fifth grades," Lucas said.

"How fast will it take us to catch them at a hundred and five?"

"Uh, about . . . five-sixths of a mile every minute . . . we're about sixteen miles behind them now . . . you take sixteen divided by five and multiplied by six . . . about nineteen and one-fifth minutes . . . more or less."

"How do you know it's five-sixths of a mile every minute?"

"Because sixty miles an hour is a mile a minute. We're going fifty miles an hour faster than they are, and that's five-sixths of sixty . . . so we catch up five-sixths of a mile every minute."

"Well, hell, even I could do that."

"Yeah, if you knew how."

JENKINS CALLED. "There's one guy in the truck. I came up fast with my high lights on and illuminated the truck, then passed him in a hurry, like I was an asshole. There's only one guy in the truck."

Lucas took the handset from Del: "Get as far out in front of him as you have to, to lose his headlights. Then find a side road and dodge off on it, until he passes. Then get behind again. Where in the hell are Jane and Sarah?"

"Jane is a mile behind Shrake, and I'm right behind her," Bradley said. "I'm going to start falling back in case she has to pass Dannon."

Shrake said, "I'm gonna have to pass in the next couple of minutes. I'm coming up on him."

Stack: "I'll tell you what—he's not going to Taryn Grant's place. Not unless he's taking the way-scenic route."

———

THAT'S THE WAY IT went for sixteen minutes. At four minutes, Shrake had to pass. He also reported one person at the wheel, and that he was sure it was Dannon. Stack moved up until she was running a half-mile behind Dannon, and Jenkins, coming off a side road, fell in behind Stack and ahead of Bradley. Bradley passed him, so that Jenkins could hang back longer. By then they were well up I-94, running parallel to the Mississippi River.

At sixteen minutes, Jenkins called to say that he could see Lucas's flashers. Lucas turned off the lights and eased off the gas. They passed Monticello, the city lights spreading off to the right, toward the Mississippi, and then plunged back into the dark. Five minutes later, he came up behind Jenkins and dropped his speed to fifty-five. They ran like that for another fifteen minutes, and as Stack was coming up on Dannon, she called and said, "I think he's getting off at the exit. . . . He's getting off. I'm going straight."

Lucas: "Jenkins, pull off and kill your lights. Sarah, keep going behind Jane, turn around as soon as you can."

As Jenkins moved to the shoulder, Lucas pulled over behind him, then fished an iPad out of the seat pocket behind Del.

Jenkins, looking at the GPS tracker, called: "He's gone right, he's headed down toward the river."

Lucas thought, *Perfect graveyard.* He called back, "Wait one," brought the iPad up, went to Google Earth, got a satellite view of the area and said, "There's no bridge down there. It's not a dead end, just a bunch of back roads."

Jenkins: "Let's go to the top of the overpass."

"Go," Lucas said, and they waited until a couple of cars passed, then ran dark to the overpass and up the exit ramp, and pulled off at the top. In the distance, probably a mile away, they could still see Dannon's taillights. He seemed to be moving slowly, tentatively. Lucas went back to Google Earth, pulled up a measuring stick. He hopped out of the Lexus and carried the iPad to Jenkins's car, and stood by the driver's-side window.

"He's about one-point-two miles in," Jenkins said, looking at the monitor for the GPS bug.

Lucas enlarged the satellite view, then stretched the measuring tape down the map. There was nothing on the map at 1.2 miles, but at 1.4, there was a minor track going off to the left, probably gravel or dirt, along the river.

They watched the monitor and the iPad, and at 1.4, the taillights disappeared, but they could see the faint streak of headlights, now running parallel to both the highway and the river. Two-tenths of a mile down the side road, Dannon stopped. Below them, on the highway, Shrake did an illegal U-turn across the interstate median, and came up the ramp; a minute later, he was followed by both Bradley and Stack.

When they were up, they got out of their cars and gathered around Lucas, who said, "We're going to head down to that intersection. About one-point-four miles. No lights. When we're there, we'll go in on foot. He's about two-tenths of a mile in, probably three or four hundred yards. I want Sarah and Jane to stay with the cars."

"I want to go in," Stack said.

And Bradley: "I do, too."

"I don't have time to argue," Lucas said. "The fact is, we'll be on foot, and you don't have the shoes for it. If he sees us coming, he could come busting out of there in that truck, and we'll be in trouble. We need somebody in the cars who can take him, if it comes to that. Jenkins, Shrake, Del, and I have all done this before, and we've all been in gunfights. You two haven't. So, you stay with the cars. End of story. Let's load up and go."

THE TWO WOMEN WEREN'T happy about it, but they did it.

Jenkins had a pair of night-vision goggles, and the most experience with them. He'd lead. All six of the cops had LED flashlights, big 135-Lumen Streamlights. They all loaded up and started down the side road, running dark, except for taillights, following Jenkins.

The countryside was densely wooded, with breaks for the occasional farmstead and backwoods house; and with the clouds, black as a coal mine. Lucas could barely see the road in front of him, and took it slowly, at twenty miles an hour, watching Jenkins's taillights, feeling for the right edge of the tarmac with his tires.

"At twenty miles an hour, how long does it take to go one-point-four miles?" Del asked.

"You'd go a mile in three minutes," Lucas said. "You'd go the rest of the way in four-tenths of three minutes. Three minutes is one hundred and eighty seconds, and one-tenth of that is eighteen seconds. Four-tenths would be seventy-two seconds. So, four minutes and twelve seconds."

"How big a grave can you dig in four minutes and twelve seconds?"

"Don't have the math on that one," Lucas said.

AT A LITTLE MORE than 1.3 miles on Lucas's odometer, they saw the road going left, which looked like a darker tunnel on a black sheet. Jenkins pulled off to the left side of the road, Lucas edged off behind him, and the others followed. They all climbed out into the cold night, and Lucas whispered, "No talking. This guy might have experience night-fighting. Spread out, don't shoot each other. Stay on the road. No noise."

The four men moved off, spread across the road like gunfighters in an old spaghetti western; and, Lucas thought, they *were* gunfighters, every one of them. Jenkins was the lead man, with two to his left, one to his right, in a V, like a bunch of Canada geese headed south.

Lucas was counting steps. Two hundred and eighty slow steps down the road, and they could hear Dannon working, the rhythmic *chh! chh! chh! chh!* of a spade digging into damp earth, but they couldn't see him.

WHEN DANNON WAS IN the army, he'd served as company level and battalion level intelligence officer. In the latter job, in Afghanistan, he'd serviced a dozen sources in villages scattered around the forward operating base. They would call into the cell number and leave messages, which the native translator would render into English. Most of it was inconsequential—this guy or that guy had come or gone, and he was Taliban or an Arab or whatever. Arabs were always interesting, because they were rare and sometimes important. Most times, they were kids from Saudi or Jordan looking to make their bones, wandering across the landscape like itinerant skateboarders; but sometimes interesting. The Americans usually tried to pick up the Arabs.

The actual pickups were done by special ops people. Dannon had gone along on a number of the operations, when there was space available—the commander encouraged staff people to get out in the weeds—and had twice been involved in firefights with the targets. Both times, they'd been kids, and both times, killed.

But.

Except for the fights themselves, it had always been high-tech: sources fingering the targets, live calls when a target was leaving a village, tracking them from gunships, then closing them down.

He'd never used a GPS tracker, and it never occurred to him that there might be one on his truck. He'd never been tailed, and though he'd watched his rearview mirror, looking for cars that were pacing him, it never occurred to him that cars that overtook him and disappeared in the distance were the watchers. He'd never thought that night-vision goggles could be used against him.

He'd never been snuck up on in the dark.

But.

He'd sat on nighttime ambushes, every sense digging into the dark, and as he dug Carver's grave, that was operating on some level. At one point, a few minutes after he started digging into the reeds in the swampland, he picked up what seemed to be a vibration. He stopped digging and walked out to the road, and peered in the dark toward the turnoff. Nothing but darkness.

He turned back, navigating with a taped flashlight, a thin needle of light showing him the path.

He worked for another five minutes, and then felt another chill. What *was* that?

There was no specific noise, other than the engines from the interstate, a mile away, but there was something under that . . . an unidentifiable pattern . . .

He didn't feel foolish at all: the special ops people always had said that when you had a feeling, pay attention to it; most times, it was nothing. The other time, if you hadn't paid attention, it would kill you. So he paid attention, sitting, no longer digging. The burial site, near where they'd put Tubbs down, was off a gravel track, down a path that led to the river, and then off the path fifteen yards.

Lots of zigs and zags.

He was invisible, he thought. He sat, listening, listening . . .

And heard the crunch of gravel.

No. Imagined he heard the crunch of gravel? He wasn't sure. He slipped his gun out of its holster, pressed the safety forward.

Duckwalked out to the path to the river.

A MINUTE OFF THE TRACK, Lucas felt Del's arm slow him down, and pull him in. They bunched up and Jenkins whispered, "His truck is twenty-five or thirty feet in front of us. I think he's off to the right, right by the truck."

Lucas said, "Keep the lights handy. Light him up if you see him."

They moved on, up to the truck; and then a few steps beyond. Lucas heard the crunch of gravel and put out a hand to Del, who was to his left, stopping him in his tracks. Del did the same, to Jenkins, and Jenkins to Shrake. They all froze, and listened, peering into the blackness.

Three of them could see nothing; but there was some kind of faint, faint noise coming from the front. Jenkins saw Dannon edge into the path, a gun in his hand.

Jenkins had his flashlight in his left hand. He pointed it at Dannon's eyes, pointed his pistol, and without warning, turned it on.

Dannon was there, thirty feet away, pinned by the dazzling light like a frog on a tenth-grader's dissection tray. Unlike those frogs . . .

Jenkins shouted, "Freeze, freeze or we'll shoot."

. . . Unlike those frogs, Dannon leaped sideways back into the swamp reeds and then, scrambling on his hands and knees, still clinging to his pistol, began running mindlessly through the brush.

The cops all turned on their lights and played them through the brush, and caught flashes of Dannon, the movement of the swamp weeds and brush as he tore through them, and Lucas shouted, "Jenkins, Shrake, Del, go after him, take care, take care . . ."

Lucas turned and in the light of his own flash, ran back up the dirt track toward the gravel road, pulled his handset and said, "Sarah, Jane, he's coming right at you. Watch out, watch out, he's on foot, I think he's coming for the road. . . ."

NOTHING AT ALL WENT through Dannon's head. He'd had some escape and evasion classes, and one of the basics was simply to put distance between yourself and your pursuer. Distance was always good; distance gave you options. He didn't think about it, though, he just ran, fast and as hard as he could, and he was in good shape.

Good shape or not, he fell three or four times—he wasn't counting—and the small shrub and grasses tore at him and tried to catch his feet; he went knee-deep into a watery hole, pulled free, and ran on, looking back once. He was out of the light, now, he was gaining on them, he was almost there . . .

And he broke free into the road. He couldn't see it, except as a kind of dark channel in front of him. The lights were now a hundred yards back, but still coming, and he ran down the dark channel. When he got far enough out front, he'd cut across country again, and then maybe turn down toward the river. . . .

He ran a hundred yards down the channel, heedless of the sounds of his footfalls, breathing hard. . . .

———

LUCAS WAS ON THE ROAD, moving faster than Dannon, but at the wrong angle—Dannon, though in the swamp, was cutting diagonally across the right angle of the gravel road and the dirt track. Lucas could tell more or less where he was because of the brilliant lights of the cops behind him, and the sound of Dannon's thrashing in the brush. Then the thrashing stopped, and Lucas stopped, trying to figure out where he'd gone.

BRADLEY AND STACK HEARD him coming. Stack whispered, "I'm going to hit the car lights."

"Okay."

Stack reached to the light switch, to the left of the steering wheel, and waited, waited, trying to judge the distance, and when it seemed that he might be close enough,

Flipped the switch.

And Dannon was there, covered with mud, clothes hanging wet from his body, a bloody patch on his head, mouth hanging open. He had a gun in his hand and as Stack stepped to the left of Bradley, he brought it up and Bradley screamed, "Drop the gun," and he didn't, he brought it higher . . .

The women shot him.

Later, it would turn out that they'd each fired four times, though neither was counting, and of the eight shots, had hit him five times.

Two of the shots would have been wounding; two of the shots would have killed him in seconds or minutes; one of them went through his throat and severed his spinal cord, and Dannon went down like Raggedy Andy.

27

ucas not only heard the gunfire, but saw it. He was at right angles to the confrontation, running back to the cars, saw the lights go on, and then behind the lights, the sound of the gunfire and the flicker of the muzzle flashes. The women were both shooting 9mm weapons, and the flashes were small, even in the dark night. He shouted, "Davenport coming in . . ."

Running as hard as he could, he was there in fifteen seconds. The two women were still by the cars, guns pointed at Dannon's body. Lucas came up, and Bradley said, her voice cool, "He had a gun, he pointed it at us."

Lucas nodded once, said into his handset, "You guys get to the closest road, he's down."

He did that as he stepped over to Dannon's body and checked it. He was on his side; blood pooling around him, his gun still gripped in his hand.

Lucas backed away, and Jenkins ran up and looked at the body.

He said, "Who . . . ?"

Bradley said, "We did."

"Jesus," Jenkins said.

Del and Shrake came up and stopped beside Jenkins; all three of them were covered with mud, their trousers wet above the knees. Del had a scrape above one eye. Lucas said to Jenkins, "Get your flashers on, block the road. Figure out what county we're in, and call the sheriff's office and get some deputies down here."

To Shrake: "Call the duty officer and get a crime-scene crew on the way. Tell them to bring lights—lots of lights. Tell them to hurry."

And to Bradley and Stack: "You two put your guns away. Decock them but leave them in the same condition, don't reload them. Stay around the car, don't approach the body."

To Del: "Come on. We've got to check on Carver."

"Hope to hell Carver's down there," Del said. "Be a hell of a note if Dannon was out digging black dirt for his flower garden."

THEY HURRIED ALONG THROUGH the night, turned the corner down the dirt track, to Dannon's truck. They shone lights in the window, without touching the truck, but it was empty. They then stepped carefully through the brush back to the spot where they'd heard Dannon digging. There was a hole in the ground, and beside it, a bulky body with a plastic bag on the head. "That's him," Lucas said. "I'm not gonna touch the bag."

"You think Tubbs is out here?" Del asked.

"I'd bet on it, but I'm not looking around here now," Lucas said, shining the light down on his shoes. The ground was damp, but not actually swampy where he was standing.

"One thing about November," Del said, shining his flash up into the sky. "No bugs."

"Yeah, that's one thing about it," Lucas said. "Let's go back and wait for the crime-scene people."

———

THEY HAD THREE SHERIFF'S cars at the scene in twenty minutes, one blocking the road, the other down by the mouth of the dirt track, one with the BCA group. The crime-scene truck arrived a few minutes after three-thirty, and took charge of the scene, along with the sheriff's deputies. They also took charge of the women's pistols.

After they'd walked the crime-scene crew through the entire action, and marked the critical bits, Lucas ordered the two women and Shrake and Jenkins back to BCA headquarters: "I want full preliminary reports from everyone, start to finish, with timelines. Right now, tonight. When you're done, cross-check them, then get some sleep. We'll meet tomorrow at one o'clock in the afternoon and figure out the bureaucratics. Jane and Sarah, you did good. The guy murdered at least three people in cold blood, and if you hadn't shot him, he'd have killed you and taken one of the cars. Nobody could have asked for more."

Lucas called the BCA duty officer and asked him to send another crew to cover Dannon's and Carver's apartments. "Seal them off at a minimum."

The four of them coughed and shuffled their feet and talked for a minute or two, before going to their vehicles, to trundle back up the road. By that time, both the area around Dannon and the area around Carver were bathed in work light, and one of the crime-scene people was making a movie of the shooting area.

Del asked, "We're staying?"

"We might have to come back, but right now, we're going to talk to Taryn Grant."

"You think she knew about this?"

"I . . ." Lucas had to stop and think. "I'd give you six-to-five that she did. No better than that. We have nothing with her name on it. If she's involved, we'll have to find something in Dannon's apartment. Probably not Carver's."

BY THE TIME THEY got back to town, it was after five o'clock, not even a hint of the dawn. They dropped off I-94 onto I-494 at the western edge of the metro area, then turned off and headed deeper west, into the lake neighborhoods. When they got to Grant's house, they found the street deserted; no well-wishers, no TV trucks. There were a few lights in the house, and two security guards at the driveway.

Lucas and Del got out of Lucas's truck and walked up the driveway. The guards moved down to block them, and Lucas pulled out his ID and said, "We're with the Bureau of Criminal Apprehension. We need to wake Ms. Grant. Now."

One of the guards looked at the ID with his flashlight and said, "You got it . . . but I think she's still awake. There are still some people here."

Del asked, "Any more of you guys around?"

"Yeah, one guy behind the house, he moves back and forth across the yard."

THEY WALKED UP TO the front door, rang the bell. Del scratched his neck and looked at the yellow bug light and said, "I *feel* like a bug."

"You look like a bug. You fall down out there?"

"About four times. We weren't running so much as staggering

around. Potholes full of water . . . I see you kept your French shoes nice and dry."

"English. English shoes . . . French shirts. Italian suits. Try to remember that."

"Makes my nose bleed," Del said.

The door opened, and Green looked out: she was still fully dressed, including the jacket that covered her gun and the fashionable shoes that she could run in.

She took a long look at Del, and asked, "Where're Dannon and Carver?"

"Dead," Lucas said. "Where's Grant?"

"In the living room."

"You want to invite us in?"

She opened the door, and they stepped inside, and followed her to the living room.

Grant was there, still dressed as she had been on the stage; she was curled in an easy chair, with a drink in her hand, high heels on the floor beside her. Schiffer was lying on a couch, barefoot; a couple of Taryn's staff people, a young woman and a young man, were sitting on the floor, making a circle. Another man, heavier and older, was sitting in a leather chair facing Grant. Lucas didn't recognize him, but recognized the type: a guy who knew where all the notional bodies were buried, a guy who could get the vice president on the telephone.

When Lucas came in, behind Green, Grant stood up, putting her drink aside, and asked, "What? What now?"

"Your pal Dannon murdered your pal Carver and took his body out in the countryside to bury it. We were tracking him, and when we approached him at the grave he was digging, he tried to shoot it out. He's dead."

There was a moment of utter silence: Schiffer seemed to be the most affected, as she got to her feet, her face gone white, a hand at her throat.

Grant recovered first, and asked, "What . . . does that mean?"

"We were hoping you could help us with that," Lucas said.

"I don't know what that means," Grant said.

"You sent me a message earlier tonight . . ." Lucas began.

Grant put up a hand: "No. No, I didn't. I already told you that."

Lucas took his phone out of his pocket, called up the message, stepped up to her and said, "Here's the message. Is this your phone number?"

She looked at the message and the number, and said, "That's not right. That's crazy."

"Is that your phone number?"

"Yes, but my phone, I can't find my phone. It's gone. Somebody took it out of my purse. Marjorie had my purse . . ."

She looked at the woman on the floor, who said, "I was really careful with the purse. It was zipped up."

Lucas said, "The call came in at ten-oh-six. You were still here at ten-oh-six, weren't you?"

Grant looked at Schiffer, who said, "Yes . . . we were still here. We left for the hotel around ten-fifteen."

Grant said, "Then the phone call came from here. My purse was back in the bedroom. In fact . . ." She looked at Schiffer. "In fact, you called me while I was back there."

They stared at each other for a moment, then Schiffer said, "That's right," dug around in her bag, pulled out her phone, and said, "I made that call at nine-fifty-eight. What's that . . . eight minutes before you got the message?"

"There was nobody in the bedroom but me. I went back there

to get ready to go," Grant said. To Schiffer: "I got the call from you . . . I put my phone back in my bag. My bag was on the chest of drawers."

Green stepped over to Grant and took her by the arm and said, "One second . . ." She pulled Grant off to one side, twenty feet away, stood with her back to Lucas and the rest of the group, and whispered directly into Grant's ear. Grant looked at her, then nodded, came back and said, "I'd like to alter that statement a bit. Doug Dannon escorted me back there. We didn't talk, I just wanted some privacy to pee. I was alone when Connie called, and I dropped my phone back in my purse and came straight out here. Then when we were ready to go, I went back and got my purse."

"Can we look at the bedroom?" Lucas asked.

Schiffer said, "Maybe we ought to have a lawyer."

Lucas: "There's a very good chance . . . actually, it's not a chance, it's a certainty, that this is a crime scene. Somebody called me on Ms. Grant's phone, who had knowledge that Dannon was planning to kill Carver. As he did. A lawyer might tell you not to talk, but he can't keep us away from a crime scene."

Schiffer shrugged, and Grant said, "I don't care, anyway. This is . . . awful. Awful! This is insane! The bedroom . . ."

She walked back toward the bedroom wing, and Lucas, Del, Schiffer, Green, and the others followed. Halfway down the hall, Lucas looked back and said, "I don't want anyone here except Ms. Grant."

Grant said to Lucas, "I want witnesses. You have lied to me and worked for Smalls since the beginning of this thing, and I wouldn't put it past you to frame me. I want witnesses. I want Connie and Alice with me."

Lucas said, "I did not . . ." Then he stopped and nodded. "Ms.

Green and Ms. Schiffer. Nobody else. Do not touch a thing. Stand in the doorway where you can see and hear, but do not touch anything. Do not touch the door or the doorknobs or anything else."

They stepped inside the bedroom and Grant pointed to her left and said, "I went in there to use the bathroom. My purse was right here, on the dresser." She pointed at the dresser. "Doug was out in the hall. Nobody could have gotten past him, without him knowing. And I don't know why a, a . . . confederate . . . of his would call to say he was planning to kill Ron. Anyway, I used the bathroom, and came out, and as I came out, the phone rang, and I talked to Connie, and then put the phone back in the purse and went out. With Doug . . ."

When they'd entered the bedroom, Del had slid off to the left to clear the bathroom. He came back and listened to Grant's narration. When she finished, he asked, "When you were in the bathroom, did you notice anything unusual? Did you look out the window?"

"Out the window? No, I didn't look out . . . Why?"

"Because the window seems to be missing," Del said.

LUCAS HAD BEEN INVOLVED in any number of clusterfucks in his working life, but the one at Grant's house was notable. They all went to look at the window, which was, without a doubt, missing. Then they trooped around to the backyard, where they found three separate sheets of glass lying under an arborvitae.

Lucas said, "Why would—"

Taryn put a hand to her lips and said, "Could they get in the safe?"

"What safe?" Del asked.

They trooped back inside, and Taryn reached behind a side table and did something, and a bookcase rotated out from the wall. They all looked at the safe, which was closed. She said, "Would you turn away for a minute?" and they did, and turned back when she said, "Okay," and turned the heavy handle that worked the safe locks.

She pulled the door open and looked into a safe that was completely empty.

In the silence, she stumbled backward, staring at the empty steel hole in the wall, and screamed, "No! No! No!"

Lucas was looking at her face when she opened the safe, and in his estimation, there was no chance that she was faking the reaction. Not even if she was crazy; not even if she'd known the safe was empty, and had rehearsed.

No chance.

LUCAS MOVED EVERYBODY out to the living room, and sat them down, and called the BCA duty officer again, and told him what had happened. He said, "You've got people spread all over the metro area."

"Leave the Dannon and Carver apartments. Seal them up—we can get to them later. Right now, I need a crew here. Get them moving."

Grant was pacing the living room, hands to her face. Everybody else sat without talking. Green went into the kitchen to get something to drink, and Lucas followed her. She handed him a personal-sized bottle of orange juice, opened one for herself, and asked, "Is there any possible way to keep me out of this? As an informant? I need the work."

"If you don't have a problem with the possibility of a little perjury," Lucas said.

"I don't, because I never told you anything meaningful," she said.

"I keep thinking, the one person who may have had access to that phone, and who might have been aware of the whole Dannon-Carver situation, and who might have been willing to warn me . . . was you."

"But I didn't. And when we give our statements, you'll find that I was right on the door when Taryn went back to the bedroom with Doug. I was monitoring the door, and the comings and goings, every minute. I couldn't have made that phone call: and I didn't."

"So you're out, if that's what the statements show," Lucas said. "I'm leaving my ass in your hands. I won't mention you, and you don't mention me, except when we spoke in public."

"Thank you."

They carried the bottles of juice back into the living room, where Grant looked at them, and muttered, almost to herself, "Almost four million."

Lucas: "What?"

"That's what they got—whoever it was. Four million. Cash, gold coins, and mostly a lot of jewelry. Diamonds, gold. The Star of Kandiyohi, which is a diamond as big as a robin's egg, a Patek Philippe watch that I got from my grandfather, worth a quarter million dollars all by itself. . . ."

Schiffer looked at her and said, "Okay. Agent Davenport has his crime scene. But you are a United States Senator-elect, and we have important issues to deal with. We need legal advice. Now."

Schiffer looked around: "Not another word, anybody. Not another word to Agent Davenport or other police officers, not until the lawyers get here."

28

Weather usually slept hard from ten o'clock at night until six in the morning. Lucas came to bed at all kinds of times, usually between midnight and three, so when he didn't come to bed on election night, she didn't miss him until she woke up at six. Then she got on the phone, a cold clutch in the stomach, and when he answered, she said, "You're not shot."

"No," he said. "But there was some shooting."

He spent five minutes telling her about it, in detail, and at the end of it, she said, "I'm revising a rhino in two hours and I'm shaking like a leaf." Translated: She was fixing a nose job that some other surgeon had messed up.

"Stop shaking," Lucas said. "I'm fine, Jenkins and Shrake are fine, Bradley and Stack are a little screwed up, but they'll be okay, and Del is good, except that he looks like a bug."

Then he had to explain that.

THE LAWYERS ARRIVED, and officially informed Lucas that there would be no further statements from the principals, until there had been extensive consultations. They said it in a long-winded way, and Lucas had to take a break from it, when a crime-scene supervisor called.

"We've been out here walking the area and we've found what looks a lot like another grave. It's about a hundred and fifty feet from the grave Dannon was digging, on the same track, on the same side of the road. We'll document it and open it."

"Do that," Lucas said. "It's Tubbs."

THE CRIME-SCENE CREW ARRIVED in force, and started by processing the window in Taryn's bathroom and the ground outside. They would get to the safe, but the supervisor complained to Lucas, "Why'd you let her open the safe? There might have been prints on the keypad."

"Given the look of the rest of it, do you really think so?" Lucas asked.

"Well, no. But . . ."

"No buts. If this was a real robbery, it was a pro. Like, a top pro," Lucas said.

"You think it wasn't real?"

"I'm not sure of anything," Lucas said. He looked at his watch: "Gotta make a call. I'll talk to you again before I leave."

THE SUN WAS UP, somewhere behind the clouds, but exactly where was hard to tell. In any case, it was light outside when Lucas wandered down to the end of the driveway and called the governor.

The governor's phone rang four times, then Henderson said, "This time of the morning, it can't be good."

"About your party's senator-elect: her top security guy murdered another one of her security people and tried to bury him by the Mississippi halfway to St. Cloud. We interrupted that and there was a shoot-out and he was killed. The crime scene has found another dug-up area nearby. I think they'll be pulling Tubbs out of there, in the next couple of hours."

After a moment, the governor laughed and said, "You are a piece of work, Lucas. You and that fuckin' Flowers, both of you. I really get my entertainment dollar's worth."

"The last person who said I was a piece of work, offered to take me to bed," Lucas said.

"Well, I'll pass on that," Henderson said. Then, after a moment of silence, the governor said, "I'll have to mediate this. I'll have to confer with other Important People. Porter, of course, is going to lay an ostrich-sized egg. I don't see how Grant can stay on as a senator, and frankly, that's about the best possible outcome I could have imagined."

"How's that?" Lucas asked.

"Guess who would appoint her replacement?" Henderson said. "I'd have Porter Smalls out of my hair and a new senator who would be wildly happy about supporting me for a better job . . . if somebody goes looking for, say, a vice president."

"That hadn't occurred to me," Lucas said.

"Because you're not a natural politician," the governor said. He laughed again. "This is the kind of thing that makes life interesting."

"Unless you're Dannon. Or Carver."

"Well, yeah, I suppose," the governor said. "I'll assign somebody to say a prayer for them."

AFTER THAT, IT WAS a lot of crime-scene stuff, lawyers and political wrangling. Tubbs was dug up and after a nasty autopsy, he was reburied. He'd been hit on the head with a heavy, rounded object like a baseball bat. Death had not been quick.

They found the smear of blood that Tubbs had left in Dannon's car. Unfortunately, the crime-scene tech who found it, and sampled it, unknowingly destroyed the scrawled TG—for Taryn Grant— that Tubbs had hoped they'd see. DNA proved that Tubbs had been in Dannon's car, but they already knew that Dannon or Carver had killed him. So Tubbs's last, fading, flickering effort came to nothing.

LUCAS GOT STATEMENTS from everybody and Alice Green had been telling the truth: at the time Grant went to the bedroom with Dannon, Green had been assigned to the door, and could be seen doing that on the security tapes. Connie Schiffer, in particular, had been curious about Grant and Dannon leaving the party, heading back to the bedroom, and had exchanged looks with Green.

One other politician, arriving late to congratulate the new senator, spoke to Green at the door, and remembered that Grant had not been in the room when he got there. He asked for her, and a moment later she reappeared from the direction of the bedroom, to give him a hug.

The tapes of the bedroom showed nothing, because the room started out dark. Then there was a flicker of light, apparently when Grant walked into the room, and she'd reached out (automatically, she said) and hit the privacy switch, which turned the cameras off. A minute later, she hit the privacy switch again (again, she said, an automatic reflex) and turned the cameras back on as she left. She left the door open, so there was a bit of light, and then a short time later, the door mysteriously closed again, killing the light. There was nothing more on the tape for several hours, when Grant got back from the hotel and hit the privacy switch on the way to the bathroom.

The next people on the tape were Grant, Lucas, Del, and the others, going down to investigate the bedroom.

All of that supported what both Grant and Green had said, except on one point: Grant hadn't been in the bedroom long enough to get to the bathroom and pee, not unless she'd set the women's North American land-speed record for micturition. Nor had she reported the cut-out windows, which seemed impossible to miss. The toilet was in a separate booth, and the window was right overhead. But she was sticking to her story, saying that she hadn't bothered to turn the light on in the bathroom and was in a hurry and simply hadn't noticed the windows. In reality, Lucas suspected she'd gone back to talk with Dannon, but didn't want to admit it, because the next thing Dannon did was kill Carver.

He also suspected the robbery had taken place when the door mysteriously closed, because that must have been when the phone was stolen; and after the party had gone to the hotel for the victory celebration, the house had been closed and the dogs turned loose.

He further suspected that Green, or possibly Carver, could have had something to do with the robbery: probably through an accomplice. He thought that because they monitored the security cameras, and if Grant had ever forgotten to turn the cameras off, could have seen her opening the safe; they probably knew something about the contents of the safe, and that it would be well worth hitting; and they knew about the security measures outside. Also, both Green and Carver had his phone number.

He still didn't understand why either one would call him with the message from "Taryn."

That made no sense at all.

ONE OF THE CRIME-SCENE crew had found what appeared to be two small imprints under the arborvitae bush below the bathroom window. One looked like an impression from the outer edge of a hand; the other just a little curve in the dirt, possibly the impression of a heel. He'd taken photos of both.

When he showed the photos to Lucas, he said, "We're not sure that they are what I think they are. I couldn't testify to it . . . I mean, I could say what I think, but any good defense attorney would tear my ass off."

"Cut the crap: What do you think?"

"The curves are small . . . like a small hand and a small heel. Like they were made by a woman."

Somebody with large balls, like an ex–Secret Service woman, Lucas thought. Could Green have cut the windows out earlier in the day, to make way for an accomplice? But that seemed unlikely. Why would she think that Grant wouldn't be going back to pee, and wouldn't notice the cut-out windows?

THE POLITICAL WRANGLING WAS more amusing than anything. The governor called, laughing again, a week after the murders hit the newspapers, and said, "Well, I called and told our senator-elect what all the Important People said, and she said I should write it all down on a piece of paper, roll it into a sharp little cone, and shove it where the sun don't shine. She's not quitting."

"Jesus, I thought she *had* to, from what I've been reading," Lucas said.

"With a billion dollars, you don't have to do much of anything you don't want to, and she doesn't want to quit," the governor said. "If she does a few million in political advertising over the next six years, nobody'll even remember this little dustup. So, we're moving right along to the important stuff, like revising the estate tax."

"That's the end of it?"

"Not quite. I've invited Grant to a little confab in my office tomorrow, with Porter Smalls. Mitford will be there, and her campaign manager, and I'd like you to sit in. And I'll get Rose Marie to come along."

"Why is that?"

"Because I want everybody clear on what happened here, and why everybody did what they did—including you and me," the governor said.

THE NEXT AFTERNOON, they all got together at the Capitol, in the governor's conference room: Henderson, Grant, Smalls, Mitford, Rose Marie, Lucas, Connie Schiffer, and Alice Green, still working as Taryn's security.

For a political gathering, there was a remarkable lack of even symbolic amity. The governor shook hands with everybody, but nobody shook hands with anybody else.

The governor sat at the head of the conference table, cleared his throat, and said, "I don't expect all of us to be pals after this, but I'd at least like to get things clear for everybody. Senator-elect Grant has, of course, made it clear that she didn't have anything to do with the rogue security people on her campaign staff, and in fact feels that she was being set up for long-term blackmail by those same people. In any case, she will not resign and will take her seat in the Senate in January."

Smalls said, "I think that—"

The governor: "Shut up for a minute, will you, Porter? Let me finish."

"I just—"

"You'll have your chance," Henderson said. He looked at Taryn Grant and asked, "Setting aside all the BS aimed at the media, am I correct that this is your position?"

Grant nodded: "Yes."

Connie Schiffer started to say, "I think we all know that Senator Smalls—"

The governor interrupted: "No. Be quiet. We don't want any of that. So we know that Senator-elect Grant will take her seat in the Senate. I'll now turn to Lucas Davenport, the lead investigator in this case. Lucas, do you have any issues that you will continue to pursue?"

Lucas said, "There are several small mysteries about the whole case that I'd like to resolve, and some minor entanglements—for example, Minneapolis still has to decide what to do about the files that were used to frame Senator Smalls. But at this moment, I see no further possibility for arrests or prosecutions involving anyone in this room. I will tell you that I suspect that Senator-elect Grant is not telling us all that we need to know to effectively close out this case. I have no proof of that, and I see no way to get any proof, unless it turns out that either Douglas Dannon or Ronald Carver has somewhere left behind some evidence of her involvement. We have been through both of their town houses, and through Dannon's safe-deposit box at Wells Fargo. We found considerable cash, but we found nothing that would implicate Senator-elect Grant in any wrongdoing."

"So you're at the end of that road," Henderson said.

"Yes, unless something extraordinary turns up, but I don't think that will happen."

Henderson said, "Okay. I want to tell everybody that I asked that Lucas be assigned to this case, because I trust him absolutely. And now I am ordering him not to speak to any media or to anyone else regarding his suspicions about anybody in this case, unless or until he has absolute proof of wrongdoing. Is that clear to everybody? Lucas?"

"That's clear," Lucas said.

Henderson turned to Smalls: "Porter."

Smalls said, "This is one of the most disgraceful moments in the history of American politics and I'm a student of that history, so I know. I was the victim of the most brutal character assassination ever carried out against an American politician, and the main financial sponsor of that assassination actually benefits, and goes to the Senate. Well, I'll tell you—there are people on both sides of the Senate aisle who are frightened by what was done here. I will go to Washington for the lame-duck session, and I will talk to my friends there."

He looked directly at Grant: "I will tell them that I think you are guilty of the murder of three people and that you were the sponsor of the child-pornography smear, and that I think a person of your brand of social pathology—I believe you are a psychopath, and I will tell them that—has no place in the Senate. And I will continue to argue that here in Minnesota for the full six years of your term, and do everything I can to wreck any possible political career that you might otherwise have had."

Grant smiled at him and said, "Fuck you."

The governor said, "Okay, okay, Porter. Now, Taryn, do you have anything for us?"

"No, not really. I'll be the best senator I can be, I reject any notion that I was involved in this craziness." She looked at Smalls: "As for you, bring it on. If you want to spend six years fighting over this, by the time we're done, you'll be unemployable and broke. I would have no problem setting aside, say, a hundred million dollars for a media campaign to defend myself."

"Fuck *you*," Smalls said. And, "By the way, I'd like to thank Agent Davenport for his work on this. I thought he did a brilliant job, even if I wound up losing."

Grant jumped in: "And I'd like to say that I think Davenport created the conditions that unnecessarily led to the deaths in this case, that if he'd been a little more circumspect, we might still have Helen Roman and Carver and Dannon alive, and might be able to actually prove what happened, so that I'd be definitively cleared."

Smalls made a noise that sounded like a fart, and Henderson said, "Thank you for that comment, Porter."

After some more back-and-forth, Henderson declared the meeting over. "We all need to go back and think about what we've heard here today, think really hard about it. We need to start winding down the war. We don't need anything like this to ever happen again."

The people at the meeting flowed out of the conference room, into the outer office, but then stopped to talk: Grant with Schiffer and Rose Marie, Smalls with Mitford. Henderson pulled Lucas aside and said, "Let's keep the rest of the investigation very quiet. Back to quiet mode."

"Not much left to do," Lucas said. "I'll let you know if anything else serious comes up, but I think it's over."

"Good job," Henderson said. "But goddamn bloody. *Goddamn bloody.*"

Lucas saw Green hovering on the edge of the gathering and waved her over. She came, looking a little nervously over at Grant, who was talking with Rose Marie and paying no attention to Green.

Lucas said, "Governor, this is Alice Green, a former Secret Service agent and Ms. Grant's security person. I think she's a woman of integrity, and if you someday have an opening on your staff for a personal security aide . . . she's quite effective."

Henderson smiled and took her hand and didn't immediately let it go. He said, "Well, my goodness, as we wind up for this upcoming presidential season, I might very well have an opening . . ."

Lucas drifted away, and let them talk.

OTHER BITS OF THE CASE fell to the roadside, one piece after another.

The Minneapolis Police Department showed little appetite for investigating itself concerning the possibility that dozens of its personnel had been viewing child porn as a form of recreation. A few scraps of the story got out, and there were solemn assurances that a complete investigation would be done, even as the administration was shoveling dirt on it. Quintana, no dummy, apologized to everybody, while hinting that he'd have to drag it all out in the open if anything untoward happened to him. He took a reprimand and a three-day suspension without pay, and went back on the job.

Knoedler, the Democratic spy, got lawyered up, and the lawyers quickly realized that everything could be explained by the Bob Tubbs–Helen Roman connection, and there were no witnesses to the contrary. They put a "Just Politics" label on it, and it stuck.

Clay, the suspect in the Roman murder, was freed, and Turk Cochran, the Minneapolis homicide detective, mildly pissed about that, gave Lucas's cell phone number to Clay and told him to check in at least once a week and tell Lucas what he was up to. Clay started doing that, leaving long messages on Lucas's answering service when the call didn't go through, which threatened to drive Lucas over the edge.

TWO WEEKS AFTER the shootings, a few days after the meeting in the governor's office, Dannon's aunt came from Wichita, Kansas, to Minneapolis, to sign papers that would transfer Dannon's worldly goods to her. She was his closest relative, as his parents had died twenty years earlier in a rural car accident, and he'd left no will that anybody could find.

The crime-scene people told Lucas that she would be at his apartment to examine it and to sign an inventory, and Lucas stopped by for one last look. A BCA clerk was there, with the inventory, and Lucas found nothing new to look at. The aunt, after signing the inventory, gave him a box covered with birthday-style wrapping paper; the box had been unwrapped, and opened.

"I think you should give this to that woman, the senator," the aunt said. Her name was Harriet Dannon.

Lucas took out a sterling silver frame. Inside was a news-style photo of Grant on the campaign, shaking hands with some young girls, with Dannon looming in the background. The frame was inscribed, "I'll always have your back. Love, Doug."

"I never thought he was a bad man," Harriet Dannon said. "But I mostly knew him as a boy. He was a Boy Scout. . . . I never thought . . ."

LUCAS DIDN'T QUITE KNOW why Harriet Dannon thought *he* should give the picture to Grant, but he took it, and back outside, thought, *Might as well.* He was not far from her house, and he drove over, pulled into the driveway, pushed the call button.

A full minute later—there may have been some discussion, he thought—the gate swung back. He got out, walked to the front door, which opened as he approached. Alice Green was there: "What's up?"

"Closing out Dannon's town house. Is Senator Grant in?"

"She's waiting in the library. With the dogs."

Lucas reached inside his sport coat and touched his .45, and Green grinned at him. "Won't be necessary," she said. And very quietly: "Thanks for the governor. That's going to work out."

"Careful," he said.

GRANT WAS IN THE LIBRARY, sitting in the middle of the couch with the two dogs at her feet, one on either side of her; like Cleopatra and a couple of sphinxes, Lucas thought.

He walked in and she asked, "What do you want?"

"I was over at Dannon's apartment, we're closing it out. He left this: I guess he never had a chance to give it to you."

She looked at the photo, and then the inscription, then tossed it aside on the couch. "That's it?"

Very cold, Lucas thought. "I guess," he said. He turned to walk away, and at the edge of the room, turned back to say, "I know god-damn well that you were involved."

She said not a word, but smiled at him, one long arm along the top of the couch, a new gold chain glowing from her neck. If a jury had seen the smile, they would have convicted her: it was both a deliberate confession and a smile of triumph.

But there was no jury in the room. Lucas shook his head and walked away.

IN THE CAR, backing out of the driveway, he had two thoughts.

The first was that Porter Smalls, in vowing to smear Grant with other members of Congress, was pissing into the wind. He could go to the lame-duck session and complain all he wanted about Taryn Grant, but nothing would be done, because Grant was a winner. In Lucas's opinion, a good part of the Congress seemed to suffer from the same psychological defects that afflicted Taryn Grant—or that Taryn Grant enjoyed, depending on your point of view. Their bloated self-importance, their disregard of anything but their own goals, their preoccupation with power . . .

Not only would Taryn Grant fit right in, she'd be admired.

The second thought: He was convinced that Grant was involved in the killings—not necessarily carrying them out, but in directing them, or approving of them. Once a psychopathic personality had gotten that kind of rush, the kind you got from murder, he or she often needed another fix.

So: he might be seeing Taryn Grant again.

He would find that interesting.

A COUPLE MORE WEEKS slipped by.

A mass shooting in Ohio wiped everything else out of the news, and the whole election war began to slip into the rearview mirror.

Flowers arrested the Ape Man Rapist of Rochester, a former cable installation technician, at the Mayo Clinic's emergency room. He'd tangled with the wrong woman, one who had a hammer on the side table next to her bed. And though the rapist was wearing his Planet of the Apes Halloween monkey head, it was no match for her Craftsman sixteen-ounce claw. After she'd coldcocked him, she made sure he couldn't run by methodically breaking his foot bones, as well as his fibulas, tibias, patellas, and femurs. Flowers estimated he'd be sitting trial in three months, because he sure wouldn't be standing.

Lucas would sit in his office chair for a while every day, and stare out his window, which overlooked a parking lot and an evidence-deposit container, and run his mind over the Grant case. He didn't really care about Grant's jewelry, but the phone call plagued him.

He kept going over it and over it and over it, how somebody else could have worked it, and then one day he thought, *Kidd could monitor the security cameras.* And he thought, *No way Kidd could get his shoulders through that bedroom window.* And Lucas thought, *Had there been a twinkle in Kidd's eye when, speaking of Lauren's previous career, he'd said, "Insurance adjuster"?*

He thought about Lauren, and he thought she was far more interesting than an insurance adjuster. She *seemed* more interesting than that. . . .

He looked up her driver's license and found she'd taken Kidd's name when they married. Without any real idea of where he was going, he idly looked up their marriage license, and found that her maiden name had been Lauren Watley.

Then he checked her employment records. . . .

And there, back, way back, he found that she'd worked as a waitress at the Wee Blue Inn in Duluth, where the owner was a guy named Weenie.

LUCAS KNEW ALL ABOUT Weenie. He was, at one time, Minnesota's leading fence and criminal facilitator. Everybody knew that, but he'd never been convicted of a crime after an arrest for a string of burglaries as a teenager, and a short spell in the youth-offender facility.

Never arrested because he only dealt with high-end stuff, the stuff taken by the top pros; he didn't deal with guns or anyone who routinely used violence. Just the good stuff. If you needed to change two pounds of gold jewelry into a stack of hundred-dollar bills, Weenie could do it for you, for twenty percent. If you needed to cut open a safe, he knew a machinist who could do that for you.

And Lauren had worked as a waitress for . . . fifteen years, sometimes, it seemed, under the name LuEllen. *Fifteen years?* Lucas laughed: that was not possible.

Not possible. He knew her *that* well.

What *was* possible was that Weenie provided her with an employment record, wrote off her salary while sticking the money in his pocket. In the meantime, she was off doing whatever she did. . . .

Lucas wasn't exactly sure what that was, but he now had an idea . . . an itch that needed to be further scratched.

A MONTH AFTER the shoot-out with Dannon, on a crisp, bright, dry December day, Lucas got in his 911 and aimed it north on I-35, and let it out a little. He went through Duluth at noon, stopped at the Pickwick on the main drag, ate meat loaf and mashed potatoes, and then cruised on up to Iron Bay, a tiny town off Lake Superior.

Iron Bay had once been the home for workers at a taconite plant, and when the plant went down, so did the town. At one time, a house could be bought for ten thousand dollars, and many had been abandoned. The town had seen better days since, but it was not yet a garden spot.

Lucas threaded his way through a battered working-class neighborhood, and finally pulled into the driveway of a small ranch-style house. A heavy old man named James Corcoran came to the door, sucking on a cigarette, and said, "That car is a waste of money, in my opinion. You shoulda gone for the Boxster. All the ride, half the price."

"Got hooked on the looks," Lucas said, checking out his car. "A Boxster is nice, but you know . . . a 911 is a 911."

"Come on in," the old man said. "You want a beer?"

"Sure."

THEY SAT IN THE living room and Corcoran, who'd once been the town's only cop, said, "So, Lauren Watley. I do remember that girl and I hope she's all right."

"Married to a millionaire artist," Lucas said.

"Good for her, good for her," the old man said. "Her dad was one of the bigger jerks in town. Smart guy, engineer at the factory, but when he lost his job, he packed up, put it all in the car, and took off. Never looked back, as far as I know. Took every last cent, too. Janice Watley woke up one morning and didn't have enough cash to buy cat food."

"How old was Lauren at the time?"

"Don't really know," Corcoran said. "Junior high school, I guess. After her old man took off, the family went on welfare, and child support, but hell, that was nothing. Then, we started having some break-ins around town. Whoever was doing it knew what was going on, who had what, and where it was. For a long time, it was only money. But then, there was a guy here who ran the only thing in town that was worth a damn, a payday loan company. He had a coin collection, and it disappeared. Probably worth fifty grand."

"You thought Lauren was doing it?"

"You know, it was one of those small-town things," Corcoran said. "Everybody knew what their situation was over there. They had *no* money. Janice couldn't find a job . . . hell, nobody could find a job after the plant went down. So they were hurting. But they weren't hurting enough. They found the money for a used car. They paid cash for things . . . and the feeling was, money was coming from somewhere."

"But there was no proof."

"No proof. Lauren got to be in high school, and then this coin collection disappeared. The owner's name was Roger Van Vechten. He sued the insurance company, because they only wanted to give him thirty thousand, and he wanted fifty. But that was later. Right after the coins disappeared, I happened to be in Duluth, for something else entirely, buying something, I can't remember what . . . anyway, I see little Lauren coming out of the Wee Blue Inn. You know the guy there . . ."

"Weenie . . ."

"Yeah. Dead now," Corcoran said. "He was the biggest fence in the Upper Midwest. Everybody knew it. The question was, what was Lauren doing coming out of the Wee Blue Inn? I thought I knew the answer to that and followed her back to Iron Bay, and we got to her house and I braced her. Made her turn her pockets out. She had two dollars and some change. I checked the car . . ."

"You had a warrant?"

Corcoran laughed, and then started coughing. When he recovered, he said, "Oh, hell, no. That was a different time, up here. I just did what needed to be done. Anyway, I checked her, and she was pissed, but she didn't have a thing. Said she went down there to apply for a waitress job. I said, 'Lauren, you ain't no waitress.' And she said, 'Jim, you never been poor.' She called me 'Jim,' when everybody else her age would have been calling me 'Mr. Corcoran.' She was fifteen and all grown up."

"I've known women like that, girls like that," Lucas said, thinking of his Letty.

"But that wasn't the kicker," Corcoran said. "The kicker was, we had some rednecks out here who made a connection down in the Cities, and got the local cocaine franchise. One day, I borrowed a couple deputies from the sheriff and we raided them, and we got a half-kilo of coke and eight thousand dollars in cash. I locked it up in the evidence cage at the police department, which was on the side of city hall. That night, somebody cracked the back door on city hall, slick as you please, broke through the drywall into the police annex, cut the lock on the cage, and took the cash and the coke. I know goddamned well it was Lauren and I didn't have one speck of evidence. I just looked at her and I could see it in the way she looked back at me: she thought it was funny. She was getting back at me for bracing her."

Lucas smiled, and said, "Yeah, I can see her doing that."

"You got something on her?" Corcoran asked.

"Exactly what you got," Lucas said. "A belief."

"And not a speck of evidence."

"Not a speck," Lucas said.

"Well, good for her," Corcoran said. "I always liked that girl."

On the way out of town, Lucas stopped at the only gas station to get a Diet Coke and whatever kind of Hostess Sno Ball imitation they had, and found himself looking at a rack of postcards.

A COUPLE OF DAYS later, Lauren and Kidd were going out for a late lunch, and they stopped in the bottom hallway to check the mail. Lauren took a postcard out of the mailbox and Kidd asked, "Anything good?"

"It's a postcard from Lucas. . . . It says, 'Glad you're not here.' " With a puzzled look on her face, she turned it over and found a photo looking out over Iron Bay and Lake Superior.

"Oh, shit," she said, stricken.

"What?"

"Lucas knows."

FIFTEEN MINUTES LATER, wrapped in warm winter jackets, she and Kidd stood side by side on the Robert Street bridge, looking down at the dark waters of the Mississippi.

Kidd said, "This is the only time since I knew you, all those years, that you ever kept anything that they could stick you with."

"Because it's gorgeous," she said. A gold watch dangled from her fingers. "It's a Patek Philippe, from 1918. I've looked it up—it could be worth anything up to a quarter million."

"And it would hang you, if anybody ever saw it," Kidd said.

"I know," she said. "But I refuse to give it back to a killer."

"It's a shame, though," Kidd said.

"Would you do it if it was a Monet?"

"Jesus Christ, no," Kidd said. "If it was a Monet . . . I'd . . . I'd . . ."

"You'd never drop it in the river," Lauren said. She relaxed her fingers, and the watch dropped like a golden streak through the gray light of winter, and a quarter million dollars disappeared into the black water below the bridge.

"That's it," Lauren said, dusting her hands off. "Not a speck of evidence, now."

"Not a speck," Kidd said, hooking an arm through hers. "C'mon, little housewifey. Let's go get a cheeseburger."

KT-151-869

IF SHE WAKES

ALSO BY MICHAEL KORYTA

IF SHE WAKES

IF SHE WAKES

MICHAEL KORYTA

HODDER

First published in Great Britain in 2019 by Hodder & Stoughton
An Hachette UK company

1

Copyright © Michael Koryta 2019

The right of Michael Koryta to be identified as the Author
of the Work has been asserted by him in accordance with
the Copyright, Designs and Patents Act 1988.

A CIP catalogue record for this title is available from the British Library

Hardback ISBN 978 1 473 61464 2
eBook ISBN 978 1 473 61467 3
Trade Paperback ISBN 978 1 473 61465 9

Printed and bound in Great Britain by Clays Ltd, Elcograf S.p.A.

Hodder & Stoughton policy is to use papers that are natural, renewable
and recyclable products and made from wood grown in sustainable
forests. The logging and manufacturing processes are expected to
conform to the environmental regulations of the country of origin.

Hodder & Stoughton Ltd
Carmelite House
50 Victoria Embankment
London EC4Y 0DZ

www.hodder.co.uk

For Pete Yonkman,
who gave me the book that gave me the book.
Many thanks for your support, motivation, and friendship.

Part One

IGNITION

I

Nineteen minutes before her brain and her body parted ways, Tara Beckley's concern was the cold.

First night of October, but as the sun set and the wind picked up, it felt like midwinter, and Tara could see her breath fogging the air. That would have been crisp New England charm on another night, but not this one, when she wore only a thin sweater over a summer-weight dress. Granted, she hadn't expected to be standing in the cold, but she had a commitment to deliver one Professor Amandi Oltamu from dinner to his keynote presentation, and the professor was pacing the parking lot of the restaurant they'd just left, alternately staring into the darkness and playing with his phone.

Tara tried to stay patient, shivering in that North Atlantic night wind that swept leaves off the trees. She needed to get moving, and not just because of the cold. Oltamu had to arrive at 7:45, and *precisely* 7:45, because the Hammel College conference was coordinated by a pleasant woman named Christine whose eyes turned into dark daggers if the schedule went awry. And Professor Oltamu—sorry, *Dr.* Oltamu, he was one of those prigs who insisted on the title even though he wasn't a medical doctor, just another PhD—occupied the very first position in the program of Christine with the Dagger Eyes, and thus he was worthy of more daggers. It was, after all, opening night of the whole silly academic show.

"We have to go, sir," Tara called to the good doctor. He lifted a hand, asking for another minute, and studied the blackness. Pre-speech jitters? Couldn't he at least have those indoors?

3

Conference coordinator Christine and every other faculty member and student who'd attended the kickoff dinner for Hammel's imitation TED Talks were already long gone, leaving Tara alone with Dr. Oltamu in the restaurant parking lot. He was an odd man who seemed like a collection of mismatched parts—his voice was steady but his posture was tense, and his eyes were nervous, flicking around the parking lot as if he were confused by it.

"I don't mean to rush you, but we really—"

"Of course," he said and walked briskly to the car. She'd expected him to ride shotgun, but instead he pushed aside her yoga mat and a stack of books and settled into the back. Good enough. At least she could turn on the heater.

She got behind the wheel, started the car, and glanced in the mirror. "All set, Dr. Oltamu?" she asked with a smile intended to suggest that she knew who he was and what he did when in truth she hadn't the faintest idea.

"All set" came the answer in the chipper, slightly accented, but perfectly articulated English of this man who was originally from…Sudan, was it? Nigeria? She couldn't recall. She'd seen his bio, of course—Christine made sure that the student escorts were equipped with head shots and full bios of the distinguished speakers they'd be picking up throughout this week of grandeur, when Hammel College sought to bring some of the world's finest minds to its campus. The small but tony liberal arts school in southern Maine was just close enough to Boston to snag some of the Harvard or MIT speakers looking for extra paid gigs, and that looked great in the brochures to donors and prospective students alike. You needed to get the big names, and Hammel managed to, but Dr. Oltamu wasn't one of them. There was a reason he was batting leadoff instead of cleanup.

This was Tara's second year serving on the student welcoming committee, but it was also her last, because she was close to an exit. She'd taken extra classes in the summers and was set to jet in December, although she could attend the official graduation day in May. She hoped to be immersed in bigger and better things by May, but who knew, maybe by then she would want to return. That wasn't hard to imagine. In fact, she was already nostalgic about Hammel, because she knew this was her last taste of it. Last autumn in Maine, last parties, last midterms, last of a lot of things.

"We are good on time, yes?" Dr. Oltamu said. He checked an impressive gold watch on his left wrist, a complement to his fine suit, if only the fine suit had actually fit him. It seemed he'd ignored tailoring, and as a result he would be presenting his speech in the sartorial equivalent of an expensive hand-me-down from a taller, leaner brother.

Presenting his speech about...

Damn all, what does he do?

"We'll be just fine," she said. "And I can't wait to hear your presentation tonight."

Presentation on...

She'd been hoping for a little help, but he twisted away and stared out the back window.

"There is a planned route?" he said.

"What do you mean?"

"From the restaurant to the theater. Everyone would drive the same way?"

"Uh, yeah. I mean, as far as I know."

"Can we go a different way?"

She frowned. "Pardon?"

"Give me the Tara tour," he said, turning back around and offering a smile that seemed forced. "I'd like to see your favorite places in the community."

"Um...well, I need to get you there on time, but...sure." The request was bizarre, but playing tour guide wouldn't slow her down. In fact, she knew exactly where she would take him—down to the old railroad bridge where she ran almost every morning and where, if she timed it right, she could feel as if she were racing the train itself. That bridge over the Willow River was one of her favorite places on earth.

"It is very beautiful here," Oltamu said as she drove.

Indeed it was. While Tara had applied exclusively to southern schools for her graduate program in a concerted effort to bust out of Maine before another February snagged her in its bleak grasp, she would miss the town. The campus was small but appealing, with the right blend of ancient academic limestone towers and contemporary labs; the faculty was good, the setting idyllic. Tonight they'd gone to a fine restaurant on a high plateau above town, and as she followed the winding roads back toward the sea, she was struck by her affection for this town of tidy Colonial homes on large, sloping lawns backed up against forested mountains that provided some of the best hiking you could ever hope to find. The fall chill was in the air, and that meant that woodstoves and fireplaces were going. This blend of colored leaves against a sunset yielding to darkness redolent with woodsmoke was what she loved about New England—the best time of day at the best time of year. She left her window cracked as she drove, not wanting to seal out that perfect autumn scent.

Dr. Oltamu had turned around and was staring behind them again, as if the rear window were the only one with a view. He'd been respectful but reserved at dinner, which was one of the reasons she couldn't remember what in the world he was there to speak about.

Oil? Energy crisis? No...

They wound down the mountain and into town. There was the North Woods Brewing Company on the left, a weekend staple for her, and there was the store where she'd bought her first skis, which had led to her first set of crutches, and there, down the hill and past the Catholic church and closer to the harbor, was

Garriner's, which had been serving the best greasy-spoon breakfast in town for sixty years. Down farther was the harbor itself, the water the color of ink now but a stunning cobalt at sunrise. Along this stretch were the few bars that Hammel could claim as its nightlife, though to most people they were nothing but pregame venues—the serious drinking was done at house parties. It wasn't a big school, and it wasn't a big town, but it was pleasant and peaceful, absolutely no traffic tonight as she drove toward the auditorium where Dr. Oltamu would address the crowd about...

Climate change?

"Lovely place," Oltamu said, facing forward again. "So charming."

"It was the perfect college town for me," she said, and she realized with some surprise that she wasn't just delivering the student-tour-guide shtick. She meant it. She could see the area just as he did: bucolic, quaint. A town designed for a college, a place for young adults to bump up against the real world, every experience there for the taking but with a kinder, gentler feel than some of the large campuses she'd visited.

"It is truly excellent when one finds where one belongs," Dr. Oltamu said as Tara drove away from the harbor. The car climbed and then descended into the valley, where the campus waited across the Willow River.

Oltamu was gazing behind them again.

"I'm looking forward to your talk tonight," she tried once more. *Your talk about...artificial intelligence?*

"I appreciate that, but I'm afraid I'll surely bore you," he said with a small laugh.

Come on, gimme some help here, Doc. "What's the most exciting part of your work in *your* opinion, then?" she asked. A pathetic attempt, but now she was determined to win the war. She would figure out what he did without stooping to ask him flat-out.

He paused, then said, "Well, the Black Lake is certainly intriguing. I've just come from there, actually. A fascinating trip.

But I doubt there are many creative-writing majors who are fascinated by batteries."

There it was! Batteries! He designed some sort of solar panels and batteries that were supposed to save fuel consumption and, thus, the earth. You know, trivial shit.

Tara was embarrassed that she hadn't been able to remember this on her own, especially since he'd somehow remembered her major from the chaotic introductions at the restaurant. Then again, he had a point—batteries were not an area of particular fascination for her. But you never knew. There was, as her favorite writing professor always said, a story around every corner.

"Where is Black Lake?" she asked, but he'd shifted away yet again and was staring intently out the back window. A vehicle had appeared in her rearview mirror in a sudden glare of lights and advanced quickly, riding right up along her bumper, its headlights shining down into the CRV, and she pumped the brake, annoyed. The taller vehicle—a truck or a van—backed off.

Tara drove beneath a sugar maple that was shedding its leaves, a cascade of crimson whispering across the hood, bloodred and brittle. No matter what warm and beautiful beach was within walking distance of wherever she was next year, she would miss autumn here. She understood that it was supposed to be a somber season, of course, that autumn leaves meant the end of something, but so far in her life, it had marked only beginnings; each fall brought another birthday, a new teacher and classmates, sometimes new schools, new friends, new boyfriends. She loved fall precisely for the way it underscored that sense of change. Change, for Tara Beckley, twenty-two years old as of a week ago, had always been a good thing.

She crested the hill, made the steep descent down Knowlton Street, and turned onto Ames Road, a residential stretch. The headlights behind them vanished, and Dr. Oltamu faced forward again.

She was just about to repeat her question—*Where is Black Lake?*—when he spoke.

"Why so dark?"

"Pardon?"

"The street is very dark."

He wasn't wrong. Ames Road was unusually dark.

"There was some fight with the property owners over light pollution," she said, a vague memory of the article in the student newspaper coming back to her. "They put in new street lamps, but they had to be dim."

She flicked on her high beams, illuminating another swirl of rust-colored leaves stirring in the road.

"I see. Now, Hammel is a walking campus, I understand? Things are close together?"

"Yes. In fact, we're coming up to a place where I run every morning. *Almost* every morning at least, unless there's a big exam or…something." Something like a hangover, but she didn't want to mention that to the good doctor. "There's an old bridge down here that crosses from campus into town, and it's for pedestrians and cyclists only. There's a railroad bridge next to it. In the morning, if I get up early enough, I can run with the train. I race it." She gave a self-conscious laugh.

In the darkness below, the old railroad bridge threw spindly shadows across the Willow River. Beside it, separated by maybe twenty feet, was the new pedestrian and cycling bridge, part of a pathway system that wound through the campus and town. Tara started to turn left at the last intersection above the bridge, but Oltamu spoke up.

"May we stop and walk?" he said.

It was such an odd and abrupt request that it took her a moment to respond. "I can show you around after your talk, but they'll kill me if I get you there late."

"I would very much like to walk," he said, and his voice now matched his tense posture. "It's my knee. Stiffens up and then I'm in terrible pain. Distracting pain."

"Um…" She glanced at the clock, doing the math and trying to imagine how she might explain this to Christine.

"Please," he said. In the mirror, the whites of his eyes stood out starkly against his dark face. "You said the bridge goes to campus, correct?"

"Yes, but we'd really be pushing it for time. I can't get you there late."

He leaned forward. "I would very much like to walk," he said again. "I would like to see the bridge. I will make it clear to anyone involved that this was my delay. But I walk quickly."

Even with that bad knee? "Sure," she said, because she was now more alarmed by the strange urgency in his request than by the specter of an angry Christine. "We can walk."

She eased the car down the hill, toward the old railroad bridge and the new footbridge. A dozen angled parking spaces waited beside a pillar with a plaque identifying the railroad bridge's historical significance. The spots were all empty now, but in the morning you'd see people piling out of their cars with dogs on leashes, or removing bikes from racks.

She pulled into one of the angled spaces, and Dr. Oltamu was out of the car almost before it was parked. He stood with his back to the river and the campus and stared up the hill. Everything there was lost to darkness. He'd wanted to see the bridge; now he faced the other way. He'd been worried about time; now he wanted to walk. He had a bad knee; now he craved exercise.

"Why don't we head across the bridge, sir," she said. But he ignored her, took his cell phone from his pocket, and beckoned for her.

"May we take a picture together? I've been asked to use social media. You know…for a broader reach. I am told photos are best for engagement. So may I? You are my Hammel escort, after all."

She didn't love the way he said *escort,* but she also wasn't going to be shy about putting an elbow into his windpipe if he tried to grab her ass or something, so she said, "Sure," and then leaned awkwardly toward him for the photo—head close, ass away—and watched their image fill the screen of his iPhone. The phone seemed identical to hers, but the camera function was different; the screen was broken into a grid of squares. He tilted the phone in a way that centered Tara in the frame, and her smile grew more pained and she started to pull away as he snapped the photo. He didn't touch her, though, didn't say anything remotely lewd, just a polite "Thank you very much," and then he turned his attention to the screen, tapping away as if he intended to crop, edit, and post the photo immediately.

"Sir, we really do need to get going."

"Yes. One moment." Head down, tapping away. Then he said, "Did you ever have a nickname?"

"Pardon?"

He looked up and smiled. "You know, something only a good friend calls you, something like that? Or were you always just Tara?"

She started to say, *Just Tara, thanks, and now let's get a move on,* but reflex took over and she blurted out, "Twitch."

"Twitch?"

"My sister, Shannon, called me that because I was a jumpy kid. I spooked easily, I guess. Scary movies, in particular—I always jumped."

When Tara was little, the nickname was just Shannon picking on her. But later on, it became affectionate. Shannon liked how much Tara cared about fictional characters, how emotionally invested she became in their stories.

"We really should be—"

There was a rustling sound behind them, and they whirled at the same time, Tara with a startled jerk that offered a live-action demonstration of the childhood nickname. Her response was still more composed than Oltamu's, though. He gave a strangled cry, stepped back, and lifted his hands as if surrendering.

Then Tara saw the dog in the bushes and smiled. "That's just Hobo."

"What?" Oltamu backed farther away.

"He's a stray. Always around the bridge. And he *always* comes out to bark at the morning train. That's how I spotted him. If you come by often enough, he'll get to know you. But he doesn't let you catch him. I've certainly tried." She knelt, extended her hand, and made a soft sound with her tongue on the roof of her mouth. Her rush to get Oltamu to the venue was forgotten in her instinct to show affection to the old stray, her companion on so many morning runs. He slunk out of the darkness, keeping low, and let Tara touch the side of his head. Only the side; never the top. If you reached for him, he'd bolt. Not far, at least not with her, but out of grasping distance. He was a blend of unknown breeds, with the high carriage and startling speed of a greyhound, the floppy ears of a beagle, and the coat of a terrier.

"He's been here for a long time," she said. "Every year people try to catch him and get him to a rescue, but nobody ever succeeds. So we just give up and feed him."

She scratched the dog's soft, floppy ears, one of which had a few tears along the edge, and then straightened.

"Okay," she said. "We've got to hurry now. I can't get you there late. So let's—"

"Hobo?" Oltamu was staring at the dog as if he'd never encountered such an animal.

"It's just what I call him. He likes to chase the train. Anyhow, we have to—"

"Stay there, please. I'd like a picture of him." He knelt. "Can you get him to look at me?" he asked as he extended his phone.

I'll tell Christine to look at his phone, Tara thought. *I have exculpatory evidence now.* "Do you see, Christine? He made me stop to take pictures of a stray dog!"

"His attention?" Oltamu said. "Please? Toward the camera?"

Tara raised her eyebrows and pursed her lips. *Oookay.* Then she turned back to Hobo and made the soft clucking sound again. He looked at her but didn't move. Oltamu was a stranger, and Hobo didn't approach strangers.

"Very good," Oltamu whispered, as entranced as if he were on a safari and had encountered a rare species. "Excellent."

The camera clicked, a flash illuminated the dog in stark white light, and Hobo growled.

"It's okay," Tara told him, but he gave a final growl, gazed up the hill at the dark street beyond, then slipped back into the trees.

"All right," Tara said, rising again. "We really *have to*—"

"I need you to do me a favor. It is very important. Crucial."

"Please, Doctor. They're waiting on you at the auditorium, so—"

"Crucial," he said, his accent heavier, the word loaded with emotion.

She looked at his earnest face and then across the river at the lights of the campus. Suddenly she felt far away from where she belonged, and very alone. "What's the favor?"

He moved toward her, and she stepped back, bumping into one of the bike racks. Pain shot through her hip. He reached out, and she recoiled, fearing his hand, but then she saw that he was extending the phone to her.

"Please put this in your car. Somewhere secure. Can you lock the glove compartment?"

She wanted to object, or at least ask him for a reason, but his face was so intense, so worried, that all she did was nod.

"Put it there, then. Please. I'm going to walk across the bridge myself. I'll find my way."

What is happening here? What in the world is he doing?

"Please," he repeated, and Tara took the phone from his hand, walked hurriedly past him, and opened the passenger door. She leaned in and put the phone in the glove box. It took her two tries to lock it, because her hand was trembling. She heard him move behind her, and she spun, hands rising, ready to fend him off, but he was just watching to see that she'd done what he'd asked.

"Thank you," he said. "I don't mean to frighten you, but that phone is very important." He looked up the hill, then back to her. "I will walk from here alone. You should drive."

She hadn't spoken throughout this, and she didn't now. She just wanted to get away from him. Driving off and leaving him here was fine by her.

"Thank you, Tara," he said. "It is important. I am sorry you are afraid."

She stood motionless, hands still raised, watching him as warily as Hobo had.

"Please go now," he said. "Take the car and go. I will walk across the bridge when you are gone."

She moved. Going around the front of the car would have been quicker, but she would have passed closer to him, so she made her way around the back. She'd just reached the driver's door when she heard the engine behind her.

She glanced in the direction of the noise with relief, glad that she was no longer alone with this bizarre man, expecting to see headlights coming on. Instead, there was just the dark street. The engine grew louder, and with it came the sound of motion, but she saw nothing, so she just stood there dumbly, her hand on the car door. Oltamu had also turned to face the sound. They were both staring into the darkness when Tara finally saw the black van.

It was running with no trace of light. It came on down the road like something supernatural, quiet and dark but also remarkably fast.

She had only an instant to move. Her guiding thought was that she wanted to be away from the car, even if that meant going into the river. Down there, she thought she might have a chance.

She was scrambling away from the CRV when the van hit it squarely in the rear passenger door, pinning Oltamu against the side of the car, and then the CRV hit her, and though she got her wish of making it into the river, she never knew it. She was airborne when the front of her skull connected with the concrete pillar that marked the railroad bridge as a historical site, and by the time she entered the water, she wasn't aware of anything at all.

2

When the flight from Portland to Detroit arrived and her asset didn't walk off the plane, Lisa Boone moved from the gate to the Delta Sky Club and ordered a Johnnie Walker Blue.

"Rocks?" the bartender asked.

"No."

"Water back?"

"No."

An overweight businessman in an off-the-rack suit with a hideously mismatched tie and pocket square turned on his bar stool and smiled a greasy, lecherous smile.

"The lady knows how to order her scotch."

Boone didn't look at him. "The lady does," she said and put cash on the bar.

"Have a seat." He moved his laptop bag off the stool beside him. The laptop bag had not one but two tags identifying him as a Diamond Medallion member. Wouldn't want your Sky Club status to slip under the radar.

"I'm fine."

"Oh, come on."

"I'm fine," Boone repeated, but already she knew this guy wasn't going to give up so easily. One didn't become a Diamond Medallion member without some dedication.

"Humor a fellow traveler," he said and patted the leather-topped stool. "I've been drinking Budweiser, but I like your style—scotch it is. Have a seat, and put your money away. I'll buy the drinks."

Boone didn't say anything. She breathed through her nose and waited for the bartender to break the fifty she'd put on the bar, and she thought of Iraq and the first fat man she'd killed. You weren't supposed to admit such a thing, but she'd always taken a little extra pleasure in killing fat men.

"I hope this doesn't seem too forward," Diamond Medallion Man said, leaning toward her and deepening his voice, "but you are absolutely stunning."

The bartender put her change down, and Boone picked up most of the bills, leaving a five behind, and turned to Diamond Medallion Man. He gave what was undoubtedly his winningest smile.

"I hope this doesn't seem too forward," Boone said, "but do you know the difference between Bud and Bud Light?"

His smile wavered. "What?"

She reached out, grasped the flesh under his chin, and pinched it hard between her thumb and index finger. "*That* is the difference," she said and released him as he went red-faced and wide-eyed. "You might consider switching it up."

She picked up her scotch and walked away from the bar, chastising herself. The fat man and the bartender were both staring, and that meant at least two people would remember her now, the polar opposite of her goal today. She'd known better, of course, should've just shrugged the lech off, but her temper could get away from her when she was forced to be passive.

All she could do right now was sit and wait and hope that her man had taken a later flight.

She went to the monitors and studied the arrival times. Maybe it wasn't trouble yet. Maybe he'd just gotten delayed or had overslept. There was not supposed to be any contact today, so even if he'd missed his flight, he wouldn't have reached out. She had no choice but to wait. The next flight in from Portland was in three hours. Then there was a final flight at nine p.m. If he wasn't on either one, it would be a very bad sign.

Of course, his last messages had been a bad sign. Cryptic and scared.

Am I being followed? If so, tell them to back off.

Nobody was following him. Nobody should have been, at least. That was by his own insistence too. He was out in the cold, unprotected, going through his last week of free movements as had long been agreed upon. He could not attract attention, and he thought that canceling an established speaking tour would launch a signal flare into the blackness.

Or what they hoped was blackness.

She wasn't allowed to call him, wasn't allowed to make contact. Just pick him up in Detroit and go from there. All week long, she'd waited as he went from stop to stop, and she'd wanted protection on him the whole time, but it had been refused. The last stop had seemed the safest, though. A small town in Maine, an hour of speaking at some overpriced liberal arts school for kids with Ivy League trust funds but SEC brains. Hardly hostile territory. One night in a hotel on campus, a drive to the Portland International Jetport that morning, then a flight bound for Los Angeles with a layover in Detroit, and in Detroit he would disappear.

But the magic trick wouldn't work if he never stepped onstage. A man who never appeared couldn't disappear.

Boone left the flight monitors and walked through the lounge, past the sitting area with the crackling electric fire and the dark paneled wood that strove for the feel of an elegant home library in a place where every minute you spent was one more than you wanted to spend, and on out to a row of chairs facing the glass walls that overlooked the concourse. She sat, crossed her legs, sipped her scotch, and stared at the crowds hurrying for the tram.

Two more flights. Two more chances.

If he didn't walk off one of those planes, she'd have to call it in. If he didn't walk off one of those planes, there were going to be big problems.

Come on, Doc, she thought. *Don't let me down now. Not so close to the finish line.*

She withdrew her secure phone from her purse, pulled up his last message, and read it again, as if it might tell her something she'd missed before.

ASK THE GIRL.

What girl? Ask her *what?*

Boone put the phone away, swirled her scotch, and silently begged the next flight from Portland to deliver her man.

3

On the day before negligent-vehicular-manslaughter charges were filed against him in Maine, Carlos Ramirez bought a plane ticket to Caracas under a name for which he had both a driver's license and passport and waited for the kid to pick him up and take him to the airport.

The kid was late, and Carlos had a feeling that was intentional. The kid looked barely old enough to buy cigarettes, and he didn't say much, but he always had this faint smile that suggested he was laughing at you, the kind of smile that made you want to check to see if your fly was unzipped or if there was food stuck in your teeth. That was annoying shit from anybody, but from a child, it was begging for an ass-beating.

Carlos didn't think he was supposed to touch the kid, though. In fact, he had a feeling that would be a terrible mistake. He didn't know why the kid was so protected, but it was clear that he was, and so Carlos dealt with that bullshit smile and the mocking eyes. He'd have to do it only once more. If the kid ever showed up in Venezuela, it would be a different story.

Twenty minutes after he was supposed to be picked up and just as he was beginning to worry that he'd miss his flight and everything would be fucked, Carlos stepped outside to have a cigarette and stare up the street, as if he could will the car into appearing.

The car was already at the curb.

He stared at it, shook his head, and muttered, "Can't you come up and knock on the damned door," under his breath.

The kid spoke from behind him.

"I was told to meet you on the porch."

He was sitting in a plastic lawn chair with his back against the house, one foot hooked over his knee, looking for all the world like an old man relaxing and watching the neighborhood pass by.

"The hell are you doing?" Carlos snapped. "How long you been here?"

The kid took his cell phone out. Studied it. "Twenty-six minutes."

"You fucking kidding me? You just sat there?"

"I was told to meet you on the porch," he repeated, unbothered, and pocketed the phone. All of his movements were slow, but there was a quality to his slender muscles that promised he could move fast if he was so inclined. He had a couple inches on Carlos and a longer reach, but Carlos would have liked nothing more than to step inside that reach and lay some good shots on his body, let the little prick understand that respect was not unimportant in this business.

Just get to the airport. Stay cool long enough to get your cash and get on the plane.

The cash was at the airport, and the kid was the ride. These were the rules.

Carlos said, "Let's get moving, you…" He stopped himself before saying *little asshole.* "Let's go."

"You?" The kid raised his eyebrows with patient curiosity, as if he weren't offended, merely intrigued. "You…what?"

"Nothing. Let's get moving. I can't miss this flight, man. You know that."

The kid didn't stand. He still had his foot resting on his knee, his posture relaxed, in total contrast to his pale blue eyes. They danced around until they locked on you, and once they did that, you wished they hadn't. It was an empty stare. Vacant. It reminded Carlos of men he'd fought in dingy gyms in Miami. They were always the guys who didn't seem to mind being hit.

The kid adjusted the bill of his baseball cap, bending it slightly with both hands. He always had that damn hat, which was jet-black with no logo and a line of metallic thread tracing the front seam. That was no doubt supposed to add flair, but instead it seemed to provide a target for anyone who wanted to stitch a line of bullets through his skull. Carlos would have happily volunteered for that task.

"I hate unfinished sentences," the kid said. "People do that all the time. Leave a thought floating in the air, and then you've got to guess at what it was going to be." He lowered his hands and his eyes flicked to Carlos and held on him in that creepy way he had, like he was deciphering something written in a foreign language. "That can cause misunderstandings."

Carlos beckoned to him with his right hand, because his right hand had risen despite himself, and now he needed to do something with it that didn't involve smacking the shit out of the kid.

"Come on. Get up. This is serious."

The kid didn't move. "Finish your thought."

"Excuse me?"

"Otherwise I'll keep guessing at what it was going to be. Then I'll be distracted on the drive. That's not safe. You, of all people, should be familiar with the risks of distracted drivers."

"You're a piece of work, man."

"Is that what you were going to say? 'Let's get moving, you piece of work'?"

"Sure."

The kid made a show of pondering this with a thoughtful frown, and then he mouthed the sentence without giving voice to the words and shook his head. "That doesn't sound right."

"How about 'you little asshole'?" Carlos said, finally losing his temper. "Does that sound better?"

The kid went back to the thoughtful frown, and then he mouthed this one too: *Let's get moving, you little asshole.* He snapped his fingers and pointed at Carlos.

"Yes," he said, smiling. "That's it. I can buy that one."

Carlos took a breath, ready to tell him to stand up or to *make* him stand up—this thing was going one way or the other—but the kid finally moved. Still with that practiced laziness, every motion slow, uncrossing his foot from his knee, standing, brushing off his pants, stretching, adjusting the ball cap. But at least he was moving.

"Let's get you out of here, sir," he said, formal as any suit-and-cap chauffeur.

"Yeah. Let's." Carlos went inside, grabbed the duffel bag that held the only belongings he was leaving the country with, and slammed the door for the last time. He was ready to be out of this shithole. Say what you wanted about Venezuela; he'd take any corner of that country over the Boston winters.

They walked down the porch steps and across the street to the kid's car. It was a rust-colored Camaro with dark-tinted windows that looked like an unmarked cop car. Or an asshole kid's car. Carlos opened the back door, threw the duffel bag in, then went around to the passenger side. The kid had the big engine growling by the time Carlos was in the passenger seat. The car was immaculate inside, absolutely devoid of personal effects except for an energy drink sitting in the cup holder, something called Bang, the word written in red on a black can. Music was playing, a high, tinkling keyboard riff over a thumping bass line that rattled the energy drink can against the cup holder. It sounded like the opening of a shitty rap song, dance-floor hip-hop, but nobody ever came on with a verse.

The kid drove them out of the neighborhood while the song played. He sipped the energy drink and set it down and it resumed rattling against the cup holder in tempo with the bass line from the song.

Bang.

When Carlos picked up the can, it was more to stop the rattling than anything else. The metallic jangle was getting in his head, bouncing around like a troublesome pinball determined to jostle every rage nerve it could find. "I bet this tastes like shit."

The kid didn't answer. He was smiling and bobbing his head to the music with a little right-to-left shimmy in his shoulders, and Carlos wanted to smash the aluminum can into his teeth. He forced himself to look down at it instead, fighting for calm.

"'Bang,'" he read from the label. "'Potent brain and body fuel.' What did you pay for this, six bucks? Potent brain and body fuel, my ass."

"Try it."

"I'd rather drink my own piss."

"Not in my car, please."

Carlos set the can down and watched it vibrate with each thumping shake of the speakers, the same riff still playing on loop.

"What is this bullshit music? Anybody ever gonna throw a verse?"

"You can if you want. I won't laugh."

"Oh, it's just the beat, eh? So you're a rapper? Cool, little man! Let me hear something. I bet you're good. Like Eminem...nah, more like Macklemore, right?"

Carlos was obviously screwing with him, but the kid didn't react, didn't lose his smile. There was a strange quality to him that didn't just unsettle Carlos; it reminded him of someone. He couldn't place it.

"What's your name, anyhow?" he said. It had honestly never occurred to him to ask. Their transactions hadn't been of the let's-get-to-know-each-other type.

"Dax."

"Dax. The hell kind of name is that?"

"Serbian. It means 'little asshole.'" He said it calmly and quietly and never looked at Carlos.

"Hilarious," Carlos said, worrying that he'd pissed the kid off and hating himself for worrying. The kid couldn't be more than nineteen, and Carlos had been in the game for twenty years and had killed fourteen men and two women and he was not about to be intimidated by some child with a weird smile.

But you are. He bothers you. He scares you.

"I don't like saying *Dax*," Carlos said, because talking made him feel better than just riding. "*Dax*. Makes me feel like I'm gagging."

"I'm sorry it doesn't roll off your tongue like *Carlos*."

"Sure doesn't. What's your last name? I'll call you that."

For the first time in their limited relationship, the kid seemed to hesitate. It was quick, just a little hitch, but it was there. It was exactly what you looked for in the ring, and when you saw it, you threw the knockout punch.

"Blackwell," the kid said then, and Carlos's knockout punch was forgotten, all his confidence sapped by this unanticipated jab.

That's it. Holy shit, that is it, he's just like them.

"Which one?" Carlos asked. He felt a cold tension along his spine.

"Pardon?"

"Which one of them are you related to?"

"Which one of who?"

"Don't be a dick. Which one of those brothers that got killed in Montana are you related to, Jack or Patrick?"

The kid glanced at him, amused. "That's a strange question."

"Why?"

"If they were brothers, and I was related to one, I'd have to be related to both. Do you follow that, Carlos? We'd all be part of the same family then. That's the way it works."

Again the urge to smack him rose, but this time it was easier to grip the armrest. The body count that Carlos had amassed would not have meant anything to Jack and Patrick Blackwell.

"I didn't know either of them had a son," Carlos said. "They didn't seem like—"

He managed to stop himself.

The kid said, "Want to finish that thought, Carlos? Or do you want me to guess?"

His eyes were on the road, and his right hand was looped over the steering wheel and he seemed perfectly relaxed, but Carlos did not like the sound of that question, so he decided to answer it without fucking around.

"They didn't seem like the family type," he said.

"Oh. All about their work, you mean?"

"I guess."

"Well, everyone has a personal life. Does that surprise you? That they would have had lives of their own and that they would have been private about those things?" He looked at Carlos, and Carlos struggled to meet his eyes, then chose instead to stare over the kid's shoulder at the construction site they were passing, the gutted remains of an old strip mall that stood waiting for bulldozers to raze it. Then he looked down at the vibrating aluminum can. *Bang. Potent brain and body fuel.* He released the armrest so that both hands were free. Suddenly, it seemed very important to have his hands free.

"No," he said. "It doesn't surprise me, and I don't really give a shit. I was just curious, that's all. I should've figured it out earlier. You remind me of them."

They'd pulled up to a stop sign. The kid smiled at him again.

"I hear that a lot," he said, and then he fired two shots from a suppressed handgun that was inside his jacket pocket. He shot left-handed, firing under his right arm without ever removing his right hand from the steering wheel, that confident in his aim, and he never lost the smile.

Then he turned the corner, pulled the Camaro to the curb, and put it in park. He left the key in the ignition and the engine running, the music still playing, those high piano notes over the low bass with no lyrics, but he took the energy drink. He sipped it while he shut the door on the music and the corpse, adjusted his baseball cap with the other hand, and walked away.

Part Two

LOCKED IN

4

The case was so simple that Abby Kaplan decided to stop for a beer on her way to the scene.

This wasn't encouraged protocol—drinking on the job could get her fired, of course—but there wasn't much pressure today. The cops had already gotten one of the drivers to admit guilt. They had a signed statement and a recorded statement. Not much for Abby to do but review their report, take her own photos, and agree with their assessment. Cut and dried.

Besides, Hammel was a forty-minute drive from the Biddeford office of Coastal Claims and Investigations, and Abby, well... Abby got a little nervous driving these days. A beer could help that. Contrary to what most people—and, certainly, the police— believed, a beer before driving could make her safer for society. It settled twitching hands and a jumpy mind, kept her both relaxed and focused. Abby had no doubt that she drove better with a six-pack in her bloodstream than most people did stone-cold sober. She was damn sure safer than most drivers, with their eyes on their cell phones and their heads up their asses.

This wasn't an argument you'd win in court, but that didn't mean it wasn't the truth.

She stopped at a brewpub not far from the Portland jetport, a place busy enough that she wouldn't stand out, and she paid cash so there would be no credit card transaction to haunt her if something went wrong. Not that anything *would* go wrong, but she'd seen the ways it could. She also made a point of tearing the receipt into bits, because cash could help you only so much; there were different kinds of paper trails. She'd worked one case where the driver had been dumb enough to leave a receipt on the console recording the five margaritas he'd knocked back just before getting behind the wheel and blowing through a stop sign. It wasn't that abnormal, really. You stopped by the body shop to take pictures of a cracked-up car and found damning evidence just sitting there in the cup holder, a tiny slip of paper with a time-and-date stamp that blew up any possible defense. Amazing. Abby had been on the fringes of the PI game for only a few months, but already she understood what sustained the profession: people lied, and people were stupid.

Oh, and one more: People sued. People *loved* to sue.

That was precisely what worried the good folks in the risk-mitigation office of Hammel College, her current client. When a world-renowned engineer was killed on your campus while in the care of a student escort, you didn't have to be paranoid to imagine the lawsuit.

Abby sat at the bar, sipped her beer, and reviewed the case file. She didn't see much for the college to worry about. The girl who'd been escorting the engineer around town had had clean blood-work—a relief to the college, since it meant no DUI claim, but not much help to the girl, because she was still lights-out, five days in a coma now. And even though she had a negative drug screen, she could still have been negligent or at fault, which could turn into an expensive wrongful-death suit, but—good news for the Hammel Hurricanes—the second driver involved had taken responsibility on the scene!

He'd given a full statement to the police that was the accident-report equivalent of tying a hangman's noose and sticking his own head through it: He'd been using his cell phone, trying to get his bearings through the phone's map application, and when he looked up, he realized that what he'd thought was a road bridge was in fact a pedestrian bridge. He swerved to avoid it—and ended up in a hell of a lot of trouble.

Mr. Carlos Ramirez of Brighton, Massachusetts, was now into the realm of criminal courts, because one person was dead and another was a vegetable and Ramirez had eliminated any compelling argument for even a shared-fault case, what was known in Maine as modified comparative negligence. A good investigator paired with a good attorney could almost always find a weasel's way into a modified-comparative-negligence ruling, but Carlos Ramirez was going to make it tough on his team.

It was Abby's job to imagine what that team was considering, though, and in this case, it would be Tara Beckley's location at the time of the accident. She was supposed to deliver her charge to an auditorium that was nowhere near where she'd parked. Some enterprising attorney might wonder whether her failure to follow the plan for the evening's keynote speaker might qualify as negligence and, if so, whether the college might be responsible for that.

After Tara had parked her CRV beside a bridge that led to the Hammel College campus, Carlos Ramirez smashed into the car, killing Amandi Oltamu and knocking Tara Beckley into the cold waters of the Willow River. A bystander on the opposite side of the river had heard the crash but hadn't seen it, and he managed to pull her out in a heroic but ultimately futile effort, because Tara Beckley was in a coma from which she was unlikely to emerge.

That left one dead man, one silent woman, and no witnesses.

I need to get my hands on her cell phone, Abby thought. Cell phones could either save you or hang you in almost any accident investigation. The beautiful simplicity of the case against Ramirez could be destroyed by something like a text message from Tara Beckley saying that her car had run out of gas or that she had a migraine and couldn't see well enough to drive. You just never knew. Dozens of apps kept tracking information that most users were blissfully unaware of; it was entirely possible that the precise timing of the accident could be established from a cell phone. And if Tara Beckley had been using the phone while she was behind the wheel, Oltamu's family might take a renewed interest in suing the college and their selected escort. Any whiff of negligence had to be considered.

Only problem: her phone seemed to be missing.

So it went into the river with her, Abby thought. *She came up, and the phone didn't.*

She drained her beer and frowned, flipping back and forth through the pages of the report. Explaining Tara Beckley's missing phone didn't seem to be difficult, but Amandi Oltamu's phone could also contain evidence, and Abby didn't see where that was either. The police report included the items removed from the car, and the coroner's report had a list of personal effects removed from the body, ranging from a wallet to a Rolex.

No phone, though.

The lead investigator was a guy with the state police named David Meredith. Abby wasn't eager to speak to police these days, considering that there were two cops in California still urging a prosecutor to press charges against her for an accident that had made her more of a celebrity than she'd ever desired to be.

The concern conjured the memory, as it always did. Luke's empty eyes, his limp hand, the soft whistle and hiss of the machines that kept him breathing. Synthetic life. And the photographers waiting outside the hospital for a shot of the woman responsible for it all: Abby Kaplan, the woman who'd killed Luke London, cut down a rising star in his prime. James Dean and Luke London, joined in immortality, young stars killed in car crashes. The only difference was that Luke hadn't been driving the car.

That was a fun little secret about his movies. He never drove the car.

Never felt any shame over that either. Luke was completely

comfortable in his own skin, happy to hand the keys over to a woman who barely came up to his shoulder, to smile that magazine-cover smile and say, "One day you'll teach me how to do it myself."

And I was going to. That was the idea, you see. It was his idea, not mine, I just happened to have the wheel, and my hands were steady, my hands were…

She shook her head, the gesture violent enough to draw a curious glance from the bartender, and Abby tried to recover by pointing at her now-empty glass, as if she'd been intending to attract attention.

One more, sure. One more couldn't hurt.

She took out her phone to call David Meredith. He was safe. Most people here were. This was why she'd come back to Maine. David Meredith knew Abby only as Hank Bauer's employee, nothing more. Hank was the closest thing Abby had to family, and he wasn't telling any tales about her return to Maine. She owed him good work in exchange, even if that meant speaking with police.

She found Meredith's number, called, and explained what she was working on.

"You guys caught that one?" Meredith said. "Good for Hank. It's easy money."

"Sure looks that way," Abby agreed. "But I'm heading out to take some pictures at the scene and see if there was anything that might be trouble for the college."

"There isn't. Tell the lawyers they can sleep easy."

"I'm curious about the phones, actually. Where are they?"

"We've got his."

"Ramirez's, you mean?"

"Yeah."

"What about hers? Or Oltamu's?"

David Meredith paused. "I'm assuming hers is in the water."

"Sure. But his?"

"The coroner's office, probably."

"The report doesn't account for it. His wallet and watch and keys and even a comb were mentioned. But there was no phone."

"So he didn't have one. Some people don't. His doesn't matter, anyhow. Now hers, I could see what you're worried about there. Was she texting or whatever. But…she was parked and out of the car. Hard to imagine a scenario where she gets blamed."

"She wasn't where she was supposed to be. That's my only worry."

"I can't help you on that one. But like you said, the wreck is simple, and Ramirez is going to be formally charged tomorrow. That'll help you. I've got to talk to the girl's family today. I'll ask about the phone, see if I can figure out who the last person to hear from her was."

"Great." Abby thanked Meredith and hung up, glad that her client was the university, faceless and emotionless, and not the family of that girl in the coma. Five days she'd been in there, alive but unresponsive. Abby didn't like to imagine that, let alone see it. That was precisely the kind of shit that could get in her head and take her back…

"I'll have one more," she told the bartender.

One more wouldn't kill her. It just might save her, in fact. Thinking about the girl in the hospital and wondering if her eyes were open or closed was not the sort of image Abby needed in her head before she got behind the wheel. Another beer would help. People didn't understand that, but another beer would *help*.

Abby was five foot three and a hundred and fifteen pounds, and two pints of Sebago Runabout Red would bring her blood alcohol content up to, oh, 0.4. Maybe 0.5, tops. Still legal. And steadier.

A whiskey for the spine and a beer for the shooting hand, her dad used to say. Abby had no idea where he'd picked up that phrase, but it had always made her laugh. He also liked to say *One more and then we'll all go,* which was even funnier because he was usually drinking alone. Jake Kaplan had been one funny guy. Maybe not in the mornings, but, hell, who was funny in the morning?

Abby sipped the pint and held her slim right hand out level above the bar.

Steady as a rock.

She turned back to the case file and flipped through it to see where the cars were impounded. Tara Beckley's CRV and the cargo van rented by Carlos Ramirez had both been hauled off by an outfit with the exquisite name of Savage Sam's Salvage.

Abby called. The phone was answered almost immediately with one curt word: "Sam."

Savage Sam? Abby almost asked, but she managed to hold that one back and explained who she was and why she was calling.

"Ayuh, I got 'em both, the van and the Honda," Sam acknowledged without much interest. "Both of 'em beat to shit, but the Honda took it worse. Those are little SUVs, but they're stout, so it must've taken a pretty good pop."

Abby thought of the photos of the bloodstained pavement and of Tara Beckley in her hospital bed, body running on tubes and machines, eyes wide open and staring at Abby.

"Yes," she said. "It did take a good pop. I'll need to see the vehicles, but I'm also interested in what you might have found in the car."

"I don't steal shit out of cars, honey."

That was an interesting reaction.

"My name is Abby, not honey, and I didn't mean to imply that you stole anything," she said. "It's just that I'm looking for a phone that seems to have gone missing and that might still be in the car."

There was a long pause before he said, "I can check it again, maybe."

First the adamant claim that he didn't steal things out of cars, now the willingness to check it again. Perhaps Savage Sam was uptight for a reason. Abby had a hunch that he was going to discover the phone—and maybe a few other valuables. She suspected this wasn't the first time he'd swept through a wrecked car in his impound lot.

"I'd appreciate that," Abby said. "Because that phone is going to be pretty important to the case, and we've got one dead and one in a coma. You know what that'll lead to—trial, lawyers, cops, all that happy crap."

She said it casually but made sure to emphasize the police and lawyers. It did not seem to be lost on Savage Sam, who said in a more agreeable tone of voice, "It's possible I overlooked somethin'."

Abby smiled. "Can happen to anyone. If you don't mind checking, that would be great. And I can keep the cops out of your hair. If they come by, they'll waste more of your time than I will, you know?"

"I'll check it, sure," Savage Sam said, now seeming positively enthusiastic about the prospect.

"Just give me a call back if you find anything."

Five minutes, she thought when she hung up. That was how long it would take Savage Sam to call back with news of the discovery of a cell phone. He probably already had it in his desk drawer, waiting on a buyer from Craigslist or eBay.

She was wrong—it took nine minutes.

"It turns out there *was* one in there," Savage Sam informed her with a level of shock more appropriate for the discovery of a live iguana in one's toilet. "Jammed down by the gas pedal and wedged just between it and the floor mat. Crazy—I *never* would've seen it unless I'd been looking for it."

Abby grinned. "I bet. Well, I'm sure glad you checked again for me."

"Yeah, happy to help."

"You're positive there was just one?" Abby said.

"Positive. What do you want me to do with it?"

"I can pick it up today, or I can have the police do it?"

"Why don't you grab it," Sam said. "I don't need to get in the middle of things."

Abby wondered just how much swag this guy sold. "I can be there just before five, if that works for you?"

"That works."

Abby paid the tab. Three beers—when had the third one snuck in there? Oh, well, she was still legal. One for the spine, one for the shooting hand, and one for the memories she'd rather not let into her head while she was behind the wheel. Clarity could be a bitch sometimes.

5

"She won't quit," Shannon Beckley insists.

Her face is hovering just inches from Tara's, but she's squinting like someone peering through a microscope, searching for something. Her voice carries conviction, but her eyes lack it. Her eyes think the search might be hopeless.

"Trust me," Shannon says.

I always trust you, Tara answers, but no sound comes out. Why isn't there a sound? Strange. She starts to speak again but Shannon interrupts. Not unusual with Shannon.

"Trust me," Shannon repeats, "this girl...will...not...quit." Shannon's green eyes are searing; her auburn hair is falling across her face, and her expression is as severe as any boot-camp drill sergeant's. Tara can smell Shannon's Aveda moisturizer, with its hint of juniper, and feel her breath warm on her cheek. She's that close, and yet Shannon's eyes suggest that she feels far away, unable to see whatever she's looking at. That's confusing, because she's looking at Tara.

Good for her if she will not quit, Tara tells her sister, and again there is no sound, but that concern is replaced by confusion. Hang on—*who* will not quit? And what is it that she's not going to quit?

Shannon is always forceful, but her face and words carry heightened intensity as she makes these stark but meaningless assertions about the girl who will not quit.

Not her eyes, though, Tara thinks. *Her eyes are not nearly so sure about things.*

Shannon leans away then, and the light that floods into Tara's face is harsh and white. At first she can't see anything because of that brightness, but then it dulls, as if someone has dialed back a dimmer switch, and she sees her mother. Her mother is crying. Rick is rubbing her shoulders. Good old Rick. Always the man with a hand for the shoulder and a comforting word. Usually the words don't mean much, silly platitudes, bits of recycled wisdom. But Tara's mother needs a steady diet of encouragement. The supportive touches and comforting words do the job she used to let the pills do.

But what is today's crisis? Tara watches her mother cry and watches Rick rub her back with a slow, circular motion that feels nearly hypnotic, and she tries to determine what the problem is, why everyone is so scared, so sad.

Oh, yeah—someone won't quit, that's the problem.

Tara's mouth is dry and her head aches and she is very tired. Too tired to deal with her mother's anxiety yet again. Let Rick deal with it. And Shannon. Shannon is here, ready to take charge, as always. Why is Shannon here? She's in her last year of law school at Stanford, and Shannon doesn't miss classes. Ever. But here she is…

Where is here? Where am I?

She knows this should matter, and yet it doesn't seem to. Between Rick's soothing and Shannon's shouting, it will all work out. Tara isn't needed for this one. She's too tired for this one.

What is this one?

The girl who won't quit. That girl is the problem. Who exactly she is and what exactly she is up to, Tara doesn't know, but the girl who won't quit is clearly causing the trouble here. Tara is too tired to join them all in their concern, though. The whole scene exhausts her and makes her strangely angry. Whoever the girl is, she needs to back the hell off and leave everyone alone. Look at them. Just look at their faces. See those tears, that fatigue, that sorrow? Back off, bitch. Back off and leave them alone.

Just go away.

Tara decides she will sleep again. Maybe while she sleeps, this relentless problem girl will finally abandon her confusing quest.

All Tara understands with certainty is that it will be better for everyone when that girl finally quits.

6

Savage Sam might've been sixty or a hundred. Either one seemed reasonable. He stood well over six feet, even with his stooped stance, and that natural forward lean paired with his unusually long arms gave the impression that he could have untied his boots without changing posture.

"I might not have been completely clear about the phone when we talked," he said when he greeted Abby at the front gate. He was carrying a shoe box.

"You don't have it?"

"Oh, no, I think I've got it."

Abby frowned. "I don't follow. Either you have it or you don't."

"Not necessarily," the old man said, and then he took the lid off the shoe box. Inside were at least a dozen cell phones as well as a heap of chargers and three GPS navigators.

"Now, before you get to thinkin' somethin' that isn't true," Sam cautioned, "I want you to know that I always hang on to them for thirty days before I sell them. A firm policy. Otherwise it'd be stealing."

"The state law is thirty days?"

Savage Sam blinked and squinted. He had bifocals tucked into the pocket of his flannel shirt but chose to squint instead, as if the glasses were a prop or he'd forgotten he had them. Or perhaps he'd swiped them out of a car and was intending to sell them later.

"It's awful close to thirty days, even if it isn't exactly that," he said. "They might've changed it."

Abby didn't think they'd changed the law regarding the presumption that whatever was in a wrecked car belonged to the car's owner, but she wasn't interested in debating the point. "That many people leave their phones?" she asked, peering into the bulging box. "Most people these days would rather cut off their hands than walk away from their phones."

"A lot of times it's probably an old phone or a backup or something. People give phones to their parents or grandparents, and the old-timers have no use for them, so they just pitch them into the glove compartment and forget about them. And you'd be surprised how many I find that are still in the boxes they came in."

It made some sense. She stared at the contents of the shoe box.

"You don't know which one came from the Honda, then?"

"Well...no. I mean, I just picked it up and threw it in there. Didn't think about it. Now, I recall it was one of the nicer ones. Probably an iPhone." His wizened thumb jammed into the box and shifted an iPhone forward, then another, and then a third. "But I don't know exactly which one. And with you saying there's police involved, and a man's been killed and all...it would probably be easier if you sorted it out."

He offered the box. Abby took it, contents shifting, and put the lid back on. If she just got them charged up and called numbers for Oltamu and Tara Beckley, the winner would ring.

"I've been here forty years and my brother's had a pawnshop for thirty-nine," Savage Sam said. "It works pretty well, you know?"

"I'd imagine so," Abby said, thinking that keeping crime in the family often did.

"I guess we were always the pack-rat kind. Hell, even the sign required a bit of scavenging."

He gestured above them, and the sign was indeed a sight to behold—a massive, old-fashioned neon marquee that would have been appropriate for a drive-in movie theater. *Savage Sam's Salvage* was lit up like the Fourth of July, even though the property didn't seem to consist of much more than an old man and a tow truck.

"It is an impressive sign," Abby acknowledged. "Mind if I ask about the name? Savage Sam?"

Sam leaned back, which brought him nearly to an upright posture, and grinned. For an instant Abby had a glimpse of what he must've looked like as a kid, one of those hell-raisers who charmed teachers and parents and then set the town on fire when the adults turned their backs.

"They misspelled it," he said, and laughed. "Was supposed to read *Sam's Salvage*. Simple. But then the sign came, two pieces, one said *Sam's*, the other said *Savage*. They forgot the *L*! I was *pissed* at first. Because the sign wasn't cheap. So I called the guy who sold it to me and gave him hell, asking what kind of idiot could screw up a sign with only two damned words. Dumb as he was, I guess I should've been grateful he got *Sam's* right. Anyhow, he sent me a replacement sign that had the mysterious missing *L*, but he didn't ask for the other one back. Shit, why should he? So I had the three of 'em, and I got to looking them over and I thought, *Why waste it?*"

Now Abby was laughing too. "So you just hung them all up?"

"Sure. I thought it was kind of catchy. By then, I was starting to like it. You know how there are always those kids with nicknames and you never had one? Or did you have one?"

Abby had earned plenty of nicknames on the speedway, some more kind than others. Even the kinder ones, like Danica, had usually been offered with a sneer.

"I'm just Abby," she told Sam, though she was remembering the Wiscasset Speedway; she'd become the first woman to win there. Someone had spray-painted *White Trash Rocket* on the driver's door before the race.

"Well, I'd always been just plain old Sam Jones, no nickname coming out of that, but then that idiot screwed up the sign and I've been Savage Sam about ever since." He laughed again. "But, hell, no reason to waste it. Like I said, my family's always been pack rats."

He seemed so happy staring at the old misspelled sign that Abby almost hated to interrupt his reverie. But she did. "The phone was in the Honda, right? Not the van?"

Sam blinked, jogged out of the past and into the present. "Yup, the Honda. I'm telling you, I never could've seen it down there if you hadn't asked me to look. You don't know which phone it is?"

"I don't. I'll have to charge them and call them, I guess. That'll take a while."

"Keep 'em all overnight, then. Just bring the rest back."

We wouldn't want those falling into the wrong hands before they hit the pawnshop, would we? Abby thought. "You're good with that?" she said. "You want to take an inventory of them or anything? A photo?"

It seemed like there should be some record of the transfer of evidence between two people who were not police, but the question apparently struck Savage Sam as an odd one. He thought it over and said, "You got a card or something?"

"Um…yeah." Abby fumbled through her purse and withdrew a business card. It had Hank Bauer's name on it; Abby had declined cards of her own on at least a half a dozen occasions because any formality suggested that this job might last for more than a few weeks. Never mind that she'd already been at it a few months. The gig was temporary, and she'd be West Coast–bound again soon, or back to Europe, maybe, or possibly Tokyo. Sure. Any day now. And until then, she had Hank Bauer's cards to hand over.

"You don't want to write down what all I'm taking?" she asked.

"This'll do." Sam pocketed the card. "Either you're gonna steal 'em or you're not." He shrugged.

With that official police business having been concluded with no police, no signatures, and the exchange of a shoe box, Abby decided to push ahead.

"You still have the cars?" she asked.

Savage Sam nodded. "Right out back. You want a look?"

"Please."

Despite his odd posture and nearsighted squint, Sam moved quickly, stepping nimbly around the piles of junk—hubcaps, a massive bag of bottles, a stack of what appeared to be truck fenders covered by a tarp—and out to the cars.

Tara Beckley's green Honda CRV was all too familiar to Abby from the photos; there was scarcely any part of the car left undamaged except for the driver's seat. Tara would have been better off if she'd stayed behind the wheel. Abby leaned down and looked at the floor mat there—it was khaki-colored, clean, and dry. The phone would've surely stood out against it. There was no trace of blood on the fabric.

The same couldn't be said for the backseat. She got only a glance at the crimson stains across the ripped upholstery before she felt dizzy, and she straightened up fast.

"He must've been driving to beat hell when he hit her," Sam said conversationally, running his long, knobby-knuckled fingers over the crumpled metal. "See the frame damage you got here? That doesn't happen at low speed. He must've been—"

"Where's the van?" Abby cut in. She hadn't intended to be rude; she simply wanted an excuse to look away from the bloodstained Honda.

"Right over here," Sam said without reproach. His interest in the Honda's former occupants and their blood was minimal.

The van was a cargo hauler with a heavy bumper that was crushed back into the hood. Damaged, yes, but nothing significant compared to the Honda.

"Those vans are big, heavy bastards," Sam said with admiration. "Wasn't even carrying a load, but it probably goes four thousand pounds empty. And as tall as it is, shit, that little car didn't have much of a chance. I heard he was using his phone or something.

Ain't surprising. You drive down the road any day of the week and pay attention, you'll see how many of these jackasses are driving with their heads down, not giving a damn about anybody on the road but... what are you looking at?"

Abby was on her knees in the gravel, one hand braced on the van. "The tires."

"They're still worth selling," Sam acknowledged. They'd probably be on their way to his brother's pawnshop before long.

And he wasn't wrong about the tires. They were certainly worth selling; the tread didn't look worn. The daylight was dying, and in the shadows, Abby couldn't find a wear-indicator bar on the tires, so she set the shoe box down and searched her purse for a coin. Sam's gnarled fingers appeared in her face, a penny held between them.

"Thanks." Abby rotated the penny so Abe Lincoln's head was pointed down and inserted the coin between the tire's tread grooves. Lincoln's head sank below the black rubber and vanished up to the shoulders. Sam was right; the tires were nearly new.

Abby sat back on her heels and stared first at the van, then at the Honda.

"I might need to come back and take some pictures," she said. "Tomorrow morning, when I return the phones?"

"I guess," Sam said. He sounded resigned to trouble. "Hell, I ought to stop taking cop tows. They ain't worth the hassle."

"I'll try to keep it from becoming a hassle for you," Abby said, no longer caring much if the old man had intended to sell the stolen phone. He'd turned it over, at least. Savage Sam of the misspelled neon signs wasn't such a bad guy. "I'll get in and out, quick and painless, I promise."

"That's what they told me the last time I had a colonoscopy," Sam said.

7

Ghosts are real.

Tara knows this because she is one.

When clarity first returns, she sees her mother, her stepfather, and her sister. She sees them and she hears Shannon's voice and thinks: *The dream is done.*

She thinks, slower and more carefully, because it is so important: *I am alive.*

There is relief with that realization, but it is a temporary relief, because she soon determines that she is invisible.

Shannon is arguing with Rick and Mom, but she is arguing on Tara's behalf, and Rick and Mom are facing Tara, staring right at her but not seeing her.

"She wouldn't quit on us, and so I am not going to listen to anyone say one word about what we must *consider*," Shannon snaps. "Because what you're *considering* is quitting on your own daughter!"

Tara looks into her mother's eyes and waits for recognition, awareness, something. *Notice me, speak to me, touch me.* But her mother just stares blankly, her eyes bloodshot and ringed by dark circles. She doesn't seem to see Tara. Rick looks at Tara as well, his bearded face doing a poor job of hiding his annoyance with Shannon. He doesn't see Tara either. She's used to being ignored by Rick—and to ignoring him—but this is different. He's looking right at her and yet for all the world he seems to be staring at a wall.

I'm invisible. Maybe I'm not alive. Maybe I'm dead, and this is what it's like?

She is a ghost. The realization is sudden and certain. It is the only explanation for her condition.

How did I die?

"It's too early to talk like this," Shannon says, and Rick closes his eyes with fatigue. Mom just keeps staring. Shannon starts to speak again, then thinks better of it, shakes her head furiously, and stalks to the window. Everyone is quiet then. Tara wants to speak but her tongue is heavy and rigid and uncooperative in her mouth, and so she lies there and tries to gather her voice.

It is then that understanding begins to come, agonizingly slowly, like filling a glass one drop of water at a time.

Mom. Rick. Shannon. A television turned to CNN, but muted. A bed with a pair of feet resting on it. Wait—those are her feet. She is in the bed. The bed is not her own. The room is not her own. Her confusingly thick tongue is not a tongue at all—it is a tube. There are more tubes in other places, and she's aware of them now, first with pain and then some shame. There are wires too, a seemingly endless amount of wires.

Hospital.

Yes, that is it. She is in a hospital, and she is not a ghost. Not just yet. What is she, though?

"Every coma is different," Shannon says without turning, her voice trembling with barely subdued anger, and in that sentence, in that single word—*coma*—Tara has her answer.

She has been in a coma. This makes sense; it's a better explanation than anything she's come up with on her own. But she is out of the coma now, because she is awake and alert and she can see and hear. Why don't they notice this? Why don't they see that she is awake?

Because you haven't said anything, dummy. Tell them!

Hello, Tara says.

No one reacts. Shannon doesn't turn; Mom's stare doesn't break; Rick's slumped shoulders don't tense.

Panic rises then, a terrible, claustrophobic panic, and this time Tara screams, determined to be heard.

I'm right here!

Nothing. Shannon stares out the window, Mom bows her head, Rick stands slumped and weary.

This time, Tara understands, though. She didn't make a sound. Her scream had produced...nothing.

Had she even parted her lips? Surely she had. She'd screamed at the top of her lungs, screamed in terror and confusion, and no one had reacted. How is this possible? Maybe there is a wall between them, some sort of glass partition, the kind with a mirror on their side like in the cop shows so she can see them but they can't see her.

This thought brings logic back to an insane world, and the terror subsides. She tells herself to sit up and figure out the two-way mirror, find that glass panel and rap on it and get their attention, let them know that she is here, she is back, awake again.

Sit up.

She thinks the words, visualizes the motion, and waits. Nothing happens. She's still lying down, and she should be upright. Just...sit up.

But she can't.

The terror is back now.

She tries again but makes no progress, and, worse, she realizes there's no sense of resistance, nothing holding her down, no weight or strap or anything that would block this simple command to her body. Even if she is injured—and she's in a hospital with tubes and IVs in her, so of course she has been injured—she should be able to fight upward.

She can issue the command, but her body can't obey it.

Paralyzed. Oh no, not that...

She starts to cry then. To cry and shake.

No tears come. No sounds.

Shannon turns and looks down at her, right into her eyes, and

Tara stares back into her older sister's loving face and pleads for help.

Shannon looks away.

"I don't want to hear any of the spiritual shit, Rick," she says. "I do not want to hear it yet."

"I'm sorry that *shit* bothers you, Shannon, but I think it's worth talking about!" Rick answers, taking a step toward her. "You need to begin to ask yourself who this is for, your sister or her body. You need to begin to consider that there is a *difference*."

"I am not *considering* a damn thing until we've seen a neurologist," Shannon says.

"Everyone says if we just keep our faith…" Mom tries timidly, but Shannon isn't having it.

"Everyone on your *Facebook page* says that. While you're making Team Tara posts and people are offering advice from their phones between bites of their bagels, I'm suggesting we consult an actual expert."

Mom winces, Rick sighs, and Shannon lifts her hands in regret. "Sorry. I'm not trying to be a bitch, Mom, I'm really not. The Facebook page is important. I get that. But I don't want us to begin premature conversations."

"Our job will be to imagine her quality of life," Rick says softly, "and you can't even reach that point until you know whether there *is* a life."

"She's breathing!" Shannon shouts. "Her heart is beating! Her eyes are open, she's *watching* us!"

Rick points at Tara, a beaded bracelet jangling on his right wrist. He is looking directly at her but seems to see only an empty bed.

"Her body is doing those things, yes. But where is Tara?" he asks in that pastoral whisper he uses so often to calm their mother. "Look into her eyes, Shannon, and then tell me. Where is *Tara* right now?"

I am right fucking here! Tara shouts.

They all turn toward her then, and for a moment she thinks she's made contact. Then she realizes they are just following Rick's outstretched hand and considering his question.

"Tell me, Shannon," he whispers, moving his hand to rub his graying beard. "Where...is...she?"

When Shannon says, "I don't know," the tears overwhelm Tara again.

No one in the room knows that she's right there, and no one in the room knows that she's crying.

8

The place where Amandi Oltamu had died was beautiful and peaceful. Crisp orange leaves glowed in the fading sunlight as they swirled across the pavement, and beneath them were glittering bits of pebbled glass that the cleanup effort had missed. The blood had been hosed off the pavement.

Abby stepped out of her car, looked at that bright, too-clean patch of asphalt, and tried to ignore the steady accelerating of her heartbeat.

Exposure therapy, that's what this job of studying car wrecks was supposed to be. You kept things from taking up damaging residence in your brain by meeting them on your own terms in small, planned doses, building up a tolerance. The mind was no different than the body—it could become immune to a bad memory just like it could to a virus.

This was what a therapist in California had told her. Granted, the therapist hadn't recommended changing careers, let alone moving back to Maine. She'd encouraged Abby to look at some pictures, that was all. And Abby had tried. But...

But the therapist hadn't killed her boyfriend in a car wreck, and once you've done that, well, those pictures can become harder to look at than most people would believe.

The job Abby had now was an almost ludicrous outgrowth of a technique she'd been asked to embrace in California, but she was the only person who understood the bridge between the two. Nobody on the West Coast knew what she was doing now, and she hadn't volunteered any of her stories to Hank or anyone else in Maine. She'd had absolutely no desire to.

Until today, at least. When Hank had given her the overview of the wreck in Hammel, Abby had almost broken and told him the details of her horror story, told him about the way Luke's hand had closed on her arm just before they left the road, told him that *maybe* his last words hadn't been *Faster, Abby,* but rather *Slow down,* told him how his eyes had seemed to track hers in the hospital even after the doctors said there was absolutely no indication of awareness. For an instant, she'd been ready to tell Hank that under no circumstances could she investigate an accident that had put someone in a coma.

She hadn't said a word, though. In the end, she'd just taken the file and headed out to do her job—with that quick stop for a beer on the way. Because the past was the past, Luke was nothing but a memory, and Abby couldn't afford to spend any more of her life with her eyes on the rearview mirror.

But now, standing here in the cold fall air with the sun setting behind the wooded hills and the smell of the sea riding the wind, she couldn't bring herself to look at the wreck photos. They would make her think of the miles of roads that lurked between here and home. Intersections and stoplights, sharp curves and banked slopes, all of those challenges so simply handled by basic instinct, and challenges that could be turned into creative triumphs if your mind was fast and your hands were steady. It was a bitch if that basic instinct ever wavered on you, but if you'd once had a fast mind and steady hands and a hundred and twenty miles per hour felt like fifty? In that case, it was worse. Deeper and darker. In that case, you began to feel like you didn't really know yourself anymore.

Focus, damn it. Focus on the job and then get out of here.

She stood at the base of the hill and looked out at the two-lane bridge that crossed the river and led to the college campus. There was a concrete pillar on the sidewalk identifying the bridge's place in the state's history. This was what Tara Beckley's CRV had struck after Carlos Ramirez, his head down and cell phone glowing, drove his van into the car.

Lives ended from mere moments of distraction. Happened all too often.

Doesn't require distraction, though. There are variations on the lost-lives theme. Stunt drivers taking famous actors out for a spin, for example. Those trips can end badly too.

Again, Abby could see Luke's hand reaching for hers.

She shook her head, then walked up the hill to put herself in the position the van's driver had been in. She took out her camera and pivoted slowly, shooting a 360-degree view. The sun was sinking fast and lights were visible on both sides of the bridge. The campus was on the western side of the river, and atop the steep hill on the east, everything was residential. If Ramirez hadn't already fallen on his sword, there might have been some mitigation from the lighting. The streetlights were toned-down replicas of old gas lamps, designed more for aesthetics than illumination.

Abby was about 280 degrees through her 360-degree turn when she lowered the camera and frowned, thinking of the massive amount of destruction done to Tara Beckley's Honda CRV. Carlos Ramirez had to have been hauling ass when he hit them to inflict that sort of damage. Down a steep hill and into those angled parking spaces…

She paced up the hill a few steps and turned to look back at the parking spots.

The wind that gusted and stirred the brittle leaves was getting colder. Abby zipped up her fleece and paced back down to the edge of the bridge and looked up at the hill, and now her old instincts were alive. This insurance investigator—could there be a less glamorous occupation?—had once been the fabled Professional Driver on a Closed Course, and while that was an adrenaline-jockey business, it was also a science-based business.

Abby Kaplan didn't need to run a calculation to know what was troubling her—the police photos didn't do justice to the hill.

That hill was much steeper than Abby had imagined. The road crested and then seemed to dive toward the river. The police had probably viewed that as a contributing factor to the wreck. Carlos Ramirez had been driving an unfamiliar cargo van, he'd been going fast, he'd been distracted, and he'd been on a dangerous slope. Check, check, check, check. All of that played well on paper. But...

How come he didn't roll it?

Abby chewed her lip and stared at that steep hill rising from the river and thought about the nearly new tires she'd seen on the van.

There were two types of rollovers, tripped and untripped. Most rollover accidents were tripped, which meant that some external object—a curb, a ditch, a guardrail—upset the vehicle's balance. The rarer untripped rollovers were the result of the battle among three cornering forces: centripetal (tire friction), inertial (vehicle mass), and good old gravity.

Untripped rollovers were caused or avoided by the driver's ability (or lack thereof) to understand and control the car. The driver was alone in that critical moment, tethered to the world by nothing but four points of rubber and her own skill.

Abby could remember standing on a course in Germany waiting to drive a Mercedes prototype while an engineer droned on about this; she kept wishing she could just get behind the wheel and *go* because her hands and eyes already understood everything the guy was babbling about.

Back then they had, at least.

He'd been talking about the CSV, or critical sliding velocity. She had started to pay more attention at that point, because he'd uttered the word that owned Abby's heart: *velocity*. The CSV formula determined the minimum lateral speed at which the vehicle would roll.

When he'd killed Amandi Oltamu and knocked Tara Beckley into a coma, Carlos Ramirez had been executing a fishhook maneuver. On test runs, that meant you followed a fishhook-shaped curve: You went straight, then turned sharply in one direction—as you'd do to avoid something in the road—then overcorrected in the other. On each run, you widened your path, steering at sharper and sharper angles, testing it until the tires howled and threatened to lift off the pavement—or until they did lift off.

Abby had executed maybe two thousand fishhook runs. She didn't need an engineering degree to see the problem with the scenario on the bridge across from Hammel College. The slope was too steep and the fishhook turn was too narrow.

He'd have rolled first. He might have hit Beckley's car, but he'd have had his van on its side by the time he did. The cargo van was too tall, its center of mass too high, to handle such abrupt cornering and remain upright.

Unless he'd never tried to turn. Unless he'd been coming straight at them, targeting them.

Abby didn't hesitate to look at the photos this time. Her curiosity had overridden her apprehension, and she was able to see past the blood on the pavement and focus on the vehicle positions.

The cargo van was upright, the CRV was upright, the damage was catastrophic, and all of that made sense until you stood down here and looked up the hill and thought about the angles.

Her phone rang, a shrill shattering of the quiet, and she closed the accident report and looked at the phone. Hank Bauer, her boss and friend and onetime sponsor, a man who'd paid the fees to get a teenage Abby Kaplan into stock-car races in Wiscasset, Scarborough, and Oxford.

"Hey, Hank."

"How's it going, Abs?"

"Fine. Actually . . . well, it's a little messed up."

"Whaddya mean?"

"Something's wrong in that report. What Ramirez said happened is impossible. It might be what he *thinks* happened, but it isn't right."

Hank's voice dropped an octave. "He smashed directly into a parked car. How wrong can he be about *that?*"

"He would have tipped that van," Abby said. "Hank, I'm telling you, there's no way he could have hit the passenger side of her car that hard if he'd swerved the way he said he did. He'd have rolled it into the river first."

"Let the police worry about Ramirez," Hank said. "I just want our girl Tara to be clean as a whistle. Okay?"

"Right," Abby said, but she didn't like it because she wanted someone who could talk on her level about this problem. She changed tack instead. "I might have good news there. I think I've got her phone."

"How'd you do that?"

Abby told him about the trip to the salvage yard, and Hank began to laugh before she was done.

"Only thing surprising about that is Sam hadn't sold it yet."

"Well, I've got a box of phones now and I don't know which is hers. I'll charge them up tonight and test them."

"Save yourself the trouble—you can ask her sister tomorrow."

"What?"

"She wants to know what you're doing, I guess. Wants to meet you. Wants to meet anyone and everyone who's involved."

"She's coming up here?"

"No, you're going down there, to the hospital in Massachusetts. Bring your treasure chest from Savage Sam along."

"The hospital? Why?" Abby felt a cold fist tighten in her gut. She did not want to go to the hospital. She most sincerely did not want to see that girl in the coma. "I'll call the sister. I don't need to go to Boston to see her in the hospital."

"You think I don't know that? I already called her. The sister is a law-school student but apparently believes she's already passed the bar and been appointed district attorney. I'm glad it's you and not me who gets the treat of meeting her in person."

"I'm not wasting a day in Boston just to explain what I'm doing."

"Like hell you're not. Billable hours! Abby, do you have any idea how much I can soak that college for? If the family wants to see you at the hospital, you go to the friggin' hospital. You can show her the phones. That won't be a waste of time. And you can take the Challenger!"

His enthusiasm made Abby close her eyes. "I'm good with the Chrysler, thanks."

"Aw, c'mon, Abs." Sorrowful now. "I bought the damned thing."

"Nobody told you to."

"Just drive it, would you? Get a taste again. See what it does for you."

"I'll think about it," Abby said, and then she hung up.

What Hank wanted her driving was a Dodge Challenger Hellcat with 707 horsepower growling under a black-on-red hood. He'd bought it for well under value after it was repossessed by a friend of his who sold cars in New Hampshire. Because Hank still believed Abby craved speed, he'd purchased the Challenger and offered it to her as a temporary "company car."

It could do zero to sixty in under four seconds, was outfitted with Pirelli racing tires, and was generally everything one could want in a modern American muscle car.

Abby hadn't had it over sixty miles an hour yet.

On a couple of occasions, Abby pretended that she'd put the car through its paces on the back roads and been duly impressed. One part of that wasn't a lie—she *did* keep it on the back roads. That was because she could avoid the anxiety of driving in traffic and at higher speeds, though, not so she could test those beautiful Pirellis on a double-S curve.

Hank wasn't wrong. Abby should have been driving it. Exposure therapy. Stare the fear down, in small doses.

Soon, she told herself.

Any day now.

She pocketed the phone and walked toward her Chrysler 300, a pleasant if somewhat staid sedan. Nothing threatening about it. Not like the Challenger Hellcat.

As she crossed the road, her right ankle throbbed, a souvenir from an early crack-up at the Oxford Plains Speedway in western Maine. She looked down and watched the way her hiking shoes flexed across the top as she walked sideways across the steep slope. The leather uppers pulled right, toward the river, while the rubber soles fought them and tugged left, biting into the pavement.

It would have rolled, she thought. *That van would have rolled.*

9

When she was a child, Tara was terrified of a house at the end of the road: 1804 London Street. It was a once-grand Victorian built by a family who'd made a small fortune in the days when Cleveland had been a manufacturing boomtown, money later tied up in a bitter feud among the siblings who'd inherited it upon their mother's death. When Tara first saw the house, it had been vacant for at least ten years, the beautiful wood trim rotting beneath peeling paint, the stonework around the gardens and the patio lost to weeds and untamed hedges. For the older kids in the neighborhood, it inspired ghost stories and fevered claims of a woman in white who appeared in the attic window. They would run onto the porch and knock on the door, just like the children in Tara's favorite book, *To Kill a Mockingbird,* and it was probably this association that gave her the bravery to finally join in the fun.

Boo Radley's home had held no terrors. Boo was simply misunderstood, and because all Tara wanted to do in life was be Scout Finch and because she liked to imagine her late father had been like Atticus Finch, she carried out a summer of replication, leaving notes and small treasures tucked in trees and under eaves on the property. However, because this was not a fictional southern town in the 1930s but a Cleveland suburb in the early 2000s, her notes were not replaced with intricate handmade delights. Instead, someone who saw her leaving the notes responded by filling her favorite hidey-hole with condom wrappers.

She stopped trying to re-create her Scout-and-Boo fantasy after that.

But still, she didn't fear the house as she once had. That was the power of imagination, the power of the mind—she'd taken ownership of the place, trading scary stories for warm ones, and with her fantasy vision, she erased the fear. The kids who mocked her might be able to replace her charm bracelets with condom wrappers, but they couldn't replace her new vision of the once-frightening abandoned house.

In her thirteenth summer, she used that power of imagination to win twenty dollars. That summer, when Mom was doing better and Shannon was distracted by the acquisition of her driver's license, a neighborhood boy named Jaylen dared Tara to go into the house alone and appear in a window on each floor, including the turret window of the supposed woman in white. If she did, he said, he'd give her twenty dollars and something she pretended she wanted nothing to do with: a kiss.

"Just the money, creep," she'd told him, but he was tall and handsome and had impossibly beautiful brown eyes and played on the basketball team, and, highly appealing to Tara, he told the most creative of the dumb scary stories about 1804 London Street. He was also black, and to Tara this seemed both exotic and undeniably Scout Finch–approved. If there was anything not to like about Jaylen, Tara hadn't yet discovered it.

He'd forced the front door open with a screwdriver, and then they'd both run away, sure there was an alarm, and hid behind a tree up the street. A few minutes went by and nothing happened, but he told her to wait awhile longer.

"It's probably a silent alarm, like they have in banks," Jaylen said, and Tara found that very wise.

No police came, though, and eventually Jaylen decided that the silent alarm must have been deactivated, probably because they weren't paying the bill, just like nobody paid to keep the lawn mowed. The house was fair game, and the dare was still on.

"You don't have to," he said when they reached the porch. His voice was soft and serious, and Tara realized that now that it had progressed from talk to possibility, he thought it was a bad idea and wanted out, the classic game of chicken that had gone too far. Facing the cracked porch steps and the tall weeds and the filthy windows with crude phrases written in the dust, Tara felt a surge of fear rise up, but she fought it down. She was Scout Finch, after all, and she could not only play with the boys but beat them at their own games. And take their money.

And, maybe, get a kiss.

"I'll wave to you from the windows," she said, and she pushed through the door and into the musty foyer. Stairs rose to the left, ascending into shadows, and in front of her a wide hallway led to what had to be the living room. To the right was a formal parlor or sitting room, old-fashioned chairs positioned around a china hutch that was filled with blue-and-white dishes and crystal glasses. In the center of the room was a puddle, and above it the ceiling sagged around a massive water stain.

The floorboards creaked like trees in a windstorm, but they held, and she reached the first window, looked outside, and saw Jaylen staring apprehensively up at the house. He appeared gravely concerned, more scared than Tara, and this gave her confidence. She grinned at him and waved. Relieved, he waved back, and then hollered that she could come out.

"You don't need to do 'em all! You win! Come back out!"

He wants that kiss, she thought.

Her confidence grew, and she shouted back that she was going to do them all, and then she walked confidently to the stairs.

The problem was the lack of light. A lot of the windows were shuttered and those that weren't were covered with years of filth, so only the dimmest light filtered in, and since she didn't know the house, each step into the darkness was a journey into unfamiliar territory. That built confusion, and confusion fed fear.

She was no longer smiling when she reached the second-floor window, and if Jaylen had yelled at her to come down again, she might have listened. But by now he seemed resigned to her determination not to quit, so he just waved back, silent and seeming very far away.

It took her some time to find the turret window. She was moving too fast, and she took wrong turns, and with each wrong turn, she felt her panic escalate. She was breathing raggedly and she was sweating even though it was cool in the house, and there was a terrible smell coming from behind one of the closed doors, and it took all of her imagination and willpower to fend off the images of a rotting corpse. She stopped, took a deep breath, and said, "Pass the damn ham, please," a Scout Finch quote that delighted her endlessly, particularly when she used it in situations where it made no sense to anyone else.

The line was a reminder of the power of imagination. There was no ghost in 1804 London Street, nothing worse in here than the lingering smell of old cigar smoke, which Tara hated because it reminded her of Mom's cigarette days. The house was as harmless as Boo Radley's home in Maycomb, Alabama, and she was as brave as Scout Finch.

She walked on down the hall through the darkness. When she finally found the turret window, she saw Jaylen pacing the yard nervously, and she had to rap on the glass with her knuckles to get his attention.

This time, instead of waving at her, he beckoned urgently, the message clear: *Get out of there!*

She was ready to go. More than ready; she'd held the panic off for as long as she could, but now the dark and the smells and all those images of what might lurk behind each closed door were piling up, gleefully crowding the space in her mind, a race to see which one would break her.

She was concentrating on staying calm and watching where she put her feet, sure that there would be rusty nails or a piece of broken glass or an ax matted with hair and blood—*Stop that, Tara, stop that!*—and in the intensity of her focus, she completely overshot the main staircase and found herself on an unfamiliar one, tighter and steeper.

For a second, she hesitated, considering going back. Then her hand brushed a cobweb and that made her give a little cry and a jerk, and the steps creaked ominously underfoot, and now she was running, but she ran down, following instinct—the front door was below her, so down was the right direction.

She'd never been in a house with two staircases, and so the idea that it might not lead to the same place as the main stairs never occurred to her. Even when she reached a landing and the staircase bent in an unexpected direction, she trusted it. She had to go down to get out, and down she went, rushing and gasping for breath and feeling her way along the wall with her hand because it was nearly full dark here, and she couldn't see anything beyond the next step.

When she arrived in the cold room that smelled of damp stone, she realized her mistake. She'd bypassed everything and gone straight from the third floor to the cellar. Something rustled in the darkness to her right, and she scampered away and smacked into the wall, then ran right into a cobweb. She screamed, tearing at the sticky threads with both hands. She was no longer Scout Finch; she was Tara Beckley, known as Twitch to her sister, and she was earning the nickname now.

She backed up; her foot skidded on something wet and slick, and then the rustling sound came again, and she whirled and shouted.

That was when she saw daylight.

There was only a faint line of it—it looked as if someone had drawn it with yellow chalk on the dark stone wall—but it was there. She stared at it, gasping and crying, and thought about her options. She could run back the way she'd come and hope to find her way out, or she could cross the darkness and trust that light, however faint.

She trusted the light.

She fell twice crossing the cellar, banging her shin painfully into something hard and metal and then scraping her forearm on a rusted pipe that seemed to be a floor support, but she made it to the other side, and there she saw that the daylight was no illusion. There was a door here. Two of them, actually, heavy steel doors that might once have met squarely in the center but no longer did, offering just enough of a gap to let the light filter through.

She found the handles and pushed, then pulled. Rust flaked off and bit into her palms, and the doors grated over the rough concrete floor, a menacing, grinding sound like the time Shannon had broken the garbage disposal by filling it with Mom's pill bottles. Her hands ached and her shoulders throbbed, but the space between the doors widened slightly, more daylight flooded in, and she felt warm air on her face, and though there was no way she could slip through and escape, she thought the gap was wide enough that she might at least be heard.

She put her face close to the door and shouted for Jaylen over and over.

No one came. She could hear birds and the faint sound of a passing car, but no one answered her.

I'm trapped, she thought. *I will be here forever, somehow I found a staircase that no one else will find, they can search the whole house but they will never find me because the staircase won't be there, it was a trap, and I—*

"Damn it, Tara, what the *hell* were you thinking?"

Her sister's voice came through the doors. Then Shannon's face was in the two-inch gap Tara had opened between the monstrous old doors, and she was staring at Tara with anger and concern.

"Are you okay?" Shannon said. "Are you hurt?"

Tara sniffled out that no, she wasn't hurt, and yes, she was probably okay, she was just scared and she wanted *out*.

"I'll get you out," Shannon said. "Let me get your dumb boyfriend. I think he's scared of me."

With the help of an aluminum baseball bat, Jaylen and Shannon were able to pry the doors far enough apart for Tara to wedge herself through and back to freedom. She was covered in cobwebs and dirt and her shin and arm were bleeding, but she was safe again.

Shannon hauled her home, lecturing her the whole way; Jaylen said good-bye and started to offer Tara a whispered apology but Shannon shot him a look, which accelerated his exit. Once the sisters got back, Shannon told their mother that the car was making a weird noise, which drew her out of the house and into the driveway and let Tara sneak in the back and get herself cleaned up before Mom saw any evidence of her bloody adventure. When she got off the pills, Mom always wanted to play the good-mother role, but by then Shannon had claimed it. Discipline was handled by big sister, period. The same with protection.

Apparently, Shannon thought the scare had been enough for Tara, because she let it drop after extracting a promise from her: *never again* would she enter that house.

Two days later, Jaylen approached Tara cautiously in the yard, glanced left and right, then said, "Your sister isn't here, is she?" When Shannon's absence was confirmed, Tara finally got the twenty dollars and the kiss. A few of the latter, in fact. It turned into a good summer, one of the better ones of Tara's childhood, and she kept her promise to Shannon. She'd never entered 1804 London Street again.

Until now.

She was locked in again, and she didn't know the way out, and all around her was fear and shadow. She was on the dark staircase that she hadn't anticipated, hadn't even known existed, and this time she didn't have the option of turning around and going back the way she'd come.

Propped up in her hospital bed, tubes running up her nose and down her throat, machines humming at her side, and her family sitting around her with no idea where she was, Tara realized that her worst fear from the cellar of 1804 had come true. She was trapped, and they would never find her.

This time, there was no thin line of light for her to chase through the blackness.

10

The neurologist's name was Dr. Pine. His house in Marblehead was everything a prestigious New England doctor's home should be—three stories painted an appropriately coastal gray-blue with gleaming white trim and plenty of windows, exquisite brickwork on the driveway and sidewalks, massive brass light fixtures styled to look like old gas lamps. Lisa Boone waited an hour before he finally arrived, pulling up to the house in an equally appropriate Range Rover. He parked in the garage and put the overhead door down behind him, so Boone walked up the brick path that ran to the door on the side of the garage and waited for him to emerge. When he saw her, he stopped short, startled, and took a step back before determining that she posed no threat—an attractive white woman, thank goodness, no danger here.

"May I help you?" he said. His voice was deeper than his stature would suggest.

"Probably not," Boone said, "but I have to try."

"Pardon?"

"You have a patient named Tara Beckley. I need to speak with you about her."

He frowned and studied her, wary now.

"I can't talk about my patients," he said, "and I'm curious why you're at my home."

"Because the United States government needs you to understand that your patient might have been a casualty of—and, if she lives, potentially a witness to—an execution killing."

His jaw didn't quite drop. His mouth parted and then closed.

He took a breath, then gave a little shake of his head and a half laugh. "I expect to encounter new things every day," he said, "but this one is really something. What branch of the U.S. government needs me to understand this?"

"May we go inside, Doctor?"

"What branch?"

"Department of Energy." She smiled. "Surprised you twice, didn't I?"

"Yes," he said. "Come on in."

She followed him up the back steps and into a kitchen with thick wooden counters and a massive center island. He pulled a stool up to the island, offered one to her, then unbuttoned his cuffs and rolled up his shirtsleeves slowly and precisely. He seemed to be moving methodically to gather his thoughts, and Boone was pleased by his demeanor. She'd expected a flood of questions, but what she needed was someone who could listen.

When he looked up again, he said, "I don't want to seem foolish or paranoid, but it would probably be prudent to ask you for some identification."

Wise man. She showed him her ID card, and he studied it with care, even tilting it so that the hologram caught the light.

"'Office of Intelligence and Counterintelligence,'" he read. "I'll admit I didn't know the DOE had their own investigations division. I'd have guessed they'd farm that out."

"Sometimes. Not always."

"So what brings the DOE intelligence division into the game?"

Boone knew he was testing her, asking a question that achieved multiple things at once. He wanted to learn how legitimate she was and how much information she'd share, and he wanted to buy himself time to consider the situation while he listened.

"The office protects vital national security information and technologies that represent intellectual property of incalculable value," Boone said in her best public-speaker-introducing-a-bullshit-politician-at-a-ribbon-cutting voice. "Our distinctive contribution to national security is the ability to leverage the Energy Department's unmatched scientific and technological expertise in support of policy makers as well as national security missions in defense, homeland security, cybersecurity, intelligence, and energy security."

"Are you required to memorize that or is it your unique sense of humor?"

"It's on the website." She shrugged.

"Nicely done. Not exactly what I was hoping for, though. Would you give me an example of your work?"

Killing a man in a hotel room in Tokyo with a garrote, Boone thought, but the first example to come to mind wasn't usually the one you should share. She said, "Serving on a joint task force with the FBI and CIA using legal vulnerabilities to motivate employees of a chemical corporation to reveal the covert sharing of patent secrets with the Chinese military." She paused. "Hypothetically. Of course."

"Of course," he said, never looking away from her.

"Do you need another?"

"I'm not sure that I do." He gave a wan smile. "'Using legal vulnerabilities to motivate,' you said? That's quite a phrase. Distill it and one might say it means *blackmailing* employees."

"One might," Boone acknowledged. "But one would be wrong."

"Sure." He nodded, studying her, and then said, "Tara Beckley was a student escort. A creative-writing major. Neither she nor her family seems to have any expertise that would interest the Department of Energy. I know far less about her charge, simply that he was a guest speaker and that he was killed. Your belief, then, is that this man was assassinated—is that the idea?"

"I wouldn't use that term, but that's the gist."

"A killing with political intent isn't an assassination?"

"You'll note that I've said nothing about politics, sir. Pardon me, *Doctor.*"

He waved that off. "No assassination, then. Fine. My understanding was that it was a car accident, and a driver admitted guilt. Rather unusual way to commit a professional execution. He even called the police himself, I believe."

"Do you know that he's dead?" Boone asked.

That stopped him.

"Police in Brighton just found his body in a car," Boone told him. "Shot twice in the head. This unfortunate development paired with his uniquely cooperative admission at the scene means there will be no investigation into the death of Amandi Oltamu now, no trial. Do you see?"

After a lengthy pause, the doctor said, "And who is Amandi Oltamu to you? What value did he have that you were hoping to use legal vulnerabilities to motivate?"

Boone smiled. "This is where we get to the unpleasant part. You have questions, I have answers, but I can't share them. And the less you know, the better for you."

His eyes narrowed. "For my safety?"

"Yes."

"So you want me to violate patient confidentiality—which means breaking the law, you know, not to mention the Hippocratic oath—and in exchange I get…nothing? Because of your deep concern for my safety, of course."

"That's the idea."

He gave that little disbelieving half laugh again, then stood up. "Mind if I pour myself a glass of wine?"

"By all means."

"Join me?"

"No, thank you."

He poured from an opened bottle of pinot noir on the counter, took a drink, then looked at the clock on the microwave. "My wife will be home in about fifteen minutes," he said. "If there is any chance that what you intend to tell me will put me in danger, well, such is life. The same philosophy does not apply to my family, though."

"I understand."

He turned back to her but didn't return to the island, just leaned against the counter.

"You don't have a witness," he said. "I can tell you that much, because you'll be able to find it out from other sources, and I can spare you that trouble, and we can spare ourselves the back-and-forth bullshit about the greater good in service of my country. That's what I'd get if I tried to hold out, right?"

Now it was Boone's turn to laugh. "Pretty much."

"Thought so."

"So there's no chance she'll regain consciousness?" Boone asked. "No chance of recovery?"

"Oh, I certainly intend to see that she has every chance at recovery. But at the moment, she is not going to offer you any help. If she has memories that could be of use to you, they're sealed up tight."

Boone nodded. "That was my understanding, but I had to try. What I need you to know is that if she wakes, she'll be not only a potential asset to me, but also likely in harm's way. I don't intend to ask you to break any laws or oaths, Doctor. What I want from you is your assurance that if anything changes with Tara Beckley, I'll be notified immediately."

"Why not ask that of her family? Why me?"

"Because I don't want to terrify them," Boone said. "And because the stakes on this require the poise of professionals. What I've heard about you suggests that you'd be good under pressure."

He tried not to look flattered, but he was. Everyone liked an ego stroke. Doctors too.

"It's beyond unorthodox," he said. "This shouldn't be my role."

Boone removed a business card from her purse and slid it across the gleaming hardwood surface of the island. "Just a phone call," she said. "If there's a change in Tara Beckley's condition, I need to know. *Tara* will need me to know. At that point, I'll deal with the family. Not until then. I wasn't fully honest with you a moment ago, Dr. Pine. I said I was holding off on contact with them because I didn't want to scare them. That's true, but it's not everything. I also can't afford too much conversation about this. You are, as you've already made clear, a man who understands the need for confidentiality, for professional silence. You know what breaking that silence can cost people."

He picked up the card and slid it into his shirt pocket. "What if there's no change in her condition?"

"Then you don't need to worry about me."

"That's not my point. If there's no change, when do you deal with the family? When do you let them know the truth about what happened to Tara?"

Boone didn't answer. She just gazed back at him, and he nodded.

"Right," he said. "That's where we'll reach the bullshit about the greater good, isn't it?"

Boone got to her feet. "You're asking questions above my pay grade, and I think you know that. What you decide to do here is up to you. But be aware that you've got something more than a patient in Tara Beckley. You might have the key to some vital intelligence."

"I have a human life. She's no different than any patient."

"Wrong. Tara is very different."

"I can't look at it that way."

"You'll need to." Boone bit her lower lip, looked at the floor for a moment, then back at him. "I'll give you this much perspective: Billions of dollars at stake, and dozens of lives. Maybe hundreds of lives. Still think she's no different than the rest?"

"What she saw is worth *that*?"

"Potentially," Boone said.

He didn't have a response.

Boone thanked him for his time and consideration and let herself out the back door. If she drove fast, she could make it to the airport and catch the last flight back to DC. Her asset was dead, the witness was unresponsive, and the Brighton cops were clueless about Carlos Ramirez. That meant that unless something changed, Lisa Boone was on to her next assignment. She'd spent nearly a year on Amandi Oltamu, but sometimes this was how it went. There was always more work, and you couldn't brood over lost causes.

But she wanted to know what he had. All this time, all this careful recruiting and secrecy, and she still didn't know what he'd been able to produce. She'd heard only his guarantees.

Still a chance, though, she thought as she pulled away from Dr. Pine's home. *If that man is one hell of a neurologist, I suppose there's still a chance.*

I I

Shannon has been in the room with Tara most of the afternoon, but she leaves when Mom and Rick return, saying she needs to answer some e-mails and study. This is no doubt true—Shannon is missing crucial days of law school—but Tara knows there are also other reasons why Shannon prefers to check her e-mail elsewhere. Shannon doesn't want to be with them because they have different opinions on what should happen to Tara.

The truth of it is obvious: Tara's mother and stepfather want to kill her.

They don't think about it this way, of course. They're wandering around the outside of 1804 London Street, calling her name and shining lights in through the filthy windows, but even if they could get through the locked doors and inside the house, they wouldn't find the staircase that leads into darkness.

No one can follow her down there.

They don't know that she's still in the house, and so they hate the house for what it represents: The house killed their daughter. It needs to be condemned, torn down, and the foundation scraped clean.

The problem with that is that Tara's body *is* the awful house.

She's listened to their halting, tearful exchanges already. The word *dignity* is Rick's mantra. They must think of her dignity. They'll be preserving her dignity by ending the feeding tubes and diapers. They have no idea that she's still here, watching them, listening to them. They have no idea what their hopelessness takes from her.

What am I taking from them, though? she thinks as she watches them. They seem so tired all the time. So beaten. All because of her.

Tell me if there's any hope, she wants to say. She begs them through her silence and her stillness to just look her in the eye and state the cold hard truth. Is Shannon delusional, or has a doctor told them that Tara might come out of this? Is there any hope that she can convey her awareness to anyone outside of her own skull? Because if not…

If not, then do it.

Their focus isn't even on her, though. No one wants to look her in the eye. Mom is usually on her iPad. She posts constantly on Facebook, updating friends, responding to well-wishers, and begging for help. She's corresponding with three doctors, two ministers, and at least one psychic—maybe more, but she shut down disclosures on that pretty quickly after Shannon's response to it. She sometimes stops and stares at Tara, but the rest of the time, she's tapping away on the iPad. She doesn't put on any makeup or do much more with her hair than run a brush through it. It hurts Tara to watch her. To feel responsible for it all.

Rick just gazes at Tara with a horrible detachment. He doesn't accept the possibility that she can see him, and he's unhappy about the time he is required to sit here and talk to her.

He will make the call, she thinks. *In the end, he will convince Mom that it's best, and then Shannon will be overruled. She doesn't get a vote, anyhow. All she can do is argue. From a legal standpoint, isn't my mother in charge of deciding to end my life?*

These are issues that the three of them surely discuss, but they never do it in front of her. And yet, as terrible as it might be to hear, she wants them to explain the situation to her. She needs to understand.

There's a soft knock. Rick stands and says, "Yes?" and the door opens.

Please be a doctor, Tara thinks. She hasn't seen the doctor since she returned to awareness, only heard her family talk about doctors.

It's not a doctor, though, or even a nurse.

It is a boy with a bouquet of flowers in hand. He's younger than her, maybe not even out of high school yet. Average height and build, but he seems carved out of something very hard, not earned muscle so much as a natural quality; his angular face is all rigid edges and crisp lines. He's dressed in old jeans and a black hoodie and a black baseball cap with a line of silver stitching down the front.

"Can I help you?" Rick says.

"Is this..." The stranger glances Tara's way. "Yeah, it's Tara's room." He says her name softly, almost reverently, and she is very confused. She has no idea who he is.

"Yes," Rick says. "And you are?"

"A friend," he says, and Tara thinks, *What? A friend? I've never seen you before.*

"Oh. Well, we've asked for some privacy from visitors, because it's very—"

"I know, and I'm sorry. I just...I had to see her. I wanted to drop these off and...I'll get out of your hair. I'm so sorry. I just had to see her."

Who are you?

"It's fine," Mom says. "That's very sweet. What's your name?"

"Justin Loveless."

Tara stares at him. No, he is not Justin Loveless. She hasn't seen Justin in months, but he doesn't look even remotely like this kid.

Is this a symptom of something? Is that really Justin? Why can't I tell that?

While she fights a rising hysteria over this disconnect, he steps farther into the room and sets the flowers down on a table already crowded with them. He turns to her then and stares into her face

77

and she feels a deep, cold fear and thinks, *He is lying,* with a sudden certainty. *He is pretending to be Justin, and he is lying. Why is he here? Who is he?*

Unlike most visitors, he isn't avoiding her eyes but looking directly into them the way Shannon does, seeking some sign of connection, of awareness. It doesn't feel affectionate, though. They are a hunter's eyes.

"Hi, Tara," he whispers.

She holds her breath. It's the first time she's realized that she can do this—the first clear connection between brain command and body response—but any joy over the discovery is drowned by the fear she feels as he studies her.

Without taking his eyes off hers, he says, "She's not responding at all? No blinks or hand squeezes or anything?"

"Not yet," Rick says. "But we're hopeful."

"Yes," the stranger answers. "Everyone is. She's so strong. She'll make it back. Are the tests encouraging, at least? I know the scans can sometimes show—"

"We're dealing with all of that as a family and with the doctors," Rick says, cutting him off. The stranger nods, accepting that, and Mom seems embarrassed.

"How do you know her, Justin?" she asks. "Do you go to Hammel?"

He straightens and looks at Mom. "I do. We were in the same a cappella group."

It is true that Justin Loveless goes to Hammel College and that Tara sang with him during her brief flirtation with the music department as a freshman, when she had visions of Broadway that were quickly crushed. But…this is not Justin Loveless.

"It's very nice of you to come," Rick says, "but we really do need to ask you to respect the family's request."

If this were a real friend, Tara would be furious at Rick's coldness, but instead she thinks, *Yes, get him, Rick, get him out of here!*

"Of course. I shouldn't have come. I just wanted to see her and tell her that I know she can make it back to us. I'm sorry to intrude, though. I really am."

"It's okay, hon," Mom says.

He gives a little nod, then says, "I'll leave now. I really appreciate you letting me say hello, though. A lot of people are thinking of her. I hope you know that."

"We do. Thank you. Hey!" Mom's face brightens. "Have you joined the Team Tara page?"

"Team Tara," he echoes. "What's that?"

"We're on Facebook, Instagram, and Twitter. I'm trying to keep everyone updated because we can't, obviously, let everyone in to visit. But we know how many kind people like you are out there, and we don't want to take that for granted."

"Team Tara. I like that. I'll sign up. I am definitely on Team Tara."

Rick clears his throat, and the stranger nods with understanding, then turns back to Tara. He leans down and puts his hand on hers. The overwhelming, irrational fear returns, amplified now by his touch. His eyes search hers.

"When you come back, Tara," he says, "I'll be here."

12

It was a two-hour drive from Biddeford, Maine, to Boston, and Abby could have driven down, talked to the sister, and been back by early afternoon, but she took the train.

Not because she couldn't handle I-95, with that press of traffic, cars squeezing you from all sides, like being caught in a tightening fist—of course she could handle that. A simple drive in traffic was no problem, but...well, maybe it was better not to rush things.

She tried not to consider how many months she'd been using that excuse. Tried not to consider that she'd come back to Maine promising herself she would be there just two weeks, that she would clear her head, get away from the tabloid photographers who wanted to run her picture beside images of gorgeous Luke London in his hospital bed, and then go back to LA.

No, she certainly wasn't rushing things.

The Downeaster left Portland at 8:15 and arrived in Boston's North Station shortly before noon, and the train gave her a way to relax after a largely sleepless night. Train travel was underrated, she thought. Sure, going by Amtrak took longer than driving, the stations weren't pristine, and you ran the risk of sitting beside a talkative stranger, but wasn't that all part of the romance of the rails? Simpler times, as Abby's dad always said during reruns of black-and-white TV shows.

It was raining when she got to Boston, and she was soaked by the time she caught a taxi driven by a man who smelled like he would have benefited from a few minutes in the downpour, perhaps with a little shampoo mixed in. But, hey, simpler times. She reached the hospital a little after one—five hours to get here for a ten-minute conversation that she could have had over the phone. The shoe box was wet now, the cardboard starting to soften and peel, but the phones inside were dry. She wished she'd thought to put them in a briefcase or something more formal.

Tara Beckley could be seen by visitors if the family and doctor approved it, but Abby made it clear to the receptionist that she did not want to see Tara.

"I'm here for her sister," she said. "Shannon Beckley. I'll wait here for her."

She sat in a vinyl-covered chair and jittered her right palm off a closed left fist as if drumming along to a song and she tried not to think of the hospital in Los Angeles where Luke had died. Abby had done a good job of making visits there. At first. Maybe not so good of a job later. But what was the point? Luke's eyes were empty, and his family's eyes were not. His mother stared at Abby with hate, his father stared at her with a naked question of *Why couldn't it have been you?,* and Hollywood magazines featuring the story piled up on the bedside table. The reporters called endlessly, and everyone advised Abby to say nothing.

She was the only one who *could* say something, though. Luke couldn't say a damn thing, couldn't defend Abby.

Would he have defended you? Sure, he would have. He'd have understood. He wanted to see how far you could push it. That was for him, not you. He loved risk, and he cast no blame.

And, yet…had he yelled at her to slow down just before the last curve? He'd said it so many times, but he'd been laughing, and it wasn't a command or even a request, just the delight of a kid on a roller coaster saying, *Slow down, slow down,* but not really meaning it. That was how it had gone. His tone hadn't shifted when Abby pegged the needle at 145. No way. That was her revisionist memory seeking to take blame, but it wasn't reality.

Slow down! His hand on her arm, tightening, his nails biting into her skin.

In a hospital three thousand miles away from that scene, the receptionist cleared her throat loudly, and Abby realized how she'd picked up the speed and volume of the drumming of her open right palm off her closed left fist. She looked like a drug addict in need of a fix. Looked like a...

Speed freak.

She flattened her hands and pressed them together as if in prayer, giving a weak smile of apology to the receptionist.

I'm not a speed freak, ma'am. If you'd watched me driving around lately, you'd know I was anything but that.

The doors between the waiting room and the long hallway opened and a tall young woman with red-brown hair and very green eyes, bright enough to stand out above the puffy purple crescents of fatigue, strode through the doorway like a marshal summoned to a fight in a saloon.

"You're the investigator?" the woman said.

"Yes. Abby Kaplan." She rose and offered her hand. The woman seemed to consider rejecting it but then shook it grudgingly. Her fingers were long and slender and strong, like a piano player's. Or like the Boston Strangler's, judging from her grip.

"What's this crap about her phone?" she said. "What does her phone have to do with anything?"

Abby saw the receptionist give a tired little shake of her head, as if she were all too familiar with this woman.

"Uh, I was just hoping to meet with the family and introduce myself and then we can get into any questions you all might have," Abby began, because she knew there was more to the family than this woman, and she figured she might find more friendliness in that group. Or in a rattlesnake den.

"You don't need to bother meeting the family," Shannon Beckley said. "I'm the family's legal representative."

"You're a lawyer?"

"I'm the closest thing they have right now," Shannon said. Contrasted against the dark red hair, her green eyes seemed aflame. "And in point of fact, I *will* be a lawyer." She paused, and her voice was softer when she said, "Maybe a little later than I'd expected now. Stanford doesn't stop. Not even for tragedy."

She gave a cold smile that made Abby pity whoever would have to face this woman in the courtroom in the years to come.

"So I'll lose a semester maybe." She shrugged, but it was forced indifference. "Whatever it takes, fine. Because that girl in there?" Shannon pointed to the closed double doors. "She and I have been through…" She caught herself, and Abby had the distinct feeling she was walling off a rise of emotion, brick by brick. She wouldn't allow herself to fall apart. Not in front of Abby, at least.

"So," she said when she'd composed herself, "tell me what you're doing, please, and why her phone matters."

Yes, the emotion was gone now, and cold steel was back in its place.

"Her mother—your mother—is here, correct?" Abby asked, not because she had any desire to speak to the mother but because she wanted to counter this woman somehow, however politely, and show that she had at least a little power in this situation.

"My mother is glued to Facebook, where she posts updates every ten minutes on a Team Tara page that my stepfather created so she'd have something to do, something that calmed her down that did not involve a tranquilizer. Do you really need to interrupt that?"

Abby remembered Luke's Facebook fan page, the blog, the Twitter account, all the endless updates fading from hopeful to resigned. She shook her head. "No. I don't need to interrupt that. I'm just trying to answer your questions, and I was told you needed to see me in person to address them."

"That's right. But your boss said you wanted to show me her phone. What's on the phone?"

"I don't know. I'm not even sure if I have it." Abby lifted the wet shoe box, feeling like a fool, and pulled back the lid. "The guy at the salvage yard gave me this. He's pulled them all out of cars. I was wondering if one of them belonged to your sister."

Shannon Beckley's eyes narrowed and she reached in the box and sorted through the phones quickly with those long, elegant fingers.

"No."

"You're sure?"

"Positive. Hers was a rose-gold iPhone in a case."

"Okay. Well, maybe one of them belonged to her passenger, then. The guy who towed the car was positive that he found one of these inside."

"What does it matter when you've got a driver whose guilt is already established?"

"I'm just trying to find out whether the phones survived the wreck," she said, and then she regretted that phrasing—*survived* was not the right word for a phone. "If one did, it might contain something useful."

"Useful to whom?"

"To...I mean, to everyone. It could provide clarification on a few points of—"

"Are you trying to get out of a claim? Is that the idea? Because I promise you, if you guys pull any bullshit to make this more expensive to my family than it already is, I will get that story on the front page of the *New York Times.*" She looked Abby up and down and then added, "Or on Fox News. Whatever hits your company harder."

"That would actually be the *Portland Press Herald,* then."

"This is funny to you?"

She was leaning in, and Abby almost stepped back but then decided not to give her the satisfaction. "No. But before you start shouting threats, you might want to remember that I'm working on her behalf."

"Oh, that is such crap. The college hired you to find out if they had any risk. That's the truth."

She wasn't wrong, of course. Abby started to offer a pat reply about how the college intended to work hand in hand with the family, but something about Shannon Beckley's heated eyes made her dispense with the bullshit. "They're going to have someone do it," Abby said. "It'll be me or it'll be somebody else, but they will have someone ask questions."

Shannon studied Abby for a moment and then said, "Come see her."

"What?"

"If you're working on her behalf, I'd like you to come see her with me. We can talk with her, right?"

Abby blinked at her. "I thought...I was told that..." Shannon waited, eyebrows raised, and Abby felt she was talking her way into a trap. "That she's nonresponsive," she finished finally. "Was I misinformed?"

"We're not sure." Shannon Beckley softened her tone. "Maybe she's hearing it all, maybe she's not. We just don't know. At first it was a medically induced coma to try to limit the swelling in the brain, but now they're bringing her back out of it, and..." She cleared her throat. "And we're waiting on more tests."

"I understand," Abby said. "And I'm sorry. I can't imagine what that's like."

Bullshit, Abby. Why lie?

For an instant, she almost corrected herself. Almost told the truth to this sleep-deprived stranger with the searing stare, almost told her that she knew the situation all too well.

All she got out, though, was a question: "Has she had an fMRI yet?"

"No, but it's scheduled."

Abby nodded. "They usually start there. Then other scans. There are lots of ways to try to determine if she's...aware of things. Different doctors have different ideas."

"Too many ideas. I've been reading about all of them, and it's exhausting. There's a university hospital nearby where they have the patient watch a movie while undergoing an MRI, and they scan the brain for an emotional response. They've had good results with that."

"Like that Hitchcock film," Abby said. Shannon Beckley looked offended, and Abby realized she thought that Abby was comparing Tara's situation to a movie and headed her off. "Some researchers use an episode called 'Bang, You're Dead' from Alfred Hitchcock's old black-and-white TV series. A kid picks up a loaded gun, and the audience knows it's loaded, but the kid doesn't know. So the audience reacts emotionally as he goes from place to place carrying what he thinks is harmless and what the audience knows is deadly. That activates different areas in the brain of someone watching it. It shows awareness."

"Tara hates anything in black-and-white. If she's not in a vegetative state now, the sight of a black-and-white TV show might put her into one." She forced a laugh that choked at the end, like an engine running out of gas, and then she looked away and tried to gather herself. Abby didn't want to offer any canned condolences or well wishes, knowing exactly how exhausting and hollow those grew, and so she tried to follow the attempt at humor.

"Tell the doctors she's got to see a favorite movie of hers, then, because you want to know if her memory is activated. That sounds legitimate."

She was kidding, but Shannon Beckley said, "You know, that's not a bad idea."

"Actually, it probably is a bad idea. The doctors have their protocols for a reason. They tend not to like input from an insurance investigator."

"I'll find a more credible source, don't worry." Shannon regarded Abby curiously. "So you've dealt with a case like hers before?"

"Not a case." Now Abby regretted telling her anything. This woman, who was just a few years younger than Abby's thirty-one, was clearly not in the Luke London fan club, because she hadn't reacted to Abby's name. But she would Google it at some point, and then she'd have new questions.

"You spend that much time reading about coma patients? It's a hobby?"

"I get a lot of newsletters, trade magazines, crap like that."

"Your *trade magazines* deal with advanced coma protocols?"

"They've got to fill space," Abby said. "Listen, let me just introduce myself and explain what we are—"

"Let's go into her room for all this talk."

The way she said it made Abby feel as if Shannon were baiting her, as if she sensed fear. "It's not my job, I mean, it's not my place to be in there."

"Actually, it's anyone's place. The doctors have encouraged us to talk to her. That's what I'm supposed to be doing right now. So join me. Who knows—maybe she'll respond to you."

Luke? Luke, baby, if you're in there...do something. Speak, blink, squeeze my hand, slap me, just do something *so I know!*

"Okay," Abby said, her mouth dry. "Sure."

She followed Shannon Beckley through the double doors that parted automatically as if hurrying out of her way.

13

The nurses think Tara is brain-dead.

They treat her as an empty shell. They adjust her in the bed to prevent sores from forming, turn her and spread her legs and clean her, unaware of the horrifying humiliation, handling her roughly and without interest, talking around her and above her. They don't bother to speak to her, to introduce themselves. She can't even be certain they're nurses. Therapists of some sort, maybe? How do you know what they are doing when they don't bother to explain it? If they have any hope for her future, they don't indicate it. All she picks up from them is apathy; all she feels is pain and shame.

A young blond woman wipes Tara's ass and complains to a gray-haired black woman about the amount of time her fiancé spends with his friends smoking cigars in the garage right below their bedroom, which fills her clothes with the awful smell.

"He just doesn't get it," she says, and then she rolls Tara back over without so much as a glance at her face, holding a soiled diaper with her free hand.

"A phase, maybe?" the black woman suggests. "Something he'll get out of his system now, and after the wedding it will be different?"

"I'd *love* to believe that. But I'm not sure that I do."

The blonde discards the diaper, peels off her gloves, and looks down at Tara without any interest, then she consults a clipboard and makes a note. Is there a box you check when you wipe someone's ass? If so, can they add that you're required to do it discreetly and with apology or compassion? Or tell the patient your damn name, at least?

The nurses finish with her, add a few more checks to the clipboard beside her bed, and then the black woman hesitates and looks down into Tara's eyes for the first time.

"This one is supposed to be on the move tomorrow."

"Yes," the blonde agrees without looking over, and then they are out of sight, crossing the room and vanishing out the door and into the hallway.

This one.

A body, nothing more. That's what Tara is to them.

Also a body that is supposed to be on the move tomorrow. Where are they taking her? And why?

Of all the agonies of her condition, none is worse than the lack of explanations. She reentered a world that has moved on without her, and because no one is aware that she's back in it, no one slows down to clarify anything. Even her most basic questions—*How long have I been here? What happened to put me in here? Is there a diagnosis? Is there a plan? Is there hope?*—are unanswered, because everyone around her has already had these conversations, probably countless times. Why go backward, then? Instead, they move forward, following a course that was charted while Tara was lost to the blackness. She doesn't know where it began, let alone where it will end.

An accident? An attack? An illness?

She has no idea. The coma she understands, but its cause remains a mystery. Was she felled by a club or a clot? Her lack of memory in this regard is terrifying. She knows who she is, where she lives, what she does, likes, hates, loves; everything related to her identity is clear. What brought her here, though…she can't even begin to retrace the steps. She remembers getting out of the shower and checking the clock, which was important because she couldn't be late for…

For what?

She has no idea. Something important and time-sensitive. Time was her primary concern.

Did they find me there in the bathroom, naked on the floor, steam still on the mirror?

Every now and then, flickers of images will rise and then sink, like leaves carried in a swift stream, but she believes those images aren't memories, just pieces of the awful nightmare she'd endured prior to waking. A stranger, a cold wind, and a wolf.

The door opens again. She feels Shannon's presence before she actually sees her. This is how it has always been with Shannon. She buzzes with a different energy than most people, moving through the world with a swirling, nearly chaotic force. It is a force that Tara clings to now, because she can feel the hope draining away from her mother and Rick. They aren't as bad as the nurses yet, and she expects they never could regard her with such indifference, but...they are drifting that way.

Shannon is with an unfamiliar young woman with short, dark blond hair and blue eyes. She is lean and slim-hipped, an almost boyish figure, though her eyes and athlete's grace would stand out if she weren't shuffling in so unhappily, like a child dragged into the principal's office. She glances at Tara only briefly, and while Tara is growing used to cursory glances, this one feels different. It isn't that the new woman sees no point in making eye contact with her; it's that she's afraid.

"Tara, I've found a new friend," Shannon says with false cheer. Shannon keeps up a steady stream of conversation most of the time she is here, and when she does finally fall silent, she usually leaves soon after. It reminds Tara of the years when they shared a bedroom—when Shannon stopped talking, it meant she'd fallen asleep.

Now Shannon rests her hand on Tara's arm. The touch is warm and kind. Tara wonders what her skin feels like to Shannon—the same healthy human warmth or the clamminess of sickness? Or something worse?

"Abby's an investigator," Shannon says. "She tells me she's working on your behalf."

Abby is holding an old, wet shoe box. She clears her throat and says, "Hello, Tara. It's good to meet you."

Tell me why you're here, Tara screams silently. Abby doesn't, but why would you tell a piece of furniture what your purpose in the room is?

Abby's attention is back on Shannon when she says, "Have the police asked you any questions about the accident?"

The accident. This is interesting. This is the first time anyone has spoken of what led her to this terrible, trapped place.

"Sure," Shannon says. "But nobody talked about her phone until your boss called me. The police said it was clear who was at fault. The driver *admitted* that at the scene. And then he repeated it, on the record."

The driver. So it was a car accident. This resonates in a way that is both exciting and troubling; it sets off a tingle of memory, but no images come forth, just a feeling of dread.

"I know that. And now he's going to hire an attorney who will find any way possible to mitigate the driver's responsibility. It's not right, but it's what happens. My job is to get out in front of that." Abby pauses, then says, "His story has some issues too."

"Do not tell me you're questioning his version of things." There's a warning in Shannon's voice.

"I'm not questioning that he was at fault."

"Good."

"But—"

"Oh, boy. Here we go."

"*But* I do not like his facts. It's clear that he hit her car, that her car was stationary, and that she was out of the vehicle. Of course he's at fault. But he's also mistaken about the details, and I don't understand why."

I was out of the vehicle. Tara feels that tingle again, stronger now, and she wants to grab Abby's hand and squeeze, wants to tell her to say more, paint a better picture, because she is close to remembering, she is very close, this woman can help Tara bridge the void.

"He's probably confused because he was staring at his damn phone," Shannon says.

Abby Kaplan shakes her head, and a muscle in her jaw flexes, as if she's grinding her teeth.

"The angles are wrong," she says softly. "The angles and the speed. He was driving terribly, yes, and he was negligent, but if he swerved like he says he did, then he should have flipped that van before he hit her."

"The police can probably explain that to you," Shannon says curtly.

Abby shakes her head, eyes distant, as if she is envisioning the scene.

Say what you're thinking! Tara screams, but of course Abby doesn't hear her.

"No, they actually can't," she tells Shannon. "They haven't driven the right kind of cars at the right kind of speeds to know what is possible and what isn't."

"And I suppose you have."

The short, slender girl looks at Shannon then, and there's a spark to her when she says, "Yes. I have." She takes a breath and the spark fades and she seems sad. "Anyhow, you don't need to worry about me messing up any claims. It wasn't your sister's fault. But…it also didn't happen the way Carlos Ramirez said it did."

"So Ramirez was confused."

"Maybe." Abby Kaplan turns to face Tara, and this time she lets her stare linger. Her eyes are on Tara's when she says, "I'm confident she would have a different memory of the way it happened."

Tara stares back at her from within her corporeal shell, trying somehow to convey how desperately she needs the facts. If someone can just walk her through it, then maybe she can remember.

"Have you talked to the other victim's family?" Shannon asks. "Oltamu's?"

"Not yet." Abby turns away from Tara.

Oltamu. Shannon says the name so casually, but it's a cataclysmic moment for Tara.

Dr. Oltamu. A visiting speaker. She was driving him from dinner to the auditorium. She was driving him and then…

A block in her memory rises again, and she has a distinct vision of a wolf with its ears pinned back and its hackles raised.

Hobo. The wolf's name is Hobo.

Why would a wolf have a name? But Oltamu is a name that registers; he is the black man with the nice smile and the expensive watch. Memories are returning now, scattered snapshots.

His name was Amandi Oltamu, and I was driving him. But who is he? Why was I driving him, and where? And what did he do to me?

Tara's mind is whirling now, trying to capture each crucial detail, knowing that she must catch them all before they escape into the blackness like fireflies and disappear for good.

"Think his family will sue the college?" Shannon asks.

"Maybe. But I don't see their case yet. The only thing that's odd is why she parked where she did."

Because he told me to, damn it, Tara thinks without hesitation. *He wanted the Tara tour.* This element is strangely vivid amid the fog of all the memories she's lost—Oltamu asked her to get out of the car. She sees the two of them walking toward a bridge and she knows that this is true. *We were both out of the car. We were both out because he wanted to walk, and I was worried about that because of the time, time was tight. But he told me that he wanted to walk, so we started to walk down to the bridge and then the wolf got us. The wolf came out of the darkness and got us.*

She knows this is madness, and it scares her that it seems so logical, so clear.

I am not just paralyzed, I am insane.

"Nobody can answer that but her," Abby Kaplan says, studying Tara's face, and again Tara feels that strange electric sense of connection just beyond her grasp, like a castaway watching a plane pass overhead. "Do you know anyone who was with her at that dinner?" Abby asks Shannon.

"A few people have reached out."

"I wonder if anyone would remember whether Oltamu had a phone on him."

"Why?"

"Because he's dead, and she can't talk," Abby says, running a hand through her hair as if to tamp down frustration. "People are on their phones all the time. He could have been using it right up until the end. And one of these"—she lifts the shoe box—"belongs to him. Unless the salvage guy kept it or sold it already. Neither would surprise me."

He took pictures with his phone, Tara tells them silently. *A selfie with me, because he needed to increase his social media presence. That was what worried him right before he died and I was erased from my own life. The last time I ever smiled, it was for a selfie with a stranger so he could improve his social media profile. If not for that, I'd have been across the bridge.*

The lucidity of this is exciting, but she knows it's still not complete. She is circling the memory like someone fumbling through a dark house searching for a light switch.

"I've wondered about *her* phone," Shannon says hesitantly, as if she isn't sure she should make this admission.

"Why?"

"Because when she drove, she put it on one of those magnet things on the dash. It wasn't there, and it wasn't in her purse. She was wearing a dress and a thin sweater with no pockets. So if it went into the river, that means she got out with the phone in her hand, as if she was using it."

Shannon pauses then, which is wonderful, because Tara is frantically snatching at all these fireflies—*phone, dress, sweater, river*—trying to capture them before they escape into the darkness.

Abby Kaplan clears her throat and says, "I hope she comes back to you soon. For her sake and yours, of course, but also because I'd like to hear what she remembers." She gives Shannon a business card, tells her to be in touch with any questions, and wishes her well, as if Shannon is alone in this struggle.

She does not look at Tara again before she leaves.

14

The untimely death of Carlos Ramirez was supposed to bring an end to a problem that should have been resolved easily, but this situation seemed determined to keep turning up like the proverbial bad penny.

Gerry Connors had dealt with such problems before, though, and he wasn't worried by this one. Not just yet, at least. The potential for concern was floating out there, simply because of the price tag on this job. The price tag, and the German's reputation. He had never met the German, but he'd heard of him, and when he did meet him, he certainly didn't want to be delivering bad news.

For this, Gerry had Dax Blackwell, and he needed him to be as good as his bloodline promised he'd be.

Gerry Connors had first made his way into organized crime in the 1990s in his hometown of Belfast, working with the IRA at a time when work was easy to come by for a man who didn't mind killings and bombings. Gerry felt no fierce loyalty to either church or state, and he hadn't met many like him in that struggle until the Blackwell brothers arrived. Two freelancers from Australia who looked like sweet lads, blond-haired and blue-eyed and innocent-faced as altar boys, they'd entered a room filled with hardened IRA men, outlined their plan, and didn't blink in the face of all the hostility and all the bloody history. Men had shouted at them, men had threatened them, and the brothers had calmly named their price and said take it or leave it.

Eventually, the boys in Belfast took it. A week after that, three members of the constabulary had been buried, the nation was in an uproar, and the Blackwells were wealthy—and long gone from the country.

They'd come back, of course. When the money was right, they returned, and during the 1990s, Jack and Patrick found plenty of work in Ireland. So did Gerry. He'd moved to America and gone into contract work, providing papers and identification for those who needed them. Soon he was providing more than papers—cars, guns, and, inevitably, it seemed, killers.

Jack and Patrick had come back around often then.

It was just after 9/11, and the business was experiencing fresh risks when Jack Blackwell requested multiple sets of identification for his newborn son. Gerry was reluctant to take on the task in those days, but he was even more reluctant to disappoint Jack Blackwell. He produced the requested birth certificates, which came from fifteen different states in America, as well as four sets of international papers, Australian, British, Dutch, and Swiss. Each was in a different name, and Jack provided all of the names, which led Gerry to wonder if they meant something to him, if they indicated something from his past life—or perhaps indicated lives he'd ended.

Gerry had no idea what the boy's real name was, but the first time he'd met him, Jack had called him Dax, and so that was what Gerry went with, even though there was no paperwork for that name. Or at least, none that Gerry had created. Knowing Jack, Gerry figured he'd likely sourced identification from more than one person.

More than a dozen years later, when Gerry had need of Jack and Patrick's services again, Jack told him they themselves were unavailable, but his son could handle the task. Gerry's first response was to laugh—a very dangerous response when one was around the Blackwells, but Gerry knew the boy wasn't even old enough to drive yet.

Jack Blackwell hadn't laughed. He'd waited until Gerry said,

"You're not serious," and then the faintest of smiles had crossed his face, and he nodded exactly once.

That was enough.

Nine days later, Dax Blackwell completed his first professional killing. Or at least, his first professional killing for Gerry Connors.

Over the years that followed, Gerry had been in touch with the boy fairly often. He had no idea where he lived or where he'd gone to school—or if he had gone to school, although he was certainly well educated, almost preternaturally bright. He also had no idea how much time the boy actually spent with his father and uncle, but based on his mannerisms and his skills, Gerry suspected that he was with them more often than not. After hearing word of Jack's and Patrick's deaths in Montana, Gerry considered offering his condolences to the boy, but he hadn't. Instead, he offered him work, and the boy accepted the job and completed it. Small-time stuff, mostly, no high-dollar work, no international work. Gerry viewed it as an internship.

The pupil flourished.

They never spoke of Dax's father and uncle formally, but they each mentioned them in passing and never referred to their deaths. Gerry followed the boy's lead in keeping discussions of them in the present tense, as if they were still there, ghosts in the room, just waiting for the call to summon them back.

And in fact, when Gerry sent for Dax, that was exactly how it felt. As the boy grew, Gerry saw more and more of those two Aussie lads who'd walked so calmly into the room of hardened IRA killers.

Yes, he felt very much like he was calling on a ghost when he sent for Dax Blackwell.

Today the ghost arrived. He entered Gerry's office in Boston's North End expecting a paycheck for a completed job, having no clue yet as to the trouble that had occurred. Carlos Ramirez had needed to kill one man and steal one phone. Somehow, Carlos

Ramirez had managed to steal the wrong fucking phone. Gerry understood this because the German had told him not to worry about a trace on the phone because it wasn't active and had no signal. The phones in Gerry's desk drawer had signals. Both of them had been ringing, and that was a problem. That was, maybe, an enormous problem, as the German was due to arrive by the weekend to pick up something for which he had already paid handsomely but that was not in Gerry's possession. The German did not travel internationally to pick up things in person that could be mailed unless the items were of the utmost importance. Based on Gerry's understanding of the German, he felt that this in-person disappointment was not the sort of thing one would want to experience firsthand.

Enter Dax Blackwell.

"The job's not done," Gerry told him as soon as the door was closed behind him.

"Not done? Did Carlos walk out of the morgue?" the kid asked as he sat down. Make no mistake, Dax carried his family's blood. Which was to say that he was empty and cold in all the right ways, but he also carried his father's smirk and his uncle's deadpan delivery. Gerry had never been a fan of those qualities.

The only thing Gerry hated more than Dax's attitude was his wardrobe. Jeans and hoodies, tennis shoes and a baseball cap. Always the fucking baseball cap. Whatever happened to gangsters with class? When did people decide they could come see him without shining their damn shoes, maybe putting on some cuff links?

But Dax wasn't a gangster, of course. You had to be patient with the young ones. When young shooters became old killers, then you could demand more from them. If they made it that far, they'd probably figured it out on their own. Right now he was an Australian version of what the cartels called a wolf boy—a teenage killer, an apprentice assassin. Wolf boys were valuable in the border towns. Why couldn't they be useful on a larger scale too?

Dax Blackwell, the Aussie lobo, descendant of ghosts.

"We are missing a phone," Gerry said, leaning back and propping his feet up on the glass-topped coffee table so the kid could get a good look at his hand-stitched, calfskin Moreschi wingtips. Put style in front of his face, maybe it'd seep through his skull.

"He gave me two. You have them."

"Neither is right. One is hers, and one is his, but neither one is right."

"Carlos's house was clean. So was his bag."

"What about his pockets?"

The kid looked nonplussed. Dax Blackwell didn't like to be asked questions for which he didn't have ready answers.

"Didn't check," he said eventually. "I hadn't been asked to. You told me get two phones; I got two phones. But I also don't think he'd have kept one unless he knew its value. Did he?"

This was both more attitude and more inquiry than Gerry wanted from the kid, but he wasn't wrong to ask the question. Carlos had no idea what the phone was worth. *Gerry* didn't know anything about the phone other than that he was supposed to hand it to the German.

One thing Gerry had learned over the years was not to ask too many questions about what went on above your pay grade—hell, not to *think* too many questions about it—and he surely did not want to begin thinking about what the German needed from this cell phone. What he *was* willing to extend his personal curiosity to, however, was what would happen if he disappointed people above his pay grade, and he didn't have to work too hard to imagine the outcome.

He needed that phone.

"Police found Carlos's body," Gerry said. "If he had the phone, it'll be in evidence lockup, and I'll get it. But I don't think he had it."

"I don't either. If he was going to make a mistake like that, he'd have done it a long time ago."

Again, more confidence than Gerry wanted to hear, more swagger, but also, again, not wrong.

"Probably. Which means it's missing somewhere between here and there."

Dax Blackwell thought about this, nodded, and then said, "He needed two phones, so he grabbed Oltamu's and grabbed the girl's. Dumb mistake, but that's probably what he did, and he didn't pause to check properly, so he missed the third. By the time they'd cleaned the scene and I picked them up by the river, the phone you needed was gone with the cars."

Now he sounded just like his old man. Jack Blackwell always got right to it, but he never showed impatience, and he never rushed.

"That phone is imperative," Gerry said. "I need it fast, and Carlos is no longer able to assist."

"I heard he was…deported, yes."

Now this was his uncle's personality, everything about it pure Patrick—no twitch of a smile, and yet you knew he'd amused himself with the comment.

"Unless you want an expedited trip to the same place, spare me the wit," Gerry said. The kid didn't so much as blink. Gerry wasn't sure whether he liked the kid's response or if it infuriated him. Composure was appropriate. But fearlessness in front of Gerry? Less appropriate.

"I'll get the phone, then," Dax said. "You should have just let me take the whole job from the start."

Gerry looked at him over the gleaming toe of the Moreschis, considered his response, and let silence ride. If it bothered the kid, he didn't show it.

"It was supposed to look like an accident, and it was time-sensitive," Dax said. "There were many better ways to do that than what he chose. He brought a brawler's touch to a finesse job."

"Just go find that fucking phone, and maybe I'll have more patience for your input in the future," Gerry said, frustration getting the better of him now, partly because the kid wasn't wrong and partly because he didn't understand one crucial element of the deal—Gerry had spared Dax's life. The German had been very clear that anyone involved with hitting Oltamu needed to be expendable. Carlos, already a risk to Gerry on other matters, had thus been ideal for the job. But Dax could've gone too. Should have, in fact, by the terms of the deal.

But he was too promising.

If I can own one of them, Gerry thought, visions of the Blackwell brothers coming back to him, *it will be worth it. If he grows into one of their kind, and he is all mine, loyal to the throne and not just the checkbook, then he will certainly be worth the trouble.*

The kid stood without being told they were done. For a moment, Gerry thought about ordering him to sit his ass back down, but what was the point?

"Go on," he said, and he waved at the door. "Get me the phone. It's an iPhone, but it has no signal. That's all I know. If the phone puts out a signal, it's the wrong one."

Dax Blackwell didn't move right away. Instead, he stood there looking at Gerry, and then he said, "The phone is one problem Carlos left behind. There might be another. Do you have an opinion on that yet?"

He meant the girl, of course.

"She's as good as gone, is my understanding."

"That's enough?"

"She's brain-dead. And even if she wakes up, what's she gonna say?"

"You don't know," Dax said. "That would be precisely my concern."

Gerry flushed and swung his feet down.

"I understand my fucking liabilities, son. I don't need your assistance with the big picture. I need you to bring me the phone. Now get out of here and do it."

He didn't like the way the kid studied him and then nodded and turned away as if he'd seen something in Gerry's anger that interested him.

No, it was more than interest, Gerry thought as he stared at the closed door, Dax Blackwell's footsteps reverberating across the tiled floor on the other side. That expression hadn't been one of intrigue or curiosity but something deeper, something darker.

Like whatever he'd seen in his boss had made him hungry.

"He's just a kid," Gerry said aloud. The words echoed in the empty room, and when they bounced back at him, they weren't reassuring. He sounded nervous, sitting in his own office and talking about his own employee. What in the hell was that about?

About the kid's old man and his uncle, of course. Jack and Patrick were long gone, yes, but they cast long shadows too, a pair of dark smiling ghosts.

The best hitters you ever saw. So trust the kid, Gerry thought. At least a little longer. He was a beta-Blackwell. But if he bloomed? Well, then.

Wouldn't that be something.

15

Dax had spent an hour the previous night listening to the idle chatter in Tara Beckley's hospital room, enough time to confirm both that they'd kept his flowers and that she remained mute, but each day had the potential for new blessings, as the Team Tara Facebook page reminded him that morning, and so he checked back in after leaving Gerry Connors's office.

The recorder he'd placed in the flower vase was of excellent microphone quality but he was disappointed with its computer interface and mobile options. He had to use the web browser to log in, and then he had to sort through multiple files that captured dialogue exchanges of longer than two minutes. He wished he'd used a better system, but Tara Beckley was only of value-added potential for Dax; she wasn't a threat. With threats, you spared no expense. The microphones he had planted in Gerry's office, for example, were cutting-edge, and he'd paid accordingly.

He sat in his car and updated himself on *A Day in the Semi-Life of Tara Beckley*. He listened to her mother talk endlessly and aimlessly, scrolled past that, found the same with the sister, and then some nurses chattering, and then...

What was this?

"Abby's an investigator. She tells me she's working on your behalf."

That was the sister talking. The investigator, when she spoke, sounded nervous. Well, no surprise there—Tara's empty-eyed stare and those tubes could be unsettling to some. Dax doubted many people had given her the kind of deep eye contact that he'd offered.

The investigator blathered on awkwardly, not saying much of

interest, but then the sister said something that made Dax sit up straight.

"Nobody talked about her phone until your boss called."

Her phone? Well, now. The investigator might be more interesting than Dax had thought.

He listened through more chatter, the investigator agreeing that Carlos Ramirez was at fault—apparently she didn't yet know that Carlos was also in the morgue—and then carrying on about how she didn't like Carlos's story. Dax had to give her some credit for this because she seemed to understand the physics of it all in a way the police hadn't, and thus she got what a colossal disaster Carlos Ramirez had been. Time-sensitive, make-it-an-undeniable-accident instructions be damned; Carlos had picked an awfully dumb way to go about the hit. Perhaps he hadn't cared because he knew he'd be out of the country by the time anyone showed real interest. That was fine, but the mess he'd made of things reflected poorly not only on Carlos but on Gerry Connors. And since Dax worked with Gerry, there was the risk of contamination. The Blackwell brand could be damaged before he'd had a chance to re-introduce it if Gerry stumbled. You had to be careful who you worked for in this business. *Independent contractors are not immune to the perils of poor management,* his father had told him often.

For a hick insurance investigator, Abby was surprisingly astute. She was also scared, it seemed, which was interesting. Information and fear didn't go together in Dax's mind—knowledge was power, the cliché promised, and so far in his young life, he'd found that to be true. Then why was this woman so nervous?

Probably it was Tara's dead-eyed stare. Abby the investigator kept pushing, though, almost grudgingly, as if she couldn't help herself.

"And one of these," Abby said, and there was a rustling sound, "belongs to him. Unless the salvage guy kept it or sold it already. Neither would surprise me."

"I've wondered about *her* phone," Shannon said.

Dax Blackwell rewound and replayed that portion.

16

Another advantage of the train—beyond the fact that it didn't make her heart thunder or her vision blur white in the corners—was that Abby could work while she traveled.

She typed up the details of the visit with Shannon Beckley (and Tara Beckley, though that felt more like a visitation, a respectful glance into the casket) on her laptop while the Downeaster rattled back north. Or, as befitted its name, back *down east,* a term that referred to prevailing summer winds along Maine's coast. In most places in America, *down* meant "south," but in southern Maine, *down* took you north.

The visit had been as pointless as Abby had promised Hank it would be—nothing that she couldn't have accomplished with a phone call. And yet she found herself more invested in the work because she'd made that pass by the casket, glanced down at the beyond-reach Tara Beckley in her comatose state.

Those eyes. Her eyes looked so damn alert...

But Abby knew they weren't. She'd been through that cruel illusion before.

Luke was famous for his face, but the audience didn't understand that his eyes were what made his face work. They were so alive, penetrating and laughing and *alive*. There was a reason he'd moved so quickly from sending in his head shots to getting auditions to being offered lead roles in blockbuster action films, and, yes, some of it was talent, and, yes, some of it was his physical beauty, but Abby knew the secret was his eyes.

When they made love, he kept his eyes closed. When they made love, she wanted to see him. Finally, one night, when he was on top of her and inside of her but somehow still absent, she'd put her hands in his hair and tugged his head back and said, "Look at me."

He'd opened his eyes then, and even in the darkness she'd felt that strange, powerful energy, the unique sense of *life* that came from within his gaze. They'd finished together, face-to-face, clenching and shuddering and gasping but never breaking eye contact, the best sex of her life by far.

"I like to see you," she'd whispered, and she bit his shoulder gently.

He'd laughed, the sound soft and low in the room, and said, "I'll remember that."

And he had. He always had.

That made those moments in the hospital even crueler.

Her phone rang, pulling her thoughts away from Luke. It was Hank, calling from the office. Abby answered just as a couple seated beside her burst into laughter.

"Where are you?" Hank asked.

"Headed back."

"Who's in the car with you?"

"Nobody." She grimaced and tried to shield the phone from the sound of the voices.

"Then who am I listening to in the background?"

"I'm on the train," Abby admitted.

"The train? Why in the hell would you take the train to Boston?"

"It gives me time to work."

"You turn a six-hour day into ten or twelve hours so you can buy time to work? I know you're a product of Biddeford public schools, Abby, but that is really bad math."

Hank had gone to Thornton Academy in Saco, which was a public school for some local residents but an in-demand private boarding school for the rest of the world, and he liked to wear it as a badge of honor. He rarely mentioned that he'd dropped out of community college shortly after his stint at Thornton.

"Funny," Abby said. "But I've got the report caught up, and I dealt with the sister and saw Tara, so I checked all the boxes you needed."

"Great. But you've got a big one unchecked that is going to stay that way—Carlos Ramirez isn't talking to you."

"Finally got smart enough to hide behind a lawyer?"

"Nope. He's dead."

"What?"

"Yup. Bullet to the brain."

"Suicide," Abby said, less a question than a statement, because it seemed to make so much sad sense—Ramirez knew he was looking at prison time, and he hadn't been able to bear that prospect.

"Nope. Caught two shots down in Brighton in the passenger seat of a stolen car. I just heard the news. Guess they found him yesterday, last night, something. But he was murdered, so whatever trouble we thought he had over that accident might have been only the surface. I wonder if they checked that van for drugs. Just because his blood was clean doesn't mean *he* was, know what I'm saying?"

The train clattered and swayed as Abby held the phone to her ear without speaking.

"Crazy shit, right?" Hank prompted.

"Yeah. Crazy." Abby wasn't sure why the news bothered her so much, why she couldn't view it with the detachment that Hank did.

"Whatever closure Oltamu's family might've felt from watching that guy go to jail is gone now, and that's a problem," Hank said. "Maybe they look elsewhere for it and sue the school. Meanwhile, my trusty investigator is worried that Ramirez didn't get his facts straight when he talked to the police, which will not make the liability folks happy. Can you get yourself in line with his statement?"

"No."

"Excuse me?" Hank sounded stunned.

"I think he lied."

"He took the blame! Why in the hell would he lie to take the blame?"

"I have no idea, Hank, but I'm sure that he didn't tell the truth. I don't care if it was because he lied or because he was confused, but he did not tell the truth. That isn't good news for your client either way."

"No, it sure isn't." Hank groaned. "Are you *positive* his version doesn't hold together?"

"Yes. And somebody is going to notice eventually, so we'd better warn people before that happens."

"Shit. You're ruining this, Abby. It was so damn simple! Wreck, fatality, confession, and then the guilty dude's dead! That's as clean as they come."

That's why this news bothers me, Abby realized as the couple next to her laughed loudly in her ear again. *Ramirez being killed makes it even cleaner.*

"Let's talk it over when I get back," she said. "Something's wrong here."

"You sure know how to spoil a good thing."

"Come on, Hank, you're an investigator! Where's your detective's gusto?"

"Gimme a break. I hold that friggin' PI license only as a necessary credential to support my career as a bullshitter."

"But this could be a break in the case. That should make your day."

"I've never desired to break open any case that wasn't filled with beers."

"Maybe you'll be able to do both for a change."

"Wouldn't that be something," Hank said dismally.

"Chin up," Abby said. "You might be a hero when this is all done. Get the key to the city or something."

"I got plenty of bowling trophies, thanks. Come by the office and we'll talk, all right?"

"It'll be late by the time I'm in."

"Because you took the friggin' train. Meanwhile the Hellcat's sitting out back."

Abby didn't respond, and Hank sighed and said, "We'll catch up in the morning, then. And I'll start looking for a new employee. 'Wanted: slow learner with lack of ambition.'"

When they ended the call, Abby didn't put her phone away. She sat there for a while as the couple beside her laughed again, that wonderful oblivious-to-everything-else laughter that came when you were so locked in with another person that the rest of the world was only peripheral. She wanted to glance at them but didn't want them to catch her staring, didn't want to intrude on that moment. Good for them if they had that connection. Hopefully they could keep it.

She found Shannon Beckley's number and called.

"This is Abby Kaplan. I'm the one who—"

"I know who you are; I saw you less than two hours ago. What do you need?"

"Have you heard about Carlos Ramirez?"

"Heard *what* about Ramirez?"

"That he's dead. He was murdered."

Abby didn't think it was easy to knock Shannon Beckley off her stride, but this seemed to do it. Abby heard her take a sharp breath before she said, "You're serious."

"Yes. Shot to death in a stolen car. I wanted to let you know."

"Why?" Shannon asked, and it was a damn fine question. Abby hadn't put the answer into words yet, not even in her own mind, but now she had to.

"Whatever Tara saw might be important," she said.

"Dangerous for her," Shannon answered. "That's what you mean."

"I don't know. But I won't rule it out. Listen, I'm not trying to scare you; you've got enough to be scared of right now. But Ramirez lied to the police. I'm sure of it. And now he's been murdered."

"It was just a car wreck," Shannon said, but she wasn't arguing. She said it in the way you did when you wanted to make something big small again.

"Maybe."

There was a moment of silence, and then Shannon Beckley said, "What are you thinking?"

"Nothing. I just wanted to let you know that this had—"

"Bullshit. You're looking at it differently than everyone else. You didn't believe him, and now that he's dead, you think that means something. So let me ask again, please—what are you thinking?"

Her tone was no longer combative or even commanding. It was lonely.

"When she comes out of it," Abby said, "be careful about the people who are around when she's asked about the accident. Be careful who asks her about it."

"*When* she comes out of it," Shannon said softly. "I like your confidence."

"She's in there," Abby said. "I'm almost positive."

"Yeah? The doctors aren't. So how do you know?"

"Because I've seen someone who wasn't. There's a difference."

I'm almost positive, she repeated to herself. But of course she wasn't. Not now when she said Tara was still in there and not back when she'd said Luke no longer was.

17

It wasn't yet five o'clock, but Savage Sam Jones figured you didn't always need to go by the book, certainly not at his age, and so he opened a PBR well before he locked the gates at the salvage yard. It was a quarter past four and he was hungry as well as thirsty and he wanted a slice or two of pizza from the corner store, but right now it would be the old, dried-out shit left over from lunch. For the good pizza, he'd have to wait until five.

Might as well wait there as here, he thought.

He'd closed the door to his office and turned to lock it, and he was standing with his keys in one hand and a beer in the other when he heard the car pull in.

Son of a bitch. There was business after all.

He left the keys in the door, set the beer down on the step, and walked toward the gate as a young guy stepped out of a Jeep and gazed at the place. That wasn't uncommon; teenagers were always coming around. They were young enough to still have an interest in working on their own cars, and they didn't have the money for new parts.

"Come on in, but don't forget it's gettin' on toward closing time," Sam hollered.

"It's not even four thirty." The kid said this in an amused voice, not confrontational, but still, it riled Sam. Who gave a damn what a kid thought closing time should be?

"Like I said," Sam told him drily as he picked up the PBR can. The kid watched him and then smiled, like he'd just learned something that pleased him.

"I don't want to impose on you, sir. I can tell you've got better things to do." This was smart-ass, but he plowed on past it so fast that Sam didn't have a chance to retort. "I'm just doing my job, which requires hassling you about a couple of cars that you towed in here from up by Hammel College a few days ago."

"Shit." Sam drank more of the beer. He was tired of those cars from the college. They were costing him more in headaches than they were worth in dollars. "They send you to take the pictures?"

The kid cocked his head. "Did who send me?"

"The gal I gave the phones to, she said she was coming back for pictures."

The kid didn't move his head, didn't change expression, didn't so much as blink, and yet Sam felt a strangeness come off him like an electric pulse.

"Who was this?"

"I don't remember," Sam said, and that wasn't a lie. He was always awful with names and even worse when he wasn't interested.

"Police?"

"Insurance, I think. She gave me a card."

Sam drained the beer and shook the empty can with regret, and he was just about to tell the kid that he had an appointment with a slice of pepperoni pizza when the kid said, "You like whiskey?"

Did Savage Sam Jones like whiskey? He almost laughed aloud. It had been a number of years since he'd heard that question. He was about to shout back, *Does Hugh Hefner like big tits?* but then he recalled his business decorum. That and the fact that Hugh was dead and this kid might not have the faintest idea who the man was or why glossy magazines had ever been needed. The damned internet had spoiled these kids.

"Does the pope shit in a funny hat?" Sam asked instead, figuring even a youngster could follow that old gem, and the kid grinned as he approached. He had a backpack slung over one shoulder and he didn't look like any trouble. Just lazy, that was all. You could tell that by the way he dressed, way he moved, everything. All these damned kids were lazy now, though. If he was here looking for car parts and asking about whiskey, why, he couldn't be as bad as most of them.

"I've got a bottle I might share with you, then," he said, and Sam squinted at him. This was more intriguing—and concerning. Was he some sort of street preacher? Was the whiskey a ruse entirely? If the kid got to carrying on about the spirit and the soul, that was not going to go well. It would go even worse if he was trying to sell some homebrew small-batch bullshit.

What he produced, though, was good old-fashioned American Jack Daniel's. It was hard to argue with that. Granted, it was a higher-dollar version, something called Gentleman Jack, but Sam had seen it at Walmart and so he knew it could be trusted.

"What do you want, son?" he said. He didn't mind the kid, and he surely wouldn't mind the whiskey, but he also didn't drink with strangers who showed up at five—well, close to five, anyhow—on a workday.

"Just a bit of your time. I can pour you a drink if you listen to me for a few minutes."

Sam looked at him and then at the bottle, and then he pictured the pizza slices spinning their slow dance in the warming oven on the corner store's counter. It would be twenty minutes at least until there were fresh slices in there.

"Who'd you say you worked for?" he asked.

"I didn't," the kid said, and smiled. "But I promise I'll be less trouble than any of the rest of them."

"Rest of who?"

"The people who are asking about those cars and the phones."

"Son, I only towed 'em in here. I didn't witness the damn wreck, and I don't have the damn phone."

"But there was a phone in the car?"

Sam wasn't sure whether he liked this kid or not. He smiled an awful lot, but the smile seemed to belong to an inside joke, which was strange considering it was only the two of them here and Sam didn't get the joke. "I don't know," Sam said. "Go call the cop who called me and ask him—"

"I don't think we should call the cops," the kid said. "I think we should have a drink and talk. Because you made a mistake, Mr. Jones. You shouldn't have given that phone away to anyone who didn't have a badge. She had to have been aware of the trouble she was getting you into, and you're telling me she didn't warn you?"

"Shit, no!" Sam was uneasy now, thinking of the number of phones he'd entrusted to the blond gal.

The kid made a disappointed sound and shook his head. "I know her type, all friendly talk, winking at you and then somehow leaving with property she doesn't have any right to, and when the cops show—and they will—the cops will have heard an entirely different story than the one you were told. There'll be petty charges, maybe, but what's petty when it's your own life and your business?"

Shit, shit, shit, Sam thought. Sam did *not* want to appear in court, and he said as much now.

The kid nodded sympathetically and said, "I think we can keep it from going that way."

"You can? What're you, my Boy Scout representative?"

The kid smiled. "You know, that's not far off, really. I was raised to know what to do in the woods, that's for sure. I can still start a fire in the rain."

"All due respect, but I wouldn't mind seeing your boss. Just to talk to somebody at the top, you know?"

"I've been involved in my father's business since I was very young," the kid said. "It's a tricky line of work, and training starts early. I worked with my father, worked with my uncle. I know I look young, sir, but I assure you I know how to handle a situation like this."

Sam thought he'd probably just heard gospel. Immature and lazy as the kid looked, he talked a mighty fine game, said the right things and said them firmly. And, hell, he was a worker. That mattered. Most kids these days didn't show any ambition at all.

"More I listen to you, and the more I think on it, you're right, it could get pretty bad," Sam said. "Got one dead and one with no more brain activity than a head of lettuce, and you just know there's going to be lawsuits coming out of that. Don't matter that the Mexican hit them, he ain't got no money, so they'll find—"

"The Mexican—" the kid began, and Sam interrupted hastily.

"I don't want you thinking I'm racist or nothing, it's just, my understanding was that he was some kind of Mexican."

"Correct," the kid said with the barest hint of a smile, most of it lost to the shadows his black baseball cap cast over his face. "He was indeed some kind of Mexican, and now he's the dead kind. He was murdered outside of Boston, I'm told."

Sam gaped. *Murdered.* That was not a word Savage Sam wanted to hear in connection to any of the cars he towed, even when they were for the police. Murder cases were unholy messes. His sister-in-law over in York County had to serve on the jury of a murder trial once, and it lasted most of a month. Now, she did say the lunches were pretty decent, and the case was interesting, kind of like TV, but Sam had no desire to get wrapped up with anything that could get him on the witness stand. Once he got to explaining those phones…

"It'll be a damned turkey shoot," he grumbled aloud. "I shouldn't have given the phones to that gal. If she was a cop, maybe. But she promised she'd get them to the police. That ain't gonna sound real good when I say it, though, is it?"

The kid gave him a sympathetic look and didn't answer. Sam lifted the PBR to his lips and then remembered it was already empty.

"What if I could get them back for you?" the kid asked. He'd walked right up to the front porch steps now. Just a child, and yet he talked with such authority that Sam might've believed *he* was a cop. "Once I understand the details of the situation, I can make sure that your property is returned and that the woman who pulled this fast one on you won't bother you anymore. By the end, she'll be more afraid of the police than you will. As she should be."

"Hell, yes, as she should be," Sam said, beginning to think it was a damned good thing that this kid had pulled in when he did. Just ten minutes later, and Sam would've been settled at his booth down at the store, a couple pieces of old pizza on paper plates in front of him.

"Let's have a drink," the kid said, "and you can talk me through it. Unless, of course, you don't drink on the job?"

Sam answered with a snort and crushed the empty PBR can beneath his dusty work boot. "I expect I can get a couple fingers of that sippin' whiskey down just fine."

The kid grinned. "I'm glad to hear it."

Sam turned to the door. The keys were still in the lock. He took them out and then swung the door open and held it so the kid could pass through.

"A few more minutes and I'd have missed you," he said. "Now I've got help *and* whiskey."

"Lucky break."

"So which side of the show are you working for? The girl's family or the dead Mexican fella's? Or the first dead guy's? Shit, almost forgot about him. Lot of death around that wreck."

"There sure was," the kid said. "Say, do you have any glasses?"

Sam got so distracted by searching for clean glasses that he forgot the kid hadn't answered the question about who he was working for. He found glasses and sat down behind the desk. The old chair wheezed beneath him, and dust rose, but the cushions were crushed down to the shape of his frame now, still plenty comfortable. Customized, you might say.

"There you go," he said, sliding the glasses across the desk. The kid poured him a nice healthy shot, three fingers, maybe four. Sam almost told him to stop, but what the hell. He didn't want to come across as a doddering old-timer who couldn't handle his liquor.

The kid sat back and capped the bottle. Sam frowned. "Ain't gonna have any?"

"Drinking on the job is high-risk, according to my father."

"Well, hell, now I feel like you're getting me drunk just to get me talkin'," Sam said, and he was only half joking.

The kid must've seen that because he said, "Tell you what—I'd do a beer if you've got any more of those around."

"Sure." Sam fetched him a tallboy can of PBR, and the kid drank this without hesitation, which put Sam at ease.

The whiskey went down with a smooth burn and a faint tang. Sam pulled the bottle closer and tilted it one way and his head the other so they aligned in a fashion that allowed him to read without his bifocals.

"Gentleman Jack," he said. "Not bad, but what was wrong with just the good old stuff? Why's it always gotta be changing?"

The kid bowed his head and said, "Ah, that's a sentimental thing, really. My father's name was Jack. He was a gentleman too. A charmer, sir. People who made it through a whole day or a whole night with him, they always loved him."

Now, this was something Savage Sam Jones could embrace, a kid who cared about his father. For all the bullshit you heard about these kids and their cell phone addictions and electric cigarettes and liberal notions, it was reassuring to know there were still some good ones.

"That's real nice," Sam said, and that's when it hit him—the kid had said his father's name *was* Jack. "Oh, man. He's gone, isn't he?"

The kid nodded.

"I'm truly sorry to hear it. I lost my old man too young too. What happened to yours?"

The kid lifted his head and stared at Sam with flat eyes. "He burned up in a forest fire in Montana."

"Shit," Sam breathed. "A real damned hero. I'm sorry for your loss, but at least you know he went down doing righteous work. I hope you think about that."

"Oh, I do, sir. I think about that often. Matter of fact..." He rose, uncapped the whiskey, and refilled Sam's glass. "Maybe a toast to him, if you don't mind? Fire season's done here, but out in California and Arizona, they've still got men on the lines."

Sam lifted his glass. "To heroes," he said. "To men like your father."

"To my father," the kid said, and he clinked his PBR can off Sam's glass and drank.

The whiskey tasted fine, but, boy, it snuck up on you too. After just two shots of the stuff—well, two pretty stiff pours—Savage Sam Jones was fighting to keep his vision clear and his words from slurring.

"So what can you tell me about this woman who came to get the phone from you?" the kid said.

Sam told him everything there was to tell. He explained his habit of scouring cars for items of potential value and his immediate quest to notify the owner when such a thing was found. He explained how if nobody claimed their shit within thirty days, then you could hardly be expected to imagine they cared about its fate, and so he'd been known to take it down to his brother's pawnshop a time or two. This kid listened respectfully and didn't give any of the wry smiles like the blond gal.

As his whiskey glass was refilled and went back down, he decided to give this polite kid with the dead-hero father a little more of the truth.

"It was actually in the glove compartment," he said. "But like I said, I always give a careful look. Situation like that, where people get hurt, people *die*? Those sentimental things sometimes really matter to people." He leaned back and waved his glass at the kid. "Hell, you know all about that, with what your dad did. You got anything like that left from him?"

The kid hesitated, and Sam wondered if it was too fresh, if he'd touched a wound that hadn't yet healed. But finally the kid nodded. "More than a few things," he said. "Most of them, I keep here." He touched his temple, then tapped his heart, and Sam nodded sagely.

"Well, sure. Of course. I just mean some people like to have a tangible..."

He stopped talking when the kid brought the gun out.

It was a revolver, a Ruger maybe, with black grips and a blackened muzzle and bore but chrome cylinders for the bullets. It was a beautiful gun, and a mean one. Any fine-looking weapon was a frightening one. People hadn't fallen in love with those friggin' AR-15s because they were ugly guns. They looked the part. Hold one and look in the mirror and you felt the part. Problem was, that got in some people's heads. Some children's heads, for that matter.

"You just carry that with you, do you?" Sam said, and he didn't like how unsteady his voice sounded. He'd been around guns all his life. Why did this one scare him?

"Yeah, I guess." The kid pocketed it again, and while Sam was glad it was out of sight, he was aware of how natural it fit in the kid's hand.

"Where are you from?" Sam asked.

"All over. Moved around a lot, growing up."

"Because of the fires," Sam said, thinking of the kid's dead father. "They don't stay in one place, nice and tidy, do they?"

The kid smiled. "No," he said. "Fires tend to move around." He started to pour again, and Sam waved him off, because at this point if he tried to drive even as far as the corner store for pizza, he'd be taking a hell of a chance. His vision was blurring in a way it usually didn't from whiskey.

"Aw, come on," the kid said. "Just one more, for my dad. His burned bones are on some mountain out there I've never seen. Right now, they're probably already under a blanket of snow. Have a drink for him, would you, sir?"

How could you say no to that? A kid asking you to toast to his dead father's bones, burned black by fire and now buried by snow, and the kid was offering his own whiskey, and you were going to say no? That didn't seem right.

"Pour it," Sam said.

The kid poured it tall again, but what the hell. If Sam needed to doze off here in the chair for an hour or two until he was ready to get behind the wheel, that was fine. He'd done it before. He saw no reason to be troubled by his heavy eyelids.

"The card?" the kid asked loudly.

"Huh?" Sam jerked upright. He realized he'd actually been on the way to sleep, and he'd let his eyes close.

"You said you couldn't remember the woman's name, the one you gave all of the phones to, but that she left a card."

"Oh, shit. Yes. Yes, she did." Sam tried to stand, but he was woozy. Damn, that new Jack Daniel's had a different kind of kick to it. Sneaky as a snake in the grass. He'd stick to the old classic in the future. He fumbled around on the shelf behind the desk and then he turned around, triumphant, the card held high.

"Here ya go." He tossed it on the desk so the kid could read it. No way Sam could pick the words out of that blur, not now.

"'Hank Bauer, Coastal Claims and Investigations,'" the kid read. "Hank was a woman?"

"No, but that's the card she left. She must work for him. She wasn't as young as you, but not very far from it either. Maybe thirty. Tiny little thing, with blond hair. She was decent, I suppose, but she might be a smart-ass. And like you said, she should've left the…the…uh…" Sam couldn't keep his thoughts steady, and he was beginning to sweat. "It should've been the police that came, is what I mean."

"Sure. Well, Mr. Jones, consider your problems solved. I'll take care of this whole matter, and I'll do it discreetly."

Sam tried to nod. Tried to say thank you. Instead he felt his eyes close, and this time he didn't fight them.

"That's some damn strong liquor," he said, and the words were hard to form and seemed to echo in his own ears.

"It's a proprietary blend," the kid said. "I add a little custom touch to it."

Wish you'd mentioned that earlier, Savage Sam Jones thought but didn't say, couldn't say. His eyes were still closed, and he felt his head lolling forward on a suddenly slackening neck.

I need some water, he thought. *I need some help.*

When Savage Sam Jones slumped forward in his chair, Dax Blackwell didn't move. He waited a few minutes, calm and patient, before pulling on thin gloves and checking for a pulse.

Nothing. The old man's flesh was already cooling. His heart had stopped.

Long after he was certain of this, Dax Blackwell kept his hand on the man's wrist and his gaze on the man's closed eyes. He studied the tableau of death where life had flourished just minutes ago, until Dax's arrival on the doorstep of this man now turned corpse.

Finally, reluctantly, he released him.

There was business to do, and time was wasting.

He kept the gloves on while he wiped down the whiskey glass and the PBR can and the desk. Sam's old chair swiveled under his weight, turning the dead man away from the door. Dax carefully turned the chair back so that his face would greet the next visitor.

When he left, he took the bottle.

18

The neurologist's last name is Pine, and if he has a first name, he doesn't offer it to Tara. He is Dr. Pine, period. He has a pleasant smile and smart, penetrating eyes and the kind of self-assured bearing that gives you confidence.

It gives Tara confidence, at least, until he asks her to blink.

"Twice for no, once for yes," he says in his deep, warm voice. They are alone in the room; Shannon objected to that, but Dr. Pine insisted, and Dr. Pine won.

He is the first medical staffer to introduce himself to Tara and explain who he is. *Hello, Tara, I'm Dr. Pine, your neurologist. We're going to need to work together to get your show back on the road, okay? This will be a team effort. But I promise you I'm going to do my part.*

All of this is so nice to hear. So encouraging. But then...

"Blink for me," he says again. "Please, Tara."

And she wants to. She has never wanted anything more in her life than to blink for this man.

She can't do it, though. She tries so hard that tears form in her eyes, but tears are always forming in her eyes, and she doubts this means anything to him. It's not crying so much as leaking, and nobody seems to notice it except Shannon and the black nurse whose name Tara still doesn't know. Sometimes they will dab her tears off her cheeks.

My sister used to call me Twitch, she thinks. *I was that jumpy. If you showed me a scary movie or slammed a door when the house was dark, I'd jerk like I'd been electrocuted. Now I can't even blink.*

Dr. Pine stares at her, says, "If you're comfortable, give me one

123

blink. If you're not comfortable, give me two," and Tara begins to feel exhausted from the strain of effort, an exhaustion that's only heightened by the outrage that there's no evidence of her effort, no sign that she's fighting her ass off in here. She doubles down on the effort of the blink, every ounce of her energy going toward her eyelids. *Come on, come on...*

And that's when her thumb twitches.

She feels a wave of elation; Dr. Pine shows nothing. He didn't see her thumb. He's watching her eyes, and so he missed the motion in her hand.

"That's okay, Tara," he says, and he pats her arm and stands up and turns his attention to his notepad.

But my thumb moved! It moved, how could you miss that, I need you to see that I can move!

Twitchy Tara the scaredy-cat girl is back and better than ever. Twitch is no longer a shame name; it's a lifeline.

Pine looks up, smiles at her, and then says, "Let's bring your family back in, shall we?"

Damn it, Doc, where were your eyes when I needed them!

But he's gone, and her thumb is still again. The lifeline lifeless. He opens the door and they all file in, Shannon in front, then Mom, then Rick with his hand on Mom's arm. Always the reassuring touch.

"Remember," he tells Mom, "the truth is always progress."

He keeps talking, his voice rising and falling with the softly melodic tone that Shannon always claims is attempted hypnosis. When she and Tara were kids, that was one of the inside jokes about Rick that kept them laughing and made his endless optimism and stream of life-lesson-inspiration bullshit tolerable. That and the way he kept Mom away from the pills. She'd been in her fourth stint at rehab when she met Rick, and nobody expected this one to work any better than the first three had. It would buy a few weeks maybe, but then Tara would come home and find her mother hadn't gotten out of bed, or Shannon would open a DVD case and Vicodin tablets would pour out.

Rick, with his relentless *What is your intention for this day?* mantras, his vegan diet, and his awful taste in music—lyrics were an unfortunate interruption of melody, he always said—connected with Martha Beckley in a way no one else had been able to, and that was enough to make him tolerable to her daughters. Because while Mom's obvious vulnerability was to medications, not men, there were always plenty of the latter. The construction accident that had claimed her husband's life, taking from Tara a father that she scarcely remembers, left Martha Beckley both a psychological wreck and a wealthy woman.

Rick has been a good influence for Mom, an absolute relief in some ways, but Tara has never completely trusted him, and she certainly doesn't like the sound of the statement *The truth is always progress.* He's preparing her mother to hear a truth that will be hard to take, and he wants her to believe that it's progress.

"Why don't we let the doctor tell us what progress is," Shannon snaps.

Get him, Shannon, Tara thinks.

Sometimes Mom will joke about her "guard daughters." Mom thinks of it as a joke, at least, but Shannon and Tara take it literally. When Dad died, their lives became a revolving door of people offering help and people seeking to take advantage. Shannon, the older and the alpha, led most of the battles. Now, voiceless, motionless, helpless, Tara can only hope that her sister redirects that same fury to fight on her behalf. *You are a redheaded Doberman,* she'd told Shannon once. It was a joke then. Now, though, she needs the guard dog.

Do not listen, Shannon. Do not let anyone convince you that I'm just a body, mindless and soulless in here. Please, oh, please do not let them convince you of that.

Dr. Pine studies the three of them and then says, "I really wish she could blink."

Tara's heart drops. Why did he have to start there? Why did he have to start with what she can't do and not with what she might be able to do—listen, watch, think! And twitch her damn thumb every now and then.

"Based on my reading, that can often take time," Shannon says. "We're not even a week into this."

"Correct. I didn't say it was cause to lose hope; I simply said that I wish she demonstrated a blink response. She's so far ahead in so many ways, you know. Breathing without assistance is, on its own, unusual in these circumstances, and encouraging. The question of awareness, however, would be helped by a blink response." Dr. Pine shrugs. "But it hardly means the battle is lost. Tara's brain was banged around the inside of her skull, quite literally pulled from its moorings. That caused bruising and swelling; blood vessels were torn and axons stretched. Critical communication regions were damaged. As you know, this is what the induced coma was designed to mitigate—it decreases the amount of work the brain has to do, which keeps the swelling down, and we have a better chance at restoring these processing areas."

"But it didn't work," Rick says, and Tara wishes that it was her middle finger that could twitch instead of her thumb.

"We don't know if it worked *yet,*" Shannon corrects, and Dr. Pine nods.

"Yes and yes. This is, of course, going to be a possibly long and certainly painful process. Each coma patient is different. Some make remarkable recoveries and fairly swiftly. Others make less complete recoveries and over much longer periods." Pause. "Others do not recover at all."

Shannon looks at Tara, and Tara does her damnedest to call up a sister-to-sister radio signal. She is certain that such a thing exists. There are some people who hear you without words. Shannon has always heard her, and Tara needs her now. Oh, how she needs her now.

"There's a coma researcher at the university hospital eleven miles from here," Shannon says. "A doctor named—"

"Michelle Carlisle," Dr. Pine finishes. "Yes. I know her well. An excellent research doctor."

It feels like there's something slightly diminishing in the way he says *research doctor,* as if he's indicating the difference between practice and theory with a mild shift in tone.

"I'd like to take Tara to see her," Shannon says.

Rick says, "I think we need to let Dr. Pine make those decisions, Shannon."

Shannon doesn't so much as glance at him. "Of course I want to consult with Dr. Pine while *we* make these decisions."

Dr. Pine adjusts his glasses and then closes his notebook. The gestures seem designed to delay the inevitable—he's going to say there's no point.

"I'm a fan of Dr. Carlisle's work," he says at last.

"It's another opinion," Mom says, "and that's good, but we haven't heard *yours* yet."

Her voice trembles, but Tara is almost painfully proud of her for speaking up.

"Every case is different," Dr. Pine says again, a hedge that no one, even Tara, wants to hear.

"Scale of one to ten," Rick says.

"Pardon?"

"On a scale of one to ten, how...how close to dead is she?"

"Rick, you *asshole,*" Shannon says, whirling on him. "What kind of question is that?"

"A fair one," he replies, standing firm. "Dr. Pine has treated hundreds of patients in similar conditions. He has an opinion, and I'd like to hear it. We all *need* to hear it."

No, we do not, Tara thinks.

Dr. Pine looks at each of them individually. Tara is last. His eyes are on hers when he says, "On a scale of one to ten, if one is the most alive, then physically she's probably a two or three. She needs assistance, of course, but her body is healthy and it will continue to survive, though obviously not to thrive, for the foreseeable future."

"And what about the soul?" Rick says, and Shannon rolls her eyes on cue.

"I think he means her mind, Doctor. Is she with us?"

More than any of you want to know, Tara thinks, because they've all had moments in front of her that she is sure they wouldn't have wanted her to witness. Moments when their love was buried beneath fatigue and frustration. She doesn't blame them for this, but it doesn't make those moments any less hurtful.

"I'd encourage more tests."

"But right now? What would you say based on the tests you've already done?" Rick presses.

"Eight," Dr. Pine answers without hesitation. "Based on what we've already done."

Eight. On a scale of one to ten, he is rating Tara's brain as far closer to dead than alive.

"Then we'll do more," Shannon says, but there's a hitch in her voice.

Everyone's faith is beginning to waver.

Not fair, Tara thinks. *I was just giving a ride to a stranger. Why isn't he trapped like this instead of me?*

But Oltamu is worse off than her, of course. Oltamu is dead; she's heard them say this.

Maybe the wolf got him.

If she could shake her head, she'd do it just to get rid of that strange recurring image of the wolf with raised hackles and narrowed eyes and pinned-back ears and exposed fangs. That wasn't real, and Tara can't afford to have any distractions in a brain that's already failing to do its job. She's got tests to take, and if she can't pass them, she's going to end up just like Oltamu.

Don't think that way. Once you start that, you're done.

A voice whispers that she is already done, that it is time to give up, give in, quit. She fights it off.

Oltamu is dead; Tara Beckley is not. Tara Beckley is alive and not only that, her thumb has twitched.

She thinks again of the cellar in 1804 London Street, where she once stood in the blackness, gasping, cobwebs on her face, tears in her eyes. She remembers that in that moment of panic, she turned her head to face that darkness directly, and she found the faintest glimmer of light. It was a long way off, and she wasn't sure that she could make it there or if freedom existed beyond it, but she had seen it, and she had tried.

There's a glimmer of light inside this vacant house too. Among all the dark hallways and unknown corridors and treacherous stairs, there are cracks and gaps. The doors might be locked, the windows sealed and shuttered, but there are always gaps.

Find one and force it open. Then someone will notice. Someone will hear.

Tara retreats into the blackness, imagining the corridor between her brain and her thumb, and she gets to work.

Part Three

ON THE BACK ROADS

19

Hank Bauer lived in what had once been a hunting camp. He'd purchased the cabin intending to keep the property's purpose intact, but then his wife learned of his affair with a waitress at Applebee's, and the hunting camp rapidly became his home. He often told this story as a cautionary tale of the risks of marriage—but never of the risks of having an affair with a waitress, Applebee's or otherwise.

Those hunting-camp days seemed long ago and far away. He felt some shame over the way his marriage had ended but no real regret for how his life had gone. He was good on his own, always had been, and the marriage and the mortgages had been the real mistakes, the steps out of character. That had been trying on a suit he knew he'd never care for even though it sure looked nice and comfortable on other men. Margaret had called him an arrested adolescent during the divorce, and he didn't disagree. His life had been mostly games and gambling, drinking and storytelling, hard rock and hangovers. It wasn't an adulthood anybody should really take pride in, but he'd learned to lose his shame over it all the same. At sixty-one, he was too old to be embarrassed. He'd had fun.

And he'd done well too. Not well enough for the mortgage in Cape Elizabeth that had scared him right into the welcoming arms of Applebee's, but well enough that it had been a long time since he'd worried about money. He'd found himself in the insurance business by accident—didn't everyone get there that way?— but the money was steady, you got to meet plenty of people, and sometimes you actually had the sense that you'd helped to ease a person's mind.

On the day that he returned to his home on twenty-seven acres of woodland and trout-brook frontage and found the kid in the black baseball cap waiting on him, Hank was largely content with his life. The only thing nagging at him that afternoon was Abby Kaplan.

He'd met Abby when she was just thirteen. Her mother had bolted after determining that raising a child was less enjoyable than being one, and so it had been just Abby and her father, who was a good man with a bad booze habit. He was also the most talented natural mechanic Hank had ever seen, probably capable of building a functioning engine out of duct tape and toothpicks if you spotted him the gasoline. Hank's first encounter with Jake Kaplan's daughter didn't have the makings of a lifelong friendship: she had stolen his car.

Hank had a ridiculous, souped-up '85 Trans Am back then, and he'd trusted Jake Kaplan to retool it. Then one day the police called to tell him they'd recovered his stolen car and had the thirteen-year-old thief in custody. The cops said she'd been doing ninety-four when they clocked her, and Hank's first question was "How was she handling it?"

He'd told the cops not to press charges, which hadn't pleased them, as they believed he was aiding and abetting the development of a local delinquent. And maybe he had been. But Abby was honest and apologetic when they spoke, ready for consequences, and Hank was struck by both the sadness of her demeanor—a good kid expecting bad things, as if that were preordained for her—and her infatuation with his old muscle car.

Jake Kaplan, a good ol' boy's good ol' boy with a worldview shaped by drunks and dropouts, didn't often mention Abby's missing mother, but that day he did.

"Abby wants to race," Jake told Hank mournfully.

"So let her race. Don't need to have a driver's license on the oval. Ed Traylor's boy was racing when he was no older than Abby."

"I can't let her do that. I'm supposed to raise a daughter to be a woman."

"Ever heard of Sarah Fisher?" Hank asked.

And so it came to pass that Hank Bauer sponsored Abby Kaplan's first foray into racing. It was curiosity and amusement at first, and it made for a damn good story; the boys at the poker games *loved* hearing about how Hank had become the sponsor for his own car thief.

Nobody chuckled after the first races, though. Hank watched her beat older men night after night, and then she went on to the bigger speedways, and when she lost, it was not to better drivers but to better cars. Hank saw that this game, like all of them, had a ceiling that could be cracked only with cash.

Coastal Claims and Investigations became a more serious sponsor then. It wasn't just because Hank liked the girl and felt bad for her; it was also because he was damn curious to see what she could do with the right machine.

What she did was win. Early, often, and then always. She smoked the drag-racing circuit through northern New England and then got onto the oval and kicked even more ass, and everybody's bet was on NASCAR or Indy when she'd fooled them all and gone into stunt driving instead. Hank had seen some version of that coming when Abby fell in love with the drift. Even winning a race didn't put the same light in her eyes that a controlled drift did—a floating test of traction and throttle that looked wildly out of control to the average spectator. If you could control it, though... well, Hank supposed it was a special kind of high.

She'd gone to a couple stunt schools, caught the right people's eyes, and ended up in Hollywood and then Europe. For a while she'd been shooting commercials in friggin' Dubai or someplace, bouncing some bastardized supercar turned SUV around a desert. She'd been all over the world driving the finest cars known to man and making good money doing it, and Hank was awfully proud of her.

And now awfully worried about what was keeping her in Maine.

The crack-up she'd had out on the West Coast would have been bad enough if the boyfriend with her had been anonymous. But he was a rising star, his face was on magazine covers, and that crush of attention had made a bad deal worse for Abby. She'd come back to Maine to clear her head, she claimed, but Hank knew better.

Abby was hiding.

Hank had practically begged his way into the Hammel College job when he learned about the girl in the coma. He thought this might be useful for Abby, if for no other reason than it would get her to open up a little, tell him what exactly was wrong so he could go about helping her. That hadn't worked out, though, and so on the day when Hank arrived at his home to find an unfamiliar white Jeep in his driveway, he was thinking that he needed to get out of this case before it became a real mess.

The white Jeep pushed those thoughts from his mind. Hank didn't have many visitors.

The rain splattered over the windshield made it look empty, but then the door opened and a kid in a black baseball cap stepped out and waited with a weird half smile. Hank got out of the car into the misting rain.

"Can I help you, fella?"

"Mr. Bauer?"

"That's right."

"My name's Matt Norris."

"Okay." Hank waited, but the kid was quiet, hands still in his pockets, odd smile still on his face.

"So you dropped by just to practice introducing yourself?" Hank said. "You did real well on the part with your name. The rest needs work."

Norris laughed softly. "No. Sorry, my mind wandered. I'm not real sure I should've come by at all." He took one hand from his pockets and adjusted the black baseball cap. "I couldn't get the cops to listen to me, though."

Hank straightened. "Cops?"

Matt Norris nodded without changing expression, as if it were perfectly normal to be standing in the rain on a stranger's property talking about the cops.

"I go to Hammel College."

Aw, shit. "Yeah? That's terrific. But Matt, buddy, I don't step in front of police, okay?"

"You're a private investigator."

"No. I'm in the insurance business."

"You have a private investigator's license."

Hank sighed and rubbed his face with a damp palm. "That's marketing crap. I'm no detective, I don't want to play one on TV or in my yard in the rain. You got something to say on that wreck, it should be to the cops, not me."

"Carlos Ramirez wasn't driving the car," the kid said. "How 'bout *that*?"

I almost went bowling, Hank thought. *It was a coin-toss decision back there at the office—head to the alley or head home. Why in the hell didn't I go to the bowling alley?*

Something told him the kid would've waited, though.

"Come on in out of the rain," Hank said with a sigh. "You're going to cause me enough trouble without giving me pneumonia too."

The kid laughed too loudly. As Hank unlocked his door and held it open for Matt Norris to pass through, he was frowning. It hadn't been that funny of a line, but from that laugh, you'd have thought the kid was at a comedy club.

Something's off with him, Hank thought, and then he closed the door to shut out the rain and the darkening sky.

20

Abby was in the shower when her phone began to ring. She let it go, but then it rang again and again, and so she shut off the water, knotted a towel above her breasts, and went out to the living room, leaving wet footprints behind.

It was Hank.

"Can't leave a message?" Abby said, the phone held against her damp cheek. "I was in the shower."

"Sorry, kid." Hank's voice was strained, as if he were calling in the middle of a workout. "Think you can stop by here?"

Abby cocked her head, shedding a spray of water from her hair to the floor. "Now? What's up?"

"I, uh...I guess that Ramirez story might have some issues. You were right, I think. Anyhow, uh, Meredith is coming by with some cop from Brighton, and they want the phones."

"They're coming by your house?"

"Yeah." There was a rustling sound, and Hank gave a quick, harsh intake of breath before he said, "And he's going to want the phones."

"Sure thing," Abby said. "Give me twenty minutes, maybe half an hour."

"Yeah. Faster the better. Thanks, Abs." Hank hung up.

Abby lowered the phone, frowning. Hank had sounded tense, worried. Cops coming to your house could do that, though, especially when one of them was from out of state and working on a murder case.

She thought about that as she toweled off and dressed in jeans, a light base layer, and a fleece. She had the window cracked to let the steam bleed out of the bathroom, and she could hear the laughter of patrons at Run of the Mill, a brewery that shared a portion of her apartment building, all of it the reimagined and re-purposed site of what had once been the Pepperell Mill, a textile mill that had at one time employed what seemed like half of Biddeford. Now it was a mixture of condos and businesses, and the roof was lined with solar panels—but the Saco River remained, and Abby enjoyed listening to the water as the town found new ways to thrive around it. The river was the constant, and the river ran steady. She appreciated that.

As she tugged a brush through towel-dried hair, she thought of the police waiting at Hank's, and when she picked up the decaying shoe box of phones and chargers, some of the cardboard flaked off in her hands. She didn't relish the idea of explaining to police from Boston that she'd transported evidence in a homicide investigation back and forth through the rain in a shoe box. She found some plastic bags and separated the phones and chargers. Savage Sam had been nearly positive that what he'd taken out of the car was an iPhone, so she separated those too, then put the iPhone chargers in with the iPhones, figuring anything that made it look more official couldn't hurt. For all of Hank's jokes about his PI license, it carried legal liability, and Abby didn't want to put him at risk.

Should've just called Meredith to begin with, she thought. But it had been Hank's idea for her to take the phones to Shannon Beckley, and back then there'd been no questions of guilt and no bullets in Carlos Ramirez's brain. Or at least nobody had known about them.

Abby found a Sharpie and wrote the date and her name and *Beckley case* on the three plastic bags. Hardly a proper evidence folder, but better than a soggy shoe box.

She left her apartment and drove away from the mill toward Hank's house, the bagged phones and chargers on the passenger seat. Usually she avoided the short stretch of turnpike that was the fastest route, but Hank had asked her to hurry, so tonight she took it. Driving was easier for her at night, regardless of traffic. She didn't feel as crowded in the dark or as exposed. There was no horizon line, and your visual range in the mirrors was limited. The blackness obscured both where you'd been and where you were going. Somehow, that containment helped dull the anxiety brought on by visible obstacles ahead, and it eased the dread of traffic rising up behind.

It was only seven miles on the turnpike before she exited onto the county roads, and she made it without incident, no dry mouth or racing pulse. Traffic was light, but it probably helped that she was distracted too. She didn't like the idea of sitting down with police on this. David Meredith was fine; Abby knew him a bit, and Hank knew him well. But homicide detectives from Boston? That was different. That brought back memories too. The detectives in California hadn't been homicide cops, but they'd felt close enough.

Clean blood isn't everything, Ms. Kaplan. We're looking at that curve and that guardrail and trying to figure out how exactly you got airborne. And you're a pretty good driver, we understand. Professional.

She turned off the county road and onto the teeth-rattling gravel that wound through the pines and bone-colored birches that surrounded Hank's place. It was beautiful country, but isolated. The deep woods were never far from you in Maine. Abby was a native Mainer, but she wasn't completely comfortable here at night. Her childhood home had had sidewalks and streetlights; this place, deserted except for snowmobile trails and tree stands, had always seemed foreign to her.

As she drove slowly through the ruts, a few untrimmed branches swiped her Chrysler, and even the high beams didn't seem to cut the darkness. There was a single light on in Hank's house, a glow from the kitchen. That was unusual, because Hank spent only as much time in the kitchen as it took him to microwave his dinner. He also didn't use the blinds, but tonight they were closed.

In the narrow driveway, Hank's Tahoe was parked behind a white Jeep. There was no room to pull up alongside or even turn around without driving onto the lawn. Abby parked behind the Tahoe, and she was about to kill the engine and get out when she felt the familiar warm buzz in her veins that had been her early-warning system for so many years, that rapid pulse of adrenaline-laced instinct that was triggered when you were doing a hundred and fifty miles per hour and saw the cars in front of you shift and knew that something was about to go wrong. That silent alarm had been Abby's gift on the track. She'd been able to tell when things were going bad just a fraction of a second ahead of most.

They're positioned wrong, she thought now.

Hank had said the police *were* coming, not that the police were already there. But the Jeep was sitting in front of the Tahoe. Unless Hank had come and gone in the twenty minutes since he'd called Abby, whoever was driving the Jeep had been here first.

She sat with the engine growling and the headlights on and stared at the cars and the house, and her hand drifted back to the gearshift. She almost put it in reverse. But what was she going to do, back out of here and call Hank from the road and say she was scared of the Jeep? Come on. She'd spent too much time thinking paranoid thoughts on the train after seeing Tara Beckley and hearing about Carlos Ramirez. Her mind was built for that now; the docs had told her this. Panic floated; panic drifted like dark smoke and found new places in the brain to call home.

Screw that. Be tough, Abby. Be who you always were.

She released the gearshift and killed the engine. While the head-lights dimmed, she grabbed the three plastic bags of cell phones and chargers, and was reaching for the door when the strange fear rose again, and she found herself shoving the bag with the iPhones under the driver's seat.

I'll say I dropped it. When I know that things are legit, I'll come back and get it.

No clean logic to the choice, just a response to that old pulse in the blood, to that fresh dark smoke drifting through her brain. *People have died and someone wants those phones. You don't just carry them through the door.*

She got out of the car with the two bags in hand, the Chrysler parked behind the two SUVs, forming a mini-caravan in the narrow driveway. She looked at the Jeep's plate—Massachusetts. Good. That was as promised. But where was David Meredith?

The rain had stopped but puddles littered the dirt driveway like land mines. Abby dodged them, crossed the yard, went up the front steps, and rapped her knuckles on the wall as she pulled open the screen door. Hank's muted voice floated out from inside.

"Yeah, Abs. Come in."

She pushed open the front door, stepped inside, looked toward the light, and saw Hank tied to a kitchen chair.

It was an old wooden straight-backed chair, and he was bound to it with thin green cord. His right arm was wrapped tight against his side, but his left arm was free, and he lifted it with his palm out, signaling for Abby to stop.

The gesture wasn't required. Abby stood frozen in midstride, staring at the scene in front of her as the screen door slapped shut behind her with a bang.

"Close the other one too," a soft voice from behind her said, and as Abby whirled toward the voice there was the distinctive metallic snap of a cocking revolver.

2 1

For a moment it was still and silent. The only light was coming from a battery lantern that threw an eerie, too-white glow over the kitchen and couldn't penetrate the shadows in the rest of the house. Whoever was speaking was standing in the hallway, no more than a silhouette against the darkness.

A silhouette and a gun.

"Abby?" the figure in the hall said. "Close the door."

Abby reached out and took the cold metal knob in her left hand and closed the door.

"Good," the man in the hall said. "Now lock it."

Abby moved faster to obey this instruction, turning the dead bolt and dropping her hand quickly to distract from the quarter turn she'd given the lock, enough to move the bolt but not enough to shoot it home. If she made it back to the door, it would open when she twisted the doorknob.

"Go into the kitchen," the man in the darkness said, and Abby obeyed again, shuffling backward, moving off the wooden floor and onto the tile of the kitchen. She glanced at the kitchen counter, expecting to see the block of knives that always sat beneath a years-old calendar that showed Abby being showered with cheap champagne by her father and Hank and Hank's then-girlfriend after Abby had become the youngest driver—and the first woman—to win at the Bald Mountain Speedway.

The calendar was there. The block of knives was gone.

"Stop," the man said, and Abby stopped and then the man walked out of the shadows and into the light and Abby saw him clearly.

He was a child, almost. Eighteen or nineteen, maybe twenty—but probably not. His boyish face was shaded by a black baseball cap with chrome-colored stitching that matched the cylinders on his black revolver, as if he'd coordinated the outfit. The gun was offset by that almost friendly face. He wore the sort of perpetual but false half smile of someone whose job required him to feign interest in the troubles of strangers, like a hotel concierge.

"Hello, Abby," he said.

"Who are you?"

"You think I'm going to give my name in this situation? Come on. Be better than that."

Abby looked at Hank. He seemed unharmed—no blood, no bruises—but absolutely terrified. He searched Abby's eyes but didn't speak and Abby saw something beyond fear in his face—apology.

"Put the bags on the counter," the kid said.

Abby did.

"You have a weapon?" the kid asked.

"No."

"You don't mind if I verify that?"

"No."

"Very gracious, thanks." The kid pressed the muzzle of the revolver to Abby's head as he patted her down with his free hand. He was wearing thin black gloves, and his touch made her skin crawl and her stomach knot, but she tried not to give him the satisfaction of a visible reaction. He took her phone and felt over her car keys but left them in her pocket.

The gun moved away from Abby's skull and then the kid stepped back, looked down at her phone, and tapped the screen. The display filled with the image on the lock screen: Luke sitting on a rock overlooking the Pacific, a smile on his face, his tousled hair blown wild by the wind.

"He was handsome, wasn't he?" the kid said, and then he tossed the phone onto the counter. "A shame what happened to him. I know the expression is 'Live fast, die young, and leave a good-looking corpse,' but he didn't really earn that live-fast idea. I mean, at least James Dean was driving, right?"

Abby's slap came without premeditation. She simply swung.

The kid sidestepped it with ease—damn, he was fast—and laughed.

"I seem to have touched a nerve," he said. "Apologies." He nodded at a chair that was pulled back from the table. "Take a seat."

"What do you want?" Abby asked.

"More original material, for one. You're asking such obvious questions: *Who are you? What do you want?* It gets tedious to be the guy with the gun. Redundant."

The kid looked so unthreatening despite the gun that Abby found herself measuring the distance between them and wondering if she should attack. She just needed to sweep that gun hand away. As long as the bullet went wide when he pulled the trigger, Abby didn't think it would be hard to take the gun from him. He was looking at her and seeing a small woman who couldn't throw a punch. She'd blackened the eyes and bloodied the noses of a few guys who'd thought that same thing.

If he tries to tie you, then do it, she told herself. *Punch, kick, bite—do anything and everything if he tries to tie you up. But not until then. As long as you can move, then just talk through whatever this is.*

"I asked you to sit," the kid said.

Abby sat. The battery lantern was on the table next to two tumbler glasses filled with whiskey, a bottle standing between them. Gentleman Jack.

She was now facing Hank, and her back was to the door. Hank's jowly face was drained of color, and he was breathing in short, audible pants. His eyes flicked away from Abby's, down and to the left, as if he were trying to see behind himself. Abby followed the look and saw that Hank's portable generator was on the floor behind his chair.

What in the hell is that doing in here? It was a gasoline-fueled backup generator, capable of producing enough electricity to run the lights, TV, and a space heater or two for a few days. The rural road wasn't a high priority for the Central Maine Power repair crews. Abby had never seen the generator inside the house, though.

Battery lantern on, generator inside? The power's out, and the kid doesn't know enough to leave the generator outdoors. But if he wants it, then he thinks we're going to be here for a while. He's not just going to take the phones and go. We're waiting on someone else.

"Get comfortable," the kid said, as if confirming Abby's thoughts. "Let's have a drink."

Abby looked at the full whiskey glass, then back at Hank's face, and shook her head. "What's in it?" she asked.

"Nothing," the kid said. "That's a fine-quality whiskey. Not cool enough for the hipsters, you know, it's not small-batch stuff, but it's awfully smooth. And the name is nice. The name is...meaningful to me."

He gave Abby a smile that looked positively warm and kind.

"Gentleman Jack," he said, and his voice went a little wistful at the end, as if they were all sharing in this strange reverie. "And double-mellowed, it says. That's a funny joke if you knew my family. But you don't, unfortunately. Nevertheless, please have a drink, Abby."

She shook her head again. The kid sighed and leveled the pistol so the muzzle was just inches away from Hank's knee.

"We can drink," the kid said, "or we can bleed."

Abby took the glass. The kid nodded in approval and then spoke to Hank without turning to him. "You too, old-timer. We're all celebrating."

Hank took the glass. His hand was shaking, and some of the

whiskey spilled over the top and dripped down the backs of his hairy fingers in golden beads. Abby saw for the first time that one of the cords binding him to the chair was actually an extension cord, and it had been cut and stripped so the bare wires glistened.

What in the hell had happened in here? What had Hank endured before making his call?

"Drink up," the kid said, and both Abby and Hank took a swallow. The whiskey had a mellow burn, but nothing about it tasted unfamiliar or tainted. Abby drank a finger of whiskey and set the glass down. Hank got less of it in, his hand still shaking; some of the whiskey dribbled from the corner of his lip and down his chin.

"Good stuff, isn't it?" the kid said. He was hardly more than a child. But Eric Harris and Dylan Klebold had been children too.

"Take the phones," Abby said. "Take them and go. We don't know what it's about. We can't begin to send anyone after you. We don't know enough to do that."

"Who else knows about the phones?"

"Nobody."

"No? Then who bagged them? They were in a shoe box before." He smiled at Abby's reaction. "Don't like that I know that, do you?"

She shrugged. "Don't care. *I* bagged them. I labeled them too."

"If I need an assistant, I'll keep you in mind. Now, again, who else has seen them?"

Abby almost answered honestly. She was afraid, both for herself and for Hank, and she had no stake in whatever insanity was transpiring around that car wreck and the lies Carlos Ramirez had told before he was murdered. *So tell the truth,* her brain commanded. But instead she said, "Nobody else has seen them."

"And how many people know you have them?"

"One. The guy I took them from."

The kid studied her intently. "You understand how imperative it is for us to be honest with each other? How badly this night might go if you make one poor decision?"

"Yes."

"Then let's try that question again. You seem to struggle with even basic addition. I didn't realize your academic record was as poor as your driving record." Whatever he saw in Abby's face then made him smile. "Yes, I've acquainted myself with your history. Mr. Bauer here has been helpful in that regard."

Abby looked at Hank, who gazed back with apology, his face sickly white.

"One more time," the kid said. "How many people know you have them?"

Again, Abby thought about telling the truth. Again, she decided against it. "Well, it would be two people, I guess," she said. She nodded at Hank. "He makes two."

"Will two become four if you think on it a little longer?"

"No. That's all."

"You sound convincing. And yet my friend Hank here said you took them to Boston. Which means you're lying to me now."

Hank's exhale whistled between his teeth. "I didn't say—"

The kid moved the gun to Hank's temple without turning his head or body, the gun landing on its target point with the accuracy and fluid speed that came only with practice or natural talent. Or—far worse for Abby—both.

"Hank?" the kid said. "I've still got the floor."

Hank was quiet. Abby tried to remember what exactly they'd said in the phone conversation they'd had when she was on the train. Did she tell him that Shannon Beckley had seen the phones? Did she say that she'd called Meredith? For that matter, *had* she called Meredith? No, Hank had called him. Right? Why couldn't she remember something so simple? She was having more trouble thinking than she should have. Her mind felt foggy and slow.

She looked at the whiskey bottle. The kid followed her eyes.

"Let's finish those drinks, shall we?" he said.

"No," Abby said.

The kid lowered the muzzle of the revolver so it nestled in Hank's eye socket.

"All right," Hank said, and he reached for the glass. His one visible eye was wide and white with panic. "Come on, Abs," he said. "Please. Just do as he says."

"Those are the words of a man who wants to see the morning," the kid said, and he smiled as Hank gulped the whiskey, sloshing more of it down his chin. "But this can't be a one-man party. Abby? It will be that glass or this gun. You pick."

Abby took the glass and drank more of the whiskey. It put a high and tight feeling in the back of her skull. It would not have been an unpleasant sensation in other circumstances. But now it was terrifying.

It's going to slow you down. Even if he didn't put anything else in it, the booze alone will slow you down if you don't do something in a hurry.

There *was* something else in it, though. She could feel that already. This was the steroid-injected version of the fear that haunted any woman who was handed a drink made by a stranger—the taste was just right, nothing there to warn you of what was on the way, of oncoming blackness and horrors that you might not remember even if you lived to see morning.

"Nothing like a little whiskey on a cool dark night," the kid said. "Tell you what, though. Let's do something about that chill in the air."

Still keeping the gun in his right hand, he reached into his back pocket with his left and pulled out a length of coiled parachute cord. The same kind that bound Hank to his chair. Abby tensed, but the kid just smiled and tossed the cord onto the counter.

"We won't need that, right? You're not running?"

"No."

"Good. It's getting cold in here. I'm going to run the space heater if you don't mind." He walked behind Hank, knelt by the generator, and flicked the battery on. Red lights glowed. He switched the revolver from his right hand to his left and jerked the starter cord. The motor growled but choked out. The cord demanded more of his attention than he wanted to give, and when his eyes darted away, Abby slipped her right hand into the pocket of her fleece and closed it around the key fob to the Chrysler. Its surface was smooth, but she was familiar with the four buttons on its face and knew which one operated the remote start. All she had to do was press it twice. The car was parked facing the house, and it would throw its lights toward the door, but, more important, the engine would turn over. She thought that would make the kid look in that direction. It would probably be a very fast look, but it would happen.

That would likely be the last chance Abby would have to move.

The generator caught on the second pull and clattered to life, belching out a cloud of exhaust. The kid plugged in a space heater, and the ceramic coils inside glowed red.

"Damn power outages," he said. "They're a bitch out here in the woods."

He straightened, reached in his back pocket, withdrew a plastic mask, and pulled it over his face. It looked like the masks the fire crews wore at the speedway when they knew the fumes and smoke might threaten their lungs.

Abby understood things then. The kid intended to get plenty of booze in their bloodstream and let exhaust fumes fill the room; when it was over, he'd untie them. They'd look like a couple of clueless dead drunks.

"It's not worth this," Abby said. "Whatever you think we understand...we don't."

"I agree," the kid said, voice muffled by the mask. "Want to stop me? Tell me the truth about who has seen those phones."

Abby said, "This was why he didn't roll the van."

"Pardon?"

"I wasn't wrong. Ramirez was attempting to hit them the whole time."

"Remarkable detective work," the kid said. "Keep this one around, Hank. She's brilliant. She walks into your house, sees you tied up by a man with a gun, and suddenly realizes that there's trouble afoot."

He took a step closer to Abby and lowered himself so he was eye level with her. "Tell me who knows about the phones."

"I already did."

The kid shrugged and adjusted the generator's choke until the engine was fighting between firing and flooding. The exhaust smoked blue in the white light of the lantern.

Her thumb tightened on the key fob, but she didn't press it yet. If the kid intended to use the gun, he wouldn't have gone through the effort of hauling the generator in here. The carbon monoxide from the generator wouldn't knock them out for a while yet, even in a small space. Abby had time. Not much; it was going to be an awfully small window of opportunity and she'd have to move awfully fast, but she still had time.

"This is a stupid idea," she said. "It won't fool anyone. You want police to believe we just got drunk and passed out with the generator running? You'll get caught. You'll go to jail."

The mask muffled his laugh. "You'd be surprised how many friends I've got around jails," he said. "Some in cells, some in uniforms."

Who the hell is this kid? "They'll be able to tell that Hank had been tied up," Abby said. "It'll be obvious." Her words came slowly and thickly, but the kid seemed to give them careful consideration. Then he spoke in a gentle voice, as if breaking news that it pained him to share.

"I don't think you two are important enough to warrant intense scrutiny from a medical examiner." He lifted his free hand, palm out, to make it clear that he'd meant no offense. "Now, I might be wrong. But...two hill-jack insurance investigators sitting in a shitty cabin, power out, heater cooking, and their blood full of alcohol? No, I don't think it's going to get the level of forensic study that you're hoping for."

"There's a generator plug on the back deck," Abby said. "Hank installed it. Nobody will believe we sat here with it inside."

The mask nodded up and down. The voice from behind it said: "Your critique is duly noted."

"It won't work," Abby said. Her tongue felt thick against the roof of her mouth. Too thick for just the whiskey.

Time's running out. The window's closing, your fuel is low, your tires are bad, and all these other assholes have more money under the hoods, but that doesn't matter because you've got reflexes, you've got instinct, you've got...

She came back to awareness with a jerk, her subconscious kicking her awake.

The kid smiled. "Getting tired, Abby?"

"No." And she wasn't anymore; that last jolt of adrenaline had cleared some of the fog, but she knew she was running out of time fast. "I'm just telling you that this won't work."

"It seems I'll have to try it simply to settle this debate."

The foggy feeling from the whiskey was blending with the acrid fumes. She stared at the bottle and wondered whether she could grab it and slam it into the kid's skull without getting shot. Wondered whether her motor skills were deteriorating as fast as her speech.

Going to have to try soon.

"How much did you already have, Hank?" Abby said, and Hank blinked sleepily at her and then refocused.

"It's a bad deal," Hank said thickly. "Shouldn't have called you. Knew better. I'm sorry."

"Don't give up yet, champ," the kid said, and his eyes flicked toward Hank.

Abby thought it was the best chance she'd get.

She punched the remote start on the key fob twice, taking care not to move the rest of her body. There was a slight lag, and then the motor growled and the running lights blinked on.

When it happened, Abby turned toward the sound with surprise, even though she'd been counting on it. It was this that sold the trick. The kid originally turned toward her, but when he saw Abby's surprise, he, too, looked toward the yard. Then he leaned across the table to push back the window blinds.

Abby rose and grabbed the neck of the whiskey bottle. She didn't pause to draw the bottle back or change its position, knowing that time was short; she simply swung it up in one continuous motion, aiming for the kid's face. She moved well despite the fogginess in her brain, and she was sure the strike was going to work.

The kid's speed was incredible.

Where his head had offered a clear shot, nothing but air waited.

Abby's momentum carried her forward. The bottle flew from her hand and shattered off the wall in a cloud of glass and whiskey, and then she fell to the floor beside Hank's chair. The kid had somehow pivoted and leaped in a single fluid motion, avoiding the contact and also maintaining his balance. He pointed the gun at Abby's face. Above the mask, his eyes were bright with amusement.

"You're quick," he said. "Better than I'd have guessed."

All of their attention was on each other, so when Hank moved, it surprised Abby as much as the kid. Hank's chair lurched sideways and the hand that had been left untied so he could drink suddenly locked over the kid's forearm.

The revolver fired; the shot went wide, the bullet sparking off the generator's engine block. Hank overbalanced and fell, but he kept his hand on the kid's arm and so they both went down while Abby tried to rise. Hank hit the floor with a splintering crack that

Abby hoped was the chair and not his arm. The kid landed on the other side of Abby, twisting while he fell, composed and nimble. He would've made a clean landing if Abby hadn't gotten in the way by sheer accident.

Her rising shoulder caught the kid's knee and knocked him off balance, and when he fell, his gun hand landed squarely on the glowing grill of the space heater.

The burn achieved what neither Abby nor Hank had been able to—it made the kid finally drop the gun. Even as he howled in pain, though, he was already reaching for the weapon with the other hand, absolutely relentless.

Hank just beat him, managing to roll onto his side and over the gun. He was still bound to the chair, his free arm dangling uselessly now, clearly broken. He couldn't have picked the gun up and fired it even if it had landed in his fingers. But he'd covered it with his body, and he looked up at Abby, his eyes wide and white, and said, "Run."

Abby scrambled to her feet and started toward Hank, but he repeated his command, and this time it was a scream.

"Run!"

Abby ran.

22

She reached the front door and turned the knob and then the door was open and she fell onto the screen door and tore it half off the hinges as she surged through it and into the cold night air.

If she'd been thinking clearly, she would have left the driveway and angled toward the trees, seeking cover immediately, but she wasn't thinking, just moving, and so she ran ten yards straight out of the door and down the wide-open drive, and it was only the sound of the growling engine on the Chrysler that brought her out of the fog.

Don't run. Drive, dummy. Driving is faster.

She had her hand on the door when a gunshot cracked and the driver's window exploded. Glass needled across her hands, and a thin line of blood ran down her index finger as she slid into the driver's seat, jammed her foot on the brake, and punched the starter button to engage the transmission of the idling car. She kept her head under the dash as she shifted into reverse and pounded the gas, focused on two things—she had to stay down to avoid a bullet, and she had to keep the wheel steady and the accelerator pinned to the floor. Hank's driveway was a straight shot through the pines and back to the rutted road; she didn't need to lift her head to drive, not yet.

She kept her foot on the gas and her bloody hands tight on the wheel, driving blind but straight.

You'll know when you hit the road. And then you'd better get your foot on the brake fast.

It seemed to take longer than it should have—driving blind

ruined distance perception—but finally she felt a thunk under the back wheels as the Chrysler left the driveway. She slammed on the brake, sending the tires slaloming through the wet dirt and gravel of the camp road, and managed to bring the car to a stop without sliding into the trees. Now she *had* to risk looking up.

No bullets came for her, and she didn't wait to give them a chance, just cut the wheel hard to the left, shifted into drive, and hit the gas again. The decision to go left was simple—the trees were thick to that side, and the right was wide open, making her an easy target. She was expecting more shots. No one fired, though. Even when she passed through a gap between the pines, no bullets came.

She should have understood that the lack of gunfire meant she'd made a mistake.

Instead, all she felt was relief. She was free. Out of sight of the house, out of pistol range, and moving under her own power.

Or the car was moving under its own power at least. Abby, maybe less so. The adrenaline was losing the battle with whatever was in her bloodstream—*That's not just whiskey; what else was in there?*—and the windshield was a mess of milky cracks that blurred the road in front of her. The combination was disorienting, and she wanted to stop, get out of the car, and put her feet on the ground.

An engine roared to life behind her.

That sound kept her foot away from the brake.

Just keep going fast, she told herself, *go far and go fast, that's all you need to do.*

But she didn't know where she was going. She'd been on the road to Hank's a thousand times, but she'd never turned this way coming out of the driveway. What was ahead of her? An intersection? There had to be. She needed a paved road; please, *please,* let there be a paved road. Give her pavement and nobody would catch her; the devil himself would not catch Abby Kaplan if she had four good tires and a paved surface.

No pavement appeared. The hard-packed dirt road got tighter and rougher. The Chrysler shimmied and shook like it was crossing cobblestones. The trees crept in, branches slapping off both sides of the car. Abby wanted to slow down. Wanted to stop.

No. Hank said to run. You've got to run.

But she couldn't remember what she was running from anymore. Her brain spun, out of sync with her eyes and her hands, and all she could hear was Hank's voice—or was that Luke's? Was that Luke telling her to go...

Faster. Faster.

Sure thing. Abby could always go faster.

She remembered her father's lullaby, the one from the old Robert Mitchum movie about an Appalachian bootlegger with a hot rod, the mountain boy who had G-men on his taillights and roadblocks up ahead. Being the motherless daughter of Jake Kaplan meant that such songs became lullabies. "The Ballad of Thunder Road" had been Abby's favorite. Her father's voice, off-key, his breath tinged with beer, singing, *"Moonshine, moonshine, to quench the devil's thirst..."* had eased her to sleep many times, the two of them alone in the trailer.

All these years later, the song could resurface clearly when she edged toward sleep.

"He left the road at ninety," her dead father crooned softly, *"that's all there is to say."*

When the Chrysler left the road, Abby had no idea if she'd missed a curve or simply driven right through a dead end. All she knew was that suddenly she was awake and the car was bouncing over uneven ground and now it wasn't branches whipping at the windows but whole trees, saplings that cracked with *whip-snap* sounds. Before she could move her foot to the brake, she hit a tree that did the stopping for her, an oak that slammed the car sideways. The airbag caught her rising body at stomach level, a gut punch that stole her breath but kept her from striking the windshield.

She sat gasping for breath and trying to clear her vision, desperate for just a little time to get her bearings.

Headlights appeared in the rearview mirror.

There was no time.

Abby got the door open and hauled herself out of the car, but her legs were wobbly and uncooperative, her vision spinning. She stumbled forward, trying to fight through the branches with her hands held up to protect her face. Her feet hit wet soil and went out from under her and suddenly she was down on her ass in the muck.

She might've stayed there, disoriented and exhausted and near the point of collapse, but she could still see the glow from the headlights, and they triggered whatever primal impulses the brain stem held on to until the very end.

Run. Flee.

She fought ahead on hands and knees, and this was a blessing in disguise because she crawled faster than she could have run. The boggy soil yielded to actual water, cold and deep enough to cover her arms to the elbows. She'd splashed into a creek, and she couldn't make sense of that. What creek? Where did it lead? She tried to remember and couldn't. Hadn't she hiked out here once with Hank and her father? Yes, absolutely. The winter before her father's heart attack. There'd been snow that day and the iced-over creek had turned into a beautiful white boulevard through the pines and birches, leading down past an ancient stone wall and on toward…

Toward nothing. There was nothing out here but trees and rocks and water. That was the point; Hank had never wanted neighbors. Abby needed a neighbor now, though. She needed anyone who could help, because something was behind her. Who or what was no longer clear. Her flight was now instinctual, not logical. Her body was working better than her brain.

That's fine, because all I need to do is keep running, she thought just before she slid over a moss-covered rock and bounced into the sinkhole below, where she lay covered in mud and decaying leaves and dampness. There, her body started to quit on her too.

She knew that she needed to get up and get moving, but this hole with its pillow of old leaves and cool moss felt comfortable, almost safe, except for the dampness. There was something about being tucked into the earth like this that felt right.

Like a grave. You are in your grave, Abby.

She thought she could still see the headlights, but it was hard to tell with the fog gliding through the trees. It was a low, crawling mist that seemed to be searching for her. She wasn't sure if the lights behind the mist were moving or stationary or if they were even out there at all. Her eyelids were heavy and her blood felt thick and slow.

She wondered how long it would take the kid to find her.

The kid. Yes, that's who you're running from. He's a killer.

And he was quick. The way he had ducked that punch? That was more than quick. So it would not take the kid long to find Abby now.

What was his name? Had he said a name? Sure, he had. Gentleman Jack.

Abby burrowed into the soft embrace of the leaves that smelled like death and waited on the arrival of Gentleman Jack.

23

Her first awareness was of the cold.

She opened her eyes and saw a moss-covered rock, beads of water working slowly but resolutely over it, following the terrain like bands of determined pioneers. Then they reached the edge and fell, manifest destiny gone awry.

Plink. Plink. Plink.

She stared at the rock and the puddle for a while without recognition of anything else. Except for the cold. That was still there, and it was intensifying. Uncomfortable but also necessary, because it was pounding clarity into her brain.

Get up. Get up and move before you freeze to death.

She struggled upright, and the motion made her dizzy and nauseated. She rested on her hands and knees, head hanging, waiting for the vomit to come, but the nausea passed and she didn't get sick. She worked a wooden tongue around a mouth so dry and swollen, it felt carpeted.

What the hell happened?

The kid.

That was what had happened. The night chase came back to her, and she was suddenly convinced that she wasn't alone here, that the kid had to be right behind her, the kid with his baby face and his grown-up gun.

There was nothing in sight but the woods, though. Abby was in a gully below a forested ridge; above, white birches and emerald pines were packed in tight, and a stream there split and ran down swales on either side of her. No sound but the running water.

She tried to walk up the hill but her feet tangled and she fell heavily and painfully onto her side. She rolled over and breathed for a while and then tried again, slower this time. Each motion required caution because her head spun and her stomach swirled. She tasted bitter bile and her throat was sore, as if she'd been retching. She didn't remember doing that, though.

The sky was bright enough to show some of the world, but not much of it. Predawn light. That meant she'd been down here for hours.

What had happened to Hank in that time?

She hobbled up the slope. Her left side and left hip hurt the worst, and she wasn't sure why. She didn't remember much about the drive, the run through the woods, or her fall. She just remembered that she'd been trying to get out in front of the kid and of whatever the whiskey had put in her bloodstream. They'd both been closing in on her fast.

And Hank had been well behind them, tied to the chair. Had he gotten loose? He'd had some time alone while the kid pursued Abby. He'd had a window for escape, if he'd been able to free himself.

She got to the top of the hill, but even from there, the Chrysler wasn't visible. Just the trees. In her running and crawling through the night woods, she'd made it farther than she'd thought. The smell of rain was heavy in the air. She could find no clear track to show her how to get back to where she'd started, and she decided that following the stream made as much sense as anything. She started along it, walking uphill, breathing hard and fighting for each step, thinking, *Maybe when I got out, that evil kid got scared and ran, and Hank's still back there, tied to the chair and hurt, maybe, but alive. Waiting for help. For me.*

When she crested the next rise, struggling to keep her footing on the slick leaves, she finally saw her car.

It was punched into an oak's trunk and wedged between pines, and she was bizarrely pleased by how far she'd made it into such dense trees before getting hung up. When she stepped closer, she could see the dangling airbag visible through the shattered glass. Everything about the car was as she remembered.

Then she saw Hank's body in the passenger seat.

Abby froze, then took a wavering step forward, knees going weak, and cried, "Hank!" Her voice was broken and hoarse. *"Hank!"*

Hank Bauer wasn't going to answer. His head lay unnaturally on his left shoulder, and the right side of his face was swollen and bruised, his eyes open but unseeing. Abby wrenched open the passenger door, and Hank's head dropped bonelessly forward, chin down on his chest, eyes still open, his neck obviously broken.

Abby stepped back and sat down in the wet grass. She rubbed a filthy hand over her face. She breathed with her eyes closed, then opened them and looked at Hank once more.

"What happened?" she said aloud.

Hank offered no insight.

The way he sat there, slumped in the passenger seat with the wound on the right side of his head and the broken neck, made it look as if he'd been in the car when it hit the tree and died on impact, when in reality he'd been dead before he was brought here.

Or maybe not.

Maybe he'd been alive and trying to stay alive by obeying orders, the kid saying, *Get in the car,* holding a gun to his head. Abby could picture him climbing into the wrecked car, hoping for mercy, only to have his skull smacked off the windshield, his neck snapped.

Abby looked up the road then, searching for either help or threat, finding neither. It was peaceful and quiet and lonely. When the wind gusted, raindrops fell from the trees like a fresh shower. Hank's house was the last one on the isolated camp road. Nobody would have heard the crash. The kid would have had time to go back and bring Hank down here and not be rushed, but still, it seemed a reckless choice because Abby had been out there in the darkness, free.

He knew you were going to be down for a while, though. He was sure of that. He wasn't rushing because he knew he didn't need to.

Thanks to whatever was in the whiskey, the kid knew he had time. Maybe he even thought Abby was dead. Plenty of time, then.

Why move Hank's body, though? Why bring him down here and put him in the passenger seat? Even if he'd thought Abby was dead, that arrangement didn't make any sense, because there was no driver.

Abby looked at the empty driver's seat, and suddenly she understood.

I didn't realize your academic record was as poor as your driving record, the kid had said.

It was Abby's car, and Abby had wrecked it. The physical evidence would say that, because it was the truth.

Hank hadn't been riding shotgun when the Chrysler went into the trees, and he hadn't broken his neck in the crash, but if the police found this scene and then found Abby dead in the woods, uninjured but with drugs and alcohol in her bloodstream, what would they think?

The kid was panicked and tried to rig the scene. A bad plan, but he needed something.

Was it that bad, though? When Abby called this in, she was going to have to tell the police that she'd been poisoned and that while she was sleeping it off in the woods, a teenager with a gun had killed Hank Bauer and belted him into the passenger seat. That was the truth, but it was going to be an awfully strange story to tell and an awfully hard story for a detective to believe. And if the detectives who heard it happened to know that Abby had ended up back in Maine working for Hank Bauer because of another night that went a lot like this one…

Just call them. Let them figure it out.

The man had been murdered, and Abby knew who'd killed him. In that case, you called the police. Period.

When she stood up and reached for her phone, she realized it was gone, and only then did she remember the kid taking it and tossing it onto the kitchen counter after he'd looked at the photograph of Luke on the home screen.

He'd known Luke was dead. He'd known what had happened. So this scenario, this scene he'd built with Hank, was maybe a little bit better than Abby wanted to imagine.

I can tell the police the truth. They'll need time to verify it, but they'll believe it.

Hank's dead eyes stared through the shattered windshield. *California isn't the only problem,* those eyes seemed to say.

True. Police would learn quickly that Abby had also been arrested in Maine, and for stealing a car from Hank Bauer, no less. Never mind that Hank hadn't pressed charges; whatever police records still existed from that, either on paper or in memory, would show yet another night very similar to this one—Hank Bauer had a fast car, Abby Kaplan had a thirst for speed, and it had ended badly.

It's easier to believe than the truth, she realized. *Either Abby Kaplan fucked up for the third time behind the wheel or a hit man disguised as a Boy Scout killed an insurance investigator in rural Maine. Which would you pick?*

She needed evidence. At least one shot had connected with the car, and it went through the driver's window. That would prove she wasn't crazy, maybe even indicate the caliber of the bullet and the distance of the shot.

She walked around the front of the car, stepping over a torn tree with white-pulped flesh protruding from shredded bark like an open fracture.

The driver's window was gone. Not just cracked with a clean hole through the center, but completely shattered. The sunroof was also demolished. So was the passenger window. Wherever the bullet might have left its mark, the kid had seen it and taken care of it.

That doesn't matter. It's a weak-ass attempt to cover things up, but it won't stick, and the faster you get the police out here, the faster you'll be done.

But she could imagine the cops' faces as she told them about the kid with the gun and the bottle of Gentleman Jack. What would they look like when she got to the part about how she'd started the Chrysler with the remote and Hank had fallen on the gun, still tied to the chair, and from there it was all question marks and darkness…

That was the truth, yes. And the truth should always be enough, yes.

But she wasn't so sure that it would be.

What does the house look like? she wondered. *If it looks like the place I left, then my story is fine. If he took the time to clean it up, though…*

She looked back at Hank. There was no need to rush for him. They didn't use sirens and flashers when they were taking you to the morgue.

Abby closed the door on her friend's corpse and walked up the road. She followed the rain-filled ruts left by her own tires until Hank's house came into view, and then she stopped and stared.

The kitchen blinds were open again. The way they always were, or always had been until last night.

Bad sign. If he took that much time to set things right…

She crossed the yard like an inmate walking to her execution. Went to the window and looked in at the kitchen.

The chairs were tucked under the table, which was bare except for a newspaper, open to the sports section. No whiskey, no tumbler glasses, no lantern. The generator was gone, and so was the space heater. The block of knives was back on the counter.

You'll have to tell them that this sociopath did all this while you were passed out in the woods. You will have to convince them of that, and you don't even know anything about him.

No, that wasn't true. Looking in at the kitchen, all traces of chaos eradicated from it, Abby felt like she knew plenty about that kid.

And all of it was terrifying.

Could she describe him? Not in much more than general terms. And the kid did not fit the story, because the story seemed to be a professional killing, and baby-faced teenagers did not carry out professional hits.

I'll need to be able to tell them who he is, but I don't know who he is. All I know is that he's fucking scary, and he wanted the phone.

He'd wanted it, yes. But did he have it? The bags of phones Abby had carried in were gone, but what about the one she'd jammed under the driver's seat? Had the kid searched the car?

Abby left the house and started back down the road, moving at a jog this time, but it was a long distance and she was hurting, so she quickly fell back to a labored walk. She opened the driver's door, avoided staring at Hank's face, and reached below the seat.

The bag was there. Three iPhones inside.

She took it out and stepped away from the car and looked up at the lightening sky—the day was moving along, and she needed to do the same. One way or the other, she had to make a decision.

It was a memory that sealed the choice. When she'd been sitting at that table trying to reason her way out of the situation, she'd told the kid that he would end up in jail. The response had been immediate, and chilling: *You'd be surprised how many friends I've got around jails. Some in cells, some in uniforms.*

Abby didn't think he'd been lying.

She looked at the dead man who'd backed her time and again throughout her life. "I'm sorry, Hank," she said. She wanted to remember some other version of Hank's face, not this death pallor and endless stare, not the broken-stem look of his neck. All she could see was that, though—that and the image of Hank's face, sweaty and scared in the lantern light, as he screamed at Abby to run.

Backing her one last time.

"Thank you," Abby told the dead man, and then she closed the door. She walked back up the lonely road to Hank's house and up the steps. The screen was damaged from where she'd blasted through it—the only physical evidence that supported her story. The knob turned freely. Once inside, she didn't waste much time looking for things the kid might've missed in his cleanup effort. She had a feeling there wouldn't be any, and she needed to move quickly.

Hank's guns were stored in a glass-doored cabinet in the living room, impossible to miss. Some people were proud of guns and wanted them as conversation pieces. The cabinet had a lock, which was better than nothing, but a lock didn't mean much when it secured thin glass doors. Abby wrapped her fist in a blanket that was draped over the back of the couch and then punched each door once, without much force. The glass shattered and she swept it away with the blanket. She took one shotgun, a black Remington over/under; one rifle, a scoped .308; and both handguns, a Glock .45 and a SIG Sauer nine-millimeter. The ammunition was stored on a shelf below the guns. She took all of it, boxes and boxes of shells and bullets, and wrapped them in the blanket with the guns.

She stepped back and looked at what she'd done and tried to find the voice in her head that would say this was a mistake. Before it could so much as whisper, though, she glanced into the kitchen and saw the tidy arrangement of chairs and tables, no trace of violence.

Friends in cells and friends in uniforms, the kid had said.

Abby picked up the blanket with the guns and the ammunition and walked out of the living room. She crossed to the kitchen counter and picked up her phone. It had a charge and a signal, but she put it in her pocket without pause. She'd make the call to police, but not from here.

She carried the guns to the door, found the basket where Hank kept odds and ends, and fished out his car keys. She was moving quickly and purposefully now, not wanting to slow down long enough to consider the reality of what she was doing. Driving away in a murdered man's car was obviously a dangerous choice.

Staying, though, seemed worse.

24

I n another life, Gerry Connors had been a bomb maker, but that was long ago. For the past two decades, he'd been a networker, a middleman. He was not a fixer, although people often thought of him as one. In reality, he put the players together, and he kept silent when silence needed to be kept. He asked only the necessary questions, and he shared only the minimum of information. He handled contacts and he handled money. For the German, he'd handled the hiring of Carlos Ramirez, but he had not told the German of the hiring of Dax Blackwell. That had been his own decision.

This now had the potential to cause real problems for Gerry.

The kid sat across from him in the dark-paneled office with his customary slouch, eyes alert but body loose, and if he was at all aware of the trouble that he'd caused, he didn't show it. If he was at all concerned about what this trouble meant to him, he certainly didn't show that. If not for the kid's lineage, Gerry might've had to view this as stone-cold stupidity, but Dax's bearing was so similar to his father's that in the midst of the frustration, there was a strange reassurance. Gerry dearly missed the kid's dad and uncle. Right now, Jack and Patrick Blackwell would have kept his pulse down. He needed Dax to do the same. Because the German had paid a lot of money for killing Oltamu and recovering the phone and doing it all quietly. Efficiently. Gerry had managed to accomplish only a third of that.

Now it was growing exponentially worse, Dax Blackwell seemed indifferent to the problem, and the German was due in town in forty-eight hours.

"There was no iPhone except her own," Dax said. "You've got what she brought in. I checked her phone. I chose to leave it behind because if she manages to make it out of those woods alive, it's going to hurt her story when they find the house clean and her phone inside. But it was not Oltamu's phone."

"Then where *is* Oltamu's phone?"

"That question would be easier for me to answer if I knew something about the situation. Like who wants it, why they want it, and who else might want it."

"That's not your fucking role!"

A shrug. "Then it'll be harder."

"You're not even sure she's dead! She saw you, and she might be able to talk!"

"Correct."

Gerry took blood pressure medication daily, and he thought that was the only thing saving him now. He breathed through his teeth and said, "You want to tell me how you're going to deal with that? If she walks out of those woods, we'll have some sketch artist's rendering of your face on every news broadcast in North America."

The kid said, "I don't think so."

"*Pardon?* You poisoned her, shot at her, and killed her boss, but you expect her to go quietly into the night?"

Dax nodded calmly. Gerry was incredulous. Every time he wanted to kill the kid, he found himself asking questions instead. He did that again now.

"Want to explain why she'd stay quiet?"

"Her personal history. She's been involved in a car wreck that left a movie star in a coma and, eventually, dead. People hate her for that. It's always amusing to me just how much people care about some asshole in a movie, but they do. Her boss, Bauer, thought the Tara Beckley case might make Abby confront those demons." He smiled at that, then said, "Sorry. That one kind of broke me up. I mean, how's it going to *help*? But Hank Bauer, may he rest in peace, didn't strike me as a particularly skilled psychotherapist. It was an effort, though. You have to appreciate friends who make an effort."

Gerry could hardly speak. The kid's attitude was that astonishing. "You talked through all this with them?" he managed finally. "You got their life stories but no phone?"

"I really only had the chance to speak with Mr. Bauer at length."

Gerry needed a drink. Needed to lie down. Hell, both. Lying down and drinking at the same time, that was what this called for. "Abby Kaplan is going to bring cops down all over this."

"I disagree. You've got to think about the story she has to tell them. You really think the police are going to buy that? I had this same conversation with her, and my guess is that it lingered. She'll think about it before she calls, at least. I'm sure of that."

He hadn't gotten the phone, he'd killed a man, and he'd left a witness alive, and if any of this bothered him in the slightest, it didn't show.

"The phone, however, remains a concern," he said.

"No shit, it remains a concern!" Gerry shouted. "*That's* what I need. I didn't ask you to kill some hick in Maine, I asked you to get the phone!"

"Well, things come up."

Things come up. Holy shit, this kid. Gerry rubbed his temples and forced himself not to shout. "You said Abby Kaplan had the phone."

"That's what I was told. She showed up in good faith for the boss with phones and chargers, like the salvage guy said she should have. They weren't in a box. When I broke into her apartment, I found the box. Empty. There were no phones in the apartment either. But it's not a lost cause. You can help me with that."

Gerry lowered his hands and stared. "*I* can help *you* with that." Another nod.

"How might I be of service to you, Dax?"

The kid ignored the sarcasm and said, "I could talk to your client."

You didn't ask to speak to the client. Ever. You pretended there *wasn't* a client.

Gerry said, "Are you out of your fucking mind?"

"I understand it's not protocol, but—"

"You *understand it's not protocol*. Well, that's reassuring. Why would you possibly need to speak to—"

"But I think it's time to consider that someone else has the phone," Dax finished. "It's difficult for me to locate that person if I don't understand the value of the phone, do you see? I've come up with an alternative, though, if you don't want me to have an open dialogue with your client."

"I do *not* want you to have an open dialogue."

"Then in lieu of that, we'll have to settle for a lesser option. Suggest to your client that he give me the phone that Carlos grabbed by mistake. Let me work off that. Oltamu's personal phone gives me a starting point."

The client did not have Oltamu's personal phone. Gerry still did. It was in the drawer just below his right hand.

"Could you do that much?" Dax asked, and there was something about his eyes that gave Gerry the uncomfortable sense that the kid knew Gerry had the phone. He was sniffing around the edges, asking questions that he shouldn't, questions that he knew better than to ask.

"You're not your father or your uncle," Gerry said.

Dax's face darkened. Barely perceptibly, but it was the first anger Gerry had ever seen him display.

"No," he said. "I'm not. I'm better than them."

Gerry snorted. "You think?"

"Unquestionably," Dax said. "They're dead."

He was giving Gerry that flat stare again, the one that sent spiders crawling into your brain.

"Think it over," he said. "I'll get back to work regardless. I will get the right phone, and I will kill Abby Kaplan if she's still alive. These things will happen, but they'll go slower if I don't have some insight into the situation. And speed's important at the moment."

He stood up, and Gerry almost told him to sit his ass back down, but what was the point? He wasn't wrong; speed was important now.

The German was coming.

25

A bby made the call from a service plaza off the turnpike where there was always plenty of traffic. She was in Hank's car, and she knew she'd have to dump that soon, but for now it was the best of bad options. She thought about calling 911, decided against it, and called David Meredith directly.

"What's up, Abby? I gather you heard about our boy Carlos. Neat twist, eh?" He was cheerful, and the disconnect was so jarring that for a moment Abby couldn't speak. David had to prompt her. "Hello? Did I lose you?"

"No, sorry. Yes, I heard about Carlos Ramirez. I've also got a lot more detail on that than you can imagine, and it's all bad. I'm going to tell it to you once, so you're going to want to take notes or record it. Recording it would be better. I won't be able to call back and go through it again, at least not right away."

Silence. Then: "Abby, what in the hell are you talking about?"

"Can you record me?"

"No. Not here. But I can call you back from—"

"Take notes, then."

"Abby—"

"Hank is dead," Abby said, and her throat tightened, but she swallowed and kept talking. "He's in the passenger seat of my car, which is wrecked in the trees at the end of his road. It looks like he died in the wreck, but he didn't. He was murdered, and I nearly was, and it's all got something to do with that accident at Hammel College. I don't know what, but it—"

"Abby, whoa, slow down here. He was *murdered*? You need to—"

"I need to talk, and you need to listen and write it down," Abby said. "I'd love to trust you, but I'm not sure that I can right now. I was pretty well set up. The story I'm about to tell you sounds crazy, but it's the truth. You need to hear it. Can you just listen?"

Another pause, and then Meredith, sounding dazed, said, "I'll listen."

"Write it down too."

She told him about the call from Hank, and her arrival at the house, and the way things had gone from there. Told him about the generator and the Gentleman Jack and how she'd started the car and, with an assist from Hank, made it out the door. Told him how many hours had passed while she lay unconscious in the woods and what she'd found upon waking.

Meredith didn't interrupt, which was a relief. Abby wasn't sure how she'd respond if the man started asking questions, if his voice held any doubt or disbelief.

"You'll find him there, and you'll think that I'm out of my mind, but do me the favor of taking a good, hard look for physical evidence that shows I'm wrong," she said. "Maybe it'll be in Hank's blood. Maybe you'll find a bullet. Maybe the kid screwed up something at the house...but I kind of doubt that. Just promise me you'll look."

"Of course we will," David said, the first time he'd spoken in several minutes. "But you've *got* to come in. You know that, Abby. Running from this thing...it's the worst choice. Nobody will believe you if you run, no matter what we find."

"I don't think that's true," Abby said. "Hank's dead, and I sound like a lunatic, telling this story. Today you'll tell me that it will all work out, but tomorrow? Then the charges come. And you'll promise me that it's still not a threat because a good attorney will work it out, but I'm not sure. Hank Bauer of Coastal Claims and Investigations was murdered over a car accident involving a girl from Hammel College and a guy from Brighton who is already dead? That's going to keep me out of jail?"

"If it's the truth, it will," Meredith said, and Abby smiled grimly. She was watching the side-view mirror, looking for police cars; her scratched and bruised face stared back at her. She reached up and pulled a pine needle from her hair.

"Get started on proving it," she said, "and then I'll consider coming in. Talk to Shannon Beckley, talk to Sam at that salvage yard, and you can verify my movements through the day. That's worth something. Then work that scene right. Look for bullets, look for damage to the generator, get them to run toxicology tests on Hank's blood that will find *anything* unusual. Get some foren-sics expert to see if he can tell whether he was tied up. Most important? Find out whose phone matters so much that people will kill over it."

She didn't say that she had the phone. All Abby understood so far about the phone was that if she'd given it to the kid last night, she'd certainly be dead by now. She wasn't inclined to hand it off to anyone else just yet.

"When I call you next," Abby said, "you can tell me what progress you've made. Then we'll talk about me coming in."

"This is a suicide move, Abby," Meredith said, and he was angry now. Fine. Let him be angry. Abby just needed him to do the work.

"Two people have been murdered over that accident already," Abby said. "I was supposed to be the third. I'm not inclined to make my location known to the world right now."

"Even if you *did* get charged, which shouldn't happen if you're telling me a legit story, then you're safer with us than on the run, hiding from killers *and* cops."

"He said he has friends in jail."

"We'll have you in protective custody."

"He said some of those friends are in uniforms."

"This is insane. If there is anything to what you're saying, then we'll find plenty of evidence to support it, and we'll do that fast."

"See, I don't like the way you phrased that. *If* there's anything to what I'm saying. Already, you're skeptical."

"That's my job."

"And that's why I called you," Abby said. "To give you a head start doing your job. I'll be in touch."

"Abby, damn it, if you—"

She disconnected, powered down her phone, and stepped out of the Tahoe. She put the phone just beneath the front tire, backed up over it, pulled out of the service plaza, and got back onto the Maine turnpike. She drove north, toward where the towns were smaller and the woods were darker.

26

Blinks are coming.

They're not all the way there yet, but not far off either. Not impossible, certainly. Tara has worked on them with ferocious intensity, and while she hasn't succeeded, something about her eye motion feels different. It's promising, at least, a sensation like a door being forced open, just like when she was in the basement of that house on London Street.

She thinks it's an upward motion. She tries to blink, she demands that her eyelids lower…and while they do not obey, her focus seems to shift. A small difference, and a dizzying sensation, but she's almost certain she's looking upward. Her eyes are so damn dry that it's hard to tell, though. They're dry even though they constantly leak with tears at the corners. People dab the tears away from time to time, but people also avoid the kind of direct, hard stare that could tell her if indeed she's making any progress here. The motion she thinks she's achieving is so slight that thorough scrutiny would be required to observe it. In the early hours, people would look hard into her eyes, searching for her as if she were submerged in dark water. Shannon. Dr. Pine. The strange boy in the black baseball cap—his scrutiny might have been the most intense of all, actually.

Those deep stares are rare now, though. Everyone has become more evasive, as if they're fearful of Tara's gaze, as if a coma is contagious. Or embarrassed by it, as if her eyes are a mirror offering an unflattering image.

If anyone would look hard now, though, they would see that

she is close to blinking. As close as you can be without succeeding, and she feels like that should be noticeable. If Shannon would just pay attention, she would notice. Tara is almost certain of this. But Shannon is immersed in a phone call, and she seems concerned.

She's holding her cell phone to her ear with her left hand and a ballpoint pen hovering above a notepad in her right, and her all-business attitude just crumbled with whatever has been said. Tara watches her face and feels a cold and certain assurance that this is the inevitable call that means the decision has been made. They are going to end her life. If life was what you called this frozen purgatory. Then Shannon speaks, and Tara realizes that it has nothing to do with her at all.

"She might have *killed* someone? The same woman I spoke to? Abby Kaplan, yes, that was her name, but what in the world..." She stops, clearly interrupted.

Tara is trying to follow the conversation, but it's confusing— Abby Kaplan was one of the two strangers who'd visited her. Older than the second one, the one who pretended to be Justin Loveless and stared into Tara's eyes like a hunter looking through a scope. That man seems right for a murderer; Abby Kaplan does not. Abby Kaplan is supposed to be part of her team, someone to help. The college hired her.

Top-notch recruiting, Hammel, Tara thinks, *put that one in your brochures.* She wants to laugh, and even though she can't, it is still a pleasant sensation. Terror is often present, and frustration is constant, but humor is beginning to appear now and then to leaven these, as if her brain has tired of the relentless sorrow. She sometimes thinks that if she could simply communicate her mere existence, the rest could be endured. She could learn to have a life with some pleasure, then. Not the life she'd imagined, of course, but still one worth living. If they just knew that she was in here. But without that...

"Her own boss?" Shannon says into the phone. "Are you kidding me? I just…no, listen, I don't give a damn about how Hammel is going to find a better firm, what does that even mean? Your first hire just killed her boss, and now you'll admit that you could have done better?"

Bless you, Shannon, Tara thinks.

The pen descends to the notepad, but no words are written, and Shannon's mouth screws tight. Then she says, "I *know* I'm not a police officer, that's not a revelatory bit of information, but I still possess common sense, and maybe I should *talk* to the police, don't you think?"

Shannon lifts the ballpoint pen away from the pad and clicks it rapidly while she listens. The sound seems large to Tara; something about that small click embeds in her brain in a different way than other, louder things. Why was that?

Suddenly, Tara's thumb twitches.

Stunned, she tries to do it again, without success. But…it just moved. She is positive of that. Now that her attention is on it and she can't replicate the feat, though, the sensation begins to feel false, a phantom movement, a cruel illusion. And yet, for an instant, she'd been *certain.* It came from the sound, almost, from watching Shannon click that pen and hearing the accompanying sound and then it was as if her muscle memory had fired and Tara had mimicked the gesture.

But she tries again and again, and her thumb rests limply against her index finger.

She's lost track of Shannon's words, but now hears her say, "Listen, I might have been one of the last people to talk to her. I sure think it would be useful if I could talk directly to the police instead of through a handler from the college."

Pause, and Tara hopes she'll begin clicking the pen again, but the pause is brief and then Shannon says, "Fine, just please give me a call back so I can explain this to my family."

Shannon disconnects, lowers the phone, and stares at the wall with an expression that Tara hasn't seen many times on her sister's face: helplessness. The only memories Tara has of this look come from early childhood, in the days after her father's death, when her mother's depression was the darkest, the battle with medications the worst; even big sister Shannon had no idea what to do.

Put down that phone, Shannon had told Tara one terrible day after Tara had picked up the phone to call 911 for their unconscious mother. Shannon's helplessness was gone from her face, replaced by fury. *If you call, they'll take us away, don't you understand that?*

Tara had put down the phone. Shannon sat with their mother until dawn, washing her face with a damp cloth and making sure that her head was tilted to the side so she couldn't choke on her own vomit. Then she made Tara breakfast and sent her to school with instructions to keep her mouth shut about the situation at home; Shannon was handling it.

She had, too. Somehow, she had handled it.

Shannon turns to her, one eyebrow cocked, and Tara could swear that they've bridged the void somehow. This happens with people occasionally, with Shannon more than anyone else and most frequently when they are alone in the room. Now Shannon looks at her and says, "I think you should have gone to a state school, *mi hermana.* You could've saved a lot of money in student loans for the same level of incompetence."

Tara laughs. She doesn't move or make a sound, of course, but she laughs, and some part of her believes that Shannon knows it.

"The college hired an investigator for your case," Shannon says, "who then apparently *killed her boss* and ran away. Talk about bringing in the best and the brightest."

She's smiling; she always seems happiest when she's being sarcastic or cutting, a trait that makes relationships a struggle for her. Then the smile fades, her focus shifts away from Tara, and it is evident that she feels like she is alone in the room again.

Which breaks Tara's heart.

"Abby seemed like she cared," Shannon says softly, clearly speaking to herself now. Then she gives a little snap-out-of-it head shake, pulls a chair to the side of the bed, sits, and looks hard at Tara's face.

"Regardless, she gave me a good idea, T. I did some reading last night, and I made some calls this morning, and I have good news—you get to watch a movie."

Watch a movie? The television is always on. Mostly, Tara hates that. If she were able to change the channel, it wouldn't be so bad, but when they leave it on just for *background noise,* like she's a nervous puppy, it's infuriating.

"Dr. Pine himself approved it," Shannon says. "Even Rick and Mom say it's worth a try. Not just a movie, though, T.—you get a field trip." She takes Tara's limp hand. Her touch is warm and wonderful. So few people are willing to let their touches linger.

My thumb can move, Tara thinks. *Do it again, damn it, do it now, you stupid thumb, while someone has the chance to notice.*

But her thumb lies motionless against Shannon's palm.

"They're going to put you in an ambulance and take you to a lab about an hour away, at a university hospital where there's a coma research program, and then they'll hook you up to even more of these…" She lifts one of the many wires that lead from Tara's body to the monitors beside the bed. "And then they're going to show you a movie and wait to see if the computers can tell whether you respond to it. Whether you can track it, whether you *feel* anything watching it." Shannon's voice wavers, and she bites her lower lip and looks away.

Tara realizes just how important this test must be. If she doesn't pass this one, if she can't somehow let these computers know that she is in here…big decisions are going to be made soon.

This may be her last chance to have a voice in them.

"I did win one battle," Shannon says, turning back to her with a sniff and that forced smile. "They usually use some crappy black-and-white film. I told them that my sister *hates* black-and-white. They didn't like the idea of changing, but I can be persuasive."

An understatement for the ages. *She could* still *sell tickets for the Titanic*, Rick had once said of Shannon.

"So I got to pick the film," she continues, squeezing Tara's hand. "And I'll give you one guess what I picked."

Something scary, Tara thinks. Shannon loves Tara's fear of horror movies, the way even the cheesy ones can make her jump, how she covers her eyes and watches them through her fingers.

"That's right," Shannon says, "your test will be a familiar one. You get to watch *Jaws*."

Well, now. Tara has long proclaimed *Jaws* to be the most re-watchable movie in history. She hasn't anticipated that being put to a coma test, though.

"You'll respond," Shannon whispers. "I know you will. When Quint starts talking about the *Indianapolis* sinking or when Chief Brody realizes his own son is on the sailboat by the shark, you'll respond. Just to the dumb music, you'll respond." She's imploring now, a hint of desperation to her words that scares Tara. This test is going to be *very* important.

"The people at the lab were encouraging," Shannon says, seemingly more to reassure herself than anything else. "They've had good results." She pauses. "Maybe I won't mention where I got the idea."

27

As Abby drove Hank's Tahoe along the turnpike, she remembered that she'd already spent some time considering life as a fugitive, thanks to Luke. One of his first leads in anything that wasn't a purely over-the-top action film where spiders fought robots was in a movie about a husband-and-wife team on the run, a Hitchcock knockoff that bombed at the box office. While he was reading the script and rehearsing, though, he enjoyed pondering the scenario.

"It's so much harder now than it would have been fifty years ago," he'd said, stretched out on the chaise longue on their cramped balcony during one of the rare hours that sunlight fell on it. "Think about it—you could pay cash for hotel rooms and rental cars and plane tickets, there were pay phones everywhere and no surveillance cameras, and you could hot-wire a car with a screwdriver."

Abby interrupted and asked him to explain that process, to tell her just how he'd go about hot-wiring a car with a screwdriver in the good old days. Luke smiled. "That was the golden age of hot-wiring! Simple! But the newer cars are tougher."

"Oh?"

"Yes." He'd nodded emphatically. "Just trust me on this."

"Certainly."

"The first thing you'd have to do if you were running from the law or people who were trying to kill you is ditch the cell phone, obviously," he went on. "They can always track those. But it's easy to get a burner phone—if you have cash. Credit cards are no good, right? And how many people have enough cash to go on the run? How much cash do you have in your wallet right now?"

Abby had four bills crumpled in her purse—and she was pleasantly surprised to discover one of them was a ten. She'd thought they were all singles.

"So there you go, thirteen dollars," Luke said. "I couldn't get far on that. They'd find me before I hit the state line. I'd run out of gas—"

"Is this in the car you hot-wired with a screwdriver?" Abby asked, and he grinned. For all of his physical beauty—and he was stunning, no question about that—he had a kid's smile, awkward and shy, and his off-the-set laugh was the same, a little too big, too high, far too likely to end with a helpless snort. Abby loved that about him. All the surprising touches that turned the movie star into a human being were reassuring. The more human he became, the more she loved him. That first day, when he'd joked to her about the grief his friends were giving him for having a woman perform his stunt driving, she'd thought he was exactly what she'd expected: good-looking and charming and arrogant and false. The first date, she'd asked herself why she was wasting her time. But soon she realized that her initial wariness about him was understandable, but it was not the truth. The truth was complicated, as it usually is, and the truth of Luke London made him easier to love than Abby wanted. Her truth was that she wanted to stay far away from actors. Her truth was that she was breaking rules for him.

"Sure it's the car I hot-wired," he said of his escape vehicle. "Because I'd have found an old car, right? As we discussed."

"Ah, of course."

"But then I run out of gas, and I've got no cash. What then? Pretend to be a homeless person?"

"It doesn't sound like it would be pretending by then."

Her pointed at her, sculpted triceps flexing under his T-shirt. "Good point! It would be method acting at its finest."

"And you suck at that."

He nodded thoughtfully. "Indeed. I'd stand out, and they'd find me."

"Who?"

"The people who are trying to kill me! So what do I do?"

"You steal," she said.

"I'd get caught. I guarantee it. I have a naturally guilty disposition when it comes to crime. One try at shoplifting, and I'm getting caught and going to jail. Which means, obviously, another inmate will be paid to kill me. Or maybe a guard. But going to jail is not hiding."

"You steal carefully, then," Abby had said. "Maybe break into a house. Just a matter of finding the right place."

Now, two years after that conversation and months after they'd taken Luke off life support, Abby drove along the turnpike and wondered where the right place was.

She had some cash—a hundred and thirty bucks, enough for a hotel room somewhere, but hotels were dangerous. Her face was going to be on the news, and this was off-season in Maine, which meant that the employees of hotels that took cash were going to have time to pay attention to their guests, learn their faces.

That was when she got it.

Off-season. The right places, she realized, were plentiful. They didn't call the state Vacationland for nothing—most people who owned property in Maine didn't stay there year-round. There were thousands of vacant houses, cabins, and cottages out there for her, and plenty of them were isolated.

She left the interstate in Augusta and moved on to the back roads. She realized only after taking the exit that the other cars hadn't made her uneasy, nor had the speed. Her mind was too busy with a real crisis to let the imaginary threats creep in. When you were fleeing a murder scene and a murderer, a traffic accident suddenly didn't seem too bad.

As she followed one of the winding country roads east toward the coast, it began to rain again. That felt good, like protective cover. She was driving east because most of the summer people clung to the coast. There were exceptions at every lake and pond, of course, but nowhere was the population of seasonal houses higher than the Midcoast. When the patio furniture was moved into storage and the lobster shacks folded up their bright umbrellas, the population of those towns fell by at least half.

How to pick the right house, though? Driving around some little coastal village and staring at houses would allow her to identify a few vacant ones, but it would also get her noticed by a year-round resident.

She stopped at a gas station with a lunch counter, a place busy enough for her to feel like she wouldn't stand out and big enough for her to suspect they'd have what she needed. Her clothes had dried but were still covered with mud, and she didn't want many people to get a look at her. She waited until an older couple got out of their car and headed toward the door, and then she got out of the Tahoe, crossed the parking lot swiftly, and walked in on their heels. They turned toward the deli counter, and Abby stepped behind one of the merchandise racks and pretended to be looking at candy while she looked around the store. Just beside the door, she saw what she wanted—a rack of real estate guides, free of charge.

She grabbed one, exited, and tried to keep her pace slow while her heart thundered and her every impulse screamed at her to run.

Nobody gave her so much as a passing glance.

She drove to Rockland and pulled off the road at a busy Dunkin' Donuts where the Tahoe wasn't likely to stand out. She'd have to change plates if she intended to keep the car, but right now her priority was finding a place where she could buy some time.

The real estate guide offered plenty of them. Abby knew what she was looking for; the keywords were *seasonal,* which meant they'd likely be empty now, and *motivated,* which meant they'd been on the market for a long time, and the neighbors were used to seeing strange cars pull in for a look.

She found both of those packaged with an even more golden word: *isolated.*

There was a seasonal property in St. George, a rural stretch of peninsula about twenty minutes from Rockland, that boasted a reduced price, motivated seller, and fifteen isolated acres.

A private oasis, perfect for artists, nature lovers, or anyone seeking beauty and seclusion!

The Realtor didn't spell it out, but the place certainly appealed to fugitives too.

Abby drove south on Route 1, then turned in South Thomaston and followed 131 through winding curves that led out of the hills and down the peninsula, the sea on one side and the St. George River on the other. Past an old dairy truck that stood on the top of a hill like it was waiting to be used for a calendar photograph, past a few houses with tall stacks of lobster traps in the yard, and then through the little fishing and tourist town of Tenants Harbor. More fishing town than tourist spot now; this was far enough out of the woods to be unappealing to the leaf peepers, so it probably ran on a short season, Memorial Day to Labor Day, for most everyone but the locals. Just before Port Clyde, the road to the *private oasis* appeared. She followed it into an expanse of ever-thickening pines and then spotted a FOR SALE sign beside a stone post onto which the house number had been carved: 117.

She followed a dirt driveway up a slope and around a curve and then the house came into view, a tall structure of shake shingles and glass that made her think of a lighthouse, everything designed vertically, with each floor a little smaller than the one below it, so it looked as if the levels had been stacked on one another. On one side of the home was a garage and on the other a small outbuilding that had probably been a studio.

She got out of the Tahoe and stood in the silent yard. A light breeze carried the smell of the nearby sea, and the scent mingled with the pines. The place did feel like an oasis, and that was good, because her adrenaline was fading and exhaustion was creeping in. She needed rest. Hopefully, David Meredith was making good on his pledge to do righteous work down at Hank's house, and when Abby woke, it would all be done, nothing left to endure but a lecture from the cops for running and then listening to news of the kid's arrest and identifying him in a photo lineup, maybe.

Sure. It would be that easy.

She tried the garage door first, and it was locked. The house was the same, but there was a Realtor's lockbox on each door. She left the one on the front door intact and hammered the cover off the one on the side door with the butt of the SIG Sauer. There was a Red Sox key ring with three keys—house, garage, and studio, all helpfully labeled.

Abby put the Tahoe in the garage, lowered the door, sealing it out of sight, and went in the house. It was a beautiful place, with gleaming wood floors and fresh white paint on the walls, so even on a gray day it seemed filled with light. There wasn't any furniture. It had been a long time since anyone lived here. From the third-floor master bedroom, you had a view of overgrown gardens that would once have been spectacular, and, just visible over the treetops, a glimmer of blue ocean. You could also see almost the entire length of the road. There were only four other homes on it, and trees screened them out.

The house was mostly empty, but in a closet she found some old drapes and a throw pillow that featured Snoopy flying a biplane. She picked a second-floor bedroom that faced away from the road and offered easy access to a porch roof. She opened the window, removed the screen, then closed it again, leaving it unlocked. If anyone showed up, at least she'd have a chance to run.

Run where?

Abby didn't have the answer to that. She was out of answers and

needed sleep in the worst way. She went back out to the garage and got the bag with the phones and carried that into the house and tucked it in one of the bathroom cabinets. Then she returned to the Tahoe and got the guns. She put the shotgun in the closet near the front door, brought the scoped rifle up to the third-floor master bedroom, and kept the handguns with her as she walked back down to the second floor. She felt nauseated and dizzy and weary. Adrenaline was an amazing thing. There was a certain gift to panic, to terror. As long as you could control it and channel it, there were fuel reserves in fear that most people didn't know existed.

She'd burned through the last of hers, though.

She lay down on the cold hardwood floor, set the guns near her hand, put her head on the Snoopy pillow, covered herself with the old drapes, and slept.

28

For as long as Tara has been awake, the hospital has seemed horrible, and yet as soon as they begin to move her, she's afraid to leave. Fortunately, she has Shannon in her ear, Shannon who, bless her, would talk to a mannequin if that was the only audience she had.

"Dr. Pine says there's no risk in moving you because your spine is stable and your heart and breathing are good, but if there's trouble, have no fear, we'll handle it—that's the best part about traveling by ambulance."

Mom shuffles numbly alongside, and now Tara is certain that they've given her mother tranquilizers. She's surprised—and angry—that Rick has agreed to it. Or does he not know? Is Tara the only one who's picking up on this because everyone else's attention is on her, not Mom? Possible.

A few people give her kind smiles as they pass, and it's both interesting and overwhelming to see the sheer size of the hospital. It occurs to her that she has no idea where this hospital is or how she got here. Ambulance, helicopter? She's always wanted to fly in a helicopter. If you're going to be airlifted to a hospital, you might as well get the view.

They descend in an oversize elevator, big enough to accommodate the gurney, and exit out onto a loading dock, and, sure enough, there's the ambulance, ready and waiting.

The fifty feet between the hospital and the ambulance are the most terrifying part of the journey. Open air isn't a relief to Tara; it's shocking and intimidating, and she misses the confines of the hospital room. *Just leave me in there and I'll get better!* But then they have her up and into the back of the ambulance and Shannon is at her side, Rick and Mom apparently driving separately. There's a young paramedic in the ambulance, an impossibly good-looking guy, and Tara would love to exchange a glance with Shannon over this.

"Tara, I'm Ron," he says as he pats her leg, and now she likes him even more—an introduction *and* a kind touch. She listens to Shannon and Ron talk for the remainder of the ride. Ron is encouraging; he's heard of the lab they're headed for, and he knows they've had great results. Dr. Carlisle is the best. Tara is in great hands with Dr. Pine and Dr. Carlisle. Shannon agrees, but mostly she's just proud of the way she convinced them to use *Jaws* for the test.

"She hates black-and-white film," Shannon tells Ron. "Even the classics. If they show her anything in black-and-white, she's not going to be more alert, trust me. She fell asleep in the first five minutes of *Casablanca*."

Not entirely true—Tara closed her eyes during the first five minutes of *Casablanca*. She didn't fall asleep until at least fifteen minutes in.

She's grateful for the conversation swirling around her, since it helps distract her from the swaying motion of the ambulance. Being inside a moving vehicle is a memory trigger—she can see Dr. Oltamu's face in the rearview mirror again and hear the urgent tension in his voice when he insisted that he needed to get out and walk.

Transition from ambulance to the university lab is quick and smooth and everyone here is friendly and smiling, far more eye contact than what she's used to at the hospital. Dr. Michelle Carlisle is leading the way. She's a tall, striking woman. She kneels to Tara's level, looks her in the eye, and introduces herself politely but formally, as if this is just a standard doctor-patient interaction.

Tara is instantly a fan of Dr. Carlisle.

"What we're going to do," the doctor explains, "is both cutting-edge and quite simple, Tara. We're going to give you the chance to watch your beloved *Jaws*"—she looks at Shannon when she says this with an expression that isn't entirely pleased—"and while you watch it, we watch you. You'll be inside an MRI scanner. I don't know if you've ever had an MRI before, but it might feel a little claustrophobic at first. Just be patient and let that pass."

Speaking as if Tara has a choice in that matter is absurd, and yet it is deeply appreciated.

"The movie plays on a scanner above you and is reflected on a mirror that you can see comfortably. While you watch, the MRI will be recording your responses in various brain areas—auditory cortex, visual cortex, parahippocampal, frontal, and parietal lobes. We'll compare your activation results to that of baseline tests, which will help us say definitively that you're alert and aware, that you're watching and engaging with the film and the story." All of this is for the benefit of Shannon, Mom, and Rick, of course, but Dr. Carlisle addresses Tara. "Well…are we ready?"

I don't know, Tara thinks. *Because there's one big question nobody has answered yet: What if your tests don't show any activation?*

Dr. Carlisle smiles as if Tara has given consent and stands. "Then let's get to it."

The doctor lied about the MRI scanner. It doesn't make Tara feel merely *a little claustrophobic.* It's petrifying.

The machine looks big enough from a distance, but when they slide Tara into it and the rest of the room vanishes from view, the rounded walls close in on her, and it's like being in a coffin. When the hatch behind her is sealed, she's instantly convinced that there's not enough air in this thing, and the panic that overtakes her is the worst since her return to awareness. Maybe worse. What if she can't breathe in here, what if she begins to hyperventilate? She

can't bang on the walls or scream or thrash; she can't do anything to let them know that she needs out.

She's Twitchy Tara again, worthy of her big sister's snarky nickname, anxiety swelling to panic when she knows it's irrational.

She's certain each inhalation is using up her oxygen supply in this coffin-like enclosure, and now she's worse than paralyzed—she's paralyzed and entombed.

Be brave, damn it!

She tries to think of 1804 London Street again, of the long journey down dark halls. She can't conjure up the image, though. And that was so long ago; that happened to a child! She doesn't need a child's courage, she needs a woman's warrior heart.

The Allagash.

The name rises unbidden in her mind, and suddenly she sees the Allagash River, the big, beautiful, dangerous river that bisects northern Maine's roadless, townless wilderness. The river flows south to north, an unusual path in North America. In her freshman year at Hammel, when she was afraid she couldn't hack it at school, couldn't make friends, couldn't survive so far away from home, Tara went alone to kayak on the Allagash. Imprudent; reckless, even. But necessary. She would make her decision there—whether to stay through the semester or go back to Cleveland and enroll somewhere local, somewhere familiar. Or maybe head west, find a school near Stanford, near Shannon.

But first, she wanted to see this river.

She was afraid that day. She saw no one. She was alone in the wilderness. But gradually, the fear faded enough that she found the beauty of the place. She paddled south against the current and then rode it back to the north, and she took the kayak out of the river as the day faded and the last of the sunlight was filtered through the pines and cast a gorgeous green-gold sparkle over the water. She knew in that moment, bone-weary but renewed, that she could take whatever challenges Hammel sent her way.

She thinks of the river now, remembering the fragrance of pine needles and the feel of the cool water and the soft cry of a loon. Remembering the green and gold light on the bejeweled surface of the river, the river that flowed north instead of south. This river that she had conquered alone.

She blinks. Not a full blink, but a Tara blink, a flick of the eyes.

The tube fills with blue light. The MRI chamber darkens, and this actually helps, because she's less aware of the squeeze of the tight space now, and she can see the movie playing on the screen.

The scene shifts to a woman running across sand dunes and alongside a battered wooden fence. A young man behind her, breathless, calling out, "What's your name again?"

Chrissie, Tara thinks before the answer comes.

She knows it all. The most re-watchable movie of all time—all due respect to *Shawshank,* but the prize has to go to *Jaws*—and the only thing Tara has to do now is watch it once more while lighting up the correct areas of her brain.

No pressure.

Chrissie and the boy keep up their stumbling run along the darkened ocean, peeling their clothes off awkwardly, and he yells at her to slow down, then tumbles drunkenly onto the dune as Chrissie dives into the lapping sea and swims out into the dark water.

Tara tracks the action, but her mind is on the first time she saw the movie, at their house in Shaker Heights back when Dad was still alive. They'd sent her to bed, saying she was too young, but Shannon had crept in and told her she could see the screen from the back of the hallway.

Just don't make any noise, Shannon had commanded. *If you make any noise, they'll know you're here.*

They hadn't known. Tara had passed that test. Now it's the same test, and she needs to fail it. *Make some noise, T.,* she tells herself. *Let them know you're here.*

Chrissie is swimming toward the buoy, alone in the sea. Smiling, tossing her blond hair. Then the camera angle changes and shows her from below. Legs dangling.

And the music starts.

The first soft notes, growing louder as the camera closes in, Chrissie floating in graceful, blissful ignorance and then—

Tara's heart thumps with Chrissie's first scream.

She's seen the damn movie a hundred times, and still she cringes, no different than that night back in the dark hallway when she was seven years old.

Chrissie thrashes, screams, cries for help. Her drunk boyfriend is passed out on the shore, waves teasing the soles of his bare feet. Out in the blue-black sea, Chrissie grabs the buoy and clings to it, a moment's safety, a last desperate chance.

Then the unseen attacker has her again, tugging her toward deep, dark water, while the only one who can save her is sprawled on his back in the sand, oblivious.

"Please help!" Chrissie screams. Her last words before she vanishes from the screen, pulled into the depths.

Good-bye, Chrissie, Tara thinks. *I heard you.*

But did her auditory cortex activate? Did Tara put out a glimmer of light for poor Chrissie?

She will know soon.

29

Abby woke before dawn, stiff and aching but rested. Reality crept back, terrible memories of the previous day, and when she sat up, her hand brushed the stock of the SIG Sauer. The touch of the gun removed the last vestiges of hope that this might have been a vivid nightmare.

A nightmare, yes. But not the kind you woke up from.

She rose and stretched, the sound of her popping joints loud in the empty house. Her throat throbbed and there was pressure behind her eyes and under her jaw that promised the arrival of a cold. Hardly a surprise; she'd spent one night bedded down in wet leaves and the next on the wood floor of an empty house. She went into the bathroom and splashed her face with water, then cupped her hands and drank. The water had a mineral taste to it, but that was fine, and the cold of it soothed her throat. She walked back out and stood on the second-floor landing. Moonlight filtered down from above, and she followed it up the stairs and into the third-floor master suite. She sat on the floor there and stared at the shadowed trees as the moonlight gave way to gray and then to rose hues and then the world was back, though it didn't feel like the world she knew. Abby was alone in a strange house in a strange town, sitting in a bedroom that contained absolutely nothing but a scoped rifle she'd stolen from a murdered friend.

How many hours had it been since she'd grudgingly boarded the train to Boston to meet with Shannon Beckley?

A different lifetime. But she'd been in this situation before, in a way. More than a few times.

The first time she'd flipped a car, it had been in New Hampshire. She'd known her tires were thin, but there were seven laps left and she was sitting in third and although her engine was overmatched by the two cars in front, she was sure she could beat them. She'd gotten outside on turn two and the car in front moved to block her while the leader shifted inside to attack the straightaway, and Abby saw a gap opening like a mistake in a chess game. It was going to be tight, and it was going to test what was left of her tires, but she could do it.

She'd made the cut to the inside and then the back wheels drifted and she knew it was trouble but she tried to ride it out, punching the accelerator, eyes locked on that closing gap. When the contact came from the back of the driver's side, she wasn't ready for it. It knocked her car to the right and then the tires were shrieking as they tried to hold on to the asphalt like clawing fingernails. Then she was airborne. And dead.

Or that's how it had felt. A detached sense of foolishness—*You had third, and third was fine*—paired with the certainty of death.

The car had flipped twice before it hit the wall, but somehow she was upright when it was done, and people were reaching for her and shouting and a stream of fire extinguisher foam was pounding against her.

She was sitting on the gurney in the back of the ambulance, the doors still open, offering a view of the track, when she thought: *This was my last race.*

She'd been wrong about that too.

Either you quit or you picked yourself up and moved on. For a long time, Abby's greatest asset had been her ability to get back behind the wheel after a wreck and feel right at home. You wrecked again; of course you did. You expected death again; of course you did.

But you kept on moving. Up until Luke, she'd always been able to do that.

Up until Luke, she'd also always been alone in the car.

She was alone again now, and there was wreckage behind her, but she knew these feelings. There were similarities between what had happened to her yesterday and what had happened to her on the track; anyone who said otherwise had never flipped a car at 187 miles per hour, never walked out of a cloud of flame.

You survived only when you kept moving. Yesterday, Abby had done that. She'd been all instinct and motion. That had felt right to her. She'd felt more right, in fact, than she had in a long time, which was a damned unsettling realization.

Today she did not feel right. She was frozen and indecisive. Did she call David Meredith to learn what they'd made of the scene, see if she could trust him? Maybe they'd found enough to back up her story already. Maybe she'd slept on the floor in a vacant house for no reason. She needed the internet, but she'd crushed her phone back at the service plaza. She'd have to risk taking the Tahoe out so she could find a Walmart and pick up a burner phone with cash.

"You're an idiot," she said aloud, voice echoing off the hardwood floors and empty walls. She shook her head, got to her feet, and went down the steps to the bathroom where she'd stowed the bag of iPhones from Savage Sam. She took them back upstairs, where she figured the signal would be best, sat down in front of a wall outlet, separated the phones and paired them with chargers. Three phones and only two chargers. She plugged two in and waited for them to power on. Only one was protected by a PIN code, but it had no signal, as if it were old and forgotten or maybe its owner had suspended service on it. It would still work if connected to Wi-Fi, though, and the PIN code would be easy enough to defeat; you just reset the phone to factory settings.

One problem there—people were being murdered over whatever was on these phones, and deleting that material didn't seem wise.

The other phone was functional but had absolutely no personal data. Maybe Savage Sam had wiped it clean in preparation for selling it? Or maybe Oltamu had wiped it clean for other reasons?

She picked up the third phone, and something felt wrong about it immediately. The weight was off. It was in a simple black case with a screen protector, and it looked for all the world like the others, but it was too heavy.

She brought the charger to the base of the phone but couldn't find the port. She turned it over, looking to see how she'd missed the charging port on a phone that looked like a twin of her own.

It wasn't there.

An electric tingle rode up her spine.

The top of the phone had a power button that looked standard. When she pressed it, the screen lit up, and the display filled with what appeared to be the factory-setting background of a new iPhone. She hit the home button, expecting to be denied access, but she was greeted with a close-up image of Tara Beckley's face. Tara was smiling uncertainly, almost warily, into the camera, and behind her was a dark sky broken by a few lights from distant buildings.

Below the photo were the words Access authentication: Enter the name of the individual pictured above.

When Abby tapped the screen, a keyboard appeared. She moved her thumb toward the *T* on it, then stopped. She wasn't sure what she was opening here. If this phone actually belonged to Tara Beckley, it was a strange and poor security feature—a selfie asking for your own name? Then there was the question of the weight, which was decidedly different from a standard iPhone's. She pulled off the case and checked the back and found no Apple logo and no serial number. If it was a phone, it was a clone, a knockoff. But if it wasn't a phone...what did it do?

It had one hell of a battery, that was for sure. It had been at the salvage yard for a week and had no charging port, and still it ran without trouble. Definitely not the iPhone of Abby's experience. But it looked like one. Would it act like one? Would it ring?

She picked up the phone that actually functioned and plugged it back into the charger. Then she went downstairs, out of the house, and into the crisp autumn day. The wind was coming in off the sea, and the smell of salt was heavy in the air. She could hear waves breaking on rocks. Down there, beyond the trees, it would be violent, but up here it sounded soothing.

She found the Hammel College case file in the backseat of the Tahoe and scanned through the loose pages and old photographs, all of it feeling surreal and distant—the idea that this had once been merely a job for Hank and her seemed impossible, laughable. It was the whole world to her now.

College administrators had provided the paperwork that had been given to the conference coordinator; it included two phone numbers for Oltamu, helpfully labeled *office* and *mobile,* and a note saying that the doctor preferred to be called before nine or after three.

Abby didn't think Oltamu would mind the disturbance anymore.

She took the contact sheet, went back upstairs, punched the mobile number into her one working phone, and called, staring at the bizarre clone phone with Tara Beckley's face on the display.

It won't ring, she thought, but then she heard ringing.

She was so surprised that it took her a moment to realize it was from the phone at her ear.

She was about to disconnect the call when the voice came on.

"Hello?" A man, speaking softly and with a trace of confusion. Or fear.

Abby looked at the phone as if she'd imagined the voice. The call was connected. She had someone on the line.

"Hello?" the man said again.

Abby brought the phone back to her ear and said, "I was looking for Dr. Oltamu."

There was a pause, and then the voice said, "Dr. Oltamu is unavailable. May I ask who's calling?"

Abby hesitated and then decided to test him. "My name is Hank Bauer."

Pause.

"Hank Bauer," the man echoed finally, and Abby thought, *He knows. The name means something to him.*

"That's right," she said.

"And what can I do for you, Hank?" A bad impression of friendly and casual.

"Dr. Oltamu is dead," Abby said. "So who are you and why are you answering a dead man's phone?"

The silence went on so long that Abby checked to see whether the call was still connected. It was. As she started to speak again, the man finally answered.

"Would this be Abby Kaplan?"

"Good guess. Now, what's your name?"

"That's not important."

"Of course not." Abby got to her feet and started pacing the empty bedroom, the phone held tightly. "Give me another name, then—give me the kid's name."

"The kid."

"That's right. Tell me who he was and I won't need your name. I want him."

Another silence. Abby glanced at the display again—she'd been on the phone for thirty-seven seconds. How long was too long to stay connected?

"Do it fast," she said.

"I've got no idea what *kid* you're asking about. Or why you called this number."

"Then why did you answer?" Abby knelt and punched the home button on the clone phone, which brought up the picture of Tara Beckley. She was ready to tell the man on the other end of the line what she had, ready to try a bargain, but she stopped herself.

She thought she understood now, understood the whole damn thing—or at least a much larger portion than she had before.

I've been there, she thought, looking at the photo. The background over Tara's shoulder showed spindled shadows looming just past her pensive, awkward smile. Shadows from an old bridge. Abby had paced that same spot with a camera. That place was where this photo had been taken. Hammel College's campus was just across the river.

"You got the wrong phone," Abby said.

"What does that mean?" the man said, but his voice had changed, and he hadn't asked the question out of confusion—he was intrigued. Wary, maybe, but intrigued.

"The one you just answered doesn't matter," Abby said. "The one I've got does. It might not even be a phone, but it's what you wanted. It's what you need now."

When the man didn't speak, Abby felt a cold smile slide over her face. "You took two of them," she said. "You took Tara Beckley's phone and Oltamu's. That was the job. Other than killing him, of course. The job was to kill him and take the phones. I don't know why, but I know that's what you were trying to do. But there were three phones, and you didn't know that. That's the problem, isn't it?"

"Why don't you explain—"

"You missed one," Abby said. "And if you want it, you're going to need to give me the kid who killed Hank. Think we can make that trade?"

"I bet if we meet in person, we can work this out. Quickly. How about that, Abby? You're in some trouble, and I can ensure that it ends. You need some serious help."

"And you need that phone. So make a gesture of good faith. Tell me his name."

Pause. "I'd be lying if I told it to you. There's my gesture of good faith. Whatever name he's going by now, I don't know it."

For the first time, Abby believed him. "I need to come out of this alive," she said.

"You will."

"I'll believe that when you tell me where to find him."

No response. Abby looked at the phone again. What if the call was being traced? How long was too long? "Make a choice," she said.

"Okay. All right. But it will take me some time. And I'll need to know you've got the phone and where you are. You tell me that, I'll put him in the same place. How you handle it then is up to you."

"What do you call him?" Abby said.

"Huh?"

"Forget his real name. What do *you* call him?"

Another pause, and then: "Dax."

"Dax."

"Yes. But it won't help you. Trust me, he's not going to be located under that name."

"That's fine. You want the phone, you'll put him where I can find him. Agreed?"

"Tell me something about the phone."

"It's a fake, for one."

She could hear the man on the other end of the line exhale. "A fake?"

"Yes. It's built to look like an iPhone, but it's not one. Now—ready to make a deal on giving me your boy Dax?"

"Yes."

"Great. Then I'll call back. From a different number."

"Hang on. Tell me where you—"

Abby cut him off. "End of round one. Answer when I call again."

"Hang on, hang on, don't—"

Abby disconnected and stood looking at the phone. Her hand was trembling. She powered the phone down. She didn't want it putting out any sort of signal.

Who the hell was that? Who answered Oltamu's phone?

Not Oltamu, that was for sure. And not a cop.

The options left weren't good.

She sat beside Hank Bauer's rifle and picked up the fake phone, trying to imagine what had made it worth killing for and what Tara Beckley had understood about it when her photo was taken. The smile was uncomfortable, forced, and the man she'd been with had been killed a few minutes—seconds?—later. Tara had been sent spinning into the river below and then rushed to the hospital, where she now lay in a coma. But there was a difference between uncomfortable and afraid, and as Abby looked at her face, she was sure Tara hadn't been scared. Not yet, at least. Maybe after, maybe soon after, but not in the moment of that photograph.

Access authentication: Enter the name of the individual pictured above.

She hesitated, then typed Tara and hit Enter.

The display blinked, refreshed, and said Access denied, two tries remaining.

"Shit," Abby whispered, and she set the phone down as if she were afraid of it.

As if? No. You are *afraid of it.*

People were being killed over this thing, and for what? Something stored on it made sense, but wasn't everything cloud-based now? What would be on the phone that couldn't be accessed by a hacker? Hacking it seemed easier than leaving a bloody trail of victims up the Atlantic coast. She stared at the device as if it would offer an answer. It couldn't. But who could?

Oltamu.

Right. A dead man.

"Why'd they kill you, Doc?" she whispered.

She couldn't begin to guess because she didn't know the first thing about Oltamu. That was a problem. Abby was out in front, but she didn't know what was coming for her.

Look in the rearview mirror, then. Pause and look in the rearview.

To get answers, she would have to start with the first of the dead men.

30

Whenever the concealed microphones in Gerry Connors's office were activated, Dax Blackwell received an alert on his phone. Generally, he chose not to listen unless Gerry was in the midst of a deal. He was always curious to determine how Gerry valued his efforts, since in Dax's business, it was difficult to get a sense of the going professional rates. There weren't many Glassdoor.com reviews for what he did.

Today he listened, tucking in earbuds. He sat in the car with an energy drink in hand and listened to Gerry Connors give his name to Abby Kaplan.

He was surprised by how disappointed he felt. He'd known Gerry was a risk, because anyone who knew how to find you was a risk, and yet he'd had as much trust in Gerry as anyone on earth since his father and uncle had been killed.

Time to put that away, though. Disappointment wasn't a useful emotion; it did nothing to help your next steps.

And why be surprised? He remembered a day at the shooting range with his uncle and father, Patrick putting round after round into the bull's-eye from two hundred yards, totally focused, eye to the scope, and Dax's father looking on with the sort of pride that Dax wanted to inspire in him. Something about watching that shooting display had made his father reflective. Jack Blackwell tended to be philosophical when guns were in hand.

But that day, as Patrick racked the bolt and breathed and fired and hit, over and over, Jack Blackwell had watched his brother with fierce pride and then looked at his son and said, "Dax, if you find one person on this earth who would never fuck you over for money or women, you'll be a fortunate man. People like that are rare."

There you had it, then. Why feel disappointment in Gerry Connors when he was doing exactly what you'd expect him to? The only question was how to respond.

Dax sipped his energy drink and played the recording once more, then sat in silence, thinking, his eyes straight ahead. At length, he picked up his phone and called Gerry.

"It's me," he said. "I'm struggling here. Our girl Abby has done a good job of hiding. Any ideas?"

31

Gerry Connors had a decision to make, and he needed to make it fast. Abby Kaplan was out there doing exactly what Dax Blackwell had predicted—avoiding police and trying to make a play on her own. The German was out there, inbound and impatient, and he didn't even know what a mess this had turned into yet. And now there was Dax Blackwell on the phone asking for guidance, and Gerry had to decide whether to set him up or give him a chance.

It seemed impossible that he'd been put in this situation by some disgraced stunt-car-driving chick turned insurance adjuster.

The most intriguing part of the whole thing was that the kid had been right. Kaplan hadn't gone straight to the cops; she'd gotten scared and run. Gerry couldn't imagine how the kid had been so damned sure of this.

Yes, you can. You have always imagined it. He's one of them.

"Gerry?" Dax said. "Are you there?"

"Yeah. I'm here. And she's not hiding. She's calling people."

"Calling who?" Dax said, and he seemed pleased by the news.

Gerry looked at Amandi Oltamu's silent phone on his desk and wondered how long it would be before it rang again…and what Abby Kaplan would have done in the meantime. Beside the phone was a notepad on which Gerry had scribbled the number she had used to call him. He looked from the phone to the notepad, drumming a pen on the desk.

Trade Dax or trust him?

"Gerry?" Dax prompted.

"She's trying to make her own way out of this," Gerry said. "She might already be with the cops, but it didn't feel like it. She says she's got the phone, although she might be bluffing. But she understands the way it went, at least. She understands what Ramirez did wrong."

Dax was quiet for a moment, then said, "How do you know this?"

There he went again, pushing, fishing.

"My client," Gerry said tightly.

"How did Abby Kaplan reach your client?"

If he'd been in the room, Gerry might've shot him. Instead he squeezed his eyes shut, took a breath, and said, "She's calling Oltamu's phone."

"And your client was dumb enough to answer it?"

"Listen, shut the fuck up and let me talk, all right? She called the phone and spun some bullshit about trading for…safety. I don't know what that means to her exactly and probably neither does she—she just knows she's in trouble."

Dax didn't say anything this time.

"I want to know where she's calling from," Gerry said.

"I'd imagine."

Gerry would have shot him twice for that.

Trade him, then. Give him up.

"How'd you know she'd go this route?" he asked, and the kid must have heard the sincerity in his voice, because for once he wasn't a wiseass when he responded.

"A lot of factors. She likes to be on the move. Has her whole life. From the cradle until I finally put her in the grave, Abby's been about motion and speed. She doesn't have a good history with police either. There are still people in California who are pushing for her to be charged in the wreck that killed the pretty-boy actor. And…" He hesitated, that brief hitch that his father had never shown, or at least had never shown to Gerry, before he said,

"I guess you could call it my own instinct. Abby's not dumb, and I saw that, but I also made sure she knew that *I* wasn't dumb. Everything that's happened since is a reaction to our understanding of each other. That seems simple, but it's not. If someone is close to a mirror, you see it."

"Close to a mirror? What the hell does that mean?"

The kid gave it a few beats before he said, "I understand her. That's all it means."

"She's an insurance investigator. If you feel like she could work with you, then I've sorely underestimated your talents."

With no trace of annoyance, the kid said, "Oh, you haven't underestimated *my* talents, Gerry. Abby Kaplan's, though? She's something more than we'd have expected."

"Because she got away from you. That's all you mean. You don't want to admit that you screwed up with her. Because she got away, we need to pretend she's something special."

Still no inflection change when Dax said, "Didn't you tell me I was right in my prediction about how she'd choose to move, Gerry?"

"*Maybe* you were."

"She's on the run and she's calling you—sorry, calling your *client*. Give me the benefit of the doubt on this one. I was right about Abby."

"After you lost her."

"Once. Yes. After I lost her once." He was unfazed. "It won't happen twice."

Gerry said, "I've got the number she called from, and that's all I've got."

"It's a start."

"You need to work fast. This is going to go in one direction or the other very quickly."

"An object in motion tends to stay in motion," Dax Blackwell said cheerfully, "unless an external force is applied to it. Let's see if we can apply a little force. What's the number?"

Gerry read it off. "See what you can do with that, and let me know in a hurry."

"If Abby calls back, is your client going to answer that phone again?"

"How the fuck do I know?" Gerry snapped.

"I suppose you don't."

"Of course I don't. Just do your job."

"Right," the kid said, and he disconnected.

Gerry looked from his own phone to Oltamu's and found himself wishing Oltamu's would ring. *I'll make that trade, Kaplan. I had high hopes for this kid, but they're vanishing fast. You call back, and I will absolutely make that trade.*

But for now...

He couldn't make the trade until Kaplan called back. In the meantime, he could give the kid a chance to clean up the mess. Keep two plays alive until the right one announced itself and then act decisively. That was how you won.

Gerry would win this yet.

32

When both doctors enter the room together, Tara knows it's bad news. They've decided on an alliance, neither wanting to make the other crush a family's hope. Teamwork, then; they'll break hearts together. At the sight of the doctors, Mom and Rick and Shannon all rise to their feet, their voices loud and chaotic and too cheerful, as if pleasantries can change the outcome. Dr. Carlisle is all warm smiles and soft tones; Dr. Pine looks like a Zen shark, a good-natured predator swimming past potential victims, not yet sure if he'll turn and devour them. He eludes Rick's awful bro-hug-handshake hybrid with grace, then walks to Tara's side and looks her in the eyes.

"When this is all over," he says, "I want you to tell me everything that was said about me behind my back."

The room goes silent, and Dr. Carlisle appears vaguely annoyed. In that expression, Tara sees the results of the test—she passed, and Dr. Carlisle wanted to make the announcement.

She passed. Tara is positive. They know that—

"She's alert," Dr. Carlisle says, the annoyed expression gone and a radiant smile in its place. "Not just alert—fully and completely aware, cognitively and emotionally. Her results are extraordinary. Not unprecedented, but close. Every lobe reacted as it should have; her visual, auditory, and processing responses to the movie were perfect." She turns to Shannon and says, "And she certainly had an emotional response to the girl at the beginning of the movie. You weren't wrong about that."

Chrissie, Tara thinks. *Why can't anyone ever remember her name?*

That's when Mom falls on her knees beside the bed and presses Tara's hand to her face, her tears soaking Tara's palm, and then Shannon is there, saying how she always knew it, but her quavering voice gives her away, and Rick is the only one who holds back, but Tara can't blame him for that, and she's grateful that he's actually pausing to thank the doctors and is touched by the emotion in his voice.

"She's hearing us?" Mom says, staring at Tara with wonder. "You're sure? Right now, she's hearing me?"

"Every word," Dr. Carlisle promises, pulling a chair up beside the bed. Dr. Pine stays on his feet, smiling but pacing. Like any shark, he must keep moving or he will die.

"And she's always heard us?" Shannon asks, and Tara wants to laugh at the poorly suppressed guilt in her voice. Shannon is probably conducting an inventory of everything she let slip in moments when she thought she was alone. No matter what confidence they all professed, none of them were sure that Tara could hear a word. Now they are getting an awareness of that ghost in the room.

"I can't tell you when she came back or whether she's been alert the entire time; all I can tell you is that she is now," Dr. Carlisle says.

"What does that mean for her prognosis?" Shannon asks. Mom looks wounded by the question, as if it's in some way undermining the joy of what they've just been told, but it is also the question Tara would ask if she had a voice.

"Entirely unknown," Dr. Pine says. "But it only helps. One of the greatest challenges in rehabilitating the brain is the constant testing and guessing it requires from the medical team, from the family, everyone. Based on Dr. Carlisle's results, Tara is going to be able to help us enormously there. She may not have her voice, but she should be able to communicate. If we know what she's experiencing, feeling, and requiring, that is a tremendous advantage in treating her successfully." His eyes are locked on Tara with excitement.

I'm an opportunity to him, she realizes. *Something he's been waiting for for maybe his whole career.* It's an odd sensation but not a bad one—he wants to see if he can bring her all the way back. That's a goal Tara can get behind.

"There may be even more reason for celebration," Dr. Carlisle says. "When reviewing the video of Tara's face during the test, Dr. Pine noticed what seems to be some oculomotor progress."

"Oculomotor?" Mom echoes tentatively.

"She can blink?" Rick asks.

"Not quite...or at least not quite *yet,*" Dr. Pine says. "But the progress she's demonstrating since our initial tests may be more useful than even Tara knows."

He's studying Tara's eyes while moving his hand in the air like a conductor. The longer he does it, the more delighted he seems.

"Vertical eye motion," he says. He sits and perches with perfect posture on a stool beside her bed; he looks like a bird of prey. "She's regained that. Consistent with locked-in syndrome."

"Locked-in syndrome?" Rick asks, and he looks at Tara with something between concern and horror. The name seems self-explanatory, and terrifying. They're all learning now what Tara has been living with for days.

"Charming name, isn't it?" Dr. Pine says. "But it's clear, at least. Tara is with us, but Tara is trapped."

Mom murmurs something inaudible and puts her head in her hands.

"Not all bad, though," Dr. Pine continues. "Locked-in syndrome prevents outbound communication, yes, but it also, perhaps, provides some protection. And now that we know she's in there, we can work to bridge the void." He studies her with a slight incline of his head, then smiles. "Excellent."

Tara tracked the motion with her eyes, and he saw it. The rush of euphoria this realization brings is almost overwhelming, and if she could cry, she would. *He sees me. He sees me!*

"Locked-in syndrome is caused by an insult to the ventral pons," he says. "But with vertical eye motion, she's not as trapped as she was before. She should be able to communicate."

An insult to the ventral pons, Tara thinks. That's the term for having your brain knocked around your skull and leaving you unable to move or speak—an *insult?* The word seems woefully insufficient.

"Essentially, her condition has caused paralysis with preservation of consciousness and retention of vertical eye movement. She has some voluntary eyelid motion, but her response to the blink requests, as you saw, showed a lack of control." He leans forward and lifts a pencil with his thumb and index finger. "But there's progress. I think Tara *is* in control of her vertical eye motion now. Aren't you, Tara? Show them."

He lifts the pencil slowly, then lowers it. Mom gasps; Rick puts a hand on her shoulder that seems designed to steady himself as much as her, and Shannon stares at Tara, enthralled.

"Oh, honey," Mom says. "Oh, baby." She's squeezing Tara's hand and blinking away tears. Dr. Pine tolerates the interruption. Behind them, Dr. Carlisle paces and smiles.

Competitive, Tara thinks. *She found me in here first. He wants me now.* That is just fine with her. The more the merrier when it comes to people invested in her return, but she wonders if they'll remember who suggested she watch *Jaws.*

Mom releases her hand, rises, gets her iPad, then rushes back, holding it with the camera lens trained on Tara. She's shaking so badly it seems unlikely she'll be able to keep it in her hands, let alone in focus. Tara wants to laugh. For years, she and Shannon made fun of Mom's insistence on capturing every family moment on film, but even *now?*

Dr. Pine says, "Tara, let's try for yes and no. When you want to indicate a *yes* response, look up once. When you want to say *no,* do it twice." He pauses and wets his lips, and for the first time Tara sees that behind the clinical demeanor, he's nervous. "Okay," he says. "Tara, do you understand what I just said?"

She looks up. Once.

"Tara, does two plus two equal ten?"

She looks up twice.

Dr. Pine lets out a long breath. "We're batting a thousand," he says. "Tara, is Shannon your sister?"

Up once.

"Am I your father?"

Up twice.

Mom is crying now, tears streaming down her face, over those purple rings below her eyes that have darkened with each day in here; her iPad shakes in her hands like a highway sign in hurricane winds.

Shannon pushes in beside Dr. Pine, kneels, and looks at Tara with a trembling smile. "Tara," she says, "did you ever quit?"

Dr. Pine looks annoyed at the intrusion, but when Tara moves her eyes upward twice and they all burst into a clumsy hybrid of tears and laughter, he smiles charitably and lets them have their moment. He keeps watching Tara, though, his focus unbroken.

"Tara," he says, "would you like to try the alphabet board?"

Up once.

He stands. "Okay," he says, "let's see what she can do."

Yes, Tara thinks. *Let's see.* It's the first time she's been given an active role—even the crucial fMRI was passive; she was shoved into a tube and shown a movie—and the opportunity is both exhilarating and exhausting. The joy that comes with being known, with being breathed back into existence in the room, is an injection of adrenaline, but the eye tests were oddly fatiguing, as if simple willpower drains her. Perhaps it does. But she's got willpower reserves they haven't seen yet, and she'll figure out how to replenish them, locked-in or not.

"This is all just a starting point," Dr. Carlisle says. "Yes/no communication is, obviously, an enormous step. But we've got an open road ahead of us now."

Dr. Carlisle begins to talk about a combination of rudimentary alphabet boards and sophisticated computer software, and Dr. Pine chimes in with a discussion of tongue-strengthening exercises—those sound like fun. Mom returns to her chair and focuses on her iPad. Tara watches in astonishment as she taps away, seemingly oblivious to the conversation around her. *Are you bored, Mom? I'm back from the dead, but you've got e-mail to check?* Then Mom rises with a smile and brings the iPad to Tara and turns it to face her.

"You have no idea how badly I've wanted to be able to post this," she says, starting to cry again.

On the screen is the Team Tara Facebook page. Mom has pinned the video of Tara's eye-motion test with a caption: *We have blessed news! Tara is awake!*

33

Back when he'd been rehearsing for the fugitive role, asking Abby countless questions about how she'd handle herself on the run, Luke had given her a simple but memorable piece of advice: "Never underestimate the helpfulness of your local library."

On her first day as a fugitive, Abby headed for the library in Rockland. In Luke's script, there'd been dialogue about big cities being better to hide in than small towns, because nobody paused to look at a stranger in a place where *everyone* was a stranger. She believed that, but big cities were hard to come by in Maine, and so she settled for Rockland, the county seat, home to the courthouse and the jail and the BMV. A regular metropolis by Maine standards, with maybe twenty thousand residents.

She parked several blocks from the library, near the harbor in a busy parking lot that was shared by two seafood restaurants and a YMCA, and she walked along the water for twenty minutes, watching her back, before she moved toward town. No one followed. In the library, she found a computer where she could sit with her back to the wall and her eyes on the door.

When she logged on to the internet, her first instinct was to read about herself. Pragmatic fugitive behavior or clinical narcissism? She wasn't sure, but a cursory review of news sites was reassuring to her invisibility, if not her ego—the reports were that Hank Bauer had died in a car accident whose cause was currently under investigation. Police in Maine were keeping Abby's story quiet for a reason, or possibly they didn't believe it, but in any case, they weren't making a big deal out of her call to David Meredith.

Not yet.

She moved on to Amandi Oltamu. There was plenty to read here, because Amandi Oltamu had been an important man, but Abby was going to need a translator to help her understand half of it.

The obituaries were helpful but vague, capturing his childhood escape from a war-torn Sudan and his education history (Carnegie Mellon and MIT) and revealing that his marriage had ended in divorce and he had no children. He was described as "renowned in his field." *Okay,* Abby thought, *let's find out some more about that field.* A few searches later she landed on a paper written by Oltamu. The title was "Improving the Coupling of Redox Cycles in Sulfur and 2,6-Polyanthraquinone and Impacts on Galvanostatic Cycling."

It wasn't a good sign that Abby was tentative on the pronunciation of two of the words in the title.

She didn't waste time attempting to wade through the entire paper. If there was a clue in that paper, Abby wasn't going to be able to identify it. Instead, she went to the Hammel College site and found a short press release on Dr. Oltamu's scheduled talk. This one was at least a bit more civilian-friendly: He was going to speak on how batteries could combat climate change. The press release didn't mention anything about teenage assassins, though. Less helpful.

Oltamu's bio on the site said that he'd consulted with the International Society for Energy Storage Research. The ISESR page noted that his work was focused on a new paradigm for battery energy storage at atomic and molecular levels.

Terrific. And tragic. He'd been doing vital work, and then he was killed. Maybe the vital work was why he'd been killed. If so, that was going to require more understanding of the topic than Abby could glean from web searches. There was a better chance of her figuring out how to jailbreak the security on that cloned iPhone than of her determining the breakthrough Amandi Oltamu had made with regard to the new paradigm of galvanostatic coupling. Or cycling. Whatever. Understanding the importance of Oltamu's work required an advanced degree, or at least the ability to pronounce *polyanthraquinone* without sounding like Forrest Gump.

Jailbreaking the device Oltamu had left behind seemed like the better option, but Abby had failed once already. She'd tried *Tara* and not *Tara Beckley,* but if *Tara Beckley* was wrong, she was down to one swing of the bat. She still didn't understand the security approach either; shouldn't it be more advanced, a fingerprint or a retina scan or facial recognition?

Maybe it was. Maybe the prompt asking for Tara's name was a ruse, and the only way the device unlocked was with Oltamu's retina. That would be a problem, considering that by now he'd been buried or cremated.

Had Oltamu been trying to protect himself at the end, adding Tara Beckley's photograph as a lock just before Carlos Ramirez drove into him? Or was Abby's instinct wrong, and Oltamu hadn't taken the picture? Even if Abby was right about the location, and she was pretty sure that she was, it didn't mean that she was right about when it had been taken. For all she knew, it was Tara Beckley's Facebook profile picture.

Bullshit it is. Not with that smile. Something was wrong when that picture was taken. She wasn't sure what yet, but she knew something was wrong.

Tara's Facebook profile was private, but Abby found an open Facebook page called Team Tara, the one Shannon Beckley had said kept her mother occupied and away from tranquilizers. Abby opened it without much hope, then froze.

The first post was a video with a caption claiming Tara was awake.

She moved the cursor to the video and clicked Play. The camera was shaking, but Tara was clear, and so were her eyes. As a doctor asked her questions, she looked up. Once for yes, twice for no. The motion was unmistakable.

Her mother wasn't being optimistic; Tara was awake and responsive.

Abby whispered, "Oh, shit," loudly enough to earn an irritated glance from an old man reading a newspaper a few feet away.

Abby lifted a hand in apology and returned her attention to the screen. The video had been posted only a few hours earlier but already it had hundreds of shares, people eager to distribute this good news far and wide.

A blessing, yes. And maybe a terrible invitation.

She logged off the computer, picked up the case file, and left the library, then walked back down to the harbor and stood about five hundred yards from the Tahoe. She pretended to stare at the sea, but she was really looking for people watching the car. There was no obvious sign of interest in the vehicle, but right now everyone felt like a watcher. Paranoia was growing. She forced her eyes away from the parking lot and looked out across the water. The wind was rising, northeasterly breezes throwing up nickel-colored clouds, as if the morning's sunshine had been a mistake and now the wind was working hastily to conceal evidence of the error.

Abby knew that making contact with Tara Beckley's family would be a suicidal move. They'd rush to the police, bring more attention, and, quite possibly, kill whatever faint hope she had of trading the phone in her pocket for evidence that exonerated her in Hank's death and for the chance to send his murderer to prison. It was too early to reach out; she'd be better off walking into the police station.

Unless the family believes you.

Unless that, yes.

She watched the ferry head out from Rockland toward Vinalhaven, and she thought of the way Tara's eyes had flicked up at the doctor's questions, the responsive motion so clear, so undeniable, and then she thought of the countless tests Luke had failed. Then she withdrew the working cell phone from her pocket, the one she'd promised herself she wouldn't use again. Just by turning it on, she was broadcasting her location.

But she had to try.

She opened the case file she'd taken into the library and flipped through it in search of another number. Not Oltamu's this time. Shannon Beckley's. She dialed.

Shannon answered immediately. "Hello?" A single word that conveyed both her confidence in herself and her distrust of others. She wouldn't have recognized the number, so she was probably already suspicious.

"This is Abby Kaplan and it is very important that you do not hang up. You need to listen to me, please. You've got to listen to me for Tara's sake."

She got the words out in a hurry. She had to keep the conversation short on this phone.

"Sure," Shannon said. "Sure, I remember you." Her voice was strained, and Abby heard people talking in the background and then the sound of a door opening and she understood that Shannon was leaving a crowded room. She was at least giving Abby the chance to speak.

"Have they told you I killed Hank Bauer yet?" Abby asked.

"They have." She spoke lightly, as if trying not to draw concern or attention, and Abby heard her footsteps loud on the tiled floor of the hospital. She was walking away from listeners.

"It's a lie. We were both supposed to die and I made it out."

"That's different than what I've heard."

"I'm sure it is. If I could explain it, I'd have gone right to the police. But Hank is dead because whoever killed Oltamu—and Ramirez, there are three of them now, all of them dead..." Her words were running away from her and she stopped and took a breath, forcing herself to slow down. "Whoever did that wants a phone. Not your sister's, and not Oltamu's real phone. One that he had with him, maybe. I'm not sure it's actually a phone; it might just be a camera designed to look like one. But I've got it."

"What does—"

"Hang on, listen to me. I just read a post from your mother's Facebook page that claims Tara is alert. I saw the video. That needs to come down."

"What? Why?"

Abby looked at how long she'd been on the call—twenty-five seconds. "I've got to hurry," she said, "and I don't have all the answers you're going to want, but you have to limit access to Tara. And you have to limit the questions she's asked. Because if she remembers what happened that night, then she's a threat to somebody. Three people are already dead, and that's just the ones I know of. I was supposed to be the fourth."

Shannon Beckley didn't speak. Abby wanted to be patient, but she couldn't. Not on this line.

"If you think I'm crazy, fine, but I'm trying to give you a chance," she said. "Trying to give *her* a chance."

Shannon's voice was low when she said, "I don't think you're crazy."

"Thank you."

"But I can't limit access to her," she said. "There are too many doctors involved, and they're not going to let me call the shots. If you think she's at risk of being…killed, then who am I supposed to tell? Who do I call?"

The wind gusted off the water, peeled leaves off the trees, and scattered them over the pavement, plastering one to Abby's leg. She stared at the bloodred leaf, then looked over to where the Tahoe was parked. A man in an L. L. Bean windbreaker walked by it without giving it so much as a passing glance, but still Abby scrutinized him.

"I don't know who you call," she said finally. "If I knew, I'd call them myself. Maybe *you* can trust the police."

"You're not sure of that, though?"

"I'm…" She'd started to say she was sure, but she couldn't. All she could think of was the way the kid had smiled when he'd spoken of friends in cells and friends in uniforms. "I'm not sure," Abby finished. "Sorry. There has to be someone to call, but I don't know who the right person is, because I don't know who I'm dealing with. I don't know what Tara saw, what she heard."

She faced the hard, cutting wind and paused again, aware that she was letting the call go on too long but no longer caring as much because an idea was forming.

"Can you ask her the first round of questions?" she said. "Without doctors around, or at least without many of them. Can you handle that?"

"Questions about what happened that night?"

"Yes. You need to do that. But they have to be the right questions. They have to… they need to be *my* questions."

"What are those?"

"I'm not positive yet. I mean, I know some, but… let me think."

"You have to tell me what to ask!"

Abby squinted into the cold wind and watched the ferry churn toward the island, its wake foaming white against the gray sea, and then she said, "Ask her if he took a picture of her. I definitely need to know that. And if he did, then ask if she gave him another name."

"Another name? What do you mean, another name?"

"I'm not sure. If she called herself Tara or Miss Beckley or whatever. Ask what he knew her by. That's really important. What would he have called her?"

"She would have been just Tara. That's it," Shannon said, her voice rising, but then she lowered it abruptly, as if she'd realized she might be overheard, and said, "Why does this matter? What do you know?"

"People are killing each other to get to a phone that was in her car," Abby said. "I have it now. It was in the box I brought down to you. I don't know what in the hell is on it, but it looks like he took her picture. It's on the lock screen now, and it wants her name. But her name doesn't—"

The phone beeped in her ear then, and her first thought was the battery was low, but when she glanced at the display, she saw an incoming call, the number blocked.

The wind off the water died down, but the chill within her spread.

"Hang on," she told Shannon Beckley, and then she ignored her objection and switched over to answer the incoming call. "Hello?"

"Hello, Abby."

It was the kid.

34

A bby didn't speak.

She stood with the phone to her ear and her head bowed, eyes focused on the single red leaf fluttering against her dirt-streaked jeans.

The kid seemed amused when he said, "You *do* recognize my voice, right? I'm usually memorable. Apologies for the arrogance of that statement."

Abby reached down and flicked the leaf free from her jeans and watched it ride away on the wind. Finally, she found her voice.

"You didn't have to kill him."

"Kill who?"

"Fuck you."

"Exactly. This is how we can go for as long as you'd like, or you can make progress. The way I understand it, you're in a bit of a bind."

He talks like an imitation of a human, Abby thought. *Like he's not entirely sure how to walk among us, but he's studied it enough to fake his way. He's got the exterior down just enough to pass. What evil is on the inside, though?*

"I'll be needing that phone, Abby," the kid said, and right then someone down on the pier shook the remains from a bag of fast food into the water, and a handful of seagulls rose in wing and full-throated voice. They danced and dived and fought for French fries and the kid said, "On the coast, are we?"

Abby paced away from the water, a pointless effort given the piercing chorus of gulls, and wished death upon the indifferent diner who'd scattered his French fries to the wind.

"Yeah," she said. "Miami. Come south."

The kid's laugh was the only genuine thing about him.

"I like you, Abby," he said. "I mean that. But we really should get down to business."

Abby looked at the phone display. Twenty seconds and running. Shannon Beckley still on the other line. But the kid wasn't wrong. Abby had to get down to business or get to a police station, one or the other, and in a hurry.

"You want the phone, and I want you in jail," she said.

"There's not much to entice me in that scenario."

"I want you in jail," Abby repeated, "but I know I might not get that."

"Wise. So what do you need instead?"

"To keep myself alive *and* out of jail."

"Typical millennial. One thing is never enough. You want free shipping too?"

"The phone keeps me alive," Abby said. "The police will too. The right ones, at least."

"Be very cautious about that. Finding the right ones isn't impossible, but it won't be easy. Not for you. That's not a bluff. That's a promise."

He said it with calm, earned confidence. If Abby weren't already scared of his reach, she'd be with the police now, and they both knew that.

"Give me a number where I can call you back," Abby said.

"Call the German. He'll get me."

The German? The guy who'd answered Oltamu's phone had sounded anything but German. A trace of Boston accent, maybe, or a hint of Irish, but not German.

"You don't know him," the kid said. "Do you?"

"No."

"Interesting. Let me ask you something, Abby—do you need *me* to go to jail or do you just need somebody other than you to go?"

"I need the right person to go."

"Then you don't need me. Not if you care about the food chain."

"You killed him."

"Think I won't be replaced, Abby? You're smarter than that. I know you are."

Abby hesitated. "Hold the line a minute."

"What?"

Abby switched calls and spoke without preamble to Shannon Beckley. "I'm going to be in touch from a different number. Keep people away from Tara. If you see a kid, somebody who looks like he walked out of the high-school yearbook, call the police."

"What are you—"

"I won't blame you if you don't trust me. But you need to." She switched calls again. "Still there?"

"Yes," the kid said. "You have a recorder going now or a helpful witness listening, maybe?"

"No. I'm going to tell you where to find me."

"Oh?"

"Yeah. Listen real close so you don't miss it."

Abby left the call connected when she tossed the phone into the sea.

Before it reached the bottom of the harbor, she was running for her car, keys in hand. Even if she'd stayed on the phone long enough for them to trace it already, she'd be gone when they got here. It was time to get moving. Instinct told her to go farther north, to seek ever-smaller towns and more isolation, but she wanted to see Shannon Beckley. There was risk in that, of course, but maybe less than she thought. And Boston was a city filled with strangers. It would be easier to blend in there. They also had an FBI headquarters, probably even CIA. She could pick her police agency instead of relying on the locals. That's what she would do. Get to Boston, get to Shannon Beckley, and then get to the FBI. When she called Oltamu's phone again, she would be with the professionals. A day ago, she'd had nothing to tell them but the wild story about Hank's house, but now she had the phone that wasn't a phone, evidence of what all this killing was about, and that changed everything. They would believe her now.

She unlocked the Tahoe, slid behind the wheel, and cranked the engine to life. Her hand was on the gearshift when she felt the cold muzzle of a revolver press the base of her neck.

She moved her eyes to the mirror, and from the backseat, the kid in the black baseball cap smiled congenially.

"Found you," he said.

Part Four

EXIT LANES

35

Abby waited on the kill shot. There was no reason for the kid to hold off on it now. Unless he had a sadistic streak, which Abby thought he probably did.

He didn't take the shot. Instead, he said, "Go ahead and put it in drive."

Abby didn't move. Why make it easy on him? If she was going to die either way, she'd make the little prick take the shot in a crowded spot, where people would hear it and respond to the sound, where maybe surveillance cameras would give the police a lead.

"Abby?"

"Do it here," Abby said. She could feel the weight of the SIG Sauer in her jacket pocket, where she'd jammed it awkwardly, more concerned about concealment than access when she'd walked into the library. An amateur playing a pro's game.

"No."

"You're going to have to," Abby said, and as she spoke, her eyes drifted higher on the mirror, and she estimated the distance to the curb and the slope that led over the jogging path and down to the boardwalk and that deep-channel harbor. If she could get it in reverse and keep her foot on the gas, she'd at least be able to take this sociopath down with her.

"You think you're done?" the kid said, sounding surprised. "That's a disappointing attitude from someone with your resilience."

It was less than thirty feet to the curb, and once she cleared that, gravity might handle the rest. If the kid fired, the bullet was going to obliterate Abby's brain and any control she had over the wheel and the gas pedal, but as long as momentum and gravity worked together, the Tahoe might make the water.

"I was thinking we could go back to the house in Tenants Harbor," the kid said, and his smile brightened when Abby's eyes returned to him. "Yes, I knew you were there. Beautiful spot. Love that detached studio too. Made me feel creative. The whole place is nice and peaceful, though, much better than this parking lot. And we'll need to pick up your guns. They're likely to concern the Realtor."

When Abby still didn't move, the kid sighed and said, "If I wanted you dead, you'd be dead by now, get it?"

Abby pulled the gearshift down. She considered reverse, passed it, and put the car into drive.

"How'd you find me?" she asked.

"Bauer's phone is in the glove box, and I enabled tracking. I did the same to yours, but you were smart enough to get rid of that one. You didn't check the Tahoe out fully, though. Poor choice, Abby."

All day and all night, Abby had believed she was off the grid, hidden. In reality, she'd been exposed and at the kid's mercy.

"Why'd you let me live?" Abby asked, pulling out of the parking lot and turning right, then left, putting them back on Route 1, headed south.

"Priorities. You were there for the taking if I needed to do it, but the phone was the bigger problem, and I didn't think you had that. Tell me, where was it?"

"Under the driver's seat. You didn't check the Chrysler out fully. Poor choice, asshole."

The kid laughed, and suddenly the pressure of the gun was gone from Abby's skull. "I like you," the kid said. "I really do."

"It's not mutual."

"I struggle at first impressions. Give me time."

"Okay," Abby said, and then she added, "Dax."

It was the only card she had to play, the only thing she knew about him that might make him pause, but he took it in stride.

"There aren't many people left who call me that, but go right ahead. It's always been my preference. And, Abby? Keep a close eye on your speed, please. You're going pretty slow, and it would be a bad day to be pulled over."

"Where am I driving?"

"I told you."

"We're really going back to the house in Tenants Harbor?"

"I think we should. We could use a private, peaceful place like that to talk."

"Not much to talk about. You've won."

"Plenty to talk about, and if you hadn't polluted Penobscot Bay with that phone, we might already understand each other better. But I've always preferred face-to-face conversations, anyhow. We're going to be together for a while. Gerry is waiting on your call, and you will need to be alive to make that. Good news for you, right?"

"Gerry?"

"That's the name of the man who answered the other phone. Gerry Connors. Crusty old bastard. I liked him. For a long time, I liked Gerry just fine."

"He's the German?"

"No. He's not. But we'll get to the German before we're done, I think. I'm pretty sure we're going to need to do that."

He shifted in the backseat, and Abby looked in the mirror again and saw that he'd hooked his right foot over his left knee, as relaxed as a passenger in a chauffeured car. Which, Abby supposed, was exactly what he was now.

"You don't work for him?"

"I did. But I think the relationship is on the rocks at this point."

"I don't follow."

"Sure you do." He leaned forward. "You've already tested him. You offered him the phone for my life once. You're going to do the same thing again."

How did he know this? He'd known Abby's location; he knew

her movements, her calls, her words. How was he so damned omniscient?

"By the way, Abby, where is the phone now?"

She could lie, but what was the point? "My jeans. Front right pocket."

The kid nodded, satisfied. He leaned back in the seat, slouched and nearly uninterested, although the gun was still pointed at Abby's back. It would be easy to spin the car and throw off his balance, and Abby thought there was a good chance she could do that and buy enough time to get out, but she couldn't imagine she'd buy enough time to get out and find cover. The kid would shoot before then. Abby could flip the car, of course, but then she was as likely to die as he was.

"Do you know what's on it?" the kid asked. "Do you actually have a clue what's on the phone?"

"No."

"It's just a phone?"

Abby hesitated but realized there was no point in holding out. "It's a fake. Looks like an iPhone, but it isn't. As far as I can tell, it's not really a phone at all."

For the first time, the kid showed real interest. He shifted into the middle of the seat, where he could keep the gun trained on Abby's head and watch all of her movements, and said, "Pass it back to me, please. I'm trusting that you won't reach for the gun in your jacket instead. Remember, you're still alive due to my choices and to yours. Make the right ones."

Abby took her right hand off the wheel, slid the phone out of her pocket, and passed it back. The kid accepted it and leaned away. For a while, he didn't so much as glance at the phone; he kept his eyes on Abby, assessing her.

"Keep driving, and you'll keep living," he said. "Can you do that? Keep driving?"

"Yes."

The kid looked away then. Down at the phone. The gun was still in his hand, but his attention was compromised.

Flip the car. Just do it, you coward, flip it and take your chances. You'll have witnesses and people calling 911 and police cars screaming out here...

She kept driving. She couldn't will herself to flip the car, even though she'd walked away from worse before. She tried to tell herself it was because of the gun in the kid's hand.

While Abby drove, the kid alternated between glancing at her and studying the phone. He never lowered the gun, keeping it in his right hand as he turned the phone over carefully in his left. When he finally spoke, it was softly, almost to himself.

"Didn't expect that."

Abby didn't respond. The kid was silent for a moment, and then he looked up and said, "You know who's on the screen, don't you?"

"Yes."

"A picture of Tara. Interesting. Any idea why that would be there?"

"No."

"But you've taken a swing at it, I see. It looks like you tried her name, maybe?"

Abby nodded.

"Do you know why that didn't work?"

"No."

"Guess." The kid slouched back against the seat, the phone in his pocket now, all of his attention on Abby. "Show me some promise, Kaplan. Offer a strong theory."

"It's all fake."

"What does that mean?"

"That the picture is pointless, maybe. A smoke screen. It's not how you unlock the phone." She glanced in the mirror and saw the kid staring intently at her.

"How do you think the phone is unlocked, then?"

"I'm not sure."

"Give me another effort. I think you're close."

"A fingerprint. A PIN number. I really don't know."

"Actually, you're very close. Not bad at all. It's biometrics, but it's not a fingerprint. The camera is real, so I'm betting on facial recognition."

"Do you think it's really Tara's face that has to be recognized, though?" They were on a narrow stretch of the peninsula now, Penobscot Bay looming to their left, the sea gray-green under the massing clouds, a tower of battered lobster traps stacked high on a weathered wharf.

"Smart question," he said, and his voice softened in a way that made her think he hadn't considered the possibility before. "Is Tara the key that opens the lock, or is she a ruse? And if she is…" He let the sentence drift, then said, "I think she's the key. Smart play by Oltamu, if I'm right. Tara Beckley would have been anonymous to anyone who took the phone. She was a stranger. That's quite brilliant, really. The problem is that she stopped being a stranger that night. But he wasn't counting on that."

Abby didn't speak, but that didn't stop the kid from talking. It seemed nothing would stop the kid from talking. He liked conversation, and he liked to watch people. He reminded Abby of some demented dentist, poking and prodding, testing nerves, coaxing a reaction.

"I wonder if he told her what he was doing," the kid mused. "Was she just a face, or does she know something? If he was feeling urgency…maybe Tara knows a lot more than we think."

"Too bad she's gone," Abby said.

"Don't rush to judgment on that. I received an encouraging update on her condition this morning."

Fuck, Abby thought, and she was so defeated by that news that she let the speed fall off. The kid leaned forward and tapped her head with the gun.

"Pick it back up. Speed limit or five miles over, no more."

Abby accelerated to five miles over the limit. She tried to look indifferent to the discussion of Tara, but all she could think about was whether the kid had heard her talking to Shannon, whether he knew what Abby had disclosed to her.

"In fact," the kid said once he was satisfied with Abby's driving, "the news about Tara is particularly encouraging after seeing this. She can move her eyes, Abby. Isn't that wonderful?"

Abby was silent.

"Okay, maybe you're not a member of Team Tara. Rather cold-hearted, but to each her own. As a proud member of Team Tara, though, I'm especially encouraged after seeing the phone, because a lot of facial-recognition systems depend on active eyes. While once she might have been useless, now…"

He let the thought hang unfinished, then said, "Do you get it yet, Abby?"

Abby didn't want to engage with him again. Each time she did, she felt like the kid was seeing more of her brain, learning her heart. It was through his strange dialogue that he opened you up somehow, laid you bare on the table and decided whether there was anything in you worth keeping alive. If he decided the answer was no, that was the end.

"I think you do, but you're in a sullen mood. Understandable. It's been a tough couple of days for you. I'll explain what you already know, then, since you're not willing to play along. If I'm right, Abby, then what we have is a lock…" He lifted Oltamu's phone. "And Tara Beckley, bless her miraculous survivor's will, is the key."

He put the phone back into his pocket, braced his gun hand on his knee, and said, "That makes our next move pretty easy, doesn't it? We'll need to bring the lock to the key. Usually it would work the other way around, but we're in very atypical circumstances. Tell you what, Abby—we're going to detour. Forget the house and turn around. Right up here will work."

He nudged Abby with the gun. They were approaching the

Tenants Harbor village center, which amounted to a general store and the post office on the left, a volunteer fire department up ahead, and the school and the library somewhere off to the right. The street was empty save for one man in a rusted pickup filling plastic gas cans at the general store's pump. He didn't even look up when Abby pulled in behind him and then backed out. She didn't leave the parking lot, though. The clouds had obscured the sun and now the first drops of rain fell, fat and loud as they splattered on the hood.

"Where am I going?" she said.

"Southbound," the kid answered. "Boston or bust."

Abby kept her foot on the brake, and this time the gun muzzle found her ribs, a jab with more force.

"Don't sit here waiting to be noticed. Get on the move."

Abby eased her foot off the brake. She wasn't sitting there hoping to be noticed or expecting to find help in this isolated fishing village.

She was thinking about I-95 southbound in the rain. They'd hit the Boston area around rush hour, although every hour seemed like rush hour in Boston. Cars and trucks squeezing you from all sides, tens of thousands of drivers oblivious to the killing power controlled by their hands and feet.

And a sociopath with a gun in her backseat.

This was the first time she'd shared a car with anyone since Luke. Always, she'd made sure to drive alone in the days after that, making any excuse. No excuse offered itself now.

"Let's go," the kid said, and Abby moved her foot to the gas.

The Tahoe rolled out of the general store's parking lot and passed the post office; the North Atlantic was visible briefly to the right, then gone. Abby drove on through the gathering gray as the coastal fog swept in. She told herself this would be fine, this was the simple part, whatever came next was the trouble.

Faster, Abby, Luke had whispered just before the end. *Faster.*

Or had it been *Slow down?* It was so damned hard to remember.

36

The hospital room is abuzz with joy, yet Shannon seems distant.

Tara doesn't understand this at all. Shannon, her champion, the one who would never quit on her, is somehow the most distracted person there. She's left the room four times now, and each time she returns, the phone in her hand, she seems farther away. She's stopped looking Tara in the eye and she seems, inexplicably, more concerned now than she was before Dr. Pine and Dr. Carlisle arrived with their good news.

What does she know that I don't?

Recovery prognosis. That has to be it. Either the doctors have been more honest with Shannon than they've been with Mom and Rick or Shannon is doing her own research. Maybe Shannon understands already what Tara fears—it would have been better if she'd failed the tests, because there's no return to real life ahead of her. Nothing but this awful limbo, only now they all know she's awake and alert, and that means they feel an even greater burden of responsibility. Endless days of one-way chatter, countless hospital bills, all to sustain an empty existence. This would defeat even Shannon's willpower.

But the doctors are excited, and the disconnect there is confusing. It's also something Tara can't focus on any longer, because Dr. Pine is demanding all of her attention. In his hands he has a plastic board filled with rows of letters, each row a different color. The first row is red, the second yellow, the third blue, then green, then white. At the end of the red row is the phrase *end of word*. At the end of the yellow row is *end of sentence*.

This is Tara's chance to speak.

"It's going to feel laborious," Dr. Pine warns, "and you might get tired. It's more work than people would guess."

He's right about that. Even the yes/no answers were draining. But Tara is a marathon runner. She knows how you keep the finish line from invading your thoughts too early.

"Do you have enough energy to give this a try?" Dr. Pine asks.

She flicks her eyes up once.

"Terrific. What I'm going to do is ask you to spell something. You get to pick what it is. You're in charge now, Tara, do you understand?"

She flicks her eyes up again and feels like she could laugh and cry simultaneously—she's paralyzed, but he's telling her that she is in charge, and right now, that doesn't seem as absurd as it should. The simple possibility of communicating is empowering, almost intoxicatingly so. Her message is within her control. Such power. So easily taken for granted.

"Tell us whatever you want to tell us," Dr. Pine says, "but I'd suggest a short message to begin. The way we get there is simple—we're going to spell it out together. That means I've got to narrow down the first letter of the word. So I'll ask whether it's red or yellow or blue. You will tell me yes or no. Once I have the color, we'll go through the letters. You'll tell me yes or no. If I'm trying to go on too long, you'll tell me that we're at the end of the word or the end of the sentence." He studies her. "It's not easy. But stay patient, and let's give it a try. Do you have a message ready for your family?"

Does she have a message? What a question. She's overflowing with messages, drowning in them. There is so much she wants to tell them that the idea of picking just one thing freezes her momentarily, but then she remembers to flick her eyes upward, because he has asked a question and is waiting on the answer. Yes, she has a message.

"Great," he says. "Now, is the first letter red?"

Two flicks. No.

"Yellow?"

No.

"Blue?"

One flick.

"Is it *I*?" No. "*J*?" No. "*K*?" No. "*L*?"

One flick. Tara is exhausted, but she has her first letter on the board.

Next letter. Not red, yellow, or blue. Green. Then she gets a break—finally, it's the first letter in the column. One flick, and she has her second letter on the board: *O*.

It's harder than any race she's ever run. She's exhausted, and the focus makes her vision gray out at the edges, blurring the columns and letters, but she's not going to quit now. Not until it's out there. Her first words, tottering forth into the world like a newborn. She has to deliver them, even if they're also her last.

L
O
V
E
End of word
Y
O
U

They're all crying now, Mom and Rick and Shannon; even Dr. Pine might have a trace of mist in his eyes, but maybe that's Tara's blurring vision.

"Tara," he says, "you just spoke. And they've heard you."

She wants to cry too. She's so tired, but she has been heard, and it is remarkable. It feels like all she has ever wanted.

"Do you have another message you want to share with us right now?" Dr. Pine asks.

Two flicks. No. She got out the one that mattered most. She can rest now.

She fades out, grateful for the break, as Dr. Carlisle begins to talk excitedly about computer software that should make this a faster process, and Rick asks if there's a more holistic approach, which makes Shannon tell him to shut up and let Dr. Carlisle finish, and Mom tells her not to talk like that. The conversation is a chaotic swirl but Tara is not put off by it because they know she's there now, they know she's hearing it all. She's so relaxed, relieved, and so, so tired. The last thing she hears before she drifts off is Dr. Pine excusing himself from the room. That makes her smile. She thinks he's happy to leave Dr. Carlisle to handle this mess.

"I have to make a phone call," he says.

Yeah, right, Doc. People have used that excuse around my family before.

The last sound she hears before sleep takes her is the soft click of the door closing behind him.

37

Boone's phone began to ring while the plane was still descending, and she caught a reproachful look from one of the flight attendants.

"Airplane mode until we're on the ground, please."

"Right," Boone said. She'd never used airplane mode in her life, preferring to have her phone flood with e-mails and messages while they eased down through the clouds. If this habit were truly dangerous, a lot of planes would be tumbling out of the sky, she thought. But why quibble with the flight attendant—Boone's business cards said Department of Energy, but her expertise wasn't really in that field.

Instead, she simply silenced the phone while pretending to put it in airplane mode. The caller went to voice mail. Boone looked at the number and didn't recognize it, but the area code was Boston's.

It's a big city, she thought, trying to tamp down the swell of hope. *Could be anyone, about anything. Could be the boneheads in the Brighton PD calling to state their unequivocal confidence that Carlos Ramirez was killed in a drug buy gone bad.*

Or it could be her one hope: Dr. Pine.

She held the phone in her lap as the plane made what now felt like an endless descent, and as the signal strengthened, the iPhone offered an awkward attempt at transcribing the voice mail. While some of it was clearly a mistake—she doubted the phrase *jazz trombone* would be involved—the first words were crystal:

Hello, this is Dr. Pine.

Son of a bitch, son of a bitch, son of a bitch. There was hope. Dr. Pine meant there was hope.

The plane finally hit Tampa tarmac, tires shrieking, cabin shuddering. Boone was in the aisle seat, still staring at her phone, and when she didn't rise instantly at the chime indicating they were now free to take off their seat belts and exit the plane, the passenger beside her cleared his throat loudly and made an impatient gesture toward the aisle, where people were attacking the overhead bins in a frenzy, as if they'd all boarded the last flight out of a failed nation-state. Actually, Boone had been on two of those flights, and they weren't all that energetic.

She unclipped her seat belt and rose, ducking her five feet ten inches to avoid the overhead bins but never taking the phone from her ear. Now she could hear what the transcription software had missed.

"Hello, this is Dr. Pine, in Boston. I trust you'll remember me. I just left a pretty jazzed-up room. Tara Beckley is alert. She has what we call locked-in syndrome. This means her ability to move and vocalize her thoughts is lost, at least temporarily, possibly forever, but her mind is intact, and she is aware. I just asked her to spell out a message to the family and she completed this task successfully. She is also capable of answering yes-or-no questions." He paused, and Boone could sense both his pride in the moment and his conflicted feelings about sharing the information.

"I'm not sure if I would have made this call if not for the mother," he continued. "She's making regular updates on social media, broadcasting Tara's condition to the world. Since it seems the news will not be hard to find, I suppose I will take a chance on telling you. If, as you once suggested, her life may be in danger...well, we're going to need to take swift action on that. I didn't know how to keep the mother from sharing this joyful news. Perhaps this is why you should have dealt with the family to begin with. At any rate, this is Tara's status at the moment. If you have any questions that don't involve a deeper invasion of my patient's confidentiality, I would be happy to answer them."

"You stupid bitch," Boone said aloud, and though the sentiment was directed at a joyful mother two thousand miles away, her seatmate clearly thought it was for him as he rushed to pull his bag out of the overhead bin. Boone ignored his umbrage while she called Pine back. *Answer, damn it. Answer.*

She was on the jet bridge being jostled by the crowd when he picked up.

"You've got to shut her down," Boone said without preamble.

"Pardon?"

"Protect that girl. Limit access to her and get the mother to pull that shit off the web."

"Isn't this *your* role?"

"Yes, it is. But I just touched down in Tampa, where I'm not even going to leave the airport, I'll just get the first flight back north. In the meantime, I need your help." She felt a rush of humid Florida air as she crossed the jet bridge and entered the terminal, and then the blast of air-conditioning washed it away and brought harsh reality along with the temperature drop. Boone was in the wrong city and she could not fix what had already happened. She said, "It's too late to pull the news down, isn't it? People will have gotten notifications as soon as she posted. They'll be sharing it. So we don't need to worry about the mother. We just have to limit the people who have access to the girl."

"This simply isn't my role," Dr. Pine said. "You need to get the police to talk with this family if they are—"

"I understand your role, and I understand mine much better than you do. Bringing police off the street and into that hospital will only make things worse. I just need to interview her. That's all. You say she's able to communicate."

"In a limited fashion, yes."

Boone fought through the crowd to a row of flight monitors and looked for the next departure to Boston. It was a three-hour wait. Not great, but not terrible either. She wouldn't be able to charter a plane much faster, and until she knew if Tara Beckley had any memory of the event, nobody was going to approve that budget item.

"Does she remember what happened?" she asked.

"I don't know. That wasn't today's priority. Again, this is simply not within the—"

"A lot of the risk depends on whether she has any memory at all of the moments around Oltamu's death," Boone said. "You need to find out if she remembers the night."

"That's *your* job!"

"And I'm going to do it. But Doctor? You're there. She's there. Her protection and her threat are both still outside the hospital walls. Want to make sure the right one gets there first? Find out if she remembers the night. I don't need you to interrogate her, I need you to assess whether she has any memory of it. It's that simple, and it's that crucial."

Silence. She thought about waiting him out but decided to press instead. "When you do that, make sure the mother is out of the room. Then call me immediately."

She hung up on his protest.

Did it matter that Tara Beckley was back? It was surprising— stunning, actually, based on the initial diagnosis—but it wouldn't mean a damn thing if she couldn't remember her ride with Amandi Oltamu. If she had any memory of that night, she would be of use. Boone was confident of that because of Oltamu's last message.

Ask the girl.

Boone walked toward the nearest Delta gate. If she could get on the next flight to Boston, she would ask the girl. And if the girl remembered?

If she woke and remembered, they'd need the best in the game. If she woke and remembered, they'd need Boone.

38

A bby did fine until they reached Portland.

Driving out of Tenants Harbor and back to Rockland, she stayed on winding two-lane country roads that were no problem, and in Rockland she picked up Route 1 heading south, although it would have been faster to take 17 west all the way to Gardiner, where she could jump on the interstate.

She was in no hurry to get on the interstate, though. She was in no hurry, period. She wanted time to think and plan, and if the kid was bothered by her choice, he didn't voice concern. Didn't voice anything at all, surprisingly. His focus was undeniable, his eyes and the muzzle of the gun returning to Abby any time she so much as shifted position, but at last, finally, he was silent.

He seemed to want this time to think too, although they were contemplating different goals. Abby wondered if he was any closer to understanding how to reach his.

Traffic was minimal on Route 1, the occasional chain of stoplights in one coastal village or another breaking things up, and the road always had a shoulder if she needed it, a place to pull over and catch her breath and focus her eyes.

They curled through Wiscasset and up the hill where, in the summer, tourists would gather in long lines outside Red's Eats waiting for lobster rolls, and then they crossed the Kennebec River into Bath, where naval destroyers rested in their berths at the last major shipbuilder in Maine, Bath Iron Works. Once they'd made five-masted schooners here; now they made Zumwalt-class destroyers at four billion dollars a ship.

The hills were lit with fire-bright colors, but clouds kept pushing in, and the rain fell in thin, windswept sheets, flapping off the windshield like laundry on a line. The pavement was wet, but the Tahoe's tires were good and the car never slipped. Abby was trying to think about the things that mattered—Tara and Shannon Beckley in Boston, the kid with the gun in the backseat, those vivid, real things—and yet her mind drifted time and again to the feel of the tires on the wet road, to the weight of the car pressing on the curves, and to the fear that she would push too far, too fast. The power of a phobia was extraordinary. *Yes, I know there's a gunman right beside me, but I think I just saw a spider in that corner…*

It was as if the brain couldn't help but yield the battlefield when a phobia appeared, no matter how irrational the fear.

Just drive, she told herself, breathing as steadily as she could. *Just drive, and keep an eye on that shoulder, and know that at these speeds, nothing that bad can happen. You're in a big car, cruising slow.*

She was through Brunswick and her mind was on the upcoming I-295 spur and its increase in speed and traffic when the kid broke the silence for the first time in nearly an hour.

"We'll need to lose the Tahoe before we hit civilization."

For a moment, Abby was ridiculously pleased, as if they were going to take the bus or the train from here while the kid held the gun on her and smiled at the other passengers in his polite but detached fashion. He added, "We should be in my car already, but I had different visions of the way this day was going to play out. An oversight on my part. Oh, well. We've got options. Stealing a car is one, but that has its own risks. The other option is at your office, I believe. The sports car. What kind is it?"

A shudder in her chest, cold and sudden, like a bird shaking water from its wings.

"You know the car I'm talking about," the kid said. "What is it?"

"Hellcat," Abby managed. Then, clearing her throat: "A Dodge Challenger. Hellcat motor."

"Nice ride. The title is in Bauer's name, but the police already searched his office, and I doubt they thought to add that plate to the mix, since the car was still there. It was pretty clear what car of his you stole after you killed him."

To Abby, the idea of shifting to the Hellcat somehow seemed worse than the lies he was telling.

"I also doubt they're waiting for you there," he continued. "Small county with limited resources, and common sense says you're not going to show up at the office. So we will."

"Back roads," Abby blurted.

"Excuse me?" The kid leaned forward, the gun's chrome cylinders bright in Abby's peripheral vision.

"I'll need to take the back roads to get there. Otherwise, we'll go through the toll. The tollbooth cameras will pick up this plate. They're wired in with state police."

She had no idea if this was true, but it sounded good.

It also apparently sounded good to Dax, because he leaned back and said, "Good call, Abby. I knew there was a reason I'd entrusted the driving to you. Take the back roads, then. We're in no hurry."

The approach allowed her to avoid the I-295 spur and stay in the thickening but slow-moving traffic, bouncing from side street to side street, grateful for the stoplights and speed limits. It added at least forty minutes to the journey, and in truth they wouldn't have had to pass through a tollbooth, but Dax evidently wasn't familiar enough with the area to know that.

Abby's focus was entirely on keeping control—of the car and of herself—until they reached the office. Then the memory of Hank's dead face, his head rolling on his broken neck, rose, and she felt sick and shamed. Not only had she been unable to save Hank; she was now chauffeuring around the man who'd killed him.

Dax was sitting tall in the backseat as they approached, head swiveling, scouting the surroundings for any watchers. There were none.

The office of Coastal Claims and Investigations had once been a hair salon, and Hank had kept some of the mirrors and one of the barber's chairs. He'd insisted the chair was comfortable and too expensive to waste, and he liked to sit in it and have a cigar while he read the paper, which always made him look like a man waiting on a ghost to cut his hair.

The building and its oversize detached garage sat alone in a large gravel parking lot surrounded by empty fields. There was a Dunkin' Donuts visible just down the road, and a gas station across from that. They were the only possible places for covert surveillance, but Abby agreed with the kid—the police would have seen no purpose for that.

"Drive past," Dax said.

Abby cruised by, came to the four-way stop with the gas station and the Dunkin' Donuts, and waited for instructions. The kid was leaning close again, the gun in Abby's ribs.

"If you saw something out of place, speak now or forever hold a hollow-point in your heart."

"Looked clear. He has security cameras, but they don't work. Just a deterrent."

"I noticed that in my previous visit, but I appreciate your honesty. Okay. Go on back."

Abby turned around in the Dunkin' Donuts parking lot and drove back to the office where she'd spent countless hours as a child talking tires and engines with Hank and her father, the office to which she'd returned when she couldn't get a job anywhere else.

"Open the garage door," Dax said.

Abby hit the button and the overhead door rolled up, exposing the low-slung Dodge Challenger with the red paint, black trim, and black hood, looking every bit deserving of the Hellcat name.

Her heartbeat quickened at the sight of it.

"Pull in."

Abby parked next to the Challenger and put the garage door

down, sealing out the daylight. She cut the engine on the Tahoe and the kid said, "Do you have keys to the office?"

"Yeah. But I've also got the keys for that car. There's no need to go inside the office."

"Actually, there is. We're going to make a phone call." He got out of the Tahoe and waved the pistol at Abby in a hurry-up gesture.

Abby got out and led the way across the narrow opening to the office. A few stray raindrops splattered off them, and the parking lot was pockmarked with puddles. A relentless gray day. The cars on the road passed quickly, everyone in a hurry to get home. Still, being there was a risk. Locals knew Hank, and locals knew that no one should be at his office.

"Let's go," the kid said, impatient, as if he was thinking the same thing.

Abby opened the side door and stepped in, entering behind a desk facing the windows. Hank's various collections of oddities filled the room—the barber's chair, an antique gas pump, a neon Red Sox sign, a gumball machine filled with gumballs that had to be forty years old.

The kid settled into the barber's chair, swiveled to face Abby, and pointed at the desk. "Pick up the phone."

"If I use that phone, it'll be traced back here."

"The guy you're calling is going to ask me to trace it, so I think we're good."

Abby looked at him, surprised, and Dax nodded. "You're calling my boss. Terms are going to be straightforward, and you're going to set them, just as you promised before. You'll give him Oltamu's phone if he gives me up. Now, you don't trust him, of course, so you'll want a nice public spot. Safety. You'll want me to come to you, not the other way around. Someplace you're familiar with, and I won't be. Someplace with good visual potential, where there might be cops I won't notice. What sounds good to you?"

Abby thought about it. "The pier at Old Orchard Beach. Wide open, plenty of people, and if I got there first, I'd be able to see everyone coming and going."

The kid smiled and pointed at Abby approvingly with the pistol. "That's not bad. It's even better because you thought of it. Now, where are you going to give him Oltamu's phone? Can't be the same place. He'll want it before he gives me up."

He said it without sorrow or anger.

This time Abby didn't have an answer.

"You're going to put it inside the mailbox of a vacant house in Old Orchard," Dax said, "and at eleven forty-five tomorrow morning, you'll text him the address. By noon, I'll need to walk onto the pier. You've got to give him time to pick up the phone. That's only fair."

"He'll think there's a trap in both places," Abby said.

"Yes. But he really needs that phone."

Abby looked at him, sitting there so at ease in the barber's chair, with the dim light filtering through the blinds and painting him in slats.

"You're going to kill him too," she said.

The kid shrugged. "Too early to say."

"No, it isn't. If he's willing to trade you for the phone, you can't overlook that. It's personal to you."

"Nothing is personal. It's a matter of price point, Abby. I feel like mine is moving north."

Abby parted her lips to say more, but the kid stopped her.

"Just make the call. The same number you did before."

Abby reached for the phone, then hesitated. "I don't know it. It's written down, but it's out in the Tahoe."

She moved for the door as she spoke. If she could get to the garage alone, if she could open the door and get behind the wheel while the kid waited in here, then maybe she could—

"Good news," the kid said. "*I* remember it."

He did, too, reciting it without taking his eyes off Abby. The gun muzzle never wavered. Outside, cars passed in the rain, but there were no lights on inside the office, no indication that anyone was inside. If people gave the place a glance, they'd think nothing was amiss. Maybe they'd mourn Hank Bauer and curse Abby Kaplan for killing him, but they would not slow.

She punched in the last of the digits, and the line hummed, and then rang. Once, twice. Then—"Hello?"

It was the same man. For a moment Abby couldn't remember what to say or how to begin. Then Dax left the barber's chair, leaned across the desk, and punched the speakerphone button. He set a digital recorder down beside the phone, then leveled the pistol at Abby's head.

Abby finally spoke. "I don't want this thing," she said to the man Dax had called Gerry. "This phone or camera or whatever. I don't want it, and I never did. It has nothing to do with me. I don't understand what it is, so I'm no threat to you once it's gone. Do you agree?"

The man said, "Yes. That's a smart choice," with enthusiasm that bordered on relief.

"But I need him," Abby said.

"I gave you his name."

"And you said that it wouldn't be worth a damn. I need *him*. Not his name, his address, or even his fucking fingerprints. I want him."

Dax smiled in the darkness. Approving of the performance. His eyes, though, weren't on Abby. They were on the phone. He was waiting to hear whether he was considered expendable.

The silence went on for a long time. Abby watched the recorder on the desk count off the seconds of silence. Eleven of them passed before the man spoke.

"How am I supposed to get the phone?"

Dax stepped away, as if he'd heard enough. He returned to the barber's chair.

Abby followed the script—the phone would be in the mailbox of a vacant house in Old Orchard, and she'd give them fifteen minutes to pick it up and get clear. The kid would need to step onto the pier at noon. Throughout her spiel, the man never interrupted, just listened. Abby could hear the faint scraping of a pen on paper.

"What's your plan for him?" he said when Abby had fallen silent.

Abby hadn't anticipated this question. She hesitated, then said, "That's my business."

"I need to know. Are you coming for him with police or..."

The answer rose forth easily this time.

"I've got something else in mind for him," Abby said. Dax lifted his head to meet Abby's eyes. He smiled at her.

"All right," the man said. "Then if I see a cop, everything's off."

"You won't see one. After what he did, I'm not worried about police. I want him."

Abby held the kid's eyes while she said that, but Dax never lost the smile. Instead, he gave a respectful nod.

It was then that Abby realized that she wasn't lying to the man on the phone. She *didn't* want police. She wanted to kill him. Or try.

"So you'll text the address at eleven forty-five tomorrow morning," the man said, "and you'd better pick a location that's close to the pier."

"Why?"

"Because I'm not going down there myself. Think I trust you? He'll get the phone, then I'll get the phone, and then I'll send him along to you. So choose your spot carefully."

"Don't worry about that," Abby said. "Just make sure he's there."

"He will be."

The kid left the chair, walked to the desk, and killed the connection. Then he set the phone back in the cradle, picked up the recorder, and put it in his pocket. The smile was still on his face, but it seemed to have been painted on and forgotten.

"Well," he said. "That's that. Nicely done, Abby. You're going to survive all of this, I think. You're earning your way out."

Abby didn't say anything. They stood looking at each other in the office that Hank Bauer had worked out of for thirty-three years, and then the quiet was shattered by a shrill ring. Abby looked at the desk phone, but Dax stepped away and reached into his pocket and withdrew his cell. Before he answered it, he lifted the revolver and put it to his lips, instructing Abby to be silent. Then he said, "Yeah?"

Abby could hear the caller's voice faintly, but she couldn't make out most of the words.

Dax said, "Old Orchard is pretty exposed. You couldn't negotiate a better spot than that?"

The voice on the other end rose a bit this time, and Abby heard the phrase *know your role*. Dax's face never changed.

"Right," he said. Then: "So we'll pull her away from the pier beforehand. You're sure that she'll go?" He listened to the caller. "Why don't I pick out the house? I can sit on it all night. Make sure it's clear."

Pause. Then: "All right. We'll ride together. I'll drive."

Pause. Then: "You're the boss. I'll be there. Let's put an end to this one. This bitch has been too much trouble already."

Pause. A smile slid back onto his face, and this time it was genuine, and it was cold. "Yes, I did allow it to happen. I realize that. But trust me—I'll end it, too." He disconnected and put the phone back in his pocket. "Get the gist, Abby?"

"He's lying to you."

Dax nodded. "In his version, *he* will pick the house. I would expect that's where you and I are supposed to die. The pier was never ideal. A vacant house, even if you pick it, is much better— provided there are no police. And you know what? I think he believed you on that. He'll check first, of course, but...he believed you. Do you know why I'm so sure?"

Abby shook her head.

"Because I believed you too," the kid said. "I don't think jail is the fit you want for me anymore. You want me to die."

He seemed to wait for a response. Abby said, "Doesn't matter either way, does it?"

"Actually, it does. You're finally growing into someone I understand."

He walked around the desk and opened the top left-hand drawer. The Challenger keys rested beside a spare set for the Tahoe and one for the office.

"Grab the winners," he said.

Abby picked up the keys. The kid faced her, gun extended, and smiled. "Now we *really* ride," he said. "But keep the race-car-driver instincts in check, okay? No flashing lights in the rearview mirror tonight."

Abby moved woodenly out of the office, across the rain-swept parking lot, and into the garage. The Hellcat sat before her, looking smug, as if it had always known Abby would return.

This time, Dax took the passenger seat and not the back. Abby slid behind the wheel. The interior lights glowed bright, then dimmed down once she closed the driver's door. She felt an immediate claustrophobia when the door was shut. When she turned the engine over, the 6.2-liter engine's growl filled the garage and put a low vibration through the base of her spine. The dash lights glowed red, her mouth went dry, and her pulse trembled.

Beside her, the kid laughed. "This is a beast, isn't it?"

Abby put the garage door up and backed out. In reverse, the car only hinted at its power. Once they were outside, though, when she shifted into drive and tapped the gas, she could feel it immediately. The car seemed to leap rather than accelerate. It was always crouched back on those beautiful Pirelli tires, just begging for the chance to spin off a few layers of rubber. At low idle, the engine offered both a throaty growl and a higher, impatient tone, a whine like a beehive.

"I'll stick to the back roads," Abby said. "Then take Route One down to Old Orchard. That's the safest way."

"We're not going to Old Orchard."

Abby looked at him. He was positioned at an angle, the gun resting on his leg, finger not far from the trigger.

"I thought that was the plan," Abby said. "The pier and the house, all that."

"That's for Gerry. Something for him to chew on while I got a sense of the world through his eyes. The actual plan is a little different. We've got a few stops to make along the way. Starting with Boston. I have to determine whether our girl Tara is really the key to the lock."

Boston. I-95 in the rain. All that traffic. Some of the bees left their hive in the engine and took up buzzing residence in Abby's brain. They brought gray light with them, clouding her vision, and their stingers injected adrenaline that rode through her veins, made her heart rate quicken and her throat tighten and her fingertips tingle.

Dax studied her and said, "While you're thinking of the chessboard, Abby, you might add this to it: People who see me are likely to die. You've probably noticed that trend by now. I'll get to Tara one way or the other, but you can help pick the path."

"Okay. Back roads are still smarter, though. If anyone is aware of this car, we'll be—"

"I'm not worried about the car. I'm worried about time. Take the interstate. It's faster, and speed's going to count for us tonight. You're just the woman for the job. I need to stay on schedule, and time's wasting, so let's go a little faster."

Faster, Luke's voice agreed from somewhere behind the droning bees.

Abby pulled out of the parking lot and drove into the darkening night.

39

The day of joy has given way to a contentious night. A show-down is brewing, and Tara doesn't understand it. Two people are determined to test her memory, and each one is determined to do it alone.

Tara imagines that Dr. Pine is used to winning these battles. He is also probably not used to having them with the likes of Shannon.

Mom and Rick conceded without argument. The doctor said it was time to see what Tara remembers about her accident, and the doctor must be right. The doctor said this should happen in private, with less "external stimuli," and, again, the doctor must be right. It's his business, after all. Mom and Rick are the type of people who trust doctors.

Shannon, though, is not having it.

"I want to be the one who asks her what happened," she insists, and she waves Rick's objection off before he can gather steam. "I agree with you that there shouldn't be a crowd in the room. So it will just be me."

"We don't have family members conduct medical tests," Dr. Pine says acidly.

"Dr. Carlisle encouraged us to engage with her. She said, in fact, that in most cases of locked-in syndrome, it is a loved one who detects progress. Not a doctor."

Ding—put a point on the board for Shannon.

"My colleague is right," Dr. Pine says, "but I'm not talking about simple engagement, I'm talking about specific memory testing, and with all due respect, I am the primary—"

"This could be traumatic for her," Shannon cuts in. "I think she'd feel less trauma if she were with someone she knows. You have no idea what she's been through in life, what fears she has, what triggers. I do. If she remembers the night, she'll share it with me."

Mom tries a timid "Shannon, let the doctor—"

"No!"

Even Tara is taken aback by the fierceness of Shannon's response. She's always been tenacious, but there's something different here, a humming tension under her skin. Shannon is afraid.

But why? What scares her about leaving Tara alone with a doctor now?

"I'm simply going to have to insist—" Dr. Pine begins, but Shannon cuts him off again.

"Ask her."

"What?"

"Ask Tara. You have a patient who can communicate her own wishes, Doctor. Let's respect those."

They stare at each other like gunslingers, and then Dr. Pine takes a deep breath and says, "Very well. We should know her opinion. I can't argue with that."

He seems disappointed and also to be speaking largely to himself. As with Shannon, there's something different about Dr. Pine's demeanor, something beneath the surface, but Tara doesn't know him well enough to guess what it is.

As he reaches for the alphabet board, Shannon turns and focuses her fierce green eyes on Tara. She doesn't say a word, but she doesn't have to. Tara feels like she's nine years old again, being quizzed by a child protective services worker about Mom's drug use. Shannon would fix that stare on her, and Tara would say what Shannon had prepared her to say. Things were under control. That was Shannon's mantra. Things were always under control. Even when things were absolute chaos, Tara believed that her big sister would wrestle it all back to order.

Dr. Pine swivels his stool to face Tara, slides closer to the bed, and extends the alphabet board. He's moving distractedly, his usual focus lost. There is definitely something else on his mind. What's going on here?

"You don't need the board yet," Shannon says. "Can't we just ask her yes or no?"

A good question, and while he seems disgusted that she's right, he nods grudgingly. "I'll ask her. You can watch. There is no deceit here, Ms. Beckley."

He focuses on Tara. "Tara, are you willing to communicate your memories of the accident with me?"

She's a ghost again; she's the thing on the other side of the Ouija board being summoned into the real world. *Are you willing to communicate?* When she and Shannon were kids, they would sneak up to the attic with a Ouija board and candles and play this game, and inevitably Tara would grow scared, and Shannon would never admit that she was moving the planchette. Mostly, though, Shannon wouldn't use those moments to scare her. The planchette's messages were always positive. *Yes,* the board would say, *Mom will get better. Yes, Daddy can hear you when you talk to him at night, and he loves you. No, they will not break up this family.*

You have to believe it, Shannon would say, *because what reason would a ghost have to lie?*

Tara, now the half-ghost, has no reason to lie. She flicks her eyes up. Yes, she is willing to communicate her memories of the accident.

"Thank you," Dr. Pine says. "Now, Tara, are you willing to be alone with me when—"

"Don't phrase it like that," Shannon snaps. "Ask her if she wants me to stay."

Dr. Pine turns and regards Shannon as if he's considering new uses for his scalpel, but he submits. "Fine. Tara—do you *need* your sister present for this?"

She doesn't need Shannon present for this. Why would she? But she remembers those looks from her big sister across the years, and she remembers the messages the Ouija board carried. She'd known that Shannon was the force that moved the planchette across the board, but she never minded because that force was love. A fierce, protective love that carried Tara through the worst of her life.

She flicks her eyes up once. Yes—she needs her sister to be present for this.

Dr. Pine seems to deflate, and Shannon offers him a tight smile. When he turns away, she gives Tara a wink and a thumbs-up.

"Maybe we all stay, then," Rick says, and Dr. Pine and Shannon answer in unison, both the word and the tone:

"No."

"I think we want to limit the stimuli and the pressure," Dr. Pine says, gentler. "But we can ask Tara again if you'd like."

"I trust your judgment," Rick says, clearly more for Shannon's ears than Dr. Pine's. "We can let you do your job."

Shannon doesn't react. Mom squeezes Tara's hand as she and Rick pass by, and then it is just the three of them: Tara, Dr. Pine on his stool beside the bed, holding the alphabet board, and Shannon standing at the foot of the bed, arms folded across her chest, eyes hard on Tara's.

"Okay," Dr. Pine says. "Let's just begin with some basics, Tara. Yes-or-no questions to start. If there is any trouble with the process or if at any point you feel you wish to stop, I want you to give me three looks upward. Do you—"

He stops abruptly because Tara's thumb twitches. This time, he sees it. Shannon does too. They both stare at her hand, then at each other, and then Dr. Pine says, "Tara, can you do that again?"

Not yet, she thinks, *but soon. I'm getting closer.* Because she knows what triggered it this time, just like with the clicking of the pen—old muscle memory, a delayed response to the thumbs-up Shannon gave her. Tara wanted to return the gesture, and she just did. Or came as close as she could, at least. There's a lag, but there's something opening too, a door between brain and body cracking open, and in time she may be able to push it wider.

She flicks her eyes up twice. No, she can't do it again. She wants to say, *Keep trying me, though,* but there's no way to do that.

"Did you feel it?" Dr. Pine asks.

One flick.

Dr. Pine reaches for a notepad and jots something down. When he turns back, he's frustrated again, running a hand over his face as if to refocus. He's conflicted in some way. Why?

"Okay, back to the memory test. Yes-or-no questions to start. Tara, do you remember anything about the night of your accident?"

One flick.

"Do you remember the man in your car?"

One flick. Oltamu, the doctor from Black Lake. Yes, she remembers.

"Do you remember the moment of the accident?"

One flick.

Dr. Pine wets his lips and shifts forward. The stool slides beneath him, moving soundlessly on the tile, bringing him closer to the bed. He lifts the alphabet board, then hesitates and lowers it again. He glances at Shannon, who is motionless, still standing with folded arms. She hasn't interrupted him yet, a surprise to Tara, so surely a shock to him.

"Tara," he says, "was it an accident?"

This sets Shannon in motion. She takes a step forward, staring at him, and says, "Why would you ask that—"

He lifts a palm. "Let her answer. It's important. Tara—was it an accident?"

She's not sure. There's no way to respond *I don't know,* though. She's supposed to answer yes or no, period, but what she remembers of the night doesn't fit neatly into either of those categories. Those memories are fragments laced with unease and an unidentifiable fear. She remembers the doctor looking behind them, over and over, remembers the way he wanted her to secure the phone, remembers the sound of an engine and terror of...of *something,* no clarity here, just an overwhelming memory of her fight-or-flight response, and she'd tried to flee.

Then there was blackness. The long dark.

Tara recalls Oltamu pressing that phone into her hand, and she thinks of the engine that roared, no lights, black on black, the vehicle seeming as much a creature of the night as the wolf. A predator.

She flicks her eyes up twice. No, it was not an accident.

This is a showstopper. Dr. Pine doesn't ask another question, doesn't really respond. Shannon, who had been advancing toward him as if to physically prevent him from asking anything, is frozen in midstride, halfway around the bed, almost like Tara was halfway around the CRV before the impact—the blackness— came. She's staring down at Tara, but when she finally speaks, the question is for Dr. Pine.

"Why did you ask that?"

"Memory assessment."

"Bullshit," Shannon says.

He turns to her and the two of them gaze at each other in a silence so loaded that it seems to have texture, like an electric fence.

"What do you know?" Shannon asks. "And who told you?"

He doesn't answer. Shannon lets her gunslinger gaze linger, then pivots away, leans close to the bed, and says, "Tara, did Dr. Oltamu take pictures of you?"

"Hang on," Dr. Pine says, but Tara responds immediately, one flick. Yes, there were pictures, the strange and awkward pictures, but how in the world does her sister know this?

"You need to step back and let me do my job," Dr. Pine says, rising from his stool as if to block Tara from Shannon's line of sight. Shannon fires off another question.

"Was there something strange about Oltamu's phone? Something different?"

The camera grid. It wasn't an iPhone camera. Not a normal one, at least.

Tara gives one flick: Yes. How does Shannon know this? How is she inside of Tara's brain, moving through the dark corridors of her memories?

Dr. Pine is now attempting to physically get between them, determined to keep Shannon from making eye contact with Tara, but Shannon evades him, prowling to the other side of the bed like a cougar stalking prey.

"Tara, do you think—"

"Stop this," Dr. Pine says, nearly hissing the words. "We're not interrogating her, that's not my role or yours, and that is *not going to*—"

Shannon speaks over him. "Tara, do you think someone killed Oltamu because of that phone?"

Because of the phone? Tara has no idea. Shannon now has access to something more than Tara's memories. Shannon is capable of passing through the locked doors and joining Tara in her lonely house of memories, and she can also move outside it. Tara can't match that; she's bound to the cellar, with no idea what is happening anywhere else. But the question Shannon posed makes sense to her, though she's never considered it in such precise terms.

Because of the phone? Maybe. Yes, maybe it was all about the phone.

She gives one flick, signaling affirmation, even though she's not sure it's correct. She knows it's possible, at least, and the recognition fills her with hot anger—she is trapped in her own body, paralyzed and mute, all because of a *phone*?

Dr. Pine doesn't lose his focus on Tara even while he's trying to shut Shannon up, and he sees Tara's eyes move, understands her answer and the weight of it. He and Shannon both do. Tara's doing more than passing awareness tests now; she's describing a murder. There is a long silence, and then Dr. Pine speaks in a soft voice.

"I think it's my turn to ask who has been talking to *you*, Ms. Beckley."

"I can't tell you that," Shannon says.

"You're going to have to."

"No." Shannon shakes her head, and Tara sees the fear lurking beneath her frustration. Shannon is scared, and Shannon is never scared. Both she and Dr. Pine seem to know more than Tara, which is infuriating, and when Dr. Pine suggests to Shannon that they step into the hall to speak in private, Tara is so outraged that she wants to scream.

No sound comes—but her thumb twitches again.

I'm building a connection, she thinks. *Restoring one, at least.* That cracked-open cellar door is swinging a little wider, scraping across the damp concrete, the rusty hinges yielding, as if pushed by a re-lentless wind that is capable of rising in sudden swift gusts.

For the first time, Tara understands the source of that wind: her own willpower. Her willpower is not gone yet, and she is certain it is capable of gathering strength. She will continue to widen the crack, keep pushing until she can slip through the gap.

"You want us to stay," Shannon says to Tara, and though it isn't really a question, Tara flicks her eyes up gratefully.

Dr. Pine is reluctant, but Shannon is firm. "If we talk, we talk in front of her. She's got to be scared in so many ways, scared of things we can't even begin to understand. We can't build more silence around her."

Thank you, sis. Thank you, thank you.

The doctor sighs, rubs his eyes, then nods once and sits heavily on the stool.

"I don't know much," he says. "That's the truth. I have been warned that Tara might have been a witness to something more than an accident. That's all." He looks up at Shannon. "You know it too."

She nods.

"Who told you?" he asks.

Hesitation. Shannon doesn't want to give up her source. She looks at Tara, considering, and Dr. Pine apparently takes her silence as a refusal to cooperate, because he gives up.

"You don't need to tell me," he says. "I probably don't even want to know."

"She's in danger," Shannon says, her voice scarcely more than a whisper. "I have been told that she is in danger. I don't know how to help her. Who to call."

"I can help you with that," Dr. Pine says.

"How?"

He leans forward, elbows on his knees, and studies Tara. When he speaks, his eyes are on her, not Shannon.

"There is an investigator with the Department of Energy who will be very interested to know that Tara has memories of the night. All of this talk about the phone and the pictures—I know nothing about that. But you're going to need someone to trust. Tara, I'm asking you this, doctor to patient—do you want to meet with the investigator?"

Department of Energy? This shouldn't make sense, and yet it touches off a faint chord of familiarity, something that Tara has either forgotten or never really paid attention to, something that once seemed trivial and was quickly shuffled off into the mists of memory.

Tara flicks her eyes up once: Yes, let's meet the investigator.

Dr. Pine says, "Okay." Then, turning to Shannon, he repeats, this time as a question, "Okay?"

Shannon looks from Tara to the doctor and nods, then stops and grabs his arm as he starts to rise.

"Hang on. What does he look like?"

"What?"

"The investigator. How old is he?"

Dr. Pine stares at her, bewildered. "The investigator is a woman. And she is probably around forty."

Shannon releases his arm, but he looks at her with narrowed eyes. "Would you like to be more candid about who's spoken to you?"

Shannon considers. "Is your response going to be any different if we talk about that now? Or are you going to make the same call?"

He acknowledges the point with a slight nod. "I'll make the call," he says. "So I might as well do it sooner than later."

When Shannon doesn't object, he leaves the room, closing the door behind him with a soft click. He forgets to take his alphabet board. Shannon looks at it, then looks at Tara, an unspoken question in her eyes.

Tara flicks her eyes up once.

Yes. Let's chat.

40

The clouds that had begun massing along the coast during the day swept in off the North Atlantic and collided with a warm front as darkness fell, and then the night was illuminated with flickering tongues of lightning as the pressure systems fought for dominance.

Abby drove southbound on I-95, trapped between and beneath the battling weather fronts. Thunder cracked and boomed and rolled to the west, and from the east, the winds continued to buffet the car.

She didn't notice the impact of the wind as much as she had before, though, when she was sitting up high in the Tahoe. She was low now, riding close to the pavement, only a few inches of steel separating her from the asphalt that was buzzing by at seventy-five miles per hour. She had the Challenger in cruise control so she could ignore the speed and focus on keeping her breathing and heart rate steady. She was grateful for the darkness, for the shrinking of the horizon, the tightening of the world.

The lightning, though, was a problem.

With each flash, the highway lit up bold and bright. With each flash, cars that were nothing but taillights in the darkness were suddenly given shape. With each flash, her breathing became harder to control.

The lightning was worse than a high sun and a clear sky. When the road came at her in flashes, unpredictable and unexpected, suddenly she couldn't work saliva into her mouth; her heart was thundering, and the breathing exercises weren't doing a damn thing. Her head felt high and light and dizzy. *Just concentrate on the tires and feel the road,* she told herself, but then a brilliant flash of lightning would paint the road white, the world would shudder with thunder, and dizziness drove through her brain and into her spine.

She was sweating, cool beads on a hot forehead, her shirt clinging damply to her back. Dax watched with curiosity but in silence. As Abby's sweating grew more noticeable and her breathing more ragged, Abby was sure he would speak, but then two things happened nearly at once: The rain began to fall in torrents, clattering off the windshield as loud as coins on a winning slot-machine pull, and the kid's phone gave a shrill chirp. Not a ring, an alert tone.

Abby had no interest in the phone. She was tunnel-vision-focused on the road, hands tight on the wheel—too tight; like an amateur, not a pro—her head forward, her hand shaking as she set the wipers to high. Even at that rate, they didn't seem to achieve much, merely adding a slashing motion across her field of vision, which was already graying out at the edges. The Pirellis held the road, but she was certain that they couldn't continue to, not in this weather. There was too much torque to the Hellcat. If she made a mistake, she'd start to skid.

But that was fine, she told herself, because she could steer out of a skid, she'd done it successfully thousands of times before.

Not always.

You just turned into it, that was all, the only requirement—turn back into it. Counterintuitive, but it worked. You regained equilibrium if you could only teach yourself to go against instinct and trust the physics. The world rewarded you for trusting physics. In time, that trust became instinct.

You'll get that instinct back. You'll get it back, and tonight's a good run, a good trial, because there's nothing to worry about out here, it's just a little rain, that's all.

As if to contradict her, the sheet lightning flashed, revealing what waited ahead—two semis, one in the left lane on its way around the slower-moving one in the right lane, passing even in this weather. There was a truck coming up behind Abby, too, one that looked to be loaded with logs from the north woods. Damn it, damn it, damn it. Why so much traffic? Why couldn't everyone get off the road and home to bed and let Abby drive to Boston with a murderer in peace?

Dax's face was lit by the display of his phone, his attention pulled away from Abby, responding to whatever that chirp had signified. Suddenly, voices filled the car.

It took Abby a moment to recognize Shannon Beckley's voice. There were several in the mix, male and female, but hers rang a clarion note that the others lacked. Shannon was asking about methods for her sister to communicate easier and faster.

Abby chanced a look in the kid's direction. He lifted his eyes immediately. He seemed preternaturally aware of Abby's movements. The gun was in his left hand, on his lap, pointed at Abby. It was always pointed at Abby.

"Checking on our girl's progress," he said cheerfully. "Sounds like it was a big day, and you and I have had our share of distractions, haven't we? I'll need to get caught up."

Shannon Beckley's voice faded, others overtaking it, but they were all discussing the same thing—Tara was awake. Tara could talk.

He bugged the hospital, Abby thought. The realization was almost enough to pull her attention away from the dizzying, sweat-inducing fear of the drive.

Almost.

It didn't last, though, because she had a car on her left now, neither trying to pass nor, evidently, aware that passing was the point in the left lane. Instead, the car just rode alongside, penning her in. She looked over and swore under her breath.

"Everything all right, Abby?"

Abby didn't answer. She accelerated, thinking that she'd pass on the right and get out in front and then maybe this moron would get the idea and shift back into the right lane. As long as she kept some clear space, some avenue of escape, she would be fine. All the way to Boston, she'd be fine.

But these idiots, calm behind their steering wheels, were sealing her in.

As she accelerated, the semi in front slowed and flashed its headlights, signaling that the truck trying to pass was clear to shift back into the right lane. The truck driver in the left lane, like the driver of the car next to Abby, didn't take the opportunity or the hint. Maybe it was the weather, this pounding rain, scaring them both off from making the simple lane shift. Maybe they were distracted. Maybe they were morons who never should have been issued driver's licenses.

None of that mattered. She was trapped.

She took a harsh breath and sat up straight, then leaned forward quickly, hunching over as if caught by a stomach cramp, because she was suddenly sure that she couldn't get air into her lungs. Or her brain. Her blood was oxygen-free, thickening and slowing, her heart thundering to try to make up for it but pushing nothing but sludge through her veins. Her vision dimmed and then came back and then went again.

The kid said, "Abby," in a warning voice, but it barely penetrated the fog.

Going to crash. I am going to crash and I'm going to take one of these poor people out with me, because there is nowhere to go, when I black out I am going to hit them or they are going to hit me and then we'll be skidding together through the night on the wet road, glass breaking and blood flowing and screams, someone will be screaming, but there is nothing I can do to stop it, because there is no…

She saw the gap in the guardrail of the median just ahead. It looked freshly cut, probably the result of an accident, some other night when they'd pulled dead bodies out of mangled cars. It was small, a narrow opening, not meant for access, but...

"He left the road at ninety, that's all there is to say," her father sang.

Faster, Luke said.

Abby pounded the accelerator; the Hellcat roared and the Pirellis spun, hunting for traction, then caught and hammered the car forward. As she shifted in front of the car on her left side, a horn blew, piercingly loud, but by then Abby was out in front and angling farther left, the guardrail looming, the gap in it no more than fifteen feet long, maybe just ten, an almost impossibly narrow target to slip through at this speed and in this rain...

She made it without creasing either side of the car. Shot the gap and pounded the brakes and brought the car to a fishtailing stop in the grassy median between northbound and southbound lanes, plowing a furrow of damp sod beneath the tires.

She fell back against the seat, gasping and half smiling, almost oblivious to the horns and the rain, aware of nothing but the victory of having gotten off the road without harming anyone.

Safe, she thought, and only then did she realize the muzzle of the gun was pressed against the side of her head.

"What are you doing?" Dax said.

"I need to breathe."

"What?"

"I just need to—"

"If you get the cops called, a lot of people are dying tonight. You'll be the first but not the last. You better back this thing up and get moving right now or I promise, Abby, you're going to—"

"I just need to breathe!" Abby screamed.

The kid pulled the gun away and stared at her. Abby shoved the gearshift into park and leaned her head back against the seat and sucked in air as sweat trickled down her face in cool rivulets. The sweat was good; the cooling was good; everything needed to cool down, it had gotten too hot in here, it had gotten dangerously hot and—

Faster. Faster! Slow down. Slow down!

It had almost gone very badly.

"You're freaking out," Dax said. "What's going on? Scared of the gun, Abby? You've done so well with it. I can't put it away. I don't think we have the necessary trust for that."

Abby didn't answer. Just closed her eyes and concentrated on that slow, sweet cooling. Tried to listen to the rain, hoping it would drown out Luke's voice. *Faster,* Luke said, then *Slow down!* he screamed.

Shut up, Abby thought. *Please, baby, just shut up for one night so I can do this thing. So I can see morning. Then come back and talk all you want and I'll listen forever, no matter how miserable it is, but for this one night, just please…be quiet. Let me drive.*

"So *this* is why Abby Kaplan came back to Maine," Dax said. "You're not hiding from media. You really can't do it anymore, can you? You lost the nerve."

Abby still didn't speak.

"What a sorry shame," Dax said. "End of a good run for you, wasn't it? But that's of no interest to me. And the longer we sit here, the more likely it is that a cop joins us." He shifted around in the darkness and leaned forward and suddenly Abby's hands, which were still on the steering wheel, were bound tight and zipped together by a plastic cord that bit into her skin.

"Get out and trade seats with me. Do it quick and do it calm, or I will shoot. There is no more patience."

Abby fumbled with the door handle, struggling with her bound wrists, then stepped out into the pouring rain. She didn't mind it. The rain was cold, and the rain was clean.

The kid pushed open the passenger door, then slid across into the driver's seat, and he lifted the gun and pointed it at Abby's face as she stood there in the downpour.

"Your choice," he said. "Die there and leave the sweet Beckley sisters to me, or get back in and ride. Good news—you don't have to drive anymore, Anxious Abby."

I got one thousand dollars, Hank Bauer had said on a humid July night at a New Hampshire speedway, *that says that little girl kicks all their asses and wins this thing.*

Abby was fifteen years old and couldn't drive legally on a highway, but she won that night on the track. Hank gave her half the money, and they'd piled into his truck with her father and driven into the night with the windows down and Green Day loud on the radio, and Abby's future was firm.

The world was hers that night, and she understood that all she needed was four good tires to take it.

She looked up the highway now, through the rain and into the blur of oncoming headlights, and then she walked around the car, past those beautiful Pirellis, and toward the passenger seat. The door was open, waiting, rain streaming down the interior panel. Lightning strobed, illuminating the car, and Abby saw the kid's cell phone. It was on the floor mat on the passenger side. He'd dropped it, maybe when he'd slid into the driver's seat or maybe when Abby had shot the gap into the median.

And I made the gap too. Not all bad. It was reaction, not strategy, but I still made it.

"Get in," Dax said, and he cocked the revolver.

Chill rain streamed down Abby's spine in ribbons. She stood there for just a second longer, just enough to make sure that the kid's focus was on her face. Then she made a show of tumbling awkwardly into the passenger seat and fell forward, almost across the gearshift, as she landed.

Dax's attention stayed on her. He did not follow the motion of Abby's right foot, did not see her lower her shoe onto the phone and slide it backward, did not hear it clatter up and over the door frame and out into the rain.

"Get off me!" he snapped.

Abby leaned back, said, "Sorry," then turned her bound wrists toward the door, grasped the handle, and slammed it shut. She moved quickly, but she got a last glimpse of the phone sitting there in the rain.

Did it matter? Probably not. For a moment, though, Abby had taken one thing from him. He wouldn't be able to play Shannon Beckley's voice for a little while. It wasn't much—wasn't anything, maybe—but it felt like a victory. She'd taken something from him.

And I made the gap. Thought I couldn't do it, thought we were going to die in the rain, maybe die with other people too, innocent strangers, all of us burning in the rain because I couldn't hold myself together. But that didn't happen. I saw the gap, and I took it.

I fucking took it.

The kid leaned toward her, shoved the muzzle of the revolver under her chin, and forced her head up. His face was shadowed by the black baseball cap, but you could still see the smile.

"Pretty-boy Luke London did a real number on you, didn't he?"

Abby went for him then. She lunged forward, trying to snap her forehead off the kid's nose, not fearing the gun any longer, scarcely aware of it.

When he hit her behind the ear with the barrel, Abby sagged and her vision went black, but she could still hear the rain.

Then he hit her again, and this time the sound of the rain went away too.

4 1

Thirty thousand feet in the sky, Boone sat in the bulkhead seat and turned her phone over and over in her hands, compulsively.

Check signal. Nothing. Of course nothing. Even cheating on airplane mode wouldn't help at this altitude.

She turned the phone, turned it, turned it…and checked again. No signal.

She was on Wi-Fi, but it wouldn't let calls through.

Land this bitch already. The thought rose with such intensity that she almost shouted it aloud. Containing frustration was always a struggle for her. Once more, she was passive, Detroit all over again, sitting at the gate and waiting, waiting, waiting. Back then, unknown to her, Amandi Oltamu was already dead, and Boone had been reduced to waiting, clueless.

Tara Beckley wasn't dead, though. She was coming back. But did she know a single thing that might help?

Boone's phone vibrated, and for a glorious second, she was sure that the signal had somehow pierced the clouds.

Wrong. It was just an e-mail slipping through on the wireless network. She knew that it wouldn't matter, but she checked it anyhow, needing something to fill her time. When she saw the sender, she caught her breath.

It was Pine.

I have been trying to call for the past twenty minutes. Your phone goes straight to voice mail. I am assuming and hoping this is because you are in the air and en route. Tara is not only alert, but she has memories of the night. Specific and clear memories. There is also a difficulty with her sister, who appears to have been contacted by someone other than you, someone with knowledge of the danger in this situation. Knowledge that I don't have. She has lots of questions about Dr. Oltamu's phone. She seemed unsurprised to learn of your agency's interest, but she will not tell me why or who has provided her with whatever information she has. It is imperative that we have guidance on this situation. I am going to give you a little time, but then I feel it's essential to contact local authorities.

Boone nearly jammed a thumb in her hurry to respond.

Keep her safe, keep her quiet, I am inbound, almost there.

She hit Send, leaned back in the seat, and stared out the window. Lightning flashed below them, entombed in the clouds, giving an otherworldly quality to the night sky.

Shannon Beckley had lots of questions about Oltamu's phone? Why? If Tara Beckley remembered the phone, that was one thing. But her sister? Who had been in contact with her sister? And if someone had told her sister so much about the situation that she understood things at the level Pine seemed to suspect, then there was a much bigger question: How was she still alive?

The intercom gave a burst of static, and Boone let out a relieved breath, anticipating the message—they were beginning their descent into Boston's Logan Airport, please fasten seat belts and prepare for landing.

"Ladies and gentlemen, you might have noticed the lightning outside your windows," the pilot began, and Boone tensed.

No, no, do not tell me we are being delayed or diverted, not tonight…

"What you're seeing," the pilot continued, "is part of a series of supercell thunderstorms that are moving north-northeast at the moment, and they're delaying operations at Boston Logan until that weather clears."

"No!" Boone said aloud, drawing stares from the flight attendants in front of her. She shook her head, closed her eyes, and clamped her molars together as the pilot kept babbling.

"We're going to be in a holding pattern for just a bit, hopefully not more than fifteen to twenty minutes," he said. "I'll let you know as soon as we get word from the folks at Logan that we are cleared for descent. We don't expect it to be a long wait, so just sit back, relax, and enjoy. The good news is that all the turbulence is below us, and the storm seems to be moving fast."

42

Blue.

Not *I*. Not *J*. Yes, *K*. One flick.

Tara is exhausted, but Shannon is pressing, and Tara won't quit on her. She's answered every question Shannon has thrown at her so far, and she's surprised at how the task is sharpening her memory, bringing images back with clarity and vividness. The growing paranoia she'd felt with Oltamu has more precision now, and she remembers a specific question he'd asked, about whether everyone took the same route from dinner to the auditorium. She'd thought he was worried about being on time, but a man worried about his destination didn't keep looking over his shoulder. He was worried about what was behind him, which meant that the place he'd come from might matter, and she remembers this name and is trying to spell it out, quite literally, for Shannon.

Red? No. Two flicks.

"Yellow?" Shannon asks, and then interrupts herself, a feat only Shannon could achieve. "Hang on, we don't need to waste your time. It's *E*, isn't it? It's Black Lake?"

Tara gives one relieved upward flick of the eyes. *You win Double Jeopardy!* Tara thinks, and she wants to laugh hysterically. She's never been so tired in her life. All she's doing is moving her eyes, and yet it drains her more than any marathon ever has.

"He came from Black Lake," Shannon repeats, and now she has her phone out, tapping into it, probably searching for the town. "Black Lake, New York? Or there's...a ghost town in Idaho. I hope he didn't come from there. Was it New York?"

Tara doesn't know, so she doesn't move her eyes. Shannon waits, then says, "Do you even know where it was?"

Two fatigued flicks.

"Okay." Shannon lowers the phone. "Did he take any other pictures?"

One flick.

"Of you?"

Two flicks.

"Someone else."

Tara hesitates, then looks upward.

"We're going to have to spell, aren't we?"

One flick.

And so they spell.

Yellow—*H*. Green—*O*. Red—*B*.

"Hobbs?" Shannon guesses.

Two flicks, more angry than exhausted now; just let her finish.

"Red?"

No. Finally, they get there. Green—*O*.

"Hobo?" Shannon says, voice heavy with disbelief. "He took pictures of a hobo?"

She looks at Tara as if she's crazy, as if this is the first clear misfiring of memory, and Tara wants nothing more than the power to reach out and strangle her. Her thumb twitches against her palm, but Shannon doesn't notice, because Shannon is watching only her eyes. This is the only window out. For now. Tara has to stay calm, stay patient, and keep working at it. It's 1804 London Street all over again—Tara trapped inside, Shannon waiting to rescue her from the outside, and the two of them working to widen the gap in the steel doors that separate them.

"A hobo," Shannon says, taking a breath. "Can you explain more than that?"

One flick.

"Spell it. Red line?"

One flick.

"A?"

Thank goodness, yes, it's finally the first column and first letter. *A* is a common letter, isn't it? How in the hell is Tara never drawing an *A* in this thing? She's got two of them in her own damned name!

"Red line?" Shannon asks, and again, this is a yes, but Tara has to go all the way to the end of the row now to get to *end of word,* and halfway through she realizes that she didn't need the stupid *A* anyhow—stick to nouns and verbs, damn it!

So over they begin, but good news—it's red again! Not *A,* not *B,* not *C,* but *D, D* for *Damn it, I want my voice back.*

Green—*O.* Yellow—*G.* Thankfully, Shannon doesn't make her indicate *end of word* again, but guesses. "A dog? That's not what you mean. Tell me that's not what you mean?"

If I could kick you, Tara thinks, *you'd have bruises for weeks. What in the hell am I supposed to do with that phrasing? "A dog? That's not what you mean. Tell me that's not what you mean?" How do you answer that with a yes or a no?*

So she doesn't answer. She waits. She's swell at waiting. She's becoming the best there ever was in the game of waiting, a natural, a pure talent.

Shannon gathers herself, finally understanding that her typical flurry of speech is not the way to go about this, and says, "Did Oltamu really take pictures of a dog named Hobo?"

She says it in the tone of voice in which you might ask someone to tell you the details of her alien abduction. Tara gives her one flick of the eyes, a flick with *attitude.*

Yes, it was a dog named Hobo, and kiss my sweet ass if you think I'm crazy.

Shannon sets the alphabet board down flat on her lap and stares at Tara as if she can't decide what to ask next. Tara wants to hold her arms up in a giant *V* for victory. She has achieved the impossible—not in coming back from a coma, not even in proving she's awake despite being paralyzed. This is a truly heroic feat: she has rendered Shannon Beckley speechless.

"You're serious. Do you think the dog matters, or am I going on a wild…" She stops herself, holds a hand up, and walks her words back. Communication with Tara favors the short-winded, which doesn't play to Shannon's strengths.

"Do you think it matters that he took pictures of a dog?"

Tara doesn't know, so she doesn't answer.

"You're not sure?" Shannon says, beginning to understand what a blank stare means.

One flick.

"Did he take any other pictures after the dog?"

Two flicks.

"Did he tell you anything about the phone?"

Tara wishes she could think of a way to communicate the odd camera and its unique grid, but she can't. Or she doesn't think she can, at least, but then Shannon does what only a sister could possibly do: she seems to slip inside Tara's mind.

"Was it a real phone?"

Two flicks.

Dr. Pine enters almost soundlessly.

"Can't you *knock*?" Shannon snaps, startled.

He takes a step forward, brow furrowed, hands clasped behind his back, as if he would have been content to remain a spectator.

"Pictures of a dog?" he says.

"That's none of your business," Shannon says. Still not trusting him. Tara understands this but she disagrees with it. Shannon hasn't trusted many people in her life, having been burned too many times, but for all of Shannon's force of personality and will, she doesn't have the most intuitive reads on people. Extroverts are too busy projecting their opinions and personalities to intuit anything submerged about anyone in their audience, in Tara's opinion. Tara, the introvert—and has there ever been a more undeniable introvert than the current model of Tara Beckley? She's the literal embodiment of the concept now. She does not see herself as superior to her sister in most ways, but she is more intuitive. Tara doesn't distrust Dr. Pine. The very tics that make Shannon nervous are the reasons Tara trusts him. He's genuinely concerned about her, and he's genuinely concerned about his ethical dilemma in this situation.

"Where's your investigator?" Shannon asks.

"En route. I couldn't speak to her, but she e-mailed from the plane. She'll be landing soon and coming directly here." He pauses. "Would you like to wait until she is here before you tell me what you've been asking Tara?"

"Yes."

"Fair enough." He paces, hands still behind his back. Outside the window, lightning strobes in dark clouds, and the wind throws raindrops at the glass like handfuls of pebbles.

"Your parents have gone to the hotel to take a short rest," he says. "I didn't object. If you wish to bring them back, though…"

"No," Shannon says, firm, and Dr. Pine seems unsurprised. He looks at Tara, and this time she answers without needing to hear the question voiced. Two flicks: no, he does not need to summon her parents. Mom is an exhausted mess, and Rick will battle with Shannon. Tara needs to save her energy for the Department of Energy—*ha! Why can't anyone hear these jokes?*—and whatever information this mysterious investigator will have. Tara wants to hear answers, and that will mean providing answers, a task that she now knows is utterly exhausting.

"You could call the local police," Dr. Pine suggests. "But you haven't done that yet. Why not?"

Shannon looks like she doesn't want to answer, but she says, "I'm not sure. I guess because I haven't had time to figure out what I would even tell them. And I've been instructed…I've been warned about trusting the wrong people."

"Warned by whom?" Pine asks gently.

Shannon shakes her head and gives a little laugh. Dr. Pine seems to read it as frustration, but it's more than that—Shannon is unsure of herself. Tara knows. Tara is just as curious as Dr. Pine, though. Where is Shannon's information coming from?

"Who have you told about the Department of Energy investigator?" Shannon asks Dr. Pine.

"Just you."

"Really?" Those dubious Doberman eyes fixed on him.

"Really."

Shannon takes a breath and leans back. "All this for a phone," she says softly. "What in the hell was on that phone?"

Even if they were using the alphabet board, Tara would have no answer for this one.

Outside, lightning strobes again, but it is dimmer, distant. The storm is clearing. Tara hopes she can take some confidence from the symbol, but she doesn't believe that. There are too many things she doesn't know, and most of them are happening outside of these walls.

43

Abby fumbled for her harness. She'd been knocked out, but her helmet was still on, and she was upright, trapped in the seat. That meant she needed to release the harness, but where was the pit crew? She needed them. Needed help.

Something wrong with her arm too. Broken, probably, and it felt like her hands were smashed together. Why couldn't she separate them?

She opened her eyes and stared at her hands as if they were unfamiliar, and only when a lightning flash lit the yellow cord that bound her wrists together did she remember where she was and that there was nobody in the pit coming for her.

But she was too upright, just like if she'd been harnessed into the seat. Why was that?

A cord was around her neck, too, that was why. She was bound against the headrest, the cord just slack enough to let her breathe but not to let her slump sideways or forward. The kid had positioned her well. He'd also put his black baseball cap on Abby's head, pulled low, shading her face. That was what Abby had confused for the helmet. To any passerby who glanced in the car, she was just a woman in a baseball cap, dozing in the dark.

Dax Blackwell looked over. "Morning, Abby."

When Abby turned, the cord chiseled across her throat. She winced, then refocused.

It was the first time she'd ever seen the kid without the baseball cap, and even in the dark, his hair was a startlingly bright blond. It was cropped close to his skull, moon-white and luminescent in the glow from the dash lights.

"Nice touch with the hat," Abby said. Her voice came out in a dry croak.

"I thought it would help. You had a little blood in your hair. Sorry about that."

The road rolled beneath them, the lights of Boston up ahead. They were still on I-95, cruising by the northern suburbs. The hospital wasn't far away.

"You're lucky you're necessary," the kid said. "I'd have very much enjoyed killing you back there, but…priorities. Nice trick with the phone too. I almost missed it."

He took one hand off the wheel and held the phone up.

Abby tried not to show her defeat. It had been the only win, the only thing she could take from the evil prick.

"Interesting developments in Tara's room," the kid said. "Investigator en route, it seems. Department of Energy, no less. Do you understand that?"

"No." Speaking made Abby's skull ache. She closed her eyes and waited out the pain.

"You've done some research on our friend Amandi Oltamu," the kid said. "Where is Black Lake? Seemed to confuse Shannon, and I don't know anything about it either."

"I don't know."

"Tara thinks Oltamu came from Black Lake, but my information said he came from Ohio. There's no Black Lake in—"

"Yes, there is." Abby's eyes opened. Suddenly she understood Oltamu. Something about him, at least. And why the Department of Energy would be interested in him.

"Siri disagrees with you," Dax said. "Surely you don't mean to tell me Siri is confused? She's a voice of reason in a mad world."

"Black Lake is not a town. Or even a lake."

The kid looked at her, interested now. "What is it?"

Abby stared straight ahead, watching taillights pull away. Dax was keeping the Challenger pinned at the speed limit, refusing to tempt police.

"It's the nickname for a place where they run cars through performance and safety tests," she said. "It's fifty acres of blacktop, and from the sky it looks like dark water—that's where the nickname comes from. You can ask a car to do anything in that space. A high-end car, tuned right, can be a lot of fun out there."

It could also be instructional, of course. The Black Lake was all about pushing limits. Sometimes you exceeded them. That was the nature of testing limits, of playing games on the edge of the deep end of the pool. Sooner or later, you slipped into it.

"Oltamu wasn't in the car business," Dax said, and Abby didn't argue, but she believed Oltamu might very well have been in the car business. He was the battery man—and every automaker on the planet was working on electric vehicles now. But if Tara was right, and Oltamu had just come from Black Lake in East Liberty, Ohio, then he'd been watching performance tests. You didn't go to the Black Lake to test a battery-charging station. You went to the Black Lake to push a car to its performance limits—or beyond.

Dax shifted lanes. Despite the late hour and the storm, traffic was thick. Welcome to Boston. Traffic was always thick.

"We've had to reroute, and I've been tempted to drive faster, but if I got pulled over, I'd have a hard time explaining you, wouldn't I?" He laughed, a sound of boyish delight. "It's a waste of the car, though."

He put on the turn signal and then shifted again, gliding left to right in a move that would attract no attention, and yet Abby could feel that he was still learning the throttle of the Hellcat, the bracing amount of torque that even a light touch on the accelerator brought. It was a waste of the car with him behind the wheel. He had no idea how to handle it, how far it could be pushed. Or how quickly control could be lost.

I made that gap in the guardrail, Abby thought dully. *That was one hell of a move. Splitting traffic with the angle and acceleration perfect, then the hard brake and turn without misjudging the tires and rolling, putting it through a gap most people couldn't hit at forty, let alone ninety, and doing it all on wet pavement…dumb, yes, and a product of panic, but…not easy to do.*

Strange and sad, how that still pleased her. It was nothing to be proud of—she'd been melting down, her nerves no longer merely fraying but collapsing like downed power lines, sparking flashes of failure.

But it was also the first time she'd taken anything remotely resembling a test of the old instinct, the old muscle memory.

The old Abby.

For a moment, the woman she'd been had surfaced again. For a moment, she'd seen nothing but that narrow target, had anticipated the speed of the cars crowding in, felt the tires exploring the pavement in a way that was as intimate as skin on skin. She'd executed the intended maneuver perfectly and in circumstances where inches and fractions of seconds mattered.

There weren't many people alive who could have pulled that off without causing a deadly pileup, and she'd landed without even scratching the paint.

And now you're riding shotgun with a killer, tied to the seat, and you didn't even succeed in taking his phone from him. Some victory, Abby.

Victories, though, like phobias, weren't always rational. Sometimes they were very internal, invisible to the outside world. Matters of willpower or control were still wins. The short-term impact didn't matter nearly as much as the fact that you'd held on in the face of adversity. A win was a win, as they said. No matter how small, no matter how private.

She watched the traffic thicken as Dax rolled southeast, and she wondered how she'd feel with the wheel in her hands again. The same old panic? Or would it be diminished by the knowledge that when things went to hell, she'd maintained enough of her old brain and body to execute the escape maneuver? Tough to call it an escape maneuver when there'd been no real external threat, nothing except the irrational dread that soaked her brain like chloroform, but the brain didn't operate strictly on facts; its fuel was emotion.

This much, Abby understood very well.

The exit for the hospital was fast approaching, maybe five miles away. She wondered what the kid's plan was and if he had any concern, any fear. He projected nothing but confidence. He was to killing what Abby had once been to driving—a natural pairing, in total harmony with his craft.

But killing Tara Beckley wasn't his goal. Not tonight, at least. He had to get Oltamu's phone to her, and she would need to be alive for that. How he intended to walk through a hospital and achieve this without attracting attention, Abby couldn't imagine.

She figured she'd be a part of it, though. There was a reason she was still alive, and it wasn't his compassion.

Dax shifted right again, decelerated, and exited. Abby didn't follow this choice; if time was now an issue, then he shouldn't abandon the interstate this far north. Then they were moving into a residential stretch, high-dollar homes on tree-lined streets. Driving farther from the hospital.

The kid pulled into a parking space on the street, tucking in behind a behemoth Lincoln Navigator, and studied the road. His eyes were on the houses, not the cars, but then he paused and checked the mirrors as well. Satisfied by whatever he saw or didn't see, he killed the engine.

"Time to start earning your keep," he said, turning to Abby. The boyish features seemed to fade, and his hard eyes dominated his face, eyes that belonged to a much older man.

"What are we doing?"

"You'll be sitting right there. But you'll be watching too." He picked up his phone from the console, tapped the screen, and then set it back down. The screen displayed a live video image of the interior of the car. Abby twisted her head, searching for the camera, the cord rubbing into her throat. She didn't see a camera, but when she looked back, she realized the video was in motion. When she stopped, it stopped.

Dax smiled. "I'll need my hat back," he said.

He took the hat off Abby's head, and the video display followed the jostling motion. He settled it back on his own head, then turned to Abby, and Abby's face appeared on the cell phone display, a clear, high-definition image. She saw there was dried blood crusted in her blond hair from where he'd hit her with the gun.

"I need to confess something," the kid said. His voice seemed to echo, but it was really coming from the phone's speaker. "Covert audio recording is illegal here in Massachusetts. This is a two-party-consent state."

He sighed, and the sigh echoed on the phone like a distant gust of wind.

"I've had to make my peace with that," he said, "because my uncle was a big fan of recording things. Knowledge is power, right? The more eyes and ears one has, the more one knows. I think my uncle would've liked this hat. I never got the chance to show it to him, but…" He shrugged. "I'm confident of his opinion."

He moved his hand to the ignition and started the engine again.

"You're about to meet the man who's responsible for the unfortunate trouble Hank Bauer encountered," Dax said, pulling away from the curb.

"You killed him," Abby said. "I don't care who paid you."

"Sure you do."

At an intersection, they paused at a stop sign, then they continued along the dark street and pulled into a driveway that was flanked by ornate brick pillars, a gate between them. Dax put the window down, punched four buttons on a keypad mounted in one pillar, and the gates parted. He drove through. The gates closed behind them and locked with a pneumatic hiss followed by a clang.

He pulled down the drive, parked, and cut the engine.

"Just sit tight," he said. "I know it's uncomfortable, but at least you'll have a view."

With that, he stepped out of the car, slammed the driver's door, and locked the car with the key fob, engaging the alarm. If Abby tried to smash the window, it was going to be loud, and the kid would have plenty of time to get outside. There was a slim chance that a neighbor might come to investigate, but probably not. Car alarms were viewed as nuisances, not cries for help. Unless Abby freed herself from the passenger seat, she wasn't going to achieve anything by breaking a window.

Dax walked around the back of the house and disappeared from sight. Abby's eyes went to the cell phone, and now she could see from Dax's point of view: a light came on in the back of the house. Dax went to knock, but the door opened before he could make contact, and a short, wiry man with graying hair and a nose crooked from a bad break stood in front of him, gun in hand.

For an instant, Abby thought this could be good news—she didn't care who this guy was; anyone who shot the kid was on her team.

But the man didn't shoot. He lowered the gun and said, "What in the fuck do you think you're doing?"

"My job," Dax said. If he was in any way troubled by the gun, he didn't show it.

"Your job? You don't come to my fucking home unless I tell you to! That's not your—"

Something moved at the edge of the frame and then came into the center. Dax was holding up Oltamu's phone. "This was my job, Gerry."

The man stared at the phone. He leaned forward, then pulled back, suspicious and confused.

"How'd you get it? Kaplan said—"

"Kaplan's trying to bluff her way back to life," Dax said. "Let me in. I don't want to stand outside and talk about this shit."

Gerry hesitated, then nodded, and stepped aside. Abby followed the bouncing path of the camera as the kid walked through a sunroom with a marble fireplace, opened another door, and stepped into a kitchen that was filled with expanses of white cabinets and stainless-steel appliances.

"You alone?" Dax asked.

"Yeah. And remember, the questions are—"

"The questions are yours to ask, right. I didn't think that one could do much harm."

Gerry paced back into the frame. His body language was tense, like a fighter's before the bell. The kid worked for him, but he didn't seem to have his employer's trust.

Maybe that was because Gerry had just arranged to kill him.

"How in the hell did you get that?" he asked.

"Kaplan's been bullshitting you the whole time. She never had it. The salvage-yard guy gave it to his brother. It was in his pawnshop. I bought it for ninety bucks. I assume I'll be reimbursed?"

"Let me see it."

Dax passed it over. Gerry set his gun down on the counter to study the phone.

Unwise, Abby thought, watching in the car. She was captivated by the scene playing out on the phone's screen, but it was time to worry about more important things—she was *literally* captive within the car, and that wasn't going to change unless she could free her neck.

She reached for the cord with her clumsy, bound hands. There was just barely enough room between skin and cord to get a grasp, and when she did, the cord had no give. She leaned forward, straining painfully, and twisted until she got her hands over her shoulder. It was an awkward movement that put pressure on her rotator cuff as well as her throat, but she was able to feel the way the cord had been looped around the headrest and knotted. The knot was a pro's work; Abby wasn't going to be able to untie it from this angle, working blind and unable to separate her hands.

There was, however, another option. She was tied to the headrest, which was a perfectly effective approach when the headrest was in place, but the headrest could be removed. It would be awkward, and it would be painful, but if she could lift the headrest out, the cord would slide off it.

She arched her back, wincing at the pain, stretched her shoulders until the tendons howled in protest, and began to hunt for the headrest release with her fingers.

44

W hen he'd seen the kid arrive at his back door—his *back* door, he didn't even walk up the front steps like a normal human—Gerry was tempted to shoot him. It had been years since he'd killed anyone, but he intended to do it in the next twelve hours regardless, and the sight of Dax seemed to portend trouble. Gerry didn't want to kill him on his own property and in a quiet neighborhood with an unsilenced weapon unless it was necessary, though.

Then he saw the phone, and killing Dax Blackwell became less of a concern. The phone was the whole point, and somehow the kid already had it.

Standing in his kitchen, Gerry was no longer thinking about the arrangements he'd made in Old Orchard or the suppressed hand-gun that was under his driver's seat, the one that already had a bullet chambered for Dax. The phone had all his attention.

It was the right phone—no signal, a clone, and with a lock screen featuring a picture of the girl. Everything about this was good news except for the last.

"How do you unlock it?" Gerry said.

"Either with facial recognition or a code name." Dax leaned laconically against the counter. "But does it matter?"

"Of course it matters!"

"Why?"

Gerry lifted his head and stared at the kid. He was standing there in the shadows, slouching and wearing his hoodie and the dumb friggin' baseball cap, same as always.

"If you can't open it, then it's not worth a shit."

"Were you hired to open it?" Dax said. "Or just provide it to your client? My understanding was that he wouldn't even want you to wonder too much about it."

Gerry's angry rebuttal died on his lips. It was a fair point. He could do more harm than good if he even told the German about the lock screen. Let the German deal with it.

"I do think it could change your price point, perhaps," the kid said.

"Change my price point."

"Sure. The girl is alive. If your client wants us to bring that phone to her, I can do it. We can unlock it, which I'd assume is your client's desire. But that's above and beyond the initial job, isn't it? Value added should not be free." He shrugged. "At least, not in my opinion. But it's your show."

Damn right it was Gerry's show. However, the kid was spot-on. The German was inevitably going to want to get the phone to the girl if this was indeed a biometric lock, and Gerry wasn't doing that shit for free. He wasn't sure that he wanted to do it at all, though. This job had been sliding sideways from the beginning.

"Maybe he wants this thing to disappear, period," Gerry said, turning the phone over on the counter. It was a perfect replica of an iPhone. "That's all he wanted for Oltamu."

"He wanted Oltamu dead. The phone, he wanted in his possession. If he'd planned on having it destroyed, he could have asked you to do it. But he didn't."

Gerry had made it his business not to ask questions that he didn't need the answers to, but the German had wanted the phone, and Gerry was curious just what was on this thing that made it so valuable. Already, the German had been willing to go to two million for the job. Gerry hadn't even had to push to get that much. How much could he get for an unlocked version?

"Call him and ask," Dax said, as if Gerry had voiced the question aloud.

Gerry looked from the phone to the gun and then up at the kid. He couldn't see his eyes because of the shadow from the black baseball cap, but his posture was the same as it always was, the slouch of a bored delinquent. In this way, he was different from both his uncle, who had a military bearing, and his father, who was always in a state of physical calm but had *presence,* a means of commanding attention and respect without any alpha-male posturing. The kid would need to grow into that or learn the hard way that he came across as more sullen than sinister. Hard men would look him over and feel like they could test him. The more that happened, the more likely it was that one of them would succeed, and Dax Blackwell would be in a coffin before he was twenty.

His mind and his hands worked fast, though. He'd killed Carlos and walked away clean; he'd eliminated a pair of difficulties in Maine; he'd called Kaplan's bluff and found the phone. While Gerry had been scrambling to deal with Kaplan, Dax had been solving problems. Maybe he was right. Maybe this was worth making a call.

"We'd have to be sure we can get to her," Gerry said.

"I can."

"Yeah? How? She's in intensive care, she's got doctors and nurses and family all over her, and there are cameras everywhere in a hospital."

"I'll get to her," Dax said, unfazed. "I look the part. A visiting friend from good old Hammel College. I don't need to stay long— I can just pass through, say a prayer, take a picture."

Gerry grinned. The kid could probably play that role just fine. He was young enough to get away with it. "Okay," Gerry said, straightening. "I'll make the call. But keep your mouth shut. He's going to need to think I'm alone."

"Sure."

It was two in the morning in Germany, but Gerry figured he'd get an answer. He wasn't even sure if his man was still in Germany.

He was supposed to be in the States by tomorrow, so maybe he was on a plane or already on the ground.

Wherever he was, he answered the phone. They used an end-to-end encryption app that allowed for texting, voice, and video calls. Virtually untraceable, and the messages vanished. The German also used a voice-distortion device, though Gerry had never wasted time on that.

"Do not tell me there is trouble," the German said. Through the distortion, he sounded cartoonish, a Bond villain.

"None on my end," Gerry said. "Maybe some on yours."

"Explain."

Gerry did. Told him that Oltamu had put a facial-recognition lock on the phone before he died, and the face wasn't his but the girl's. He could get to the girl, he said, or he could hand the device off and let other people deal with it. He didn't care; his work was done.

There was some swearing, and then some silence. Gerry was beginning to think he'd made a mistake by allowing the kid to goad him into this when the German said, "Do you know it will work? She is in a coma. Will it work with someone who is in a coma?"

Gerry looked at Dax, who nodded, pointed at his eyes with two fingers, then moved his fingers up and down.

"It should," Gerry said. "She's got eye movement."

Dax gave him a thumbs-up. The kid was so damned cocky. He was also awfully good. In fact, after Dax's work on this job, Gerry's faith in him was renewed. The kid was more than a beta-Blackwell; he was the real deal.

And to think, Gerry had planned to kill him. What a waste that would have been.

"If it can be done safely," the German said, "then do it. Otherwise, back off."

"Fine," Gerry said. "And how much is that worth to you?"

Another pause. Then: "Half."

Half was a million. If Dax Blackwell could walk into that hospital, hold the phone up to Tara Beckley's face, and unlock it, Gerry was three million dollars richer.

"Fine," he said again, but he saw Dax shake his head and gesture upward with his thumb. He wanted Gerry to go higher. The *balls* on this kid. Gerry didn't respond, just glared at him, and Dax shrugged and jammed his hands back into the pockets of his hoodie.

"Has to happen fast," the German said.

"It will. Or if it isn't doable, I'll back off."

"We meet at the same place and same time, no matter what. Don't risk anything that compromises that. I won't wait."

"You won't have to."

They disconnected. Gerry put his phone in his pocket, looked at Dax Blackwell, and smiled. He was feeling warm toward the kid, and why not? He'd just made Gerry an extra million bucks. "It's on," he said. "Think you can get to Tara Beckley without trouble?"

"Yes."

"Don't push it."

"Of course not. What about Kaplan? She's still out there. She doesn't have the phone, but she's still a threat. Somebody ought to meet her in Old Orchard, right?"

"Ought to be you. You're the one she's seen, the one she wants."

"It's personal to her, huh?"

Gerry was still riding the buzz of an extra million, and problems seemed to be solving themselves, so he nodded. "Yeah, her bullshit was that she'd trade the phone for you."

Dax said, "I don't recall you mentioning that."

Gerry hesitated, realizing that he hadn't brought that up before, then shrugged. "Wouldn't have mattered much. We'd have taken her tomorrow and gotten the phone. Now it's even easier. Cleaner."

"Because we have the phone." Dax was watching him intently.

"Right," Gerry said. "So tomorrow, it can be quick. No need to waste time. Just clip her and move on."

"Where will you be?"

Gerry frowned. "Taking the phone in."

"Where?"

"The hell business is that of yours?"

"Abby Kaplan wants to see you. Maybe we should both be there."

No, Abby Kaplan wanted to see the kid. The kid would go there and kill her. Or possibly he'd go there and fail, but Gerry had trouble believing that. If the bitch actually appeared, the kid would handle her. And if Abby Kaplan was somehow leagues better than anticipated and had arranged for cops all over the pier, well, Gerry still wasn't overly concerned about that. Dax didn't seem like the talking-to-cops type, and if it turned out he was, Gerry had silenced people in prisons before.

"Let me handle my shit," Gerry said, "and you handle yours."

He didn't like the way the kid was looking at him. It was that clinical, under-the-microscope stare, penetrating and yet distant, the look that his father and uncle wore so naturally. The look they'd given those hard boys in Belfast all those years ago.

As if reading his thoughts, Dax said, "I've cleaned it all up pretty well so far. Things had the potential to get out of hand, and now they're back in my control. Do you still think my father and uncle would have done it better?"

"They couldn't have done it any better than this," Gerry said, "and there were two of them."

Dax's face split into a wide smile beneath the shadow cast by his baseball cap.

"You're right," he said. "Since there's just me, I've got to be twice as good, don't I? Nobody in my corner. They were good, but there were two of them. I'm solo. I have to reach their level and then push beyond it."

"You're on your way," Gerry told him, unsettled by the conversation, by the way the kid happily measured himself against dead men. He nodded at Oltamu's cloned phone, which was still sitting on the counter. "But you got some work left to do. Let's not waste time."

"They liked you," Dax said, as if he hadn't heard the instruction. "They didn't like many people either. But my father once told me that there were only two things I could trust. One of them was Gerry Connors."

This was oddly flattering. Gerry had looked out for the kid. Giving him chances, bringing him along in the business. And now, he'd decided to let him live. He'd extend their relationship; grow it, even. It wasn't too late for that.

"Glad to hear I earned their trust," Gerry said. "Who was the second man?"

"What?"

"You said he told you to put your trust in two things."

"Oh." Dax laughed. "I confused you, sorry. The second one wasn't a person."

Gerry cocked his head and frowned. A question was rising to his lips when Dax Blackwell said, "It was this," and then there was a clap and a spark of light that seemed to come from within the kid's black hoodie, and suddenly Gerry was down on the floor, hot blood pumping out of his stomach. He put a hand to the wound and let out a high moan that brought the taste of blood into his throat and mouth. He looked at the counter and saw his gun sitting there, out of reach.

Dax took a black revolver with gleaming chrome cylinders out of his hoodie pocket and waved it in the air like a taunt. Or a reminder.

It was this. Gerry saw that gun and remembered where he'd seen it before: Jack Blackwell's hand.

Of course, he thought, the pain not yet rising, the panic not rising, nothing rising but the taste of blood and the sense of inevitability. *Of course Jack would have told the boy to trust the gun above all else.*

Dax knelt beside him and brought his face down low. This close, Gerry could finally see his eyes beneath the shadows of the baseball cap. They were a light blue, and the expression in them could almost pass for compassionate. Gerry needed some compassion now. Just a trace of it. He needed the kid to understand that they could make this right. They could get Gerry patched up, could save his life, and if that happened, he would never turn the kid in, would never try to get revenge for this. He'd never even speak of it. If the kid just gave him life, there would be no end to Gerry's kindness.

He opened his mouth to speak, to convey his promise, but all that left his lips was a warm stream of blood.

Dax Blackwell looked down at him sadly, and then he leaned even closer, his eyes still on Gerry's, his gaze unblinking.

"I want you to know," he said, "how much I've appreciated the opportunities."

When Gerry opened his mouth to beg for his life, Dax shoved the gun between his lips and pulled the trigger once more.

Gerry Connors died on his kitchen floor, three thousand miles and thirty years from the place where he'd first met the Blackwell family.

Part Five

THE LONG WAY HOME

45

Abby had succeeded in lifting the headrest to its fully extended position, which required bracing her feet on the front of the seat and arching and twisting her back like an Olympic diver attempting a half gainer. She could feel the release buttons, but removing the headrest entirely required more pressure and a lifting motion, a feat that was not easy to execute when you were tied to the damned thing and each lift strangled you and each push at the release buttons numbed already clumsy fingers.

She was close, though. She was very close, and she was so intent on the task that she'd almost forgotten about the scene playing out on Dax's phone.

Then came the gunshot.

She spun at the sound and slipped, and the headrest slid back into place. She could hear it clinking down, level by level, lock by lock, like an extension ladder closing.

"Shit!" she cried, the cord tight against her throat, her swollen fingers numb, all of her gains lost. She could see the display of the phone again, though, and so she was looking at it when a man's horrified face came into view, the man Dax had called Gerry. Gerry's lips parted, and blood ran over them and down his chin. Abby stared at the image in horror, and when the revolver appeared from offscreen and slipped between the man's bloodied lips, she closed her eyes, a reflex action.

"I want you to know," Dax said, "how much I've appreciated the opportunities."

She didn't see the second shot, but she heard it. The sound was loud on the phone, but out here in the driveway, beyond the walls of the brick house, it was softer, swift and insignificant.

That was how a human life could end. Neither with a whimper nor a bang—just a muffled pop that wouldn't turn any heads in the neighborhood. The night didn't pause for the kill shot. The night carried on.

The night always would.

Abby sat in the passenger seat, breathing hard, eyes squeezed shut, sweat on her brow from the exertion of her work on the headrest. She'd been so close. A fraction of an inch away, a few more seconds, that was all she'd needed, but now she would have to start over, and without even opening her eyes to check the phone display, she knew that time was short.

It was. She opened her eyes in time to see the kid moving for the door, and then she didn't require the display anymore, because she could see Dax emerging from the shadows. He was walking at a leisurely pace, no sign of panic or even concern. There was a brown paper bag in his hand. The gun he'd just killed with was nowhere to be seen.

He used the key fob to unlock the Challenger, and too late Abby wondered whether there was any sign of her nearly successful effort to free herself. Dax opened the door, dropped into the driver's seat, and looked her over quickly but carefully, but if he saw anything that troubled him, he didn't show it.

"Sorry you had to watch that," he said, apparently attributing Abby's sweat to fear over what she'd seen play out on the phone. "Remember, the man was going to kill you too."

When Abby didn't answer, Dax lifted a hand in an *It's all right* gesture and said, "No thanks needed. Happy to help."

He tossed the brown paper bag into the backseat. It landed heavily, and Dax registered Abby's response to the sound.

"There's a wallet, a watch, a gun, a phone, and two hundred thousand dollars cash in there," he said. "I'm afraid Gerry was robbed. But good news—if anything happens to me, all of that is yours."

He picked up the phone from the center console and closed out of the concealed-camera application. The video disappeared, and audio replaced it—the feed from Tara Beckley's hospital room. Abby recognized Shannon's voice and a lower, male voice that she thought was the doctor who'd been with them previously. They were making small talk now, long pauses between comments.

Dax listened thoughtfully, then said, "Killing time."

It was a common expression, and yet when it left his mouth, Abby thought he meant that the hour of murder was upon them again.

"They're waiting on the cavalry to arrive," Dax said. "Which means we can get there first."

With that, he backed out of the driveway. This time, the gates opened automatically. Abby still hadn't spoken. She stared at the gates as they closed again.

"Onward!" Dax said jauntily, and he pulled onto the street. "It's your time now, Abby. Are you ready to own the moment? A lot of people will be counting on you."

He had a heavy foot on the gas pedal, was doing forty-five in a thirty-miles-per-hour zone and gaining speed. The Hellcat's power could sneak up on you if you were distracted, and the kid was distracted. The cheerful mask was a false front, and his voice was no longer his natural taunt but something he was ginning up because he needed to feel that old confidence. Abby was confused. She had no sense that killing bothered Dax, and yet something about this one had rattled him.

"Who was he?" Abby said.

"No one of significance to you."

"But he knew your father." This much Abby had heard while she strained at the cord around her throat. Talk of a father and an uncle. That had mattered to him in a real way, one that his masks could not fully conceal. The car was still gaining speed, roaring down the residential street at more than fifty, and he had no idea.

"You're going too fast," Abby said.

He registered the speed with surprise and eased off the accelerator.

"Good eye," he said, the forced cheerful demeanor back. "You're a fine partner, Abby. Don't ever let me forget to acknowledge that."

The weakness is family, Abby thought, watching him, and then: *One of them was named Jack. That person matters to him. And this last murder wasn't like the rest. For a reason involving family, it was different.*

Had he killed a family member back there? It seemed possible; with him, any horror seemed possible. But Abby didn't believe that was it. The dead man had been important to him, but he wasn't family.

The kid hooked a left turn and then they were on a four-lane street, leaving the neighborhood, and up ahead, the lights of the interstate showed.

Abby leaned back against the headrest to let the cord loosen as much as possible and felt the thrum of the big engine work into her spine. Only hours ago, that had driven panic through her, but now she felt the connection again.

She knew that the headrest would come off. She'd been close to getting it, and she would be faster the next time.

If she survived until the next time.

"Where are we going?" she asked. "Or have you killed enough people for one day?"

"We're not done," the kid said. His voice was a monotone, as if he couldn't muster the energy to do his typical upbeat act. "You're going to see Tara. If things go well, you might live a little longer. So might Tara."

When Dax shifted onto the interstate ramp, the Pirellis spun on the wet pavement, and the Challenger fishtailed briefly. He got it under control fast, and he didn't react with fear or even surprise. He might not understand the car, but he understood power, and he learned quickly.

46

Boone wanted her own car, but asking for assistance from her employers would break the silence around Tara Beckley, and adding more actors to the mix, even a simple driver/bodyguard who understood rank and wouldn't ask questions, felt risky right now. The operations protocol around Oltamu had been silence, and though he was dead, she didn't think that protocol should be.

The rental counter would waste time, and Uber would not, so when she made it to the ground, she went against her strongest instincts and sacrificed control for speed. The plane had circled for twenty-five minutes while the storm lashed the New England coast beneath it, but it had finally landed, and now all that was left between her and Tara Beckley was fifteen miles. She summoned the Uber, and when it arrived, she stepped off the curb, got into the car, handed the driver—a too-friendly chick with dyed-pink hair—a hundred-dollar bill, and told her to start moving fast and keep moving fast.

"I don't want to get a ticket," the girl protested. She had approximately twenty piercings and fifty tattoos, but she didn't want to challenge a speed limit?

"If you get a ticket, I'll pay it," Boone said.

"It still affects my Uber status! They'll know if I—"

"Then you won't get a ticket," Boone snapped. "I can make it disappear. Trust me on this, would you? Any cop who stops us will let us go in a hurry." The girl, mouth open, looked at her in the mirror, and Boone said, "Keep your eyes on the damned road."

Boone texted Pine while they pulled away from Logan. She told him she was en route and asked if anything had changed. Pine said no. Boone asked where the family was. Pine said the sister was present but the mom and stepdad were in their hotel room; did she want them? Boone said no. She just wanted the girl. Tara might or might not have the answers, but the parents definitely didn't.

Get rid of the sister, Boone texted.

Can't be done, Pine replied.

What do you mean, it can't be done? Boone wrote.

You'll learn, Pine responded.

47

Tara rests while Dr. Pine and Shannon talk about inconsequential things; everyone is waiting on the arrival of the investigator who will make sense of it all. Tara knows that will require conversation again, the exhausting process on the alphabet board. Dr. Carlisle has promised they'll experiment with computer software soon, but that's not going to help Tara now. She's got to rely on her eyes, nothing else, and she's got to call up the stamina to make it through. Last mile, running uphill. She's been here before.

But she hasn't, of course. She has never had to face that last mile suffering the relentless pain of tubes jammed into various orifices or the maddening cruelty of paralysis. There is no analogy in the world that applies here. She's not invisible any longer, but she's also no closer to leaving this bed or even making a sound than she was when she woke up.

Don't let yourself think that way. Be strong.

She's tired of being strong, though. Tired of how much everyone cares about Oltamu and his fucking phone. He's dead, but Tara isn't, and maybe she's worse off than him. Endless days like this, endless expenses…what if there's no finish line? What if this is it?

Remember your thumb.

Yes. Her thumb. Capable of spasmodic twitching. What a win!

You take your wins where you can find them, though. Water could erode rock, drop by drop.

She tunes out the conversation around her and focuses on the channel between brain and thumb. Visualizes it, imagines it like

311

a river, sees her force of will like a skilled rower pulling against the current, forcing her way upstream. Brain to thumb, no turning back, and no portages around treacherous water. You had to beat the current.

The visual takes clearer shape, and she can see a woman who is like her but who is not her, a different version of Tara, more dream than memory, but so tenacious. The rowboat becomes a kayak, and though real Tara is awkward with a kayak paddle, dream Tara is not. She's strong and graceful, fighting a current that flashes with green-gold light just beneath the surface. As she paddles, the river widens, and the current pushes against her, and then, impossibly, it reverses direction and begins guiding her downstream, an aid rather than an enemy now.

Make it to the thumb. Make it there, and once you know the way, you will make it again. Once you know you can go that far whenever you like, then try another river in another direction. We'll explore them all, run them to the end. We have nothing but time.

She could swear she feels a tightening in her thumb, a faint pulse of muscle tension.

Yes, it can be done. It's long and hard but it can be done. Keep riding the current, keep steering, keep—

"She's on her way," Dr. Pine says, and at first Tara is convinced that he's speaking about her, that he's somehow aware of her journey downriver. Then she sees that his eyes are on his phone.

"Fifteen minutes," he reports. Then he looks at Tara. "Do you want your parents here?"

The two eye flicks are necessary, but they also take her away from the river, and she feels a loosening of tension in her hand. She was so close. Why did he have to interrupt?

No matter. She's found the way once, and she will find it again. Over and over, however long it takes. The water was not so bad. Eventually the current had shifted to help her, and whatever produced that green-gold hue beneath the surface was good. She's not sure why she's so sure of that, but she knows beyond any doubt that it is a good sign.

I'll be back, Tara promises herself, and then she gives Pine her attention again. He smiles in what is supposed to be a reassuring fashion, but she can tell that he's nervous. Who can blame him? It's not enough to be tasked with bringing a patient back from the dead; now he's supposed to see that the patient provides witness testimony to some sort of government agent? Even for a neurologist, this can't feel like another day at the office.

She'd like to smile back at him and let him know that she's grateful for all he's done and that she felt better the moment he walked into the room, looked at her with those curious but hopeful eyes, and introduced himself. And used her name. Sometime soon, when she has the computer software that makes all of this less of a chore, she will let him know how much that mattered. Small things, quiet things, but he gave her dignity when others did not.

Shannon isn't offering any smiles. She's not even offering her attention. She's glued to her own phone and seems distressed. Tara watches Shannon tap out a text message and send it, but she can't read the message because Shannon is shielding the phone with her free hand. It's an unsubtle way of making it clear that she doesn't want Pine to see it. Once the message is sent, she stands up, her chair making a harsh squeak on the tile.

"I'll be right back."

Pine turns and stares at her. "Where are you going?"

Shannon gives him an icy look. "Is that your business?"

"Right now, I feel that it is, yes. We're fifteen minutes away from—"

"I know! Trust me, I am aware. I just need to…breathe for a few seconds. Okay?"

Pine doesn't like it, but he decides not to fight it. He seems to think Shannon is on the verge of a panic attack, which would be a logical assumption if he were dealing with anyone other than

Shannon. Tara knows better. Shannon has no fight-or-flight response; it's only fight with her. If she were flooded with adrenaline, she'd refuse to leave the room. So what in the hell is going on, and why won't she meet Tara's eyes?

Then she's gone. Without a look back.

48

I nside the Challenger, Dax and Abby listened to the exchange in the hospital room. Dax nodded, pleased, and said, "Attagirl. Way to stand your ground."

Abby, still bound to the passenger seat of her dead friend's car, said nothing. They were parked on the fourth floor of a five-floor garage attached to the hospital, and most of the spaces around them were empty, as were many on the third level, which connected to the hospital through a walkway. There should be little if any traffic up here.

When Dax had parked, he'd sent a text message to Shannon Beckley, making sure that Abby saw each word. He identified himself as Abby, and from there the text was simple: he told her the car he was in and where it was parked in the hospital garage, then said he would give Shannon Oltamu's phone provided she came alone.

It was, Abby had to admit, a smart choice. Shannon wanted the phone, and she knew Abby had it. Any other tactic—threatening her, for example—might not have rung true. But the promise of the phone was tempting, particularly with the DOE agent on the way, and the situation made sense. As far as Shannon knew, Abby was doing what she'd said she would: reaching out to her from another phone number and offering what help she could from her own perilous position in the world.

Shannon should have no reason to doubt her.

"You're going to have the opportunity to make some noise, I suppose," Dax said, pocketing the phone and turning to Abby.

"You could scream, kick the horn. I don't know what all has run through your head, but I'm sure you've had ideas, and I can promise you that all of them are bad. Right now, she's got the chance to walk in and out of this garage alive and unhurt. Don't ruin that for her, Abby."

He studied Abby's eyes for a moment, then nodded once, opened the driver's door, and slipped out. They were parked beside a large panel van with a cleaning company's logo, and he vanished on the other side of that. Abby watched him go and then turned to her right, where the stairwell was.

Shannon Beckley should come from that direction. Maybe alone, maybe not. If she walked through the door with a cop in tow, Abby didn't think it would take long for the shooting to start.

Shannon came alone. She'd moved fast too, because the wait hadn't been long. The stairwell door opened and there she was, tall and defiant, or at least trying to look defiant, though you could see her nerves in the way she scanned the garage even after she'd observed the Challenger parked where she'd been told it would be. She hesitated, and Abby saw her glance back at the stairwell door as it clanged shut behind her, but then she steeled herself and started toward the Challenger with long, purposeful strides.

She made it halfway there before the kid got her.

Abby hadn't seen him move. She'd thought he was still waiting on the other side of that van, but he must have crawled under it or around it, because he emerged from behind a pickup truck that was parked four empty spaces from the Challenger, now on Abby's right instead of her left. Shannon Beckley was walking fast, her eyes on the Challenger, and she might have glimpsed Abby's face through the darkly tinted glass because she seemed to squint just before Dax rose up beside her.

She had time to scream, but she didn't. Instead, she tried to fight and run at the same time, stumbling backward while throwing a wild right hook. If she'd stepped into the punch, she might've landed it; she had a fast hand. But because she was trying to both attack and flee, she missed the punch, and then Dax had her. He caught her right wrist, spun her, twisted her arm up behind her back, and clapped his gloved left hand over her mouth.

Abby jerked forward instinctively as if to help. The cord bit into her throat and forced her back. She reached for the headrest release, but before she could even find it, they were walking her way, Dax whispering into Shannon's ear with each step. When they arrived beside the car, he released her and drew the gun. He did this so quickly that it was pressed against the back of Shannon's skull before she had time to react to being free. She stood still, staring through the window at Abby, close enough now to see the cord around her throat.

"Open the driver's door," Dax said to Shannon. His voice was soft but menacing, like early snowflakes with a blizzard behind them.

Shannon walked around the back of the car and opened the driver's door, and then she and Abby were briefly face-to-face with no glass between them.

"I'm sorry," Abby said. The words sounded as hollow to her as Shannon's expression told her they felt.

"Backseat," Dax said, folding the driver's seat forward and allowing access to the back. Shannon hesitated, and he cocked the revolver. She crawled into the backseat, scrambled across the leather, and crouched in the far corner. Dax followed, swinging the door shut behind him and sealing them all inside, Abby tied to the front passenger seat, Shannon and Dax and the gun in the back.

"All together now," he said. "Terrific. This thing is close to done, Shannon. Closer than you think. You've got a big job to do, though. You've got to get our beloved little phone to your sister and unlock it and bring it back. You've got to do that quickly and without anyone else seeing it. Otherwise, the killing starts fast."

Shannon had been staring at Abby, but now she looked back at Dax and seemed to be sizing him up. Other than having the gun, he didn't appear all that imposing. Abby remembered the night she'd made the same mistake.

"You need to listen to him," Abby said. "And not for me. I'm not worried about myself anymore. But you need to listen to him because you need him to go away fast."

"That's excellent advice," Dax said. "Abby's been along for the ride for a while now. She's seen some things. I'd trust her wisdom if I were you."

Shannon Beckley looked at Abby and then back at Dax, and Abby knew her mind was whirling, and she was almost positive she knew what she was thinking.

"When the Department of Energy agent gets to the room, she isn't going to be able to help," she said, and Shannon's eyes widened. "Nobody in that room can help, because he can hear you. He's listening to the hospital room. Has been."

She'd taken this chance expecting retribution from Dax, expecting maybe even a bullet, but instead she received a smile.

"That's right," Dax said. "But we won't need to worry about ears anymore. Shannon's going to give us eyes too."

He took off the black baseball cap and extended it to her. She recoiled and smacked against the door. But she had nowhere to run, and it was far too late for that anyhow.

"The agent is en route," Dax said. "My understanding is that she's very close. That puts some added pressure on you, Shannon. I'm sorry about that, but…" He shrugged. "I'm not the one who sent for her. It's your turn to wear the black hat."

Abby watched in the mirror. Shannon took the hat from his hand like she was accepting a snake, then put it on. She pushed her hair behind her ears and settled it down. It looked natural enough. Looked good, even. But it wouldn't look right to the doctor who was in that room.

"Why'd she leave and put on a hat?" Abby said.

"Good question," the kid answered, not looking at her. "Why'd you do that, Shannon?"

Silence for a moment, then Shannon said, "I don't know."

"I think you do. I think you get migraines from the lights in the hospital. Stress and bright light? That can definitely bring on a headache. You took some Excedrin, you put on a hat, and now you want everyone to just shut the hell up about you and focus on your sister. I think everyone is ready to focus on Tara."

He reached into his pocket and withdrew Oltamu's phone. When he tapped the display, Abby watched Shannon's face change. She understood the picture. Or at least, she wasn't confused by it.

"You're going to need to hold this up to her eyes," Dax said, "and hope that it unlocks. It asks for a name, but I think that's bullshit. It just needs her eyes. If I'm wrong, though…there'll be a lot riding on Tara figuring out what to do then. Because I know your mother and stepfather are in room four eighty-one in the hotel next door, and they'll die fast if you make a bad choice."

He pressed the phone into her hand. Her hand was trembling, but only a little.

"You can save a lot of lives tonight," Dax told her.

"They'll be watching me," Shannon said. "At least, Pine will be. The doctor. How do you expect me to explain this to him?"

"Convincingly," Dax said. "That's how I expect you to do it. I'm not a fan of scripts. People get hung up on them, they forget their lines, and then things go to hell fast. I like quick thinkers with room to be creative. Maybe you want a word in private with your sister. Maybe you're angry with Dr. Pine. I don't know. But I think you'll figure it out. And Shannon? Make it believable. Because if that phone finds its way back to my hand, your family stays alive. If it doesn't…" He inclined his head toward the front seat. "Ask Abby what happened to the last person who disappointed me today."

Shannon didn't look at Abby. She put Oltamu's phone in her pocket and said, "May I go now?"

"You in a hurry?"

"Yes. I don't want any strangers around. Let me go now, before the detective or agent or whoever gets here."

"Wise," Dax said, and then he moved back, keeping the gun pointed at her, opened the door, and stepped outside. He lowered the gun and kept it down against his leg as she climbed out. He actually offered her a hand, looking like a high-school kid with his prom date. She ignored it and climbed out alone. She ignored the gun too. She ignored everything and just started walking toward the stairwell.

"He sees and hears you," Abby called after her. She knew how pathetic the warning sounded, but she was terrified for Shannon. She was going to try something. Abby was sure of that. She might not have a plan yet, but this woman was absolutely going to try something.

Dax leaned on the roof of the car and sang, "'He sees you when you're sleeping. He knows when you're awake. He knows if you've been bad or good, so be good, for goodness' sake!'"

The stairwell door opened and clanged shut, and Shannon Beckley was gone.

49

Pine wasn't as helpless over the sister as he'd claimed because when Boone arrived, he came down to meet her and said that the sister was gone and it was just Tara now.

"Shannon will come back," he said. "I'd be stunned if she didn't. Maybe we should wait."

"We are not waiting," Boone said. "Less is more, Doctor, when it comes to time and witnesses in this scenario."

She didn't give him a chance to consider that, just walked in front of him and down the corridor as if she knew where she was going. Using motion to push past hesitation was one of her favorite techniques, and it worked. Pine reacted as most men in positions of authority did and quickened his pace in an attempt to not only catch up to her but make it seem as if he were actually leading the way, that the rush had been his idea all along.

The corridor ended in a T, and Pine turned left and exchanged quick greetings with two nurses in the hall. If they had any interest in Boone, they didn't show it. She was just another stranger here to look at the brain-dead girl, evidently. Pine had done a good job of shutting down the chatter about Tara Beckley's return to consciousness in his own hospital, at least. The girl's mother had carried news outside the walls, but inside, it was business as usual. For the first time, Boone was pleased that she'd gotten here so late; the hospital was quieter at this hour.

"The process will seem simple to you," Pine said. "It will seem easy, even. She moves her eyes to give you answers—what could be less taxing, right? But I warn you that it is a laborious process for her. We've pushed her hard already today. At some point, the fatigue will catch up to her. Remember that as you phrase your questions."

"I tend to be concise," Boone said, which was certainly not a lie.

"It's not about being concise. You can talk all you want. What you need to consider is how many words are required for her to respond. You want to cut that down, down, down. As much as possible, use yes-or-no questions. When she has to spell out a word, make that word count."

They had reached room 373.

"Omit needless words," he admonished her, and then he opened the door.

50

*O*mit needless words." *Dr. Strunk is here!* Damn it, if Tara could only speak, she would say that to see whether Dr. Pine is enough of a writing geek to laugh. She expects that he is. Aren't all doctors well read? Their patients hope so, certainly.

As Dr. Pine ushers the new woman in, Tara finds herself thinking that she looks forward to having a real conversation with him at some point. She likes him and trusts him, and she suspects that he has good stories. In a business like his, how could you not? Tara wants to become one of his best stories.

A success story.

"Hello, Tara," he says, "your guest has arrived." He pauses, and then, as if reading her thoughts, he adds, "I'm sure Shannon will be here in a moment. But would you like to wait for her?"

Tara has no idea what bug crawled up Shannon's ass to send her rushing out of here, but she's comfortable with Dr. Pine and certain that Shannon will return soon. Then they will all get the lecture on how they shouldn't have started without her. But in the meantime, why not get to it?

She flicks her eyes up twice. No need to wait.

The woman with Dr. Pine is tall and lean, well muscled. A workout junkie, probably. Not a runner, though. Or at least, not just a runner. She likes free weights. Her shoulder muscles are defined under her tight-fitting black top, and Tara is surprised and somewhat disappointed that she's not wearing a jacket. She'd expected a jacket that might conceal a gun. Having never met a Department of Energy agent before, she allowed her imagination to go wild, and she should have known better. This is a notepad-and-laptop kind of law enforcement agent, not a gun-belt type. But, hey, she's clearly strong.

"Tara, it's very nice to meet you," the woman says, walking closer, every movement balanced and her focus on Tara total. "Dr. Pine was explaining how I can make this as easy as possible for you. I'll respect his guidance on that. I understand that yes-or-no questions are best, and I am going to stick to those as much as I can, but occasionally, I might need to ask you to spell. Do you understand all of that?"

Tara flicks her eyes up once, thinking, *Say your name, damn it.* At some point, she's going to have to take the time to get that sentence out so Dr. Pine knows how important it is to her. Common courtesies like introductions make her feel more human, less like a spectacle, some tourist attraction or circus freak, the Amazing Locked-in Woman, five dollars for five minutes of her incredible nonverbal communication.

The woman sits on the stool that Dr. Pine usually claims, and for some reason this bothers Tara. *Let the medical professional run the show, lady.* But there's no one in the room who matters to the woman except Tara.

Until the door swings open, and there is Shannon, dressed like a hostage negotiator. What in the world is she doing in that dumb black baseball cap?

"Sorry I'm late," she says in an odd, too-loud voice. "I was getting a bad headache. The stress and the lights…" She waves her hand at the overhead fluorescents. "I was afraid it would become a migraine."

The agent seems less than delighted to have Shannon join the party but accepts it with a thin smile and nod. "No problem. I was just about to ask Tara a few simple questions, and then I hope I can bring an end to your stress. At least this additional aspect of it." She rises from the stool and offers her hand, and Tara thinks, *Sure, the walking-talking girl gets an introduction.*

"Shannon Beckley," Shannon says, still too loud, as if she wants to be heard three rooms away. Her eyes are skittering all around the room, like someone taking inventory after a burglary.

"Nice to meet you, Shannon. I'm Andrea Carter, with the Department of Energy."

Well, Tara thinks, *at least we now have a name.*

And then, as Tara stares at her sister, something troubling overtakes her: She has seen that hat before. She's seen that hat in this room, when the Justin Loveless impostor showed up with the flowers.

What in the hell is happening?

5 1

Inside the Challenger, Dax and Abby sat side by side, like part-
ners, and watched the video feed on the phone. It had been a
disorienting show so far, with Shannon Beckley's head creating the
effect of a Steadicam in a horror movie. Now things finally slowed
down, and room 373 took on clarity: Tara in the bed, the doctor
named Pine standing in the corner, and the DOE agent sitting on a
stool at the bedside. Abby couldn't see her face, just the back of her
head, blond hair against a black shirt, but then she turned to the
door, and Abby waited with the sensation of a trapped scream for
Shannon Beckley to say the wrong thing, to doubt the killing ca-
pacity of the kid who'd sent her in there. She might think calling
911 would be the right move, and then she would learn swiftly and
painfully that such a mistake would be measured in lost lives.

Instead, she nailed it—voice too loud and a little unnatural,
but the rest was right. The bit about the stress and the migraine
worked well enough. Abby exhaled, feeling like the first step was
a good one, but Dax went rigid.

What did he see that I didn't? Abby wondered.

Dax picked up the phone and used his fingers to change the
zoom. The agent's face filled the screen.

"Well, now," he said, and other than during the initial moments
after his last murder, it was the first time he'd sounded unsteady to
Abby.

"What is it?" Abby said. She wasn't expecting an answer, but
she got one.

"That's not a DOE agent," Dax said. "That's Lisa Boone."

"Who is Lisa Boone?"

"She worked with my father a few times. He thought she was very good." Dax finally looked away from the screen, met Abby's eyes, and realized the message meant nothing to her. His gaze was steady when he said, "That means she's a professional killer."

52

Shannon stands there wearing the black hat, the hat that Tara hasn't thought about on this day of developments, her future opening in front, her attention being directed to the past, pulling her in opposite directions. The young man with the hunter's eyes and the black hat seemed a forgotten player to her.

Now he is back. Tara knows this, and Shannon must too.

I could have warned her, Tara thinks.

Shannon says, "I don't want to interrupt this. I really don't. Trust me, I understand the importance. But I would like to have a few words alone with my sister before we begin any interviews."

Agent Andrea Carter is not happy with this. She rises, and for the first time Tara can see the intimidation evident in that lean, well-muscled frame. She moves with a menacing grace, like the instructor in the one self-defense class Shannon made Tara take before she went off to college. *For frat parties,* Shannon explained. *And pay attention to the groin shots.*

"We're not stopping now," Agent Carter says. "This is a lot bigger than this room, Ms. Beckley. This is more crucial to more people than you can possibly fathom."

"I'm not asking anyone to stop, just to give me a minute alone with my sister," Shannon says, and if she's intimidated by Carter, she doesn't show it. In fact, her bearing seems oddly helped by the strange hat, all that flat black beneath the lighter silver thread that draws the eye above the brim.

"You've had plenty of time to discuss this," Agent Carter says. "Tara just gave me consent in front of her doctor. I will not waste her time or put her at risk, but I will also not be interrupted. If you'd like to—"

"Hang on." This is from Dr. Pine, and Shannon and Agent Carter seem surprised that he is still in the room. He and Shannon have clashed from the start, but he's looking at her intently, seeing the insistence in her eyes, and when he looks back at Tara, he takes a protective step in her direction.

"This isn't your jurisdiction," he says, pointing at Agent Carter with his right index finger. "And it isn't your decision." He points at Shannon with his left. "This is my hospital, Tara is my patient, and she and I will make these decisions together. Tara gave consent to an interview, yes, Agent Carter. She also has the right to have a few private words with her sister beforehand."

"I'm not trying to stop you," Shannon says again. "But the private words…I need them." She looks at Tara, trying to convey how badly she needs these words, but the look is unnecessary, because Tara knows the hat.

Dr. Pine pivots, looks at Tara. "It's your call, Tara. I'm going to ask you two yes-or-no questions. First: Would you like a private word with your sister at this point?"

One flick. Yes. Very much so. Because that hat…

"I'm going to—" Agent Carter starts, but Dr. Pine cuts her off with a wave of his hand.

"Second: Once you've concluded that exchange with Shannon, are you willing to continue the interview with Agent Carter?"

One flick.

Andrea Carter's chest rises and falls with a frustrated breath. She's been overruled by the locked-in girl, and she doesn't like that at all. Tara finds a strange pleasure in this. She can't move or speak, but she can control the room. It's a sense of power she hasn't felt in a long time.

"Make it quick, Ms. Beckley," Agent Carter snaps. "There's a lot riding on this."

Commands like this usually don't sit well with Shannon, but tonight she barely seems to register the tone, just gives a half nod and keeps her eyes straight ahead. As Dr. Pine passes by Shannon on his way out, she whispers, "Thank you, Doc." He almost stumbles, he's so surprised.

"Of course," he answers, and then he and Agent Carter are out the door. It closes behind them with a soft click, and the Beckley sisters are alone. With their respective questions. Tara knows hers— *Where did the hat come from, and what does it mean, and did he hurt you?* but she can't voice any of those, so she has to trust her sister. She's back in that basement at 1804 London Street again, steel doors between them, a thin band of light, and a lifetime of trust.

The doors are heavier here, the band of light narrower, but the trust has only deepened.

"Tara," Shannon whispers, "I need your help right now. For both of us. And for Mom and Rick. I need you to understand that without me saying much more. I need you to trust me."

Tara gives her one flick.

Shannon smiles awkwardly. Her grateful smile, the least natural, the most heartbreaking.

"Everything that you've been through," she says, "and I need you to save us all. No pressure, T."

Then she reaches into her pocket and pulls out her phone.

No, wait. It's not her phone. It's a black iPhone without a case. Tara understands immediately: It is Oltamu's phone. Somehow, Shannon has come into possession of this oddly desired item, and it has something to do with the reason she's wearing the black hat and is afraid.

Tara's pulse begins to hammer. Not since they sealed her in the tube so she could demonstrate proof of life has she felt an adrenaline rush like this.

"Do you know what this is?" Shannon whispers, her voice so low it's scarcely audible.

One flick.

"Okay. I don't know if this will work, but I need you to try." She taps the screen with her finger and then turns the display to Tara. The blackness has been replaced with an image: Tara standing uneasily beside Dr. Amandi Oltamu above the Willow River, the spindly shadows of the railroad bridge visible just beyond them.

The last memory Tara has of when her body was her own.

For a moment, her vision grays out, and she's afraid she's doing something that would seem impossible—can a paralyzed patient faint? She's about to. But then there's gold-green beneath the gray, and she sees the girl in the kayak, sees the river wide and rushing and the girl riding it out, riding the current into that shimmering gold-green mist, and Tara knows the mist this time—it is spray from a waterfall. There's a waterfall up ahead, but the girl in the water is paddling straight for it, and she is unafraid.

Suddenly all of that is gone and the room is back and the phone is before Tara once more. Shannon's face is hovering just behind it, her eyes darkened by the terrible black baseball cap.

"I'm going to turn this around now and try to capture your face. Just like a camera. It's locked, and you...you might be able to open it. You understand what I mean?"

One flick. Tara grasps the idea, and, bizarre as it sounds, she thinks she even understands it. The odd photos, the way Oltamu gave her the phone...nothing was accidental. Not those choices, and not the choices of the man who drove into the two of them just seconds later.

All part of competing plans. Tara is the pawn in the middle. She has been turned into a human key.

Shannon wets her lips, breathes, and turns the phone around. Tara wants to adjust her head to face the small camera lens, but of course she can't do that. She has to trust that Shannon will get it right.

It takes longer than it should, and Tara is sure it's a failure, but then Shannon arches up a little and changes the angle, pointing the camera down at Tara's eyes from above, and Tara can tell from the way her body relaxes that she has the result she wanted.

"Okay," she says. "That's good, and bad. Take a look."

She turns the phone back to Tara. It says FRS verified and there is a green check mark. But just below that, there's a red X and a white box beside the command Enter name of FRS-verified individual to complete authentication.

FRS. Facial-recognition scan? That seems right, but it wasn't enough to unlock the device. The name prompt remains.

"Do I just try yours? First and last? First only?" Shannon's voice is rising now, and her attention is totally on the phone, and that can't happen, because Tara knows what she needs to enter, Tara knows this and has to speak it and—

The gray-out comes again, and then the green-gold mist, and Tara is riding the waterfall, tumbling and falling to an endless depth, spiraling down through the green-gold liquid light...

When she comes back, it's with a vengeance—her thumb twitches, yes, but so do two of her fingers. A rapid twitch, a plucking gesture, like a child's frantic grab at a firefly.

She's not immediately sure that it was real, but then she sees Shannon staring at her right hand in shock, and the shock confirms the sensation.

Tara is opening the channel. Tara is forcing her way back into the world.

"Did you feel that?" Shannon asks.

One flick.

"Can you do it again?"

She can't. Not yet. But maybe soon...Tara opts not to respond to that question. She doesn't know the answer yet. Her control of her own body no longer belongs to the land of yes-or-no answers. What an amazing thing that was. She wishes Dr. Pine had seen it. And Mom, Rick, all of them. But at least Shannon was here. At least Shannon saw.

"I tried your name," Shannon says then, and Tara remembers the phone, the reason for all of this. "It says 'access denied.' I've got only one try left." Her voice quavers. "T., do you have any idea what he called you?"

One flick.

"You're sure?" Shannon says.

One flick.

"Can you spell it?"

One flick.

Shannon reaches for the alphabet board with a trembling hand.

53

Her hand moved. Abby thought it was an optical illusion, some disruption of the camera's feed, but then Shannon Beckley's questions turned it into reality.

Tara can move. Maybe not consistently, but she can move.

"The name matters," Dax said. "Shit. That slows us down. That might derail the whole thing, actually. Because if Tara doesn't know what he put in there..."

He rubs his thumb over the stock of the revolver distractedly, a circular motion. Abby watches him and thinks about Tara's hand, that sudden twitch. She's coming back. Maybe. Or was it just a spasm? Regardless, it was something more than Luke had ever managed. Tara has vertical eye motion, and one of her hands can move. She's not only still alert in there, she's progressing.

"Boone is in play," Dax said, uninterested in everything else, his attention lost to the blond woman who'd left the room. "But who put her in play? Not Gerry. I'm sure of that."

Abby didn't respond. Her attention was focused on the screen. All the things that had mattered just seconds ago seemed less consequential.

Tara can make it back, she thought. And then: *If nobody kills her first.*

54

Pine wanted privacy. He took Boone down the empty corridor that smelled of a disinfectant tinged with juniper and then turned into a small office. A desk took up all of one wall, and the other walls were lined with filing cabinets and bookshelves. The only chair was the one facing the desk, but he offered it to her. She sat, although she didn't want to. She was buzzing with anger and energy, too close to be wasting more time now.

"If that sister tries to talk Tara out of cooperating, I'm not going anywhere. I hope you understand that. It matters—"

"Too much," Pine finished for her with a weary nod as he closed the door. "I get it, I get it. I also think I'm going about this wrong."

Boone cocked her head. "Meaning?"

"Something's wrong with Shannon."

"The sister. You're worried about her?"

"Yes." He looked at her defiantly. "I am worried about them all. But as I tried to explain to you, she knows a lot. She knows more than I do. She won't tell me how, but she knows more than I do, and I have no idea who is giving her that information. Her behavior has changed since you arrived, but it's not about you. I think she's hearing something."

Boone started to rise. "You believe all this, but you let her sit in there alone?"

Pine blocked her. "Yes! She deserves that. And I deserve a hell of a lot more than I've been given. You tell me how much is at risk here, but not what. I *understand* confidentiality, trust me. It has been my business and my life. I respect it. But this is..." He searched for the words. "Already operating at a level of secrecy that I'm not comfortable with. That I never should have allowed."

"Dr. Pine?" Boone's voice snapped like a whip. "Do not make a mistake at this stage. I will talk to that girl tonight. I don't care if I have to get a DOJ order to make it happen, I will—"

"That's exactly what *should* happen!" he fired back. "I want the damned order! I want the right security. I want the administrators of this hospital to be made aware of all possible risks. There are many patients here besides Tara Beckley. You're acting as if they're not a concern. I can't do that."

Boone was sitting on the edge of the chair, muscles tensed, eyes on Pine's. She made a show of slackening. Easing back into the chair. Giving him a posture of thoughtful consideration that bordered on the verge of concession.

"I have an acquaintance with the special agent in charge of the FBI field office in Boston," he said. "Her name is Roxanne Donovan. You know her, I assume. Or of her?"

"Yes," Boone lied.

"Perfect. Then let me call her. Let me bring someone into this building whom we both know, whom we both trust, and proceed from there. I can't let all this"—he waved a hand toward the closed door that led to the hallway—"continue in silence. Tara Beckley has experienced enough damage from silence. I won't let the same thing happen to others. Or let any more of it happen to her."

Boone steepled her fingers and rested her chin on them. Thoughtful. Then, with a sigh, she said, "I'll make the call," and she reached into her pocket as if going for a cell phone. She stopped before withdrawing anything, paused as if reconsidering, and looked at his desk phone, which was just past her left shoulder.

She said, "No, actually, you should make the call. From the hospital, and on speaker, so I can hear it. You can call Donovan. No one else. And no details should be shared before I have clearance to share them. Can you get her here with that much? Is your relationship that strong?"

"Roxanne Donovan will be here immediately when she understands the stakes," Pine said confidently. "Can I at least share your name?"

"By all means."

"Thank you," he said, an exhale of relief following his words. He leaned forward and reached past her shoulder for the desk phone. He had his hand on the receiver and his focus on the keypad when Boone withdrew the syringe from her pocket, flicked the cap off with one snap of her thumbnail, and drove the stainless-steel needle into the hollow at the base of Pine's throat.

His eyes went wide and white and he reached for his throat, but the needle was already gone, and Boone was up and had her hand over his mouth. He tried a punch then, but she blocked it easily with her left arm. She held him upright as he stumbled backward, kept him from falling, from making any noise. He looked at her with a cocktail of horror, accusation, and shame before his eyes dimmed completely. She watched him see his mistake and consider its ramifications just before his heart stopped.

Then she eased him into the desk chair. His head slumped forward onto the desk, his cheek on the keyboard, depressing keys, but they made no sound. It looked natural enough for a man who'd suffered a massive coronary, so she didn't adjust his position. A standard autopsy would show a heart attack, and only if the coroners had reason to look very, very carefully would they find any evidence to suggest otherwise.

If that happened, Boone would be long gone.

She was pleased to find that the office door had a push-button lock. It wasn't much of a security feature, but it would delay the discovery. She doubted any of the night nurses would want to disturb a doctor of Pine's stature if he'd closed and locked the door.

He had big things to work on, after all; he'd brought a woman back from the beyond.

Boone locked the door behind her and walked briskly back to room 373. The clock was speeding up now, and the time for games and lies was gone.

55

Twitch? You told him your nickname was Twitch?"

Shannon seems either disbelieving or disturbed. Tara—fighting for patience because Shannon doesn't understand how hard it is to keep battling this current, to keep the channel open, commanding her eyes to answer properly even while her own mind races with unanswered questions that she can't voice—gives one flick of the eyes. Yes, Twitch.

"If the facial recognition worked," Shannon says, "maybe this will too."

Her voice is doubtful but she turns her attention to the phone and taps the name into the display. She's holding her breath.

"It worked," Shannon says, and Tara adds this to her growing collection of points of light. Everything is progress right now. Everything is trending the right way.

Tara and Shannon are so focused on each other that neither one notices she's no longer alone in the room.

Then Andrea Carter says, "I'll need to see that."

How long she's been standing there, Tara has no idea, but it can't have been long. Shannon has her back to the door, but Tara thinks she would have glanced right eventually. Carter's face is a hostile mask. Apparently she feels Shannon has held her at bay long enough. Dr. Pine isn't with her.

Shannon rises from the stool, lowering Oltamu's phone and pressing it against her leg.

"Do you mind?" Shannon says. "I'd asked for just a little bit of privacy. If you could just give me a few more..."

339

Tara is watching Shannon, so she doesn't understand why her voice trails off, why her eyes go wide. Then Tara looks back at Andrea Carter and sees the knife.

It's a small knife but it seems to be all blade, a curved piece of metal with a razor edge, a crescent-moon-shaped killing tool. She's holding it in her right hand, down against her leg, in a posture that mirrors Shannon's with the phone.

"You need to be very quiet," Carter says, "and you need to give me that."

She advances with her eyes on Shannon, her movements sleek as a panther. Tara wants to scream but can't; Shannon could and won't. In fact, Shannon's face seems oddly unsurprised, as if she's been anticipating something like this. "What's your real name?" she says.

Carter is only a stride from her now, and she moves the knife out and to the side, the curved blade glistening, and extends her left hand, palm up. "The phone."

Shannon doesn't hesitate, and Tara is relieved. There's something in this woman's eyes that promises violence. Her eyes remind Tara of the eyes of the boy in the black hat. The hat that is now on Shannon's head. They must belong together, this woman and the boy. But why, oh, why is Shannon wearing the hat?

56

Dax was very still, his thumb on the revolver's cylinder, his eyes unblinkingly focused on the video display, even his breathing so restrained that it was scarcely noticeable.

That's Lisa Boone. She worked with my father. She's a professional killer.

In those short sentences, he told Abby more about himself than he had in all the terrible hours they'd spent together. It explained the bizarre pairing of youth and skill, emptiness and professionalism, brutality and calculation. Abby knew his world now, and his world explained him. An assassin's son was just right. Nature and nurture.

She found a strange comfort in this idea, as if there might be a rationality to him where before she'd seen only a sociopath.

Then again, she was still bound to the passenger seat, and less than an hour had passed since Dax had committed a murder. You took your reassurances where you could find them, but this one was a hell of a stretch.

When Lisa Boone stepped back into the frame, alone this time, no doctor at her side, Dax tensed and reached for the door handle, then stopped himself, lowered his hand, and relaxed back into the seat.

He knows it will be easier to take it from her once she's outside, Abby thought. Entering the hospital was a risk that Dax clearly intended to avoid—he'd gotten Shannon to make the actual room call, and that was, Abby realized with dismay, a smart move. Right now, however capable a killer Lisa Boone was, she was a full step behind him, and he was patient enough to realize that as long as he had the upper hand, forcing the action was unnecessary. He saw more of the board than she did.

None of that was reassuring.

Abby watched the camera shift and weave as Boone approached and took Oltamu's phone from Shannon Beckley's hand. Then she walked backward, sure-footed and graceful, to the door. Only when she was there, with plenty of distance between herself and Shannon, did she glance at the phone.

For all of Abby's horror, some small part of her just wanted to know—what was on it?

Whatever it was, it didn't please Boone. Her face twisted in anger, and she said, "What is this?"

Offscreen, speaking from behind—and below—the camera, Shannon Beckley said, "How do I know?"

"Because you just said *it worked*. The facial recognition and then you put in her nickname and said that it worked. I heard you and watched you."

"It did work. I thought it did. It changed screens, at least. The old screen was her. Once I held it up to her eyes and put in that nickname, it reloaded and the screen changed."

She was speaking too loud, as if trying to draw people's attention. Lisa Boone said, "Keep your voice down."

Shannon went silent. Boone looked at the phone once more, studied it, then said, "It changed from her face to *this*?"

"Yes."

Beside Abby, Dax sighed and said, "I'd like to know what *this* is."

An instant later, Boone said, "Then what in the fuck is this?"

Dax spread his hands and gave a theatrical nod, like *Thank you!*

"I don't know," Shannon said, voice softer now.

"Does she?" Boone asked.

Shannon didn't respond. Boone advanced, phone in one hand, knife in the other.

57

Tara hasn't seen the image yet, but she has an idea of what the woman with the knife is looking at. In fact, she's pretty sure she knows exactly what it is.

Andrea Carter is moving toward her, and Shannon steps protectively between them, and then the knife is nearly at her throat, the movement so swift and sudden that Tara scarcely registers the fact that her hand twitches again.

Carter speaks with the blade pressed against Shannon's neck.

"There's a way to do this without your sister dying," Carter says. "But you need to cooperate."

Shannon gives a strange, high laugh that surprises Tara as much as it apparently surprises Carter.

"Step back," Carter says, "and shut up."

Please listen, Tara urges silently. *Do what she says, because I can answer her next question, I already did, I told you what he took pictures of, and then he was dead, so I know he didn't take any more. I can answer her questions, and she will leave.*

But will she leave? As Shannon moves away, taking two steps toward the foot of the bed, Tara watches Carter and is not so sure. If Tara doesn't answer her questions, then they both have to die. But if she does...what changes? Is there really any way this woman is leaving them alive?

"Show Tara the phone," Shannon says, and she looks at Tara for the first time, and there's a knowingness to the gaze. Tara thinks, *I am right about what's there, and Shannon remembers what I said.*

The woman turns the phone display to her then, and, sure enough, there he is: Hobo.

"What is the dog's name?" the woman asks.

Tara looks at Shannon. Flicks her eyes up once. Yes, tell her. What is the point in protecting this? *Saving our lives, that's the point.* But Tara's instinct says that talking is better. It's a strange instinct for a woman who can't speak, and yet there it is.

"What does that mean?" Carter asks. "The way she looked at you. Her eyes moved up. That's a yes. What is she saying yes to?"

Her voice tightens with anger, and Tara is terrified of what will happen if Shannon lies or resists, but for once, she doesn't.

"She's saying yes to me because she wants me to tell you who the dog is," Shannon says.

"You know?"

Shannon nods.

"Say it."

"Hobo," Shannon says, once again in a loud voice, but this time the woman doesn't tell her to lower it. She just stares at her as if she's making a very dangerous joke.

"Hobo."

Shannon nods again.

"How do you know that?"

"Because she told me. Earlier. When the doctor and I were asking her about her memories of the accident. Before it happened, Oltamu took a picture of her and a picture of Hobo."

Andrea Carter eyes Shannon, then Tara. She sees either no indication of a lie or no reason for them to lie. She flips the phone over in her hand, and taps on it with her thumb.

"Doesn't work," she says, but her voice is troubled and she keeps staring at the screen.

"I think," Shannon says cautiously, "that's because you'll need the dog's eyes."

The woman looks at Shannon as if she wouldn't mind gutting

her with that knife right here. Suddenly, Tara has a terrible fear for Dr. Pine. Surely she wouldn't have killed him in a hospital.

But where is he?

Dead, she thinks. The fear turns into a certainty, and that grows into a certainty over how this will end. She and Shannon will die too. All for something Tara will never understand, all for whatever is on this stranger's phone. Damn it, don't they at least deserve to know what they're dying for?

"That's how it worked with her," Shannon says. "Facial recognition first, then name."

The woman looks at the display again, and Tara thinks she must be seeing a message that confirms this, because she seems even more frustrated by the device than by Shannon.

"That's insane," she says. "For a dog? It won't work. The technology doesn't exist."

"Actually," Shannon says, "they use it on pet doors. I saw an ad for one."

"I don't have time for this bullshit. *You* don't have time to do this."

"Google it," Shannon says. "You can buy pet doors that open with facial recognition. I don't know why. To keep out raccoons or whatever, I have no idea. But I am telling you, the way it worked with her was to get the facial-recognition lock first, then put in the name. The dog is named Hobo. I am positive."

They stare each other down for a moment. Finally Andrea Carter says, "Where is the dog?"

"He was up there by the bridge. Where Oltamu died. She says he is a stray."

"You're lying," Carter says, but it's more hopeful than forceful.

"Ask her," Shannon says.

Carter turns to Tara. "Is she lying?"

Tara flicks her eyes twice. No, Shannon isn't lying.

Carter pauses, seems to fight down building rage, and then says, "Will the dog be up there? Is he easy to find?"

Hobo is not particularly easy to find, and he certainly won't be for a stranger, but Tara sees more hope for them in that lie than in the truth, so she gives one flick—yes.

"He took a picture of you and asked for a nickname," Carter says. "And then he took a picture of the dog and asked for the dog's name?"

One flick. Yes. Growing more certain with each answer that she's sealing their fates, but not seeing any way out. The world is an extension of her body now—a trap with no escape.

"Was that the last picture he took?" Carter asks.

Tara's thumb jerks. Carter and Shannon both see this.

"What does that mean?" Carter asks warily.

"Nothing. It's a spasm."

But Shannon is wrong. That thumb twitch means everything. It means the girl fighting against the current has found the green-gold waters again, the secret channel where the water rotates and then the current becomes friend and not foe. It is so much more than a spasm. It is Tara coming back. Finding her way through dark halls and riding dark waters, chasing thin bands of light.

"Just use your eyes this time. *Was that the last picture he took?*" Carter repeats.

Tara sees it then, as if the last twitch of her thumb were a courier arriving with critical news, a message Tara should have understood already: She has power here. She has control of the situation in a way none of them suspect she does.

Yes, she is motionless and mute, locked in. But now she recognizes the strength in this. The only move that can save them will come because of her condition. She can buy Shannon time, at least. She can do that much.

She flicks her eyes twice, telling this awful woman, *No, it was not the last picture he took.*

Tara can't do many things, but she can still think, and she understands the dilemma she's placing the woman with the knife in now—the lie is worth the risk, because Tara knows what's coming.

Sure enough, the question arrives like a hanging curveball, belt-high.

"Did he take another one of you?" Carter says.

One flick, and Tara swats it out of the park.

Yes, she lies, *he took one more of me. And you know what that means, bitch? You can't kill me yet. You'll need my eyes again. Think about it. Won't work with a dead face. Or at least, you're not sure that it will. And you can't take me to Hammel with you, so that means you've got to come back to find me, dead or alive. I'll be harder to find if I'm dead, and you'll have to trust that the phone will recognize my face if I am. I don't think it will.*

There's a pause that seems endless but that can't be more than five seconds. Those seconds feel like the countdown before an explosion, though. The crescent-moon blade glimmers, Andrea Carter stands with every muscle taut, and Shannon looks as paralyzed as Tara.

"Here's how we're going to handle this," Carter says at last. "Shannon and I are going for a ride. Together. We will find the dog and test your story, Tara. If it works, and no one follows us, then Shannon will drive back to you. If it doesn't, or if you somehow send someone after us? Well, I suppose you'll have plenty of time to think about that in the days to come."

Shannon is looking at Tara with an expression that Tara remembers well—quiet and restrained, thoughtful. A quiet Shannon is something to worry about, because on the rare occasions that she swallows her anger and retreats, she is lost to thoughts of settling the score. This is good, because it means she knows that Tara lied and that the phone will prove that. Tara bought her time, but Shannon will be alone when the lie is discovered.

"All right," Andrea Carter says, and the blade disappears into a black handle that vanishes into her hand. "Then we'll ride,

Shannon. You'd better hope your sister understands the stakes. People will ask her questions about me. Her answers are going to decide your life."

Shannon doesn't respond to that. She just looks at Tara.

"You know how much I love you?" she says.

Almost too late, Tara remembers to look upward once.

Shannon nods and turns away. She opens the door and steps out with Andrea Carter walking just behind her, the knife not visible but not far away.

58

"Brilliant play!" Dax shouted at the video like a color commentator breaking down a playoff game. "She's caught lovely Lisa, do you see that, Abby? Do you understand? Lisa *can't* kill Tara now. Not if she's going to need her again. That's ingenious. It might even be true that she'll need Tara again, but I doubt it. Boone probably doubts it too. What can you do, though? You can't pick the girl up and take her with you. So you take the sister and hope that keeps her quiet. But Tara called the shot on that one. Good for her."

He spoke with true admiration, although Abby had no doubt that he would still kill Tara himself without hesitation or pity.

No one had passed them in the garage since they arrived, and only two cars had pulled out from the floors below. A hospital never shut down, but it had quiet hours, and they had arrived in the midst of them. When Shannon Beckley exited room 373 and began her walk out of the hospital with Lisa Boone alongside her, the camera showed a quiet hallway ahead. They avoided the main lobby and entered a side stairwell.

Dax started the car.

He backed out of the parking space and started down toward the garage exit, driving slowly, unhurried as always and seemingly sure of his choice. His treasured phone, the item worthy of all this bloodshed, was in the hands of an apparent rival, but he seemed unbothered.

They passed an elderly couple walking to a Buick, and if the pair had looked into the Challenger, they might have noticed the cord around Abby's neck, but they did not look.

"Are you following them?" Abby asked. Once she'd hated listening to the kid's incessant talk, but now she wanted to know. It felt, surreally, as if a part of her were rooting for Dax now. Shannon Beckley seemed more likely to die at Lisa Boone's hands than his at this moment, and he was the only person who knew enough to intercede. Other than Tara, of course, mute and trapped.

"That wouldn't be smart," Dax said.

"You're giving up? Just letting her take it?" Abby had a horrible thought: What if this Lisa Boone worked with Dax? What if his surprise at her presence was simply because she'd been unannounced, not because he viewed her as a rival?

Then he said, "Oh, we're certainly not going to do that. Come on, Abby! We've come too far to give up now."

"Then what are you doing?"

If the questions bothered him, he didn't show it. He put his window down, fed a ticket and a credit card into the automated garage booth, and the gate rose. He took the credit card back, put the window up, and pulled away, out of the lights of the garage and back into darkness.

"It would be a mistake to follow her," he said. "Boone is too good. At least, that's my understanding. It's a long drive, and she'd see us, and she would have the advantage then. Right now we have the advantage, Abby, don't you see? We know where they're going. And we can watch them."

On the cell phone's display, the camera was bobbing along, Shannon Beckley still on foot, walking across the street and toward a parking lot on the other side of the hospital. Lisa Boone was not in the frame.

"Correct me if I'm wrong," Dax said, "but haven't you been to the accident site?"

Abby didn't answer right away. She was seeing the idea coalesce. It was a very simple trap, but a trap set for an assassin. She couldn't imagine how anyone was going to make it out of this night alive. Dax might. Or Boone might. One or the other had to win. But as for Abby and Shannon Beckley?

He'll get out of the car, she thought. *He'll have to, down there. And when he does, he's going to leave you here. You'll need to be a lot faster with that headrest than you were last time.*

"Haven't you?" Dax repeated, an edge to his voice now.

"Yes," Abby said. "I've been there."

"Then you'll guide me and tell me what to expect when I get there. It's important that you remember it accurately. If I lose my advantage, well, that could become an ugly situation for everyone." He caught a green light and turned left, heading for the interstate. "We'll need to drive a bit faster too. Boone won't want to take risks, but I don't think she's inclined to waste much time."

Once they were all on the highway, the camera's livestream began to fade in and out, but they weren't missing much. Just the open road in front of Shannon Beckley, the same open road that was in front of Abby. Dax paid the video feed no mind, but Abby watched, trying to identify mile markers and signs that would show her how far behind Boone and Shannon were. She guessed they were maybe ten minutes behind when Dax exited the interstate and began following the winding county roads that led to Hammel.

They were in the hills now, and a low fog crept through bare-limbed trees and settled beneath those that still had their leaves. A few houses had Halloween decorations up, and jack-o'-lanterns with rictus smiles sat on porches or beside mailboxes. The wind shivered dead leaves off skeletal branches. Autumn charm was dying; winter was on its way.

Dax drove with his right hand only, the gun in the door panel, close to his left hand, which rested on his thigh. Abby watched him bring that left hand up time and again on curves. Usually he didn't bring it all the way to the wheel, but Abby knew that the Hellcat was still foreign to him, and even though he wasn't driving recklessly, he was uneasy about that power and handling. Didn't trust himself with the car yet.

Watching his weakness gave Abby a feeling of strength that would have seemed absurd to any spectator—one person had the gun and the wheel, and the other was tied to the passenger seat. And yet, as a passenger, able to watch the way Dax handled the car and the uncertainty he brought to it, she felt her confidence grow. That uncertainty was a small thing, but it was a weakness. If Abby could get the wheel back, he'd be gone. The gap she'd found in her panic on the rain-swept highway when she'd sliced through the semis and cars and glided through the break in the guardrail seemed to have carried some of her old brain back into her body. A door had opened in that moment. If she got behind the wheel, she could find it again. She could kick that door down if it didn't open willingly.

All she needed was the chance.

She looked back down at the phone's display. They'd lost the signal, and Shannon Beckley's camera was gone. No surprise, not in these hills. Dax wasn't pushing the speed too much, and Abby expected that the women behind them wouldn't be either. They were clones—one killer, one hostage, nobody looking to attract police attention. That would give Dax his five- or maybe ten-minute lead at Hammel. What would he do with it? Abby thought he would leave the car. He would expect the car to attract attention that a man on foot in the darkness would not.

If I get five minutes alone, I'll get that headrest off. I know how it's done now. Feet on the dash, back arched, start with the left side...

She just needed those minutes.

"Turn left here," Abby said.

Dax seemed surprised by the instruction, but he slowed.

"The signs say the college is to the right."

"We'll save a few minutes this way. Minutes matter now, don't they?"

Dax turned to her, looking even younger and less hostile without the hat. Just a boy out for a ride in a muscle car.

"Yes," he said. "Minutes matter."

He turned left.

They wound through a residential stretch with Abby calling out directions, and then they turned on Ames Road and started a steep descent. The darkness was lifting in that barely perceptible way of predawn, not so much a brightening as a fading of the blackness.

"The railroad bridge is at the bottom of the hill," Abby said. "Parking is on the left. There won't be any cars down there now, probably."

She thought about saying more, adding something about how they'd stand out to Lisa Boone if they parked down there, but she caught herself. Let him reach that conclusion on his own. He'd be suspicious if Abby offered too much help.

The transmission downshifted on the steep grade, an automatic adjustment that took the driver out of the equation and that Abby had always hated but that Dax seemed to prefer. You could switch the Challenger to a bastardized version of a manual transmission, no clutch pedal but paddle shifters. He hadn't done that once, though.

Scared of the power, Abby thought, and again the ludicrous confidence rose. *I can beat him if he just gets out of the car.*

The headlights pinned the railroad bridge below them, the angled steel beams throwing shadows onto the dark river. Abby looked at the place and tried to remember what it had felt like when she'd paced this pavement with a camera in hand and confusion rising. That's all it had been then—confusion. Carlos Ramirez's story, so clean and simple, wasn't accurate. Carlos, the second person to die. Hank, who'd wanted nothing but easy money and a chance for Abby to face down her demons, was the third. Gerry, the man who'd died on his kitchen floor, the fourth.

Will I be the fifth? Shannon Beckley the sixth? How many more die before it's done?

"Do you know what's on Oltamu's phone?" Abby asked.

Again, Dax seemed startled by the sound of her voice. He hesitated, then said, "I don't. Should be interesting, don't you think? A lot of people seem willing to go to extreme lengths just to have it in their hands."

"What if it's nothing?"

Dax laughed. "I hardly think that's an option."

"It may be. He could have wiped the data. You don't know."

"No. All those locks on an empty phone? There's something there."

"It will involve batteries," Abby said. "And I think it might involve cars. He came from the Black Lake. He watched testing."

Dax seemed more intrigued now, but he was also in the place where he had to set the trap, and he wasn't going to divide his focus.

"When I find out," he said, pulling into one of the angled spaces in the spot where Amandi Oltamu had died and Tara Beckley had nearly been erased from existence, "you'll be the first to know. You've earned that much, Abby. I'll tell you before I kill you. That's a promise."

He was surveying the area, taking rapid inventory, his mind no longer on Abby but on the possibilities waiting here in the darkness above the river. The possibilities, and the pitfalls.

"Did you see the dog when you were here?" he asked.

"I did not."

"But our girl Tara believes he will appear. Hobo. There's a lot riding on a stray dog named Hobo." He went silent, drumming his fingers on the steering wheel and staring into the dark woods where birches swayed and creaked.

"Boone needs the phone to be opened," he said at length. "Interesting. Gerry's German friend seemed to think it was worth trying to open it, but it wasn't a priority. So our buyer wants to kill the phone, and hers wants to see it."

He looked at Abby again. "You're right—I'm awfully curious about what's on it."

He dropped his right hand onto the gearshift, put the car in reverse, backed out, whipped the car around, and drove up the hill again. Abby tried to stay expressionless, tried not to let her relief show.

Dax was going to park the Challenger where it wouldn't stand out, and that meant he would need to leave the car. The options, then, were to keep Abby in the car or bring her along. The latter carried more risk.

There's a third option. He kills you here. He doesn't need you anymore.

At the crest of the hill on Ames Road, where more houses began to appear, Dax turned the car and parallel-parked in a spot between streetlights where the Challenger would be obscured by shadows. He cut the engine and the lights. Paused and assessed. Nodded, satisfied. He took the cell phone, its screen filled with the image of the weaving night road that Shannon Beckley was driving just behind them, and slipped it into his pocket.

"Now, Abby, I'm afraid we're going to have to separate for a time. I'll miss you, but it's for the best. You'll have nefarious ideas in my absence, I'm sure. Things you could do to hurt me and, in your noble if dim-witted mind, help Shannon." He plucked the gun from inside the door panel, and for an instant Abby could see the barrel being shoved through the lips of the man named Gerry just before the kill shot was fired and thought the same was coming for her.

Then Dax switched the gun to his right hand and reached for the door handle with his left.

"Before you make any choices," he said, "I want you to consider this—I've kept you alive, and Lisa Boone is unlikely to do the same. You want me dead, and that's fine. If I'm dead, though? She's the last one left. I'm not sure I'd choose that if I were you."

With that, he opened the door and stepped out into the chill night. He'd disabled the interior lights, and when he closed the door, he did it softly. Then he started down the hill at a jog, moving swiftly and silently.

Abby watched until he vanished into the woods. Then she braced her feet on the dashboard, took a deep breath, and arched her aching back to extend the reach of her bound hands as far as possible. She found the headrest releases quicker this time, and she set to work.

59

Boone hadn't been planning on a hostage, but that didn't mean she was unprepared for one. She was always prepared for such a contingency.

She used plastic zip-tie cuffs on Shannon Beckley's wrists and a single piece of duct tape over her mouth, things that could be removed quickly in the event of trouble, but she used real cuffs to bind Shannon's left ankle to a bar beneath the passenger seat. There would be no runaways on Boone's watch.

Satisfied, she drove away in the girl's rented Jeep. In the backseat, Beckley seemed composed enough; she was avoiding hysteria, at least, which was a help. Boone would have no trouble silencing her if it came to that, but she also needed to keep her alive until all sequences of locks had been defeated. Tara Beckley had managed to claim an infuriating amount of control. For a quadriplegic who couldn't speak, an astounding amount of control, actually. Even if they found the fucking dog and the lock actually opened, Boone would still have to make her way back to Tara once more and deal with the challenges of the hospital without her helpful aide Dr. Pine. Shannon Beckley could be key to gaining access during the daylight hours, when the hospital was more active and the parents would be in the room, and Boone feared that the waking vegetable that was Tara Beckley could cause more trouble if she didn't see proof of life of her sister. She could hold out. In fact, Boone suspected that she would, and she understood why—Tara didn't have much left to lose.

Then again, there were the parents to consider.

Maybe Shannon wasn't so vital after all.

All this would be decided after they left Hammel. For now the task was dictated by the image on the phone. Her current pursuit was ludicrous—this was a multimillion-dollar job in service of billions, and Boone was chasing a stray dog named Hobo. In her varied and diverse career, leaving corpses in more than a dozen countries, she'd never felt more absurd, and yet a part of her admired Oltamu. Somehow he'd felt the hellhounds closing in, and his response had been as resourceful as anyone's could be in that moment. Nobody was going to get the intelligence he'd collected simply by picking up his phone. He'd played a risky game and lost it, but he'd made a fine effort all the way to the end.

Ask the girl, he'd instructed Boone, presumably having no idea just how difficult that would be. The doctor had come through, the girl had come through, and now the locks were turning, albeit slowly.

The drive ate away at hours Boone couldn't afford to lose, and with the night edging toward dawn, she had to will herself to keep her speed down and use the time to consider what lay ahead. Pine was going to be a problem. People would find him soon enough, and while it would take a first-rate medical examiner to determine that he hadn't died of natural causes, it would also inevitably cause chaos in the hospital. The place wouldn't be nearly so quiet when Boone returned.

Chaos, though, could be used as a shield. It was all a matter of timing. The dog had to be dealt with, then Tara Beckley. Step by step. Unless, of course, Tara Beckley was lying, and there was no third lock. In that case, Boone could leave her sister's body behind and be out of the country before Tara blinked her way through the alphabet board with any message that police might believe.

They reached the outskirts of Hammel, passed signs for the college, and then the winding New England road crested and dropped abruptly, a steep hill descending toward the river.

This was the place.

She slowed and checked the mirrors. No one had been behind them for long throughout the drive, and no one was now. To the right and to the left were peaceful houses with tree-lined lawns, windows dark, a porch light or outdoor floodlight on here and there. The streetlights were designed for form rather than function, and they cast only a dim glow over the sidewalks, where dead leaves swirled in the wind. Three cars on the curb to her right, one car and one truck to the left. None of them looked like police vehicles, but there was one that didn't fit the neighborhood—a souped-up Challenger with a vented hood and wide racing tires. It was parked at the end of the street and in the shadows. Boone gave it a careful look as she passed, but the windows were deeply tinted and she couldn't make out anything. Some professor's midlife-crisis car, she decided, and drove on.

At the bottom of the hill, angled parking spaces lined the left-hand side, all of them empty, and then there was an ancient railroad bridge. Beneath it, the river was a dark ribbon, swollen from recent rains. The current would be strong. If Tara Beckley had gone in the water today, she likely wouldn't have been rescued. That would have cost Boone some serious money. Tara's miraculous recovery to waking-vegetable status had the potential to be very, very lucrative. Instant-retirement money, vanish-to-your-own-island money, though Boone had no intention of retiring. When you loved your work, why stop? And hers wasn't a profession you left easily. Those who remained alert to every motion in the shadows stayed alive; those who didn't died. There was no retreat. This was the journey of any apex predator.

She pulled into one of the angled parking spaces on the river's eastern shore, cut the engine, and said, "It's going to be very unfortunate for your family if the dog isn't here."

The threat had nothing behind it, though. The dog was Boone's problem and one that couldn't readily be solved with or without the Beckleys. Either the girl was right or she was wrong. The dog would be here or he wouldn't be.

"Sit tight, Shannon," she said. She popped the door open and stepped out into the night.

For a few seconds, she just stood there, surveying the scene. The lonely lamps in the area, too dim, cast the only light on either side of the bridge. The next street lamp was all the way at the top of the hill, where the houses began. No one had built down here, prob- ably due to flood risk. The river was high and felt close, the low whisper of moving water almost intimate in the darkness.

To her left, a jogging path curled into the trees, went up a small rise, and then vanished, probably running parallel to the river. To her right, the bridge loomed high and cold above the water, the old steel girders giving the wind something to whistle through. It was a long bridge, maybe two hundred feet, spanning a narrow river below. She saw now that there were actually two bridges—the old railroad bridge, set higher, the tracks running on banked gravel when they crossed the river, and slightly below it, a newer pedes- trian bridge, connecting the jogging paths on eastern and western shores. On the other side of the river, ornate lamps threw muted light onto the path as it led through a thicket of pines and on to- ward the campus. She could see the brighter lights of the buildings beyond, maybe a quarter of a mile off.

It was a dark and quiet spot. It suited her.

Satisfied that she was alone, she moved away from the car. She had the knife in her left hand and the gun holstered behind her back. She left Oltamu's phone in the car, unconcerned about that for now. Priority one was ensuring that she was alone and knew the terrain.

She walked toward the pedestrian bridge, thinking of how far a stray dog might have gone in all this time. He could be in a shelter or dead, hit by a car. What were the odds of finding him?

She went farther out onto the bridge, pivoted, and looked back down at the parking lot. Shannon Beckley's rental Jeep was a dark silent shape in the place where her sister had once posed for Amandi Oltamu, clueless to all that was headed her way.

A dog, Boone thought with disgust. *Amandi, you took it a step too far.*

Somewhere to the west, behind the cold, freshening wind, a train horn sounded, soft and mournful, like something out of another time. Maybe the girl hadn't lied. Maybe the dog would appear for the morning train as promised. Maybe—

"Hobo."

The sound of the dog's name came at her so softly that at first she didn't believe it was real, as if the voice had come from within her own mind. Then it came again, clearer now.

"Hobo! Hey, buddy. C'mere. C'mon out."

Someone at the other end of the bridge was calling to the dog. Boone stared in that direction, trying to make out a shape, but it was too far off. Branches cracked, and bushes shook, and somewhere on the western bank of the river, the voice said, "Good boy! Eat up, chief."

A male voice, young and foolish. A Hammel student, probably. Another fan of a stray dog that the kids had adopted like a mascot.

Or a trap? Had Tara managed to communicate quicker than Boone had anticipated?

Boone considered this and dismissed it. If the girl had been able to summon police this quickly, they wouldn't have been the kind of police who would set a trap. They'd have raced up with sirens blaring, county mounties with big guns and small brains, looking for a heroic moment.

"Good boy," the voice said again, and again the bushes rustled, and this time Boone spotted the point of motion.

She drew her gun with her right hand and her knife with her left. Ordinarily she wouldn't have considered this—you fired with two hands unless you had no choice. But she didn't want to make any more noise than she had to, and then there was the special consideration of the dog.

Oltamu's phone was back in the Jeep. She considered returning for it but pressed ahead. She wanted to get a clearer view of what she was dealing with. She crossed the pedestrian bridge silently and swiftly, walking to the place where the bushes rustled. It was just below the pines, close to the water's edge. As Boone neared the end of the bridge, the boy made one of those annoying clucking/cooing sounds that people used around animals and babies. It sounded as if he was trying to win the dog's allegiance and hadn't yet succeeded. This was a bad sign. If the animal was that skittish, Boone might have to risk a gunshot. But then, trying to get his eyes lined up for the camera presented its own challenges. How much fight would the dog have left, and how fast would Boone lose the opportunity to capture the life left in his eyes? Too many unknowns. Perhaps if she recruited the help of this kid who knew the dog, she could—

"Put the gun on the ground and then take two steps back, Boone."

She knew better than to whirl at the sound. She was surprised by the voice, yes, but Boone had been surprised before, and she knew that you lived when you listened, stayed calm, and waited for the opportunity to correct your mistake. Clear head, fast hands. These were her gifts, and they weren't gone yet.

"The gun," he repeated.

Only the gun. This alone was a reassurance. If he hadn't noticed the knife, then he was already on his way to death.

She knelt, taking care to let her left hand hang naturally, drawing no attention to the knife curled against her palm, and set the gun on the asphalt in front of her, then straightened and took two steps back as instructed. The voice had come from behind her and to the right. She looked that way, finally.

He was standing on one of the iron spans that held up the railroad bridge. That put him above her and shielded by the shadow

from the bridge, his face obscured. She saw him only as a silhouette, framed above the dark rushing water.

"Hi, Boone," he said.

The voice was vaguely familiar, but she couldn't place it. Youth-
ful but with a lilt to it, a thread of taunt, that evoked someone she'd
once known.

"Who are you?" she said.

"Call me Hobo." His hand moved in the darkness, and on the
west bank of the river, bushes shook. He had some sort of a line
attached to them, designed to draw her attention. An amateur's
gambit, one that she should have spotted immediately, but she'd
been so certain she was out in front that she hadn't feared the trap.
How did he know the dog's name? Who was he, and how had he
known that she would arrive in this place, on this mission?

"Who's your client?" he said.

Boone didn't respond.

The man shifted, his shadow unspooling like a piece of the bridge
coming to life, and the bushes shook once more. He thought that was
cute. Boone was pleased to see it. He had one hand busy with that
trick. That he would face her down with one hand occupied told
her that she didn't need to worry about placing that voice; he was a
stranger. He knew her name, but he did not truly know Boone.

"My client is an Israeli," she said, turning her body to him and
squaring her shoulders. "But I don't know his name."

He moved farther out on the steel beam, and she saw that there
was a gun in his right hand but that it was held down against
his leg. How foolish was he? How did one come to know Lisa
Boone's name and not know enough to keep one's gun pointed at
her heart? She was almost insulted.

He stood there watching her from what he thought was a clever
hiding spot but was really just a convenient place for him to die. The
dark river below waited to carry his body away when he fell. His
left hand still held the cord that he'd tied to the bushes, and his right

hand held the gun with its muzzle pointed at the river. He was out on the center of the beam now. It couldn't have been much more than ten inches wide, and yet he never looked down, had moved with smoothness in the night. What he lacked in brains he made up for in composure and balance. It was a dangerous high-wire act out there. Boone's own balance was also perfect, though, and she had a stable platform beneath her. She would have to throw the knife left-handed, but this was why you practiced with your left hand and in the dark. She was not worried about accuracy.

"You'd better remember the client's name," he said, "because Tara Beckley can't blink that one out for me."

Again, the voice sounded familiar, and Boone probably could have made the connection if she'd allowed her focus to drift. But she wouldn't. Not as she slowly, almost motionlessly, thumbed the knife blade open in her cupped left hand.

"I don't have names," she said. "I only have phone numbers."

"You'll have to do better than that."

"Deal," Boone said, and when she threw the knife, she was almost sad that he'd end up in the river, because she wanted to see his face.

She was down on her back before she understood that she'd been shot.

How? How did he beat me? Did I miss? I've never missed.

Her knife was gone, but where was her gun? Somewhere below her and to the left. She told herself to reach for it, but the command couldn't bring strength. She lay there tasting her own blood and watched her killer jump nimbly from the railroad bridge span down to the footbridge, a treacherous leap in the dark but one he made without hesitation. He caught the railing on the footbridge with his left hand, then swung himself up and over.

She saw then that she had not missed with the knife. The blade was embedded in the back of his right hand. His shooting hand. He'd brought the gun up just fast enough. Fraction-of-a-blink speed. That was the separation between life and death. Before this, Boone had always been the winner in this contest.

Who are you? She tried to ask it but couldn't. No words came. She watched him advance, and her vision grayed out, and she hoped that she would last long enough to know who it was.

He'll get the phone, Boone thought numbly, aware that it was no longer a concern to her yet still disappointed. It had been worth so much.

He came on patiently, without firing again even though that would have been the smart play, and Boone had the sense that he wanted her to know him too. When he was close enough to be seen, though, she realized something was wrong. In the confusion brought on by darkness and imminent death, he looked like a child.

He'd shot like a pro, though. Boone's knife was still embedded in the back of his right hand, blood running down his fingers and falling to the pavement in fat drips. He hadn't paused to address the knife yet, and Boone knew that he wouldn't until he was certain that she was dead. There weren't many in her business with that level of focus.

So who had gotten her?

She blinked and studied him. The boyish face was a lie; she knew his voice, knew his motions, knew his pale hair in the moonlight. Knew him because he'd shot fast and straight even with a knife embedded in his gun hand.

"Hello, Boone," he said. He blurred before her eyes, and in the moment of double vision, she seemed to see two of him smiling down at her, and then she knew them. They came in a pair, always. Her brain whispered that this was impossible, but she couldn't remember why. She squinted up at her killer.

"Jack?" she whispered.

"No," the boy said, "but close enough."

Then came the fulfillment of a promise that Boone had understood for many years now: the last thing she saw was the muzzle of a gun.

60

Abby was halfway down the hill, moving quietly but awkwardly, still trying to get her circulation flowing, when she heard the clap of the gunshot.

The sound came from the far side of the bridge, close to the western shore. She had no idea if Dax had killed or been killed.

She also knew that it didn't matter. She'd escaped the car, the headrest coming free with one spine-popping twist, but Shannon Beckley was, presumably, still trapped in hers. Abby stopped in the blackness beneath a twisting oak limb and took gasping breaths of the chilled autumn air. She looked behind her, out to where the woods promised cover and the houses promised help, and then back down at the Jeep, where Shannon waited alone for whoever had survived the shooting on the bridge.

Abby's hands were still bound at the wrists. She could run but not fight. They wouldn't pursue her. Dax wouldn't, at least, and the woman he'd called Lisa Boone was of his breed. They'd calculate risk and reward, and they'd run.

But they wouldn't leave Shannon Beckley behind. The witness who couldn't run or hide was the witness who would be eliminated.

Abby started downhill again, moving quietly, chasing the shadows. The bridge was bathed in blackness, but as she watched, a figure leaped from the upper bridge, beneath the railroad tracks, and landed on the footbridge, catching the rail with his left hand. In that moment when he flickered through the night, Abby knew who'd come out victorious in the showdown between assassins.

Dax hadn't wasted his advantage. Those early minutes in the darkness, all-seeing and all-knowing as he waited for an unprepared adversary, had been put to good use.

His attention was diverted from the car now, though. The bridge crowned above the river, and the shooting had taken place near the opposite shore, which meant his view of the parking lot would be minimal. Abby stayed as low as she could, approaching the Jeep, and just before she reached for the door handle, she felt the overwhelming certainty that it would be locked and she would have come down here for no reason but to guarantee her death.

Right then, there was another clap on the bridge. A second shot.

She knelt and turned her hands palms up, like a beggar, and got her fingertips under the door handle. She pulled, bracing for the interior lights that would come on like a prison guard's searchlight, pinning her escape attempt.

The door opened, and darkness remained.

She's just like him, Abby realized. The woman named Boone had shut off the automatic lights. She was just like him, favoring control at all times.

And she was dead now.

Abby leaned into the car. Shannon Beckley was in the backseat, a strip of duct tape over her mouth. Her hands rested in her lap, bound with zip-ties, similar to Abby.

"We need to run," Abby whispered. "Can you—"

She didn't need to finish the question; Shannon was already shaking her head. She moved her foot and Abby heard a metallic jingle, looked down, and saw that Shannon was cuffed to something beneath the seat. Maybe to the seat itself.

Shit, shit, shit.

Shannon made a jutting motion with her chin, a series of upward nudges, like a cat seeking attention, and Abby understood what she meant. Shannon was telling her to run. To save herself. Just as Hank once had, and back then Abby had listened and lived.

Abby shook her head. She stayed in place, heart skittering, trying to keep her breathing as silent as possible while she looked around the car for any help, any weapon. There was nothing—except for a phone in the cup holder.

She reached for it excitedly, fumbling with her bound hands, and only when she'd secured it in her grasp did she recognize that it wasn't a source of help at all. It wasn't even a phone. It was Oltamu's fake.

She dropped the phone with disgust, then jerked with surprise when Shannon Beckley kicked the back of the passenger seat, hard. Abby looked up into her fierce eyes and watched Shannon look pointedly at the center console.

Abby found the latch, lifted the console cover, and saw Shannon's cell phone resting there.

Beside the phone was a set of car keys with a Hertz keychain.

Abby grabbed them and swung into the driver's seat. She reached for the door handle with her bound hands and eased it shut, not quite latching it for fear of making noise. Just before she put her foot on the brake pedal, which would flash the telltale lights illuminating her escape attempt, she checked the mirror.

Dax was at the top of the bridge and walking their way.

Better hurry, she told herself, but she didn't move. Instead she watched him walking confidently down the center of the bridge, a gun in each hand, and she saw that he was indifferent to the Jeep, indifferent to the darkness, indifferent to everything. In his mind, the threat had been eliminated, and the rest would be easy. Abby could start the Jeep now, well within pistol range, and hope he wouldn't hit the tires. If he did, though...

She looked up the long, steep hill ahead and saw how it would end—the Jeep grinding to a pained halt on shredded rubber. He'd close on them easily enough then. This wasn't like Hank's house, where Abby had been able to get into the pines and be protected from the gunfire. She would be driving down the length of target range for him and counting on him to miss.

He wasn't going to miss.

"Get down below the windows," Abby whispered to Shannon Beckley. "Fast."

Shannon's eyes were wide above the strip of duct tape, but she didn't hesitate in following the instructions. She slid off the seat and into an awkward ball on the floor of the car. She was tall, and the space wasn't large, but she was bound to the car only by one foot, and she was flexible enough to burrow down tightly.

"Good," Abby whispered. "Stay down. No matter what. I'm going to kill him now."

Abby checked the mirror once more, then slid down in the driver's seat, low enough to bring the back of her head almost level with the steering wheel. She lost sight of Dax in the rearview mirror but found him in the side-view.

He was almost off the bridge. From there it was twenty or twenty-five paces to the Jeep. Unprotected ground. For her, and for him.

If she got him, it would be over. If she missed...

The ignition lag will be the moment you lose advantage, she thought. *That half-second hitch between engine cranking and engine catching. He's very fast.*

He'd shoot before he moved. She was almost certain of that. He'd shoot before he moved, and he would expect whoever was driving the Jeep to be in flight mode, not fight mode. He counted on fear.

He wouldn't be getting any more of that from Abby.

He walked on with a fast but controlled stride. Refusing, as always, to be rushed. Abby bit her lip until blood filled her mouth. Her hands trembled just below the push-button ignition; her foot hovered above the brake pedal, calf muscles bunched, threatening to cramp.

Down he came. Stepping off the bridge without pause. He didn't so much as glance up the road at the car from which she'd escaped. His eyes were locked dead ahead, and she was sure that he was looking right into the side-view mirror and seeing her eyes. The guns dangled in his hands, and the second of them was proof of Boone's death, as sure a trophy as if he'd carried her scalp back.

Thirty feet away now. Abby almost pressed on the brake but managed to hold off.

Twenty feet. Close enough? No. He would have to be almost to the vehicle. Then, she just had three simple steps—press the brake and the ignition, shift from park to reverse, and hit the gas.

Oh, and duck. That was key.

Fifteen feet, ten…

Abby slammed her foot onto the brake pedal and punched the ignition simultaneously. The dash lights came on, and then, with what felt like excruciating slowness, the engine growled.

She ripped the shifter from park to reverse as the back window imploded, and then she hit the gas. Three shots were fired, maybe more. The Jeep ripped backward, and then there was an impact on the left side, glancing, almost imperceptible, but she knew what it was because there'd been only one thing between her and the bridge.

Got him. Got the bastard!

The gunfire was done, and the bridge and the river beyond had to be avoided, so she switched from gas pedal to brake and jerked the Jeep to a stop.

No more shots. Not a sound except for the engine.

She poked her head up and searched for him. The headlights showed a short expanse of grass and then the trees, the jogging path a ribbon of black between them. Empty.

She looked sideways and found him.

He was down in the grass behind the parking lot, fighting to rise to his feet.

He didn't make it. He got halfway up and then fell to his knees. His hands were empty, and his left arm dangled unnaturally across his body, broken. He patted the grass with his right hand, searching for a gun, and Abby pushed herself all the way up in the driver's seat, thin slivers of glass biting through her jeans. She let go of the wheel and used her bound hands to knock the gearshift into drive.

Kill him.

As if he'd heard the thought, Dax looked up at the Jeep. Before Abby could reach for the steering wheel, he lurched upward again. This time he made it to his feet.

Then he turned and ran.

She was so astonished that she left her foot on the brake. She sat motionless, watching him go. His run was awkward; he was hurting badly. But he moved fast for a wounded man. He was panicked.

You coward, she thought. Somehow, she'd expected he would fight until the end. She was almost disappointed to see him run.

But there he went, laboring up the hill toward the Challenger. Did he think Abby was still inside that car and that Shannon Beckley had driven the Jeep into him, or had he seen Abby's face in the instant before she hit him? She hoped he had. She wanted him to know who'd gotten him. In any case, he'd know soon enough, when he found the Challenger empty. He was covering ground surprisingly fast despite his injuries, running on adrenaline. Running on fear. He was scared of her, and that filled her with a savage delight.

The train whistle shrilled to the west. To the east, at the top of the hill near the Challenger, the sky was edging from black to gray. Dawn almost here. Daylight on the way, and Dax on the run.

She'd won.

Abby twisted and looked into the backseat.

"You okay?"

Shannon nodded. Her cheek was bleeding where a ribbon of glass had opened it up, but she seemed unaware of the wound.

"He's gone," Abby said. "He's running away."

Two flashes of light came from up the hill, and she looked that way to see the Challenger's headlights come on as the Hellcat engine growled to life, started with the remote as Dax limped that way. She watched him reach the car, fumble with the door, and then fall into the driver's seat. He'd have a chance to escape now, and she almost wanted to pursue him.

She knew better, though. Let him run, and let the police catch him. He wouldn't make it far. What Abby needed to do was get help on the way. She would go to one of the houses up the road and call for...

"Oh, shit," she said, in a flat, almost matter-of-fact voice.

The Challenger was in motion, but it wasn't turning around. He was headed down the hill, not up it.

The kid wasn't fleeing. He was coming back to finish the fight.

61

E ven as she hammered the accelerator, Abby knew there was
no real gain to making the first move. She was backed in
against the river, and her options were minimal—she could swerve
left or right, trying to evade him, or drive straight at him. The Jeep
had the advantage if she chose the latter, but that didn't make her
feel confident. A head-to-head crash would do more damage to the
Challenger than the Jeep, yes, but there was hardly a guarantee of
disabling the driver.

I already hit him, she thought numbly. *I broke the bastard's arm, I
won, so why won't he quit?*

Beneath that thought, though, ran a soft, chastising whisper that
told her she should have known better.

The cars would meet about halfway up the hill. Abby was bracing for the collision and thinking too late that she needed to yell
out some word of warning to Shannon when Dax cut the wheel
and brought the Challenger smoking in at an angle, and she realized what he was trying to do—block the road.

Easy enough. She swerved right, and the front end of the
Challenger clipped the edge of the Jeep's bumper, an impact that
felt barely more solid than when she'd hit Dax. The Jeep chunked
off the pavement and back onto it and then she was past him, open
road ahead.

But the open road didn't mean much to her. Not in the Jeep,
not with him in the Hellcat. Ahead of Abby, Ames Road climbed
up, up, up. It wasn't a long distance, but it was steep, and distance
was relative. The Hellcat went from zero to sixty in a breathtaking

3.6 seconds, absurd for a factory car, and the opening acceleration wasn't even its strongest point. The Hellcat was truly special when it was already rolling. It could go from thirty to fifty or fifty to seventy in a heartbeat. The quarter-mile stretch ahead would take the Challenger maybe twelve or thirteen seconds.

She chanced a look in the mirror and saw the door open. Watched as he leaned out and picked up a handgun from the pavement.

"Fuck," Abby said. Her voice was too calm; disembodied. She couldn't see Shannon Beckley in the mirror. Shannon was still wedged down on the floor, where Abby had told her to hide back when she thought she could win this thing, a minute before that felt like a decade ago now. The rest of the race invited no such illusions. She'd hit him, yes; hurt him, yes; but he hadn't stopped, and now he was outthinking her. Now he was in the superior car *and* he was armed, and whatever injuries he'd sustained suddenly seemed insignificant.

She glanced at Oltamu's phone. What if she threw it out of the car? Would he stop to get it just as he had the gun? It was all he wanted, after all.

Not anymore, she thought grimly, remembering the way he'd fought to his feet, his arm dangling broken in front of his body, useless. No, he wouldn't settle for the phone anymore. He'd take it, but he was coming for blood now.

Behind her, the Challenger's huge engine roared, the Pirellis burned blue smoke, and the headlights swerved and then steadied, pinning Abby.

The top of the hill might as well have been five miles out.

The Hellcat roared up with astonishing closing speed.

He can't even drive it, Abby thought. That didn't seem fair, somehow. To lose to him when he couldn't even handle that car was a cruel joke.

Then beat him, Luke said, or maybe it was Hank, or maybe it was Abby's father. Hard to tell, but Abby understood one thing—the voice was right.

In a decade of professional stunt driving, Abby had asked the finest cars in the world to do things that most people thought couldn't be done. Not on that list, though, was a controlled drift uphill with her hands tied together.

She wanted to use the hand brake, but that would require briefly taking her hands off the wheel, and instinct told her that that would end badly no matter how fast she moved. The Jeep sat up high, and if she didn't have full control of the wheel, the jarring counterforce of the hand brake would likely flip the car.

Just fishhook it, then. Nice and easy. Maybe he'd overcompensate, flip his own car, break his own neck.

Sure.

The headlights were filling the Jeep with clean white light, the broken glass glistening and the roar of the Hellcat almost on top of them, and suddenly Abby knew what he would do.

He'll be cautious, Abby thought, and she had the old feeling then, the swelling confidence that came up out of the blood, cool as a Maine river at night. She had watched Dax drive that car for hours now. He didn't understand the car, but he respected its power. So he wouldn't risk flipping it; he'd overshoot instead.

A tenth of a mile from the crest of the hill, Abby said, "Hang on," as if Shannon Beckley could do anything to prepare, and then she jammed her foot on the brake and spun the wheel through her fingers, passing it as rapidly as possible, like paying out rope, left hand to right hand, feeding it, feeding it, feeding it as the world spun around them.

I needed the hand brake, she thought, but she was wrong. They hadn't been going fast enough, and the hill worked in her favor. Physics came to her rescue as she shifted from brake to gas and pounded the pedal again. All around them was the sound of shrieking rubber as the tires negotiated with, pleaded with, and finally begged for mercy from the pavement.

The pavement was benevolent.

It granted the skid. The Jeep didn't roll.

Beside them, the Challenger smoked by in a roaring blur.

Abby was already accelerating back downhill by then.

She chanced a glance in the mirror only when she was sure the Jeep was running straight. The fishhook had been a simple stunt—awkward and lumbering by any pro's standard, actually—but it had been enough. The kid had had a choice: try to match it or ride by and gather himself. He'd opted for the latter.

Dax was executing a three-point turn to counter. In a *Challenger Hellcat,* he was executing a three-point turn to catch up to a Jeep. Abby wanted to laugh. *We can do this once more,* she thought, *or twice more, however long it takes, back and forth, but he's not getting a clear shot. Not as long as I have the wheel.*

She actually might have laughed if she hadn't looked ahead and seen the headlight from the train.

It was running northwest to southeast, cutting through Hammel and across the bridge on its dawn run, out of the night and toward the sunrise.

Up at the top of the hill, where the Challenger was executing its awkward turn, bells were clanging and guard arms lowering to block traffic on Ames Road. The train would soon take over that task. The train would block them above, the river already blocked them below, and Abby and Shannon would be sealed in the middle with Dax and his gun.

Abby brought the Jeep to a stop, twisted, and looked at Shannon Beckley. She'd clambered off the floor and back into the seat. Blood from the cut sheeted down her cheek, but her eyes were bright above it. Abby looked down at the handcuff that chained Shannon to the vehicle. Only one of them could walk away from this.

I'll take the phone, she thought, *I'll take the phone and I'll make him negotiate. Just like with the man named Gerry.*

The man he'd killed.

The negotiating hour was past.

She looked down the hill. Ahead of her, there was only the parking lot, the river, and the railroad bridge.

And, now, the train.

She looked back at Shannon Beckley, expecting to see Shannon staring ahead. But she was staring right at Abby. Scared, yes, but still with a fighter's eyes.

"I have to try," Abby said.

Shannon nodded.

Abby started to say, *It might not work,* but stopped herself. That was obvious.

Behind them, Dax had the Challenger straightened out and was facing her once again.

Abby let her foot off the brake and started downhill. The wheel slipped in her bloody hands and pulled left, but she caught it and brought it back. Behind, the Hellcat roared with delight and gained speed effortlessly, a thoroughbred running behind a nag. Abby didn't look in the mirror to see how fast Dax was pushing it. Her eyes were only on the bridge and the train. The train was slowing, navigating the last bend ahead of the bridge, and its whistle cried out a shrill warning, and the bells tolled their monotonous lecture of caution.

She fed the wheel back through her blood-slicked palms, bringing the car to the right when the road curved left, toward the parking lot. She pounded the gas as they banged over the curb and off the road and then headed for the short but steep embankment that led up to the train tracks. The Jeep climbed easily, and at the top of the embankment was the first of Abby's final tests—if she got hung up on the tracks, it was over.

The front end scraped rock and steel as the Jeep clawed up

onto the berm, and she managed to negotiate the turn, praying for clearance. She had just enough. The Jeep was able to straddle the rails, leaving the tires resting on the banked gravel and dirt on either side.

Behind and below her, Dax brought the Hellcat around in a slow, growling circle, like a pacing tiger. She knew what he was assessing—the Jeep sat high, able to clear the rails, and its wheelbase was wide enough to straddle them. The Challenger sat low, a bullet hovering just off the pavement. It would hang up on the tracks, leaving it stranded.

Dax didn't seem inclined to try pursuit. The car idled; the door didn't open; no gunfire came.

He watched and waited.

He thinks I've trapped myself, Abby realized.

And maybe she had. Squeezed from multiple sides now, she could go in only one direction: straight toward the train.

She kept expecting a gunshot but none came, and she realized why—he didn't think she'd try it. His brake lights no longer glowed, which meant he'd put the Challenger in park—he was that confident that Abby was done.

She looked away from him and fixed her eyes ahead, staring down the length of the railroad bridge, where, just on the other side, the huge locomotive was negotiating its last turn and entering the straightaway of the bridge. How far off? A hundred yards? Maybe less. It couldn't be more. If it was more...

I've just got to run it as fast as I can, that's all there is to it, she thought. When it came down to the last lap, when the rubber was worn and the fuel lines were gasping for fumes, there was no math involved, no calculations, no time.

You finished or you didn't. That was all.

Abby put her foot on the gas.

62

She was doing forty when she reached the bridge and she knew that she had to get up to at least sixty, maybe seventy, to give them any chance. But she also had to hold the car straight, and the gravel banks were built to keep the rails in place, not provide tire traction. It was a bone-rattling ride and one that made acceleration painfully slow.

The train was some thirty yards away from the bridge now. Thirty yards of opportunity remained for her to decide if it was a mistake and bail out. Ditch the Jeep, and then Abby could run, even if Shannon could not. With the diesel locomotive's headlight piercing the fractured windshield and the train's whistle screaming, it was easy to believe bailing was the right move.

Behind and below them, though, Dax waited.

He thinks I'm choosing my own way to die, Abby realized.

She kept her foot on the gas.

In front of her, the train straightened out until the diesel locomotive was facing her head-on. In the backseat, Shannon Beckley moaned from behind the tape. Abby was aware of a flicker of open grass to her right, a place where she could ditch the Jeep without falling into the river below.

Last chance to get out…take it.

She tightened her grip on the wheel. The last chance fell behind. Then they were on the bridge, and out of options.

A brightening sky above and a dark river below. A whistle shrilling, a headlight pounding into her eyes. The bridge seemed to evaporate into a tunnel, and though she wanted to check the speedometer to see whether she'd gotten up to seventy, she couldn't take her eyes off that light.

She would never remember the last swerve.

There was no plan, no target, nothing but white light and speed and the question of whether she could make it. Then, suddenly, the gap appeared, and instinct answered.

Daylight.

Chase it.

She slid the wheel across blood-soaked palms, and the daylight was there, and then the daylight was gone, and then came the impact.

A bang and a bounce and blackness. *I thought it would feel worse than that. That wasn't bad at all, for being hit by a train,* she thought, and then the furious scream of the whistle brought her back to reality. She was facing a wall of grass. It took her a moment to realize that it was the bank on the far side of the river.

The engineer was trying to slow the train, but with that much mass and momentum, it didn't happen fast. The locomotive was across the bridge and headed uphill before the cars behind it began to slow. A timber train, flatbed cars loaded with massive white pine logs from the deep northern woods.

Abby looked in the mirror. The Challenger was in the parking lot, facing her, idling. It no longer looked so smug. In fact, it looked impotent.

She knocked the gearshift into park, then reached out her bloody fingers, gripped the edge of the tape covering Shannon Beckley's mouth, and peeled it away. "You okay?"

Shannon nodded, as if unaware that she could speak now, then said, "Yes." Paused and repeated it. "Yes. I think so."

Abby opened the driver's door and stumbled out into the morning air. The train was still easing to a stop beside them, each car clicking by slower than the last. In the pale gray light, she could see the Challenger's door swing open, and she thought, *After all that, he's still going to shoot me.*

The kid limped around the front of the idling car. He eyed the pedestrian bridge below the train. Abby looked in the same direction, and for the first time, she saw Boone's body. Dax started to limp ahead.

He's still coming, she realized with numb astonishment. He would cross that bridge once more, even after all of this. All for a...

She turned back to the car and reached for Oltamu's phone. Her hands hovered just above it, then drifted left, and she popped the center console open and found Shannon Beckley's phone.

It took her two tries to grasp it in her bloody fingers, and by the time she had it and stepped away from the car, the kid was at the foot of the bridge.

"Dax!" she screamed.

He looked up. He was limping badly, and his left arm hung awkwardly, obviously broken but disregarded, like a dragging muffler. The gun was in his right hand, but she was too far away to fear being shot.

"Go get it!" Abby shouted, and then she pivoted back and whirled forward and sent Shannon Beckley's phone spinning into the air. It sailed in a smooth arc out above the river and then down into it.

Dax watched it splash and sink.

He stood there and looked at the water, and then, finally, he lifted his head to face Abby.

Duck, she commanded herself, but her body didn't obey. She just stood there on the other side of the river, hands bound in front of her, blood running down her arms.

The kid raised his gun. Abby waited for the shot.

None came. Instead, he held it across his forehead, and for a bizarre moment she thought he was going to take a suicide shot. Then she realized that he was offering a salute. He held the pose for a moment, then turned and limped back to the car. As the train whistle shrieked again, he backed the Challenger out and pulled up the hill. The train had stopped before blocking the road, granting him an escape route.

Abby stood where she was until the car crested the hill and vanished, then she sank down into the grass.

She looked back at the bridge, at that narrow window between train and steel girder, and wondered how wide it had been when she slipped the Jeep through. She stared at that for a long moment, and then she struggled upright and went to Shannon Beckley. Abby extended her wrists.

"Can you untie me?"

Shannon looked at Abby's face, then down to her hands. "Yes," she said simply, and she went to work on the knots with nimble fingers. It didn't take her long. Abby watched the cord fall away, and she remembered the strangling cord at her throat, her feet on the dash and her back arched. She flexed her fingers, then reached out and plucked the black baseball cap off Shannon Beckley's head. She studied it and found the pinhole-size camera hidden just beneath the bill, beneath the odd silver stitching that drew the eye of the observer toward the top of the hat. Was he watching? No. But he would go back. He would go back to study what he'd missed.

She was sure of that.

Abby angled the bill of the cap at her face and then lifted her middle finger up beside it. Then she stepped back from the Jeep, turned, and pulled her arm back, prepared to fling the hat as far into the river as she could.

"The police will need it," Shannon Beckley said.

Abby stopped. Sighed and nodded. Yes, they would. But *damn*, how much she wanted to watch it drown.

She tossed the hat on the driver's seat. Sirens were approaching from somewhere on the campus and somewhere on the other side of the river. She ignored them, studying the plastic zip ties that held Shannon's wrists together.

"I'll need to cut that. You have anything that will work?"

"Get the phone," Shannon said.

Abby was puzzled. Shannon had seemed so composed, but maybe she was delirious. Abby wasn't cutting those ties with a phone. "No," Abby told her patiently and began to root around in the console in search of a better tool.

"Get the phone," Shannon said, each word firm as a slap, and when Abby looked up, she saw that Shannon was staring over her shoulder. Abby turned and saw the dog crouched at the tree line, head up, ears back, wary but intrigued.

She picked up Oltamu's phone and walked away from the car. The sirens were growing louder, and someone was screaming at her from across the river, but she didn't look away and neither did the dog. Abby went as close as she dared and then sat in the grass and extended a bloody hand.

"Hobo," she said. "Come see me."

63

Tara has been many things and is becoming many more. Each day seems to bring a new identity.

First she was the vegetable, the brain-dead girl, and then she was the locked-in girl, and then, within hours of learning that Shannon was alive, Tara was the Coma Crime Stopper.

This is because of the story Shannon told, giving credit to her sister's nonverbal lie.

People look at her and think she's helpless. But from that bed, she saved me without speaking a word.

The media loved that quote. They directed feature coverage to Tara on every network. Their attention, as is its way, swells and breaks. A van with bombs is found in DC, and a hurricane is howling toward Texas. The Coma Crime Stopper is forgotten.

Then the contents of the phone are revealed.

Photos, files, videos of an electric vehicle produced by a company called Zonda, which is the name of an Argentinean wind that blows over the Andes Mountains. Most of the files are complex equations or sets of computer algorithms, an FBI agent from Boston named Roxanne Donovan tells Tara and her family. The photos and videos are mostly of cars on fire. Zonda prototypes.

The product of German design, American manufacturing, and international investing, Zonda is on the verge of being about so much more than cars. The company has already agreed to a multibillion-dollar contract with one of the world's largest airplane builders, military contracts are expanding, and, one week after a woman with a knife arrived to talk to Tara Beckley—and kill her—the company was to have its initial public offering. All has been trending positively for Zonda with the exception of one troublesome engineer who, in the months before the IPO, began to reach out to a handful of select individuals, informing them of rumors and promising documentation. What he could show, he told them, was the equivalent of the Volkswagen diesel-emissions scandal that cost the company billions in fines and led to the criminal indictments of nine executives. One of the world's most exciting young companies had been built on a carefully protected lie, and he was prepared to share evidence of that or remain silent about it—whichever was more profitable.

"I'd love to tell you that Amandi Oltamu was noble," Roxanne Donovan says to Tara. "But our early information suggests that he was only looking for a payday."

This disappoints Tara. Donovan is right; Tara wants him to be noble. She wants to have his death and her own suffering wrapped in righteousness.

She won't get what she wants.

"He made at least three offers," Donovan continues. "Two were to people who had stakes in the company. Extortion efforts, basically. When those demands weren't met, he went in a different direction. He contacted a rival."

The rival, it seemed, had gotten in touch with a woman named Lisa Boone.

The source of the baby-faced kid in the black hat is less clear. He is the son of a killer, seventeen or eighteen or possibly nineteen years old, and Roxanne Donovan will say only that the Bureau is working on leads, many of them generated by interviews with Abby Kaplan. Lisa Boone is dead, shot on the railroad bridge over the Willow River where Tara had once nearly died herself, but the young killer is missing. The best lead there, Donovan tells them, involves a rural airport in Owls Head. An isolated hangar on the Maine coast, it serves as a touchdown point for the private-jet set.

On the morning after the killing on the bridge, a small jet from Germany landed in Owls Head and refueled. Its lone passenger was an attorney from Berlin. The plane took on another passenger at Owls Head, a young man with a limp and one arm in a sling. The aircraft then flew to Halifax, and from Halifax to London, changing flight plans each time. Upon the plane's arrival in London, the young passenger from America disembarked after informing the pilot that the German attorney was sleeping and wasn't to be bothered. By the time the pilot discovered the man wasn't sleeping but dead, the unknown American was gone.

While Tara was a feature story, the death of Dr. Pine received sidebar coverage. She thinks this is a crime, that all the nobility Oltamu lacked, Pine had shown.

She hopes that his family will come to see her. On the day that she lifts her right thumb on command for the first time, she uses Dr. Carlisle's computer software to compose a short letter to Dr. Pine's family. It is the first writing she's done in this condition, and the words don't come as easily as she'd like, but would they ever for a letter like this?

The Coma Crime Stopper isn't sure.

What she is sure about is that the task of calling up the words is good for her. When she closes her eyes after that first bit of strained writing, she sees more of the green and gold light, sparklers and starbursts of it illuminating new rivers and tributaries, uncharted waters.

She writes again the next day.

Dr. Carlisle's prognosis becomes a bit less guarded in the following days. More enthusiasm bleeds through, perhaps more than she'd like to show. Tara exchanges e-mail with a woman who recovered from locked-in syndrome and who has just completed her third marathon since the injury. She is an outlier, of course. But Tara watches videos of her race over and over.

She must become an outlier too. She owes them all this much.

She owes Pine, obviously, but also Shannon, Abby Kaplan, and so many more. People she never met. A man named Hank Bauer. A man at a junkyard where her devastated Honda still rests.

She knows the journey ahead is long, and a good outcome is not promised. But she has so much fuel to carry her through it.

Weary but hopeful, she closes her eyes, flexes her thumb, and searches for those green-gold glimmers in the dark.

64

"We'll find him," the investigator from Scotland Yard promised Abby after three hours of taped interviews and the review of countless photographs taken from surveillance cameras around the city of London, Abby having been asked to search the crowds for a glimpse of Dax.

When she considered Dax's destination, the city that shared Luke's last name, she couldn't help but feel that it was a taunt. His silent response to the raised middle finger she'd offered that black hat. Somehow, she is sure that he saw that.

He was not in any of the photographs.

"How will you find him?" Abby asked the investigator.

"The way it's always done: Patience and hard work. We'll follow his patterns, learn who he trusts, and find him through them or when he makes a mistake. It will happen."

Abby wasn't so sure. She didn't think the kid trusted anyone. And while she knew the kid made mistakes, she felt as if he would make fewer of them by the day, by the hour. Each moment was a learning experience.

Abby remembered the salute he'd given her in the dim dawn light across the river, just before the kid got back into Hank Bauer's Challenger and disappeared. He'd been in three countries since then, and no one had caught him yet.

"He's adaptive," Abby said. "And I think he has big goals."

The man from Scotland Yard didn't seem interested in Abby's opinion. "He's no different from the rest of his family," he said. "Which means that, sooner or later, he'll end up dead or in jail. We'll see to that."

Abby wondered how long it had taken Scotland Yard to see to that for the rest of the kid's family, but she didn't ask. The last question she asked was the one she felt she already knew the answer to.

"What was his father's name?"

"He had a dozen of them."

"The most common one, then. What did most people call him?"

The investigator hesitated, then said, "Jack."

Abby nodded, remembering the bottle of poisoned whiskey that the boy had presented to Abby and Hank on the night they'd met.

"And the last name?"

"Blackwell."

"Blackwell," Abby echoed. It seemed right. It suited the family.

"He's quite dead," the Scotland Yard man said in a nearly chipper voice.

Abby looked at the photographs of the boy contract killer, and again, she wasn't sure the investigator was right. The man named Jack Blackwell might be dead, but his legacy was alive and well, moving through Europe like a ghost.

If he was even still in Europe.

"I'll tell you this," the Brit continued, "you're bloody lucky—and so is Shannon Beckley—that you can drive like that. Put anyone else behind the wheel out there, and you're both in the morgue."

"You're right," Abby said, and for the first time she did not doubt the accuracy of the man's statement.

Abby had needed the wheel for this one.

"Not making light of it," the Brit said, "but it seems to have been rather fortunate for your reputation too, based on what I've seen."

"Excuse me?"

"The Luke London thing."

The Luke London thing. Ah, yes. When she didn't respond, just stared evenly at him, he shifted awkwardly.

"I just mean in the media. Plenty of kindness from the same folks who crucified you before. Changes the narrative, right?"

"No," Abby said. "It doesn't."

The man looked at her curiously. Abby said, "It all happened. Nothing's replaced by anything else. They fit together."

"Sure," the Brit said, but he didn't understand, and Abby didn't try to clarify. The wins were the wins, the wrecks were the wrecks, as Hank Bauer used to say. They all worked together. The only risk was in expecting that one or the other was promised to you. Neither was. When the starting flag was waved, all you ever had was a chance.

"I won't waste it, though," Abby said, and this seemed to please the Brit; this part he thought he followed.

"Good," he said, and he clapped Abby on the shoulder and promised her that they'd be in touch soon. Abby was going to be important when they got the Blackwell lad in a courtroom.

Abby assured him she'd be ready for that moment. Then she left to drive to the hospital, where Shannon Beckley waited with her sister. Tara had therapy today. Tongue-strengthening exercises. Dr. Carlisle thought she was coming along well enough that spoken conversation might be possible sooner rather than later. She wouldn't make any bolder predictions, but she'd offered this much encouragement:

She fights, and so she has a chance.

It was, Abby thought, a patently obvious statement, and yet it mattered.

She drove south to Massachusetts alone.

The coastal Maine sun was brighter than the cold day seemed to allow, an optical illusion, the sky so blue it seemed someone had touched up the color, tweaking it beyond what was natural. The Scotland Yard man had taken longer than expected, and rush-hour traffic was filling in. Abby drove at seventy-five in the middle lane, letting the impatient pass her on the left and the indifferent fall behind to the right.

Her hand was steady on the wheel.

65

The girl in the kayak is testing new waters. There are channels all around her, currents previously unseen that are now opening up, and some are less inviting than others, as dark and ominous as the mouth of a cave. Others show promising glimmers of brightness but are lost quickly behind gray fog. Still, she knows they are out there, and she has the paddle, and she has the will. She knows that she must be both patient and aggressive, traits that seem contradictory only if you have never run a long race.

She pushes east through fogbound channels, and then the current catches her and carries her, turns her east to south, and the fog lifts and gray light brightens, brightens, brightens, until she is flying through it and there are glimmers of green and gold in the spray.

Satisfied, she coasts to a stop. Pauses, savoring the beauty of it all, savoring the chance.

When she's caught her breath, she paddles back upstream. The current spins and guides her, north to south first, then south to north. These are unusual waters, but she's learning them, learning when to fight them, when to trust them. Each day she travels a little farther and a little faster.

She dips the blade of the paddle and holds it against the gentle pressure, bringing the boat around in a graceful arc. Now she faces the dark mouth of one of the many unknown channels looming ahead. So much of the terrain is unknown, but none of it is unknowable.

There is a critical difference in that.

She paddles forward boldly into the blackness, chasing the light.

ACKNOWLEDGMENTS

Let's start off with readers, librarians, and booksellers—who should always be first when it comes to author gratitude.

The team at Little, Brown and Company is the best. Thanks to Joshua Kendall, Michael Pietsch, Reagan Arthur, Sabrina Callahan, Craig Young, Terry Adams, Heather Fain, Nicky Guerreiro, Maggie (Southard) Gladstone, Ashley Marudas, Shannon Hennessey, Karen Torres, Karen Landry, and Tracy Roe. Everyone involved in the process of taking the book into the world is deeply appreciated.

Much gratitude to Richard Pine and the team at InkWell Management, and to Angela Cheng Caplan. Lacy Whitaker has done her best to make me presentable to the social-media world, which is no small task.

Thanks to Dr. Daniel Spitzer for his guidance and expertise.

Early readers who suffered painful drafts are always appreciated—Christine Koryta, Bob Hammel, Pete Yonkman, and Ben Strawn provided invaluable feedback and support. My parents always do, and always have.

And thanks to the Blackwell family. You're the gift that keeps on giving.

ABOUT THE AUTHOR

Michael Koryta is the *New York Times* bestselling author of fourteen novels, most recently *How It Happened*. Several of his previous novels—among them *Last Words, Those Who Wish Me Dead,* and *So Cold the River*—were *New York Times* Notable Books and national bestsellers. His work has been translated into more than twenty languages and has won numerous awards. Koryta is a former private investigator and newspaper reporter. He lives in Bloomington, Indiana, and Camden, Maine.